Mistress
of the
Empire

Also by Raymond E. Feist and Janny Wurts

Daughter of the Empire
Servant of the Empire

Also by Raymond E. Feist

Magician
Silverthorn
A Darkness at Sethanon
Faerie Tale
Prince of the Blood

Also by Janny Wurts

Sorcerer's Legacy
Stormwarden
Keeper of the Keys
Shadowfane
Master of Whitestorm

Mistress ✳ of the ✳ Empire

Raymond E. Feist

and

Janny Wurts

A Foundation Book · Doubleday

NEW YORK   LONDON   TORONTO   SYDNEY   AUCKLAND

A FOUNDATION BOOK
PUBLISHED BY DOUBLEDAY
a division of Bantam Doubleday Dell
Publishing Group, Inc.
666 Fifth Avenue, New York, New York 10103

FOUNDATION, DOUBLEDAY, and the portrayal of the
letter F are trademarks of Doubleday, a division of
Bantam Doubleday Dell Publishing Group, Inc.

Book Design by Tasha Hall

Library of Congress Cataloging-in-Publication Data
Feist, Raymond E.
    Mistress of the empire / by Raymond E. Feist &
Janny Wurts. — 1st ed.
        p.   cm.
    "A Foundation book."
    I. Wurts, Janny. II. Title.
PS3556.E446M57   1992
813'.54—dc20   91-24511
                                                    CIP
ISBN 0-385-24719-2

1   3   5   7   9   10   8   6   4   2

FIRST EDITION

This book is dedicated to
Kyung and Jon Conning,
with appreciation for giving us insights and friendship

Acknowledgments

In the course of five years, in writing three novels together, we are indebted to the following people without whose contributions the work would have not been as rewarding, for either ourselves or the reader. Our thanks:

To the Friday Nighters, who started it all way back when R.E.F. asked where Midkemia was, thereby making it impossible not to write the story.

To our editors along the way, Adrian Zackheim, Jim Moser, Pat LoBrutto, and Janna Silverstein, for turning us loose.

To Elaine Chubb for continuity and finish.

To so many people at our publishing houses who care more than the job requires and work above and beyond the call of duty, those gone on to other places and those still with us.

To Jonathan Matson for being more than an agent.

To Mike Floerkey for technical suggestions, and for spreading the word.

And to Kathlyn Starbuck and Don Maitz for putting up with R.E.F. and J.W. respectively while we were impossible to live with for the last six years. The fact we're still married speaks volumes for your patience and love.

Raymond E. Feist
Janny Wurts

San Diego, CA / Sarasota, FL
June 1991

Mistress
of the
Empire

1. Tragedy

The morning sun shone.

Dew bejeweled the lakeshore grasses, and the calls of nesting shatra birds carried sweetly on the breeze. Lady Mara of the Acoma savored the air, soon to give way to the day's heat. Seated in her litter, her husband at her side and her two-year-old son, Justin, napping in her lap, she closed her eyes and breathed a deep sigh of contentment.

She slipped her fingers into her husband's hand. Hokanu smiled. He was undeniably handsome, and a proven warrior; and the easy times had not softened his athletic appearance. His grip closed possessively over hers, his strength masked by gentleness.

The past three years had been good ones. For the first time since childhood, she felt safe, secure from the deadly, unending political intrigues of the Game of the Council. The enemy who had killed her father and brother could no longer threaten her. He was now dust and memories, his family fallen with him; his ancestral lands and magnificently appointed estate house had been deeded to Mara by the Emperor.

Superstition held that ill luck tainted a fallen family's land; on a wonderful morning such as this, misfortune seemed nowhere in evidence. As the litter moved slowly along the shore, the couple shared the peace of the moment while they regarded the home that they had created between them.

Nestled between steep, stone-crested hills, the valley that had first belonged to the Minwanabi Lords was not only naturally defensible, but so beautiful it was as if touched by the gods. The lake reflected a placid sky, the waters rippled by the fast oars of a messenger skiff bearing dispatches to factors in the Holy City. There, grain barges poled by chanting slaves delivered this year's harvest to warehouses for storage until the spring floods allowed transport downriver.

The dry autumn breeze rippled golden grass, and the morning sun lit the walls of the estate house like alabaster. Beyond, in a natural hollow, Force Commanders Lujan and Xandia drilled a combined troop of Acoma and Shinzawai warriors. Since Hokanu would one day inherit his father's title, his marriage to Mara had not merged the two houses. Warriors in Acoma green marched in step with others in Shinzawai blue, the ranks patched black, here and there, by divisions of insectoid cho-ja. Along with the Minwanabi lands, Lady Mara had gained an alliance with two additional hives, and with them the fighting strength of three more companies of warriors bred by their queens for battle.

An enemy foolish enough to launch an assault would invite swift annihilation. Mara and Hokanu, with loyal vassals and allies, between them commanded a standing army unsurpassed in the Nations. Only the Emperor's own Imperial Whites, with levies from other houses under his sovereignty, would rival these two armies. And as if fine troops and a near-impregnable fortress did not in themselves secure peace, the title Servant of the Empire, bestowed upon Mara for her services to Tsuranuanni, gave her honorary adoption into the Emperor's own family. The Imperial Whites were as likely to march in her defense, for by the honor central to Tsurani culture, insult or threat to her was as an offense visited upon the Light of Heaven's blood family.

"You seem delightfully self-satisfied this morning, wife," Hokanu said in her ear.

Mara tilted her head back into his shoulder, her lips parted for his kiss. If, deep in her heart, she missed the wild passion she had known with the red-haired barbarian slave who had fathered Justin, she had come to terms with that loss. Hokanu was a kindred spirit who shared her political shrewdness and inclination toward innovation. He was quick-witted, kind, and devoted to her, as well as tolerant of her headstrong nature, as few men of her culture were inclined to be. With him, Mara shared voice as an equal. Marriage had brought a deep and abiding contentment, and though her interest in the Great Game of the Council had not lessened, she no longer played out of fear. Hokanu's kiss warmed the moment like wine, until a high-pitched shout split the quiet.

Mara straightened up from Hokanu's embrace, her smile mirrored in her husband's dark eyes. "Ayaki," they concluded simultaneously. The next moment, galloping hoofbeats thundered down the trail by the lake.

Hokanu tightened his arm around his wife's shoulder as the two of them leaned out to view the antics of Mara's older son and heir.

A coal-black horse burst through the gap in the trees, mane and tail flying in the wind. Green tassels adorned its bridle, and a pearl-stitched breastplate kept the saddle from sliding backward along its lean length of barrel. Crouched in the lacquer-worked stirrups was a boy, recently turned twelve, and as raven-haired as his mount. He reined the gelding into a turn and charged toward Mara's litter, his face flushed with the thrill of speed, and his fine, sequin-stitched robe flying like a banner behind.

"He's becoming quite the bold rider," Hokanu said admiringly. "And the birthday present appears to please him."

Mara watched, a glow of pleasure on her face, as the boy reined in the mount upon the path. Ayaki was her joy, the person she loved most in life.

The black gelding tossed its head in protest. It was spirited, and eager to run. Still not entirely comfortable with the huge animals imported from the barbarian world, Mara held her breath in apprehension. Ayaki had inherited a wild streak from his father, and in the years since his narrow escape from an assassin's knife, a restless mood sometimes claimed him. At times he seemed to taunt death, as if by defying danger he could reaffirm the life in his veins.

But today was not such a moment, and the gelding had been selected for obedience as well as fleetness. It snorted a gusty breath of air and yielded to the rein, falling into stride alongside Mara's litter bearers, who overcame their inclination to move away from the large animal.

The Lady looked up as boy and horse filled her vision. Ayaki would be broad shouldered, the legacy of both his grandfathers. He had inherited the Acoma tendency toward leanness, and all of his father's stubborn courage. Although Hokanu was not his blood father, the two shared friendship and respect. Ayaki was a boy any parent could be proud of, and he was already showing the wits he would need when he reached adulthood and entered the Game of the Council as Lord of the Acoma in his own right.

"Young show-off," Hokanu teased. "Our bearers might be the only ones in the Empire to be granted the privilege of sandals, but if you think we should race you to the meadows, we'll certainly have to refuse."

Ayaki laughed. His dark eyes fixed on his mother, filled with the elation of the moment. "Actually, I was going to ask Lax'l if I might try our speed against a cho-ja. It would be interesting to know whether his warriors could overtake a troop of the barbarians' cavalry."

"If there was a war, which there is not at the moment, gods be praised," Hokanu said on a note a shade more serious. "Take care you mind your manners, and don't offend Force Commander Lax'l's dignity when you ask."

Ayaki's grin widened. Having grown up around the alien cho-ja, he was not at all intimidated by their strange ways. "Lax'l still has not forgiven me for handing him a jomach fruit with a stone in it."

"He has," Mara interjected. "But after that, he grew wise to your tricks, which is well. The cho-ja don't have the same appreciation of jokes that humans do.'' Looking at Hokanu, she said, ''In fact, I don't think they understand our humor.''

Ayaki made a face, and the black curvetted under him. The litter bearers swerved away from its dancing hooves, and the jostle disturbed young Justin. He awakened with a cry of outrage.

The dark horse shied at the noise. Ayaki held the animal with a firm hand, but the spirited gelding backed a few steps. Hokanu kept a passive face, though he felt the urge to laugh at the boy's fierce determination and control. Justin delivered an energetic kick into his mother's stomach. She bent forward, scooped him up in her arms.

Then something sped past Hokanu's ear, from behind him, causing the hangings of the litter to flutter. A tiny hole appeared in the silk where Mara's head had been an instant before. Hokanu threw his body roughly against those of his wife and foster child and twisted to look in the other direction. Within the shadows of the bushes beside the path, something black moved. Instincts honed in battle pressed Hokanu to unthinking action.

He pushed his wife and younger child out of the litter, keeping his body across them as a shield. His sudden leap overturned the litter, giving them further cover. ''The brush!'' he shouted as the bearers were sent sprawling.

Guards drew their blades in readiness to defend their mistress. But seeing no clear target to attack, they hesitated.

Mara exclaimed in puzzlement from beneath a tangle of cushions and torn curtains, over the noise of Justin's wails. ''What—''

To the guards, Hokanu shouted, ''Behind the akasi bushes!''

The horse stamped, as if at a stinging fly. Ayaki felt his gelding shudder under him. Its ears flattened, and it shook its heavy mane, while he worked the reins to soothe it. ''Easy, big fellow. Stand easy.'' His stepfather's warning failed to reach him, so intent was he on steadying his mount.

Hokanu glanced over the litter. The guards now rushed the bushes he had indicated. As he turned to check for possible attack from the other quarter, he saw Ayaki frantically trying to calm a horse grown dangerously over excited. A sparkle of lacquer in the sunlight betrayed a tiny dart protruding from the gelding's flank. ''Ayaki! Get off!''

His horse gave a vicious kick. The dart in its hide had done its work, and nerve poison coursed through the beast's bloodstream. Its eyes rolled, showing wide rings of white. It reared up, towering, and a near-human scream shrilled from its throat.

Hokanu sprang away from the litter. He grabbed for the gelding's rein, but slashing hooves forced him back. He dodged, tried another grab, and missed as the horse twisted. Familiar enough with horseflesh to know this animal had gone berserk, he screamed to the boy who clung with both hands locked around the beast's neck.

"Ayaki! Jump off! Do it now, boy!"

"No," cried the child, not in defiance, but bravely. "I can quiet him!"

Hokanu leaped for the reins again, frightened beyond thought for his own safety. The boy's concern might have been justified if the horse had simply been scared. But Hokanu had once seen the effects of a poison dart; he recognized the horse's shivering flesh and sudden lack of coordination for what they were: the symptoms of a fast-acting venom. Had the dart struck Mara, death would have taken seconds. In an animal ten times her size, the end would be slower, and brutally painful. The horse bellowed its agony, and a spasm shook its great frame. It bared yellow teeth and fought the bit, while Hokanu missed his grip. "Poison, Ayaki!" he shouted over the noise of the frantic horse. Hokanu lunged to catch the stirrup, hoping to snatch the boy clear. The horse's forelegs stiffened, bracing outward as the muscles locked into extension. Then its quarters collapsed, and it toppled, the boy caught like a burr underneath.

The thud of the heavy body striking earth mingled with Mara's scream. Ayaki refused to leap free at the last. Still riding his horse, he was swept sideways, his neck whipping back as the force of the fall threw him across the path. The horse shuddered and rolled over upon the boy.

Ayaki made no sound. Hokanu avoided a hedge of thrashing hooves as he darted around the tormented animal. He reached the boy's side in a bound, too late. Trapped under the weight of dying, shivering horseflesh, the child looked too pale to be real. His dark eyes turned to Hokanu's, and his one free hand reached out to grip that of his foster father's a heartbeat ahead of death.

Hokanu felt the small, dirty fingers go limp inside his own. He clung on in a rage of denial. "No!" he shouted, as if in appeal to the gods. Mara's cries rang in his ears, and he was aware of the warriors from her honor guard jostling him as they labored to shift the dead horse. The gelding was rolled aside, the rush of air as its lungs deflated moaning through its vocal cords. For Ayaki there would be no such protest at shattering, untimely death. The gelding's withers had crushed his chest, and the ribs stood up from mangled flesh like the broken shards of swords.

The young face with its too white cheeks stared yet, open-eyed and surprised, at the untroubled sky overhead. The fingers that had reached out to a trusted foster father to stave off the horror of the dark lay empty, open, the scabbed remains of a blister on one thumb a last testimony to diligent practice with a wooden sword. This boy would never know the honors or the horrors of a battle, or the sweet kiss of his first maid, or the pride and responsibility of the Lord's mantle that had been destined one day to be his.

The finality of sudden ending left pain like a bleeding wound. Hokanu knew grief and stunned disbelief. His mind worked through the shock only out of reflex trained on the fields of war. ''Cover the child with your shield,'' he ordered. ''His mother must not see him like this.''

But the words left numbed lips too late. Mara had rushed after him, and he felt the flurry of her silken robes against his calf as she flung herself on her knees by her son. She reached out to embrace him, to raise him up from the dusty ground as if through sheer force of love she could restore him to life. But her hands froze in the air over the bloody rags of flesh that had been Ayaki's body. Her mouth opened without sound. Something crumpled inside her. On instinct, Hokanu caught her back and bundled her against his shoulder.

''He's gone to the Red God's halls,'' he murmured. Mara did not respond. Hokanu felt the rapid beat of her heart under his hands. Only belatedly did he notice the scuffle in the brush beside the trail. Mara's honor guard had thrown themselves with a vengeance upon the black-clothed body of the assassin. Before Hokanu could gather the wits to order restraint—for, alive, the man might be made to say which enemy had hired him—the warriors made an end of the issue.

Their swords rose and fell, bright red. In seconds Ayaki's killer lay hacked like a needra bullock slaughtered in a butcher's stall.

Hokanu felt no pity for the man. Through the blood, he noted the short black shirt and trousers, the red-dyed hands, as the soldiers turned the body over. The headcloth, which hid all but the eyes of the man, was pulled aside to reveal a blue tattoo upon the left cheek. This mark would only be worn by a member of the Hamoi Tong, a brotherhood of assassins.

Hokanu stood slowly. It did not matter that the soldiers had dispatched the killer: the assassin would have died gladly before divulging information. The tong operated to a strict code of secrecy, and it was certain the murderer would not know who had paid his leader for this attack. And the only name that mattered was that of the man who had hired the Hamoi brotherhood's services.

In a cold corner of his mind, Hokanu understood that this attempt upon Mara's life had not come cheaply. This man could not have hoped to survive his mission, and a suicide killing would be worth a fortune in metal.

"Search the corpse, and track his path through the estates," he heard himself saying in a voice hardened by the emotions that seethed inside. "See if you can find any clues to who might have hired the tong."

The Acoma Strike Leader in command bowed to the master and issued sharp orders to his men.

"Leave a guard over the boy's body," Hokanu added. He bent to comfort Mara, unsurprised that she was still speechless, fighting horror and disbelief. Her husband did not fault her for being unable to keep composure and show proper Tsurani impassivity. Ayaki had been all the family she had known for many years; she had no other blood kindred. Her life before his birth had already been jarred by too much loss and death. He cradled her small, shivering body against his own while he added the necessary instructions concerning the boy.

But when the arrangements were complete and Hokanu tenderly tried to draw Mara away, she fought him. "No!" she said in strangled pain. "I will not leave him here alone!"

"My Lady, Ayaki is beyond our help. He already stands in the Red God's halls. Despite his years, he met death courageously. He will be welcomed." He stroked her dark hair, dampened with tears, and tried to calm her. "You would do better inside with loved ones around you, and Justin in the care of his nurses."

"No," Mara repeated, a note in her voice that he instinctively knew not to cross. "I won't leave."

And though she did after a time consent to have her surviving child sent back to the estate house under protection of a company of warriors, she sat through the heat of the morning on the dusty soil, staring at the stilled face of her firstborn.

Hokanu never left her. The stinks of death did not drive him away, nor the flies that swarmed and buzzed and sucked at the eyes of the seeping corpse of the gelding. Controlled as if on a battlefield, he faced the worst, and coped. In quiet tones he sent a runner slave to fetch servants, and a small silk pavilion to offer shade. Mara never looked aside as the awning was set up above her. As though the people around her did not exist, she sifted torn earth through her fingers, until a dozen of her best warriors arrived in ceremonial armor to bear her fallen son away. No one argued with Hokanu's suggestion that the boy deserved battlefield honors. Ayaki had died of an enemy's dart, as surely as if the poison had struck his own flesh. He had refused to abandon his beloved horse, and such courage and responsibility in one so young merited recognition.

Mara watched, her expression rigid as porcelain, as the warriors lifted her son's body and set it on a bier bedecked with streamers of Acoma green, a single one scarlet, in acknowledgment of the Red God who gathers in all life.

The morning breeze had stilled, and the warriors sweated at their task. Hokanu helped Mara to her feet, willing her not to break. He knew the effort it took to maintain his own composure, and not just for the sake of Ayaki. Inside his heart he bled also for Mara, whose suffering could scarcely be imagined. He steadied her steps as she moved beside the bier, and the slow cortege wound its way downslope, toward the estate house that only hours earlier had seemed a place blessed by felicity.

It seemed a crime against nature, that the gardens should still be so lush, and the lakeshore so verdant and beautiful, and the boy on the bier be so bloody and broken and still.

The honor bearers drew up before the front doorway used for ceremonial occasions. Shadowed by the immense stone portal stood the household's most loyal servants. One by one they bowed to the bier, to pay young Ayaki their respects. They were led by Keyoke, First Adviser for War, his hair silvered with age, the crutch that enabled him to walk after battle wounds cost him a leg unobtrusively tucked into a fold of his formal mantle. As he intoned the ritual words of sympathy, he looked upon Mara with the grief a father might show, locked behind dark eyes and an expression like old wood. After him waited Lujan, the Acoma Force Commander, his usual rakish smile vanished and his steady gaze spoiled by his blinking to hold back tears. A warrior to the core, he scarcely managed to maintain his bearing. He had taught the boy on the bier to spar with a sword, and only that morning had praised his developing skills.

He touched Mara's hand as she passed. "Ayaki may have been only twelve years of age, my Lady, but he already was an exemplary warrior."

The mistress barely nodded in response. Guided by Hokanu, she passed on to the hadonra next in line. Small, and mouse-shy, Jican looked desolate. He had recently succeeded in intriguing the volatile Ayaki with the arts of estate finance. Their games using shell counters to represent the marketable Acoma trade goods would no longer clutter the breakfast nook off the pantry. Jican stumbled over the formal words of sympathy to his mistress. His earnest brown eyes seemed to reflect her pain as she and her husband passed on, to her young adviser Saric, and his assistant, Incomo. Both were later additions to the household, but Ayaki had won their affection no less than the others'. The condolences they offered to Mara were genuine, but she could not reply. Only Hokanu's hand on her elbow kept her from stumbling as she mounted the stair and entered the corridor.

The sudden step into shadow caused Hokanu to shiver. For the first time, the beautifully tiled stonework did not offer him the feeling of shelter. The beautiful painted screens he and Mara had commissioned did not warm him to admiration. Instead he felt gnawing doubt; had young Ayaki's death been an expression of the gods' displeasure, that Mara should claim as spoils the properties of her fallen enemies? The Minwanabi who had once walked these halls had sworn blood feud against the Acoma. Eschewing tradition, Mara had not buried their natami, the talisman stone that secured the spirits of the dead to life's Wheel as long as it stood in sunlight. Could the lingering shades of vanquished enemies visit ill luck on her and her children?

Afraid for young Justin's safety, and inwardly reprimanding himself for giving credence to superstitions, Hokanu focused upon Mara. Where death and loss had always hardened her to courage and action, now she seemed utterly devastated. She saw the boy's corpse into the great hall, her steps like those of a mannequin animated by a magician's spell. She sat motionless at the bier side while servants and maids bathed her child's torn flesh, and robed him in the silks and jewels that were his heritage as heir of a great house. Hokanu hovered nearby, aching with a sense of his own uselessness. He had food brought, but his Lady would not eat. He asked for a healer to make up a soporific, expecting, even hoping, to provoke an angry response.

Mara dully shook her head and pushed the cup away.

The shadows on the floor lengthened as the sun crossed the sky, and the windows in the ceiling admitted steepening angles of light. When the scribe sent by Jican tapped discreetly on the main door a third time, Hokanu at last took charge and told the man to seek out Saric or Incomo, to make up the list of noble houses who should be informed of the tragedy. Plainly Mara was not up to making the decision herself. Her only movement, for hours, had been to take the cold, stiff fingers of her son in her own.

Lujan arrived near dusk, his sandals dusty, and more weariness in his eyes than he had ever shown on campaign. He bowed to his mistress and her consort and awaited permission to speak.

Mara's eyes remained dully fixed on her son.

Hokanu reached out and touched her rigid shoulder. "My love, your Force Commander has news."

The Lady of the Acoma stirred, as if roused from across a great distance. "My son is dead," she said faintly. "By the mercy of all the gods, it should have been me."

Rent to the heart by compassion, Hokanu stroked back a fallen wisp of her hair. "If the gods were kind, the attack should never have happened." Then, as he saw that his Lady had slipped back into her stupor, he faced her officer.

The eyes of both men met, anguished. They had seen Mara enraged, hurt, even in terror of her life. She had always responded with spirit and innovation. This apathy was not like her, and all who loved her feared that a portion of her spirit might have perished along with her son.

Hokanu endeavored to shoulder as much of the burden as possible. "Tell me what your men have found, Lujan."

Had Mara's Force Commander been a more tradition-bound man, he would have refused; while Hokanu was a noble, he was not master of the Acoma. But the Shinzawai faction of the household was sworn to alliance with the Acoma, and Mara was in no condition to make critical decisions. Lujan released an almost imperceptible sigh of relief. The strengths of the Shinzawai heir were considerable, and the news Lujan brought was not cheering. "My Lord, our warriors searched the corpse to no avail. Our best trackers joined the search and, in a hollow where the assassin had apparently been sleeping, found this."

He offered a round shell token, painted scarlet and yellow and incised with the triangular sigil of House Anasati. Hokanu took the object with a touch that bespoke disgust. The token was the sort a Ruling Lord might give a messenger as proof that an important errand had been carried out. Such a badge was inappropriate for an enemy to entrust to an assassin; but then, the Lord of the Anasati made no secret of his hatred for Mara. Jiro was powerful, and openly allied with houses who wished to abolish the Emperor's new policies. He was a scholar rather than a man of war, and though he was too clever to indulge in crude gestures, Mara had once slighted his manhood: she had chosen his younger brother for her first husband, and since that day, Jiro had shown open animosity.

Still, the shell counter was blatantly unsubtle for a working of the Great Game. And the Hamoi Tong was too devious a brotherhood to consent to the folly of carrying evidence of which Lord or family might have hired it. Its history extended back for centuries, and its policies were cloaked in secrecy. To buy a death from it ensured absolute discretion. The token could be a ploy designed to throw blame upon the Anasati.

Hokanu raised concerned eyes to Lujan. "You think Lord Jiro was responsible for this attack?"

His query was less a question than an implied expression of doubt. That Lujan also had reservations about the placement of the token was evident as he drew breath to reply.

But the name of the Anasati Lord had pierced through Mara's lethargy. "Jiro did this?" She spun from Ayaki's body and saw the red-and-yellow disk in Hokanu's hand. Her face contorted into a frightening mask of fury. "The Anasati shall be as dust in the wind. Their natami will be buried in offal, and their spirits be consigned to the dark. I will show them less mercy than I did the Minwanabi!" Her hands clenched into shaking fists. She stared without seeing between her husband and her Force Commander, as though her detested enemy could be made manifest through the force of her hatred. "Not even that will pay for the blood of my son. Not even that."

"Lord Jiro might not be responsible," Lujan offered, his usually firm voice torn by grief. "You were the target, not Ayaki. The boy is the nephew of the Anasati Lord, after all. The tong assassin could have been sent by any of the Emperor's enemies."

But Mara seemed not to hear. "Jiro will pay. My son will be avenged."

"Do you think Lord Jiro was responsible?" Hokanu repeated to the Force Commander. That the young Anasati heir still felt as he did, even after inheriting the mantle and power that had been his father's, bespoke stubborn, childish pride. A mature mind would no longer nurse such a grudge; but in vain arrogance, the Anasati Lord might well wish the world to know whose hand had contracted for Mara's downfall.

Except that since Mara was Servant of the Empire, her popularity was too widespread. Fool Jiro might be over slighted manhood, but surely not so much that he would invite the Emperor's wrath.

Lujan turned dark eyes toward Hokanu. "That bit of shell is all the evidence we have. Its very obviousness might be subtle, as if by calling attention to House Anasati we might dismiss them at once and look elsewhere for the culprits." Fury coiled beneath his words. He, too, wanted to strike in anger at the outrage that had been committed. "It matters very little what I think," he finished grimly. For honor demanded that he do his Lady's will, absolutely and without question. If Mara asked him to muster the Acoma garrison and march suicidally to war, he would obey, with all his heart and will.

Dusk dimmed the skylights in the great hall. Servants entered on quiet feet and lit the lamps arrayed around Ayaki's bier. Scented smoke sweetened the air. The play of warm light softened death's pallor, and shadow veiled the misshapen lumps of the injuries beneath the silk robes. Mara sat alone in vigil. She regarded her son's oval face, and the coal-dark hair that, for the first time she could remember, had stayed combed for more than an hour.

Ayaki had been all of her future, until that moment of the gelding's crushing fall. He had been her hopes, her dreams, and more: the future guardian of her ancestors and the continuance of the Acoma name.

Her complacence had killed him.

Mara clenched white fingers in her lap. She never, ever, should have lulled herself into belief that her enemies could not touch her. Her guilt at this lapse in vigilance would follow her all her days. Yet how bleak any contemplation of tomorrow had become. At her side lay a tray with the picked-over remains of a meal; the food had no taste that she could recall. Hokanu's solicitude had not comforted; she knew him too well, and the echoes of her own pain and anger she could sense behind his words galled her into deeper recriminations.

Only the boy showed no reproach for her folly. Ayaki was past feeling, beyond reach of sorrow or joy.

Mara choked back a spasm of grief. How she wished the dart had taken her, that the darkness which ended all striving could be hers, instead of her son's. That she had another, surviving child did not lessen her despair. Of the two, Ayaki had known the least of life's fullness, despite his being the elder. He had been fathered by Buntokapi of the Anasati, whose family had been an Acoma enemy, in a union from which Mara had derived much pain and no happiness. Political expediency had led her to deeds of deceit and entrapment that to her maturer view seemed no less than murder. Ayaki had been her atonement for his father's wasteful suicide, brought about by Mara's own machinations. Although by the tenets of the Game of the Council she had won a telling victory, privately she considered Buntokapi's death a defeat. That his family's neglect had made of him a tool for her to exploit made no difference. Ayaki had offered her a chance to give her first husband's shade lasting honor. She had been determined that his son would rise to the greatness that Buntokapi had been denied.

But the hope was ended now. Lord Jiro of the Anasati had been Buntokapi's brother, and the fact that his plot against her had misfired and resulted in a nephew's death had shifted the balance of politics yet again. For, without Ayaki, the Anasati were free to resume the enmity quiescent since her father's time.

Ayaki had grown up with the best teachers, and all of her soldiers' vigilance to protect him; but he had paid for the privileges of his rank. At nine he had nearly lost his life to an assassin's knife. Two nurses and a beloved old household servant had been murdered before his eyes, and the experience had left him with nightmares. Mara resisted an urge to rub his hand in comfort. The flesh was cold, and his eyes would never open in joy and trust.

Mara did not have to fight down tears; rage at injustice choked her sorrow for her. The personal demons that had twisted his father's nature toward cruelty had inspired melancholy and brooding in Ayaki. Only in the past three years, since Mara's marriage to Hokanu, had the sunnier side of the boy's nature gained ascendancy.

The fortress of the Minwanabi, Ayaki had been fond of pointing out, had never been so much as besieged; the defenses here were impregnable to an enemy. Moreover, Mara was a Servant of the Empire. The title carried favor with the gods, and luck enough to ward away misfortune.

Now Mara berated herself for allowing his childish, blind faith to influence her. She had used traditions and superstitions to her advantage often enough in the past. She had been a vain fool not to see that the same things could be exploited against her.

It seemed an injustice that the child should have paid, and not her.

His small half brother, Justin, had helped lighten Ayaki's bleak spells. Her second son was the child of the barbarian slave she still loved. She had only to close her eyes for an instant and Kevin's face came to mind, nearly always smiling over some ridiculous joke, his red hair and beard shining copper under Kelewan's sun. With him she had shared none of the harmonious rapport she now enjoyed with Hokanu. No, Kevin had been tempestuous, impulsive, at times passionately illogical. He would not have hidden his grief from her, but would have freed his feelings in an explosive storm; in his intense expression of life she might have found the courage to face this outrage. Young Justin had inherited his father's carefree nature. He laughed easily, was quick to get into mischief, and already evidenced a fast tongue. Like his father before him, Justin had a knack for snapping Ayaki out of his brooding. He would run on fat legs, trip, and tumble over laughing, or he would make ridiculous faces until it was impossible to be near him and stay withdrawn.

But there would be no more shared laughter for Ayaki now.

Mara shivered, only that moment conscious of the presence of someone at her side. Hokanu had entered the chamber in the uncannily silent manner he had learned from the foresters on the barbarian world.

Aware that she had noticed him, he took her cold hand into his warm one. "My Lady. It is past midnight. You would do well to take some rest."

Mara half turned from the bier. Her dark eyes fastened on Hokanu's, and the compassion in his gaze caused her to dissolve into tears. His handsome features blurred, and his grip shifted, supporting her body against his shoulder. He was strong in the sparely muscled way of his father. And if he did not kindle the wild passion that Kevin had, with him Mara shared an effortless understanding. He was husband to her as Ayaki's father had never been, and his presence now as grief crumbled her poise was all that kept her from insanity. The touch that sought to soothe her sorrow was that of a man well capable of command on the field of war. He preferred peace, as she did, but when the ways of the sword became necessary, he had the courage of the tigers that inhabited the world beyond the rift.

Now, belatedly, the Acoma would need those skills in battle.

As tears rinsed Mara's cheeks, she tasted bitterness that knew no limit. The guilt inside her had a name she could use as a scapegoat. Jiro of the Anasati had murdered her son; for that, she would destroy his house beyond the memory of the living.

As though he sensed the ugly turn of her thoughts, Hokanu shook her gently. "My Lady, you are needed. Justin cried all through his supper, asking what had happened to his mama. Keyoke called each hour for instructions, and Force Commander Lujan needs to know how many companies should be recalled from garrison duty at your estates near Sulan-Qu."

In his inimitably subtle way, Hokanu did not argue the necessity for war. That brought relief. Had he offered questions, had he sought to dissuade her from vengeance against Jiro upon grounds that a single shell token offered too scanty evidence, she would have turned on him in a fury. Who was not with her at this moment was against her. A blow had been struck against the Acoma, and honor demanded action.

But the form of her murdered son sapped her will; life in any form seemed sucked dry.

"Lady?" prompted Hokanu. "Your decisions are necessary for the continuance of your house. For now you are the Acoma."

A frown gathered Mara's eyebrows. Her husband's words were truth. Upon their marriage, they had agreed that young Justin would become the Shinzawai heir after Hokanu. Fiercely, suddenly, Mara wished that promise unspoken. Never would she have agreed to such a thing had she realized Ayaki's mortality.

The circle closed again. She had been negligent. Had she not grown dangerously complacent, her black-haired son would not lie in state inside a circle of death lamps. He would be running, as a boy should, or practicing the skills of a warrior, or riding his great black gelding faster than the wind over the hills.

Again Mara saw in her mind's eye the arc of the brute's rearing form, and the terrible, thrashing of hooves as it toppled. . . .

"Lady," chided Hokanu. Tenderly he pried her fingers open, and endeavored to stroke away her tension. "It is over. We must continue to strive for the living." His hands brushed away her tears. More spilled between her eyelids to replace them. "Mara, the gods have not been kind. But my love for you goes on, and the faith of your household in your spirit shines like a lamp in the darkness. Ayaki did not live for nothing. He was brave, and strong, and he did not shy from his responsibilities, even at the moment of his death. As he did, so must we, or the dart that felled the horse will deal more than one mortal blow."

Mara closed her eyes, and tried to deny the oil-scented smoke of the death lamps. She did not need reminding that thousands of lives depended upon her, as Ruling Lady of the Acoma; today she had paid for the proof that she did not deserve their trust. She was regent for a growing son no longer. There seemed no heart left in her, and yet she must prepare for a great war, and achieve vengeance to keep family honor, and then produce another heir.

Yet the hope, the future, the enthusiasms, and the dreams she had sacrificed so much for had all gone to dust. She felt numbed, punished beyond caring.

"My Lord and husband," she said hoarsely, "attend to my advisers, and have them do as you suggest. I have not the heart to make decisions, and the Acoma must make ready for battle."

Hokanu looked at her with wounded eyes. He had long admired her spirit, and to see her beautiful boldness overcome by grief made his heart ache. He held her close, knowing the depth of her pain. "Lady," he whispered softly, "I will spare you all I can. If you would march upon Jiro of the Anasati, I will stand at the right hand of your Force Commander. But sooner or later, you must put on the mantle of your house. The Acoma name is your charge. Ayaki's loss must not signify an ending but create a renewal of your line."

Past speech, beyond rational thought, Mara turned her face into her husband's shoulder, and for a very long time her tears soaked soundlessly into the rich blue silk of his robe.

2. Confrontation

Jiro frowned.

Though the unadorned robe he wore was light and the portico around the courtyard adjacent to his library was still cool at this early hour, fine sweat beaded his brow. A tray of half-eaten breakfast lay abandoned at his elbow, while he tapped tense fingers on the embroidered cushion he sat on; his eyes unwaveringly studied the game board spread at his knees. He considered the position of each piece singly, and sought to assess the probable outcome of each move. A wrong choice might not seem immediately obvious, but against today's opponent the consequences were apt to prove ruinous several moves later. Scholars claimed the game of shāh sharpened a man's instincts for battle and politics, but Jiro, Lord of the Anasati, enjoyed puzzles of the mind over physical contests. He found the game's intricacies hypnotic for their own sake.

His skills had surpassed those of his father and other teachers at a precociously early age. When he was a boy, his older brother, Halesko, and younger brother, Buntokapi, had often as not pummeled him for the contemptuous ease he displayed in defeating them. Jiro had sought older opponents, and had even contended against the Midkemian traders who visited the Empire more and more often, seeking markets for their otherworld goods. They called the game chess, but the rules were the same. Jiro found few in their ranks to challenge him.

The one man he had never defeated sat opposite him, absently scanning through an array of documents piled meticulously around his knees. Chumaka, First Adviser to the Anasati since Jiro's father's time, was a whip-thin, narrow-faced man with a pointed chin and black, impenetrable eyes. He checked the game board in passing, now and again pausing to answer his master's moves. Rather than being irritated by the absentminded fashion in which his First Adviser routinely defeated him, Jiro felt pride that such a facile mind served the Anasati.

Chumaka's gift for anticipating complex politics at times seemed to border on the uncanny. Most of Jiro's father's ascendancy in the Game of the Council could be credited to this adviser's shrewd advice. While Mara of the Acoma had humiliated the Anasati early in her rise to greatness, Chumaka had offered sage counsel that had sheltered family interests from setbacks in the conflict that had followed between the Acoma and the Minwanabi.

Jiro chewed his lip, torn between two moves that offered small gains and another that held promise of long-term strategy. As he debated, his thoughts circled back to the Great Game: the obliteration of House Minwanabi might have proven a cause for celebration, since they had been rivals of the Anasati—save that the victory had been won by the woman Jiro hated foremost among the living. His hostility remained from the moment Lady Mara named her choice of husband, and picked his younger brother, Buntokapi, as her consort over Jiro.

It did not matter that, had his ego not suffered a bruising, Jiro would have been the one to die of the Lady's machinations, instead of Bunto. Enamored though he was of scholarly thought, the last surviving son of the Anasati line stayed blind to logic on this point. He fed his spite by brooding. That the bitch had cold-heartedly plotted the death of his brother was cause for blood vengeance; never mind that Bunto had been despised by his family, and that he had renounced all ties to the Anasati to accept the Lordship of the Acoma. So deep, so icy was Jiro's hatred that he preferred obstinate blindness to recognition that he had inherited his own Ruling Lordship precisely because Mara had spurned him. Over the years his youthful thirst for retribution had darkened into the abiding obsession of a dangerous, cunning rival.

Jiro glared at the shāh board but raised no hand to advance a player. Chumaka noticed this as he riffled through his correspondence. His high brows arched upward. "You're thinking of Mara again."

Jiro looked nettled.

"I have warned you," Chumaka resumed in his grainy, emotionless voice. "Dwelling on your enmity will upset your inner balance and ultimately cost you the game."

The Lord of the Anasati indicated his contempt by selecting the bolder of the two short-range moves.

"Ah." Chumaka had the ill grace to look delighted as he removed his captured minor player. With his left hand still occupied with papers, he immediately advanced his priest.

The Anasati Lord chewed his lip, vexed; why had his First Adviser done that? Enmeshed in an attempt to fathom the logic behind the move, Jiro barely noticed the messenger who hurried into the chamber.

The arrival bowed to his master. Immediately upon receiving the languid wave that allowed him to rise, he passed the sealed packet he carried to Chumaka.

"Your permission, master?" Chumaka murmured.

"The correspondence is coded, is it not?" Jiro said, not wanting the interruption as he pondered his next move. His hand lingered between pieces while Chumaka cleared his throat. Jiro took this for affirmation. "I thought so," he said. "Open your dispatches, then. And may the news in them for once dull your concentration for the game."

Chumaka gave a short bark of laughter. "The more scurrilous the gossip, the keener I will play." He followed Jiro's indecision with an amusement that almost, but not quite, approached contempt. Then he flipped over the pouch and used the one thumbnail he left unbitten for the purpose to slit the tie.

As he thumbed through the papers inside, his brows arched. "This is most unexpected."

The Lord of the Anasati's hand hung in space. He looked up, intrigued by the novelty of his First Adviser's surprise. "What?"

Servant to two generations of Ruling Lords, Chumaka was rarely caught out. He regarded his master, speculation in his eyes. "Pardon, my Lord. I was speaking of this." He drew a paper from the pouch. Then, as his peripheral sight took in the piece under Jiro's poised hand, he added, "Your move is anticipated, master."

Jiro withdrew his hand, caught between irritation and amusement. "Anticipated," he muttered. He lounged back on his cushions to settle his mind. From this changed vantage, the game board showed a different perspective: a trick picked up from his father at an early age.

Chumaka tapped a leathery cheek with the document that had caused the interruption and smiled in his enigmatic way. Typically, he would point out a mistake; but in shāh he would not advise. He would wait for Jiro to pay the consequence of his moves. "This one," he muttered, making a mark upon the parchment with a small quill.

Jiro furiously reviewed strategy. Try as he might, he found no threat. "You're bluffing me." He went on to move the piece in dispute.

Chumaka looked faintly disgusted. "I don't need to bluff." He advanced another piece and said, "Your warlord is now guarded."

Jiro saw the trap his First Adviser had set: its subtlety infuriated. Either the master would surrender the center of the board and be forced to play a defensive game, or he would lose his warlord, the most powerful piece, and exchange position for a weakened offensive capacity. Jiro's forehead creased as he considered several positions ahead. No matter how many combinations he imagined, he discovered no way to win. His only hope was to try for a stalemate.

He moved his remaining priest.

Chumaka by now was engrossed in reading. Still, at his Lord's reply, he glanced down, captured the priest with a soldier, and paradoxically allowed his master to free his warlord.

Warned to caution by the reprieve, Jiro sought to extrapolate as far ahead as possible. Too late, his mind gave him insight: he saw with disappointment that he had been manipulated to the very move his First Adviser had desired. The hoped-for stalemate was now forfeit, with defeat simply a matter of time. Prolonging the match never helped; Chumaka seemed at times to be impervious to human mistakes.

Sighing in frustration, the Lord of the Anasati resigned by turning his emperor over on its side. "Your game, Chumaka." He rubbed his eyes, his head aching from the aftermath of tension.

Chumaka gave him a piercing glance over his letter. "Your play is steadily improving, Lord Jiro."

Jiro let the complement soothe the sting of yet another defeat. "I often wonder how you can play so brilliantly with your mind on other matters, Chumaka."

The First Adviser snapped the document into folds. "Shāh is but one aspect of the prepared mind, my Lord." Holding his master's attention with heavy-lidded eyes, he added, "I hold no trick of strategy but of knowing my opponent. I have observed you all your life, master. From your third move I could sense where you were probing. By your sixth move I had eliminated more than four fifths of the total possibilities in the game."

Jiro let his hands fall limp to his lap. "How?"

"Because you are like most men in the gods' creation, my Lord. You can be depended upon to act within a pattern determined by your individual character." Chumaka tucked the parchment in a capacious pocket of his robe. "You spent a peaceful night. You ate well. You were relaxed. While you were focused, you were not . . . hungry. By the third move I extrapolated that your game would reflect directness, and . . . not boldness and risk." Paying Jiro his undivided attention, he summed up, "The secret is to ferret out the clues that will reveal the thoughts of one's opponent. Learn his motives, know his passions, and you need not wait to see what he does: you can anticipate his next move."

Jiro gave back a humorless smile. "I hope that one day a shāh master may visit who could humble you, Chumaka."

The First Adviser chuckled. "I have been humbled many times, my

Lord. Many times. But you have never seen it.'' His gaze flicked over the disarranged players in satisfied reminiscence. ''Play with those who do not know you as I do, and you will emerge victorious. In truth, you have an enviable gift for strategy. I am not a better shāh player, master.'' The First Adviser selected another paper from his pouch as he finished his rumination. ''But I am a far better student of you than you have ever been of me.''

Jiro felt discomforted that anyone, even a servant as loyal as Chumaka, would have subjected him to so detailed a scrutiny. Then he caught himself short: he was fortunate to have the man as a high officer. Chumaka's job was to act as adviser, confidant, and diplomat. The better he knew his master, the better he would serve the Anasati. To hate him for his supreme skill was a fool's measure, the mistake of a master too vain to admit shortcoming. Jiro chastised himself for selfish, unworthy suspicions and said, ''What has you so engrossed this morning?''

Chumaka shuffled through the pouch, selected several more missives, and pushed the shāh board aside to make space to array the papers around his knees. ''I have been pursuing that lead we had into the Acoma spy network, and keeping watch upon the contacts, as you requested. News has just arrived that I'm attempting to fit in.'' His voice fell to a mutter intelligible only to himself as he reshuffled his piles, then became clearer as he thought aloud: ''I'm not quite yet sure . . .'' He twitched another paper from one pile to the next. ''Forgive the disarray, master, but such visualizations help me keep track of relationships. Too often one is tempted to consider events in a straight line, in a particular order, when actually life is rather . . . chaotic.'' He stroked his chin with thumb and forefinger. ''I have often thought of having a table constructed of sticks, so I might place notes at different heights, to further dramatize interconnections. . . .''

Experience had taught Jiro not to be nettled by his First Adviser's idiosyncrasies. He might grumble over his work, but he seemed to produce the most valuable results at such times. The Anasati spy network that Jiro had spent all the wealth he could spare to expand was providing more useful information each year. Other great houses might employ a spy master to manage such an operation in his own right; yet Chumaka had argued against allowing another to oversee his works. He insisted on firsthand control of those agents he had placed in other houses, guild halls, and trading centers. Even when Tecuma, Jiro's father, had ruled House Anasati, Chumaka had occasionally left the estate to oversee some matter or another in person.

While Jiro showed a young man's impatience at his First Adviser's foibles, he knew when not to interfere. Now, while Chumaka pored over the gleanings of his agents, the Lord of the Anasati noticed that some of the reports on the stacks dated back as much as two years. A few seemed nothing more than the jottings of a grain factor's secretary who used the margins to figure his accounts. "What is this new information?"

Chumaka did not glance up. "Someone's tried to kill Mara."

This was momentous news! Jiro sat up straight, irked that he had not been told at once, and maddened that some other faction, rather than the Anasati, had discommoded the Lady. "How do you know this?"

The wily Chumaka hooked the folded paper out of his robe and extended it toward his master. Jiro snatched the message and read the opening lines. "My nephew Ayaki's dead!" he exclaimed.

The Anasati First Adviser interrupted before his master could launch into a tirade. "Official word will not reach us until tomorrow, my Lord. That gives us today and tonight to weigh the manner in which we shall respond."

Distracted from chastising his officer for withholding information unnecessarily, Jiro diverted to consider the course of thought Chumaka desired: for politically, the Anasati and the Acoma had been bitterest enemies until Mara's marriage to Buntokapi; since Bunto's ritual suicide, her heir Ayaki represented a blood tie between the two houses. Family duty had provided the only reason for suspension of hostilities.

Now the boy was in Turakamu's halls. Jiro felt no personal regret at the news of his nephew's death. He knew anger, that his closest male kin should have been born to the Acoma name; he had long chafed under the treaty that compelled him as Anasati to provide the Acoma with alliance in the cause of that same child's protection.

That constraint was ended at long last. Mara had signally failed in her duty as guardian. She had gotten the boy killed. The Anasati had the public excuse, no, the honorable duty of exacting reprisal for the boy's untimely end.

Jiro could barely keep from reveling in the knowledge that he could at last begin to avenge himself on Mara. He asked, "How did the boy die?"

Chumaka shot his master a look of unveiled rebuke. "Had you read to the end of what you hold, you would know."

Lord Jiro felt moved to assert himself as Ruling Lord. "Why not tell me? Your post is to advise."

The hot black eyes of the First Adviser dropped back to his papers. He did not show any overt irritation over Jiro's correction. If anything, he replied with unctuous complacence. "Ayaki died of a fall from a horse. That's made public. What is not widely known, what has been garnered by our agent near her estates, is that the horse died as well. It fell and crushed the child after being struck by a poisoned dart.''

Jiro's mind pounced on pertinent bits of earlier conversation. ''A tong assassin,'' he surmised, ''whose intended target was Lady Mara.''

Chumaka's expression remained ferociously bland. ''So the paper in your hand spells out clearly.''

Now Lord Jiro inclined his head, half laughing in magnanimous spirits. ''I accept the lesson, First Adviser. Now, rather than your using this news as a whip to instruct me, I would hear what conclusions you have drawn. The son of my enemy was nevertheless my blood kin. This news makes me angry.''

Chumaka gnawed on the thumbnail he did not keep sharpened. His eyes stopped tracking the cipher on the page in his hand as he analyzed his master's statement. Jiro showed no outward emotion, in traditional Tsurani fashion; if he said he was angry, he was to be taken at his word. Honor demanded the servant believe the master. But Jiro was less enraged than excited, Chumaka determined, which did not bode well for Mara. Young yet at ruling, Jiro failed to grasp the longer-range benefits of allowing the alliance between Anasati and Acoma to dissolve into a state of laissez-faire.

The silence as his adviser pondered rasped at Jiro's nerves. ''Who?'' he demanded peevishly. ''Which of Mara's enemies desires her death? We could make ourselves an ally out of this, if we are bold.''

Chumaka sat back and indulged in a deep sigh. Behind his pose of long-suffering patience, he was intrigued by the unexpected turn events had taken, Jiro saw. The Anasati First Adviser was as enamored of Tsurani politics as a child craving sweets.

''I can conceive of several possibilities,'' Chumaka allowed. ''Yet those houses with the courage to act lack the means, and those with the means lack courage. To seek the death of a Servant of the Empire is . . . unprecedented.'' He chewed his thin lower lip, then waved one of the servants over to stack the documents into piles to be gathered up and conveyed to his private quarters. To Jiro's impatience, he said at last, ''I should venture a guess that Mara was attacked by the Hamoi Tong.''

Jiro relinquished the note to the servant with a sneer. ''Of course the tong. But who paid the death price?''

Chumaka arose. ''No one. That's what makes this so elegant. I think the tong acts for its own reasons.''

Jiro's brows rose in surprise. ''But why? What has the tong to gain by killing Mara?''

A runner servant appeared at the screen that led into the main estate house. He bowed, but before he could speak, Chumaka second-guessed the reason behind his errand. "Master, the court is assembled."

Jiro waved the servant off as he rose from his cushions. As master and First Adviser fell into step toward the long hall in which the Lord of the Anasati conducted business, Jiro surmised aloud, "We know that Tasaio of the Minwanabi paid the Hamoi Tong to kill Mara. Do you think he also paid them to attempt vengeance upon her should he fall?"

"Possibly." Chumaka counted points on his fingers, a habit he had when ordering his thoughts. "Minwanabi revenge might explain why, seemingly from nowhere, the tong chose to act after months of quiet."

Pausing in the shadow of the corridor that accessed the double doors of the great hall, Jiro said, "If the tong acts on behalf of some pledge made to Tasaio before his death, will it try again?"

Chumaka shrugged, his stooped shoulders rising like tent poles under his turquoise silk robe. "Who can say? Only the Obajan of the Hamoi would know; he alone has access to the records that name deaths bought and paid for. If the tong has vowed Mara's death . . . it will persevere. If it merely agreed to make an attempt on her life, it has fulfilled its obligation." He gestured in rueful admiration. "The Good Servant has her luck from the gods, some might argue. For anyone else, an agreement to send an assassin is a virtual guarantee of success. Others have avoided the tong, once, even twice before; but the Lady Mara has survived five assassins that I know of. Her son was not so lucky."

Jiro moved on with a step that snapped on the tiles. His nostrils flared, and he barely saw the two servants who sprang from their posts to open the audience hall doors for him. Striding past their abject bows, Jiro sniffed. Since getting his First Adviser to act with proper subservience was a waste of time, he sniffed again. "Well, it's a pity the assassin missed her. Still, we can seize advantage: the death of her son will cause much confusion in her household."

Delicately, Chumaka cleared his throat. "Trouble will transfer to us, master."

Jiro stopped in his tracks. His sandals squeaked as he pivoted to face his First Adviser. "Don't you mean trouble for the Acoma? They have lost our alliance. No, they have spit on it by allowing Ayaki to come to harm."

Chumaka stepped closer to his Lord, so the cluster of factors who awaited Jiro's audience at the far end of the hall might not overhear. "Speak gently," he admonished. "Unless Mara finds convincing proof that it is Tasaio of the Minwanabi's hand reaching from the halls of the dead in this matter, it is logical for her to place blame upon us." Acerbically he added, "You took pains when Lord Tecuma, your father, died to make your hostilities toward her house plain."

Jiro jerked up his chin. "Perhaps."

Chumaka did not press chastisement. Caught up again in his innate fascination for the game, he said, "Her network is the best I've seen. I have a theory: given her adoption of the entire Minwanabi household—"

Jiro's cheeks flushed. "Another example of her blasphemous behavior and contempt for tradition!"

Chumaka held up a placating hand. There were times when Jiro's thinking became clouded; having lost his mother to a fever at the tender age of five, as a boy he had clung irrationally to routine, to tradition, as if adherence to order could ward off the inconsistencies of life. Always he had tended to wall off his grief behind logic or unswerving devotion to the ideal of the Tsurani noble. Chumaka did not like to encourage what he considered a weakening flaw in his Lord. The ramifications of allowing such traits to become policy were too confining for his liking. The perils, in fact, were paramount; in a bold move of his own, Chumaka had taken in more than two hundred soldiers formerly sworn to Minwanabi service. These were disaffected men whose hatred of Mara would last to their dying breath. Chumaka had not housed such for his own entertainment; he was not a disloyal man. He had secretly accommodated the warriors in a distant, secret barracks. Tactful inquiry had shown Jiro to be adamant in his refusal to consider swearing them to Anasati service; ancient custom held that such men were anathema, without honor and to be shunned lest the displeasure of the gods that had seen the unfortunate house fall be visited upon their benefactor. Yet Chumaka had refrained from sending these men away. He had no hope of a change in attitude from his master; but a tool was a tool, and these former Minwanabi might someday be useful, if the Ruling Lord of the Anasati could not be weaned from his puerile hatred of Mara.

If the two Houses were going to be enemies, Chumaka saw such warriors as an advantage to be held in trust for the day their service might be needed. Mara had proven herself to be clever. She had ruined one house far larger than her own. Guile would be needed to match guile, and Chumaka was never a man to waste an opportunity.

Indeed, he saw his secret as a loyal act, and what Jiro did not know could not be forbidden.

The warriors were not all. Chumaka had to restrain himself from the desire to rub his thin hands together in anticipation. He had spies as well. Already a few factors formerly in the Minwanabi employ were now working on behalf of the Anasati and not the Acoma. Chumaka gained the same pleasure in co-opting these people to his master's service that he might in isolating an opponent's fortress or priest upon the shāh board. He knew that eventually the Anasati would benefit. Then his master must see the wisdom of some of Mara's choices.

And so the Anasati First Adviser smiled, and said nothing; to a fine point, he knew just how far he could go in contradicting Jiro. Pressing his Lord toward his meeting with the factors, he said quietly, "Master, Mara may have flouted tradition by taking on responsibility for her vanquished enemy's servants, but rather than merely removing her greatest enemy, she has gained immeasurable resources. Her strength has grown. From being a dangerous player in the Game of the Council, at one stroke Mara has become the single most powerful Ruling Lord or Lady in the history of the Empire. The Acoma forces, alone, now number more than ten thousand swords; they surpass several smaller clans. And Clan Hadama and its allies together rival the Emperor's Imperial Whites!" Chumaka turned reflective as he added, "She could rule by fiat, I think, if she had the ambition. The Light of Heaven is certainly not of a mind to oppose her wishes."

Disliking to be reminded of the Lady's swift ascendance, Jiro became the more nettled. "Never mind. What is this theory?"

Chumaka raised up one finger. "We know Tasaio of the Minwanabi employed the Hamoi Tong. The tong continues to pursue Mara's death." Counting on a second finger, he listed, "These facts may or may not be related. Incomo, Tasaio's former First Adviser, was effective in discovering some or all of the Acoma agents who had infiltrated the Minwanabi household. There was a disruption after that, and a mystery remains: our own network reported that someone killed every Acoma agent between the Minwanabi great house and the city of Sulan-Qu."

Jiro gave an offhand wave. "So Tasaio had all her agents killed as far as he could trace her network."

Chumaka's smile became predatory. "What if he didn't?" He flicked up a third finger. "Here is another fact: the Hamoi Tong killed those servants inside the Minwanabi household who were Acoma agents."

The Lord's boredom intensified. "Tasaio ordered the tong—"

"No!" Chumaka interrupted, verging on disrespect. Swiftly he amended his manners by turning his outburst into prelude for instruction. "Why should Tasaio hire the tong to kill his own staff? Why pay death price for lives that could be taken by an order to the Minwanabi guards?"

Jiro looked rueful. "I was thinking carelessly." His eyes shifted for-

ward to where the factors were fidgeting at the delay, as Lord and adviser
continued to equivocate just inside the doorway.

Chumaka ignored their discomfort. They were underlings, after all,
and it was their place to wait upon their Lord. "Because there is no
logical reason, my master. However, we can surmise: if I were the Lady,
and I wished to insult both the tong and Tasaio, what better way than to
order the tong, under false colors, to kill her spies?"

Jiro's expression quickened. He could follow Chumaka's reasoning on
his own, now he had been clued in to the first step. "You think the
Hamoi Tong may have cause to declare blood debt toward Mara?"

Chumaka's answer was a toothy smile.

Jiro resumed walking. His steps echoed across the vast hall, with its
paper screens drawn closed on both sides, and its roof beams hung with
dusty war relics and a venerable collection of captured enemy banners.
These artifacts reminded of a time when the Anasati were at the forefront
of historical battles. Theirs was an ancient tradition of honor. They would
rise as high again, Jiro vowed; no, higher yet. For Mara's defeat would be
his to arrange, a victory that would resound throughout the Empire.

He alone would prove that Mara had incurred the gods' displeasure in
granting reprieve to conquered enemy servants. Singlehandedly, he would
exact vengeance for her flouting of the old ways. She would look into his
eyes as she died, and know: she had made her worst mistake on the day
she had chosen Buntokapi for her husband. Unlike the grand Minwanabi
great hall that Mara had inherited, the Anasati great hall was as reassuring
in its traditional design as the most time-honored ritual in the temple.
Jiro luxuriated in this; no different from the halls of a hundred other
Ruling Lords, this chamber was nevertheless unique; it was Anasati.
Along both sides of a center aisle knelt petitioners and Anasati retainers.
Omelo, his Force Commander, stood at attention to one side of the dais
upon which Jiro conducted the business of his court. Arrayed behind him
were the other officers and advisers of the household.

Jiro mounted his dais, knelt on the Lord's cushions, then settled back
on his heels as he adjusted his formal robe. Before he signaled his hadonra
to begin the day's council, he said to his First Adviser, "Find out for
certain if the tong pursues Mara on its own. I would know, so we can
make better plans when this news of Ayaki's death becomes official."

Chumaka clapped his hands, and a servant came to his shoulder. "Have
two runners in my quarters by the time I reach them." While the servant
bowed and hastened away, he made his own obeisance to the master.
"Lord, I shall begin at once. I have some new sources that may provide us
with better information." Then, seeing the hardened glint in Lord Jiro's

eyes, Chumaka touched his master's sleeve. "We must show restraint until Mara's messenger reaches us with formal announcement of Ayaki's death. Speak now, and your staff will gossip. We would ill be served by giving our enemy proof that we have spies in sensitive places."

Jiro snapped away from Chumaka's touch. "I understand, but do not ask me to be complacent! All in Anasati service will mourn. Ayaki of the Acoma, my nephew, has been slain, and every man of ours who is not a slave will wear a red band upon his arm in token of our loss. When this day's business is finished, you will ready an honor guard for travel to Sulan-Qu."

Chumaka bit back annoyance. "We attend the boy's funeral?"

Jiro bared his teeth. "He was my nephew. To stay home when his ashes are honored would be to admit responsibility or cowardice, and we are guilty of neither. He may have been the son of my enemy, and I may now destroy his mother without constraint, but he shares Anasati blood! He deserves the respect to which any grandson of Tecuma of the Anasati is entitled. We shall carry a family relic to be burned with him." Jiro's eyes flashed as he finished, "Tradition demands our presence!"

Chumaka kept his reservations about this decision to himself as he bowed in acknowledgment of his master's wishes. While it was a First Adviser's place to shepherd his Lord through decisions that affected house policy, Chumaka was wont to chafe at the more mundane responsibilities of his office. The Game of the Council had changed dramatically since Mara of the Acoma first entered the arena; yet it was still the game, and nothing in life captured the adviser's fascination like the puzzle of Tsurani politics. Taut as a coursing hound, he rose up in excitement for the chase.

Almost happy despite the prospect of unfortunate developments on the horizon, the First Adviser left the great hall, muttering over the lists of instructions he would need to dispatch with his runners. Substantial bribes would be necessary to pry loose the information he desired, but if the gathered bits of intelligence could prove his morning's theory, the gains would outweigh the cost. As Chumaka paused for the servants to open the door to let him out, his lips reflected an unholy smile.

Years had passed since he had tested his wits against a worthy opponent! Lady Mara was going to afford him much amusement if Lord Jiro's obsession could not be cooled, and the Anasati marked her house for ruin.

Mara tossed fitfully in sleep. Her sounds of distress tore at Hokanu's heart, and he wished to do something, to touch her, to speak soft words, to ease her agony. But she had slept very little since Ayaki's death. Even the restlessness of nightmares offered some release. To waken her was to force her to awareness of her loss, and to the crushing necessity of bearing up under the strain.

Hokanu sighed and regarded the patterns that moonlight cast through the screens. The shadows in the corners seemed to loom darker than ever before; not even the presence of doubled sentries at each door and window could recover the lost sense of peace. The heir to the Shinzawai and husband to the Servant of the Empire now found himself a man alone, with nothing but his wits and his love for a troubled woman. The predawn air was cool, unusual for lands in Szetac Province, perhaps owing to the proximity of the house to the lake. Hokanu arose and slipped on the light robe he had cast off the night before. He tied the sash then took a stance overlooking the sleeping mat with his arms crossed tightly against his chest.

He kept vigil while Mara tossed in the bedclothes, her hair like a patch of lingering night in the slowly brightening air. The coppery moonlight faded, washed out by early gray. The screen that opened upon the private terrace had turned slowly from black to pearl.

Hokanu restrained an urge to pace. Mara had woken during the night, sobbing in his arms and crying Ayaki's name. He had held her close, but his warmth would bring her no comfort. Hokanu's jaw tightened at the memory. A foe he would willingly face in battle, but this sorrow . . . a child dead as his potential had barely begun to unfold . . . There was no remedy under sky that a husband could offer. Only time would dull the ache.

Hokanu was not a man who cursed. Controlled and taut as the pitched string of a harplike treble tiral, he allowed himself no indulgence that might in any way disturb his wife. Silently, dangerously graceful, he slid aside the door just enough to pass through. The day was too fair, he thought as he regarded the pale green sky. There should have been storms, strong winds, even lightning and rain; nature herself should rail at the earth on the day of Ayaki's funeral.

Across the hill, in the hollow before the lakeshore, the final preparations were being carried out. The stacked wood of the pyre arose in a ziggurat. Jican had made free with Acoma wealth, on Hokanu's order, and made sure that only aromatic woods were purchased. The stink of singed flesh and hair would not offend the mourners or the boy's mother. Hokanu's mouth thinned. There would be no privacy for Mara on this most sad occasion. She had risen too high, and her son's funeral would be a state rite. Ruling Lords would converge from all parts of the Empire to pay their respects—or to further their intrigues. The Game of the Council did not pause for grief, or joy, or any calamity of nature. Like rot unseen under painted wood, the circumstances that had created Ayaki's death would repeat themselves again and again.

A dust cloud arose on the northern skyline; guests already arriving, Hokanu surmised. He glanced again at his wife, reassured that her dreams had quieted. He stepped quietly to the door, spoke to the boy runner, and arranged for the Lady's maids to be with her when she wakened. Then he gave in to his restlessness and strode out onto the terrace.

The estate was beginning to stir. Jican could be seen crossing at a half run between the kitchen wing and the servants' quarters, where laundry girls already hurried between guest chambers with baskets of fresh linens balanced on their heads. Prepared for state visitors, warriors in dress armor marched to relieve the night watch. Yet, amid the general air of purpose, two figures walked by the lake, keeping pace with each other, but apparently on no logical errand beyond a morning stroll. Suspicion gave Hokanu pause, until he looked closer and identified the pair. Then curiosity drew him across the terrace and he descended the stairs that gave access to the grounds below.

Following quietly between the rows of akasi flowers, Hokanu confirmed his first impression: Incomo and Irrilandi moved ahead of him at their unhurried pace, seemingly lost in thought. The former First Adviser and the former Force Commander to Tasaio of the Minwanabi did not wander aimlessly.

Intrigued by what these two enemies turned loyal servants might be doing out so early on this sad day, Hokanu slipped silently after.

The pair reached the edge of the lake, and the reed-frail adviser and leathery, battle-muscled warrior both knelt upon a little rise. Past a notch between the scrolled eaves of the great house and the hill it fronted, the first pink clouds drifted in the sky, their undersides heating to orange as the rays of a sun not yet visible gilded their edges.

Both men sat as if praying. Hokanu noiselessly drew nearer. For several minutes the Lord and the two servants abided in frozen tableau. Then daybreak pierced the gloom, and a sunbeam fanned across the sky, catching in a crystalline formation at the peak of the rise. There came a flash that dazzled. Warmth and first light bathed the secluded quiet, and the dew sparkled, touched to gemlike brilliance. Then Irrilandi and Incomo bowed until their heads touched the earth, repeating faint words that Hokanu could not make out.

For that brief instant, the son of the Shinzawai was nearly blinded by the unexpected flash; then it was gone as the angle of the rising sun changed.

The two men completed their strange rite and stood. The war-wary eyes of Irrilandi were first to pick out a discrepancy in the morning quiet. He saw the Lord who waited nearby, and bowed. "Master Hokanu," he said. Caught short, Incomo repeated the gesture.

Hokanu motioned both servants back toward the house. "I could not sleep," he said ruefully. "I observed you walking and came to see what brought you here."

Irrilandi gave a Tsurani shrug. "Each day before sunrise we give thanks."

Hokanu's silence begged for a further explanation, though he did not look at either man but studied his bare feet as he stepped through dew-damp grass.

Incomo cleared his throat in what might have been embarrassment. "We come here each day to witness the day's beginning. And to give thanks, since the Good Servant came to us." He regarded the great house, with its high, peaked gables, stone pillars, and the screen lintels tied now with red bunting in respect for Turakamu, the Red God, who would welcome Ayaki's spirit into his keeping during the day's rites. Incomo elaborated for Hokanu's benefit. "When our Lady brought about Tasaio's ruin, we expected death or slavery. Instead we were given the gift of days: another chance to serve and gain honor. So each sunrise we offer a prayer of thanks for this reprieve, and for the Good Servant."

Hokanu nodded, unsurprised by the devotion of these high officers. As Servant of the Empire, Mara was beloved by the masses. Her own staff served her with an affection that bordered upon awe. Indeed, she would need such support for her house to recover from this loss. A ruler disliked by his people might expect a blow of this magnitude to cause hesitation in his staff, as servants from the highest positions down to the meanest slave fretted over whether heaven had withdrawn the luck of the house. Even without divine disapproval, mortal enemies would seize upon opportunity and strike where the ranks were most confused. And so the superstition fed upon the results, since a house weakened would suffer setbacks, and so seem to be in the disfavor of the gods.

Hokanu felt irritation. Too many events in this Empire twisted in upon themselves, until centuries of unbending customs led their society toward stagnation and entropy.

This inbred cycle he and Mara and Ichindar, the Emperor of the Nations, had dedicated themselves to overturn.

Ayaki's untimely end was more than sorrow and grief; it could become a major setback and be turned into a rallying cry for all those Ruling Lords who were disgruntled by recent changes. If the Acoma showed any sign of irresolution, there would be strife, and at the heart of the faction that had begun to form in rigid adherence to old traditions, the Anasati voice would be loudest.

The funeral guests would not be here to observe the ashes of the departed as they spiraled in their smoky ascent to heaven; no: they would be watching one another like starving dogs, and Lady Mara would be subjected to the most thorough scrutiny of all. Weighed down by dread, for he knew his Lady was too lost in her pain to handle peripheral matters, Hokanu pushed open the ornamental gate and started across the garden. He forgot the two men who walked with him until Incomo said, "First Adviser Saric has all in readiness, master. Entertainments have been arranged to divert the guests, and the honor guards of all but the greatest Ruling Lords will be quartered in the garrison across the lake. The pyre has been soaked in oils, and all has been done to keep the ceremony as brief as possible."

Hokanu found no reassurance in Incomo's words; that the adviser felt need to stress such points bespoke a sharing of concern. The game would go on, whether or not Lady Mara could rally and cope.

"We shall not stint in our honors to the departed young master," added Irrilandi, "but it is my suggestion that you stay by your Lady's side, and be prepared to interpret her instructions."

Politely, tactfully, the high officers of House Acoma acknowledged that their mistress remained incapacitated. Hokanu felt a surge of gratitude to these men, who were quietly and staunchly prepared to cover for her lapse. He tried to reassure them that House Acoma would not flounder with the currents of misfortune like some rudderless ship. "I shall be with my Lady. She is touched by your devotion and would have me say that you should not hesitate to approach if you have any difficulties or concerns."

A knowing glance passed between master and servants. Then Irrilandi bowed. "More than a thousand soldiers have made prayers to Turakamu to take them in the young master's place."

Hokanu nodded in respect. Those soldiers would wear arms throughout the funeral ceremony in token of their vow, a strong deterrent to any visiting Lord who might contemplate causing trouble, in breach of Acoma hospitality.

The number was a great honor to Ayaki; the men's dedication also demonstrated that barracks rumor recognized the political ramifications of what was far more than a personal tragedy. The Lords who came today would gather and circle like jaguna, the eaters of dead meat, to see what prizes could be snatched from the teeth of misfortune.

Hokanu received the departing bows of the two officers, then looked over his shoulder at the lake, where barges were now heading rapidly toward the docks. Banners flew from their poles, and the chant of the oarsmen carried across the water. Very shortly now the quiet estate would become a political arena. Hokanu considered the great stone house that had been the hall of the Minwanabi for centuries. The place had been designed as a fortress, but today even enemies must be invited inside. The priests of Chochocan, the Good God, had blessed the estate, and Mara had seen the Minwanabi natami placed in a dedicated glade, so that a once great house should be remembered. Yet despite these measures and the assurances of the priests that the Good Servant's acts had earned divine favor, Hokanu swallowed back a feeling of dread. The depths of the eaves seemed to hold shadows in which the spirits of enemies peered out in silent laughter at Mara's grief.

Hokanu wished for a moment he had overridden her bold choice and opted to adhere to the customs of conquest that would have seen this house torn down, each stone carried to the lake and thrown into the deep, each timber and field burned, and the soil of all these lush acres sown with salt. Unlucky ground should nurture nothing, according to the ways adhered to over the centuries, that the cycle of cursed events might be broken for eternity. Despite the beauty of this estate, and the near-impregnable location of its grounds and holdings, Hokanu repressed the premonition that he might be doomed never to find happiness with Mara as long as they lived under this roof.

But this was an ill time to brood, with the state guests already arriving. The consort to the Servant of the Empire stiffened his shoulders, prepared for the coming ordeal. Mara must show the proper Tsurani bearing in the face of her overwhelming grief. The death of her father and brother, who were warriors, had been one thing; the loss of her own child, far worse. Hokanu intuitively sensed that this was the ugliest fate that could have befallen the woman he loved more than life. For her he must be strong today, armor against public dishonor, for while he was still the dedicated heir of the Shinzawai, he embraced Acoma honor as if it were his own.

Secure in his resolve, he returned to the terrace outside his Lady's sleeping quarters. As the screens were not yet opened, he knew that the servants had allowed her undisturbed rest. He slid the panel soundlessly in its track and entered. He did not speak but let the gentle warmth of daylight fall upon his wife's cheek.

Mara stirred. Her hands closed in the twisted sheets, and her eyes fluttered open. She gasped and pushed herself up. Her eyes swept the room in terror until Hokanu knelt and captured her in his embrace.

Her complexion looked as if she had not slept at all. "Is it time?"

Hokanu stroked her shoulder, as servants who had waited outside hurried in at the sound of their mistress's voice. He said, "The day begins."

Gently he helped raise his Lady to her feet. When he had steadied her, he backed away and gestured for the servants to perform their offices. Mara stood with a bleak expression as her maids bustled to arrange her bath and her dress. Hokanu endured the sight of her lackluster manner without showing the anger in his heart. If Jiro of the Anasati was responsible for causing this pain to his Lady, the heir to the Shinzawai vowed to see the man suffer. Then, recalled to his own state of undress by the admiring stare of one of Mara's handmaids, he put aside thoughts of revenge. He clapped for his own servants, and suffered their fussing in silence as they arrayed him in the formal robes required for Ayaki's funeral.

The throng mantled the hills surrounding the Acoma estate house, clothed in the colors of a thousand houses, with red sashes, red ties, or red ribbons worn in homage to the Red God, brother to Sibi, who was Death, and lord of all lives. The color also symbolized the heart's blood of the boy that no longer flowed to clothe the spirit. Six thousand soldiers stood in columns flanking the hollow where the bier awaited. In front, in polished green armor, stood the Acoma warriors who had dedicated their lives; behind these, the ranks in the blue of Mara's Shinzawai consort; and after them, the gold-edged white of the Imperial Guard sent by Ichindar to carry the Emperor's condolences. Next came Kamatsu of the Shinzawai, Hokanu's father, and then the families who made up the Hadama Clan, all who had blood ties to the dead boy. After them, in a great, sprawling crowd, stood the houses who had come to pay their respects or to indulge in the next round of the Great Game.

The warriors were statue-still, heads bowed, shields held with edges resting upon the ground. Before each lay a sword, point facing the bier, empty scabbard placed crosswise beneath. Behind the soldiers, up the hillside, members of the household kept a respectful distance from the line of march, for the great of the Empire had come to bid farewell to a boy.

Trumpets blew to begin the procession. In the shade of the outer portico where the Acoma advisers and officers gathered to march, Mara fought the weakness in her knees. She felt Hokanu's grip on her elbow, but the meaning of the sensation did not register. The eyes half-hidden behind her red veil of mourning were locked on the litter that held her motionless son. His body was encased in fine armor; his white hands clasped the grip of a rare metal sword. The hand that had been crushed in the fall was decently clothed in a gauntlet; the mashed chest, hidden behind a breastplate and shield emblazoned with a shatra bird in rare gold leaf.

To the eye, he seemed a sleeping warrior, prepared at a call to arise and fight in the glory and honor of his youth.

Mara felt her throat close. No prior event, not placing the mementos of her father and brother in the family's glade to mourn them, not enduring her first husband's brutality, not losing the first man with whom she had discovered the passion of love, not the death of her beloved foster mother—nothing compared to this moment for sheer horror.

She could not believe, even now, far less accept the finality of her firstborn's death. A child whose life had made hers endurable, through her unhappy first marriage. An infant whose carefree laughter had weaned her from despair, when she had faced enemies greater than the means of her house to defend. Ayaki had given her the courage to go on. Out of stubbornness, and a fierce desire to see him live to carry on the Acoma name, Mara had accomplished the impossible.

All would be consigned to ashes, this day. This accursed day, when a boy who should have outlived his mother would become a pillar of smoke to assault the nostrils of heaven.

A step behind Mara, Justin fretfully asked to be carried. His nurse cajoled him to stand, hushing his noise. His mother seemed deaf to his distress, locked as she was in dark thoughts. She moved like a puppet to Hokanu's guidance as the retinue prepared to start forward.

Drums beat. The tattoo thrummed on the air. An acolyte clad in red thrust a dyed ke-reed into the Lady's unfeeling hands; Hokanu's fingers clasped hers, raising the reed with her lest she drop the religious symbol.

The procession moved. Hokanu gathered her into the crook of his arm and steadied her into the slow march. To honor her loss, he had forsaken the blue armor of the Shinzawai for the green of the Acoma and an officer's helm. Vaguely Mara knew he grieved, and distantly she sensed the sorrow of the others—the hadonra, who had so often shouted at the boy for spilling ink in the scriptorium; the nurses and teachers, who had all borne bruises from his tantrums; the advisers, who had sometimes wished for a warrior's sword to knock sense into the boy's mischievous head by whacking the flat on his backside. Servants and maids and even slaves had appreciated Ayaki's quick spirit.

But they were as shadows, and their words of consolation just noise. Nothing anyone said or did seemed to penetrate the desolation that surrounded the Lady of the Acoma.

Mara felt Hokanu's hand gently upon her arm, guiding her down the low stairs. Here waited the first of the state delegations: Ichindar's, clad in blinding white and gold. Mara bent her head as the regal contingent bowed to her; she stayed silent behind her veils as Hokanu murmured the appropriate words.

She was moved on, past Lord Hoppara of the Xacatecas, so long a staunch ally; today she presented to him the manner she would show a stranger, and only Hokanu heard the young man's graceful expression of understanding. At his side, elegant as always, the dowager Lady of the Xacatecas regarded the Good Servant with something more than sympathy.

As Hokanu made his bow to her, Lady Isashani lingeringly caught his hand. "Keep your Lady close," she warned while she outwardly maintained the appearance of offering a personal condolence. "She is a spirit still in shock. Very likely she will not recognize the import of her actions for some days yet. There are enemies here who would provoke her to gain advantage."

Hokanu's politeness took on a grim edge as he thanked Lord Hoppara's mother for her precaution.

These nuances passed Mara by, as well as the skill with which Hokanu turned aside the veiled insults of the Omechan. She made her bows at her Lord's cue, and did not care as she roused whispers in her wake: that she had shown more obeisance than necessary to Lord Frasai of the Tonmargu; that the Lord of the Inrodaka noticed that her movements lacked her characteristic fire and grace.

She had no focus in life beyond the small, fragile form that lay in final rest upon the litter.

Plodding steps followed in time to the thud of muffled drums. The sun climbed overhead as the procession wound into the hollow where the pyre had been prepared. Hokanu murmured polite words to the last and least of the Ruling Lords who merited personal recognition. Between the litter and the pyre waited one last contingent, robed in unadorned black.

Touched by awe, Hokanu forced his next step, his hand tightening upon Mara. If she realized she confronted five Great Ones, magicians of the Assembly, she gave no sign. That their kind was above the law and that they had seen fit to send a delegation to this event failed to give her pause. Hokanu was the one to ponder the ramifications, and to connect that of late the Black Robes seemed to have taken a keener interest than usual in the turnings of politics. Mara bowed to the Great Ones as she had to any other Lord, unmindful of the sympathy offered by the plump Hochopepa, whom she had met at the occasion of Tasaio's ritual suicide. The always awkward moment when Hokanu faced his true father was lost on her. The icy regard of the red-haired magician who stood behind the more taciturn Shimone did not faze her. Whether hostile or benign, the magicians' words could not pierce through her apathy. No life their powers could threaten meant more than the one Turakamu and the Game of the Council had already seen fit to take.

Mara entered the ritual circle where the bier lay. She watched with stony eyes as her Force Commander lifted the too still form of her boy and laid him tenderly on the wood that would be his final bed. His hands straightened sword and helm and shield, and he stepped back, all his rakishness absent.

Mara felt Hokanu's gentle prod. Numbly she stepped forward as around her the drums boomed and stilled. She lowered the ke-reed across Ayaki's body, but it was Hokanu's voice that raised in the traditional cry: "We are gathered to commemorate the life of Ayaki, son of Buntokapi, grandson of Tecuma and Sezu!"

The line was too short, Mara sensed, a vague frown on her face. Where were the lists of life deeds, for this her firstborn son?

An awkward stillness developed, until Lujan moved at a desperate glance from Hokanu and nudged her around to face the east.

The priest of Chochocan approached, robed in the white that symbolized life. He shed his mantle and danced, naked as at birth, in celebration of childhood.

Mara did not see his gyrations; she felt no expiation for the guilt of knowing her laxity had caused disaster. As the dancer bowed to earth before the bier, she faced west when prompted, and stood, dull-eyed, as the whistles of Turakamu's followers split the air, as the priest of the Red God began his dance for Ayaki's safe passage to the halls of the Red God. He had never needed to represent a barbarian beast before, and his idea of how a horse might move had been almost laughable had it not ended in the fall to earth that had crushed so much young promise.

Mara's eyes stayed dry. Her heart felt hardened to a kernel incapable of being renewed. She did not bow her head in prayer as the priests stepped forward and slashed the red cord that bound Ayaki's hands, freeing his spirit for rebirth. She did not weep, or beg the gods' favor, as the white-plumed tirik bird was released as symbol of the renewal of rebirth.

The priest of Turakamu intoned his prayer for Ayaki. "In the end, all men come before my god. The Death God is a kind Lord, for he ends suffering and pain. He judges those who come to him and rewards the righteous." With a broad wave of his hand and a nod of his skull mask, the priest added, "He understands the living and knows of pain and grief." The red wand pointed to the armored boy on the pyre. "Ayaki of the Acoma was a good son, firmly upon the path that his parents would have wished for him. We can only accept that Turakamu judged him worthy and called him so that he might be returned to us, with an even greater fate."

Mara clenched her teeth to keep from crying.

What prayer was there to be said that would not be tainted with rage, and what rebirth beyond being son of the Light of Heaven himself could await that was more honorable than heirship of the Acoma? As Mara shivered in pent fury, Hokanu's arms closed around her. He murmured something she did not hear as the torches were lifted from their brackets around the circle and the aromatic wood was set alight. A cold band twisted itself around her heart. She watched the red-yellow flames lick upward, her thoughts very far from the present.

As the priest of Juran the Just approached to give her blessing, only Hokanu's surreptitious shake prevented her from screaming curses at him, demanding to know what sort of justice existed in a world where little boys died before their mother's eyes.

The flames crackled skyward, then sheeted over the pyre with a roar of disturbed air. The treated wood spared the sight of the boy's body twisting and blackening in its embrace. Yet Mara looked upon the sight with every fiber of her body braced in horror. Her imagination depicted what lay at the heart of a brightness too dazzling for sight; her mind supplied the screams the boy had never uttered.

"Ayaki," she whispered. Hokanu's hold upon her tightened with enough force to recall her momentarily to propriety: to the stiff-faced mask that as Servant of the Empire she was expected to show in public grief. But the effort of holding her features immobile was enough to cause her to tremble.

For long minutes the crackle of flames vied with the voices of the priests who chanted their various prayers. Mara fought to control her breathing, to stave off the monstrous reality of her dead child vanishing into a roil of smoke.

For the death rite of one of lesser station, this would be time for the guests to file away, leaving those closest to the departed to a time of private mourning. But with the passing of the great, such courtesies were forborne. Mara was allowed no reprieve. At the forefront of the public eye she remained, while the acolytes of Turakamu threw consecrated oil upon the flames. Waves of heat rolled off the pyre, reddening Mara's skin. If she shed any tears, they dried upon her cheeks in the face of that cruel furnace. Above writhing curtains of flame, the thick black smoke coiled skyward to draw notice from heaven that a spirit of high honor had departed.

The sun added to the blaze, and Mara felt sick and dizzy. Hokanu turned his body to shade her as he could. He dared not glance at her too often in concern, for fear of betraying her weakness, while the time dragged by as torture. Nearly an hour passed before the flame subsided; then more prayers and more chanting followed as the wood coals were spread to cool. Mara all but swayed on her feet when the priest of Turakamu intoned, "The body is no more. The spirit has flown. He who was Ayaki of the Acoma is now here," he said, touching his heart, "here"—he touched his head—"and in Turakamu's halls."

The acolytes braved the smoking embers as they picked their way to the heart of the mound of decimated fuel. One used a square of thick leather to drag out the warped blade of Ayaki's sword, quickly passing the bundle to another who waited to quench the hot metal in wet rags. Steam rose to mingle with the smoke. Mara endured with deadened eyes as the priest of Turakamu employed an ornate scoop to fill the waiting urn with ashes. More wood than boy, the remains would become the symbol of the body's interment in the glade of his ancestors. For the Tsurani believed that while the true soul traveled to the halls of the Red God, a small part of the spirit, the shade, would rest alongside its ancestors within the stone that was the natami of the house. The essence of the child would thus return in another life, while that which made him Acoma would remain to watch over his family.

Hokanu steadied his wife as two acolytes arrived before her. One offered the sword blade, which Mara touched. Then Hokanu took the twisted length of metal while the other acolyte surrendered the urn. Mara accepted the ashes of her son in trembling hands. Her eyes did not acknowledge what she held but remained fixed upon the scattered, charred wood that remained in the circle.

Hokanu touched her arm lightly and they turned as one. The drums boomed out as the procession veered around and resumed its march toward the Acoma contemplation glade. No impression of the walk registered upon Mara beyond the stony cold of the urn in her hands, warmed at the base by the ashes inside. She set one foot before the other, barely aware of her arrival at the scrolled gateposts that marked the glade entrance.

The servants and Hokanu paused in deference to her; for the only one not of Acoma blood who was permitted to step through the arch and make his way along the stone path that led within was the gardener whose life had been dedicated to tend the glade. Here even her husband, who was still a Shinzawai, could not enter, upon pain of death. To allow any stranger admittance was to offer insult to the shades of Acoma ancestors, and to bring lasting disharmony to the peace that abided in the natami.

Mara stepped away from Hokanu's embrace. She did not hear the murmur of the nobles who watched, pitying or predatory, until she had moved beyond sight behind the hedges. Once before, upon her family's old estate, she had undertaken the terrible task of consecrating the shades of close family to the natami.

The size of this garden disoriented her. She paused, the urn clutched to her breast in stunned incomprehension. This was not the familiar glade of her childhood, where she had gone as a tiny girl to address the shade of her mother; this was not the known path where she had narrowly escaped death at the hands of a tong assassin while mourning her father and brother. This place was alien, vast, a wide park, in which several streams meandered. For a second a shadow crossed her heart as she wondered whether this garden that had been home to Minwanabi shades for so many centuries might reject the aspect of her son.

Again in her memory she saw the horse fall, a blackness like evil stamping out innocent life. Feeling lost, she gulped a breath. She chose a path at random, only vaguely recalling that all of them led to the same site where the ancient rock, the natami of her family, rested at the edge of a large pool.

"I did not bury your natami deep below the Acoma's," she said aloud to the listening air; a smaller voice inside her warned that she talked out of madness. Life was mad, she decided, or she would not be here making empty motions over the remains of her young heir. Her extraordinary display of graciousness in insisting that the Minwanabi natami be taken to a distant place and cared for, so that the shades of the Minwanabi might know peace, at this moment seemed empty folly.

She did not have the strength in her to laugh.

Mara curled her lip at the sour taste in her mouth. Her hair smelled of sweet oil and greasy smoke. The stench turned her stomach as she knelt on the sun-warmed ground. Next to the natami a hole had been dug, the damp soil piled to one side. Mara placed the fire-warped sword that had been her son's most prized possession in the cavity, then tipped the urn to let his ashes pour over it. With bare hands she sifted the earth back into the hole and patted it down.

A white robe had been left for her beside the pool. On its silk folds lay a vial, and nearby, the traditional brazier and dagger. Mara lifted the vial and removed the stopper. She poured fragrant oils upon the pool. In the shimmers of fractured light that played upon its surface, she saw no beauty, but only the face of her son, his mouth wide with suffering as he struggled to draw his last breath. The rituals gave no release but seemed a wasting wind of meaningless sound. "Rest, my son. Come to your home soil and sleep with our ancestors."

"Ayaki," she whispered. "My child."

She gripped the breast of her robe and pulled, tearing the cloth from her body, but unlike years before, when she had performed the ritual for her father and brother, no tears followed the violence. Her eyes remained painfully dry.

She plunged her hand into the almost extinguished brazier. The sting of the few hot cinders remaining was not enough to focus her thoughts. Grief remained a dull ache inside her as she smeared the ashes across her breasts and down her exposed stomach, to symbolize that her heart was ashes. In truth, her flesh felt as lifeless as the spent wood of the pyre. She slowly lifted the heirloom metal dagger, kept sharp for this ceremony over the ages. For the third time in her life, she drew the blade from its sheath and cut herself across the left arm, the hot pain barely felt in the fog of her despair.

She held the small wound over the pool, letting drops of blood fall to mix with the water, as tradition required. For more than a minute she sat motionless, until nature's healing stanched the flow. A scab had half dried before she absently tugged at her robe, but she lacked the fierceness of will to fully sunder the garment. In the end, she simply dragged it over her head. It fell to earth, one sleeve soaking up oil and water from the pool.

By rote, Mara unfastened her hairpins, loosening her dark locks over her shoulders. Anger and rage, grief and sorrow should have driven her to pull upon her tresses, yanking handfuls loose. Her emotions only smoldered sullenly, like a spark smothered by lack of air. Boys should not die; to grieve for them in a fullness of passion was to abet the acceptance of their passing. Mara twisted at a few tangles, outwardly listless.

Then she settled back upon her heels and regarded the glade. Such immaculate beauty, and only she among the living could appreciate it.

Ayaki would never perform the death rite for his mother. Hot tears erupted unbidden and she felt something of the hardness wedged within break loose. Mara sobbed, abandoning herself to an outpouring of grief.

But unlike before, when such release brought clarity, this time she found herself driven deeper into chaotic thought. When she closed her eyes, her mind whirled with images: first Ayaki running, then Kevin, the barbarian slave who had taught her of love, and who had time and again risked his life for her. She saw Buntokapi, sprawled on the red length of his sword, his great ham fists quivering closed as the life left his body. Again she acknowledged that her first husband's death would forever be marked against her. She saw faces: her father and brother, then Nacoya, her nurse and foster mother.

All of them offered her pain. Kevin's return to his own world was as painful a loss as death, and not one other had died as nature intended; all had been casualties of twisted politics, and of the cruel machinations of the Great Game.

The horrid certainty would not leave her, that Ayaki would not be the last boy to die for the empty ambitions of the nation's Ruling Lords.

That reality struck like torture: that Ayaki would not be the last. Howling in hysteria born of agony, Mara threw herself headlong into the pool.

The wetness swallowed her tears. Her sobs were wrenched short by a gasp as cold water sucked into her nostrils, and life recalled her to its own. She crawled back on dry earth, choking. Water streamed from her mouth and hair. She dragged in a hacking breath, then reached mechanically for the robe, its whiteness marred by dirt and sweet oil.

As if she were a spirit wearing the body of a stranger, she saw herself drag the fabric over her wet flesh. The hair she left bunched under the collar. Then the body that felt like a living prison gathered itself up and trudged back toward the entrance to the glade, where thousands waited with eyes hostile or friendly.

Their presence took her aback. In this Lord's fatuous smile and that Lord's leering interest, she saw the truth confirmed: that Ayaki's death would happen again and again, and other mothers after her would howl useless outrage at the injustices of the Great Game. Mara glanced down to shut away the acknowledgment of futility. One of her sandals was missing. Mud and dust caked her bared foot, and she hesitated, debating whether to look for the lost footwear, or to fling the remaining sandal into the hedge.

What did it matter, a far-off voice reasoned inside her. Mara watched her misshod feet with fey detachment as the person that was herself left the glade. Passing between the shielding hedges, she did not look up as her husband hurried forward to take up his station at her elbow. His words did not soothe. She did not want to return from her inward retreat to work at sorting their meaning.

Hokanu shook her gently, forcing her to look up.

A man in red armor stood before her; thin, elegant, poised, he carried his chin at an arrogant angle. Mara stared at him, distracted. His eyes narrowed. He said something. The hand that held some object in it gestured, and something of the biting scorn that underlay his manner came through.

Mara's gaze sharpened. Her eyes focused on the device upon the young man's helm, and a deep quiver shook her.

"Anasati!" she said, a bite like a whip's crack to her voice.

Lord Jiro gave back a chilly smile. "The Lady deigns to acknowledge me, I see."

Wakened to a slow, spiraling rage, Mara stiffened.

She said nothing. Hokanu's fingers wrenched unobtrusively at her wrist, a warning she did not acknowledge.

Her ears rang to a sound like a thousand enraged sarcats spitting in defiance, or torrents of storm-swollen rivers crashing down jagged rock.

Jiro of the Anasati raised the object he held, a small puzzle cleverly cut to a pattern of interlacing wooden hoops. He inclined his head in a formal bow, saying, "My nephew's shade deserves remembrance from the Anasati."

"Remembrance!" Mara said, in a high, tortured whisper. Inside her mind, her spirit howled: Anasati remembrance had sent her firstborn to a bed of ashes.

She did not remember moving; she did not feel the wrench of tendons as she yanked free of Hokanu's restraint. Her scream of rage cut across the gathering like the sound of a drawn metal sword, and her hands rose like claws.

Jiro leaped back, dropping the puzzle in horrified astonishment. And then Mara was on him, clawing to reach his throat through the fastenings of his armor.

Those Lords standing nearest exclaimed in shock as this small woman, unarmed, dirty, and wet, threw herself at her former brother-in-law in a fit of pure fury.

Hokanu sprang with all his warrior's quickness, fast enough to catch Mara back before she drew blood. He smothered her struggling body in his embrace.

But the damage by then was irrevocable.

Jiro glared around at the circle of stunned onlookers. "You all bear witness!" he cried in an indignation that held an undertone of wild joy. Now he had the justification he had long wished for, to see the Lady Mara ground under his heel in utter defeat. "The Acoma have offered the Anasati insult! Let all present be informed that alliance is dead between our two houses. I claim my right to expunge this shame to my honor, and blood will be called for in payment."

3. War

Hokanu acted.

While Mara beat her fists in mindless fury against his breastplate, the warriors of her honor guard closed in a tight ring to shield their Lady's hysteria from public view. Hokanu called urgently for Saric and Incomo.

One glance at their distraught mistress was sufficient to convince the two advisers: grief and nerves had overwhelmed her. She was past recognition of individual faces, and obviously beyond any capacity to issue a public apology to Lord Jiro. It had been the sight of him that had set off this breakdown. Even should reason return to her before the guests departed, it would not be wise to encourage a meeting between injured parties so she might ask forgiveness. Worse damage might result. The two advisers, one old and practiced, the other young and talented, could see that already the scope of the trouble her lapse had created was widening. It was too late, now, to mend the past.

Hokanu realized that he should have heeded Isashani's warning more closely, but he must not allow regret for his miscalculation to hamper the need for fast decisions. "Saric," he rapped out, "issue a statement. Tell no falsehoods, but select your words to insinuate that our Lady has fallen ill. We need immediate tactics to soften Jiro's accusations of insult, which will certainly come within hours, and to find a sane reason to dismiss the state guests."

The dark-haired First Adviser bowed and ducked away, already composing his words of formal announcement.

Unasked, Force Commander Lujan stepped to the fore. Despite the Ruling Lords who crowded against his warriors to gape at the prostrate Mara, he did not turn his face from her shame, but stripped off bracers, sword, and belt knife, then bent to lend his aid to subdue Mara's struggles without causing her bruises. With a glance of profound relief, Hokanu continued with instructions to Incomo. "Hurry back to the estate house. Assemble Mara's maids, and find her a healer who can mix a soporific.

Then see to the guests. We need help from what allies we have left to avert an outbreak of armed hostilities.''

"Lord Hoppara and the Xacatecas forces stand with you," announced a husky female voice. The tight ranks of honor guard swirled aside to admit the elegant, yellow-and-purple-robed form of Lady Isashani, who had used the almost mystical effect of her beauty and poise to gain passage between the warriors. "And I can help with Mara."

Hokanu assessed the sincerity of the concern in her exotic dark eyes, then nodded. "Gods pity us for my lack of understanding," he murmured by way of apology. "Your house has all our gratitude." Then he turned the charge of his Lady over to the feminine wisdom of the Xacatecas dowager.

"She has not gone mad," Lady Isashani answered, her fine hand closing over Mara's in comfort. "Sleep and quiet will restore her, and time will heal her grief. You must be patient." Then, back to the hardcore immediacy of politics, she added, "I have set my two advisers to waylay the Omechan and the Inrodaka. My honor guard, under Hoppara, will find ways to interpose themselves where they will most hamper other troublemongers."

Two fewer enemies to concern them; Hokanu tossed back a harried nod. Mara had staunch friends against the vicious factions who sought to pull her down. She was beloved by many in these nations. It tore his heart not to be able to stay at her side when she was in such a terrible state. He forced his gaze away from the small cortege that formed to convey his distraught Lady to the comfort of the estate house. To let his heart rule him at this time was fool's play. He must harden himself, as if he stood on the brink of deadly combat. There were enemies in plenty who had attended Ayaki's last rites precisely to grab advantage from an opportunity like this. Mara's insult to Jiro was by now past forgiveness. Bloodshed would result—that was a forgone conclusion—but only a fool would initiate an assault in the heart of Mara's estate, with her army gathered to pay honor to Ayaki. Once beyond the borders of the Acoma lands, Mara's enemies would start their mischief.

Hokanu moved now in an attempt to stave off immediate war. The Acoma stood to be ruined if he misstepped; not only that, but the warriors and resources of the Shinzawai might be sucked into gainless strife also. All that had been won in the past three years to secure centralized rule for the Emperor might be thrown away at a stroke.

Council must be called, to see what could be done to stave off more widespread disaster. Those Lords who held allegiance to neither Mara nor

Jiro would have to be wooed, cajoled, or threatened, so that those openly opposed to her would think twice before challenging the Good Servant.

"Lujan," Hokanu called over the rising tumult to the Acoma Force Commander, "arm the garrison, and call up the most level-headed of your officers. No matter what the provocation, at all costs set your patrols to keep the peace."

The high green plumes of the officer's helm bobbed acknowledgment over the chaos. Hokanu spared a moment for thanks to the gods that Mara had chosen her staff for intelligence and sense. Cool heads were their only hope of extricating House Acoma from devastation.

Saddened by this turn of affairs, Hokanu directed the honor guard to march back to the estate house. Had Mara been less herself, and more the pliant wife that so many Empire women became as a result of their traditional upbringing, she would never have been strong enough to have attended a full state funeral for a son cut down by assassins. As Ruling Lady, and Servant of the Empire, she was too much in the public eye, denied even the human frailties that any lesser mother might be forgiven.

Caught up in the heated core of intrigues, Lady Mara was forced into a role that made her a target.

A frantic hour later, Mara lay on her sleeping mat, stupefied by potions administered by the priest of Hantukama, who had appeared as if by magic to offer his skills. Isashani had the household well in hand, and the short hadonra, Jican, was as busy as three men, quelling wild rumors among the servants.

Hokanu found himself alone to deal with the decisions that must be made in behalf of House Acoma. He listened to the reports of the Acoma retainers. He took notes for Mara to review, when she was restored and capable. He marked which guests stood by her, and which were outspoken against her. Most had the dignity to stay silent, or else they were too shocked to frame any hostile response. All had expected to spend the day in quiet contemplation, then to be hosted by the Servant of the Empire at a formal evening meal. Instead, they were already returning home, appalled by an unforgivable act authored by a woman who held the highest office in the land, short of the Emperor's throne. More than one delegate of great houses had stopped by, ostensibly to pay their respects, but except for the Lord of the Keda, Hokanu had murmured empty thanks to men eager to catch any hint that House Acoma stood weakened. Lord Hoppara and the Lords of Clan Hadama were doing a fine job of moving through the crowds of departing guests, toning down the damage of Mara's act against the Anasati by whatever expedient they could find.

Many who were all too ready to be outraged by the breach of protocol became more inclined to overlook a grieving mother's outburst after one of the Hadama Lords or Lord Hopara had finished speaking to them.

Another noble frustrated in his attempts to reach the inner apartments had been the Lord of the Anasati. Jiro had stiffly insisted that the insult to his person was irreparable. A pack of supporters had clustered at his heels as he was turned away from Mara's door. They had found a common rallying point, and even those who had counted Mara a friend would be hard pressed to ignore a personal attack; for an enemy, it was impossible. In Tsurani culture, forgiveness was simply a less shameful form of weakness than capitulation. All in the course of seconds, the Lady had changed political opponents into allies of deadly enemies.

Jiro had not sued for public apology; indeed, he had surrounded himself with Lords whose disgruntlement with Ichindar's reformed powers of rule was most vociferous. Saric and Incomo shared the conclusion that the Anasati Lord was deliberately discouraging conciliatory overtures, choosing to place blame for the scandal squarely upon the Acoma. Jiro's loud complaints reached any who hovered within earshot: that he had come to his nephew's funeral under what was understood as a traditional truce by all who attended, and had endured physical attack, humiliation at the hands of his host, and public accusation. As much as any ruler understood or sympathized with the source of Mara's irrational act, none could deny that deadly insult had been given, with no atonement offered. Any attempt to deflect the accusation by pointing out Mara's present inability to offer a rational apology was ignored by the Anasati.

The hall of the Acoma had grown stifling, its screens drawn closed against the prying eyes of the curious, its doors guarded by the scarred veterans of past wars. These men did not wear the brightly lacquered ceremonial armor but field trappings well tested by previous engagements. Sitting upon a lower, less formal dais that was deserted in Mara's absence, Hokanu quietly requested opinions on the day's events.

That the closest, most loyal Acoma officers chose to respond to a consort who was not their sworn house Lord showed their immeasurable regard for Hokanu's judgment. If the honor of these men's vows was not his to command, they awarded him their absolute trust to act as needed in their mistress's behalf. Touched as he was by their devotion, he was also disturbed, for it signified how deeply they understood Mara's peril. Hokanu prayed that he was up to the task.

He listened in grave stillness as Force Leader Irrilandi and Keyoke, Adviser for War, reviewed the strength of the garrison, even as Force Commander Lujan readied the Acoma forces for battle. As if in emphasis, old Keyoke thumped his crutch against the stump of his lost leg. "Even if Jiro knows he will be defeated, he has no choice: honor requires he answer public insult with bloodshed. I doubt he will settle for a contest of champions. Worse, if Mara's cries of accusation were heard by any beyond those close by, her implication that Jiro hired the Hamoi Tong to kill Ayaki could be taken as an insult to the Ionani that can only end in a Call to Clan."

Absolute stillness followed this statement, making the footfalls of rushing servants echo through the hall. Several of those at the table turned to listen to the calls of house officers, gathering their masters' families into personal litters for a quick departure, and a few looked at one another and shared a common understanding: a Clan War would rip the Empire asunder.

Into the face of such grim musing, Saric ventured, "But who could take such a concept seriously? No tong dares reveal its employers, and what evidence we found to link the Anasati to the attack is hardly compelling, given the Hamoi Brotherhood's clandestine practices. I'm more inclined to suspect it's an intentional false trail."

Incomo nodded, wagging a crooked finger. "The evidence of Jiro's hand in Ayaki's death is *too* neat. No tong survives to win itself wealthy clients by being this imprudent. And the Hamoi is the most powerful tong because its secrets have never been compromised." He scanned the faces around the table. "After—what? five attempts upon Mara?—they suddenly allow one of their own to be caught with proof of Anasati participation? Unlikely. Certainly questionable. Hardly convincing."

Hokanu regarded the advisers with a flash in his eyes as dire as light on barbarian steel. "We need Arakasi back." The gifts of the Acoma Spy Master were many, and his ability to read through the snarl of politics and individual greed of the Nations' myriad Ruling Lords at times approached the uncanny. "We need him to pursue this evidence that supports Jiro's guilt, for the boy's true murderer lies behind it." Hokanu sighed. "Meantime, speculation is leading us nowhere. With Tasaio of the Minwanabi gone, who dares seek the death of the Servant of the Empire?"

Saric scratched his chin in the gloom. Not without sympathy, he said, "Master, you are blinded by love for your wife. The common folk of the nations may regard her as a talisman, but her exalted station invites jealousy from other hearts. Many would see the Good Servant on her way to Turakamu's halls, simply because of her breaks with tradition, and her climb to a rank unmatched by any previous Warlord. Also, there are many who see their house status lessened, and their ambitions curtailed, because she is favored by Ichindar. They would seek Mara's dishonor . . . if they dared.''

Hokanu looked impatient. "Then who would dare?"

"Of us all, Arakasi might know." Glancing at Incomo, Saric tactfully phrased the question that played upon his restless mind. "Is there any reason to think that your former master might be reaching from the land of the dead to strike a blow in vengeance?"

As Keyoke's eyes hardened at this possibility, the former First Adviser to the Lord of the Minwanabi, now Second Adviser to the Lady of the Acoma, cleared his throat. He unflinchingly met the distrust that focused on him. "If so, I was no part of such a plot. But Tasaio was a secretive man, and dangerous. Many times he was wont to make arrangements outside my knowledge. I was often dismissed when most Lords would have commanded my attendance. The Obajan of the Hamoi Tong was seen to pay a personal visit to Tasaio. My impression at the time was that the event involved unanswered questions over the murder of Acoma spies then in Minwanabi service." Incomo's long face showed unguarded distaste as he concluded, "Threats were exchanged, and a bargain struck. But no man alive overheard the words that passed between the Obajan and Tasaio. I can only relate that never in life did I observe the Lord of the Minwanabi so balked in his plans that he lost himself to a display of wild anger. Tasaio was many things, but he was seldom without control."

To this, Saric added speculative observation. "If the former First Adviser of the Minwanabi cannot know for certain that Tasaio left orders for vengeance should he fall, I offer that we waste ourselves in guesswork. More to the point, Tasaio was not a man who ever for a moment considered defeat—as tactician he was unmatched. Given that he believed until the end that he was free to crush our Lady in open war, why should we assume that he took the coward's path and paid death price for Mara when he gave no credence to the chance she might survive him? We should more nearly be examining the ranks of Jiro's enemies. Mara is one of the few Rulers in the Nations with strength enough to engage him without stalemate; with imperial support behind her, discord between Acoma and Anasati is the more likely to lead to setbacks for Lord Jiro."

"And yet the Anasati Lord seems eager enough to take what provocation fate and our misfortune have offered," Hokanu broke in. "He does not shrink from conflict. That does little to excuse him from culpability in the matter of Ayaki's murder. Until my wife is able, I will presume to make this decision. Order the garrison to make ready to march. There must be war, and we dare not be caught unprepared."

Keyoke silently inclined his head. He would not accord the situation the formality of spoken word, since this he could only do before his Lady. Yet his acquiescence in the matter showed unswerving support. Saric, who was younger and less bound to the old traditions, inclined his head in a gesture very close to the bow an adviser would offer his sworn Lord. "I shall make formal declaration of war upon the Anasati. When Jiro responds in kind, we shall march."

Keyoke glanced at Irrilandi, who nodded to indicate his own endorsement of what would soon occur. Most Tsurani bloodshed was committed surreptitiously, with ambush and raid, and without public acknowledgment of responsibility. But formal battle between houses was a time-honored, ceremonial event. Two armies would meet upon a field at an agreed-upon time, and one would leave victorious. No quarter was asked or given, save in rare circumstances, and again by formal rules of conduct. History held record of battles that had raged for days; it was not uncommon for both houses to be destroyed in the process.

Then Hokanu sought one further step. "I ask that we notify Clan Hadama."

Saric raised his eyebrows, deeply concerned, but also intrigued by the subtleties of the suggestion. "You provoke an Anasati Call to Clan?"

Hokanu sighed. "I have an intuitive feeling—"

But Keyoke broke in with a rare interruption that supported Hokanu's hunch. "Jiro is no warrior. He has Omelo for Force Commander, and though a good enough field general in his own right, he does not excel at large-scale engagements. A Call to Clan is the best hope Jiro has to keep his house and army intact. We do not provoke what is likely a foregone conclusion."

"More," Incomo added. "Lord Jiro is a scholar at heart. He sneers at the coarseness of armed conflict. He wishes reason to declare against Mara, and has nurtured a hatred of her that extends back into his youth. But he prefers hidden attacks, and cleverness. He is a master of shāh. Remember that. He will seek to ruin by subterfuge, not raw force. If we do call a Clan War first, then the possibility exists that Clan Ionani will not permit an Anasati interest to drag them to destruction. We are more than Jiro's match in open combat. If his clan members are behind his obsessive desires enough to escalate by accepting his slight of honor for their own, Clan Hadama will answer."

Hokanu weighed this without much hope or enthusiasm. Whether Clan Ionani moved against them or not Lord Jiro had managed to set himself at the spearhead of other factions that had cause to undermine Mara's strength. That his was not the only mind to perceive past this personal spat to deeper, more lasting discord had been evident by the number of

Ruling Lords who turned out for Ayaki's funeral. The High Council might be abolished, but its tradition of contention continued in secret, ferocious intensity, whenever excuse existed for the Empire's nobles to gather. That the Black Robes had sent a contingent of five to the rites showed that their trend of intervention in the arena of intrigue was far from ended since Ichindar's ascension to centralized power.

At last Hokanu concluded, "We may have strength and allies enough to crush the Anasati, but at what cost? In the end, it may not change things. We can only hope that a swift, bloody clash on the battlefield will contain the damage and split the traditionalists before they can ally and organize into a united political party."

"Master Hokanu," Saric interjected at the naked look of sorrow that appeared on the Acoma consort's face, "the course you have chosen is the best we have available. Rest assured that your Lady could do no better, were she capable of hearing our counsel. Now go, attend to her, for she needs you at her side. I will instruct the scribes to prepare documents and arrange for messengers to convey them to Lord Jiro's estates."

Looking haunted despite relief at this unstinting statement of support, Hokanu left the hall. His stride was a warrior's, purposeful and quick; his hands were a worried husband's, balled into helpless fists.

Saric remained, as the other Acoma officers broke the circle and departed from the hall. Left alone in the breezeless shadows, he slapped his fist into a hand grown uncalloused since his promotion from a warrior's ranks. He ached for the friends he had left in the barracks, and for the woman he had been called to serve, who had wholly won his support. If the Acoma acted quickly enough to end this dispute, the gods would be granting a miracle. Too many disgruntled Lords remained with too few responsibilities since the disbanding of the High Council. Peace left them too much space for mischief. The old political parties had broken up, their reason for existence canceled by Ichindar's new rule.

The Empire was quiet, but far from settled; the climate of unrest that had three years been held in abeyance was ripe for renewed civil war.

Though Saric appreciated his Lady's brilliance in changing the only society he had ever known, he regretted the disbanding of the Warlord's office and the power of the High Council, for at least then events could be interpreted according to centuries of precedents set by the forms of the Great Game. Now, while the old ways were still followed by the houses of the Empire, the rules were forced into change.

Speculation was becoming too uncertain, Saric decided with a grimace of disgust. He left the deserted hall, heading for the quarters he had chosen when Mara had come to occupy the former Minwanabi estate. En route to his suite of rooms, he sent Mara's runner to fetch a scribe to attend him. When the man arrived with his satchel of ink and pens, the Acoma First Adviser's instructions were clipped: "Prepare notice for our factors and agents. If Arakasi makes his presence known anywhere in the Nations, inform him he is to return home at once." The scribe sat upon the floor without comment, but he looked troubled as he placed a wooden lap board upon his knee. Quickly putting pen to parchment, he started to compose the first document.

"Add this, and use the number seven cipher," Saric concluded, pacing the floor in an agitation that had no other outlet. "Our Lady is in deadly danger."

The chime sounded, and a puff of disturbed air winnowed the silken hangings that walled the great gathering hall in the City of the Magicians. Shadows cast by the flickering flames of the oil lamps wavered as a magician appeared upon the pattern in the center of the floor. He stepped off briskly. Hard on his heels, two colleagues appeared in rapid succession. These were followed by others, until a crowd of black-robed figures congregated on the benches surrounding the walls. The huge, leather-hinged doors creaked wide to admit others who chose not to convey their bodies to the meeting by arcane means.

The Hall of the Assembly filled swiftly and quietly.

The delegates converged from all walks of the City of the Magicians, a complex of buildings and covered terraces, towers and galleries that made a maze-like warren of an entire island. Located in the midst of a great lake in the foothills of the High Wall, the northern mountains of the Empire, the City of the Magicians was unapproachable by any means but magic. Black Robes in distant provinces teleported to the site, responding to the call to Assembly sent out that morning. Gathered together in sufficient number to form a quorum, the magicians constituted the most powerful body in Tsuranuanni, for they existed outside the law. No one, not even the Emperor, dared gainsay their command, which had carried absolute privilege for thousands of years of history.

Within minutes the benches were packed to capacity. Hodiku, a thin, hook-nosed man of middle years who by preference spent most of his time in study within the Holy City, walked to the First Speaker's position, at the center of the patterned tile floor. His voice extended across the cavernous hall seemingly without effort. "We are called together today so that I may speak for the Good of the Empire." The routine greeting was met with silence, for all matters requiring convocation of the Assembly of Great Ones related to the state of the Empire. "Today the Red Seal upon the inner sanctum of the Temple of Jastur was broken!"

The announcement caused a shocked stir, for only when formal warfare was announced between houses or clans were the arched doors to the central chamber of the Temple of the War God thrown open to allow public entry. Hodiku raised his arms to encourage a return to order. "Mara of the Acoma, as Lady of her house and Warchief of Clan Hadama, does pronounce war upon Lord Jiro of the Anasati!"

Astonished exclamations swept the chamber. While a cadre of the younger magicians stayed abreast of current events, they were not among the majority. These newly sworn Black Robes had joined the Assembly during the upheavals caused by the force known as the Enemy that had endangered both their own world of Kelewan and that of Midkemia, beyond the rift. The massive threat to two civilizations had necessitated a move by the magicians to aid the Emperor Ichindar to seize absolute rule of the Nations, that internal bickering might not weaken the land in time of larger crisis. The newest of the mages might be enamored of using their powers to influence the sway of events. But to the elders of the Assembly, who were set in their individual ways and courses of scholarly study, intervention in Tsurani politics was looked on as bad form; a bothersome chore only performed at dire need.

To a still-smaller faction, headed by Hochopepa and Shimone, once close acquaintances of the barbarian magician Milamber, the recent departures from traditional rule were of interest for deeper reasons. Exposure to Midkemian thought had prompted them to view the affairs of Tsuranuanni in a changed light, and since the Lady Mara was currently the linchpin of Ichindar's support, these war tidings were of particular concern.

An old practitioner of Tsurani politics of every stripe, Hochopepa raised a chubby hand to his face and closed his dark eyes in forbearance. "As you predicted," he murmured to the reed-thin, ascetic Shimone. "Trouble, when the nations can least afford the price."

Taciturn as ever, Shimone made no reply, but watched with hawk-keen scrutiny as several of the more impulsive magicians surged to their feet, indicating their desire to speak. Hodiku singled out a young Black Robe named Sevean and pointed. The one selected stepped forward onto the central floor while the others sat.

Barely a year past his initiation to mastery of magic, Sevean was fast on his feet, quick-spoken, and inclined to be impulsive. He would leap to outspoken conclusions where other, more seasoned colleagues would wait to hear the thoughts of less experienced members before revealing their opinions. He raised a voice too loud by half for the sensitive acoustics of the hall. "It is widely believed that Jiro had a hand in the death of the Good Servant's son."

Which was no news at all; Shimone turned his mouth down in a faint curl of disgust, while Hochopepa muttered just loud enough for half the room to hear, "What, has he been listening in on Isashani's sitting room again, taking in the social gossip?"

Shimone gave no answer to this; like many of the elder magicians, he considered using powers to look in on the affairs of individual nobles as the lowest level of crass behavior. Sevean was embarrassed by Hochopepa's remark and by the harsh looks from several of the elder members. Left at a loss for words, he curtailed his speech, repeating, "It is widely believed."

More magicians vied for the First Speaker's attention. Hodiku made a choice among them, and as a slow-spoken, ponderously built initiate droned out his irrelevant viewpoint, more experienced magicians spoke quietly among themselves, ignoring all but the gist of his speech.

A mage two seats to the rear of Hochopepa and Shimone, whose name was Teloro, inclined his head toward the others. "What is the real issue, Hocho?"

The plump magician sighed and left off twiddling his thumbs. "The fate of the Empire, Teloro. The fate of the Empire."

Teloro bridled at this vagueness. Then he revised his first impression: the stout magician's bearing might betray no concern, but his tone rang with deep conviction.

Both Shimone and his stout companion seemed fixed on a discussion at the other side of the hall, where several magicians held private counsel. As the current speaker sat, and a round-shouldered man from this whispering cadre stood up, Teloro heard Hochopepa mutter, "Now we'll begin to see how this round of the game is to be played."

Hodiku motioned to the man, who was slender, with brown hair trimmed above his ears in the Tsurani fashion called a warrior's cut. The style was an odd affectation for a Black Robe, but by any measure Motecha was a strange magician. He had been friends with the two brothers who had actively supported the old Warlord, but when Elgoran had died and Elgohar had left to serve upon the Midkemian world, Motecha had conspired to maintain an appearance of distance between himself and the two brothers.

The attention of Shimone and Hochopepa intensified as Motecha opened. "Is there no end to Lady Mara's ambition? She has called a Clan War over a personal insult *she* delivered, as Lady of the Acoma."

Hochopepa nodded as if in confirmation of a hunch. "So Motecha has made alliances with the Anasati. Odd. He's not an original thinker. I wonder who put him up to this?"

Shimone held up his hand. "Don't distract with chatter. I want to hear this."

Motecha waved a ringed hand, as if inviting rebuttal from his colleagues. But he was not as magnanimous as his gesture suggested, since he rushed on to cut off any interruption. "Obviously not. The Good Servant was not satisfied with flouting tradition by co-opting her former enemy's forces—"

"Which we conceded was a brilliant move," interjected Hochopepa, again just loud enough to make the speaker stumble. Teloro and Shimone repressed amusement. The stout magician was a master at embarrassing colleagues that he deemed in need of having their pomposity punctured. As Motecha seemed ready to depart from his prepared remarks, Hochopepa added, "But please, I didn't mean to interrupt; pray continue."

Motecha was nonetheless thrown off stride. He brushed lamely past his hesitation, saying, "She will crush the Anasati—"

Representing the more seasoned members of the Assembly, Fumita stood. At Hodiku's nod of acknowledgment he said, "Forgive the interruption, Motecha, but an Anasati defeat is neither assured nor even likely. Given the well-documented assessment of the forces available to both sides, it is a given that Jiro must counteract with a Call to Clan. Alone, Anasati's war hosts are no match for Lady Mara's, and she has spoken boldly by raising Clan Hadama. This has already cost her politically. She will lose powerful allies—in fact, two will be forced by blood ties to take the field against her on Jiro's behalf—and while the Acoma are awesome in wealth and power, the two clans are closely matched."

Hochopepa grinned openly. Motecha's thinly veiled attempt to stir the Assembly on behalf of the Anasati was now crushed. Rather than sit down, Fumita continued. "There is another issue here that must be addressed."

Motecha jerked his chin and conceded the floor in disgust. Since he moved away, and no other Great One stood to claim the floor, Hodiku merely waved at Fumita to continue. "While matters of honor are deemed inviolate, we must consider: will this clash of clans so weaken the internal structure of the Empire that its stability is set at risk?"

A murmur stirred the Assembly, but no one thrust to the fore to debate the issue. Clan Ionani and Clan Hadama were large factions, yes, but neither commanded enough followers to upset civil order irretrievably. Hochopepa knew his ally Fumita stalled for time; the underlying concern behind this tactic was wider than the settlement of one house's personal honor over insult. The worst was already halfway realized: that the conflict of the Anasati and the Acoma would create a polarization of factions who opposed Ichindar. Disorganized dissenters already rallied behind Jiro's cause, forming a traditionalist party that could throw serious opposition against the Empire's new order. Though they were not yet incensed enough to contribute to the bloodshed, were there still a High Council left with power to act, there could be no doubt that if a vote were held at this minute, Lord Jiro would hold enough support to take the Warlordship. There were magicians who had regarded Ichindar's rise to power as an impious expedient: that the balance should be returned to the time before the Enemy, with the Light of Heaven's office restored to the old ways. Hochopepa led a small contingent that welcomed change; he paid scant heed to Fumita's stalling, but instead watched to see where Motecha would gravitate. To his colleague he confided, "Ah, there's the hand behind Jiro's cause."

With a slight nod of his head, he indicated the magician Motecha now spoke with, an athletic-looking man just out of youth, unremarkable save for the red hair that showed around the edges of his black cowl. He had thick brows, an expression that approached a scowl, and the carriage of a man who tended to fidget with excess nerves.

"Tapek," Shimone identified. "He's the one who burned up a building while practicing for his mastery. Came into his talents very early, but took a long time to learn restraint."

Hochopepa's mild face furrowed in concern. "He's no friend of Jiro's. I wonder what his stake in this is?"

Shimone gave the barest lift of shoulders, as close as he ever came to the enigmatic Tsurani shrug. "His kind gravitates toward trouble, as floating sticks will draw toward a whirlpool."

On the floor, debate continued. Careful to keep his tone neutral lest someone point out his personal ties to Hokanu and Mara's house, Fumita offered up his conclusion. "I believe that if Clans Ionani and Hadama destroy each other, we shall be faced with both internal and external perils." He held one finger aloft. "Can any doubt that whoever survives, that house will be so weakened that others will instantly fall upon it?" He raised a second finger, adding, "And can any gainsay that enemies outside our border will take advantage of our internal dissension to strike?"

"My turn to contribute to the general excess of hot air," Hochopepa muttered, and promptly stood. At the cue, Fumita sat with such abruptness that nobody else could rise to his feet in time to prevent Hodiku's indication that the stout magician had the floor.

Hochopepa coughed to clear his throat. "My learned brother makes a strong brief," he said, warming up to a virtuoso speech of confusing pomposity. "But we must not blind ourselves with rhetoric."

Shimone's lips twitched at this half-lie. His fat companion paced heavily to and fro, meeting the eyes of all the magicians in the front rows to draw them to attention. "I would like to point out that such clashes before have not spelled the end of civilization as we know it!" He nodded for emphasis. "And we have no intelligence to indicate that those upon our borders are poised to strike. The Thuril are too busy with trade along our eastern frontier to seek struggle so long as we give them no cause. They can be a hard lot, but profit is bound to seem more attractive to them than bloodletting; at least, that seems to be the case since the Alliance for War desisted in their attempt to conquer them." A murmur of disapproval disturbed the shadowy hall, for the attempt to annex the Thuril Highlands as a new province had ended in disgrace for the Empire, and it was considered bad form to recall the defeat. Hochopepa's scruples did not restrain him from using this point to unbalance his opposition. He simply raised his sonorous voice enough to be heard above the noise. "The desert men of Tsubar have sworn binding treaty with the Xacatecas and Acoma on behalf of the Empire, and we have had no resumption of conflict in Dustari."

That this was in part to Lady Mara's credit was not lost on the Assembly. A smile spread across Hochopepa's round face as the tumult died back to respectful stillness. "By any measure, the Empire is peaceful to the point of boredom." In a dramatic shift, his smile fled before a scowl, and he shook a finger at the gathering. "Need I remind my brothers that the Servant of the Empire is counted a member of the Imperial House by adoption? An odd convention, I know, but a tradition." He waved to single out Motecha, who had sought to discredit Mara. "Should we be so rash as to do anything on behalf of the Anasati, the Emperor could conceivably consider this an attack upon his family. And, more to the point, Elgohar and I witnessed the last Warlord's execution. At his hanging . . ." He paused for effect, and tapped his temple. "Let me see if I can recall our Light of Heaven's exact words upon that occasion of a magician acting in conspiracy with council politics. Oh yes, he said, 'If another Black Robe is ever discovered involved in a plot against my house, the status of Great Ones outside the law will end. Even should I be forced to pit *all the armies of the Empire* against your magic might, even to the utter ruination of the Empire, I will not allow any to challenge the supremacy of the Emperor again. Is that understood?' ''

Sweeping a dire glare over the assembly, Hochopepa said, ''I assure you all, Ichindar was sincere. He is not the sort to threaten violence lightly. Our previous Emperors may have·been content to sit by, dividing their time between holy devotions in the temples and begetting heirs upon their assorted wives and mistresses''—he let his voice rise again— ''but Ichindar is not one! He is a ruler, not some divine puppet wearing the costume of religious office!''

Lowering his voice, forcing every magician present to strain with undivided attention to hear him, Hochopepa summed up. ''We who attended the Good Servant's son's funeral know full well that Mara's lapse was born of overwhelming grief. Now she must bear up to the consequences of her shame. From the moment she assaulted Jiro with her bare hands, this conflict was inevitable. As our charge is to preserve the Empire, I strongly doubt we can justify pursuing any activity that might find us all'' —shaking the hall with a thunderous bellow—''opposing the armies of the Empire in the field over a matter of personal insult!'' Quietly, reasonably, he resumed, ''We should win, of course, but there would be very little Empire left to preserve after that.'' He ended with a dismissive wave of his hand. ''That was all I had to say.'' And he sat.

Silence lasted only a moment before Tapek shot to his feet. Hodiku granted him a nod, and his robes swirled to his agitated stride as he stalked onto the floor.

His face was pale as he surveyed the gathering, silently gripped by reflection. ''We have heard enough of Lady Mara. The wronged party, I must point out, is Lord Jiro. He did not initiate hostilities.'' Tapek raised his arms. ''I bid you all to consider direct evidence instead of words for a change!'' He made a sweeping gesture that carved out a frame upon the air. An incantation left his lips, and in the space before him light gathered. A rainbow play of colors resolved into a sharply defined image of a room lined with books and scrolls. There, clad in a robe elegant in its simplicity, paced Lord Jiro in a rare state of agitation. Seated on a cushion in one corner, barely out of the path of his master's temper, was Chumaka, his leathery face carefully expressionless.

''How dare the Lady Mara threaten me!'' Jiro ranted in injured fury. ''We had nothing to do with the death of her son! The implication that we are a house so honorless as to strike down a boy who shares Anasati blood is preposterous! The evidence planted on that tong assassin is a transparent effort to discredit us, and because of it we are faced with Clan War!''

Chumaka steepled his fingers, adorned with rings of carved corcara that he had yet to remove since the funeral. "Clan Ionani will recognize these wrongs," he said in an effort to restore his master to calm. "We will not march unsupported to the field of war."

"War!" Jiro whirled, his eyes narrowed with disgust. "The Lady is nothing if not a coward to initiate this call to arms! She thinks to best us without dirtying her hands, using sheer numbers to annihilate us. Well, we must fall back on our wits and teach her a lesson. Clan Ionani may support us; all to the good. But I will never forgive that such a pass has become necessary. If our house emerges from this heavy-handed attack, be sure that the Acoma will have created an enemy to be feared!"

Chumaka licked his teeth. "The political arena is stirred to new patterns. There are advantages to be gained, certainly."

Jiro flung around to face his First Adviser. "First, damn the bitch, we have to escape with our hides from what will amount to wholesale slaughter."

The scene cut off as Tapek clapped his hands and dispersed the spell that had drawn it. He flung back his flame-colored bangs, half sneering at the oldsters in the gathering who had stiffened in affront at his intrusion into the privacy of a noble citizen.

"You go against tradition!" cried a palsied voice from a rear bench. "What are we, meddling old women, to stoop to using arcane arts to spy? Do we peek into ladies' dressing chambers!" His opinion was shared by several of the greyer-headed members who shot to their feet and stalked out in protest.

Tapek yelled back. "That's a contradiction of ethics! What has Lady Mara made of tradition? She has dared to meddle, I say! Do we wait and pay the price of the instability she may create in the future? What morals will stop her? Has she not demonstrated her lack of self-control in this despicable attack against Lord Jiro?"

At this inflammatory remark, even Shimone looked disturbed. "She lost a child to a horrible death!" he interrupted. "She is a woman and a human being. She is bound to have faults."

Tapek stabbed both hands over his head. "An apt point, brother, but my concern is not for the Lady's shortcomings. She has risen to a dizzying height by anyone's measure. Her influence has grown too great, and her powers too broad. As Warchief of the Hadama and Lady of the strongest house in the Empire, she is preeminent among the Ruling Lords. And as Servant of the Empire, she holds dangerous sway over the masses. I submit the point that she is only human! And that no Ruling Lord or Lady should be allowed to wield so much influence throughout the Empire! I claim we should curb her excesses now, before the trouble grows too large to contain."

Hodiku, as First Speaker, stroked his chin at the turn the discussion had taken. In attempt to soothe the uneasiness that stirred through the gathering, he appealed to Hochopepa. "I have a question for my learned friend. Hocho, what do you suggest we do?"

Leaning back, making every effort to appear casually unconcerned by resting an elbow upon the riser behind him, Hochopepa said, "Do? Why, I thought that should be obvious. We should do nothing. Let these contentious factions have their war. When their slights of honor are sated with bloodshed, it will be an easy enough matter to pick up the pieces."

Voices rang out as another dozen magicians rose, seeking recognition. Shimone sighed audibly. "You're not going to get your way on this one, Hocho."

The stout magician set his chin in his palms, dimpling both cheeks. "Of course not," he whispered. "But I wasn't about to let that hot-headed boy run off unconstrained." Outside the law, each Great One was free to act as he saw fit. Anyone could by his own judgment intervene against Mara should he deem his action in the best interest of the Empire. By taking the issue of noninterference to the floor of the Assembly, Hodiku had made it a matter for quorum consensus. Once an accord was made formal, no member would willingly defy the final decision. Since quick resolution was beyond hope, Hochopepa changed his goal toward forcing due process to instill tempered judgment. The stout magician adjusted his robes around his girth in resignation. "Now, let's get to the meat of the matter by letting these hotheads rant themselves hoarse. When they run out of steam, we'll show them the only reasonable choice, and call a vote, letting them think the idea was theirs in the first place. It's safer to let Tapek and Motecha think they are leading the Assembly to consensus than to leave them free to initiate regrettable action on their own."

Shimone turned a sour eye upon his portly companion. "Why is it that you always seek the solution to everything through inexhaustible sessions of talk?"

"Have you a better idea?" Hochopepa shot back in sharp reproof.

"No," Shimone snapped. Unwilling to bother himself with further speech, he turned his attention back to the floor, where the first of many speakers vied to continue the debate.

*   *   *

The early sun heated the great command tent. The half-gloom inside smelled of the heavy oils used to keep the hide waterproof and of the grease used to supple the straps of armor and scabbards. The scent of lamp oil was absent, as the Lady had declined the need for light. Dressed in ornamental armor and helm crowned with the plumes of the Hadama Clan Warchief, Mara sat on fine silk cushions. The flaps of the tent's entrance were lashed back, and the morning outside edged her stiff profile in light. Behind her, his gauntleted hand upon her shoulder, Hokanu surveyed the army arrayed in ranks across the broad vale below.

The mass of waiting warriors darkened the meadow across the entire vista, from the vantage point on the hill behind: spears and helms in their neat rows too numerous for counting. The only visible movement was caused by the wind through the officers' plumes, which were many colors besides Acoma green. Yet the stillness was deceptive. At any second, every man-at-arms of Clan Hadama stood ready for attack, to answer their Warchief's call to honor.

Mara seemed an ornament carved of jade in her formal armor. Her face was the expressionless façade expected of a Tsurani War Chief. Yet those advisers who attended her observed in her bearing a brittleness, as if her stiff manner were all that contained the seething emotions inside. They moved and spoke quietly in her presence, as if the chance-made gesture or the wrongly inflected word might jar her control and the irrational rage she had unleashed upon Lord Jiro might hammer past her barriers and manifest itself again.

In this setting, with the vast armies at her command spread in offensive readiness, she was unpredictable as the thunderhead whose lightnings have yet to be loosed. A formal declaration of war meant putting aside cunning and strategies, forgoing guile and reason, and simply charging across an open field at the foe named in ceremony in the Temple of Jastur.

Across from the Hadama war force were raised the banners of Clan Ionani; like Lady Mara, Lord Jiro sat with the Ionani Warchief upon the crest of the opposite hill, proud as befitted their lineage, and of no mind to forgive a slight of honor from the Lady of the Acoma. Beyond the tight-ranked warriors of the Ionani, the command tent flew the ancient scarlet-and-yellow Anasati war banner on a standard set next to the black-and-green tent of Lord Tonmargu, Warchief of the clan. The placement of colors symbolized an age-old affirmation that the slight to the Anasati had been accepted by all the clan houses, to be resolved by bloodshed that would count no cost in lives.

To die was Tsurani; to live in dishonor, cowardice deemed worse than death.

Mara's eyes registered the details, yet her hands did not shake. Her thoughts were walled off in a cold place that even Hokanu could not penetrate. She who had deplored war and killing now seemed eager to embrace raw violence. Bloodshed might not bring her son back, but the heat and horror of battle could maybe stop her thinking. She would know a surcease from pain and grief until Jiro of the Anasati was ground to a pulp in the dust.

Her mouth hardened at the bent of her thoughts. Hokanu sensed her tautness. He did not try to dissuade her, knowing by instinct that no consolation existed that could move her. He stayed by her, quiet, tempering her decisions where he could.

One day she might waken and accept her tears for what they were. Until time might begin to heal her, he could only give unstinting support, knowing that anything less might drive her to more desperate measures.

With true Tsurani impassivity, Hokanu followed the distant panoply as several figures left the Hadama lines and approached the ranks of the Ionani. Lujan led the party, sunshine glancing off his armor and lighting the tips of his officer's plumes to emerald brilliance. At his shoulder walked his two Force Leaders, Irrilandi and Kenji, and behind, according to rank, the Force Commanders of the other houses of Clan Hadama. A scribe came last, to record the exchange as this delegation met its opposite in the center of the chosen site of battle, following tradition. A discussion would set the conditions of the coming war, the limits of the field, the hour of commencement, and the possibility, if any, that quarter could be offered or accepted. But Mara had ended hope of the last. When Keyoke, her Adviser for War, had broached the subject of quarter, her eyes had flashed hot anger as she pronounced, "No quarter."

That the houses of Clan Ionani had seen fit to become involved had moved her not a hairsbreadth. They could stand or fall with Jiro, and she would not be alone in enduring the atrocities inherent in the Game of the Council.

The lines were now drawn, the stakes set. None could dispute the word of Mara, as Warchief. Hokanu glanced around the command tent, as much to steady himself as to assess the mood of those present. Keyoke wore armor rather than the adviser's garb his position entitled him to; Saric, who had fought in the Acoma ranks before rising to high office, had also donned armor. With battle about to rage, he felt naked wearing only thin silk on his back.

Old Incomo yet wore his robes. More at home with his pen than his eating knife, he stood with his hands locked at his sash, his leathery features drawn. Though as seasoned in his way as a field general, he was unschooled in the arts of violence. Mara's call to Clan was no sane act, and since she had heretofore been the soul of gentleness and reason, her venomous embracing of Tsurani ritualized vengeance left him inwardly terrified. But his years of experience as adviser to the Minwanabi enabled him to stand firm in obedience.

Every man and woman of the Acoma, and of all the houses of Clan Hadama, waited upon the gods' will today.

Trumpets sounded and the high, curving war horns blew. Drummers beat a tattoo as the delegations of Ionani and Hadama parted company, turned about, and marched back to their ranks. The drumbeat quickened, and the fanfare assumed a faster tempo. Lujan took his place in the center ranks; Irrilandi and Kenji marched to the right and left flanks; and the other officers assumed position at the heads of their house armies. Early sun glanced off the lacquered edges of shields and spears and lit the rippling movement of thousands of warriors drawing sword from sheath.

The banners snapped in a gust, and streamers unfurled from the cross-posts, red for the Death God Turakamu, whose blessing was asked for the slaughter about to begin. A priest of the Red God's order stepped onto the narrow strip of earth between the armies and chanted a prayer. The swell of sound as the warriors joined in seemed like the tremor that preceded cataclysm. Beside the priest stood another, a black shrouded sister of Sibi, She Who Is Death. The presence of a priestess who worshipped Turakamu's elder sister affirmed that many men were fated to die on this day. The priest completed his invocation and cast a handful of red feathers into the air. He bowed to the earth, then saluted the priestess of the Death Goddess. As the religious representatives withdrew, the warriors raised their voices to shouts. Cries and insults shattered the morning as men reviled their enemies across the field. Unforgivable words were exchanged, to seal their dedication to annihilating combat: to win or to die, as honor dictated; to stiffen the will lest any soldier be tempted to turn craven. The Tsurani code of honor was inflexible: a man would earn his life through victory, or his disgrace would extend past the Wheel of this life, to cause misery in the next.

Mara regarded the scene without passion. Her heart was hard. This day, other mothers would know what it was to weep over the bodies of slain sons. She barely noticed when Hokanu's fingers settled on the shoulder plates of her armor, as his own heart began to pound in anticipation.

The heir to the Shinzawai had the right to stand apart, for he had no blood ties to either Hadama or Ionani, but as husband to the Good

Servant, he felt obliged to supervise this slaughter. Now, with the excitement of the warriors reaching a pitch to quicken the blood, a darker part of his nature looked forward to the call to charge. Ayaki had been loved as his own, and the boy's loss quickened him to share his Lady's rage. Logic might absolve House Anasati of the tong's hiring, but the thirst of his aroused emotion remained unslaked. Whether or not Jiro was guilty, blood must atone for blood.

A runner sent by Lujan arrived at the command tent. He bowed to earth, silent until the Lady waved. "Mistress, Warchief of Clan Hadama, Ionani Force Commanders have given agreement. Battle shall commence when the sun rises to a height of six diameters over the eastern horizon."

Mara scanned the heavens, assessing. "That means the signal to charge will be sounded in less than a half hour." She snapped a nod of approval. Yet the delay was longer than she desired: Ayaki had received no such reprieve.

Minutes passed slowly. The soldiers continued to cry insults until their voices grew hoarse. The sun inched higher, and the air heated with the day. All in the command tent leashed in fraying nerves, until the touch of an alighting fly was enough to snap the gathering atmosphere of pent force.

Hokanu's impatience mounted. He was ready to draw blade and see the edge drink blood. At last the sun reached its designated position. No signal passed between the high officers in the command tent. Keyoke sucked in a quick breath in concert with Mara's lifted hand. Lujan, on the field, raised his bared sword, and the trumpets pealed out their call to war.

Hokanu had drawn his own sword without conscious thought. The battle might finish without his ever facing an enemy, for his place was beside his Lady. No Ionani warriors would breach the honor guard who surrounded the command tent lest Clan Hadama be routed, yet he, and beside him Saric, were both ready.

The notes of the fanfare seemed drawn out to eternity. In the distance, at the head of the army, Lujan waited with his blade poised high, glittering like a needle in sunlight. Across the field the Ionani commanding officer held a like pose. When the weapons of both men fell, a flood of screaming soldiers would charge across the narrow strip of meadow, and the hills would echo with the clash of swords and the cries of war.

Hokanu snatched breath to mutter a hurried prayer for Lujan, for the brave Acoma Force Commander was almost certain to die. The press of soldiers on both sides made it unlikely any in the first five ranks would survive the initial strike. The two great armies would grind themselves against each other like the teeth on opposing jaws, and only the warriors in the rearmost ranks might see who emerged victorious.

The moment of suspension ended. Men finished their last silent appeals to the gods for honor, victory, and life. Then Lujan's sword quivered in the stroke of descent.

As warriors shifted forward onto the balls of their feet, and banners stirred in the hands of bearers who lifted the poles from the earth, thunder slammed out of the clear green sky.

The concussion of air struck Mara and Hokanu full in the face. Cushions flew, and Hokanu staggered. He dropped to his knees, the arm not holding his weapon catching Mara into protective embrace. Incomo was flung back, his robes cupped like sails, as the command tent cracked and billowed in the gust. Keyoke stumbled backward into Saric, who caught him, and nearly went down as the crutch fetched him a blow across the legs. Both Acoma advisers clung to each other to keep their footing, while, inside the tent, tables overturned and charts depicting battle tactics flapped and tumbled into the tangle of privacy curtains that crashed across Mara's sleeping mat.

Through a maelstrom of dust devils, chaos extended across the field. Banners cracked and whipped, torn out of the bearers' hands. A cry went up from the front ranks of both armies as warriors were cast to the ground. Their swords stabbed earth, not flesh. Thrown into disarray by the whirlwind, the warriors behind tripped over one another until not one was left able to press forward to engage the fight.

In the breach between the lines appeared several figures in black. Their robes did not stir, but hung down in an uncanny calm. Then the unnatural winds abated, as if on command. Men on both sides blinked dust-caked lashes. They saw Great Ones come to intervene, and while their weapons remained in their hands, and the bloodlust to attack still drove them, none arose, nor did any make a move to overrun the magicians who stood equidistant between the armies. The downed warriors stayed prone, their faces pressed to the grass. No command from master or mistress could drive a man of them forward, for to touch a Great One was to invite utter ruin, if not commit offense against the gods.

Mara regarded the Black Robes that had balked her vengeance with hostile eyes. The straps on her armor creaked as she arose to her feet. Her hands clamped into fists, and muscles jumped in her jaw. Softly, she said, ''No.''

A strand of loose hair slipped from beneath her helm, and her

Warchief's plumes trembled like reeds before a breeze. A heartbeat later, another Great One materialized before the open flap of her tent. His robe seemed cut from night itself, and though he was slender with youth, there was nothing young about his eyes. They held a light that seemed to blaze in contrast to his dark skin and hair. His voice proved surprisingly deep. "Lady Mara, hear our will. The Assembly forbids this war!"

Mara turned pale. Rage shook her, to be constrained from fulfilling her Call to Clan War. Never had she imagined that the Assembly might intervene against her given will. She was as helpless to protest this development as her former enemy, Tasaio of the Minwanabi, had been, for to be forbidden the traditional means of vengeance for Ayaki's murder was to forfeit Acoma honor. To withdraw without bloodshed from this confrontation would disgrace her far more than any shame the Anasati might fall heir to. *Her* son was the one left unavenged; Lord Jiro would be given the victory. He would gain esteem for his courage, having come to the field prepared to engage in battle to defend his honor, but it was not his son or his family ancestors whose shades would be diminished for being deprived of blood price for a murder. As the accuser who had not prosecuted her claims by strength of arms, the Lady of the Acoma would forfeit much of the veneration due her rank.

Mara found her voice. "You force me to dishonor, Great One."

The magician dismissed her remark with haughty calm. "Your honor, or lack of it, is not my affair, Good Servant. The Assembly acts as it will, in all cases, for the Good of the Empire. The carnage of Clan conflict between Hadama and Ionani would weaken the Nations and leave this land vulnerable to attack from outside our borders. Therefore, you are told: no force of the Acoma or of the Anasati or their clans or allies may take the field to oppose the other for this or any other matter. You are forbidden to make war against Lord Jiro."

Mara held herself silent by force of will. Once she had stood witness when the barbarian Black Robe Milamber, had torn open the skies above the Imperial Arena. The powers unleashed on that day had killed, and shaken the earth, and caused fire to rain down from the clouds. She was not so far gone in grief to lose reason and forget: the magicians were the supreme force within the Empire.

The young, nameless magician looked on in arrogant silence as Mara swallowed hard. Her cheeks flushed red, and Hokanu, at her shoulder, could feel her trembling with suppressed rage. Yet she was Tsurani. The Great Ones were to be obeyed. She gave a stiff nod. "Your will, Great One."

Her bow was deep, if resentful. She half turned toward her advisers. ''Orders: withdraw.'' In the face of this command she had no choice. Though Ruling Lady of the greatest house in the Empire, though Servant of the Empire, even she could but bow to the inevitable and ensure that no lapse of dignity could compound this enforced dishonor.

Hokanu relayed his Lady's orders. Saric shook off a stunned stillness and hastened to rouse the signal runners outside the tent from their abject prostration. Keyoke readied the signal flags, and, as if grateful to be excused from the presence of the one dark-robed form in the command tent, messengers snatched up green and white flags and hurried off to the knoll to wave the command for withdrawal.

On the field, amid the kneeling mass of his warriors, Lujan saw the signal. He cupped his hands to his mouth and shouted, and around him the other Force Commanders of Clan Hadama called orders to retreat. Like a wave held in check, the men gathered up their swords and spears, slowly stood, and pulled back into family groups. Movement surged through their ranks as they formed up, and began the march back up the hillsides toward their respective masters' encampments.

The armies poised to clash rolled back from each other, leaving the meadow trampled in the sunlight. The magicians between the hosts oversaw the retreat, then, their office completed, disappeared one by one, relocating upon the hill near the Ionani command tent.

Intent on her bitterness, Mara barely noticed the magician still before her, nor Hokanu at her side, dispensing instructions to dismiss Clan Hadama's forces homeward to their respective estate garrisons. Her eyes might view an ending of war, but their hardness did not relent. Honor must be satisfied. To fall upon her family sword was no just reparation for Ayaki's life. The public disgrace remained, not to be forgotten. Jiro would use such shame to ally enemies against her house. Shaken to reassume her responsibilities, she could only atone for her error. No choice remained, now, but to use intrigue to resolve the death and the insult between herself and the Anasati. The Game of the Council must now serve, with plots and murder done in secret, behind a public front of Tsurani propriety.

A disturbance arose outside the command tent, a flurry of raised voices, and Keyoke's rising clearest in astonishment. ''Two companies from the extreme left flank are moving!''

Mara hurried into the open, fear dislodging her thoughts of hatred. She stared out over the valley in horrified disbelief to see the leftmost element of the Hadama forces countermand orders and surge forward.

The magician who had followed at her elbow hissed affront, and more of his fellows appeared out of empty air to join him.

Mara fought panic at the new arrivals. If she did not act, the Great Ones would take issue at her side's disregard of orders. In another moment her house, her clan, and every loyal servant of the Acoma might lie dead of the magicians' wrath.

"Who commands the left?" she cried in shrill desperation.

Irrilandi, now arrived on the hilltop, called answer. "That's a reserve company, mistress. It is under charge of the Lord of the Pechta."

Mara bit her lip in furious thought: Pechta was a lord but lately come to his inheritance. Barely more than a boy, he commanded out of deference to his rank, not through skills or experience. Tsurani tradition gave him the right to a place at the forefront of the ranks. Lujan had compensated as best he might, and set the boy over an auxiliary unit, which would be called upon only when the battle's outcome was decided. But now either his youth or his hot blood invited total disaster.

Keyoke considered the situation in the valley with the eyes of a master tactician. "The impetuous fool! He seeks to strike while confusion occupies the Anasati side of the line! Didn't he see the Great Ones? How could he ignore their arrival?"

"He's bereft of his senses." Hokanu gestured to the runners, who had reached even the farthest sections of the lines. "Or else he can't read the command flags."

Saric raced off to dispatch more runners, while on the field several older commanding officers broke away from the press of retreating warriors and hurried to converge on Lord Pechta's moving banners.

On the hill, Lady Mara looked on in horror as two full companies of men in Lord Pechta's orange-and-blue-plumed armor moved forward to attack the Anasati right flank. The soldiers in red and yellow on the far hillside swirled in an about-face, preparing to meet the charge. Their commander's shouts floated on the wind as he exhorted each warrior to keep his head. They were seasoned troops, or else their fear lent them prudence. They held in compliance with the Great Ones' edict, and did not rush forward to answer Lord Pechta's provocation.

Keyoke's sinewy hands whitened on his crutch. "He's wise, that Anasati Strike Leader. He will not violate the order to withdraw, and should our men under Pechta keep coming, they will be attacking uphill. He has time to wait, and perhaps maintain the truce."

The words were spoken for the benefit of the Black Robes, who had banded together in a disturbed knot. Frowning under ink-dark hoods, they watched the Pechta forces race headlong up the rise on the Ionani side of the vale.

One spoke, and two vanished with a whipping snap of air.

Mara's servants threw themselves prone in abject fear, and more than one veteran turned white. Lujan looked sick and Keyoke like chiseled rock.

On the field, the two Black Robes reappeared before the charging forces. Tiny as toys, yet menacing in that smallness, they threw up their hands. Green light sparked from their fingertips, and a searing flash erupted in the path of the running warriors.

The eyesight of every watcher was dazzled.

Left blind by the afterimage, Mara was forced to blink tears from her stinging eyes. Moments passed before she recovered clear vision. She forced herself to face front, and gasped.

At first glance nothing appeared wrong. Lord Pechta's soldiers no longer ran; they still stood upright, their orange armor bright in the sunlight and their plumes twisting in the breeze. More careful study showed that their quietness masked a tableau of horror. The hands that still clutched weapons writhed and twitched, the flesh slowly blistering. Faces contorted in nightmarish, silent agony. Their skin raised up in pustules, then darkened, blackened, and crisped. Smoke curled on the wind, stinking of scorched carrion. Flesh cracked and oozed blood that boiled away into steam.

Mara's belly clenched with nausea. She sagged back, caught by Hokanu, who shared her tortured horror. Even the battle-hardened Keyoke looked ill to his very core.

There came no screams from the field. The victims stood arrested as puppets as their eyes burst and empty sockets seeped. Their tongues became thick purple obscenities protruding from mouths that could not emit even a single strangled cry. Hair smoked and fingernails melted, yet the soldiers lived, their jerks and quivers clearly visible to the stunned observers upon the distant hilltops.

Saric choked back a gasp. "Gods, gods, they are surely punished enough."

The magician first appointed to Mara's tent turned toward the adviser. "They are only punished enough when *we* decide to allow them their crossing to Turakamu."

"As you will, Great One!" Saric immediately prostrated himself, his face pressed to the dirt like a slave's. "Your forgiveness, Great One. I regret my outburst, and apologize for speaking out of turn."

The magician deigned no reply, but stood in cold silence as the Pechta warriors continued to suffer on the field. Burnt flesh peeled from their bodies, to fall smoking to the ground. The men at last began to topple, first one, then another, until all two hundred warriors lay tumbled, blackened skeletons, on untouched grass, still clad in gleaming armor. The orange-and-blue Pechta banner lay before them, the tassels fluttering in wind that carried barely a signature of smoke.

The young magician at length stood apart from his fellows and addressed the Lady Mara. "Our rule is absolute, Good Servant. Let your people remember. Any who defy us invite instant oblivion. Is that understood?"

Mara fought back her sickness, croaked a whisper. "Your will, Great One."

Another magician separated himself from the group. "I am not yet satisfied." He regarded Mara's officers, all on their feet except for Saric. They might appear uncowed, as Tsurani propriety demanded, yet not one did not tremble with terror. This brave front seemed to increase the Black Robe's displeasure. "Who defied us?" he inquired of his colleagues, ignoring Mara.

"Young Lord Pechta," came the reply, cold and to the point. A third voice arose from the Black Robes, this one more temperate. "He acted upon his own, without his Warchief's permission or approval."

The second magician, a sharp-eyed man with a shock of red hair that escaped the edges of his hood, shifted his regard to Mara. "His dishonor does not end here."

The magician who seemed to mediate called out again. "Tapek, I said Lady Mara had nothing to do with the defiance."

Tapek returned a shrug, as if irritated by a fly. "As Lord Pechta's Warchief, she is responsible for the conduct of all forces under her command."

Mara lifted her chin. Her mind stilled with a horror of recognition: these Black Robes might order her dead, with no more concern than they had showed for Tasaio of the Minwanabi, whose suicide had resulted from their bidding. Her officers looked arrested with terror. Keyoke showed nothing beyond a hardness around his eyes that no one living had ever seen.

Hokanu made an involuntary jerk forward, but was stopped by Lujan's rock-hard grip upon his arm.

The onlookers, to a man, held their breath. Should the Black Robes order her destruction, no sword, no plea, no power of love might prevent them. The loyalty of thousands of servants and soldiers who would gladly give their lives in her place would avail her nothing.

While the red-haired Tapek studied the Lady with a snake's heartless regard, the young magician said, "Is Lord Pechta still alive?"

Lujan reacted instantly, dispatching a runner to the field. Minutes passed. Tapek shifted in impatience, while out at the scene of the carnage the messenger conferred. A flag was brought to signal. It dipped and waved in code, while Lujan interpreted. "All who attacked are dead." He dared raise his eyes to the Great Ones as he concluded, "Lord Pechta was leading his men. His body is ashes and bones, with the rest."

The first magician nodded curtly. "The obliteration of the offender is ample punishment."

The third magician from the group affirmed, "So be it."

Mara felt faint with relief, until Tapek stepped sharply toward her. Deep in the shadow under his hood, his heavy eyebrows drew up in displeasure. His eyes were pale, cold as the depths of the sea, and menace edged his tone as he said, "Mara of the Acoma, the House of Pechta is no more. You shall see that all of that line are dead before nightfall. The estate house and barracks will be burned, and the fields fired. When the crops are destroyed, Acoma servants shall salt the earth, that nothing shall grow on the land. All soldiers sworn to the Pechta natami are to be hung. You will leave their remains to rot in the wind, and never offer them haven as you have other warriors of conquered houses. All Pechta free servants are now slaves, given over to the service of the Emperor. All Pechta holdings now belong to the temples. The Pechta natami is to be broken by hammers and the fragments buried, never to know the sun's warmth, never more to secure Pechta spirits to the Wheel of Life. From this night unto eternity, that house no longer exists. Let its ending signify this: no one may defy the will of the Assembly. No one."

Mara forced her knees not to give way. She used every shred of her strength to draw breath and find her voice. "Your will, Great One."

She bowed. Her armor dragged at her shoulders, and the plumes of her helm seemed to weigh down her neck, yet she lowered herself until her knees and forehead touched soil, and the feathers of a Hadama Warchief became sullied with dust.

The young magician inclined his head in perfunctory acknowledgment of her obeisance, then withdrew a round metal device from his robe. He depressed a switch with his thumb. A whining sound cut the stillness. With an audible pop and an inrushing of air, the Black Robe vanished.

Tapek lingered, studying the woman who was folded on the ground at his feet. His lips twitched as if he enjoyed her groveling. "See that the object of this lesson is well learned by all others in your Clan, Good Servant. *Any* who defy the Assembly will face the same fate as the Pechta." He withdrew another of the round devices and a moment later disappeared. The other Black Robes vanished after him, leaving the hilltop bare but for the circle of Mara's shocked officers.

Below, shouts rang across the vale as officers called orders to confused soldiers. Warriors crowded back up the hillsides, some in a hurry to put space between themselves and the carnage wrought by magic, others reluctant to turn their backs upon the enemy, who marched to the same edict given to Lady Mara. Saric gathered himself to his feet, while her Force Commander helped his Lady, in the encumbrance of her armor, to do the same. Hoarsely she said to Lujan, "Hurry and dispatch more messengers. We must make haste to disperse the clan, lest further mishap provoke an incident."

Swallowing hard, and still feeling sickened, Mara gestured to Saric. "And, Gods grant us mercy, order this terrible thing done: obliterate the Pechta."

Saric nodded, unable to speak. He had a gift for reading character, and the memory of Tapek's intensity gave him chills. Mara had been dealt the worst punishment imaginable: the utter destruction of a loyal clan family for no worse offense than youthful impetuosity. All for his mistress's Call to Clan, the young Lord had died in lingering agony; before nightfall his young wife and baby sons would be dead, as would cousins and relations who bore his name. That Mara must herself be the instrument of that unjust decree cut through her grief for Ayaki. For the first time since the great black gelding had toppled upon the body of her son, her eyes showed the spark of awakened feeling for others beyond herself.

Saric saw this as he trudged off to complete the horrifying task set the Acoma by the Great Ones. Hokanu observed it, too, as he steadied his Lady's steps on her return to the command tent. The fires of the Assembly's magic had cauterized the wounds to her spirit. In place of the obsession for revenge against Jiro, a fierce anger now commanded her mind.

Mara had recovered herself. Hokanu knew bittersweet relief at the change. He regretted the Pechta's loss; but the woman he loved was once again the most dangerous player of the Game of the Council the Empire had ever known. With a gesture, she dismissed the servants who rushed to neaten the disorder left in the tent. When the last of them had retreated a discreet distance away, she called Irrilandi to unlace the door flaps and restore her a measure of privacy.

Keyoke entered as the last flap slapped down. He performed a servant's task of lighting the lanterns, while Mara paced. Vibrant, even jagged with nerves, she regarded those of her house who were present, arrayed in a semicircle before her. Her voice seemed flat as she said, "They dare. . . ."

Keyoke stiffened. He glanced askance at Hokanu, who stood as mute as the others. Mara reached the fallen tangle of her privacy curtains, then spun around. "Well, they will learn."

Irrilandi, who knew her moods less well than the others, gave her a fist-over-heart salute. "Lady, surely you do not speak in reference to the magicians?"

Mara seemed tiny in the lantern light that held the shadows in the cavernous tent at bay. A moment passed, filled by the muffled shouts of the officers still mustering troops outside. Bowstring-taut, Mara qualified. "We must do what has never been done since the Empire came into existence, my loyal friends. We must discover a way to evade the will of the Great Ones."

Irrilandi gasped. Even Keyoke, who had faced death through a lifetime of campaigns, seemed shaken to the core. But Mara continued grimly, "We have no choice. I have shamed the Acoma name before Jiro of the Anasati. We are forbidden expiation by means of war; I will not fall upon my sword. This is an impasse for which tradition has no answer. The Lord of the Anasati must die by my design, and I will not stoop to hiring assassins. Jiro has already used my disgrace to whip up enemies. He has turned the dissatisfied Lords in the Nations into a cohesive party of traditionalists, and Ichindar's reign is imperiled along with the continuance of the Acoma name. My only heir is dead, so my ritual suicide offers us no alternative. If all that I have lived to achieve is to be salvaged, we must spend years in the planning. Jiro must die by my hand, if not in war, then in peace, despite the will of the Assembly of Magicians."

4. Adversity

Someone moved.

Atop a stack of baled cloth, partially hidden by the cant of a crooked bale, Arakasi heard what might be the grate of a footstep on the gritty boards of the floor. He froze, uneasy at the discovery he was not alone in the murk of the warehouse. Silently he controlled his breathing; he forced his body to relax, to stave off any chance of a muscle cramp brought on by his awkward position. From a distance, his clothing would blend with the wares, making him seem like a rucked bit of fabric fallen loose from its ties. Up close, the deception would not bear inspection. His coarse-woven robe could never be mistaken for fine linens. Mindful that he might have trapped himself by taking refuge in this building to shake a suspected tail, he shut his eyes to enhance his other senses. The air was musty from spilled grain and leakage from barrels of exotic spices. The scents of the resins that waterproofed the roof shingles mingled with those of moldered leather from the door hinges. This particular warehouse lay near enough to the dockside that its floors submerged when the river crested in spring and overran the levee.

Minutes passed. Noise from the dock quarter came muffled through the walls: a sailor's raucous argument with a woman of the Reed Life, a barking cur, and the incessant rumble of wheels as needra drew the heavy drays of wares away from the riverside landings. The Acoma Spy Master strained to sort the distant hubbub; one by one, he tagged the sounds, while the day outside waned. A shouting band of street urchins raced down the street, and the bustle of commerce quieted. Nothing untoward met his ears beyond the calls of the lamplighters who tended the street at the end of the alley. Long past the point where another man might conclude he had imagined the earlier disturbance—that what seemed a footstep was surely the result of stress and imagination—Arakasi held rigidly still.

The flesh still prickled warning at the base of his neck. He was not one to take chances. Patience was all, when it came to any contest of subterfuge.

Restraint rewarded him, finally, when a faint scrape suggested the brush of a robe against wood, or the catch of a sleeve against a support beam. Doubt fled before ugly certainty: someone else was inside the warehouse.

Arakasi prayed silently to Chochocan, the Good God, to let him live through this encounter. Whoever had entered this dark building had not done so for innocent reasons. This intruder was unlikely to be a servant who had stolen off for an illicit nap in the afternoon heat, then overslept through supper into night. Arakasi mistrusted coincidence, always; to presume wrongly could bring his death. Given the hour, and the extreme stealth exhibited by his stalker, he had to conclude he was hunted.

Sweating in the still air, he reviewed each step that had brought him to this position. He had paid an afternoon call upon a fabric broker in the city of Ontoset, his purpose to contact a factor of a minor house who was one of his many active agents. Arakasi made a habit of irregular personal visits to ensure that such men remained loyal to their Acoma mistress, and to guard against enemy infiltrations. The intelligence network he had built upon since his days as a servant of the Tuscai had grown vast under Acoma patronage. Complacence on his part invited any of a thousand possible mishaps, the slightest of which could spell disaster for his Lady's welfare.

His visit today had not been carelessly made; his guise as an independent trader from Yankora had been backed up by paper work and references. The public announcement of the Assembly's intervention between the Acoma and the Anasati had reached this southern city days later; news tended to travel slowly across provinces as the rivers fell and deepwater trade barges were replaced by landborne caravans. Aware that Lady Mara would require his updated reports by the fastest possible means to guard against possible countermoves by the Anasati or other foes made bold by the Assembly's constraints, Arakasi had shortened his stay to a hurried exchange of messages. On leaving the premises, he had suspected he was being followed.

Whoever had tailed him had been good. Three times he had tried to shed his pursuit in the teeming crush of the poor quarter; only a caution that approached the obsessive had shown him a half-glimpsed face, a tar-stained hand, and twice, a colored edge of sash that should not have been repeated in the random shuffle of late-day traffic.

As well as the Spy Master could determine, there were four of them, a superbly trained team who were sure to be agents from another network. No mere sailors or servants in commoners' clothing could work with such close coordination. Arakasi inwardly cursed. He had blundered into just the sort of trap he had set for informants himself.

His backup plan could not be faulted. He had quickly crossed the busy central market, where purchase of a new robe and sudden movement through an inn packed with roisterers had seen the trader from Yankora vanish and a house messenger emerge. His skill in altering his carriage, his movements, the very set of his bones as he walked had confused many an opponent over the years.

His back trail had seemed unencumbered as he jogged back to the factor's quarters and let himself in through a hidden door. There he had changed into the brown of a common laborer, and taken refuge in the warehouse behind the trade shop. Crawling atop the cloth bales, his intent had been to sleep until morning.

Now he cursed himself for a fool. When those following had lost sight of him, they must have dispatched one of their number to backtrack to this warehouse, on the off-chance he might return. It was a move that a less cocky man might have anticipated, and only the gods' luck had seen the Acoma Spy Master inside and hidden before the enemy agent slipped in to wait and observe. Sweat trickled down Arakasi's collar. The opponent he faced was dangerous; his entrance had almost gone undetected. Instinct more than sure knowledge had roused Arakasi to caution.

The gloom was too deep to reveal his adversary's location. Imperceptibly slowly, the Acoma Spy Master inched his hand down to grasp the small dagger in his belt. Ever clumsy with handling a sword, he had a rare touch for knives. If he had clear view of a target, this nerve-rasping wait might be ended. Yet if a wish was his for the granting, he would not ask the Gods of Tricks and Fortune for weapons, but to be far from here, on his way back to Mara. Arakasi had no delusions of being a warrior. He had killed before, but his preferred defense relied more on wits, surprise tactics giving him the first strike. This was the first time he had been truly cornered.

A scuffle sounded at the far end of the warehouse. Arakasi stopped breathing as a loose board creaked, pulled aside to allow a second man to slip inside.

The Spy Master expelled his pent air carefully. The hope of a stealthy kill was lost to him. Now he had two enemies to consider. Light flared as a hand-carried lantern was unshuttered. Arakasi squinted to preserve his night vision, his situation turned from tense to critical. While he was probably concealed from the first agent, the new arrival at the back of the warehouse could not help but discover him as he walked past holding a light.

Out of alternatives, Arakasi probed for the gap that should exist between the stack of bales where he rested and the wall. Cloth needed space for air circulation, lest mildew cause spoilage in the dark. This merchant was not overly generous in his habits; the crack that met the Spy Master's touch was very narrow. Prickling in awareness of his peril, he slid in one arm to the shoulder and wiggled until the bale shifted. The risk could not be avoided, that the stack might topple; if he did not act, he was going to be discovered anyway. Forcing himself flat against the wall, and nudging on the bale, Arakasi wedged himself into the widening gap. Splinters from the unvarnished boards gouged into his bare knees. He dared not pause, even to mouth a silent curse, for the light at ground level was moving.

Footfalls advanced on his position, and shadows swung in arcs across the rafters. He was only halfway hidden, but his position was high enough that the angle of illumination swept above him; had he waited another heartbeat, his movement would have been seen. His margin for error was nonexistent. Only the steps of his adversary covered the slither of his last furtive shove as he nestled downward into the cranny.

A mutter arose from beyond the bale. "Look at that!" As if summarizing an inspection, the man rambled on, "Tossing good cloth as if it were straw bales, and unworthy of careful packing . . . Someone should be beaten for this—"

The musing was interrupted by the original stalker's whisper. "Over here."

Arakasi dared not raise himself to risk a glance.

The lantern crept on in the hand of its unseen bearer. "Any sign of him?"

"None." The first stalker sounded irritable. "Thought I heard something a bit ago, but it was probably vermin. We're surrounded by grain warehouses here."

Reassured enough to be bored, the newcomer lifted his lantern. "Well, he's around somewhere. The factor's slave insisted he'd come back and gone into hiding. The others are watching the residence. They'd better find him before morning. I don't want to be the one to tell our master he's escaped."

"You get wind of the gossip? That this fellow's been seen before, in different guise? He's got to be a courier, at least, or even a supervisor." Cheerfully the stalker added, "He's not from this province, either."

"You talk too much," snapped the lantern bearer. "And you remember things you should forget. If you want to keep breathing, you'd best keep that sort of news to yourself. You know what they say, 'Men have throats and daggers have sharp edges.' "

The advice was received with a sigh. "How long must we keep watch?"

"Unless we're told to leave, we'll stay until just before daybreak. Won't do to be caught here, and maybe killed by guards as common thieves."

An unintelligible grumble ended the conversation.

Arakasi resigned himself to a long, uncomfortable wait. His body would be cramped by morning, and the splinters an additional aggravation, but the consequences if he should be captured did not bear examination. The loose tongues of his trackers had confirmed his worst surmise: he had been traced by another spy net. Whoever commanded the pair who hunted him, whoever they reported to, the master at the top of their network worked for someone canny, someone who had constructed a spy system that had escaped notice until now. Arakasi weighed this fact and knew fear. Chance and intuition had spared him when intricate advance precautions had failed; in discomfort, in warm darkness, he agonized over his assessment.

The team who sought to capture him were skilled, but not so polished that they refrained from indulging in idle talk. It followed that they had been set to catch what their master presumed must be a low-ranking link in the operation he sought to crack. Arakasi suppressed a chill. It was a mark of the deep distrust that drove him, that he preferred when he could to accomplish occasional small errands in person. His unseen enemy must have the chance to know who he was, how highly he was placed, or the name of the mistress he reported to. Possibly he faced the most dangerous opponent he had ever encountered. Somewhere Lady Mara had an enemy whose subtleties posed a threat greater than anything she had confronted in her life. If Arakasi did not escape alive from Ontoset, if he could not get a message home, his mistress might be taken unwarned by the next strike. Reminded by the ache in his chest that his breathing had turned swift and shallow, the Spy Master forced control.

His security had been compromised, when he had no inkling of impending trouble. The breach spoke of intricate planning. The factor's second role must have been discovered; precisely how could not be surmised, but a watch had been set over the traffic at Ontoset's docks closely enough to differentiate between regular traders and those who were strangers. That the team that lay in had been clever enough to see through two of Arakasi's disguises, having marked him as a courier or supervisor, boded ill.

Arakasi counted the cost. He would have to replace the factor. A certain slave was going to die of what must seem natural causes, and the trade shop must be shut down, a regrettable necessity, for while it doubled as part of his network, it was one of the few profitable Acoma undertakings used by the spy ring. It paid for itself and provided extra funds for other agents.

Grey light filtered through a crack in the wall. Dawn was nigh, but the men showed no sign of stirring. They had not fallen asleep, but were waiting against the chance the man they sought might show himself at the last hour.

The minutes dragged. Daybreak brightened outside. Carts and wagons rumbled by, the costermongers bringing produce to be loaded at the riverside before the worst of the heat. The chant of a team of barge oarsmen lifted in tuneless unison, cut by the scolding of a wife berating a drunken husband. Then a shout raised over the waking noise of the city, close at hand, and urgent. The words were indistinct to Arakasi, wedged behind muffling bales of linen, but the other two men in the warehouse scrambled immediately into motion. Their footfalls pattered the length of the building, and the board creaked aside.

Most likely they made good their escape; were they clever, they might have used the sound of their leaving as opening gambit for a ruse. A partner could yet be lingering to see if their quarry flushed in response.

Arakasi held still, though his legs were kinked into knots of spasming muscle. He delayed a minute, two, his ears straining for signs of danger.

Voices sounded outside the doubled door, and the rattle of the puzzle lock that held the warehouse secure warned of an imminent entry. Arakasi twisted to free himself, and found his shoulders wedged fast. His arms were pressed flat to his sides; his legs had slipped too low to gain purchase. He was trapped.

He knew galvanic desperation. Were he caught here, and arrested as a thief, the spy who had traced him would hear. A corrupt city official would then receive a gift, and he would find himself delivered to his enemy. His chance to make his way back to Mara would be lost.

Arakasi jammed his elbows against the bale, to no avail. The gap that pinned him widened, only causing him to fall deeper into the cleft. The board walls added the sting of new splinters to his wrists and forearms. Silently swearing, he pushed and slipped inexorably beyond hope of unobtrusive extrication.

The warehouse doors crashed open. The Spy Master could do nothing now but pray for a chance to innovate as an overseer bellowed, ''Take all those, against that wall.''

Sunlight and air heavy with the scent of river mud spilled into the warehouse; a needra lowed, and harness creaked. Arakasi deduced that wagons waited outside to be loaded. He weighed his choices. To call attention to himself now was to chance that no one from the enemy net waited outside, a risk he dared not take. He could be followed again, and luck would not spare him a second time. Then all debate became moot as a work team hurried into the warehouse, and the bale that jammed his body suddenly moved.

"Hey," someone called. "Careful of that loose bit up there."

"Loose bit!" snapped the overseer. "Which of you dogs broke a tie when the bales were stacked and didn't report the lapse?"

A muddle of disclaiming replies masked Arakasi's movement as he flexed aching muscles in preparation for his inevitable discovery.

Nothing happened. The workers became involved with making excuses to their overseer. Arakasi seized the moment to lever himself upward. His thrust jostled the cloth that had been shifted, and it overbalanced and tumbled downward to land with a resounding thump against the floor.

The overseer yelled his displeasure. "Oaf! They're heavier than they look! Get help before you go trying to push them about from above."

So, Arakasi concluded: the factor must have realized his dilemma and arranged a possible cover. No space remained for mistakes if the impromptu salvage was to work. Hastily he threw himself prostrate. With his face pressed to the pile of cloth where he perched, he mumbled abject apologies.

"Well, hurry along!" the overseer cried. "Your clumsiness is no excuse to lie about in idleness. Get the wagons loaded!"

Arakasi nodded, pushed himself off the stack, and fought against the unsteadiness of stiff muscles to keep his feet. The shock was too much, after hours of forced inactivity. He bent before he collapsed, leaning against the fallen bale and stretching as if examining himself for injuries. A worker eyed him sourly as he straightened. "You all right?"

Arakasi nodded vigorously enough to shake loose hair over his features.

"Then lend a hand," the worker said. "We're almost done at this end."

Arakasi did as he was bidden and caught the end of the fallen bale. In tandem with the worker, he joined the team doing the loading. Head down, hands busy, he used every trick he knew to alter his appearance. Sweat dripped down his jaw. He smeared the trickle with his hands, rubbing in dust and dirt to darken the thrust of his cheekbones. He ran his fingers through the one lock of hair kept dyed since a scar had turned it white, then smudged artfully to extend shadow and lend the illusion of shortening his chin. He lowered his brows in a scowl, and thrust his bottom teeth against his upper lip. To an onlooker he should seem noth-

ing more than a worker of little intelligence; as he hefted his end of the
cloth he stared directly ahead, doing nothing that might identify him as a
fugitive.

Each pass from warehouse to wagon scraped his nerves raw. By the
time the wagons were loaded, he had singled out a loiterer in the shadows
of the shop front across the street. The man seemed vacant-eyed, a beggar
left witless by addiction to tateesha; except that his eyes were too focused. Arakasi repressed a shiver. The enemy was after him, still.

The wagons were prepared to roll, the workers climbing on board.
Mara's Spy Master hoisted himself up onto the load as if expected to, and
elbowed the man next to him in the ribs.

"Did the little cousin get that robe she wanted?" he asked loudly.
"The one with the flower patterns on the hem?"

Whips cracked, and a drover shouted. The needra leaned into their
traces, and the laden wagons groaned into movement. The worker
Arakasi had addressed stared back in frank surprise. "What?"

As if the big man had said something funny, Arakasi laughed loudly.
"You know. Lubal's little girl. The one who brings lunches down to
Simeto's gang at the docks."

The worker grunted. "Simeto I've heard of, but not Lubal."

Arakasi slapped his forehead in embarrassment. "You're not his friend
Jido?"

The other man hawked dust from his throat and spat. "Never heard of
him."

The wagons had reached the corner of the alley and swung to negotiate
the turn. Urchins blocking the way raised curses from the lead drover,
and the overseer waved a threatening fist. The children returned obscene
gestures, then scattered like a startled flock of birds. Two mangy hounds
galloped after them. Arakasi dared a glance back at the factor's residence.
The tateesha halfwit still drooled and watched the warehouse doors,
which were being closed and locked by a servant.

The ruse, perhaps had worked.

Arakasi mumbled words of apology to the man he had bothered, and
rested his head on crossed elbows. While the wagon rolled, jostling over
the uneven paving and splashing through the refuse that overflowed the
gutters by the dockside, he smothered a sigh of relief. He was not clear of
danger, nor would he be safe until he was miles removed from Ontoset.
His thoughts turned to the future: whoever had arranged the trap at the
factor's would presume that his net was discovered. He would further
surmise that his escaped quarry must guess that another organization was
at work. Logic insisted that this unseen enemy would react with counter-

measures to foil just the sort of search that Arakasi must now launch. Ring upon ring of confusion would befuddle the trail, while the Ontoset branch of the Acoma network was left a total loss. Its lines of communication must be dissolved without trace. Two more levels of operation would have to be engaged, and swiftly: one to check for leaks in the branches in other provinces, and another to sift through a cold trail to try and ferret out this new enemy.

The difficulties were nearly insurmountable. Arakasi had a touch for difficult puzzles, true enough. But this one was potentially deadly, like a sword edge buried in sand that any man's foot might dislodge. He brooded until the wagons pulled up at the docks. Along with the other workers, he jumped down onto the wharf and set hands to a hoist. One after another, the cloth bales were dragged from the wagon beds and loaded into waiting nets. Arakasi shoved on the pole with the rest when the hoist was full, lifting the cargo high and swinging it onto the deck of the barge warped alongside. The sun rose higher, and the day warmed. At the first opportunity, he slipped away on the excuse that he needed a drink of water, and vanished into the poor quarter.

He must make his way out of Ontoset without help. To approach any other link in his net was to risk being rediscovered; worse, he might lead his pursuit to a fresh area of endeavor, and expose still more of his undercover workings. There were men in this city who would harbor fugitives for pay, but Arakasi dared not approach them. They could be infiltrated by the enemy, and his need to escape might connect him irrefutably to the incident at the warehouse. He wished for a bath and a chance to soak out the splinters still lodged under his skin, but he would get neither. A slave's grey clothing or a beggar's rags must see him past the city gates. Once outside the walls, he must hole up in the countryside until he could be certain he had made a clean break. Then he might try the guise of a courier and hasten to make up for his delay.

He sighed, discomforted by the extended time he would be traveling, left alone with conjecture. He held troubled thoughts, of an unknown antagonist who had nearly taken him out of play with one move, and that enemy's master, an unseen, unassailable threat. With Clan War between Mara and Lord Jiro decreed forbidden by the magicians, his beloved Lady of the Acoma was endangered. As opportunists and enemies banded into alliances against her, she was going to need the best intelligence to ward from her yet more underhanded moves in the murderous intrigues of the Great Game.

* * *

The tailor allowed the robe's silken hem to fall to the floor. Pins of finely carved bone were clenched between his teeth; he stepped back to admire the fit of the formal garment commissioned by the Lord of the Anasati.

Lord Jiro endured the craftsman's scrutiny with contained disdain. His features expressionless, he stood with his arms held out from his body to avoid a chance prick from the pins that fastened the cuffs. His posture was so still that the sequins sewn in the shape of killwings that adorned the front of the robe did not even shimmer in the light that fell through the open screen.

"My Lord," lisped the tailor around the pins pinched between his teeth, "you look splendid. Surely every unmarried noble daughter who beholds your magnificence will swoon at your feet."

Jiro's lips twitched. He was not a man who enjoyed flattery. Careful with appearances to the point where the unperceptive might mistakenly think him vain, he well knew the value of clothing when it came to leaving an impression. The wrong raiment could make a man seem stupid, overweight, or frivolous. Since swordplay and the rigors of battle were not to Jiro's taste, he used every other means to enhance his aspect of virility. An edge could be gained, or a contest of wits turned into victory more subtle than any coarse triumph achieved on the fields of war.

Proud of his ability to master his foes without bloodshed, Jiro had to restrain himself not to bridle at the tailor's thoughtless compliment. The man was a craftsman, a hireling barely worth notice, much less his anger. His words were of less consequence than the wind, and only chance had caused him to jar against a memory Jiro yet held with resentment. Despite his closest attention to manners and dress, Lady Mara had spurned him. The awkward, coarse-mannered Buntokapi had been chosen over him. Even passing recollection caused Jiro to sweat with repressed fury. His years of studied effort had availed him not at all, when all of his wits and schooled charm had been summarily dismissed by the Acoma. His ridiculous—no, laughable—lout of a brother had triumphed over him.

Bunto's smirk was unforgiven; Jiro still stung from remembered humiliation. His hands closed into fists, and he suddenly had no stomach for standing still. "I don't like this robe," he snapped peevishly. "It displeases me. Make another, and have this one torn up for rags."

The tailor turned pale. He whipped the pins from his teeth and dropped to the parquet floor, his forehead pressed to the wood. "My Lord! As you wish, of course. I beg humble forgiveness for my lack of taste and judgment."

Jiro said nothing. He jerked his barbered head for a servant to remove the robe and drop it in a heap underfoot. "I will wear the blue-and-red silk. Fetch it now."

His command was obeyed in a flurry of nervousness. The Lord of the Anasati seldom punished his slaves and attendants, but from the day he assumed his inheritance he had made it clear that anything short of instant obedience would never be tolerated.

Arriving to make his report, First Adviser Chumaka noted the near-frenzied obsequious behavior on the part of the servants. He gave not a twitch in reaction; wisest of the Anasati retainers, he knew his Lord best of all. The master did not appreciate overdone obeisance; quite the contrary. Jiro had matured as a second son, and he liked things quiet and without fanfare. Yet since he had inherited a ruler's mantle without having been groomed to expect the post, he was ever sensitive to the behavior of his underlings toward him. Should they fail to give him his due respect as Lord, he would notice, and take instantaneous issue.

The servant who was late to speak his title, the slave who failed to bow without delay upon presentation, were never forgiven their lapse. Like fine clothing and smooth manners, traditional Tsurani adherence to caste was part and parcel of how Ruling Lords were measured by their peers. Eschewing the barbaric aspects of the battlefield, Jiro had made himself a master of civilized behavior.

As if a robe of finest silk did not lie discarded like garbage under his sandaled feet, he inclined his head while Chumaka straightened up from his bow. "What brings you to consult at this hour, First Adviser? Did you forget I had planned an afternoon of discourse with the visiting scholars from Migran?"

Chumaka tipped his head to one side, as a hungry rodent might fix on moving prey. "I suggest, my Lord, that the scholars be made to wait while we take a short walk."

Lord Jiro was vexed, though nothing showed. He allowed his servants to tie his robe sash before he replied. "What you have to say is that important?" As all who were present well knew, Jiro held afternoon court to attend to business with his factors. If his meeting with the scholars was delayed, it would have to wait until morning, which spoiled his hour set aside for reading.

The Anasati First Adviser presented his driest smile and deftly handled the impasse. "It pertains to Lady Mara of the Acoma, and that connection I mentioned earlier concerning the vanquished Tuscai."

Jiro's interest brightened. "The two are connected?"

Chumaka's stillness before the servants provided its own answer. Excited now, Lord Jiro clapped for his runner. "Find my hadonra and instruct him to provide entertainment for our guests. They shall be told that I am detained and will meet with them tomorrow morning. Lest they become displeased by these arrangements, it shall be explained that I am considering awarding a patronage, if I am impressed by their worthiness in the art of verbal debate.''

The runner bowed to the floor and hurried off about his errand. Chumaka licked his teeth in anticipation as his master fell into step with him toward the outer screen that led into the garden.

Jiro seated himself on a stone bench in the shade by a fish pool. He trailed languid fingers in the water while his attention to Chumaka sharpened. ''Is it good news or bad?''

As always, the First Adviser's reply was ambiguous. ''I'm not certain.'' Before his master could express displeasure, Chumaka adjusted his robe and fished a sheaf of documents out of a deep pocket. ''Perhaps both, my Lord. A small, precautionary surveillance I set in place identified someone highly placed in the Acoma spy network.'' He paused, his thoughts branching off into inaccessibly vague speculation.

''What results?'' Jiro prompted, in no mood for cleverness that he lacked the finesse to follow.

Chumaka cleared his throat. ''He eluded us.''

Jiro looked nettled. ''How could this be good news?''

Chumaka shrugged. ''We know he *was* someone of importance; the entire operation in Ontoset was closed down as a result. The factor of the House of Habatuca suddenly became what he appeared to be: a factor.'' As an afterthought, he said, ''Business is terrible, so we may assume that the goods being brokered by this man were Acoma, not Habatuca.'' He glanced at one of his documents and folded it. ''We know the Habatuca are not Acoma minions; they are firmly in the Omechan Clan, and traditionalists whom we might find useful someday. They don't even suspect this man is not their loyal servant, but then they are a very disorganized house.''

Jiro tapped his chin with an elegantly manicured finger as he said, ''This factor's removal is significant?''

Chumaka said, ''Yes, my Lord. The loss of that agent will hamper Acoma operation in the East. I can assume that almost all information coming from that region was funneled through Ontoset.''

Jiro smiled, no warmth in his expression. ''Well then, we've stung them. But now they also know we are watching them with our own agents.''

Chumaka said, ''That was inevitable, my Lord. I am surprised they hadn't been aware of us sooner. Their network is well established and practiced. That we observed them undetected as long as we did was something close to miraculous.''

Seeing a gleam in his First Adviser's eyes, Jiro said, ''What else?''

''I said this was related to the long-dead Lord of the Tuscai, from years before you were born. Just before Jingu of the Minwanabi destroyed House Tuscai, I had unearthed the identity of one of the dead Lord's key agents, a grain merchant in Jamar. When the Tuscai natami was buried, I assumed the man continued his role as an independent merchant in earnest. He had no public ties to House Tuscai, therefore no obligation to assume the status of outcast.''

Jiro went still at this implied, venal dishonesty. A master's servants were considered cursed by the gods if he should die; his warriors became slaves or grey warriors—or had, until Lady Mara had despicably broken the custom.

Chumaka ignored his master's discomfort, caught up as he was in reminiscence. ''My assumption was incorrect, as I now have cause to suspect. In any event, that wasn't of significance until recently.

''Among those who came and went in Ontoset were a pair of men I know to have served at the grain merchant's in Jamar. They showed me the connection. Since no one beside Lady Mara has taken grey warriors to house service, we can extrapolate that the Spy Master and his former Tuscai agents are now sworn to the Acoma.''

''So we have this link,'' Jiro said. ''Can we infiltrate?''

''It would be easy enough, my Lord, to fool the grain merchant, and get our own agent inside.'' Chumaka frowned. ''But the Acoma Spy Master would anticipate that. He is very good. Very.''

Jiro cut off this musing with a chopping motion.

Brought back to the immediate issue, Chumaka came to his point. ''At the very least, we've stung the Acoma by making them shut down a major branch of their organization in the East. And far better, we now *know* the agent in Jamar is again operative; that man must sooner or later report to his master, and then we are back on the hunt. This time I will not let fools handle the arrangements and blunder as they did in Ontoset. If we are patient, in time we will have a clear lead back to the Acoma Spy Master.''

Jiro was less than enthusiastic. ''We may waste all our efforts, now that our enemy knows his inside agent was compromised.''

''True, my master.'' Incomo licked his teeth. ''But we are ahead in the long view. We know the former Tuscai Spy Master works now for Lady Mara. I had made inroads into that net, before the Tuscai were destroyed. I can resume observation of the agents I suspected as being Tuscai years ago. If those men are still in the same positions, that simple fact will confirm them as Acoma operatives. I will set more traps, manned by personnel whom I will personally instruct. Against this Spy Master we will need our best. Yes.'' The First Adviser's air became self-congratulatory. ''It is chance that led us to the first agent, and almost netted us someone highly placed.''

Chumaka wafted the document to fan his flushed cheeks. ''We now watch the house, and I am certain our watchers are being watched, so I have others watching to see who is watching us. . . .'' He shook his head. ''My opponent is wily beyond comprehension. He—''

''Your opponent?'' Jiro interrupted.

Chumaka stifled a start and inclined his head in respect. ''My Lord's enemy's servant. My opposite, if you will. Permit an old man this small vanity, my Lord. This servant of the Acoma who opposes my work is a most suspicious and clever man.'' He referred again to his paper. ''We will isolate this other link in Jamar. Then we can pursue the next—''

''Spare me the boring particulars,'' Jiro broke in. ''I had thought I commanded you to pursue whoever is trying to defame the Anasati by planting false evidence on the assassin who killed my nephew?''

''Ah,'' Chumaka said brightly, ''but the two events are connected! Did I not say so earlier?''

Unaccustomed to sitting without the comfort of cushions, Jiro shifted his weight. ''If you did, only another mind as twisted as yours would have understood the reference.''

This the Anasati First Adviser interpreted as a compliment. ''Master, your forbearance is touching.'' He stroked the paper as if it were precious. ''I have proof, at last. Those eleven Acoma agents in the line that passed information across Szetac Province who were mysteriously murdered in the same month—they were indeed connected with five others who also died in the household of Tasaio of the Minwanabi.''

Jiro wore a stiff expression that masked rising irritation. Before he could speak, Chumaka rushed on, ''They were once *Tuscai agents,* all of them. Now it appears they were killed to eradicate a breach in the Acoma chain of security. We had a man in place in Tasaio's household. Though he was dismissed when Mara took over the Minwanabi lands, he is still loyal to us. I have his testimony here. The murders inside Tasaio's estate house were done by the Hamoi Tong.''

Jiro was intrigued. ''You think Mara's man duped the tong into cleaning up an Acoma mishap?''

Chumaka looked smug. ''Yes. I think her far too clever Spy Master made the error of forging Tasaio's chop. We know the Obajan spoke with the Minwanabi Lord. Both were reportedly angry—had it been with each other, Tasaio would have died long before Mara brought him down. If the Acoma *were* behind the destruction of their own compromised agents, and they used the tong as an unwitting tool to rid themselves of that liability, then grave insult was done to the tong. If this happened, the Red Flower Brotherhood would seek vengeance on its own.''

Jiro digested this with slitted eyes. ''Why involve the tong in what seems a routine cleanup? If Mara's man is as good as your ranting, he would hardly be such a fool.''

''It had to be a move of desperation,'' Chumaka allowed. ''Tasaio's regime was difficult to infiltrate. For our part, we placed our agent there before the man became Lord, when he was Subcommander in the Warlord's army invading Midkemia.'' As Jiro again showed impatience, Chumaka sighed. How he wished his master could be schooled to think and act with more foresight; but Jiro had always fidgeted, even as a boy. The First Adviser summed up. ''Mara had no agents in House Minwanabi that were not compromised. The deaths therefore had to be an outside job, and the tong's dealings with Tasaio offered a convenient remedy.''

''You guess all this,'' Jiro said.

Chumaka shrugged. ''It is what I would have done in his position. The Acoma Spy Master excels at innovation. We could have made contact with the net in Ontoset, and traced its operation for ten years, and never once made the connection between the agents in the North, the others in Jamar, and the communication line that crossed Szetac. To come as far as fast as we have is more due to luck than to my talents, master.''

Jiro seemed unimpressed by the topic that enthralled his First Adviser. He seized instead on the matter closest to Anasati honor. ''You have proof that the tong acts on its own volition,'' he snapped. ''Then in planting evidence of our collusion in Ayaki of the Acoma's assassination, the Hamoi has sullied the honor of my ancestors. It must be stopped from this outrage! And at once.''

Chumaka blinked, stopped cold in his thinking. He quickly licked his lips. ''But no, my worthy master. Forgive my presumption if I offer you humble advice to the contrary.''

''Why should we let the Hamoi Tong dogs shame House Anasati?'' Jiro straightened on the bench and glared. ''Your reason had better be good!''

''Well,'' Chumaka allowed, ''to kill Lady Mara, of course. Master, it is too brilliant. What more dangerous enemy could the Acoma have, other than a tong of assassins? They will spoil her peace past redemption, at each attempt to take her life. In the end, they will succeed. She must die;

the honor of their brotherhood demands it. The Hamoi Tong does our work for us, and we, meantime, can divert our interests into consolidation of the traditionalist faction.'' Chumaka wagged a lecturing finger. ''Now that war has been forbidden to both sides by the magicians, Mara will seek your ruin by other means. Her resources and allies are vast. As Servant of the Empire, she has popularity and power, as well as the ear of the Emperor. She must not be underestimated. Added to the advantages I have listed, she is an unusually gifted ruler.''

Jiro spoke in swift rebuke. ''You sing her praises in my presence?'' His tone remained temperate, but Chumaka held no illusions: his master was offended.

He answered in a whisper that no gardener or patrolling warrior might overhear. ''I was never overly fond of your brother Bunto. So his death was of little consequence to me personally.'' While Jiro's face darkened with rage, Chumaka's reprimand cut like a knife: ''And you were never that fond of him, either, my Lord Jiro.'' As the elegant, stiff-faced ruler acknowledged this truth, Chumaka continued. ''You overlook the obvious: Mara's marriage to Bunto instead of you saved your life . . . my master.'' Short of wheedling calculation, the First Adviser finished, ''So if you must entertain this hatred of the Servant of the Empire, I will seek her destruction with all my heart. But I will proceed calmly, for to let anger cloud judgment is not merely foolish—with Mara, it is suicide. Ask a shade gleaner at the Temple of Turakamu to seek communion with Jingu, Desio, and Tasaio of the Minwanabi. Their spirits will confirm that.''

Jiro stared down at the ripples of water turned by the orange fish in the pool. After a prolonged moment he sighed. ''You are right. I never did care for Bunto; he bullied me when we were children.'' His hand closed into a fist, which he splashed down, scattering the fish. ''My anger may be unwarranted, but it burns me nonetheless!'' He looked up again at Chumaka, his eyes narrowed. ''But I am Lord of the Anasati. I am not required to make sense. Wrong was done to my house and it *will* be redressed!''

Chumaka bowed, clearly respectful. ''I will see Mara of the Acoma dead, master, not because I hate her, but because that is your will. I am ever your faithful servant. Now we know who Mara's Spy Master is—''

''You know this man?'' Jiro exclaimed in astonishment. ''You've never once said you knew the identity of the Tuscai Spy Master!''

Chumaka made a deprecatory gesture. ''Not by name, nor by looks, curse him for the brilliant fiend he is. I have never knowingly met him, but I recognize the manner of his craft. It has a signature like that of a scribe.''

"Which is far from solid evidence,'' Jiro was fast to point out.

"Final proof will be difficult to get if I have recognized the same man's touch. Should this former Tuscai Spy Master have taken Mara's service, the gods may smile upon us yet. He may be a master of guile, yet I know his measure. My past knowledge of the Tuscai operation in Jamar should enable us to infiltrate his operation. After a few years we may have access to the man himself, and then we can manipulate the intelligence in Mara's net as we desire. Our intent must be made behind diversionary maneuvers to disrupt Acoma trade and alliances. Meanwhile the Tong will be seeking Mara's downfall as well.''

"Perhaps we could encourage the Brotherhood's efforts a bit,'' Lord Jiro offered hopefully.

Chumaka sucked in a quick breath at the mere suggestion. He bowed before starting to speak, which he did only when alarmed. "My master, that we dare not try. Tong are tight-knit, and too deadly at their craft to meddle with. Best we keep Anasati affairs as far removed from their doings as possible.''

Jiro conceded this point with regret, while his First Adviser proceeded with optimism. "The Hamoi Brotherhood is not one to act in hot blood; no. Its works on its own behalf have ever been slow-moving, and cold. Traffic has passed between the Hamoi and Midkemia that I did not understand as it occurred; but now I suspect it has roots in a long-range attempt to hurt the Acoma. The Lady has a well-known weakness for barbarian ideas.''

"That is so,'' Jiro conceded. His temper fled before thoughtfulness; he regarded the play of the fish. No adviser of any house was more adept than Chumaka at stringing together seemingly unrelated bits of information. And all the Empire had heard rumors of the Lady's dalliance with a Midkemian slave. That was a vulnerability well worth exploiting.

Cued by the softening of his master's manner, and judging his moment with precision, Chumaka said, "The Anasati can bear the tiny slight in the manner of the bungled evidence. Fools and children might believe inept information. But the wiser Ruling Lords all know that the tong keeps close guard on its secrets. The powerful in the Nations will never seriously believe such transparent ploys to link your name with a hired killer. The Anasati name is old. Its honor is unimpeachable. Show only boldness before petty slurs, my master. They are unworthy of a great Lord's attention. Let any ruler dare come forward to suggest the contrary, and you will correct the matter forcefully.'' Chumaka ended with a quotation from a play that Jiro favored. " 'Small acts partner small houses and small minds.' "

The Lord of the Anasati nodded. "You are right. My anger tends sometimes to blind me."

Chumaka bowed at the compliment. "My master, I ask permission to be excused. I have already begun to consider snares that may be set for Mara's Spy Master. For while we appear to blunder about with the one hand revealed in Ontoset, that will draw the watchful eye away from the other, silently at work in Jamar to bring the dagger to the throat of the Lady of the Acoma."

Jiro smiled. "Excellent, Chumaka." He clapped in dismissal. While his First Adviser bowed again and hurried away, muttering possible plots under his breath, the Lord remained by the fish pool. He considered Chumaka's advice, and felt a deep glow of satisfaction. When the Assembly of Magicians had forbidden war between his house and Mara's, he had been covertly ecstatic. With the Lady deprived of her army, and the clear supremacy she held by force of numbers on the battlefield, the stakes between them had been set even.

"Wits," the Lord of the Anasati murmured, stirring the water and causing the fish to flash away in confused circles. "Guile, not the sword, will bring the Good Servant her downfall. She will die knowing her mistake when she chose my brother over me. I am the better man, and when I meet Buntokapi after death in the Red God's halls, he will know that I gave him vengeance, and also ground his precious House Acoma under my heel into dust!"

Arakasi was late. His failure to return had the Acoma senior advisers on edge to the point where Force Commander Lujan dreaded to attend the evening's council. He hurried to his quarters to retrieve the plumed helm he had shed during off-duty hours. His stride was purposeful, precise in balance as only a skilled swordsman's would be; yet his mind was preoccupied. His nod to the patrolling sentries who saluted his passage was mechanical.

The Acoma estate house had as many armed men in its halls now as servants; privacy since Ayaki's murder was next to nonexistent, particularly at night, when extra warriors slept in the scriptorium and the assorted wings of the guest suites. Justin's nursery was an armed camp; Lujan reflected that the boy could hardly play at toy soldiers for the constant tramp of battle sandals across the floors of his room.

Yet as the only carrier of the Acoma bloodline, after Mara, his safety was of paramount concern. Lacking Arakasi's reliable reports, the patrols walked their beats in uncertainty. They were starting at shadows, half drawing swords at the footfalls of drudges secreted in corners to meet with sweethearts. Lujan sighed, and froze, shaken alert by the sound of a sword sliding from a scabbard.

"You there!" shouted a sentry. "Halt!"

Now running, Lujan flung himself around a corner in the corridor. Ahead, the warrior with drawn sword crouched down, battle-ready. He confronted a nook deep in shadow where nothing appeared to be amiss. From behind, the tap and shuffle peculiar to a man moving in haste on a crutch warned that Keyoke, Mara's Adviser for War, had also heard the disturbance. Too long a field commander to ignore a warrior's challenge, he also rushed to find out who trespassed in the innermost corridors of the estate house.

Let it not be another assassin, Lujan prayed as he ran. He strained to see through the gloom, noting that a lamp that should have been left burning was dark. Not a good sign, he thought grimly; the council suddenly deferred by this intrusion now seemed the kinder choice of frustrations. Snarls in trade and the uneasy shifting of alliances within Ichindar's court might be maddeningly puzzling without Arakasi's inside knowledge. But an attack by another tong dart man this far inside the patrols was too harrowing a development to contemplate. Though months had passed, Justin still had nightmares from seeing the black gelding's fall. . . .

Lujan skidded to a stop by the sword-bearing warrior, his sandal studs scraping the stone floor. "Who's there?" he demanded.

Old Keyoke thumped to a halt on the warrior's other side, his dry shout demanding the same.

The warrior never shifted his glance, but made a fractional gesture with his sword toward the cranny between two beams that supported a join in the rooftree. A long-past repair had replaced a rotted section of wood. The estate house Mara and Hokanu inhabited was ancient, and this was one of the original sections. The slate scored white by Lujan's battle sandals was close to three thousand years old, and rubbed into ruts from uncounted generations of footsteps. There were too many corners to shelter intruders Lujan felt as he looked where his sentry pointed. A man lurked in the shadow. He stood with hands outstretched in submission, but his face was suspiciously smudged, as if he had used lamp soot to blacken the telltale pallor of his flesh.

Lujan freed his sword. With inscrutable features, Keyoke raised his crutch, thumbed a hidden catch, and drew a thin blade from the base. For all that he had lost one leg, he balanced himself without discernible effort.

To the intruder now faced with three bared blades, Lujan said curtly, "Come out. Keep your hands up if you don't want to die spitted."

"I would rather not be welcomed back like a cut of meat at the butcher's," replied a voice rust-grained as neglected iron.

"Arakasi," Keyoke said, raising his weapon in salute. His ax-blade profile broke into a rare smile.

"Gods!" Lujan swore. He reached out barehanded and touched the sentry, who lowered his blade. The Acoma Force Commander shivered to realize how near Mara's Spy Master had come to dying at the hands of a house guard. Then relief and a countersurge of high spirits made him laugh. "Finally! How many years have Keyoke and I attempted to set unpredictable patrols? Can it be that for once, my good man, you failed to walk right through them?"

"It was a rough trip home," Arakasi conceded. "Not only that, this estate has more warriors on duty than house staff. A man can't move three steps without tripping over someone in armor."

Keyoke sheathed his concealed blade and replaced his crutch beneath his shoulder. Then he raked his fingers through his white hair, as he had never been able to do when he was a field commander, perpetually wearing a battle helm. "Lady Mara's council is due to begin shortly. She has need of your news."

Arakasi did not reply, but pushed out from behind the posts that had hidden him from sight. He was robed as a street beggar. His untrimmed hair was lank with dirt, and his skin was ingrained with what looked like soot. He smelled pervasively of wood smoke.

"You look like something dragged out by a chimney sweeper," Lujan observed, gesturing for the sentry to resume his interrupted patrol. "Or as if you had been sleeping in trees for the better part of a seven day."

"Not far from the truth," Arakasi muttered, turning an irritated glance aside. Keyoke disliked waiting for anyone; now free to indulge the impatience he had repressed for years while commanding troops, he had stumped on ahead toward the council hall. As if relieved by the old man's departure, Arakasi bent, raised the hem of his robe, and scratched at a festering sore.

Lujan stroked his chin. Tactfully he said, "You could come to my quarters first. My body servant is practiced at drawing a bath on short notice."

A brief silence ensued.

At last Arakasi sighed. "Splinters," he admitted.

Since one terse word was all he was likely to receive in explanation,

Lujan surmised the rest. "They're infected. That means not recent. You've been too much on the run to draw them out."

Another silence followed, affirming Lujan's surmise. He and Arakasi had known each other since before House Tuscai had fallen, and had shared many years as grey warriors. "Come along," the Force Commander urged. "If you sit in Lady Mara's presence in this state, the servants will need to burn the cushions afterward. You stink like a Khardengo who lost his wagon."

Not pleased to be compared with an itinerant family member that traveled from city to city selling cheap entertainment and disreputable odd jobs, Arakasi curled his lip. "You can get me a metal needle?" he bargained warily.

Lujan laughed. "As it happens, I might. There's a girl among the seamstresses that fancies me. But you'll owe me. If I ask her for the loan of such a treasure, she is bound to make demands."

Aware that few young maids in the household would not willingly jeopardize their next station on the Wheel of Life for the promise of Lujan's kisses, Arakasi was unimpressed. "I can as easily use one of my daggers."

His apparent indifference set Lujan on edge. "The news you bring is not good."

Now Arakasi faced the Acoma Force Commander fully. Light from the lamp down the corridor caught on his gaunt cheekbones and deepened the hollows under his eyes. "I think I will accept your offer of a bath," he responded obtusely.

Lujan knew better than to tease that his friend the Spy Master also looked as if he had not eaten or slept for a week. The observation this time would have held more truth than jest. "I'll get you that needle," he allowed, then hastened on in an attempt to ease Arakasi's ruffled pride through humor. "Though you certainly don't need it, if you're carrying your knives. I doubt my sentry understood when he held you at swordpoint that you could have killed and carved him before he had a chance to make a thrust."

"I'm good," Arakasi allowed. "But today, I think, not that good." He stepped forward. Only now it became apparent that he was far from steady on his feet. He awarded Lujan's startled gasp of concern his blandest expression of displeasure and added, "You are on your honor not to allow me to fall asleep in your tub."

"Fall asleep or drown?" Lujan quipped back, extending a fast hand to assist the Spy Master's balance. "Man, what have you been up to?"

But badger though he might, the Force Commander received no explanation from the Spy Master until the bath was done, and the helm retrieved, and the council was well on into session.

Keyoke was already seated in the yellow light cast by the circle of lamps, his leathery hands crossed on the crutch across his knees. Word of Arakasi's homecoming had been sent to the kitchens, and servants hurried in with trays laden with snacks. Hokanu attended at Mara's right hand, in the place normally occupied by the First Adviser, while Saric and Incomo sat in low-voiced conference opposite. Jican huddled with his arms around his knees behind a mountainous pile of slates. Bins stuffed with scrolls rested like bastions at either elbow, while his expression looked faintly beleaguered.

Arakasi ran his eyes quickly over the gathering and surmised in his dry way, "Trade has not been going well in my absence, I can see."

Jican bristled at this, which effectively canceled anyone's immediate notice of the Spy Master's ragged condition. "We are not compromised," the little hadonra swiftly defended. "But there have been several ventures in the markets that have gone awry. Mara has lost allies among the merchants who also have Anasati interests." In visible relief, he finished, "The silk auctions did not suffer."

"Yet," Incomo supplied, unasked. "The traditionalists continue to gain influence. Ichindar's Imperial Whites more than once had to shed blood to stop riots in Kentosani."

"The food markets by the wharf," Arakasi affirmed in spare summary. "I heard. Our Emperor would do more to stop dissension if he could manage to sire himself an heir that was not a daughter."

Eyes turned toward the Lady of the Acoma as her staff all waited upon whatever she might ask of them.

Thinner than she had been on the occasion of Ayaki's funeral, she was nonetheless immaculately composed. Her face was washed clean of makeup. Her eyes were focused and keen, and her hands settled in her lap as she spoke. "Arakasi has revealed that we are confronted by a new threat." Only her voice showed the ongoing strain she yet hid behind the Tsurani façade of control; never before Ayaki's loss had she spoken with such a hard-edged clarity of hatred. "I ask you all to grant him whatever aid he may ask without question."

Lujan flashed Arakasi a sour glance. "You had already dirtied her cushions, I now see," he murmured with injured irritation. Keyoke looked a touch disgruntled. The discovery was belated that the patrol which had finally caught the Spy Master lurking in the corridors had done so only after he had held a conference with the mistress, undetected by any. Aware of the byplay, but obliged by code of conduct to ignore it, the other two advisers inclined their heads in acceptance of the mistress's wishes. Only Jican fidgeted, aware as he was that Mara's decree would create additional havoc in the Acoma treasury. Arakasi's services came at high costs of operation, which caused the hadonra unceasing, hand-wringing worry.

A breeze wafted through the open windows above the great hall of the Acoma, carved into the side of the hill against which the estate house rested. Despite the brilliance of the lamps, the room was thrown into gloom in the farthest corners. The cho-ja globes on their stands stayed unlit, and the low dais used for informal conference remained the only island of illumination. Those servants in attendance waited a discreet distance away, within call should they be needed but out of earshot of any discussion. Mara resumed. "What we speak of here must be kept in our circle alone." She asked Arakasi, "How much time do you need to spend upon this new threat?"

Arakasi gave a palms-upward shrug that revealed a yellow bruise on one wristbone. "I can only surmise, mistress. My instincts tell me the organization I encountered is based to the east of us, probably in Ontoset. We have light ties between there and Jamar and the City of the Plains, since the cover was a factor's business. An enemy who discovered our workings to the west would see nothing beyond coincidence in the eastern connection. Yet I do not know where the damage originated. The trace could have started somewhere else."

Mara chewed her lip. "Explain."

"I did some cursory checking before I returned to Sulan-Qu." More nervelessly cold than Keyoke could be before battle, the Spy Master qualified. "On the surface, our trading interests seem secure to the west and north. The recent expansion I have regrettably been forced to curtail was located south and east. Our unknown opponent may have stumbled onto some operation we just set in place; or not. I cannot say. His effect has been felt very clearly. He has detected some aspect of our courier system, and deduced enough of our methods to establish a network to observe us. This enemy has placed watchers where they are likely to trap someone they hope they can trace back to a position of authority. From this I extrapolate that our enemy has his own system to glean advantage from such an opportunity."

Hokanu settled an arm around Mara's lower back, though her manner did not indicate she needed comfort. "How can you be certain of this?"

Baldly Arakasi said, "Because it is what I would have done." He smoothed his robe to conceal the welts the splinters had marked on his shins. "I was almost taken, and that is no easy feat." His flat phrases implied a total lack of conceit as he raised one finger. "I am worried because we have been compromised." He lifted a second finger and added, "I am relieved to have made a clean escape. If the team that gave me chase ever guessed whom they had cornered, they would have taken extreme measures to be thorough. Subterfuge would have been abandoned in favor of my successful capture. Therefore, they must have expected to net a courier or supervisor. My identity as Acoma Spy Master most likely remains uncompromised."

Mara straightened in sudden decision. "Then it seems a wise course to absent yourself from this problem."

Arakasi all but recoiled in surprise. "My Lady?"

Misinterpreting his reaction for hurt feelings that his competence lay questioned, Mara attempted to soften her pronouncement. "You are too critical to another problem that needs attention." She waved her dismissal to Jican, saying, "I think the trade problems can wait." While the little man bowed his acquiescence and snapped fingers to call his secretaries to help gather his tallies and scrolls, Mara commanded all the other servants to leave the great hall. When the great doubled doors swept closed, leaving her alone with the inner circle of her advisers, she said to her Spy Master, "I have something else for you to do."

Arakasi spoke his mind plainly. "Mistress, there exists a great danger. Indeed, I fear the master in command of this enemy's spy works may be the most dangerous man alive."

Mara betrayed nothing of her thoughts as she nodded for him to continue.

"Until this encounter I had the vanity to consider myself a master of my craft." For the first time since discussion had opened, the Spy Master had to pause to choose words. "This breach in our security was in no way due to carelessness. My men in Ontoset acted with unimpeachable discretion. For that reason, I fear this enemy we face could possibly be my better."

"Then I am decided on the matter," Mara announced. "You shall turn this difficulty over to another that you trust. That way, if this unspecified enemy proves worthy of your praise, we suffer the loss of a man less critical to our needs."

Arakasi bowed, his movement stiff with distress. "Mistress—"

Sharply Mara repeated, "I have another task for you."

Arakasi fell instantly silent: Tsurani custom forbade a servant questioning his sworn ruler; and moreover, the Lady's mind was set. The hardness in her since the loss of her firstborn was not to be reasoned with; this much he recognized. That Hokanu sensed it also was plain, for even he refrained from speaking out against his Lady's chosen course of action. The uncomfortable truth remained unsaid: that no one else in Arakasi's vast network was either careful or experienced enough to counter a threat of this magnitude. The Spy Master would not disobey his mistress, though he were in mortal fear for her safety. All he could do was work in convoluted patterns, obeying her command in the literal sense, but evading what he could through general action. For the first, he must ensure that the man placed in nominal charge of digging out this new organization could report to him on a regular basis. Disturbed as he was that Lady Mara should dismiss this dire threat with such ease, he respected her well enough to at least hear her reasons before he came to judgment against her. "What is this other matter, my Lady?"

His attentive manner smoothed Mara's sharpness. "I would have you discover as much as may be learned about the Assembly of Magicians."

For the first time since taking service with Mara, Arakasi seemed startled by her audacity. His eyes widened and his voice dropped to a whisper. "The Great Ones?"

Mara nodded toward Saric, since the slant the explanation must take had been his particular study.

He spoke up from the far side of the circle. "Several events over the last few years have caused me to question the Black Robes' motives. By tradition we take for granted that they act for the good of our Empire. But would it not shed a different light on things if, in fact, that were not so?" Saric's wry humor dissolved before a burning intensity of unease as he added, "Most critically, what if the Assembly's wisdom is pointed toward their own self-interest? The pretext is stability of the nations; then why should they fear the Acoma crushing the Anasati in the cause of just revenge?" The Acoma First Adviser leaned forward with his elbows braced on crossed knees. "These magicians are hardly fools. I can't believe they don't realize that by allowing the Lord who murders by treachery to live unpunished, they plunge the Empire into strife most extreme. An unavenged death is an express contradiction of honor. Without the political byplay of the High Council, deprived of the constant give-and-take between factions as a leavening agent, we are left with every house cast adrift, dependent upon the goodwill and promises of others to survive."

To her Spy Master, Mara qualified, "Within a year's time, a dozen houses or more will cease to exist, because I am forbidden to take the field against those who would return us to the Warlord's rule. I am rendered powerless in the political arena. My clan cannot raise sword against the traditionalists, who now use Jiro as their front man. If I cannot make war upon him, I can no longer keep my pledge to protect those houses who are dependent upon Acoma alliance.'' Shutting her eyes for a moment, she seemed to gather herself.

Arakasi's regard of his Lady sharpened as he understood something: she had recovered from her mourning enough to have regained reason. She knew in her heart that the evidence against Jiro was too obvious to take seriously. But the cost of her loss of control at the funeral must be met without flinching: she had shamed her family name, and Jiro's guilt or lack of it was moot. To admit his innocence now was to make public admission of her error. This she could not honorably do without a worse question arising. Did she believe her enemy was clean of Ayaki's blood, or was she simply backing down from exacting retribution for Ayaki? Not to avenge a murder was an irrevocable forfeit of honor.

Regret as she might the heat of her rage and her wrong thinking, Mara could do nothing but manage the situation as if all along she believed in the Anasati's treachery. To do other was not Tsurani, and a weakness that enemies would immediately exploit to bring her downfall.

As if to escape distasteful memories, Mara resumed, ''Within two years, many we would count allies will be dead or dishonored, and many more who are neutral might be persuaded or driven by political pressure into the traditionalist camp. The depleted Imperial Party will face off, but, without us, with the disastrous probability that a new Warlord will reinstate the Council. Should that sad day dawn, the man to wear the white-and-gold mantle would be Jiro of the Anasati.''

Arakasi rubbed his cheek with a knuckle, furiously thinking. ''So you think the Assembly may be tinkering in politics for reasons of its own agenda. It is true that the Black Robes have always been jealous of their privacy. I know of no man who has entered their city and spoken of the experience. Lady Mara, to pry into that stronghold will be dangerous, and very difficult, if not outright impossible. They have truth spells that make it impossible to insinuate someone into their ranks. I have heard stories . . . though I might not be the first Spy Master to attempt an infiltration, no one who crosses a Great One with deceit in his heart lives to a natural end.''

Mara's hands twisted into fists. ''We must find a way to know their motives. More, we must discover a way to stop their interference, or at least to gain a clear delineation of what parameters they have set us. We must know how much we may accomplish without raising their wrath. Over time, perhaps a means can be found to negotiate with them.''

Arakasi bowed his head, resigned, but already at work on the grand scale the problem required. He had never expected to live to old age;

puzzles, even dangerous ones, were all the delight he understood, though the one his Lady had proposed was all too likely to invite a swift destruction. "Your will, mistress. I shall begin at once to realign the interests of our agents to the northwest." Negotiation was a futile hope, one Arakasi rejected at the outset. To bargain at all, one must have either force to command, or a persuasive reward as enticement. Power and popularity Mara had, but he, too, had witnessed the display of a single magician's might when the Imperial Games had been disrupted by Milamber. Lady Mara's thousands of warriors, and those of all her friends and allies, were as nothing compared to the arcane forces the Assembly commanded. And what in the world under heaven could anyone have that a Great One could desire and not simply take for the asking?

Chilled, Arakasi considered the last alternative to effect coercion: extortion. If the Assembly held a secret that it would sell favors to keep any others from knowing, something it would be willing to grant concessions for, to ensure Mara kept her silence . . . The very idea was folly. The Great Ones were above any law. Arakasi judged it more likely that even should he be lucky enough to find such a secret, the Black Robes would simply seal Mara's permanent silence by putting her horribly to death.

Saric, Lujan, and Keyoke understood this, he sensed, for their eyes were upon him most closely as he rose and made his final bow. This time, Mara dared too much, and they all feared for the outcome. Cold to the core of his spirit, Arakasi turned away. Nothing about his manner indicated that he cursed a savage fate. Not only must he sidetrack what instinct warned might be the most perilous threat to target Lady Mara so far, but he would even have to abandon any effort at effecting a countermeasure. Whole sections of his vast operation must be rendered dormant until after he had cracked an enigma no man had ever dared attempt. The riddle waited to be unraveled, beyond the shores of a nameless body of water, known only as the lake that surrounds the isle of the City of the Magicians.

5. Machinations

Two years passed.

No renewed attempts to assassinate the Lady of the Acoma came, and while all remained watchful, the sense of immediate risk had diminished.

The tranquillity that settled over the estate house as predawn light rinsed the sleeping chamber was all the more to be treasured. Pressures brought on by recent unfavorable developments in trade and the friction between political factions steadily brought more stresses to bear upon House Acoma's resources.

But now, only patrols were stirring, and the day's messengers bearing news had yet to arrive. A shore bird called off the lake. Hokanu tightened his arms around his beloved Lady. His hands touched the ivory-smooth skin over her belly and a slight fullness there alerted him. Suddenly the mornings she had closeted herself away from him and even her most trusted advisers made sense. An ecstatic flush of pleasure followed the obvious deduction. Hokanu smiled, his face pressed into the sweet waves of her hair.

"Have the midwives told you yet whether the new Acoma heir is to be a son or a daughter?"

Mara twisted in his arms, her eyes wide with indignation. "I did not tell you I was pregnant! Which of my maids betrayed me?"

Hokanu said nothing; only his smile widened.

The Lady reached down, grasped his two wrists, which were locked around her still, and concluded, "I see. My maids were all loyal, and I still cannot keep any secrets from you, husband."

But she could; as clear as the rapport between them could be, there were depths to her that even Hokanu could not fathom, particularly since the death of her firstborn, as if grief had laid a shadow on her. Although her warmth as she laid her face against her husband was genuine, and her pleasure equally so as she whispered formally into his ear that he was soon going to be a father by blood, as well as through adoption, Hokanu sensed a darker undertone. Mara was troubled by something, this time not related to Ayaki's loss, or to the Assembly's intervention in her attempt to bring vengeance on Jiro. Equally, he sensed that this was not the moment to broach any inquiry into her affairs.

"I love you, Lady," he murmured. "You had better accustom yourself to solicitude, because I'm going to spoil you shamelessly every day until the moment you give birth." He turned her in his arms and kissed her. "After that, we both might find I had acquired a habit too fine to break."

Mara snuggled against him, her fingers trailing across his chest. "You are the finest husband in the Empire, beloved—far better than I deserve."

Which was arguable, but Hokanu held his peace. He knew she loved him deeply and gave him as much care and satisfaction as any woman was capable of; the profoundly sensed certainty that something indefinable was missing from her side of the relationship was a feeling he had exhausted himself trying to fathom. For the Lady never lied to him, never stinted in her affections. Still she had moments when her thoughts were elsewhere, in a place he could never reach. She needed something his instincts warned him he lacked the means to provide.

A pragmatic man, he did not try to force the impossible, but built upon their years together a contentment and a peace that were enduring and solid as a monument. He had succeeded in giving her happiness, until the dart struck the horse that killed her son.

She shifted against him, her dark eyes apparently fixed upon the flower garden beyond the opened screen. Breezes caused her favorite kekali blossoms to nod, and their heavy perfume swirled through the chamber. Far off, the bread cook could be heard berating a slave boy for laziness; the sounds of the dispatch barge being loaded at dockside reached here, strangely amplified by still water and the mist-cloaked morning quiet.

Hokanu caught Mara's fingers and stroked them, and by the fact that they did not immediately respond knew she was not thinking of ordinary commerce.

"Is it the Assembly on your mind again?" he asked, knowing it was not, but also aware that an oblique approach would break the cold space around her thoughts and help her make a start at communicating.

Mara closed her grip on his hand. "Your father's sister has two boys, and you have a second cousin with five children, three of them sons."

Unsure where this opening was leading, but also catching her drift, Hokanu nodded. He reflexively followed up on her next thought. "If something were to happen to Justin before your child was born, my father could choose among several cousins and relations to find a successor after me for the Shinzawai mantle. But you should not worry, love; I fully intend to stay alive and keep you safe."

Mara frowned, more troubled than he had originally guessed. "No. We've been through this. I will not see the Acoma name merged with that of the Shinzawai."

Hokanu drew her close, aware now of what lay beneath her tenseness. "You fear for the Acoma name, then. I understand. Until our child is born, you are the last of your line."

Her tenseness as she nodded betrayed the depths of a fear she had wrestled with and kept hidden for the intervening span of two years. And after all she had gone through to secure the continuance of her ancestors' line, only to suffer the further loss of her son, he could not fault her.

"Unlike your father, I have no remaining cousins, and no other option." She sucked a quick breath, and plunged ahead to the heart of the matter.

"I want Justin sworn to the Acoma natami."

"Mara!" Hokanu said, startled. "Done is done! The boy is almost five years of age and sworn already to the Shinzawai!"

She looked stricken. Her eyes were too large in her face, and her bones too prominent, the result of grief and morning sickness. "Release him."

There was an air of desperation about her, of determined hardness he had seen only in the presence of enemies; and gods knew, he was not an enemy. He stifled his initial shock, reached out, and again drew her against him. She was shaking, though her skin was not chilled. Patiently, carefully, he considered her position. He tried to unravel her motivations and achieve an understanding that would give him grounds to work with her; for he realized, for his father's sake, that he would be doing no one any favors by changing Justin's house loyalty—least of all the boy. By now the child was old enough to begin to comprehend the significance of the name to which he belonged.

The death of an elder brother had fallen hard enough on the little one without his becoming the pawn of politics. Much as Hokanu loved Mara, he also recognized that Jiro's enmity was more threat than he would wish to place on the shoulders of an innocent child.

The rapport shared between the Lady and her consort cut both ways; Mara also had the gift of tracking Hokanu's inner thoughts. She said, "It is a lot more difficult to murder a boy who is able to walk, talk, and recognize strangers than an infant in a crib. As Shinzawai heir, our new baby would be safer. A house, a whole line, would not be ended by one death."

Hokanu could not refute such logic; what cost him peace and prevented his agreement was his own affection for Justin, not mentioning that his foster father, Kamatsu, had come to dote on the boy. Did a man take a child old enough to have tasted the joys of life, and thrust him into grave danger? Or did one set an innocent infant at risk?

"If I die," Mara said in a near whisper, "there will be nothing. No child. No Acoma. My ancestors will lose their places on the Wheel of Life, and none will remain to hold Acoma honor in the eyes of the gods." She did not add, as she might have, that all she had done for herself would have gone for nothing.

Her consort pushed himself upright against the pillows, drew her to lean against him, and combed back her dark hair. "Lady, I will think on what you have said."

Mara twisted, jerking free of his caress. Beautiful, determined, and angry, she sat up straight and faced him. "You must not think. You must decide. Release Justin from his vows, for the Acoma must not go another day without an heir to come after me."

There was an edge of hysteria to her. Hokanu read past that to another worry, one she had not yet mentioned, that he had missed in the turmoil. "You are feeling cornered because Arakasi has been so long at the task you set him," he said on a note of inspiration.

The wind seemed to go out of Mara's sails. "Yes. Perhaps I asked too much of him, or began a more perilous course than I knew when I sent him to attempt to infiltrate the affairs of the Assembly." In a rare moment of self-doubt, she admitted, "I was hot-headed, and angry. In truth, things have gone more smoothly than I first feared. We have handled the upsurge of the traditionalist offensive without the difficulty I anticipated."

Hokanu heard, but was not deceived into belief that she considered the affair settled. If anything, the quiet times and the minor snarls that erupted in trade transactions were harbingers of something deeper afoot. Tsurani Lords were devious; the culture itself had for thousands of years applauded the ruler who could be subtle, who could effect convoluted, long-range plotting to stage a brilliant victory years later. All too likely, Lord Jiro was biding his time, amassing his preparations to strike. He was no Minwanabi, to solve his conflicts on the field of war. The Assembly's edict had effectively granted him unlimited time, and license to plot against the Acoma through intrigue, as was his penchant.

Neither Mara nor Hokanu chose to belabor this point, which both of them feared. An interval of quiet stretched between them, filled with the sounds of the estate beginning to wake. The light through the screen changed from gray to rose-gold, and birdsong filtered in over the call of officers overseeing the change in the guard—warriors who had not patrolled so near the estate house before Ayaki's death.

Unspoken also was the understanding that the Anasati might in fact have been the target of the faked evidence carried by the tong. Jiro and the old-line traditionalists wished Mara dead, which made his enmity logical. Yet a third faction might be plotting unseen, to create this schism between the Acoma and Anasati alliance that had been sealed with Ayaki's life. The attempt had been against Mara; had she died according to plan, her son would have inherited, as heir. Hokanu in the vulnerable position of regent, would have been left to manage a sure clash between the Acoma, in an attempt to retain their independence as his Lady would have desired, and the Anasati, who would seek to annex that house on the strength of their blood tie to the boy.

But if the contract with the tong that had seen Ayaki killed had not been under Jiro's chop, all that had transpired since might be playing into the hands of some third party, perhaps the same Lord whose spy net had breached Arakasi's security.

"I think," said Hokanu with gentle firmness, "that we should not resolve this issue until we have heard from Arakasi, or one of his agents. If he has made headway in his attempt to gain insight into the Great Ones' council, his network will send word. No news is best news, for now."

Looking pale and strained, and feeling chilled as well, Mara nodded. The discomforts of her pregnancy were shortly going to make conversation difficult, in any event. She lay, limp in her husband's arms, while he snapped his fingers and called for her maids. It was part of his singular devotion that kept him at her side through her early hours of illness. When she offered protest that he surely had better things to do with his time, he only smiled.

The clock chimed. Mara pushed damp hair from her brow and sighed. She closed her eyes a moment, to ease the ongoing strain of reviewing the fine print of the trade factor's reports from Sulan-Qu. Yet her interval of rest lasted scarcely seconds.

A maid entered with a tray. Mara started slightly at the intrusion, then resigned herself to the interruption as the servant began laying out a light lunch on the small lap table beside the one she had left cluttered with unfinished business.

As the mistress's regard turned her way, the maid bowed, touching forehead to floor in obeisance very near to a slave's. As Mara suspected, the girl wore livery trimmed in blue, Shinzawai colors.

"My Lady, the master sent me to bring you lunch. He says you are too thin, and the baby won't have enough to grow on if you don't take time to eat."

Mara rested a hand on her swollen middle. The boy child the midwives had promised her seemed to be developing just fine. If she herself looked peaked, impatience and nerves were the more likely cause rather than diet. This pregnancy wore at her, impatient as she was to be done with it, and to have the question of heirship resolved. She had not realized how much she had come to rely upon Hokanu's companionship until strain had been put upon it. Her wish to name Justin as Acoma heir had exacted a high cost, and she longed for the birth of the child, that the altercation with Hokanu could be set behind them both.

But the months until her due date seemed to stretch into infinity. Reflective, Mara stared out the window, where the akasi vines were in bloom and slaves were busy with shears trimming them back from the walk. The heavy perfume reminded her of another study, on her old estate, and a day in the past when a red-haired barbarian slave had upset her concept of Tsurani culture. Now Hokanu was the only man in the Empire who seemed to share her progressive dreams and ideas. It was hard to speak to him, lately, without the issue of progeny coming between.

The maid slipped out unobtrusively. Mara regarded the tray of fruit, bread, and cold cheeses with little enthusiasm. Still, she forced herself to fill up a plate and eat, however tasteless the food seemed on her tongue. Past experience had taught her that Hokanu would come by to check on her, and she did not wish to face the imploring tenderness in his eyes if she followed her inclinations and left the meal untouched.

The report that had occupied her was far more serious than it appeared at first glance. A warehouse by the river had burned, causing damage to the surplus hides held off the spring market. The prices had not been up to standard this season, and rather than sell the leather at such slight profit, Jican had consigned them for later delivery to the sandalmaker's. Mara frowned. She set her barely touched plate aside, out of habit. Although it was no secret that, of all the houses in the Empire, hers was the only one to provide sandals for its bearer slaves and field hands, until now the subject only made her the butt of social small talk. Old-line traditionalist Lords laughed loudly and long, and claimed her slaves ran her household; one particularly cantankerous senior priest in the temple service of Chochocan, the Good God, had sent her a tart missive cautioning her that treating slaves too kindly was an offense against divine will. Make their lives too easy, the priest had warned, and their penance for earning heaven's disfavor would not be served. They might be returned on the Wheel of Life as a rodent or other lowly beast, to make up for their lack of suffering in this present life. Saving the feet of slaves from cuts and sores was surely a detriment to their eternal spirits.

Mara had returned a missive of placating banalities to the disaffected priest, and gone right on supplying sandals.

But the current report, with her factor's signature and impression of the battered chop used on the weekly inventories, was another matter. For the first time an enemy faction had sought to exploit her kind foible to the detriment of House Acoma. The damaged hides would be followed, she was sure, with a sudden, untraceable rumor in the slaves' barracks that she had covertly arranged the fire as an excuse to spare the cost of the extra sandals. Since possession of footwear gave not only comfort, but also considerable status to the slaves in Acoma service, in the eyes of their counterparts belonging to other houses, the privilege was fiercely coveted. Though no Tsurani slave would ever consider rebellion, as disobedience to master or mistress was against the will of the gods, even the thought that their yearly allotment of sandals might be revoked would cause resentment that would not show on the surface but would result in sloppy field work, or tasks that somehow went awry. The impact on Acoma fortunes would be subtle, but tangible. The sabotage to the warehouse could become an insidiously clever ploy, because in order to rectify the shortage of leathers, Mara might draw the attention of more than just an old fanatic in the temple likely to write a protest to her. It could be seen in certain quarters that she was vulnerable, and temples that were previously friendly to her could suddenly become "neutral" to a point just short of hostility.

She could ill afford difficulties from the priesthood at this time, not with the Emperor's enemies and her own allied in common cause to ruin her.

The lunch tray remained neglected as she took up clean paper and pen and drew up an authorization for the factor in Sulan-Qu to purchase new hides to be shipped to the sandalmakers. Then she sent her runner slave to fetch Jican, who in turn was ordered to place servants and overseers on the alert for rumors, that the question of footwear for the slaves might never become an issue.

By the time the matter was resolved, the fruit sat in a puddle of juices, and the cheeses had warmed on the plate in the humid midafternoon air. Involved with the next report in the file, this one dealing with a trade transaction designed to inconvenience the Anasati, Mara heard footsteps at the screen.

"I am finished with the lunch tray," she murmured without looking up.

Presuming the servant would carry out the remains of her meal with the usual silent solicitude, she held her mind on its present track. But however many caravans were robbed, however many Anasati hwaet fields burned, no matter how many stacks of cloth goods were diverted on their way to market or ships were sent to the wrong port, Mara found little satisfaction. Her heartache did not lessen. She gripped the parchments harder, searching the penned lines for some way to make her enemy feel her hatred in the place that would hurt the most.

Hands reached over her shoulder, pulled the report from her grip, and gently massaged her neck, which had grown sore from too little movement. "The cooks will be asking to commit suicide by the blade when they see how little you cared for their lunch tray, my Lady," Hokanu said in her ear. He followed the admonition with a kiss on the crown of her head, and waited while Mara reddened with embarrassment at mistaking him for a servant.

She went on to ruefully regard the uneaten meal. "Forgive me. I became so involved that I forgot." With a sigh, she turned in her husband's embrace and kissed him back.

"What was it this time, more mildew in the thyza sacks?" he asked, a twinkle in his eyes.

Mara rubbed her aching forehead. "No. The hides for the sandalmaker's. We'll purchase replacements."

Hokanu nodded, one of the few men in the Empire who would not have argued that sandals for slaves were a waste of good funds. Aware how lucky she was to have such a husband, Mara returned his embrace and heroically reached for the food tray.

Her husband caught her wrist with a firmness beyond argument. "That meal is spoiled. We'll have the servants bring a fresh tray, and I'll stay and share it with you. We've spent too little time together lately."

He moved around her cushion, his swordsman's grace as always lending beauty to what Mara knew were a lethal set of reflexes. Hokanu wore a loose silk robe, belted with linked shells and a buckle inlaid with lapis lazuli. His hair was damp, which meant he had come in from the bath he customarily took after working out with his officers.

"You might not be hungry, but I could eat a harulth. Lujan and Kemutali decided to test whether fatherhood had made me complacent."

Mara returned a faint smile. "They are both soaking bruises?" she asked hopefully.

Hokanu's reply was rueful. "So was I, until a few minutes ago."

"And are you complacent?" Mara pressed.

"Gods, no." Hokanu laughed. "Never in this house. Justin ambushed me twice on the way to my bath, and once again when I got out." Then, unwilling to dwell on the subject of the son that had become a bone of contention between them, he hurried to ask what kept the frown line between her eyes. ''Unless you're scowling to test my complacency also,'' he ended.

Mara was surprised into a laugh. ''No. I know how lightly you sleep, dear heart. I'll know you're getting complacent on the night you stop starting up and tossing pillows and bedclothes at the slightest hint of a strange noise.''

Happy to see even a moment of mirth from her, Hokanu clapped for a servant to attend to the spoiled lunch tray, and to send to the kitchen for a fresh one. By the time he had disposed of even so brief a detail, he looked back at Mara and, by the faraway look in her eyes, knew he had lost her to contemplation. Her hands had tensed in her lap, interlocked in the habitual way she assumed when thinking upon the task she had laid for her Spy Master.

His hunch was confirmed presently when she said, ''I wonder how far Arakasi has gotten in his attempt to infiltrate the City of the Magicians.''

''We shall not discuss the question until after you have eaten,'' Hokanu said in mock threat. ''If you starve yourself any more, there will be nothing left to you but an enormous belly.''

''Filled with your son and future heir!'' Mara retorted, equally playful, but not at all her usually perceptive self, by her reference to a sensitive topic.

Hokanu let the reference pass, in favor of keeping her peaceful enough to enjoy the fruits and light breads and meats he had sent for. On second thought, Arakasi's attempt upon the security of the Assembly of Magicians was probably a safer choice of conversation.

Arakasi at that moment sat in a noisy roadside tavern in the north of Neshska Province. He wore the striped robe of a free caravan drover, authentically scented with needra, and his right eye seemed to have acquired a cast. The left squinted to compensate, and also to disguise the tendency it had to water at the burning taste of the spirits reputedly brewed by Thūn from tubers that grew in the tundra. Arakasi wet his tongue again with the vile liquor, and offered the flask to the caravan master he had spent the last hours attempting to cajole into intoxication.

The caravan master had a head for spirits like a rock. He was a bald man, massively muscled, with a thunderous laugh and a regrettable tendency to slap his companions on the back: probably the reason why the benches on either side of him stayed empty, Arakasi reflected. He had bruises across his rib cage from being slammed against the table edge by the man's boisterous thumps. He could have chosen a better subject to pump for information, he realized in hindsight. But the other caravan masters tended to band together with their crews, and he needed one who stood apart. To insinuate himself among a tight-knit group, and to pry a man away from his fellows, was likely to take too much time. He had the patience, had many times spent months gaining the confidence of targeted individuals to gain the intelligence Mara required. But here, in the deserted northern tavern, a man with close friendships would be apt to remember a stranger who asked things that a local driver would already know.

"Argh," the huge caravan master bawled, entirely too loudly for Arakasi's liking. "Don't know why any man would choose t'drink such piss." The man hefted the flask in one ham fist and squinted dubiously at the contents. "Tastes poisonous enough to sear out yer tongue." He ended his diatribe by taking another huge swallow.

Arakasi saw another comradely slap coming, and braced his palms against the plank table barely in time. The blow struck him between the shoulder blades, and the trestle shook, rattling cheap clay crockery.

"Hey!" shouted the owner of the hostelry from behind the counter bar. "No brawling in here!"

The caravan master belched. "Stupid man," he confided in a spirit-laden whisper. "If we were of a mind to wreck things, we'd heave the tables through the walls and bring the stinkin' roof down. Wouldn't be losing much. There's web-spinners in the rafters and biting bugs in the loft bedmats, anyway."

Arakasi regarded the heavy lumber that made up the trestle's construction, and conceded that it could serve as a battering ram. "Heavy enough to crack the gates to the City of Magicians," he murmured on a suggestive note.

"Hah!" The burly man slammed the flask down so hard the boards rattled. "Fool might try that. You heard about the boy who hid out in a wagon, last month? Well, I tell you, the servants of those magicians searched through the goods and didn't find the kid. But when the wain rolls through the arches of the gates nearside o' the bridge to the island, well, this beam of light shoots down from the arch an' fries the cover off the wool bale the boy was huddled in." The drover laughed and hit the table, causing the crockery to jump. "Seven hells! I tell you. The magicians' servants are all running around yelling out a warning, shoutin' death 'n' destruction. Next we know, the boy's ahowlin' loud enough to be heard clear to Dustari, and then he's sprintin' down the road back into the forest like his butt's on fire. Found him later, hiding out in a charcoal burner's shed. Not a mark on him, mind, but it was days before he'd stop crying.'' The caravan master put his finger to his temple and winked knowingly. ''They scrambled his head, you see. Thought he was being eaten by fire demons or some such.''

Arakasi digested this while the caravan master took another pull from the flask. He wiped his lips on his hairy wrist and peered at Mara's Spy Master. His voice lowered to a tone of menace. ''Don't even joke about trying to cross the gate to the magicians' city. Mess with the Assembly, and all of us lose our jobs. I've got no wish to end my life as a slave, none at all.''

''But the boy who tried to sneak in as a prank did not lose his freedom,'' Arakasi pointed out.

''Might as well have,'' the caravan master said morosely. He drank another draught. ''Might as well have. He can't sleep for getting nightmares, and days he walks around like one already dead—still got a scrambled head.''

Lowering his voice out of fear, the caravan master said, ''I hear they have ways of knowing what's in the minds of those who try to come to the island. 'Cause it was this prankish lad, they let him live. But I've heard tales that if you mean them harm''—he held his hand out, thumb turned down—''you find yourself at the bottom of that lake.'' Now whispering, he went on, ''The lake bottom is covered with bodies. Too cold down there for them to bloat up and rise. The dead just stay down there.'' With a nod to affirm his statement, the caravan master concluded in normal tone. ''Magicians don't like to be messed with, there's a fact.''

''Here's to letting them be.'' Arakasi hooked back the flask and drank in an unusual fit of pique. The assignment Mara had set him was damned near impossible. Caravans traveled only as far as the gate to the river bridge. There the crews surrendered their reins to servants from the inner city, and each load was vigorously searched before the goods rolled forward. The bridge did not go all the way across the lake, but ended in a water landing, where inbound supplies were offloaded into boats, and inspected a second time. Then polemen ferried them across, into the City of the Magicians.

This was the third man to relate the fate of intruders: no one infiltrated the City of Magicians, and any who tried were transported magically to a watery grave or else driven mad.

Confronted by a bleak conclusion, Arakasi sucked from the flask to fortify himself. Then he surrendered the remains of the liquor to the hairy caravan master, and slipped unobtrusively out to use the privy.

* * *

In the stinking dimness of the road hostel's privy, Arakasi studied the coarse board walls where passing caravan teams had scribbled or scratched a motley assortment of initials, derisive comments on the quality of the hostel's beer, or the names of favored ladies of the Reed Life left behind in bordellos to the south. Among them was the mark he sought, done in white chalk: a simple stick figure, standing. By the drawing's knees was what looked to be a stray line, as if the artist's hand had skipped a beat, in his haste. But seeing this, Arakasi closed tired eyes and breathed a sigh of relief.

His agent, who happened to be a charcoal burner's errand boy, had been by, and the news was good. The warehouse operation where he had nearly been netted by enemies had been out of the message network for two and a half years and at long last the dyer across the street had promoted his eldest apprentice. The tradesman's son who applied for the now vacant position would be an Acoma agent. At last Arakasi could begin to rebuild his network. The warehouse had been operating solely as a business since the disaster of his near capture. The proprietor had accepted his demotion from spy to business factor with stone-faced resignation. Both he and Arakasi were anxious to start laying off various staff members and stevedores, but this could not be done in too much haste; the men were valuable, some useful as agents in some better distant post, but not if the trade house was still under enemy scrutiny. And, judging by the smoothness of the net that had nearly caught him, Arakasi dared not assume otherwise. Slowly, painstakingly, he must come at the problem from another angle. An agent at the dyer who could observe who still watched the warehouse would tell him much.

Abruptly aware that he must not spend overlong in the privy, he performed the expected ablutions and departed through the creaky wooden door. It occurred to him, on unpleasant intuition, that the vacancy in the dyer's shop might not be so fortuitous, after all. If he were that clever enemy, might he not be trying to set his own agent into the position? What better way to keep watch on the warehouse, after all, since loiterers and beggars on corners were far more conspicuous as plants.

Chilled by cold certainty, for he believed his enemy to be as clever as himself, Arakasi cursed and spun around. Muttering as if he had forgotten something, he barged past the drover's boy who crossed the yard toward the privy, and slammed back in through the door.

"There it is, gods be praised," he muttered, as if misplacing important items in stinking public facilities were an everyday occurrence. With one hand he twisted a mother-of-pearl button off his cuff, and with the other he erased the head of the chalk figure and scratched an obscene mark beside it with his nail.

He hurried out and, confronted by the furious boy whose errand he had interrupted, shrugged. He flashed the button in apology. ''Luck charm from my sweetheart. She'd kill me if I lost it.''

The drover's boy grimaced in sympathy and rushed on toward the privy; he'd had more of the hostel's beer than was healthy, by the look of him. Arakasi waited until the door banged fully closed before he slipped off into the wood by the roadside. With any luck, the charcoal burner's lad would happen by within the week. He would see the altered chalk mark, and the obscenity that signaled for an abort on the placement of the agent as dyer's apprentice. As Arakasi moved soundlessly through tree needles, under an unseasonally grey sky, he ruminated that it might indeed be more profitable to have the lad who finally took the apprenticeship watched; if he was innocent of any duplicity, no harm would result, and if he was a double agent, as Arakasi's intuition told him, he might lead back to his master. . . .

Later, Arakasi lay belly down in dripping bushes, shivering in the unaccustomed chill of northern latitudes. Light rain and a wind off the lake conspired to make him miserable. Yet he had spent hours here, on several different occasions. From this vantage point in the forest, on a jutting peninsula, he could observe both the bridge gate and the boat landing where servants loyal only to the magicians loaded inbound goods into skiffs and ferried them across to the city. He had long since concluded that a smuggled entry by way of the trade wagons was a doomed enterprise. The caravan master's tale had only confirmed his suspicion that inbound goods were also surveyed by magical means for intruders. What he looked for now was a way to gain entrance to the city by stealth, avoiding the apparently all-seeing arch over the bridgeway.

The isle lay too far across the water to swim over to it. From where Arakasi hid, its buildings appeared blended together into a mass of pointed towers, one of which was tall enough to pierce into the clouds. Through the ship's glass he had bought from a shop on the seacoast, he could make out steep-walled houses and looping, arched walkways that cut through the air between. The lakeshore was crammed with stone-fronted buildings, oddly shaped windows, and strange arched doorways. There were no walls and, as far as he could tell, no sentries. That did not rule out defenses of arcane means; but plainly the only way an intruder might enter the city was a night crossing by boat, and then the scaling of some garden wall, or seeking some cranny to gain access.

Arakasi sighed. The job was a thief's work, and he needed a boat in a place where there were neither habitations nor fishing settlements. That meant smuggling one in on board a wagon, no easy task where inbound caravans were comprised of men who all knew one another intimately. Also, he would require a man trained in stealth, and such were not found in honest trades. Neither problem promised a fast or an easy solution. Mara would have a long wait for information that might, in all honesty, be impossible to acquire.

Ever a practical man, Arakasi arose from his damp hollow and turned into the forest. He rubbed a crick in his neck, shook moisture from his clothing, and made his way back toward the road hostel. As he walked, he pondered deeply, a habit that more times than not had given rise to accurate intuition. He did not press the issue that immediately frustrated him, but pursued instead another problem, one that had not seemed significant at first, but was becoming an increasing aggravation.

Try as he might, he could not seem to get a start at placing new agents in the Anasati household. Only one operative remained active, and that one was elderly, an old confidant of Jiro's father's that the young Lord had taken a dislike to. The servant had been relegated to a position of little importance, and what news he heard was only slightly more informative than street gossip. For the first time, Arakasi wondered whether his failed attempts to replace that agent might be significant beyond coincidence.

They had appeared innocuous, certainly, each of seven tries foiled by what had seemed ill luck or poor timing: Jiro in a temper, a factor in too belligerent a mood to grant an old friend favors; and most lately, an illness of the stomach that prevented a trusted servant from making a recommendation for recruiting a newcomer.

Arakasi stopped dead, unmindful of the rain, which had begun to fall much harder. He did not feel the cold and the wet that slid in droplets down his collar, but shivered instead from inspiration.

He had been a fool, not to suspect sooner. But chance may not have been behind such a string of seemingly unrelated misfortunes. What if, all along, his attempts to infiltrate the Anasati household had been blocked by a mind more clever than his own?

Chilled to the bone, Arakasi started forward. He had long admired the enemy's First Adviser, Chumaka, whose flair for politics had benefited the

Anasati since Jiro's father's time. Now Arakasi wondered whether it was Chumaka's cleverness he fenced with, as unseen antagonist.

The thought continued, inexorably: was it possible that an Anasati presence was behind the byplay at the silk warehouse? The elegance of this possibility appealed to Mara's Spy Master. One gifted enemy made more sense than two unrelated foes with equal brilliance.

Deeply disturbed, Arakasi hurried his step. He needed to get himself warm and dry, and to find a comfortable corner where he could think undisturbed. For each balked effort showed that he faced a rival equal to his best efforts. It was distressing to consider that a connection might exist between such a man and Mara's gravest enemy, even more by the possibility that this rival might exceed his talents.

Getting a spy into the City of the Magicians was an impossible enterprise and its importance paled to insignificance before the threat posed to Mara's spy network by Jiro's adviser. For Arakasi had no illusions. His grasp of the Game of the Council was shrewd and to the point. More than a feud between two powerful families was at play here. Mara was a prominent figure in the Emperor's court, and her fall could touch off civil war.

6. Gambits

Chumaka frowned.

With increasing irritation, he scanned the reports stuffed between the sheafs of notes he had prepared for his master's forthcoming court session. The news was none of it good. He raised a hand and chewed a fingernail, frustration making him savage. He had been so close to tracing the Spy Master behind the original Tuscai network! It had been predictable that the net in Ontoset would be shut down as a result of the bungling chase at the silk warehouse. But what made no sense at all was that after a passage of time approaching three years, the seemingly unrelated branch in Jamar should still be kept dormant as well.

Those ruling houses who undertook the trouble and expense of spy nets tended to become addicted to them. It was simply inconceivable that any Lord grown accustomed to staying informed by covert means should suddenly, for the discovery of one courier, give up his hard-earned advantage. Lady Mara most of all; she was bold or cautious as circumstance dictated, but never one to be unreasonably fearful. The death of her son could not have changed her basic nature so radically. She could be depended upon to use every means at her disposal, and never be deterred by one minor setback. Chumaka flinched slightly as tender flesh tore under the worrying gnaw of his teeth. He blotted the bleeding hangnail on his robe and shuffled his papers into order in disturbed preoccupation. The situation bothered him. Each day Jiro was closer to demanding his answers outright. The First Adviser to House Anasati was loath to admit he was growing desperate. He had no choice but consider the unthinkable: that this time he might have run up against an opponent who outmatched him.

The idea rankled, that any mind in the Empire could outmaneuver Chumaka.

Yet such a possibility could not be dismissed. In his gut he knew that the network was not disbanded, merely dormant or turned toward an unexpected quarter. But where? And why? Not knowing was costing

Chumaka sleepless nights. Black circles and pouches under his eyes gave his already angular visage a careworn look.

The scrape of oiled wood roused Chumaka from distressed reverie. Already servants were pulling aside the screens in the grand hall in preparation for Jiro's public court. Omelo had the Lord's honor guard in place beside the dais, and the hadonra was overseeing disposition of his factors and secretaries. Within minutes, those allies or houses seeking court with the Lord of the Anasati would be arriving, escorted to their places in order of rank. Lord Jiro would enter last, to hear petitioners, exchange social chat, and, sometimes, negotiate new business.

Chumaka snapped the papers in his hand into a roll and stuffed them into his satchel. Muttering, he stalked to the dais to be sure his preferred cushions were arranged to his satisfaction. The list of Jiro's guests was a long one, and this court could last into the evening. A skinny man with lanky bones, Chumaka liked plenty of padding under his rump through extended sessions. Physical aches he regarded as a distraction to his thinking, and with this rival Spy Master so far adept at eluding him, he could not afford to miss any nuance of what transpired.

The grand hall slowly filled. Servants hurried in and out bringing refreshments and directing the placement of fan slaves. The day outside was hot, and Jiro's subtle habit was to be sure his guests were cool and comfortable. He catered to them to extend their patience, and they, believing he spoiled them to win their favor, felt their egos stroked enough that they often granted him concessions more magnanimous than they had intended at the outset.

Lord Jiro entered with little fanfare. His scribe called out his name, and only two warriors marched on either side, a half step behind their master. Today his clothes were simply cut, though sewn of the finest silk. He chose carriage and clothing that were rich but not ostentatious, and that could be interpreted as firm and manly, or boyishly innocent, depending on the advantage he wished to press. Chumaka regarded the ambivalent effect and stroked his chin, thinking: were Jiro not chosen by the gods to wear the Anasati mantle, he might have made a superb field agent.

Then such frivolous speculation was cut short as the young master ascended the dais. His warriors flanked him as he took his place on his cushions and made formal pronouncement. "The court begins."

Then, as his steward moved among the guests to announce the first on the roster, Jiro leaned over to confer in quiet tones with Chumaka. "What need I pay close attention to this day, my First Adviser?"

Chumaka tapped his chin with a knuckle. "To endeavor to compromise the Xacatecas' support of Lady Mara, we'll need allies. More to the point, we'll need their wealth. Consider the offer of the Lord of the Matawa to ship our grains to the south in exchange for certain concessions." He pulled the appropriate note from the many sheaves that jammed his satchel and swiftly scanned the lines. "The Lord wishes a favorable match for his daughter. Perhaps that bastard nephew of your cousin's might suffice? He's young, but not ill-favored. Marriage into a noble house would redirect his ambition and, down the line, provide us with another ally." Chumaka lowered his voice as others began to approach the dais. "Rumor has it that this Lord Matawa is trading with Midkemians from the city of LaMut."

Jiro heard this with a look askance. "Rumor? Or the gleanings of one of your listeners?"

Chumaka cleared his throat, keeping this point deliberately ambiguous. "I remind my Lord that many of those involved in LaMutian merchant consortiums were born in Tsuranuanni, and they may provide us with the same advantage the Acoma enjoy in their exclusive trading concessions." He finished in a thick whisper, "Mara anticipated well when she got her dispensation from the Keeper of the Imperial Seal. She acted on an outside guess and tied up the obvious goods coming through the rift from Midkemia. But because she moved on the generalities of a wild hunch, she didn't anticipate everything. There are a half-dozen items we can import that would make us rich, and while Mara might successfully block Anasati attempts to traffic goods from Midkemia, there's little she can do to prevent the LaMutians from selling across the rift to the Lord of the Matawa."

Jiro smiled. "How badly does Lord Matawa wish an exclusive shipping license? And how ugly is his daughter?"

Chumaka smiled broadly. "His daughter takes after a mother who looks like a dog, a particularly ill-aspected dog, in fact. There are two younger sisters also. Both of these have crooked teeth, and only the eldest can be given away with the title. Their father needs a bigger treasury if his youngest children are to escape the fate of becoming the consorts of low-born merchants. That means the Lord of the Matawa desires this trading concession very badly indeed."

As a delegate from the most minor house approached the dais and gave his bow of respect, Jiro concluded his conference with Chumaka. "Your counsel seems sound. I will proceed to make the Lord of the Matawa a happy man."

He faced politely forward to hear his first petitioner, when a disturbance at the rear of the hall turned half the heads in the room. A florid man in a purple robe had thrust his way past the door servants. These were slaves, and in fear of their master's displeasure, they cast themselves face down in obeisance at their lapse. The man who had intruded paid no heed but rushed headlong into the hall, ignoring the astonished protest of the Anasati house servants in relentless pursuit on his heels. He swept past the seated rows of Jiro's guests, with no more heed of them than if he had been alone in the great hall. Striding directly down the long approach to the dais, and causing the war banners to swing in the rafters in a wake of disturbed air, he skidded to a stop before Jiro. Too agitated for manners or ceremony, he shouted, "Do you have any idea of what she has done!"

The delegate he had displaced looked ruffled; Jiro himself was discommoded, but he covered this with a swift glance at Chumaka, who murmured the appropriate name behind his hand in a tone only his master could hear.

To control this startling confrontation, Lord Jiro said in his chilliest tone, "Welcome, Lord Dawan. You seem . . . discommoded."

The thick-necked man thrust his head forward, looking like a needra bull attempting to shove through a fence to reach a cow in full season. Nearly spitting with anger, he waved both hands in the air. "Discommoded? My Lord, I am ruined!"

Aware of muttering in the hall, as Lords and delegates were made to wait through this blatant breach of good manners, Jiro raised a placating voice. "Lord Dawan, please, be seated lest your distress cause you to be overcome by the heat." At a signal from their Lord, Anasati servants rushed forward to bring the distraught man cold refreshment.

Disdaining to appear to show favoritism, Lord Jiro spoke quickly, aware he must bridle the other petitioners' resentment, and to quickly assess whether he could gain impromptu advantage from the interruption. Dawan of the Tuscobar was an occasional business associate and an unsure ally. Jiro's inability to win him clearly to his cause had been an irritation, but the inconvenience was minor. The far-reaching ramifications of this byplay were anything but small. House Tuscobar held influence with the Lord of the Keda, whose support in any confrontation with Mara would net the Anasati a solid advantage. Jiro judged the alliance would be critical in the future, when the traditionalist plot to reinstate the High Council finally met with success.

Above the disgruntled murmurs of his petitioners, Lord Jiro called, "Let all who seek aid of the Anasati take heed. My house listens with sympathy to the difficulties of established friends. My Lord of the Tuscobar, what has happened?"

The heavyset Lord took a swallow from the glass of cold juice he had been handed by Jiro's staff. He gulped in an effort to compose himself. "My entire fleet, carrying every last grain of my year's harvest, was sunk!"

Jiro's eyes widened in astonishment. "Sunk? But how?"

"Some malignant spell spun by that witch," Dawan answered.

"Witch?" Jiro raised his eyebrows.

Dawan set his juice aside in favor of the wine offered by a hovering servant. He drank deeply and wiped his mouth before he felt fortified enough to qualify. "Mara of the Acoma. Who else? Everyone knows that as Servant of the Empire she has unlimited luck, and the gods' favor. She has ruined me by sending false directions to my fleet master, ordering him to ship this year's harvest to Dustari instead of the grain market at Lepala!" Lord Dawan nearly wept in frustration as he said, "That would have been bad enough. I would merely have been reduced to penury. But an unseasonal storm hit a week out of Jamar, and every last ship was sunk! I am ruined." He eased his sorrows by taking another heroic drink of wine. "I swear by my ancestors, Jiro: I will never again shirk my support of your efforts to end this woman's evil influence."

Jiro rested his chin on his fist. After deep thought, he said, "I thank you for acknowledging the risk inherent in Lady Mara's departures from tradition, but had you said nothing, I would still help an old family friend." He turned at once to Chumaka. "Have our hadonra write a letter of credits for Lord Tuscobar." To Dawan he added, "Freely borrow as much as you need. Take as long as you wish to repay us, on whatever terms you think fair."

Dawan stiffened, the wine forgotten as he regarded Jiro with suspicion. "Interest?"

As if granting largesse to the needy were a daily occurrence, Jiro waved his hand. "None! I will make no profit from a friend's misfortune." Quietly he added, "Especially if that distress is caused by my enemy."

Dawan rose. He made an extravagant bow. "Jiro, let everyone present stand as witness! You are a man of unceasing nobility and generosity. Your ancestors look down and are proud." He bowed again, belatedly deferential to the patience of the others awaiting the Anasati Lord's attention. "And I beg forgiveness for interrupting this worthy gathering."

Jiro rose. Indicating Chumaka should join him, he personally escorted the Lord of the Tuscobar to a side door, where he murmured in comradely farewell, "Nonsense. There is nothing to forgive. Now, retire to one of my baths and refresh yourself. Remain for the evening meal, even spend the night if you'd like and return home tomorrow." He appointed a slave to lead the flattered and slightly intoxicated Lord of the Tuscobar away.

As he moved to return to his dais, playing the role of magnanimous Lord to perfection, Chumaka murmured, "It's strange, don't you think? Why would Mara wish to harm a fence-sitter like Dawan? This makes no sense by any measure."

Jiro glanced at his First Adviser in immense amusement. "But she didn't. I arranged the forger myself. It was I who sent those false orders to Dawan's shipmaster."

Chumaka bowed low, chuckling silently. Quietly, so not one of the petitioners could hear, he said, "You surprise me, my Lord. You are growing into a seasoned player, both in shāh and in the Game of the Council. How did you contrive to cast blame on Mara?"

Jiro seemed smug. "Our hadonra spread rumors, at my order. Dawan and others were made aware of the insults and misdeeds done us by the Lady over the past several years. I merely copied her methods and let Dawan draw his own conclusions." Stepping decisively back toward the dais, he added, "Oh, and by making sure Dawan heard that Acoma grain is being shipped this season to the markets at Lepala."

Chumaka flushed with obvious pleasure. "Admirable, my master. Clever enough to have been an idea I wish I had thought of first."

As the Lord and his First Adviser mounted his dais, they shared the identical thought: each considered himself fortunate to have the other, for they worked remarkably well together. When the old High Council was restored and the secret of Mara's spy net was cracked, then would the Lady have cause to worry, for not even the formidable luck of a Servant of the Empire was going to spare her house from destruction.

Mara paced in frustration. For weeks the coolness between herself and her husband separated them like a wall. Hokanu's resistance to her desire to see Justin renounce his ties to Shinzawai to become the Acoma heir was understandable. Hokanu's affections were as deep as if the boy had been his own. Ayaki's death had turned him more protective as a parent, and, reminded of that loss, Mara felt bitterness that never seemed to lessen.

She paused between restless steps, one hand on the screen that over-looked her private garden. Oh, for one hour with old Nacoya and her wisdom, she wished in vain. Her onetime nurse, foster mother, and First Adviser had always offered insight straight to the heart of any difficulty. Even when Mara had refused advice or persisted in taking risks unaccept-able to the old woman, Nacoya had always seen clear and true. In matters of the heart, her perception had been unmatched. Mara sighed. It had been Nacoya who had noticed her mistress's growing affection for the barbarian slave Kevin, long before Mara admitted the possibility of love to herself. The old woman's counsel was sorely needed now. Mara attempted to conjure Nacoya's voice, but the beloved woman's shade rested far away this day.

A kick inside her belly ended her reverie. She gasped, pressed a hand to her swollen middle, and met the discomfort with a smile. Her unborn child had the strength of a barbarian tiger cub. Surely Hokanu would feel differently when he beheld his newborn first child. The pride of fatherhood would soften him, and he would cease his stubbornness and give in to her demand that Justin be named Acoma heir. The flesh that was of his own blood would make him understand that this was the gods' will, that this babe whose begetting they had shared was the proper heir to the title Lord of the Shinzawai.

Mara leaned against the lintel of the screen, anticipating the happiness of the occasion. She had borne two children, one by a man she loathed and another by a man she adored. Both little ones had given her something completely unexpected; what had begun as a duty of honor in the begetting of Ayaki, the necessity of ensuring Acoma continuance, had been transformed to a joyous reality as she came to love the heir for whom she labored. It was her offspring that would inherit the greatness of the Acoma. Once a child was held, his baby laughter giving her delight, never again could family honor seem a distant, abstract thing.

Mara keenly awaited the moment when Hokanu would feel this magic for himself. The birth of their son would bring them closer and end this cold contention of wills. Peace would return between them, and both Acoma and Shinzawai children would grow into the greatness of their future.

While Mara had never been consumed by passion for the man she cherished as husband, she had come to rely on his closeness. His understanding was a comfort, his wisdom a shelter, his wit a relief from danger and worry, and his quiet, intuitive understanding a tenderness she could not live without. She missed him. His love had become the linchpin of her happiness, all unnoticed until she had been forced to go without. For while he was ever close by, he was increasingly absent in spirit. More deeply than she could have imagined, that lack caused her pain.

The reminders were unceasing; the casual touch of his hand to her face that had not happened as she wakened; the slight upturning of his mouth that indicated humor during court that today had been nowhere in evidence. They no longer shared their afternoon tray of chocha, while Hokanu scanned reports from military advisers and she reviewed the commerce lists from far-flung trading factors presented daily by Jican. Their relationship had grown silent and strained and though Hokanu had made no issue of the matter, he had extended his practice at arms to keep busy through the hours they had once spent in companionship. No sharp words were exchanged, nor anything close to heated argument, yet the disagreement over Justin's heirship was a presence that poisoned everything they did. Mara stroked the taut flesh over her womb, praying this estrangement would end once their new son was born.

Besides Nacoya, Hokanu was the only soul she had met who could follow her thoughts without misunderstandings. Another kick slammed her innards. Mara laughed. "Soon, little one," she whispered to the baby.

A servant who waited in attendance started at the sound of her voice. "Mistress?"

Mara stepped heavily away from the screen. "I want for nothing but this child, who seems as anxious as I am to see himself born."

The servant tensed in alarm. "Should I call for—"

Mara held up her hand. "No, there is time yet. The midwife and the healer say another month at least." She furrowed her brow. "But I wonder if perhaps this baby could be early."

A polite knock sounded at the inner doorway. Mara pulled her robe more comfortably over her gravid body, and nodded for the servant to open the screen to the hall. Jican, her hadonra, bowed from outside the portal. "Mistress, a trader is here seeking permission to bargain."

That Jican would trouble her for a matter he would normally attend to himself, was unusual. He had managed her vast holdings long enough that he could anticipate almost any decision she might make, even those he disagreed with. Anxious to know what had arisen, Mara said, "What do you wish?"

Always diffident in situations outside of the ordinary, Jican replied carefully, "I think you should see this man's wares, mistress."

Glad for the diversion on yet another afternoon without Hokanu's company, Mara clapped for her maid to bring her a robe more suitable for a stranger's company. Tucked into a long-sleeved, loose-waisted garment of shimmering silk, she motioned for her hadonra to lead the way. The guest trader waited in the shaded, pillared hall in the wing that housed the scribes. Mara and Jican passed through the cavernous corridors that tunneled partially through the hillside from the sunny quarters she shared with Hokanu. Made aware by Jican's quick step that he was fidgety, Mara asked, "Are the wares this trader offers something special?"

"Perhaps." The little hadonra gave a sideways glance that confirmed his uneasiness. "I think your judgment is needed to appraise this man's offer."

Years of his loyal service had taught Mara to heed her hadonra's hunches. When he did not immediately launch into a description of the offered goods, the Lady was moved to prompt, "What else?"

Jican halted. "I . . ." Uncertainty blossomed into hesitation. He bobbed an apologetic bow, then blurted, "I am not sure how to treat this man, mistress."

Familiar enough with the hadonra's foibles to realize that questions would distress him further, Mara simply strode on in receptive silence.

In another few steps, the explanation was forthcoming. Jican said, "Because he is . . . was Tsurani."

Mara pondered this detail. "From LaMut?" LaMut was ruled by Hokanu's brother, and most trading delegations from the Kingdom included a former Tsurani soldier, to act as translator.

Jican nodded, transparently relieved he had not needed to coach her further. "A Tsurani who prefers Kingdom ways."

The reason for the hadonra's uneasiness was plainer: while Mara might bend tradition and swear masterless men to Acoma service, the concept of anyone preferring to remain without house ties on a foreign world—no matter that one of them was Hokanu's brother, Kasumi—was too alien to understand, even for her. And that such a man headed the trading delegation made negotiations more delicate than usual.

The long, interior corridor opened at last into a colonnaded portico that fronted the south side of the estate house. The gravel path leading to the main doorway ran alongside, and there, shaded by ancient trees, waited the visiting merchant's retinue, a small group of bearers and ten bodyguards. Mara's eyes widened. She did not note at first that there were more guards than usual because they were so tall! More careful study revealed them to be Midkemians all, a rare enough detail that the sentries on duty at the estate entrance stared surreptitiously as they kept watch. Scraps of a conversation in foreign speech reached Mara's ears, and the accent, so familiar, made her pause a fraction between steps. Memories of Kevin of Zūn flooded through her, until Jican's hand-wringing impatience recalled her to present obligations. Mastering herself instantly, she hastened on into the service wing, toward the hall where the merchant awaited.

That man sat correctly beneath the informal dais she used while negotiating with outsiders. Sacks and carry boxes of sample wares were arrayed by his side, while his hands rested in plain sight upon his knees. He wore a splendid silk robe, recognizably of foreign manufacture: the sheen was different, and the dyes blended in patterns never seen in Tsuranuanni. The effect was bold, just barely short of insolent, Mara decided, watching the man through narrowed eyes as she approached. Although this man had presented himself as a merchant, he outfitted himself as befitted the highest Ruling Lord of the Empire. Yet the man was no noble; in place of the customary house chop embroidered on sash or shoulder, the barbarous symbol of LaMut, a doglike creature called a wolf, was displayed. The man was arrogant, Mara decided as she allowed Jican to help her up the shallow stair and to her cushions.

Still, the stranger had impeccable manners. When the Lady was comfortable, he bowed until his forehead touched the mat upon which he knelt. He paused long enough to imply deep respect, while Jican gave his name to the mistress. "My Lady, this is Janaio, of the city of LaMut."

Janaio straightened with grace and smiled. "Honors to your house, Good Servant. Are you well, Lady Mara?"

Mara inclined her head. "I am well, Janaio of . . . LaMut."

A detail leaped out at her. This man wore gold! Mara pinched back a breath of undignified surprise. By imperial edict, all jewelry and personal effects made of metal were carefully cataloged upon entry through the rift from Midkemia. Traders from the barbarian world were often outraged as their boots were confiscated and plain sandals loaned to them while they embarked on their travels within the Empire; but the impounded items were always returned when they left. The imperial treasury had learned a rough lesson when the first entourage of Midkemians returned home without their boots, and the economy of Lash Province had been turned on its head by the iron nails drawn from the soles and changed for centis.

The trader fingered the chain about his neck. "I have given surety that I will not leave this behind, Lady Mara," he said, in response to her notice. This reminded her of his Tsurani origins, as no barbarian would have been trusted to keep his word in the face of temptation. Midkemians professed no belief in the Wheel of Life, so honor did not bind them to fear loss of the gods' favor.

Mara maintained an outward calm. The man was bold! While such an ornament might be a modest possession for a wealthy man beyond the rift, in Kelewan it was equal to the income of a minor house for a year. As well this man knew. His public display of such treasure was a calculated ostentation. Mara waited in reserved expectancy to see just what this trader wished to gain with his bargaining.

When she had determined that a suitable interval had passed to remind him of his place, she asked, "Now, what may I do for you?"

The man did not miss nuance: that the Tsurani phrase was translated from the King's Tongue. Mara's clever opening informed him without undue fuss that she had arranged affairs with Midkemian traders before. He gave her back impeccable Tsurani protocol. "I am a modest broker in certain spices and delicacies, mistress. Given my history"—he gestured broadly—"I am advantageously placed to know those products unique to my adopted homeland that would prove profitable in the Empire."

Mara nodded, conceding his point. Janaio resumed in ingratiating fashion. "But rather than waste your valuable hours speaking, I would beg your indulgence to let my wares speak for themselves."

Stirred to curiosity, Mara said, "What do you propose?"

Janaio indicated the various carry boxes and sacks at his elbow. "Here I have samples. As it is near the hour when many within the Empire cease activities to indulge in a cup of chocha, perhaps you would care for something more exotic?"

Unhappily reminded that Hokanu customarily shared such a moment to take refreshment with her, Mara repressed a sigh. She was tired, and in need of a nap, for the baby inside her interrupted her sleep at nights. "There is little time for this."

"Please," Janaio said quickly. He bowed in attempt to ease her mind. "I will not keep you overlong. You will be rewarded, both in pleasure and in riches, I assure you."

Jican bent close to his Lady. "Let me call for a food taster, mistress," he advised.

Mara regarded her hadonra closely. He also was intrigued; but more, he had something else to tell about this mysterious trader from beyond the rift. She reached down and drew out the fan tucked behind her sash. Flipping it open and using it to hide her lips from her visitor, she whispered, "What else should I know of this man?"

Jican looked uncomfortable. "A suspicion," he murmured so that only she could hear. "I received word from a factor who is friendly to us. This Janaio has also made overtures to the Lord of the Matawa."

"Who is a firm supporter of the traditionalists and Jiro." Mara fluttered her fan. "Do you think he hopes that our rivalry will help him to drive a tough bargain?"

The hadonra pursed his lips, thinking. "That I cannot say. It is possible. Should he have wares of unusual worth, the house that gains concessions will benefit greatly."

That settled Mara's mind on the matter. She must not allow the fatigue of pregnancy to cede any advantage to the Anasati uncontested. She clapped for her runner and dispatched him to the kitchens to fetch a cook who would serve her as taster. She also asked for Saric and Lujan, since further counsel might be required of them later.

Janaio met her precautions with obsequious approval. "Most wise, Lady Mara. Though I assure you, my intentions are only honest."

Mara crossed her hands over her middle without comment. No precautions were too stringent when she was so near to term with Hokanu's child. She waited, unresponsive to Janaio's attempts to make conversation, until her adviser arrived at her summons.

Saric's look of surprise as he entered revealed he had taken the man to be Midkemian, sporting Empire fashion. One glance at the Acoma First Adviser caused Janaio to straighten where he sat. As if his instincts warned that Saric's insights were to be respected, he crisply listed his sureties. "For the sake of easing your worry, great Lady, since the food-stuffs I carry are so exotic that no one in this land will be familiar enough with their taste to detect any tampering, I propose that I share each cup with you."

Unimpressed by gold chain and grand rhetoric, Saric met this pronouncement with a lack of expression. He watched intently as the trader made a display of pushing back his sleeves, to show that he wore no ring or bracelet, and that nothing was contained within his robe. "If you will have your servants prepare hot water, three pots, and cups from your own stores, I will provide the ingredients. Then you may choose which cup I am to taste and which you will." Smiling in the teeth of Saric's quiet, he said, "If it please you, Lady, I will bear the risk equally."

Intrigued in spite of her First Adviser's reserve, Mara said, "What are you attempting to bring to our Empire?"

"Fine beverages, mistress. A wonderful assortment of flavors and pungent drinks that will astonish your palate. Should this venture prove profitable, and I assure you it will, then I will also bring exotic wines and ales to the Empire from the finest vintners and brewers in the Kingdom of the Isles."

Mara weighed her impressions. No wonder this man had remained on Midkemia. He might have served as a house soldier before the final battle of the Riftwar, but he was a born merchant. She cast a sidelong glance as Lujan arrived and marched smartly to take his place behind her. If fate had cast him on the other side of the rift, given his glib tongue and facile mind, he might perhaps have been the one to sit here, selling exotic wares.

The surmise was somehow reassuring. Still, it was not her nature to trust readily, particularly when Saric had given no word in favor of this stranger's proposal. Mara chose to challenge the connection with her Anasati enemy. "What was your arrangement with the Lord of the Matawa?"

Janaio flashed her a grin in the manner of a born Midkemian. Where another Tsurani ruler might be put off by such openness, Mara had known Kevin too well to misunderstand; if anything, the foreign manner-ism set her at ease. Janaio went on, "You heard about my talks, but I assure you they are no secret. The wares I carry are luxuries and need delicate handling and skillful negotiators to place them in the proper markets. I would be a poor merchant if I failed to examine all options. The Lord of the Matawa has sent many emissaries through the rift seeking to establish a brokerage."

Mara's lips thinned as she pondered the implications of this. Jican whispered something to Saric, who nodded and quietly touched her arm. "My Lady, we know that the Matawa wish to make inroads in your trade market. They cannot disturb your imperial patent that gives you exclusive license for certain items, but they hope to become a rival presence to lure any nonexclusive trade they can wean away from our factors. They could legally establish exclusive trade rights beyond the rift, where we have no control. Arakasi's report holds that funding for the venture might well come from Jiro."

Sick that politics should increasingly come to drive even the most innocuous of ventures, Mara inclined her head to Janaio. "Send for what you need."

Her servants were devotedly efficient. Proud to uphold their Lady's honor, they swiftly brought in trays with several pots and porcelain cups. A slave hurried after, bearing a kettle of steaming water.

Janaio set out his various packets and vials with a theatrical flourish. "First," he announced, "something pungent and savory." He poured water into one of the small pots and dropped in a small pouch. "This delicacy grows on a shrub in the southern part of the Kingdom, mistress. The leaves are costly to dry and ship, and because they are susceptible to mold, only the very wealthy can afford to buy the small supply that reaches the northern lands. For this reason, the drink I prepare has not gained much popularity in my city of LaMut. Once you have tasted, I think you must agree that this is likely due to lack of familiarity." He raised the top of the pot, sniffed at the steam, and closed his eyes. "I believe you will concur that this fine beverage will find approval from Tsurani nobles of taste."

With this, he poured, filling the room with an exotic, spicy scent. When three cups were full, he nodded to Mara's servant, who lifted the tray and bore it to the dais for the Lady to choose her preference. She motioned for the slave who had carried the pot to taste one. The servant handed her one of the pair that remained, and bore the tray back to Janaio.

The merchant lifted his cup, saying, "Sip cautiously, lest you scald your tongue, mistress."

The alien aroma fascinated Mara. Unlike anything else she had known, she found it wildly enticing. She sipped the brew. The first taste was acrid and strange, yet bracing and flavorful. She considered a moment, then said, "I suspect a little honey would cut the bitterness."

The trader smiled. "You skip ahead of me, Good Servant. In Midkemia we also use white sugar made from a plant called beets. Some folk prefer a dash of milk; yet others, the juice of a tart fruit similar to the Kelewanese ketundi."

Mara sipped again and found her appreciation increasing. "What do you call this?"

The man smiled. "It is tea, Good Servant."

Mara laughed. "Many things are called 'tea,' Janaio of LaMut. What is the herb you have brewed?"

The merchant gave back a Tsurani shrug. "That is the name of the herb, or rather the leaves of the shrub. When someone in LaMut says 'tea,' this is what they speak of, not the blends of plantstuffs steeped in hot water you drink here. Yet of this delicacy there are a multitude of varieties as well, robust, subtle, sweet, and bitter. One selects to suit the occasion."

Now fascinated, Mara nodded. "What else?"

Janaio selected another pot from the Acoma supply and prepared a second hot beverage. "This is a far different drink."

A black liquid that smelled rich and heady was presently handed to Mara. This time, Jican supplanted her taster, his excitement overcoming caution. Mara could barely wait for her hadonra to try his share before she sipped at her sample. The drink was bitter and yet piquant. "What do you call this? It reminds me vaguely of chocha."

Janaio bowed at her evident pleasure. "This is coffee, mistress. And like the tea, it has a thousand different cousins. This you drink grows on plants high upon the hillsides of Yabon. Good, robust, but hardly a delicacy." He clapped, and one of his servants brought forth another basket, smaller, and tied with festive ribbons. "Let me offer a gift. Here are a dozen samples for you to consume at your leisure. Each is clearly labeled as to the type of bean used to make the drink and instructions for preparation."

Mara set aside her half-empty cup. While this sampling was diverting her from her troubled marriage, the day was waning while she tarried. She was reluctant to forgo the hour she always spent with her son while he took his supper. Justin was recently five years of age, too young to understand delays.

Sensing her impatience, Janaio raised a hand in appeal. "The most astonishing drink remains yet to be sampled." Quickly, before the Lady could rise and take her leave, he asked her servant, "Please, may I have needra milk?"

Mara might have taken issue at this man's presumption, except that Midkemians could be expected to act impetuously. She hid her tiredness and motioned for the servant to run the requested errand. In the interval, Saric bent close to his Lady's ear. "Don't miss the subtleties," he advised. "This man was Tsurani born. He apes Midkemian brashness, almost as if he knows that you had a fondness, once, for such behavior. I do not like the smoothness of this play upon your sympathies, my Lady. You will be cautious, please?"

Mara tipped her fan against her chin. Her adviser was right to wish restraint. "This Janaio drinks from the same pot as I. Surely there will be no harm in enduring one more sample. After that the interview will be ended."

Saric returned a half nod, but a glance exchanged with Jican caused the little hadonra to pause. When the servant returned with a small pitcher of milk, Jican suggested that he also would like a cup to taste, separate from the slave that would continue to perform his office.

"But of course," Janaio agreed in pleasant tones. "You are a shrewd man, who wishes to understand every nuance of the trade your house may undertake." While Mara's counselors looked on in wonderment, the trader poured equal portions of milk and hot water into the final pot. His chain sparkled as he leaned toward his basket, speaking all the while. "Occasionally, you may wish to use only milk, as it gives added richness to this drink."

His preparations were completed with yet more flourish than before. Again he passed the tray of filled cups to the servant, indicating Mara should choose hers first. She did not, but waited until Jican and the taster had selected. The smell of this drink was intoxicating. The little hadonra shed his anxiety and sipped. He recoiled with a smothered yelp as he burned his tongue.

The trader had the grace not to laugh. "My apologies, my Lady. I should have thought to warn: this drink is served very hot."

Jican recovered his aplomb. "My Lady," he said excitedly, "the taste of this rarity is incredible."

Both hadonra and Lady looked at the slave who served as taster. More careful than Jican, he had not burned his tongue, and he was slurping the drink with such evident relish that Mara motioned for the servant to pass her the tray.

As she chose from the last two cups, Janaio said, "If coffee reminds you of chocha, then this wonder may remind you of the chocha-la you make for your children. But I humbly submit, that chocha-la is to chocolate as my humble station is to your grandeur."

Mara sipped and closed her eyes at the marvelous taste. Unable to hide her surprise and pleasure, she sighed in pure happiness.

Grinning, Janaio accepted the last cup from the tray and drank deep. "This is chocolate, mistress."

Unable to help herself, Mara thought of Kevin, who had commented on more than one occasion that he missed the chocolate sweets of festivals in his homeworld. At last she understood.

Blinking back the moisture that gathered in her eyes, and passing off the indiscretion as if she avoided steam from the cup, Mara said, "This is a wonderful thing."

Janaio set aside his emptied cup and bowed. "I wish permission to be granted exclusive license to import, mistress."

Mara shook her head with open regret. "I cannot grant that, Janaio of LaMut. My patent from the Imperial Government is limited to certain items."

Obviously disappointed, the trader gestured expansively. "Then perhaps a trading agreement. If exclusivity is beyond your means, then at least let me broker through the mightiest trading house in the Empire."

Mara drank more of the delightful liquid, recalled to caution at last. "What of the Matawa?"

Janaio gave a deprecating cough. "Their offer was insulting, no, demeaning, and they lack the experienced factors you have in your employ. They require interpreters, still, to transact business, an uneasy situation for one in the luxury market, as I am. I desire no avenue that is ripe for misunderstanding, or even the outside chance of exploitation."

Savoring the dregs of her drink, Mara said, "That much I can grant."

Regret tinged her tone as she added, "I can't limit others in bringing these beverages to us, but perhaps some shrewd buying in LaMut might hamper others from competing effectively against our interests." Then, content to entrust the disposition of final details to Jican, she prepared to take her leave.

The trader bowed, touching his forehead to the ground. "Mistress, your wisdom is legendary."

Mara stood up. "When we are both made rich from the importation of chocolate to our Empire, then I will accept the compliment. But now other matters require my presence. Jican will draw up the documents sealing the partnership you request."

While servants hurried in to collect the dirtied cups, and Jican's brow furrowed as he confronted the intricate issues of trade, Mara left the room, helped by Lujan and Saric.

Outside, screened from view by the gloom of an inner corridor, Saric turned a sour eye on his mistress. "You took grave risks, my Lady. Any trader from Midkemia who was originally Tsurani-born could once have been sworn to the Minwanabi."

Left short-tempered from missing her rest, Mara answered tartly. "You all saw. He drank equal portion." Then she softened. "And those rare drinks have made me feel wonderful."

Saric bowed, his silence indicative of displeasure.

Mara moved on toward the nursery, where, even one wing distant, enraged yells could be heard from Justin. Her sigh turned into a laugh. "I am late, and the servants plainly have their hands full." She laid a hand on her uncomfortably swollen middle. "I am anxious for this baby to get himself born, though with another, there will none of us get any peace." She headed in the direction of Justin's ruckus with a girlish smile. "I may well come to miss being pampered when once again I must sit without the aid of two healthy young men."

Lujan grinned in sly appreciation, his expression mirrored by Saric. "Hokanu will do his best, I am sure, to keep you with child indefinitely."

Mara laughed, the bitter undertone not missed by her counselors. "He will, I am sure, if we can be made to agree that Justin should be the Acoma heir."

"Stubborn," Saric mouthed to his cousin over his Lady's bent head.

Past nightfall, the trader called Janaio of LaMut returned with his retinue of hired Midkemian guards to a deserted warehouse in the city of Sulan-Qu. The hour was late. The wicks in the lamps in the rich quarter had burned low, while in the crumbling tenements near the riverside only the setting quarter moon cast any light. The streets lay under inky darkness, wreathed with mist off the Gagajin. Where once the disreputable population of the city had preyed as they pleased on what traffic dared to move abroad without guard, now the Emperor's patrols drove Kentosani's malcontents and vagrants into the deepest back alleys. The only skulkers in the open were the mongrel dogs, scavenging garbage from the markets.

Though calm by the standards of Tsuranuanni, to Midkemian ears the city was far from peaceful. Even from inside the warehouse, the shouts of a madam of the Reed Life could be heard insulting a client who had been rough with one of her girls. Dogs barked, and a wakeful jigabird crowed. Somewhere nearby, an infant wailed. The mercenaries hired to attend Janaio's retinue shifted uneasily, the dank mud of the river flats an alien smell in their nostrils. They did not know why they had been brought to this empty, half-rotted building; nor did they understand precisely why they had been paid to cross the rift. Their employer had interviewed them carefully and required that they speak no Tsurani. But work in the Kingdom had slowed since the battle at Sethanon, and for men with few ties to home, the offered money had been good.

The bearers put down their bundles and waited for orders, while the bodyguards maintained their formation behind Janaio. Without sound, silk cords with weighted ends suddenly coiled down from the rafters. They caught and whipped tight, each encircling the throat of an unwary barbarian soldier.

Assassins in black followed, leaping from their unseen perches and using their weight and momentum to jerk the guards off their feet. Four men's necks snapped instantly, while the others hung kicking and gagging as they were hoisted and slowly strangled.

The bearers watched in horror as the Midkemian mercenaries died. Wide-eyed, frozen in terror, they knew better than to dare raise an outcry. Their fear was short-lived. Two more black-clad assassins flitted out of the shadows and moved through their unarmed ranks like wind through standing rushes. In less than a minute, Janaio's ten bearers lay dead, blood from their slashed throats pattering on the wood floor. The assassins who held the armed guards aloft released their cords. Dead Midkemians thumped in sprawled heaps, here one with his knuckles crumpled under his hip, and there another with his bitten-through tongue oozing blood through his beard.

Janaio removed his rich clothing and tossed it amid the corpses. One of the black-clad assassins bowed to him and offered a small bag. From this

Janaio withdrew a dark robe and cast it over his shoulders. Quickly he took a vial from his pocket and lathered sweet-smelling ointment upon his hands. The grease dissolved a layer of concealing paint; were there more light, the red dye and tattoo of a Hamoi assassin would now be revealed.

From the thickest gloom of a corner a deep voice said, "Is it done?"

The man who was no trader, who called himself Janaio for convenience, bowed his head. "As you commanded, honored master."

A heavy-set man with a too-light tread stepped from concealment. His person clicked and clinked as he moved, as bone ornaments dangling from leather thongs jostled against the instruments of death he wore affixed to his belt. His robe was studded with bosses cut from the skulls of victims; his sandals had straps of cured human flesh. He cast no glance at the bodies littering the floor, though he disdained to step in the puddles. The Obajan of the Hamoi Tong nodded, the scalplock that hung from his otherwise shaved head twisting down his back. "Good." He raised a hugely muscled arm and plucked a vial from the breast of his robe. "You are certain she drank?"

"As did I, master." The erstwhile trader bowed low yet again. "I placed the potion in the chocolate, knowing that drink to be the most irresistible. Her hadonra escaped, by luck of a burned tongue. But the Lady drank hers to the dregs. She swallowed enough slow poison to kill three men." This speech ended, the assassin licked his lips. Anxious, sweating, he controlled his nerves and waited.

The Obajan rolled the vial containing the antidote for the rare poison mixed with the chocolate between his thick palms. He watched with stony gaze as the eyes of his minion followed it; but the afflicted held in his desperation. He did not crack, and beg.

The Obajan's lips parted in a smile. "You did well." He surrendered the vial, which was colored green, symbol of life. The man who had called himself Janaio of LaMut took the promise of reprieve in shaking hands, snapped off the wax seal, and drank the bitter draft down. Then he smiled also.

A second later, his expression froze. Fear touched him, and what at first appeared to be a spasm of uncertainty. His eyes widened as pain stabbed through his abdomen, and he glanced down at the emptied vial. Then his fingers lost their grip. The container with its false offer of life dropped and his knees wobbled. A groan escaped his lips. He fell to the floor, doubled over.

"Why?" His voice emerged as a croak, pinched between spasms of agony.

The Obajan's reply was very soft. "Because she has seen your face, Kolos, as have her advisers. And because it suits the needs of the Hamoi. You die with honor, serving the tong. Turakamu will welcome you to his halls with a great feast, and you will return to the Wheel of Life in a higher station."

The betrayed man fought his need to thrash in agony. Dispassionately the Obajan observed, "The pain will pass quickly. Even now life is departing."

Beseeching, the dying man rolled his eyes up to seek the other's face in the darkness. He fought a strangled, gasping breath. "But . . . Father . . ."

The Obajan knelt and laid a red-stained hand upon the forehead of his son. "You honor your family, Kolos. You honor me." The sweating flesh under his touch shuddered once, twice, and fell limp. Over the stink as the bowel muscles loosened in death, the Obajan stood up and sighed. "Besides, I have other sons."

The master of the Hamoi Tong signaled, and his black-clad guard closed around him. Swiftly, silently, they slipped from the warehouse at his order, leaving the dead where they lay. Alone amid the carnage, unseen by living eyes, the Obajan took a small bit of parchment from his robe and cast it at the feet of his murdered son. The gold chain on the corpse would draw the notice of scavengers; the bodies would be found and pilfered, and the paper would surface in later investigation. As the Tong chief turned on his heel to leave, the red-and-yellow chop of House Anasati fluttered down onto floorboards sticky with new blood.

The first pain touched Mara just before dawn. She awoke curled into a ball and stifled a small cry. Hokanu jerked out of sleep beside her. His hands found her instantly in concerned comfort. "Are you all right?"

The discomfort passed. Mara levered herself up on one arm and waited. Nothing happened. "A cramp. Nothing more. I am sorry to have disturbed you."

Hokanu looked at his wife through the predawn greyness. He stroked back her tangled hair, the smile that had been absent for so many weeks lifting the corners of his mouth. "The baby?"

Mara laughed for joy and relief. "I think. Perhaps he kicked while I slept. He is vigorous."

Hokanu let his hand slide across her forehead and down her cheek, then softly let it rest on her shoulder. He frowned. "You feel chilled."

Mara shrugged. "A little."

His worry deepened. "But the morning is warm." He brushed her temple again. "And your head is soaked in perspiration."

"It is nothing," Mara said quickly. "I will be all right." She closed her eyes, wondering uneasily whether the alien drinks she had sampled the evening before might have left her indisposed.

Hokanu sensed her hesitation. "Let me call the healer to see to you."

The idea of a servant's intrusion upon the first moment of intimacy she had shared with Hokanu in weeks rankled Mara. "I've had babies before, husband." She strove to soften her sharpness. "I am fine."

Yet she had no appetite at breakfast. Aware of Hokanu's eyes on her, she made light conversation and ignored the burning tingle that, for a moment, coursed like a flash fire down her leg. She had pinched a nerve from sitting, she insisted to herself. The slave who had served as her taster seemed healthy as he carried out the trays, and when Jican arrived with his slates, she buried herself in trade reports, grateful, finally, that the mishap over the cramp before dawn seemed to have banished Hokanu's distance. He checked in on her twice, as he donned his armor for his morning spar with Lujan and again as he returned for his bath.

Three hours later, the pain began in earnest. The healers hurried to attend the Lady as she was carried, gasping, to her bed. Hokanu left a half-written letter to his father to rush to her side. He stayed, his hand twined with hers, and flawlessly kept his composure, that his white fear not add to her distress. But herbal remedies and massage gave no relief. Mara's body contorted in spasms, wringing wet from the cramps and pains. The healer with his hands on her abdomen nodded gravely to his helper.

"It is time?" Hokanu asked.

He received a wordless affirmative as the healer continued his ministrations, and the assistant whirled to send Mara's runner flying to summon the midwife.

"But so early?" Hokanu demanded. "Are you sure nothing is amiss?"

The healer glanced up in harried exasperation. His bow was a perfunctory nod. "It happens, Lord Consort. Now, please, leave your Lady to her labor, and send in her maids. They will know better than you what she needs for her comfort. If you cannot stay still or find a diversion, you may ask the cooks to prepare hot water."

Hokanu ignored the healer's orders. He bent over, kissed his wife's cheek, and murmured in her ear, "My brave Lady, the gods must surely know how I treasure you. They will keep you safe, and make your labor light, or heaven will answer to me for their failing. My mother always said that babes of Shinzawai blood were in a great rush to be born. This one of ours seems no different.'' Mara returned his kindness with a squeeze of her hand, before his fingers were torn from hers by servants who, at the healer's barked directive, firmly pushed the consort of the Acoma out of his own quarters.

Hokanu watched his wife to the last instant as the screens were dragged closed. Then, abandoned to himself in the hallway, he considered calling for wine. He instantly changed his mind as he recalled Mara's telling him once that her brutish first husband had drunk himself into a stupor upon the occasion of Ayaki's birth. Nacoya had needed to slap the oaf sober to deliver the happy news of a son.

Celebration was called for, certainly, but Hokanu would not cause Mara an instant of unhappy memory by arriving at her side with the smell of spirits on his breath. So he paced, unable to think of any appropriate diversion. He could not help listening avidly, to identify each noise that emerged from behind the closed screens. The rush of hurried steps told him nothing, and he worried, by the quiet, what Mara might be enduring. He cursed to himself and raged inwardly that the mysteries of childbirth held no place for him. Then his lips twitched in a half-smile as he decided that this ugly, twisting frustration of not knowing must be very near what a wife felt when her husband charged off into battle.

In time, his vigil was disrupted as Lujan, Saric, Incomo, and Keyoke, arrived in a group from the great hall, where Mara had not appeared for morning counsel. One look at Hokanu's distraught manner, and Incomo grasped what no servant had taken time to inform them of. ''How is Lady Mara?'' he asked.

Hokanu said, ''They say the baby is coming.''

Keyoke's face went wooden to mask worry, and Lujan shook his head. ''It is early.''

''But these things happen,'' Incomo hastened to reassure. ''Babies do not birth by any fast rule. My eldest boy was born at eight months. He grew healthy and strong, and never seemed the worse.''

But Saric stayed too still. He did not intervene with his usual quip to lighten the mood when the others grew edgy with concern. He watched Hokanu with careful eyes, and said nothing at all, his thoughts brooding darkly upon the trader who had worn fine gold as if it were worthless.

Hours went by. Neglected duty did not call Mara's counselors from their wait. They held together, retiring in unstated support of Hokanu to the pleasant chamber set aside for the Lady's meditation. Occasionally Keyoke or Lujan would dispatch a servant with an order for the garrison, or messages would come from Jican for Saric to answer, but as the day grew hot, and servants brought the noon meal at Hokanu's request, none seemed eager to eat. News of Mara's condition did not improve, and as the afternoon wore on toward evening, even Incomo ran out of platitudes.

Fact could no longer be denied: Mara's labor was proving very difficult. Several times low groans and cries echoed down the hallway, but more often Mara's loved ones heard only silence. Servants came in careful quiet and lit the lamps at evening. Jican arrived, chalk dust unscrubbed from his hands, belatedly admitting that there remained no more account scrolls to balance.

Hokanu was about to offer companionable sympathy when Mara's scream cut the air like a blade.

He tensed, then spun without a word and sprinted off down the corridor. The entrance to his Lady's chamber lay half-opened; had it not, he would have smashed the screen. Beyond, lit to clarity by the brilliance of lamps, two midwives held his wife as she convulsed. The fine white skin of her wrists and shoulders was reddened from hours of such torment.

Hokanu dragged a sick breath of fear. He saw the healer bent on his knees at the foot of the sleeping pallet, his hands running red with her blood. Panic jolted him from concentration as he glanced up to ask his assistant for cold rags, and he saw who stood above him in the room.

"Master, you should not be here!"

"I will be no place else," Hokanu cracked back in the tone he would have used to order troops. "Explain what has gone amiss. At once!"

"I . . ." The healer hesitated, then abandoned attempt at speech as the Lady's body arched up in what seemed a spasm of agony.

Hokanu raced at once to Mara. He shouldered a straining midwife aside, caught her twisting, thrashing wrist, and bent his face over hers. "I am here. Be at peace. All will be well, my life as surety."

She wrenched out a nod between spasms. Her features were contorted in pain, the flesh ashen and running with perspiration. Hokanu held her eyes with his own, as much to reassure her as to keep from acknowledging damage he could do nothing about. The healer and midwives must be trusted to do their jobs, though his beloved Lady seemed awash in her own blood. The bedclothes pushed up around her groin were soaked in crimson. Hokanu had seen but had not yet permitted himself to admit the presence of what the sobbing servants had been too slow to cover up: the tiny blue figure that lay limp as rags near her feet. It was now only a torn bit of flesh, kicked and bruised and lifeless.

Anger coursed through him, that no one had dared to tell him when it happened, that his son, and Mara's, was born dead.

The spasm passed. Mara fell limp in his grasp, and he tenderly gathered her into his arms. She was so depleted that she lay there, eyes closed, gasping for breath and beyond hearing. Swallowing pain like a hot coal, Hokanu turned baleful eyes toward the healer. ''My wife?''

The servant quietly shook his head. In a whisper, he said, ''Send your fastest runner to Sulan-Qu, my Lord. Seek a priest of Huntukama, for'' —sorrow slowed him as he ended—''there is nothing more I can do. Your wife is dying.''

7. Culprit

The runner swerved.

Only half-mindful of the fact that he had narrowly missed being run down, Arakasi stopped cold in the roadway. The sun stood high overhead, too close to noon for an Acoma messenger to be moving in such haste unless his errand was urgent. Arakasi frowned as he recalled the courier's grim expression. Fast as reflex, the Spy Master spun and sprinted back in the direction of Sulan-Qu.

He was fleet of foot, and dressed as a small-time merchant's errand runner. Still it took him several minutes to overtake the runner, and at his frantic question the man did not break stride.

"Yes, I carry messages from House Acoma," the runner answered. "Their content is not your business."

Fighting the heat, the dusty, uneven footing, and the effort it took to flank a man who did not wish to be delayed, Arakasi held his ground. He studied the runner's narrow eyes, full nose, and large chin and out of memory sought the man's name.

"Hubaxachi," he said after a pause. "As Mara's faithful servant, it is certainly my business to know what need sends you racing for Sulan-Qu at high noon. The Lady does not ask her runners to risk heat stroke on a whim. It follows that something is wrong."

The runner looked over in surprise. He identified Arakasi as one of Mara's senior advisers, and at last slowed to a jog. "You!" he exclaimed. "How could I recognize you in that costume? Aren't those the colors of the Keschai's traders' association?"

"Never mind that," Arakasi snapped, short of both wind and temper. He tore off the headband that had misled the servant. "Tell me what's happened."

"It's the mistress," gasped the runner. "She's had a bad childbirth. Her son did not survive." He seemed to gather himself before speaking the next line. "She's bleeding, dangerously. I am sent to find a priest of Hantukama."

"Goddess of Mercy!" Arakasi almost shouted. He spun and continued at a flat run toward the Acoma estate house. The headband that had completed his disguise fluttered, forgotten, in his fist.

If the Lady's fleetest runner had been sent to fetch a priest of Hantukama, that could only mean Mara was dying.

Breezes stirred the curtains, and servants walked on silent feet. Seated by Mara's bedside, his face an impassive mask to hide his anguish, Hokanu wished he could be facing the swords of a thousand enemies rather than relying upon hope, prayer, and the uncertain vagaries of healers. He could not think of the stillborn child, its lifeless blue form wracked in death. The babe was lost, gone to Turakamu without having drawn breath. The Lady lived yet, but barely.

Her face was porcelain-pale, and the wraps and cold compresses the midwives used to try to lessen her bleeding seemed of little avail. The slow, scarlet seep continued, inexorably. Hokanu had seen fatal wounds on the battlefield that bothered him less than the creeping, insidious stain that renewed itself each time the dressings were changed. He bit his lip in quiet desperation, unaware of the sunlight outside, or the everyday horn calls of the dispatch barge that brought news from Kentosani.

"Mara," Hokanu whispered softly, "forgive my stubborn heart." Though not a deeply religious man, he held with the temple belief that the wal, the inner spirit, would hear and record what the ears and the conscious mind could not. He spoke as though Mara were aware and listening, and not statue-still in a coma on the bed.

"You are the last Acoma, Lady, all because I would not yield to your request to swear Justin in as your heir. Now I regret my selfishness, and my unwillingness to concede the danger to the Acoma name." Here Hokanu paused to master the unsteadiness in his voice. "I, who love you, could not conceive of an enemy who would dare reach past me to strike you down. I did not allow for nature herself, or for the perils of childbirth."

Mara's lashes did not stir. Her mouth did not tremble or smile, and even the frown between her brows was absent. Hokanu fingered her dark, loose hair, spread over the silken pillows, and battled an urge to weep. "I speak formally," he added, and now his voice betrayed him. "Live, my strong, beautiful Lady. Live, that you might swear in a new heir for the Acoma over your family natami. Hear me, beloved wife. I do this moment release Kevin's son, Justin, from his obligations to House Shinzawai. He is yours, to make strong the Acoma name and heritage. Live, my Lady, and together we will make other sons for the future of both our houses."

Mara's eyes did not open to the light of her victory. Limp beneath the coverlet, she did not stir as her husband bowed his head and at last lost his battle to hold his tears. Neither did she start at a near-silent step and a voice like silk that said, "But she does have an enemy who would strike her down, and the child in her womb as well, in cold blood."

Hokanu coiled like a spring and turned to confront a shadowy presence: Arakasi, recently arrived from the message barge, his eyes impenetrable as onyx.

"What are you talking about?" Hokanu's tone was edged like a blade. He took in Arakasi's dusty, exhausted, sweating appearance, and the rust-and-blue headband still clenched in a hand that shook. "Is there more to this than a bad miscarriage?"

The Spy Master seemed to gather himself. Then, without flinching, he delivered the news. "Jican told me as I came in. Mara's poison taster did not awaken from his afternoon nap. The healer saw him and says he appears to be in a coma."

For an instant Hokanu seemed a man made of glass, his every vulnerability evident. Then the muscles in his jaw jerked taut. He spoke, his voice unyielding as barbarian iron. "You suggest my wife was poisoned?"

Now it was Arakasi who could not speak. The sight of Mara lying helpless had unmanned him, and he could only mutely nod.

Hokanu's face went white, but every inch of him was composed as he whispered, "There was a spice dealer from beyond the rift who came yesterday, offering Mara trade concessions on exotic drinks brewed from luxury herbs and ground plantstuffs from Midkemia."

Arakasi found his voice. "Mara tasted them?"

Her consort choked out an affirmative, and, as one, both men sprang for the doorway.

"The kitchens," Hokanu gasped as they almost bowled over the midwife who had returned to change Mara's compresses.

"My thought exactly," Arakasi said, swerving to avoid the runner slave who waited at his post in the hallway. "Is there any chance the utensils may not have been washed?"

The estate house was huge, with rooms jumbled together from centuries of changing tastes. As Hokanu ran full tilt through the maze of servants' passages, archways, and short flights of stone stairs, he wondered how Arakasi could know the shortest route to the kitchens, since he was so seldom home; and yet the Spy Master ran without taking any cue from Mara's consort.

As the two crossed a foyer that had a five-way intersection between wings, Arakasi unerringly chose the correct doorway. Hokanu forgot his fear enough to be amazed.

Even through his concern, Arakasi noticed. "Maps," he gasped. "You forget, this was once the dwelling of Mara's greatest enemy. It would be a poor Spy Master who did not know the lay of such a man's house. Agents had to be told which doors to listen at, not to mention the time that a guild assassin had to be given explicit directions as to which five servants were to be killed—"

Arakasi broke off his reminiscence. His eyes turned deep with thought.

"What is it?" Hokanu demanded as they ran down a stone-flagged portico, silk curtains rippling with the wind of their passage. "What are you thinking? I know it pertains to Mara."

Arakasi shook his head in a clipped negative. "I had a hunch. When I can substantiate it, I will tell you more."

Respectful of the man's competence, Hokanu did not press for answer. He poured his heart and energy into running, and reached the kitchen a half step ahead of the Spy Master.

Startled servants looked up from preparing supper for the field hands. Wide-eyed, they took in the disheveled presence of the master, then instantly fell prostrate upon the floor.

"Your will, master," cried the head cook, his brow pressed to the tiles.

"Dishes, cups," Hokanu gasped disjointedly. "Any utensil my Lady used when the foreign spice dealer was here. Have everything out for the healer's inspection."

The back of the chief cook's neck turned white. "Master," he murmured, "I have already failed in your request. The cups and the dishes from yesterday were cleaned and put away, as always, at sundown."

Arakasi and Hokanu exchanged harried, desperate glances. What garbage had not been thrown to the jigabirds would have been burned, to discourage insects.

No trace remained of what variety of poison the spice seller from Midkemia might have carried. And unless they could discover what potion had stricken Mara, there could be no hope of finding an antidote.

Instinctively knowing Hokanu was on the verge of explosive, useless action, Arakasi gripped him hard by the shoulders. "Listen to me!" the Spy Master said in a tone that made the prone servants flinch upon the floor. "She is dying, yes, and the baby is dead, but all is not yet lost."

Hokanu said nothing, but his body stayed taut as strung wire in Arakasi's grasp.

More gently, the Spy Master continued. "They used a slow poison—"

"They wanted her to suffer!" Hokanu cried, anguished. "Her murderers wanted us all to watch, and be helpless."

Daring unspeakable consequences, both for laying hands on a noble and also for provoking a man near to breaking with fury and pain, Arakasi gave the master a rough shake. "Yes and yes!" he shouted back. "And it is that very cruelty that is going to save her life!"

Now he had Hokanu's attention; and much of that warrior's rage was directed at himself. Sweating, aware of his peril, Arakasi pressed on. "No priest of Hantukama can be found in time. The nearest—"

Hokanu interrupted. "The bleeding will take her long before the poison is finished working."

"Pity her for it—no," Arakasi said brutally. "I spoke with the midwife on the way in. She has sent to Lashima's temple for golden crown flower leaves. A poultice made from them will stop the bleeding. That leaves me a very narrow span of time to track the spice merchant."

Reason returned to Hokanu's eyes, but he did not soften. "That merchant had barbarian bearers."

Arakasi nodded. "He dressed ostentatiously, also. All that gold would have drawn notice."

Through his overwhelming concern, Hokanu showed surprise. "How did you know? Did you pass the man on the road?"

"No." Arakasi returned a sly grin as he released his hold on Mara's consort. "I heard the servants gossiping."

"Is there any detail you don't miss?" Mara's husband said in wonder.

"Many, to my everlasting frustration." Arakasi glanced, embarrassed, toward the floor, both he and the master that moment recalling that the kitchen staff still abased themselves at their feet.

"For the good gods' sake!" Hokanu exclaimed. "All of you, please, get up and go about your duties. The mistress's ills are not your fault."

While the slaves and servants arose from the floor and turned back to tasks at chopping block and cooking spit, Arakasi dropped to his knees before Hokanu. "Master, I request formal leave to pursue this seller of alien spices and find an antidote for my Lady Mara."

Hokanu gave back the curt nod a commander might give a warrior on the field. "Do so, and waste no more time on obeisance, Arakasi."

The Spy Master was back on his feet in an eye's blink and moving for the door. Only when he was safely past, at one with the shadows in the corridor, did his rigid control slip. Openly anxious, he considered the probabilities of the situation he had not disclosed to Hokanu.

The spice seller had been conspicuous indeed, with his barbarian bearers and his ostentatious jewelry; and certainly not by chance. A man born in Kelewan would never wear metal on a public roadway without a driving reason. Already Arakasi knew that the man's trail would be easy to follow: for the man had intended to be tracked. The Spy Master would find only what the man's master wished, and the antidote for Mara would not be part of that knowledge.

In the portico between the great hall and the stairways to the servants' quarters, Mara's Spy Master broke into a run. Already he had a suspicion: he expected to find the spice seller and his bearers all dead.

In a tiny, wedge-shaped room in an attic over the storerooms, Arakasi opened a trunk. The leather hinges creaked as he rested the lid against the thin plaster wall, then rummaged within and pulled forth the hwaet-colored robes of an itinerant priest of a minor deity, Alihama, goddess of travelers. The fabric was smudged with old grease stains and road dust. Swiftly Mara's Spy Master flung the garment over his bare shoulders, and fastened the cord loops and pegs. Next he dragged up a cracked pair of sandals, a purple-striped sash, and a long, hooded headdress with tassels. Lastly he selected a ceramic censer, strung with earthenware bells and twine clappers.

His guise as a priest of Alihama was not complete; but as Spy Master, he added seven precious metal throwing knives, each keenly balanced and thin as a razor. Five of these he tucked out of sight under the broad sash; the last two were slid between the soles of his needra-hide sandals, under rows of false stitching.

When he passed through the doorway from his narrow dormer room, he walked with a lanky, rolling stride and peered about carefully as he took the stair, for one of his eyes appeared to have developed a cast.

So thorough was his transformation as he made his exit from the estate house that Hokanu nearly missed him. But the broad, gaudy sash caught the Shinzawai heir's eye, and since he had seen no priest of Alihama being fed in the kitchens, he realized with a start that Arakasi had almost slipped past him.

"Wait!" he called.

The Spy Master did not turn but continued to shuffle down toward the landing, with intent to catch the next dispatch barge to Kentosani.

Dressed in the high boots and close-fitting breeches that Midkemians wore while riding horses, Hokanu had to run in discomfort and catch up. He caught the Spy Master by the shoulder, and was startled into a warrior's leap back as the man whirled under his touch, almost too fast for credibility.

Arakasi's hand fell away from his sash. He squinted walleyed at Hokanu and said, soft as velvet, "You startled me."

"I see that." Uncharacteristically awkward, Hokanu gestured toward the priest's robe. "The barge and the roads on foot are too slow. I am coming with you, and both of us are going to ride horses."

The Spy Master stiffened. "Your place is by your Lady's side."

"Well I know it." Hokanu was anguished, and his hand twisted and twisted at the leather riding crop thrust through his sash. "But what can I do here but watch as she wastes away? No. I am coming." He did not say what lay upon both of their minds: that Arakasi was an Acoma servant. As Mara's consort, Hokanu was not his legal master; Arakasi's loyalty was not his to command. "I am reduced to asking," he said painfully. "Please, allow me to come along. For our Lady's sake, let me help."

Arakasi's dark eyes assessed Hokanu without mercy, then glanced away.

"I see what it would do to you to refuse your request," he said quietly. "But horses would not be appropriate. You may travel, if you wish, as my acolyte."

Now Hokanu was sharp. "Outside of these estates, how many have seen a horse from the barbarian lands beyond the rift? Do you think anyone will have eyes for the riders? By the time they have finished staring at the beasts, we will have passed by in a great cloud of dust."

"Very well," Arakasi allowed, though the incongruity between his costume and Hokanu's preference for transport worried him. All it would take was one clever man to connect his face with a priest who behaved outside of doctrine, and with an exotic creature from beyond the rift, and all of his work would be compromised. But as he considered the risks to Mara, he realized: he loved her better than his work, better than his own life. If she died, his stake in the future, and in the formation of a better, stronger Empire, was as dust.

On impulse, he said, "It shall be as you wish, my Lord. But you will bind me to the saddle, and I shall be driven before you as your prisoner."

Hokanu, already starting briskly for the stables, glanced in surprise over his shoulder. "What? For your honor, I could never abuse you like that!"

"You will." In a stride, Arakasi caught up with him. The cast was still in his eye; it seemed no distraction could make him break out of his disguise. "You must. I will need these priest's robes for later; thus, we must tailor our circumstances to fit. I am a holy man who was dishonorable enough to try thievery. Your servants caught me. I am being escorted back to Kentosani to be delivered to temple justice."

"That's reasonable enough." Hokanu impatiently waved away the servant who hurried to open the gate, and climbed the fence to gain time. "But your word is sufficient. I will not see you bound."

"You will," Arakasi repeated, faintly smiling. "Unless you want to stop six times every league to pick me up out of the dust. Master, I have tried every guise in this Empire, and more than a few that are foreign, but I sure as the gods love perversity never tried straddling a beast. The prospect terrifies me."

They had reached the yard, where at Hokanu's orders a hired Midkemian freeman stood with two horses, saddled and ready for mounting. One was a strapping grey, the other chestnut, and though they were less spirited than the flashy black that had belonged to Ayaki, Hokanu watched Arakasi eye the creatures with trepidation. Through his worry for Mara, still he noticed: the Spy Master's squint stayed pronounced as ever.

"You're lying," the Shinzawai accused, affection in his tone robbing the words of insult. "You have ice water for blood, and if you weren't so inept with a sword, you would have made a formidable commander of armies."

"Fetch out some rope," Arakasi replied succinctly. "I am going to instruct you how sailors make knots, Master Hokanu. And for both of our sakes, I hope you will tie them tightly."

The horses thundered in a gallop, dust billowing in ocher clouds on the air. Traffic on the roadway suffered. Needra pulling goods wagons huffed and shied in a six-legged scramble for the safety of the verge. Their drivers shouted in rage, and then in awed fear, as the four-legged beasts from beyond the rift shot past. Runners sprang aside, wide-eyed, and trade caravans scattered out of formation, their drovers and road masters gaping like farmers.

"You've never had these creatures off the estates," Arakasi surmised in a tight voice. Bound by his wrists to the saddle horn and by his ankles to a cord that looped underneath the gelding's girth, he endured indescribable discomfort as he tried to keep his posture and his dignity. His priest's robe flapped like a flag against the restriction of his sash, and the censer whacked him in the calf at each thrust of the gelding's stride.

"Try to relax," Hokanu offered in an attempt to be helpful. He sat his saddle with what seemed liquid ease, his dark hair blowing free and his hands steady on the reins. He did not look like a man chafed by blisters in unmentionable places. If not for his concern for his wife, he might have enjoyed the commotion his outlandish beasts were causing on the roadway.

"How do you know to start in Kentosani?" Hokanu asked as he drew rein along a forested stretch of roadway to give the horses a breather.

Arakasi closed his eyes as he endured the jolt while his gelding responded to the jerk on the leading rein and shifted from canter, to a long trot, and finally to a smoother walk. The Spy Master sighed, knocked the censer away from his bruised ankle, and gave a sideways look that spoke volumes. But his voice held no disgust as he answered Hokanu's question.

"The Holy City is the only place in the Empire that already has Midkemians in residence, where Thuril and even desert men walk about in native costume. I expect that our spice dealer wished to be conspicuous, and then blend his trail into one more difficult to follow, so that we find him, but not too soon. For I believe he has a master who gave him his orders concerning your Lady, and that man, that enemy, will not want to keep his secrecy."

The Spy Master did not add a second, more telling conjecture. Best not to voice his suspicions until he had proof. The two men rode on in silence, beneath a canopy of ulo trees. Birds swooped from the branches at the sight and smell of the alien beasts. The horses switched at flies, and ignored them.

Hokanu's comfort in the saddle stayed deceptively at odds with the emotion he wrestled inside. At each bend in the road, under the shadow of every tree, he imagined threat. Memory haunted him, of Mara's pale face against the pillow, and her hands so unnaturally still on the coverlet. Often as he chastised himself for the worry that wasted his energy, he could not marshal his thoughts. He fretted in his warrior's stillness that he could do nothing more than provide horses to hurry Arakasi on his errand. The Spy Master was competent at his art; companionship in all likelihood hindered his work. Yet, had Hokanu remained behind, he knew the sight of Mara lying helpless would have enraged him. He would have mustered warriors and marched against Jiro, and be damned to the Assembly's edict. A frown marred his brows. Even now he had to restrain himself from grasping his crop and lashing the animal under him. To give free rein to his inner rage, his guilt, and his pain, he would make the beast gallop until it dropped.

"I am glad you are with me," Arakasi said suddenly, unexpectedly.

Hokanu recoiled from his unpleasant thoughts and saw the Spy Master's enigmatic gaze fixed upon him. He waited, and after an interval filled with the rustle of wind through the trees, Arakasi qualified.

"With you along, I cannot afford to be careless. The added responsibility will steady me, when, for the first time in my life, I feel the urge to be reckless.'' Frowning, self-absorbed, Arakasi regarded his bound hands. His knuckles flexed, testing the knots. ''Mara is special to me. I feel for her as I never did for my former master, even when his house was obliterated by his enemies.''

Surprised, Hokanu said, ''I did not realize you had served another house.''

As if wakened to the fact that he had shared a confidence, Arakasi shrugged. ''I originally established my network for the Lord of the Tuscai.''

''Ah.'' Hokanu nodded. That stray fact explained much. ''Then you took service with the Acoma at the same time as Lujan and the other former grey warriors?''

The Spy Master nodded, his eyes following every nuance of Mara's consort's bearing. He seemed to arrive at some inner decision. ''You share her dreams,'' he stated.

Again Hokanu was startled. The man's perception was almost too keen to be comfortable. ''I want an Empire free of injustice, sanctioned murder, and slavery, if that is what you refer to.''

The horses plodded on, making confusion of an approaching caravan as drovers and the reinsman of a cook wagon all started shouting and pointing. Arakasi's quiet reply cut without effort through the din. ''Her life is more important than both of ours. If you go on with me, master, you must understand: I will risk your life as ruthlessly for her as I would my own.''

Aware somehow that the Spy Master spoke from the heart, and that he was uncomfortable sharing confidences, Hokanu did not attempt a direct reply. ''It's time for us to move out again.'' He thumped his heels into his gelding's ribs, and dragged both mounts to a canter.

The back alleys of Kentosani reeked of refuse and runoff from the chamber pots of the poor. Spy Master and Shinzawai Lord had left the horses in the care of a trembling hostel owner, who bowed and scraped and stuttered that he was unworthy of caring for such rare beasts. His face showed stark fear as the pair left; and the stir the horses' presence caused among the hostel's staff masked Arakasi and Hokanu's departure. Every servant was still outside, along with every patron, staring and pointing at the Midkemian horses as stablehands used to dull-tempered needra fumbled with the much more active animals.

In a change of roles like irony, now the Spy Master affected the upper hand, and Hokanu, wearing only his loincloth, played the part of a penitent on a pilgrimage as the priest's servant, to appease the minor deity he had reputedly offended. They blended into the afternoon crowd.

On foot instead of carried in a litter, and for the first time in his life not surrounded by an honor guard, Hokanu came to realize how much the Holy City had changed since the Emperor had assumed absolute rule in place of the High Council. Great Lords and Ladies no longer traveled heavily defended by warriors, for Imperial Whites patrolled the streets to keep order. Where the main thoroughfares had generally been safe, if crowded with traffic—farm carts, temple processions, and hurrying messengers—the darker, narrow back lanes where the laborers and beggars lived, or the fish-ripe alleys behind the warehouses at the wharf, had not been a place for a man or woman to venture without armed escort.

And yet Arakasi had a knowledge of these dim byways acquired years before Ichindar's abolishment of the Warlord's office. He led a twisted path through moss-damp archways, between tenements too close-packed to admit sunlight, and, once, through the malodorous, refuse-choked channel of a storm culvert.

"Why such a circuitous route?" Hokanu inquired in a pause when a shrieking mob of street children raced by, in pursuit of a bone-skinny dog.

"Habit," Arakasi allowed. His smoking censer swung at his knee, its incense only a partial palliative against the assault of stinks from the gutter. They passed a window where a wrinkled crone sat peeling jomach with a bone-bladed knife. "That hostel where we left the beasts is an honest enough house, but gossipmongers congregate there to swap news. I didn't wish to be followed; when we left there was an Ekamchi servant on our tail. He saw the horses at the main gate, and knew we were of the Acoma or Shinzawai households."

Hokanu asked, "Have we lost him?"

Arakasi smiled faintly, his slim hand raised in a sign of benediction over the crown of a beggar's head. The man was wild-eyed and mumbling, obviously touched to madness by the gods. With a twirl of the cord that spun the censer and clouded the air with incense, the Spy Master replied, "We lost him indeed. Apparently he did not wish to soil his sandals in the garbage pit we crossed two blocks back. He went around, lost sight of us for a second . . ."

"And we ducked through that culvert," Hokanu concluded, chuckling.

They passed the shuttered front of a weaver's shop, and paused at a baker's, while Arakasi bought a roll and spread sā jam in zigzags across the buttered top. The bread seller attended another customer and waved to his apprentice, who showed the apparent priest and penitent into a curtained back room. A few minutes later, the bread seller himself appeared. He looked the pair of visitors over keenly and finally addressed Arakasi. "I didn't recognize you in that garb."

The Spy Master licked jam off his fingers and said, "I want news. It's pressing. A spice seller ostentatiously dressed, and wearing metal jewelry. He had barbarian bearers. Can you find him?"

The bread seller scrubbed sweat off his fat jowls. "If you can wait until sundown, when we toss the dough scraps out for the beggar children, I could have an answer for you."

Arakasi looked irked. "Too late. I want the use of your messenger runner." Like sleight of hand, a twist of parchment appeared in his fingers. Perhaps the Spy Master had hidden it all along in his sleeve, Hokanu thought, but he could not be sure.

"Get this delivered to the sandalmaker's on the corner of Barrel Hoop Street and Tanner's Alley. The proprietor is Chimichi. Tell him your cake is burning."

The bread seller looked dubious.

"Do this!" Arakasi said in an edged whisper that raised hairs on Hokanu's neck.

The bread seller raised floury hands, palms out in submission, then bellowed for his apprentice. The boy left with the parchment, and Arakasi paced like a caged sarcat the entire interval he was gone.

The leather worker Chimichi proved to be a whip-thin man with desert blood, for he wore sweat-greasy tassels with talismans under his robe. His lank hair fell into his eyes, which were shifty. His hands had scars that might have been made by a slip of the knife at his craft, but more likely, Hokanu thought, from their number and location, by the skilled hand of a torturer. He ducked through the curtain, still blinking from sunlight, a roll decked with jam in the precise pattern of Arakasi's gripped in one fist.

"Fool," he hissed at the priest. "You risk my cover, sending an emergency signal like that, and then summoning me here. The master will see you burn for such carelessness."

"The master will certainly not," Arakasi said drily.

The leather craftsman jumped. "It's you yourself! Gods, I didn't recognize you in those temple rags." Chimichi's brows knotted into a scowl worthy of his Tsubarian heritage. "What's amiss?"

"A certain spice seller, decked with a gold chain, and carried by Midkemian bearers."

Chimichi's expression lightened. "Dead," he stated flatly. "His bear-

ers with him. In a warehouse on Hwaet Broker's Lane, if the footpad who
tried to exchange chain links for centis at the money changers can be
relied on to tell the truth. But that such a man had gold at all belies the
chance he fabricated his tale.''

"Does the imperial patrol know about the corpses yet?'' Arakasi broke
in.

"Probably not.'' Chimichi laid his roll aside, and rubbed a jammy
knuckle on his apron. The deepset, shifty eyes turned to the Spy Master.
"Ever see a money changer report what he didn't have to? The taxes on
metals are not small, these days, with our Light of Heaven needing to
increase his army against the threat of the hard-line traditionalists.''

Arakasi cut short the man's rambling with a raised hand. "Seconds
count, Chimichi. My companion and I are going on to that warehouse to
inspect the bodies. Your task is to stage a diversion that will occupy the
Emperor's patrol long enough to see us in and out of the building. I don't
want an Imperial White left free to investigate those murders before-
time.''

Chimichi flipped back dark hair to reveal a grin, and startlingly perfect
white teeth. The front ones had been filed into points, deep desert fashion. "Keburchi, God of Chaos,'' he swore in evident delight. "It's been a
long time since we had a good riot. Life was starting to get boring.''

Yet by the time he had finished his sentence, he was speaking to an
empty room. He blinked, startled, and muttered, "The man's mother
was a damned shadow.'' Then his face knitted in concentration. He hurried off about the business of turning an ordinary, peaceful day of business
in the trade quarter into unmitigated chaos.

Dusk fell, deepening the gloom in the already dim warehouse. Hokanu
crouched beside Arakasi, a burning spill in his hand. Outside, shouts and
the sounds of breakage echoed from the adjacent streets; someone howled
obscenities over the din of shattering crockery.

"The wine merchants' stores,'' Hokanu murmured. "In a very few
minutes we're going to have company.'' He paused to shift the rolled
cloth spill, which had burned nearly down to his fingers. "The doors on
this building were not very stout.''

Arakasi nodded, his face invisible beneath his priest's cowl. His fingers
moved, furtively fast, over the body of the bearer, which was well past
rigor mortis and already starting to bloat. "Strangled,'' he murmured.
"All of them.''

He slipped forward through the dark, while lines of bright light from wildfire or torches shone through the gaps in the wall boards. His concentration never wavered.

Hokanu flinched as the flame in his hands crept lower. He shifted grip, and lit the last wad of linen he could spare from his already scanty loincloth. By the time he looked up, Arakasi was searching the spice seller's corpse.

The man's chain and fine silk robes were all gone, looted by the footpad Chimichi had mentioned. The illumination cast by the spill picked out enough details to establish that the man had not died by strangulation. His hands were contorted, and blind, dry eyes showed rings of white. The mouth hung open, and the tongue inside had been bitten through. Blood blackened the boards and his still combed and perfumed beard.

"You've found something," Hokanu said, aware of Arakasi's stillness.

The Spy Master looked up, his eyes a faint glint under his hood. "Much." He turned over the man's hand, revealing a tattoo. "Our culprit is of the Hamoi Tong. He bears the mark. His posing as a man in residence across the rift speaks of long-range planning."

"Not Jiro's style," Hokanu summed up.

"Decidedly not." Arakasi squatted back on his heels, unmindful of the bang of a plank striking the cobbles close outside the warehouse. "But we're meant to think so."

Out in the night, a sailor cursed, and somebody else roared back in outrage. The din of an irate populace surged closer, overlaid by the horn call of one of the Emperor's Strike Leaders.

Hokanu also had discarded the parchment with the Anasati seal as a plant. No son of Tecuma's, and no Lord advised by a devil as clever as Chumaka, would ever condescend to the obvious. "Who?" Hokanu said, the sharpness of his desperation cutting through. Every minute that passed increased the chance that he would never again see Mara alive. Memory of her as he had left her, pale, unconscious, and bleeding, all but paralyzed his reason. "Can the tong even be bought to do more than assassinate? I thought they took on their contracts in anonymity."

Arakasi was once again busy sorting through the spice seller's underclothes. The fact they were fouled in death did not deter him, nor did the stench upset his thoughts. "The telling word, I suspect, is 'contract.' And does any hard-line traditionalist in this Empire have riches enough to toss golden chains to beggars just to make sure we have a trail to follow?" His hands paused, pounced, and came up with a small object. "Ah!" Triumph colored the Spy Master's tone.

Hokanu caught a glimpse of green glass. He forgot the stink of dead men, hitched closer, and thrust the spill toward the object that Arakasi held.

It proved to be a small vial. Dark, sticky liquid coated the inside; the cork, had there been one, was missing.

"A poison vial?" Hokanu asked.

Arakasi shook his head. "That's poison on the inside." He offered the item for Hokanu to sniff. The odor was resinous, and stingingly bitter. "But the glass is green. Apothecaries generally reserve that color container for antidotes." He glanced at the spice seller's face, frozen in its hideous rictus. "You poor bastard. You thought you were being given your life at your master's hand."

The Spy Master left off his musing and stared at Hokanu. "That's why Mara's taster never suspected. This man ingested the very same poison that she did, knowing it was a slow-acting drug and sure that he was going to get the antidote."

Hokanu's hand trembled, and the spill flickered. Outside, the shouts reached a crescendo, and the snap and rattle of swordplay drew closer.

"We must leave," urged Arakasi.

Hokanu felt firm fingers close over his wrist, tugging him to his feet. "Mara," he murmured in an outburst of uncontrollable pain. "Mara."

Arakasi yanked him forward. "No," he said sharply. "We have hope now."

Hokanu turned deadened eyes to the Spy Master. "What? But the spice seller is dead. How can you claim we have hope?"

Arakasi's teeth flashed in fierce satisfaction. "Because we know there's an antidote. And the poison vial has a maker's mark on the bottom." He tugged again, hauling a numbed Hokanu toward the loosened board by the dockside through which they had originally made entry. "I know the apothecary who uses that stamp. I have bought information from him in the past." The Spy Master bent and ducked out into the steamy, odorous dusk of the alley behind the fishmonger's. "All we have to do is avoid this ruckus that Chimichi started for our benefit, find the man, and question him."

8. Interrogation

Hokanu ran.

The streets were a bedlam of noise and fleeing citizens, with Arakasi a shadow among them distinguishable only by his voluminously flapping priest's robe. Hardened to a warrior's fitness as he was, Hokanu was not accustomed to bare feet. After stubbing his toes on raised bits of cobblestone, sliding precariously through slime in the gutters, and once landing heel first on a broken bit of crockery, he would have welcomed even ill-fitting sandals despite the resulting blisters. Yet if Arakasi was aware of his difficulty, he did not slacken pace.

Hokanu would have died rather than complain. Mara's life was at stake, and every passing minute made him fear that she might already be beyond help, that the hideous slow-acting poison might have damaged her beyond healing.

"Don't think," he gasped aloud to himself. "Just run."

They passed a pot seller's stall, the proprietor rushing about in his nightshirt, shaking a fist at passersby. Arakasi pressed the Shinzawai to the right.

"Warriors," he murmured, scarcely out of breath. "If we go straight, we'll run right into them."

"Imperials?" Hokanu obeyed the direction change, a grimace on his face as his toes squished through something that stank of rotted onions.

"I don't know," Arakasi replied. "The light plays tricks and all I see are helmet plumes." He took a deep breath. "We won't stay to find out."

He ducked left into an alley yet more narrow and noisome than the last. The sounds of the riot were fading, replaced by the furtive skitter of rats, the dragging steps of a lame lamplighter on his way home from work, and the creak of a costermonger's cart being hitched to a bone-skinny needra.

Arakasi drew up his hood and ducked into a moss-crusted doorway. "We're here. Mind the portal—the arch is very low."

Hokanu had to bend over to enter. Beyond lay a cramped courtyard, choked with weeds and what looked to be a physician's garden, over-grown with medicinal herbs. There was a fish pool at the center, also overrun with weeds and sedges; Hokanu stole a moment to wash his feet. The water was piss-warm, and noisome. He wondered in disgust if people or dogs had used the spot for a privy.

"That was originally a cistern," Arakasi whispered, as if in answer to his thought. "Korbargh dumps his wash water in it, by the smell."

Hokanu wrinkled his nose. "What sort of a name is Korbargh?"

"Thuril," the Spy Master answered. "But the fellow's no native of the Highlands. By blood, I'd say he has more of the desert in him. Don't be deceived. He's smart, and he speaks as many tongues as I do."

"How many is that?" Hokanu whispered back.

But Arakasi had already raised his hand to knock at the plank that served Korbargh as front door.

The panel opened with a jerk that caused Hokanu a start.

"Who's there?" A gruff voice snarled from within.

Unfazed, Arakasi said something in the gutturals of the desert tongue. Whoever he addressed tried to yank the door closed, but the stout wood jammed ajar as the Spy Master shoved his censer in the opening. "Let us in t'see your master, skulking dwarf, or your tongue I'll have out'f your face!" he said in a gutter Tsurani dialect used by thieves and beggars. His tone was one that Hokanu had never heard from him, but that made his flesh crawl.

The dwarf said something back that sounded like an obscenity.

"Not good enough," Arakasi replied, and with a swift inclination of his head invited his supposed penitent to help him storm the door.

Frantic with concern for his wife, Hokanu fell to with a will. He slammed his shoulder against the panel with such force that the dwarf was knocked backward, and the leather hinges burst inward. Over a boom of downed wood, Arakasi and Hokanu fetched forward into what appeared to be a foyer, tiled in terra-cotta, and decorated with friezework left over from times when the neighborhood had been more prosperous. The dwarf was yammering in a mixture of languages, that his fingers felt crushed, and his head was bruised by the door bar, which had been kicked from its brackets, and now lay in splinters on the floor.

"It was rotten anyway," Hokanu observed, scraping splinters from his shoulder. "In no condition, certainly, to keep out as much as a rat."

A touch from Arakasi urged quiet. Hokanu obeyed rather than bridle at the presumption. As a huge, toweringly muscled stranger in a robe embroidered in li birds entered, the Shinzawai noble's eyes widened. "Desert blood, did you say?" he murmured sotto voce.

Arakasi disregarded the comment and instead said something in desert tongue to the dwarf, whereupon the creature stopped howling, scrambled to his feet like a hunted gazen, and fled through a nook in a side wall.

"Gods above," boomed the giant in the effeminate robe. "You're no priest."

"I'm glad you see that," said the Spy Master. "It saves us unnecessary preamble." He moved as though to push back his hood, and his sleeves fell back, revealing a crisscross of leather ties. The knife sheaths they secured were empty, their contents a silver flash in Arakasi's hands as he lowered his arms.

Hokanu's gasp of surprise that Mara's Spy Master should own weapons of precious metal was canceled by a bull bellow from Korbargh. "So! You're the one who killed my apprentice."

Arakasi licked his teeth. "Your memory works well, I see. That's good." His knives might have been gripped by a stone statue, they were so steady. "You'll recall, then, that I can strike you through the heart before you can think, let alone run." To Hokanu the Spy Master said, "Unwind my belt and tie him, wrist and ankle."

The giant drew breath to protest, and quit at a twitch of Arakasi's wrist. Hokanu took the greatest care not to come between the two as he unknotted the priestly cincture; it was braided needra hide, and tougher than spun cordage. Hokanu tied the knots tightly, fear for Mara canceling any mercy he might have felt for the man's comfort.

A huge wooden beam braced the ceiling, with horn hooks inset for hanging the oil lamps preferred by the rich; they held only cobwebs now, but unlike the leather loops used by the poor for the same purpose, they had neither rotted nor weakened.

Following Arakasi's glance, Hokanu almost smiled in vindication. "You wish him strung up by the wrists?"

At Arakasi's nod, the giant screeched in a tongue Hokanu did not recognize. The Spy Master replied in equally guttural accents, then switched language out of politeness to his master. "There is no help for you, Korbargh. Your wife and that lout of a bodyguard you send with her are detained. There is a riot going on, and Imperial Whites are out in force, barricading off the streets where she was shopping. If she is wise, she will shelter the night in a hostelry and return home in the morning. Your servant Mekeh is currently hiding under the ale barrel in your back shed. He saw how your last apprentice died, and as long as I am here, he will not dare to show his face, even to summon help for you. So I ask, and you will answer, what the antidote was that should have filled the vial my companion will show you."

Hokanu hauled the cord taut, half hitched it secure, and produced the green flask retrieved from the dead trader in the warehouse.

Already pale from having his arms wrenched upward, Korbargh turned white. "I know nothing of this. Nothing."

Arakasi's brows rose. "Nothing?" His tone sounded regretfully mild. "Ah, Korbargh, you disappoint me." Then his expression hardened and his hand moved, fearfully fast.

Steel arced in a blur across the room. The blade grazed past Korbargh's cheek, shearing off a lock of greasy hair, and stuck with a thunk in the support beam.

In changed intonation, Arakasi said, "There are three ciphers, in desert script, on that vial. The hand is your own. Now speak." As the prisoner raised his chin for renewed denial, Arakasi interrupted. "My companion is a warrior. His wife is dying of your evil concoction. Shall he describe his more inventive methods of extracting information from captured enemy scouts?"

"Let him," Korbargh gasped, afraid but still stubborn. "I won't say."

Arakasi's dark eyes flicked to Hokanu. He gave a half-smile that was mercilessly cold. "For your Lady's sake, tell the man how you make prisoners talk."

Grasping the Spy Master's drift, Hokanu set his shoulder against the wall. As if he had all the time in the world, he described methods of torture cobbled together from hearsay, old records found in the Minwanabi house as it was being cleansed for Mara's arrival, tales told to unsettle new recruits, and a few things he improvised. Since Korbargh did not appear an imaginative man, Hokanu lingered with unholy relish over the grisly bits.

Korbargh began to sweat. His hands worked at his bonds, not out of hope of escape, but in mindless, desperate fear. Gauging his moment to a nicety, Hokanu turned to Arakasi. "What method should we try first, do you think, the heated needles or the levers and ropes?"

Arakasi scratched his chin, considering. His eyes seemed to caress the alchemist's quivering body. Then he smiled. "Well," he drawled. His eyes were ice. "You want to know what I think?"

Korbargh bucked against his bonds. "No!" he said hoarsely. "No. I'll tell you what you wish to know."

"We're waiting," Hokanu cut back. "I think that tapestry rod in the next room would serve very nicely as a lever. And I know where we can find those flesh-eating insects close by—"

"Wait! No!" Korbargh screamed.

"Then," Arakasi interjected reasonably, "you will tell us the recipe for the antidote that should have gone in this vial."

Korbargh's head twitched frantic affirmative. "Leaves of sessali steeped in salt water for two hours. Sweeten the mixture with generous amounts of red-bee honey so your Lady doesn't vomit the salty herbs. A small sip. Wait a minute. Another. Wait again. Then as much as she can take. The more she swallows, the faster she'll heal. Then, when her eyes clear and the fever leaves her, a small cup of the mix every twelve hours for three days. That's the antidote."

Arakasi spun to face Hokanu. "Go," he said curtly. "Take the horses and run for home. Any healer will have sessali herb in his stores, and for Mara, time is of the essence."

Anguished, Hokanu glanced at the strung-up figure of Korbargh, sobbing now in hysterical relief.

"I will pursue his connections," Arakasi said urgently, and found himself addressing empty air. Hokanu had already disappeared through the broken door.

Night air wafted through the opening. Down the block, two drunken comrades reeled homeward, singing. Someone threw a pot of wash water out of a window, the splash of its fall broken by a startled yelp from a street cur.

Arakasi stood motionless.

Unnerved by the silence, Korbargh stirred in his bonds. "Y-you are g-going to let me g-go?" He finished on a note of crispness. "I did tell you the antidote."

A shadow against the darkened wall, Arakasi turned around. His eyes gleamed like a predator's as he said, "But you haven't said who purchased the poison, in the bottle disguised as an antidote."

Korbargh jerked against his bonds. "It's worth my life to tell you that!"

Cat-quiet, Arakasi stepped up to his prisoner and wrenched the knife out of the beam; of incalculable value in the metal-poor culture of Kelewan, the blade flashed in the dimness. The Spy Master fingered the steel, as if testing the edge. "But your life is no longer a bargaining point. What has yet to be determined is the manner of your death."

"No." Korbargh whimpered. "No. I cannot say any more. Even were you to hang me, and the gods cast my spirit off the Wheel of Life for dishonor."

"I will hang you," Arakasi said quickly, "unless you talk: that is certain. But a blade can do hurtful damage to a man, before a rope is used to dispatch him. The question is not honor or dishonor, Korbargh, but a merciful end, or lingering agony. You know the drugs that can bring blissful death." Touching the tip of the knife to the fat of his prisoner's upper arm, he said, "And you know which drugs on your shelves make you writhe in torment for a very long time before death, drugs that heighten pain, keep you alert, and make time seem to pass slowly."

Korbargh hung from his wrists, his eyes huge with fear.

Arakasi tapped his knife point, thoughtful. "I have all the time I need, but none I'm willing to waste listening to silence."

"My wife—" began the desperate poison seller.

The Spy Master cut him off. "If your wife gets home before you have told what I need to know, she will join you. Your bodyguard will die before he can cross the portal, and you will watch me test my methods on her. I will dose her with drugs to keep her conscious, then carve the flesh from her body in strips!" As the big man began to weep with terror, Arakasi asked, "Will your dwarf apprentice sack your house, or give you both an appropriate funeral rite?" Arakasi shrugged. "He'll steal everything worth selling, you know." Looking around, he added, "Given your location and your clientele, I doubt anyone will be quick to report your murder to the City Watch. It's possible no priest will ever say a prayer for either of you."

Korbargh snarled something unintelligible, and Arakasi stopped threatening. He stepped forward, grasped the hem of his captive's robe, and cut away a strip of fabric. The cloth was not silk, but the weave was fine, and ribbon embroidery adorned the hem. Arakasi expertly twisted the length into a gag. Before he could bind it over Korbargh's mouth, the huge man gasped and pleaded.

"What are you, a fool? If you gag me before your fiendish tortures begin, how can I give what you wish, even if I were of a mind to talk?"

Arakasi never paused, but jammed the cloth between the poison merchant's teeth. As the larger man bucked and twisted, the Spy Master tied the ends with knots as secure as any sailor's. "I am anything but a fool," he said in a voice of velvet consonants.

Arakasi left the bound man to dash upstairs. He returned with several vials which he held before Korbargh's eyes, one at a time. "Tai-gi root, to heighten perception and pain," he began. "Powder from ground jinab bark, which will keep a man awake for a week. Sinquoi leaves, which will make time pass slowly. You will shortly discover that I know these as well as any healer. And I was instructed in the use of knives by an expert. You will not be permitted to scream when the agony starts, and if you wished to spare yourself pain and speak first, you have forfeited that chance already.'' With a gentleness that inspired shudders, the Spy Master loosened Korbargh's robe. He bared a hairy expanse of sā drinker's belly to the night air, then turned away and disappeared briefly into the next room.

Korbargh thrashed against his bonds like a hooked fish. He stopped when he had exhausted himself, and was hanging limp when Arakasi returned, bearing the oil lamp used to illuminate the desk when the hired clerk came to do the accounts, and the basket the day servant used for sewing.

Mara's Spy Master placed these items on a small table, which he lifted and set to his left. Then he removed the knife from his sash, and squinted to check the edge for flaws. It being a metal blade, the razor-sharpness of the weapon shone balefully perfect.

The poison merchant moaned into his gag as Arakasi said, ''I will begin without using the drugs. You may imagine how this will feel after I administer them.'' He moved forward and, stroking carefully, opened the top layer of skin from his victim's navel slantwise toward his groin. Blood pattered onto the tiles, and Korbargh gave a muffled shriek. He kicked and flopped.

''Keep still,'' Arakasi cautioned. ''I despise a messy job.''

His victim was in no position to heed, but the Spy Master seemed not to care. His quick hand compensated for Korbargh's jerks and jumps. He made another light cut and removed a triangle of skin, which he tossed aside. Then he nicked through the fat layer beneath and, as if he were performing dissections at a physician's college, bared the muscle below.

''Will you talk now?'' Arakasi said conversationally.

Korbargh jerked his head in the negative. He was dripping sweat, along with his blood, and his hair and beard were soggy. He moaned into his gag, but the look in his eyes stayed belligerent.

Arakasi sighed. ''Very well. Though I warn you, the pain has hardly begun yet.'' His knife hand moved, in utmost precision, and the muscle of his victim's abdomen parted.

Korbargh gave a muffled screech. Unheeding, the Spy Master picked out the severed veins and tied them off with thread. Then his blade set to work on the bared entrails beneath, and the blood ran faster.

The floor underfoot grew slippery as in a slaughterhouse, and the air took on the same reek. Korbargh lost control of his bladder, and rank wetness added to the puddle.

''Now,'' said Arakasi, his shadow straightening with him as he looked up into the poison seller's face, "have you anything constructive to say? No? Then, I fear, we will have to work next on the nerves."

The knife dipped into living tissue, separated a nerve sheath, and scraped, very gently.

Korbargh thrashed, unable to howl. His eyes rolled, and his teeth pierced deep into the sour cloth of the gag. Then he fainted from the pain.

Some dim time later, his head snapped back as a pungent aroma filled his nostrils. As he blinked away confusion, strong hands poured foul-smelling liquid between his lips while clamping his nostrils closed, forcing him to swallow. Pain redoubled to blinding agony, and his mind became gripped by horrible clarity.

"You will speak now," Arakasi suggested. "Else I will continue this until morning." He wiped his sticky blade, fastidiously tucked it into his sash, and reached up to loosen the knots that prevented Korbargh from speech. "Then when your wife arrives, I will begin on her, to see if she knows anything."

"Demon!" gasped the wounded man. "Devil! May you rot in body and mind, and come back next life as a fungus!"

Arakasi, looking bland, reached into the gore of his handiwork and tweaked.

Korbargh released an air-shattering scream.

"The name," the Spy Master pressed, relentless.

And words tumbled out of Korbargh's mouth, giving him the name that he sought.

"Ilakuli," Arakasi repeated. "A rumormonger who can be found on the Street of Sorrowful Dreams."

The poison seller gave a miserable nod. He had begun to sob, his face like yellow grease. "I think he was of the Hamoi Tong."

"You think?" Arakasi sighed as if correcting a child. "I know so."

"What of my wife?"

"The tong may seek her out. That is a risk you knew when you agreed to sell to them. But I will be hours gone when she returns, so in that, she's safe." Arakasi reached up very swiftly and cut Korbargh's throat.

He jumped back as blood sprayed, and his victim kicked his last in this life. Arakasi immediately snuffed the wick of the oil lamp. Merciful black-ness fell and hid the carnage in the foyer.

Arakasi worked on in the dark, his hands now trembling in spasms. He pulled Korbargh's robe closed and tied the sash, so that the young wife would not be greeted with the full grisly details of the night's events upon her return in the morning. The Spy Master cut down the body and laid it in a posture of repose on the floor. About the blood he could do nothing. His earlier search for the lamp had revealed that the household kept no wash water to hand. He wiped his fingers as best he could upon a tapestry, a prayer mat being the only other choice that would serve for a towel. Then, in the corner of Korbargh's bedchamber, he succumbed to his nerves at last. He knelt clutching an unemptied night jar and vomited violently.

He retched long after his belly was emptied. Then, unwilling to pass through the foyer again, he made his exit through a window.

The streets were all but deserted, the riot long since quelled. A few stragglers hastened homeward, and more shadowy figures lurked in the darkened alleys. A shivering, bedraggled priest had nothing of value to rob; Arakasi was left alone. The night wind in his face helped to steady him. A brief stop by an ornamental pool in the entry of what was probably a brothel allowed him to rinse the rest of the gore from his hands. Blood was still crusted beneath his fingernails, but right now he lacked the stomach to use his knife to scrape them clean. He jogged, and to drive back the nightmares that lingered from Korbargh's foyer, he turned his mind to the information he had sickened himself to win.

Ilakuli he had heard of; and there was a man in the city who would know his whereabouts. Arakasi hurried into the night.

Hokanu ran on foot. His two spent mounts jogged at his side on leading reins, their chests lathered, and their distended nostrils showing scarlet linings. Fear for Mara's life kept him on his feet, long after muscle and sinew were exhausted. He still wore the loincloth of a penitent. Of the clothing he had recovered from the inn, he had paused only to lace on his sandals. The rest he had stuffed into the roan gelding's saddlebags, never mind that he looked like a beggar, half-naked, and coated with dirt and sweat.

His sole concern was the recipe for the antidote that offered the last hope for his wife.

Mist clung in the hollows, rendering trees and landmarks ghostly in the predawn gloom. The prayer gate to Chochocan hulked up out of whiteness like something from the spirit lands ruled by Turakamu, God of the Dead. Hokanu raced under its spindle arches, barely aware of the painted holy figures in their niches, or the votive lamp left lit by a passing priest. He stumbled on, caring only that this gate marked the beginning of the end of his journey. The borders to the estate lay over the next set of hills, and through a defile guarded by his own patrols. A runner would be posted there, along with a trusted officer and another man trained as a field healer. With any luck, he would have the herb for the antidote in his stores; and every Lord's kitchen stocked red-bee honey.

Hurting in every joint, and gasping in the extremity of exertion, Hokanu hoped the Good God would forgive him for neglecting the prayer of passage the gate was intended to inspire. He lacked the breath for speech, and he knew if he stopped he would fall prone and pass out. Immersed in a misery of tiredness, Hokanu crossed through the arch into the pearly mists beyond.

The horses sensed the ambush before he did.

The big roan gelding plowed to a stop, snorting, and the mare shied. Jerked forward by the sudden halt, Hokanu gasped in frustration. But the arrow fired from a thicket by the roadway missed him by inches, clattering harmlessly on the verge.

Instantly, he banged the gelding with his elbow, sending it into a maddened pirouette. The snorting mare curvetted into its quarters, and the gelding let out a squeal and a kick. Hokanu snatched his sword from the saddle scabbard. Under cover of the milling animals, he doubled back into the arch of Chochocan's prayer gate.

Hokanu dared not assume there would be only one ambusher. He offered a brief prayer to the Good God that, whoever they were, they would not be familiar with horses from the barbarian world, for the beasts offered his only chance of staying alive.

Still tied together by their leading rein, his mounts thrashed before the archway, the gelding determined to land a defensive bite or kick, and the panicked mare spinning, jerking, and rearing, in an effort to bolt. Hokanu chanced that no assassin born on Kelewan would dare those stamping, striking hooves to rush the archway and take him. The ambusher's only option was to flank him through the entrance on the other side, and praise be to Chochocan, whatever dead Minwanabi Lord had raised this offering to the god had spent with a lavish hand. This gate was massive, built of stone and timbers, with flying buttresses to support its great height. It had intricate carving, rare gilt spires, and a multiplicity of interior vaulting, niches, and prayer nooks. Six archers could conceal themselves inside and seriously impede traffic: no doubt the real reason behind the ancient Lord's gesture of devotion.

Hokanu could only be grateful for such impiety now, as he left the shield of the frightened horses and climbed the fluted scrollwork, then hauled himself hand over hand along a beam below the rafters. He swung himself up and ducked into a nook that held a painted face of felicity. Gasping silently from overexertion, Hokanu pressed himself into the shallow shadow. He lay back against the side of the nook, eyes blindly open, while his body took in air. A moment passed like eternity. As the dizziness left him, the Shinzawai noble noticed that the face above him was hollow. The backside was built like an embrasure, with holes drilled through the eyes from which a man in concealment could observe anyone who entered the prayer gate, coming or going.

Had Hokanu not been breathless, and in deadly danger from an assassin, he might have laughed aloud. Within the Empire, not even religion was free of the Game of the Council; obviously, past Minwanabi Lords had stationed watchers here to give warning of arrivals to the estate, and also to spy upon traffic and commerce that chanced by upon the road. Whatever subterfuge had been launched from this place in the past, Hokanu seized the advantage of the moment. He grasped the support beam that held the mask in its niche, pulled himself up into its hollowed back, then looked out the eye holes.

The mare and the gelding still spun, now hopelessly entangled in the leading rein. One or the other had kicked a support post, for there was a hoof-shaped depression in one of the caryatids that supported the entry arch. Suddenly the animals turned as one, the gelding with a snort. Both stared into the night, tense, ears forward listening. Warned by the horses, Hokanu saw movement in the shadows beyond the prayer gate.

Black-clad figures stalked there, spread out in flanking formation. The three in the lead carried bows. Two more followed, as rear guard, and to the profound relief of the man they hunted, all of them scanned the prayer gate's crannies and corners at ground level.

The mare sighted the men before the gelding. She flung up her head with such force that the rein snapped, and with a whistling snort she bolted back down the roadway. Fear drove her to a gallop, a horse's instinct guiding her back toward home and stable. The marauders in black leaped out of her path and re-formed. The more phlegmatic gelding watched, ears and tail tautly lifted. Then he shook out his mane, rubbed an itch in his neck against the arm of the dented caryatid, and trotted a short distance away, dropping his nose to graze by the roadside.

In the night-damp cavity of the prayer gate, all fell suddenly silent; Hokanu knew a stab of dismay. His starved lungs still labored from his run, and an effort to quiet his breathing left him dangerously dizzy. Left with an ugly decision, he chose to be discovered and to fight, rather than to pass out and allow enemies to take him unconscious.

His five attackers heard him immediately. They stiffened like dogs pointing game and faced their quarry's hiding place. Then two slung their bows across their shoulders. The three others arrayed themselves in defensive formation, while the lead two began to climb.

Hokanu turned his sword and flung it like a javelin. The weapon caught the bulkier man through the throat, piercing him down behind the breastbone, through the heart. Silenced before he could scream, he fell with a dull thud that made the gelding start and look up. Hokanu was peripherally aware of the horse moving nervously around the pillar beyond the gateway; more immediately, he flung himself down and back into cover as three arrows whizzed toward his hiding place.

One smacked wood with a thunk, while two others chiseled splinters out of the fortune mask's ear, and deflected on, to imbed themselves in the timbers behind. Hokanu grasped the knife he had kept hidden in his loincloth. He shoved back, as far into the cranny as his size would allow, and reached up left-handed to wrench one of the arrows from the wood.

A black-clad figure emerged, an outline against the dark bulk of the beams that braced the interior of the prayer gate. Hokanu's thrown knife caught him in the neck, and he toppled back with a gurgling sound. His companion was not fool enough to follow, but ducked, unslinging his bow. Hokanu saw the weapon tip gleam in the gloom. His skin prickled with his awareness that an arrow would soon fly to impale him. He flipped the shaft in his hand around in position to stab, and prepared to rush the archer.

A gruff voice called from below. "Don't hurry. Keep him pinned. Oridzu will climb up the other statue and fire on him from above."

With a wretched, sinking feeling, Hokanu realized his cover would only protect from a sally from below; on either side, the towering likenesses of the god offered the perfect tactical advantage upon his position. Should he attempt to hide from whoever climbed, he would clearly be vulnerable to bow fire from below. Uglier, and most cruelly final: knowledge of the antidote that might save Mara would die with him. Arakasi would have no cause to doubt that he had made it through. Hokanu cursed the haste that had caused him to leave Kentosani without taking the extra minutes to assemble an escort. Even had he lacked the time to requisition soldiers from his father's or Mara's town house, he might at least have hired on mercenaries. Any sort of armed backup might have foiled the assassins' ambush.

But he had forgone the escort of warriors in favor of the speed he could make alone, mounted on the exotic Kingdom horses. The creatures could outrace the swiftest runners, and Hokanu had placed his wife's peril ahead of his own.

Now Mara would pay for his folly. She would die, the last of the Acoma, never knowing how near the man who loved her had come to getting the antidote to her.

As the furtive sounds of men moving reached Hokanu's ears, he cursed. Not one but both of the surviving assassins were climbing the statues. He would be fired on from either side, and given the bent of Minwanabi minds, he did not put it past the dead Lords to have placed concealed embrasures behind the other carvings in the prayer gate. He might be picked off without ever seeing his attackers.

Desperate, cornered, and trembling with exhaustion and rage, Hokanu grasped the arrow that was his sole weapon. He prepared to rush the one man who held him pinned. He would die, but perhaps he could take another of his enemies to the halls of Turakamu with him.

But as he tensed to shove off from the wall, an arrow hissed out. He ducked flat, too late. The shaft smacked into his hip and imbedded with a thump and dull agony into the bone.

Hokanu's lips peeled back in a silent snarl of agony. Animal hurt and white-hot anger burned him to preternatural clarity of mind. He caught the shaft and snapped it off. The resulting agony caused him to recoil involuntarily. A second shaft cracked wood where his torso had been. Braced on one knee, and weeping tears of pain, he scrabbled with blood-ied fingers for some purchase point to hold himself upright. Shock made his leg useless, and the one not wounded seemed cramped.

By some miracle, his hand closed over a smoothed end of wood that had been rounded to the form of a handle. Hokanu grimaced at the jolt. He used his last strength to haul his crippled body upright, and cried out as the handle turned with a creak and gave way downward.

It was not fixed, he realized in panic. He barely heard the thunk as another arrow bit wood beside his ear. Overwhelmed beyond recovery, he felt himself sliding downward, as a section of wall gave way—

Of course! he thought, and in the rush of adrenaline that followed, he laughed aloud. The nameless old Minwanabi Lord had built his spies an escape hatch, and he had accidentally discovered the release. The trapdoor opened outward, dragging him from darkness, and a crossfire of enemy shafts, into a dawn like a new pearl.

His feet were snapped helplessly off the beam as the doorway gaped wide, leaving him hanging by the release lever, in the air. The drop was nothing for a healthy man, a mere dozen feet. But with an arrowhead in his hip, Hokanu feared the shock of the fall might kill, or cause him to faint. He flung away the useless arrow he was holding, kicked, wrenched, and scrabbled, but failed to gain a second handhold. His wound hurt mightily, and his eyes still watered maddeningly.

A black-clothed warrior arrived behind the niche he had just vacated. He moved gloved hands, notched another arrow, and began a steady draw.

Gasping, Hokanu looked down, to see a ring of other enemies converging from the roadside. All that held them back from an open rush was the gelding, innocuously cropping grass with its reins trailing. The horse was harmless, but the assassins remained wary from the display of equine irritation they had just witnessed. The animal saw the approaching assassins and ambled away from them, until he stood directly below Hokanu.

"Chochocan bless you," Hokanu half sobbed. He let go.

His stomach turned with the plunge, and the slam as his body struck the saddle all but undid him. The torment in his hip became eclipsed by the insult to his manhood. The gelding grunted, ripped up its head in astonishment, and stumbled to its knees under the impact.

"Run, you meat for dogs!" Hokanu screamed, as much to relieve his own agony as to motivate the horse. He flung forward, gripping the mane in both fists. Though his seat was halfway out of the cantle, and one leg trailed down the gelding's flank, he pounded with the heel that still functioned and drove the horse to its feet.

That moment the archers began to fire. Struck in neck, shoulder, and croup, the gelding bucked, but fortune still smiled on Hokanu; the movement threw him upward and allowed him to hook the saddle flap with his good leg, keeping his seat. The gelding exploded into a gallop toward home.

The pounding threatened to shake Hokanu loose. He clung, dizzied and deafened by pain. His hands stayed locked white-knuckled in the horse's mane, and his blood dripped and flung away on the wind, mingled with that of his mount. He tried, but could not balance his seat. His lame hip prevented him from centering himself in the saddle. He had not come this far, he thought with clenched teeth, only to spoil things by falling off.

But inexorably, he slipped to the side, until his ankle dragged in the dust. He clung now by only his knee, and the gelding had begun to crow-hop. One, two, three gyrations, he hung on. And then his hands wrenched free. His body arced out into air—

And was caught, roughly, and unceremoniously ripped from the follow-through of inertia by a pair of gauntleted hands.

"Damn!" Hokanu yelled, and struck earth. Agony tore from him a shattering cry. The air went black, then blindingly white, and he heard voices shouting.

One of them was Lujan's.

"Assassins," he gasped out. "On my tail."

"Already dead, my Lord," said Mara's Force Commander crisply. "Hold still, you're bleeding."

Hokanu forced his eyes open. The sky seemed to swim above him, incongruously green and clear of mist. Sunrise threw golden light on the faces of his own patrol.

"We saw the mare come tearing in, riderless," someone was saying. "We assumed trouble on the road. Was Arakasi with you?"

"No," Hokanu gasped. "Kentosani. Just listen." And he managed through his pain to recite the recipe for the antidote that was the only hope to save Mara.

With the practiced efficiency of a field commander, Lujan ordered his swiftest warrior to strip off his armor and run to the healer with the instructions Hokanu had just given. As the man hurried away, and through the exploding bustle of activity as escort was arranged, Hokanu clung grimly to consciousness.

More men were sent for a litter to carry the Lady's wounded consort back to the estate house, while Hokanu's vision swam from patchy black to painful sharpness. He heard cloth tear, felt air against his inflamed skin as Lujan bared his wound.

"My Lord," said the Acoma Force Commander, "you are going to need this arrowhead cut out very quickly if the flesh is not to suppurate."

Hokanu mustered a dogged breath. "You will have nothing done with that arrow," he grated. "Not until I am back at my Lady's side, and I have seen her restored by the antidote with my own eyes."

"Your will, my Lord." The Acoma Force Commander arose, all brusqueness and hurry. "Strike Leader," he shouted to his sub-officer, "pick four men, and make up a stretcher! My Lord Hokanu would be at his Lady's side as swiftly as possible!"

9. Miracle

The sky dimmed.

Servants entered on quiet feet to close the screens and light the lamps in Mara's chamber. They finished their task and silently bowed to their mistress, who lay unmoving and wax-pale upon her cushions. Then they departed, leaving Hokanu alone with his vigil, in a quiet that ate at his nerves.

Seven hours had passed since the antidote had been administered, and his Lady showed no improvement. Her eyelids did not flicker in dreaming, and her breathing neither quickened nor changed. As twilight deepened beyond the screens and the gloom encroached, isolating husband and wife in a wan circle of lamplight, Hokanu knew doubt. What if Korbargh had lied, had misled them by giving a false antidote? What if the ambush at the prayer gate had delayed his arrival those critical few minutes, and the medicine had reached Mara too late? What if the gods had turned against them, and all that they did in life was made futile by a forgone conclusion of fate?

The ache of his arrow wound and the unrelenting worry over Mara's condition wore Hokanu to distraction. Agonizing over the need to act, to do something where nothing more could be done, he reached out and gathered up Mara's hand. Was it his imagination, or was her flesh a shade less clammy? Or was his own stressed body growing feverish and dry, as the untended arrowhead in his hip began to fester? Doubts chased the tails of uncertainties, and to break the cycle of useless worry, Hokanu tried speech.

"Mara," he began. The emptiness of the room only underscored his loneliness. "Mara." In vain he searched for something to say; but the words had all been said, the endless apologies, the affirmations of love. That petty politics should place at risk a woman who, by herself, held so much life within her served only to emphasize the fundamental wrongness of Tsurani society: a wrongness Mara had dedicated herself and her Acoma line to change. Hokanu closed his eyes against tears, unsure whether his weakness stemmed from deep and heartfelt regret or from weakness inspired by his wound.

How long he sat unmoving, fighting emotions unworthy of the woman who battled against death on the mat, Hokanu could not have said. Except when he raised his head at the sound of the knock upon the door, the dark beyond the screens had deepened with the fullness of night.

"Enter," he called, dizzied from the sudden move he had made at the interruption. He realized he had not eaten since the day before; surely that was the cause.

Lujan entered and bowed briskly. Although he would normally be off duty at this hour, taking his ease at the evening meal, tonight he still wore his armor and the plain sword he preferred for field service. Dusty, smelling of sweat, he straightened up, regarded the master with a penetrating stare, and compressed his lips into a line while he awaited permission to speak.

Hokanu gave a listless wave.

"Lord?" The tone of question was most unlike the Acoma Force Commander.

Sure a tactful inquiry concerning his own health would follow, Hokanu stiffened. His hand tightened over Mara's, and he said crisply, "You have a report to make?"

Lujan's chin jerked up at the reprimand. "I took the liberty of sending out a scouting detail, under Force Leader Irrilandi." The former Minwanabi Force Commander had been detailing patrols over the hills beyond these estates for more years than Lujan had been alive.

Hokanu nodded for the Acoma officer to continue.

Lujan said, "The patrol turned up a small force armed for a foray. There was a confrontation. Most of the enemy lie dead, but two were taken alive. One had a loose tongue. It would appear that the five archers who ambushed you were only advance scouts. They were sent to reconnoiter the roadway to select the site for a more decisive ambush. But they had not expected you to be mounted and traveling at such speed. They were caught off guard, and had to improvise. The other men, disguised as bandits, were not in place, and plainly only the gods' favor spared your life."

Half-muddled by discomfort from his wound, Hokanu nodded. "Did you find out who sent the murdering dogs?"

Lujan hesitated before he replied. His eyes remained on the master, naked with worry, as he hooked his thumbs in his baldric. "Jiro," he snapped at last. "The proof is incontrovertible. The Anasati Lord was behind this."

Hokanu blinked to clear his head. "Then he will have to die."

"No. Husband, you must not even voice such a notion. How can we go against the edict of the Assembly of Magicians?'' murmured a weak voice from the cushions.

Both Lujan and Hokanu whirled around.

Mara's eyes were open and lucid in her drawn face. Her fingers tightened shakily inside her husband's grip. ''How can we kill Jiro when the Great Ones have forbidden our blood feud?''

''Thank the Good God!'' Hokanu exclaimed. He bent over his wife and kissed her cheek, though the motion left him dizzy. ''Beloved, how do you feel?''

''Annoyed,'' Mara confessed. ''I should have known better than to taste that chocolate. My greed to gain a trade monopoly nearly became my undoing.''

Hokanu stroked her hand. ''Rest now. We are lucky to have you with us.''

Mara's brow puckered into a frown. ''The baby? What has become of our son?'' But the anguish on Hokanu's face told her all she needed to know. She braced herself and closed her eyes. ''Two sons,'' she whispered. ''Two sons dead, and we can spill no blood in retribution.'' The phrase seemed to exhaust the last of her resources, for she drifted away into sleep, a flush of anger still staining the pallor of her cheeks.

Servants descended in force upon the sick chamber the instant the Lady stilled into slumber. A healer with a satchel of remedies directed them to air Mara's bedding, and to turn down the wicks in the lamps. Lujan did not wait for orders, but stepped forward, caught Hokanu in his strong arms, and lifted the master bodily from Mara's side.

''Force Commander!'' snapped the Shinzawai irritably. ''I can walk on my own, and as of this moment you are dismissed.''

For answer, he received Lujan's most disarming grin. ''I am my Lady's man, Master Hokanu. Tonight I will take no orders from a Shinzawai. If you were one of my warriors, I would forbid you outright to move with such a wound. And truth to tell, I fear my Lady's wrath the more. I will have you off to visit the surgeon to have that arrowhead removed. If you were to die of Jiro's plots while Mara slept, that would be doing her no service.'' His tone was almost insolent, but his eyes spoke heartfelt thanks to the man who had saved the woman who was paramount in both their lives.

The surgeon set aside bloodstained instruments, looked up from his work, and met Lujan's eyes. Lamp light burnished the sweat-streaked planes of his face, to reveal a strained expression. "No, the light is quite sufficient," he said hoarsely. "I can see well enough to work."

"Then the prognosis is not good," Lujan whispered back. His hands stayed steady and firm on Hokanu's leg, an assurance to the injured man as much as a restraint to keep an inopportune flinch from disrupting the healer's touch. Dosed with sā wine laced with a narcotic herb to dull pain, Hokanu might not realize where he was or what was happening well enough to hold his honor and keep motionless. Still, no matter how muddled the consciousness of a man became, his spirit would remain aware. If the news was going to be bad, Hokanu's wal, his inner self, did not need to hear before he was sufficiently recovered to maintain self-control.

Yet either Lujan's words were not quiet enough, or the wounded man was unwilling to relinquish consciousness enough to be spared. Hokanu weakly raised his head. "If there is something wrong, I'll hear of it now."

The healer wiped his hands on a cloth. He mopped his brow also, though his infirmary was not hot. He turned worried eyes to Lujan, who nodded, then looked back at Mara's consort. "The arrowhead is removed, master. But it was deep into the bone, and your attempts to move and run caused much damage. Tendons and ligaments are severed, some frayed beyond my skills to sew back." He did not add that the wound was deep, and the lacerations invited infection. He would pack the tears with poultice, but that was all he could do.

"Are you telling me I won't walk again?" Hokanu's voice did not quaver, but held only the sharpness of command.

The healer sighed. "You will walk, master. But you will never lead a charge onto a battlefield again. You will limp, and your balance will be compromised. In combat, any competent enemy would see your lameness and kill you easily. My Lord, you must never don armor again." He shook his grey head in sympathy. "I am sorry. That is the best I can promise."

Hokanu turned his face toward the wall, utterly still. Not even his hands tensed into fists; his rage, or his pain, stayed hidden. But Lujan, who was a warrior also, knew his mind: that he was yet his father's heir, and had stood as Shinzawai Force Commander. It was an ill thing for a man in line for the mantle of a great house to become a cripple. Lujan noticed the barest tremor in the sinews under his hands. He felt his heart wrench, but dared not offer sympathy, for fear that Hokanu's desperately held dignity would break down.

And yet the man that Mara had married showed once again the sternness of his fiber. "Get on with your work, healer," he said. "Sew up what you can, and for the love of the gods, give me no more medicinal wine. I would be aware when my Lady wakes, and not half out of my head with self-pity brought on by drink."

"Shift the lamp, then," muttered the surgeon. "I'll have this over with as quickly as may be."

"Good servant, in that I may be of assistance," said a quiet voice from the doorway.

The surgeon started in surprise, his hand half extended toward his tray of instruments; Lujan all but released hold of Hokanu's leg in his initial annoyance. "I told the guard on this corridor that the master was not to be disturbed. For any reason." He half turned, drawing breath to dress down the lax soldier, and checked, appalled.

The wizened man in coarse brown robes who stood at the edge of the lamp light was no servant but a priest of Hantukama, the God of Healing. Lujan had seen his like once before, on the day Keyoke's life had been saved from multiple battle wounds and a leg amputation gone septic. He recognized the stranger's order by the shaved semicircle at the back of his head, and by the intricate braid that trailed from his nape. Mindful of how difficult it was to gain the services of such a priest, Lujan bowed as deeply as the lowliest scullion to atone for his thoughtless address.

"Forgive me, good priest, for my ill manners. In my mistress's name, you are welcome here, my brutish behavior a pitiful reflection on the honor of this house."

The priest stepped forward, silent on bare feet. His sun-browned face showed no affront but only deepest sympathy as he touched the warrior's shoulder. "With master and Lady both hurt, you would be a poor guardian if you did not seek to spare them from intrusions."

Lujan spoke with his face still pressed to the floor. "Good priest, if you have come to help, my feelings are of no consequence before the needs of my master and Lady."

Now the priest frowned, a fearful expression on a face that habitually was serene. His hand tightened, in surprising strength, and he raised Lujan from his posture of submission. "On the contrary," he snapped. "The spirit and the feelings of any man are equal in the sight of my god. You are forgiven your lapse of manners, worthy warrior. Go now. Leave me to my business with your master, and mind your post by the door with all vigilance."

Lujan snapped the priest a salute, hand over heart, and stepped out as ordered. The surgeon gave a hasty half bow, and made as if to follow. But the priest waved for him to stay as he stepped to Hokanu's bedside. "My novice is but a boy, and too tired from travel to assist. He sleeps, and if I am to be of service to my god, I will need help."

The priest set down his satchel. He took the sick man's sweating fingers into his own and looked into Hokanu's eyes. "Son of my god, how are you?"

Hokanu inclined his head, the best he could manage for courtesy. "I do well enough. Blessings of your god, and Chochocan's favor for guiding you to this house." He drew a difficult breath and forced his voice steady over his pain. "If I may presume, I would ask that you look after my Lady. Her need is greater than mine."

The priest pursed his lips. "No. I say not"—he held up a hand, forestalling Hokanu's protest—"and it is my judgment to make. I have seen the Good Servant already. I traveled here in answer to her need, for her sacrifice and her love for her people are recognized by the followers of my god. But she is mending well enough without Hantukama's blessing. You brought the antidote in good time."

Hokanu closed his eyes, his relief palpable. "I am grateful to hear she will be well again."

"She will be well." The priest paused, his face suddenly careworn. As if he chose his words carefully, he added, "But you should know, as her consort, that she will bear only one more child. The poison caused damage, and that was the best the healing powers of my god would allow."

Hokanu's eyes flicked open, black in the flicker of lamp light. His warrior's composure held, and nothing of his anguish leaked through, that his Lady could not have the many children she craved, to secure both her line and his also. "That is enough, then, good priest."

A silence fell over the chamber, with the surgeon standing motionless in respect for his master's feelings. The hiss of the oil lamp blended with the whisper of the breeze beyond the screen and, farther off, the tramp of a warrior answering the change of the watch. With summer past, the amphibious creatures were silent on the lakeshore; only insects sang in the soft warmth of the night.

Out of that stillness, and the peace that ruled the late hour, the priest of Hantukama spoke. "Master Hokanu, that is not enough."

The eyes of Mara's consort focused with an effort, through the dulling effects of drugged wine. He looked at the slender, wizened little priest, and pulled himself half-upright. "What more would you ask of me that I have not already given?"

The priest of Hantukama sighed and returned a thin smile. "It is that you give too much, son of my god. Your love and devotion to your Lady consume all that you have and all that you are. For her, the heir to the Shinzawai has risked the wholeness of his leg, and for her, he would lay down his life to spare her own. I say, as the voice of my god, that this is too much."

Now Hokanu's cheeks flushed red in anger. "What honor would I have if I saved myself before Mara?"

The priest pressed him back against his cushions with a touch that was gentle but firm. "She does not need your rescue," he said, inarguably blunt. "She is Servant of the Empire and Lady of the Acoma. She has her own strength. She needs you as confidant and companion beside her, not as a shield before her."

Hokanu drew breath to argue. The priest gave him a sharp shake that made him gasp in discomfort. "You are no less than she in the eyes of this Empire and my god. The continuance of this nation, and the better life for all promised by the Light of Heaven, rely upon you, as heir to the House of Shinzawai, as much as on her. You are a major player in this changed Game of the Council. This you must understand."

Too weakened to argue, Hokanu sank back. "You sound as if you know the future," he said tiredly. "What is it you see that we do not?"

But the priest would not say. Instead he stepped from Hokanu's shoulder, and laid his hands on the flesh at either side of the wound on Hokanu's hip. Softly, firmly, he addressed the surgeon. "Open my satchel, good healer. If this man is to rise without a limp, there is a long night's work ahead, and a need to invoke the blessing of my god."

Word of the ambush against Hokanu and the certainty of Mara's recovery caught up with Arakasi on a river barge bound downriver from Kentosani. The messenger who brought the news arrived just past dawn, during a stop to load fresh fruit. He boarded with the slaves carrying the baskets of jomach, and slipped unobtrusively forward to the huddled mass of deck passengers who bought their comfortless passage for a centi each. The barge was crowded with three families of migrant fruit pickers, two scabby beggars who had been run out of Kentosani for plying their craft without license from the Emperor, and a guild runner with a swollen ankle bound south to ask charity of an uncle while his injury healed.

Arakasi was seated between two lashed casks, his dark hood drawn over his face. Since he was as dirty as the beggars, and looked as shifty as a street thief, the peasant mothers with their fretful infants and gaggle of skinny children had given him wide berth. The newcomer found enough space to squeeze down beside him, and whisper news from the Acoma estate.

Eyes closed, head lolling against a barrel, the Spy Master appeared asleep; he had charcoal under his fingernails and an untended scab on his chin. He smelled as though he had not bathed in a sevenday. But his ears heard well. After a moment through which he thought furiously, he grumbled sleepily, rolled on his side, and returned the barest breath of a whisper.

"I will not be getting off at the river fork. Tell the connection there to convey my regards to our master and mistress. If I am needed, have the net ask after me from the jewel setter adjacent to the trophy stuffer's shop in Sulan-Qu. You'll know the place by the harulth skull on the signpost."

The messenger touched the Spy Master's wrist in confirmation. Then he made a noise of disgust, leaned over toward the nearest of the passengers, and began to proselytize for an obscure priesthood of Lulondi, God of Farmers.

"Be off, pest," snapped the bothered victim. "I don't love vegetables, and the flies are bad enough on this journey without your carping on top of them!"

The messenger bowed, carelessly banging an elbow into the knee of a peasant wife. She cursed him, lashed out a foot, and caught him a blow in the shins.

The disturbance brought the attention of the barge master. "Hey there! Mind you stay quiet, or I'll heave the lot of you overboard."

The farm wife returned loud protest. "This scum is here soliciting, and did you get a coin for his passage, anyway?"

The barge master scowled, tramped forward, and peered at the prostrate man the farm wife pointed her calloused finger at.

"You! Vermin-carrying, sores-ridden wretch! Have you a centi to pay for your space?" The barge master held out his hand, sweating in his annoyance.

The man he singled out muttered pitiably. "For the goodness of Lulondi's blessing, I ask that you let me stay."

The barge master scowled and snapped his fingers. "I'll show you Lulondi's blessing." At his signal, two polemen arose from their resting place by the rail. Muscled like wrestlers, they came forward on bandy legs and bowed before their master. "Heave him off," the barge master ordered in disgust. "And none too gently, either, since he thought to stow away."

Identical grins spread across the faces of the polemen. They grabbed their victim by the wrists, raised him, and tossed him over the side.

He landed with a smack and a splash of dirty water that all but swamped the fruit seller's dugout, tied alongside for the transfer of goods. The slaves whacked him away with their paddles, and the barge crew, the deck passengers, and bystanders gathered on the shore all laughed as the wretch kicked free of the strangling folds of his cloak and swam like a river rodent for dry land.

"Lulondi's blessing, indeed," harrumphed the barge master. He whirled, his mind back on business, and stepped over a snoring Arakasi without so much as a glance.

Two days later, Mara's Spy Master disembarked in Sulan-Qu. He made his way across the riverfront, unobtrusive in the noon shadows. The streets were nearly deserted, the shops closed in siesta. What few loiterers were about either slept in the shade of the window awnings and balconies or poked through the refuse in the gutters, in search of a crust to eat. Arakasi made his way to the House of Seven Stars, a brothel that catered to wealthy nobles with odd tastes. There, under a back-door arch adorned with kissing cherubs, he knocked in a prescribed sequence. The panel opened, and an immensely fat woman hung with beads and corcara necklaces pulled him inside.

"Gods," she murmured in a voice as deep as a man's, "do you always have to come here smelling like a sewer? We have clients upstairs who might be offended."

Arakasi flashed a grin. "Now, Bubara, don't tell me you've used up all the bath water with the kekali leaves and citrus so early in the day?"

The madam grunted through her nose. "Hardly. The girls and boys have to smell sweet." She twitched a flabby arm through a curtain, and a naked deaf-mute child with skin the color of chocha-la beans scurried out and bowed before her.

She motioned toward Arakasi and nodded.

The little boy looked at the dirty visitor, cocked his head to one side, and grinned in delighted recognition. Unmindful of the smell, he took the charcoal-marked hand and led the Spy Master off.

Arakasi tousled the boy's hair and from some hidden pocket produced a cho-ja–made candy. The boy smiled, showing a pathetic expanse of gums where teeth should have been at his age. He made soft moans of pleasure and bowed his forehead to his fists repeatedly as a gesture of thanks.

As an afterthought, Arakasi added two shell coins. "Somebody should buy you some clothing," he muttered and caught the boy by the elbow, tugging him upright as he made to prostrate himself on the floor. He patted the boy again on the head and waved him off, as he had been this way many times and knew which room he sought.

He moved off down the corridor, touched a section of carving that unlatched a hidden door, and climbed the narrow, shadowy stair beyond to a cubbyhole under the eaves, while, behind him, the little boy clutched his treasured gifts and groveled upon the pretty carpets for long, unnoticed minutes.

In the cramped chamber, under the heat of shingles ablaze under the noon sun, Arakasi picked from an assortment of carry boxes and chests which held garments of all types, from beaded, glittering robes to field workers' smocks. He selected an orange-and-purple livery and a dusty pair of sandals with a hole in the toe of the left one's sole. Then he bundled his unwashed robes in another chest that held what looked to be beggar's rags, and, clad in nothing but his dirt and a soiled loincloth, made his way back downstairs to avail himself of the madam's bath.

An hour later, he was on his knees in the offices of the moneylenders' guild, a scrub brush and bucket in hand. Afternoon trade had resumed, and if he spent overlong cleansing the tiles around the desk of the clerk by the aisle, no one commented. Merchants tended to kick him out of their path as they came and went, particularly if repayment of their loans were behind schedule, or if their need for credit had resulted from misfortune: a caravan load lost to bandits or a silk shipment spoiled by damp weather.

Arguments tended to flare in the heat of afternoon, and no one noticed that the servant muttered under his breath as he scrubbed the tiles.

Except the clerk, who, as he copied rows of figures, held his head tilted to one side.

". . . hafta track in dog dung," Arakasi grumbled. "Should be a law against letting the pets of the ladies defecate in the streets." He sniffed, cursed his aching back, and in exactly the same singsong tone added, "Offends my nose, it does, and did you notice whether the red boy took out any notes that might have been for blood money? Crap in the wash water again, and I'm tired of refilling my bucket."

The clerk scrubbed sweat from his brow, picked a slate off a corner of his desk, and made a notation. Then he shuffled it into another stack, smeared with erasures and chalk dust, and lashed out with a foot, catching the floor scrubber a hard blow in the ribs. "Here, you. Clean these."

Arakasi tugged his forelock and pressed his nose to the wet tiles. "Your will, sir, master, your will." He accepted the pile of slates, shuffled off to fetch a rag, and began the appointed task. His muttering continued, the inflection even as ever as he came to the slate with the blurred notation. At the sight of the figures there, with dates noted in code to one side, he could barely keep his wipe rag steady. Three flicks of his wrist, and the slate was empty, the figures and dates committed to memory. His appearance remained innocuously bland, but his heartbeat doubled.

For "red boy" was his code name for Anasati, and the clerk, a carefully placed agent. The numbers exchanged had revealed large sums in metal, taken out by the Anasati First Adviser. They had not been for trade purposes; those the hadonra would have signed for, and most would have been in notes to merchants that handled regular transactions. One of the sums had been borrowed just before the time of Arakasi's near-disastrous exposure in the silk warehouse. Could the events have been connected? And the other two, recently dated, might have been payments to the Hamoi Tong, blood money for specified assassinations.

Arakasi polished the last slate and shuffled back to the clerk's desk. He resumed mopping the floor, and roundly cursed when the clerk tossed a bit of thyza paper at the waste bin and missed. The crumpled scrap landed on Arakasi's cleaned tiles. He retrieved it, bowed obsequiously, and deposited it within the waste barrel. But a second scrap of paper twisted inside remained in his palm, and vanished into a fold of his loincloth.

He endured the cuffs and blows of the merchants as he scrubbed his way across the aisle, until he reached haven in a far corner.

Just before closing time, when voices were loudest and tempers most frayed, an ostentatiously dressed merchant stopped by the desk of the clerk who was Arakasi's agent. He flicked a swift glance about the shop, saw that all on the floor were occupied, and made an inquiry.

The apparently flustered clerk dropped his chalk. Arakasi dipped his scrub brush into his bucket and started on a new section of floor, but his bent head was angled so that he caught a clear view of the exchange at the clerk's desk under his arm.

The two men spoke for a few minutes. Shell counters changed hands, invisibly to anyone who happened to be standing, but not to a servant bent down on the floor. The merchant glanced to left and right, his eyes bright with exhilaration.

Arakasi, muttering, repressed a frown. Where have I seen that man before? he thought. Where? And in time the answer came to him, who was adept at separating details from circumstance, no matter how incongruous they might have seemed.

He knew, with a thrill of excitement, that the man dressed as the gaudy merchant was none other than Chumaka, the Anasati First Adviser.

"Chochocan's favor," he grumbled. "Damned floor goes on forever." He dragged his bucket to one side, half blocking the doorway that led to the privy. A moment later, he was rewarded by another blow in the ribs, as the clerk who hastened to nature's call tripped over him.

"Damn you for a wretch!" He bent to deliver another punitive blow, and, between curses, said breathlessly, "The merchant wanted to know if anyone had made inquiry into the Anasati accounts. I told him several shifty and questionable men had offered me bribes to that effect, just to make him worry."

Arakasi choked back a grin, and pressed his face to the floor in a slave's bow of apology. "Sorry, sir, master, I'm sorry. That's damned interesting news, and forgive me for my clumsiness, I beg you."

"You aren't forgiven!" shouted the clerk. "Get out on the street and scrub the stoop! And make sure no street brats have made water on the pillars on the alley side, while you're at it."

Arakasi bowed and scraped, and backed hastily out the door. But though he detailed his sharpest squad of street children to seek out the merchant's trail, no trace of Chumaka could be found.

By sundown, Mara's Spy Master was forced to concede the man's cleverness. It also left him worried. He felt cold to discover a man who could match his skills at subterfuge in the camp of an enemy. For not only was Jiro sworn to destroy Mara, he was the most dangerous member of the traditionalist faction that sought to bring down the Emperor. Others might be more public in their opposition, but Arakasi had no doubt that Jiro sought advantage by letting others voice his desires. What progress had been made to change a governance fallen to stagnation and decay remained threatened. As evening fell, Arakasi hastened through darkening streets toward the House of Seven Stars. He must go there and shift identity, then return to his mistress straight away. For although he had run into a dead end in his lead to root out the Hamoi Tong, he had other disquieting news to report, concerning political affairs within the Empire. Still more upsetting was his chance discovery that Chumaka, First Adviser to Jiro of the Anasati, had somehow discovered a need to guard his tracks.

Which of his agents, Arakasi wondered in anxiety, had been found out?

10. Interval

Mara fretted.

The debilitating effects of her poisoning passed too slowly for her liking. Two months since the event, and still she was too weak to travel. She regarded the afternoon sunlight that striped the carpet in her study, and frowned. She ought to be in the Holy City, attending the semiannual convocation of the Emperor's advisers. Frasai of the Tonmargu, the Imperial Overlord, had lost his health; some whispered in corners that he was becoming senile. The rumors were baseless, but even in his vigorous years as Clan Warchief, the Lord of the Tonmargu had ruled with an uncertain hand, trying to please divergent factions. Mara worried. With Frasai's authority crumbling, and the Imperial Chancellor, Hokanu's father, Kamatsu, hampered on all sides by traditionalist attacks that threatened not only his own prosperity, but that of his allies and supporters, this autumn's meeting could easily become a battleground.

The bloodier days when the Game of the Council had been played under rule of a Warlord were still too recent to be forgotten.

Mara hit her thin fist on her writing desk in an unwonted display of frustration, and rose to pace. That she was too weak to walk without the aid of a cane made her flush with annoyance. The servants who attended her needs, and even the runner boy by the doorway, turned their faces away from the emotions that played with embarrassing plainness across their Lady's face.

But today, she was too exasperated to waste effort keeping up a proper Tsurani façade. Kevin the barbarian, had he been there, would have teased her for that. Mara felt a pang in a place she had thought hardened over with callus. "Damn the man," she muttered, and banged down her cane for emphasis.

A gentle voice chided from the doorway. "The Empire won't fall apart, just because its favorite Servant is too unwell to go to council." Clad in little more than an overrobe dampened from sweat from his arms

· practice, Hokanu stepped in, the limp in his stride nearly gone. As Mara rounded on him in a fury, he caught her wrists. She had no strength; his fingers could circle her bones like shackles, she was so thin, and he had to take care not to bruise her. He spoke again with a firmness that of necessity he withheld from his grip. "My Lady, Lord Hoppara will have things well in hand. The council will not go to pieces because you're not there."

She looked up, her eyes snapping. After a moment, she said, "Stop treating me as though I were made of glass. You and I know the traditionalists will be vicious in their plotting, and not half of what happens will take place in the council chamber. Bargains will be made, terms set, and conditions agreed upon, and many who would otherwise act with caution will not, *because I am not there!*"

Hokanu smiled, freed one of her wrists, and straightened a fallen wisp of her hair. As he wound it back under what he guessed was the correct jade pin, he hid his pain that her dark locks had lost their shine, and her skin no longer had the luster of corcara shell. Her dancer's litheness had gone, through her weeks in a sickbed. She still looked peaked, and not even Lujan could get her to rest through the heat of the afternoons. "Imperial politics aside, pretty bird, I've taken the liberty of assembling your maids. You have a visitor."

"Dear gods, state clothing?" Mara's fury changed course toward annoyance. "I'll suffocate. Whose father has come this time, hoping to touch my robe hem to gain the luck to find auspicious husbands for his five ill-favored daughters?"

Hokanu laughed, clasped her waist, and lifted her wholesale into his arms. "How bitchy we are today. Did you know that Jican was approached by a merchant who offered him metal for your cast-off clothing? He wanted to sew the rags into ribbons to sell for souvenirs."

Mara stiffened in affront. "Jican didn't tell me that!"

"He knew," Hokanu began, and grunted as the wraith-like woman in his arms caught him in the diaphragm with an elbow. He shifted her out of reach of a stiffening bruise gained at sword drill, and manfully continued speaking. "Your hadonra didn't tell you. He knew you'd ask to have the poor man whipped off the estates, and he deemed that inappropriate hospitality, even for a rude schemer."

As her husband stepped into the hallway, Mara said a word that certainly would have tarnished the reverent image of her held by the commoners. Then she poked her husband in the arm. "So who is this visitor that Jican and you have decided it's safe for me to see?"

A grin spread across Hokanu's handsome face. "You'll want your makeup. It's Lady Isashani of the Xacatecas."

"Here?" Mara's voice was shrill with dismay. She reached up and worriedly began to pat at her hair.

Since that was the first moment anyone had seen her have a care for her personal appearance since her miscarriage, Hokanu silently thanked the provocative beauty who waited in Mara's best sitting room. Maybe after today the Lady of the Acoma would hear sense, and stop spending the reserves she needed for healing on frazzled nervous energy. The healing priest had judged that the antidote had rescued Mara from the very gates of the Red God's hall, and that with rest and a calm mind, it would take three months for her bodily recovery, then another to regain her full strength. But Mara's emotional state after the death of another baby and a near-miss on her own life had been anything but restful. Hokanu feared it would be longer than three months before his wife became her former self.

An emphatic squirm from his wife reminded Hokanu painfully that her fitness had not been the only one to suffer. If he did not sweat through a hot bath, and soon, he was going to be wretchedly stiff. She interpreted his grimace, as she was wont to do.

"You must not be long at your bath, dear man. If Isashani's come, there will be subtleties and intrigues about her as thick as perfume. It will take a handsome face to flatter the information out of her, and since I'm not male and a favorite of hers, you are placed on your honor as Acoma consort to attend."

Hokanu was neither so tired from his exercise, nor so deaf to nuance, that he did not hear the underlying fear in his Lady's voice. "What troubles you, Lady? Normally you would be delighted by a visit by Lady Isashani."

Mara looked up at him, her eyes black in the thicker gloom of the hallway. "The Great Game," she murmured. "It turns too often toward bloodshed, and once more there are rumors of a plot against the Emperor."

Hokanu's face went hard. "I'll be there. But after my bath, and after you women have a chance to renew your acquaintance." Dangerous politics might be the reason behind the Xacatecas dowager's visit; but Hokanu was damned if he would forfeit the chance to have Mara benefit from the former Ruling Lady of the Xacatecas' shrewd insight and wit.

Mara looked like a lost waif in the enveloping weight of her finery. She entered the sitting room with small, demure steps, not for the sake of dainty appearance, but because of weakness. The luster of her emeralds and jade outshone her eyes, and the bow she gave the tall woman who awaited her presence in purple-and-gold robes was of necessity shallow and brief. Prolonged obeisance of any form would have seen her on her knees on the floor, and stubborn pride prevented her from having a serving man along to steady her.

Lady Isashani of the Xacatecas arose from her cushions in a sweep of fine silk and perfumes. Her eyes were rich brown, and exotically slanted. Her hair had silver mixed in with its auburn, and the thyza powder she had used to burnish her distinctive cheekbones must have been mixed with sparkling bits of ground shell. The effect glittered with tiny points of light, and enhanced the milk-and-rose skin that had retained its glow of youth as if by a magician's spell. Renowned for her beauty, feared for her shrewdness, and acknowledged as a matchless manipulator, the dowager Lady of the Xacatecas hurried forward and supported Mara's elbow.

"You're obviously not hale, my dear." Her voice was fine-grained, mellow as the tone of a treasured old instrument handed down through generations of players. "And formalities are wasted between friends."

Mara sank gratefully into deep cushions. Her own voice sounded dry as the scratch of sand as she opened with the time-honored words of greeting toward one of higher social position. "Welcome to my house, Lady. Are you well?"

Isashani inclined her head, a saucy smile dimpling her cheeks. "I thank the Good Servant for the undeserved courtesy," she answered, her tone one of genuine pleasure at Mara's reversal of their ranks. While she was Mara's senior in age and experience, she was but a former Ruling Lady and Mara was Servant of the Empire. "I do well enough, but you look like hwaet gruel left in the sun for the livestock. My dear, have you given up eating altogether?" That her words were direct as a spearcast did not surprise Mara, but that bluntness had unbalanced many an opponent of House Xacatecas whose wits were left muddled by the Lady's alluring loveliness.

Mara dropped her eyes from the dazzle of gleaming violet silk trimmed expensively with gold thread, and as quickly glanced away from the tray of sweetmeats and sliced fruits left by the servants for her guest's refreshment. She evaded. "You surely didn't come here to hear me complain of my health." In fact, nourishment held no savor. The poison had left her stomach nervous and delicate.

The reply from the Lady came barbed as a riposte. "I certainly didn't come here to indulge you by watching you sulk."

Mara repressed a flinch. From anyone else she must interpret such rebuke as an insult; but Isashani's deep eyes held sympathy that stung her like a slap because it was genuine. She sighed, and emotion that had hardened since her miscarriage eased a little. "I'm sorry. I didn't realize my mood was so transparent."

"Sorry won't suffice." Isashani reached out a perfectly groomed hand, selected a plate, and served up a portion of the fruit. "Eat, or else I'll call your maids and have them bundle you straight off to bed."

She would, too, Mara thought, and her perfidious maids would probably obey without pause to question that the wish of their mistress might not be in accord. Isashani handled authority like an irascible field general, and folk in her presence tended to march to her tune, and think the better of their actions afterward. Since Mara did not feel strong enough to argue, she began to nibble a slice of jomach. She, too, could be direct. "Why did you come?"

Isashani gave her back a look that measured; then, as if reassured that Mara's inner fiber was not as depleted as her physical resilience, she poured herself chocha from the pot upon the snack tray. "Lord Jiro of the Anasati has made overtures toward my late husband's oldest bastard son." Her voice was hard as rare barbarian steel, at odds with her fragile beauty.

Mara set aside her half-eaten fruit slice, unthinking. A frown marked her brow. "Wenaseti," she said, quietly questioning.

An elegant nod from her guest confirmed that this was the name of the bastard in question; Isashani returned a small smile in salute. That Mara knew the name at all was impressive, since the late Lord Chipino had sampled concubines and courtesans like fine wines. His bastards were numerous as vermin, and though all had been raised in evenhanded fairness by House Xacatecas, their temperaments and characters varied like weather. The old Lord had shared his sheets as readily for beauty as for brains, and though none of the mothers he got with child had been able to successfully challenge Isashani's preeminent position as Lady and wife, some had been bitter in their defeat, and had taught their resentment to their offspring. The current heir, Hoppara, relied on his dowager mother's shrewd grasp of family politics to keep his sprawling collection of siblings and bastard relations in line.

"It is our great good fortune," Isashani added with a spark to her eye that suggested a sharpness of circumstance smoothed over, "that Wenaseti is a son loyal to his bloodline. Jiro was rebuffed."

Mara's frown did not ease, and the glint in Isashani's glance did not soften. As second-in-command to Lord Frasai as Imperial Overlord, Lord

Hoppara of the Xacatecas held a pivotal position in the Emperor's court. That he was young for such a powerful post made him vulnerable; his staunch advice and quick perception often stiffened Lord Frasai's suggestible nature to take action in time to avert setbacks from the traditionalist factions that sought to undermine reform and reinstate the abolished office of Warlord.

Lord Hoppara removed meant a key defense lost: a dangerous step closer to bloodshed and the barely stayed threat of civil war. Something in Isashani's mien gave warning.

Mara said, "You've had an assassination attempt."

Isashani's face went motionless as porcelain. "Several."

Mara closed her eyes. She felt weak to her core, pressed of a sudden by a weariness that made her long to give up the greater fight, and to narrow her hopes and her efforts toward Acoma survival in the face of perils that closed like a ring of naked swords. Yet she was Servant of the Empire, and no longer the inexperienced girl torn from service to Lashima's order to take over a beleaguered house. The enemies of the Emperor were Acoma foes also; for she was as the king post that holds the weight of a great roof. To bring down Imperial rule, Jiro and his allies must first cut off her support.

The thought that followed hard after was that the Hamoi Tong had been far too successful in its assassination attempts against friends and allies and family. For as long as Jiro ruled, the Anasati would continue to stoop to the hiring of assassins; the tong had become a liability no longer safe to ignore. Mara would never forget the horror of near strangulation, or the pain of the miscarriage brought on by poison. For the rest of her days she would suffer grief for Ayaki's death. Wrapped in bleak thoughts, Mara was made aware of Hokanu's entrance only by Isashani's words of formal greeting.

She opened her eyes to see her husband bowing over the Lady of the Xacatecas's hand. He was self-conscious as a boy, an odd mien for a man who had commanded armies in the name of his Emperor, and whose own social grace had made Mara the envy of unmarried daughters of great houses. Yet Isashani's skills at confounding men were so facile that it was rumored she was secretly a witch who manipulated her admirers through enchantment. Hokanu was one of her favorites, and her soft, bantering flattery set him at his ease at once. Men she did not care for had been known to stay tongue-tied in her presence for remarkable intervals of time.

Still half-dazzled by Isashani's charm, Hokanu took a seat beside his wife. He folded Mara's hand inside his own and said, "We also are weary of playing mo-jo-go against the tong." He referred to a card game often played for heavy stakes. "Really, it would be a relief to us all if Ichindar would sire a son. A male heir to the imperial throne would do much to damp the fires of the traditionalist faction."

Isashani's dark eyes flashed amusement. "It has been a dull few years for matchmaking, I'll agree, with every highborn son taking concubines instead of wives, in the hope of winning an imperial daughter for marriage. The parties are getting quite vicious, with so many unwed girls spitting at each other like sarcat cubs."

From there the subject turned to the trade war between a consortium from the Omechan Clan and a Kanazawai Clan group, which was causing Hokanu's father setbacks in the resin market. Frustrated by the resultant shortage in the production of laminated hide, the armorer's guild was on the verge of joining the fray, with the shipmasters and stevedores in Jamar upset by embargoes that disrupted sailing schedules. Since the Acoma had needra hides mildewing in warehouses in Sulan-Qu, and the Anasati did not, the consensus was that Jiro's allies were behind the disturbance. It did the Omechan no good to recall that their own disunity had provided the opening that had given the Emperor absolute power to begin with.

Afternoon blended into evening. As Mara's weariness became evident, and she excused herself to retire, Isashani at last took her leave. Seated in her litter in the dooryard, with her bearers in place to depart, she raised her dark eyes to Hokanu and planted one last barbed comment. "Really, young master, you had better take pains to see that your wife eats, or the gossip will go round that you are starving her to an early grave, in the hope of joining the circle of suitors who pant after Ichindar's eldest daughter."

Hokanu's eyebrows rose as though he had been sword-pricked. "Lady, is that a threat?"

Isashani smiled with poisonous sweetness. "Depend on it. My late husband was fond of Mara, and I don't want his shade out to haunt me. Also, my Hoppara would probably challenge you to a duel of honor over the issue, were he to see your Lady so sad. After her heroics during the Night of the Bloody Swords, he compares all the young women he meets to her."

"Indeed." Hokanu's voice turned serious. "No man in the Empire cares more for our Good Servant than I. And your visit has done more for her than you can possibly know."

*   *   *

Lady Isashani's visit at least inspired Mara to resume normal care for her appearance. She called upon the skills of her maids, and if at first her improved complexion was solely attributable to makeup, Hokanu was careful not to badger her. If she still kept long hours over her reports, she at least made an effort to eat more; and once she took up the practice of meditating in a small boat upon the lake, her pallor disappeared soon after.

"It's very hard to worry with the water all around, peaceful under the sky," she said, stepping ashore one evening when the afterglow of sunset turned wavelets and landscape all to gold. Holding her in his embrace, Hokanu hated to disrupt the moment. But soon enough she would find out, and unless he wished to provoke an explosion, he dared not hold back fresh news.

"Arakasi is back."

"So soon?" Mara lifted her face, kissing her husband's lips with the absentee air of one already preoccupied. "He must have heard of the attempt on Lord Hoppara before I sent out my summons."

The moment of warmth was cut short as the Lady hastened to meet her Spy Master. Hokanu accompanied her into the estate house, through hallways dimmed with evening shadows, and past the servants who dispersed to light oil lamps. Faintly, from one of the courtyards, came the echoes of Justin's happy shouts.

"What's got the little one all stirred up?" Mara asked.

Hokanu put his arm around her shoulder. "A new game. Your Adviser for War laid a bet with the boy that he could not be ambushed unawares. Justin has taken to lurking behind the furniture, and the servants won't use the back hallways anymore, for fear of being set upon."

"And Keyoke?" Mara turned the last corner and passed the length of another corridor tiled in old, worn mosaic. "Has he been caught?"

Hokanu laughed. "Several times. His hearing is not what it once was, and his crutch makes him easy prey."

Mara shook her head. "Just so Justin doesn't terrorize him. The old campaigner has received scars enough in Acoma service without getting battered in his twilight years."

But Keyoke, Hokanu knew, did not mind his bruises in the least, for Justin held the affection of the grandson the old man had never had.

The couple reached the doorway to Mara's study. There Hokanu lifted his arm and gave his wife a questioning glance. The servants had not reached this hallway yet, and the lamps were still unlit. Mara's face was a pale oval in the shadows, and her expression was unreadable. After a moment she said, "Stay with me this time. Lady Isashani's news has left me unsettled, and I would like your counsel."

Hokanu heard the worry in her voice. He asked, "Should I send for Saric and Incomo?"

Mara returned a shake of her head. "No. They would not condone what I plan, and I see no need to endure their criticism."

Suddenly cold, there in the warm darkness, with the calls of the servants near to hand, and the smells of supper wafting from the kitchen, Hokanu reached out and tipped Mara's chin up with one finger. "Just what are you thinking, pretty Lady?" His tone was at odds with the apprehension that bound his breath.

Mara answered after a pause. "I am thinking that the Hamoi Tong has made trouble for far too long. I have lost a son and an unborn child to it. I would not see Lady Isashani suffer the same loss, and I owe her late husband, Lord Chipino, at least that much."

Hokanu released a sigh, distressed by the strain that came between them over the subject of children. "It is not the tong but the enemy who employs it that is to be feared."

Mara gave back a fractional nod. "I know. That is why I am going to ask Arakasi to penetrate its headquarters and steal its records. I will know its employer, and have his plots out into the open."

"His name is probably Anasati," Hokanu said.

"One of his names." Mara's tone was ominous. "I would know the others as well, that no more parents lose young heirs to the cause of murderous politics. Come, let us go and charge Arakasi to undertake this difficult task."

Hokanu could only nod as he escorted his wife into the hall leading to her study. He held respect close to awe for the Spy Master, since watching him act on the night they had sought the antidote. Yet even for a man of his gifts of guile and disguise, to infiltrate the Hamoi Tong was asking the impossible. Hokanu had no argument for the notion that his Lady was sending her Spy Master off to die at a time when she most needed his services.

Arakasi departed his Lady's study preoccupied. Talk had left his voice hoarse. This night's report had been extensive, the end result of many months of labor in the field. The Spy Master had pushed his agents hard, had exhorted them to seek out answers even in the face of the dangers posed by Jiro's First Adviser, Chumaka. Two men had forfeited their cover to gain information, and had chosen suicide by the blade rather than face inquisition and torture, and risk betraying their mistress. And although they had winnowed out several traditionalist plots and shifts in old alliances against the Emperor, they had come no nearer to setting a name to the employer who had sent the Hamoi Tong against Mara.

More disquieting news than the late failed attempt against Lord Hoppara was that several other attempts had been foiled by Arakasi's agent in the Xacatecas household. Twice she had been ''clumsy'' around the cooks, and spilled dishes of food she suspected had been poisoned.

That report had caused Mara to flinch openly. Her face had paled, and then flushed with a depth of anger Arakasi had never seen. Her words still rang in his memory, edged with a grief that never left her since Ayaki's loss. ''Arakasi,'' she had said, ''I ask that you find a way to steal the records of the Hamoi Tong. These attacks against us, and now the allies of our Emperor, must be brought to a stop. If more than the Anasati are behind them, I would have you find out.''

Arakasi had accepted the command, fist over heart in a soldier's salute. After months of attempts to penetrate the Anasati accounts, and three unsuccessful tries to place new agents on Jiro's estate, he regarded the order to go directly after the tong almost as a relief. Arakasi had conceded from frustration that Chumaka was by far the most clever opponent he had ever faced. But even as brilliant a player of politics as the Anasati First Adviser would not anticipate a move as foolhardy as attempting to challenge the assassins. And while Chumaka might not know Mara's Spy Master by name, he was developing an understanding that let him anticipate Arakasi's methods. A dose of the unexpected, especially if no clear motives could be discerned, might throw Chumaka off balance for a while.

Quiet as shadow, and deep in his own thoughts, Arakasi turned, keeping to the dimmer passageways out of habit. This narrow hall crossed the oldest part of the estate house. The floors were built on two heights, legacy of some forgotten Lord who had believed he should always stand above his servants. He, or perhaps one of his wives, had also been a devotee of bric-a-brac. The walls held cavernous niches for statuary and artworks. Arakasi personally thought the things a liability, since some were large enough to harbor an assassin, or a large child.

Consequently, he was not taken entirely off guard when an earsplitting yell sounded at his back, and someone gave an athletic leap with intent to hammer him down from behind.

He spun, light and fast, and found himself with an armload of six-year-old, kicking and cross that his surprise attack had been anticipated.

Mara's Spy Master blew a lock of reddish gold hair out of his lips and said equably, "Do I look so much like Keyoke today that you saw fit to test my reflexes?"

Young Justin giggled and squirmed, and managed to raise the toy sword carved from wood and inlaid with lacquer disks. "Already killed Keyoke twice today," he crowed.

Arakasi's brows rose. He shifted his grip, surprised at the strength required to restrain the energetic little boy. Certainly he was his father's son, with his impertinent attitude and legs long as those of a corani, an antelope-like creature renowned for its fierce speed. "How many times did Keyoke kill you today, imp?"

Justin looked sheepish. "Four." He added a rude phrase in the barbarian tongue, most likely overheard from a soldier in the barracks who had been close to Kevin on the campaign in Dustari. Arakasi took mental note that the boy had ears as quick as his wits; the child was not too young to eavesdrop on his elders. "I have the feeling it's after your bedtime," the Spy Master accused. "Do your nurses know you're awake?" And carefully he began to walk in the direction of the child's quarters.

Justin shook back a curly mop of hair. "Nurses don't know where I am." He smiled proudly, then looked dismayed as doubt crept in. "You won't tell them? I'll get punished for certain."

A gleam lit Arakasi's dark eyes. "There are terms," he said in all seriousness. "You will have to make a promise in exchange for my silence."

Justin looked solemn. Then, as he had seen the soldiers do at dice to seal a debt, he raised his closed fist and touched thumb to forehead. "I keep my word."

Arakasi choked back a grin. "Very well, honorable young master. You will not make a sound when I slip you into your sleeping quarters, and you will lie on your mat without moving, with your eyes closed, until you wake up, and it is morning."

Justin gave a howl of betrayal. So like his father, Arakasi thought, as he lugged the protesting boy off to the nursery. Neither would Kevin accept protocols, or propriety. He was honest when it was a frank embarrassment, and lied whenever it suited him. He was anathema to any well-run Tsurani household, but life had certainly been less entertaining since his departure through the rift gate back to Midkemia. Even Jican, who had been the butt of more than his share of Kevin's jokes, had been known to remark wistfully on his absence.

In true form, Justin ceased his outcry on the threshold of his own room. His tantrum was not worth continuing at the risk of wrath from his nurses. He held to his warrior's word as Arakasi slid him into his blankets; but he did not close his eyes. Instead he glared in outraged indignation as Arakasi stood by, until at last he lost his battle with fatigue and slipped into the deep and healthy sleep of a young boy.

That he would have sneaked out of his chambers had Arakasi not stood by to enforce his warrior's given word, the Spy Master had no doubt. In many ways, the boy was more Midkemian in manner than Tsurani, a trait his mother and foster father encouraged.

Whether his un-Tsurani bent would prove an asset in adulthood, or whether it would leave the Acoma name and natami vulnerable to Jiro and his allies, could not be foretold. Arakasi sighed as he slipped through the screen and made his way across moonlit gardens. Reaching the quarters he used on his rare stays at the estate, Arakasi changed out of his most recent disguise, that of an itinerant peddler of cheap jewelry. He bathed in water gone tepid, unwilling to waste time to have servants make the tub hot, and thought as he sponged away road grime.

The only written records of contracts held by the Hamoi, or any other tong, would be in the possession of the Obajan himself. Only one trusted successor, usually a son, would know where those scrolls were secreted, against the possibility of the Obajan's accidental demise. For Arakasi even to locate the records would require him to come within touching distance of the leader of the Red Flower Brotherhood, the most powerful tong in the Empire.

Arakasi rubbed dye from his hair, his vigorous scrubbing as much a release from frustration. To gain the heart of the tong would be far more difficult than his past forays into the imperial palace.

Of the risks, Arakasi had said nothing. He had but to look at Mara's wan face to know that more worries would further delay her slow return to health. If she knew the risks behind the order she had just delivered, she would be strained enough without anyone seeming to call her judgment into question.

Arakasi settled back, unmindful that the last warmth had fled from the water. He reflected on his encounter with Justin. Mara's worry would revolve around the well-being of her surviving child, Arakasi knew. His shared duty was to see that the boy survived to reach adulthood. This moment, that meant finding means to bring down the most dangerously guarded man in the Empire: the Obajan of the Hamoi Tong.

That any sane man would have regarded the task as an impossibility bothered Arakasi not at all. What troubled his devious mind was that for the first time in his long and varied career he had no clue about where he should start. The location of the Brotherhood of Assassins' headquarters was a closely held secret. The agents who took payment for commissions were not easy marks, as the apothecary he had once tortured in a back alley in Kentosani had been. They would commit suicide—as they had, many times in history—before revealing the next in their chain of contacts. They were as loyal to their own murderous cult as any of Arakasi's agents were to Mara. Troubled, Arakasi slipped out of the tub and dried off. He dressed in a simple robe. For almost half the night, he rested in a near-meditative state, sifting his memory for facts and faces that might lend him a starting connection.

A few hours before dawn, he stood up, did some stretching exercises, and gathered together those things he felt he would need. He exited the estate house without drawing notice from the sentries. Hokanu had once joked that, one day, a warrior might accidentally kill Mara's Spy Master should Arakasi continue to skulk about the estate at night. Arakasi had replied that a guard who slew him should be promoted, as he would have rid Mara of an ineffective servant.

Dawn found Arakasi on the far side of the lake, walking steadily as he took his own counsel. Plans were formulated, reviewed, and discarded, but he felt no despair, only a quickening sense of challenge. By sundown, he was at the river, melding with travelers waiting for a commercial barge, another nameless passenger on his way to the Holy City.

11. Bereavement

Months passed.

The bloom at last returned to Mara's cheeks. Spring came, and the needra gave birth to their calves, and the barbarian mares delivered seven healthy foals to add to the stables. With Lujan's permission, Hokanu had appropriated two patrols of swordsmen and, into the summer, proceeded to teach them to ride, and then to drill on horseback in formation.

The dust from such maneuvers overhung the fields in the dry heat, and the lakeshore in the late afternoons became boisterous with the laughter and chaffing as off-duty comrades watched the chosen few swim their barbarian beasts, or sluice the sweat of workout off glossy hides. More than riders and horses emerged wet, some days when the play got rough. From the terraced balcony that Tasaio of the Minwanabi had once used to oversee field tactics, Mara often watched. She was attended by maids, and her young son, and increasingly often by her husband, still wearing his riding leathers, saber, and quirt.

One afternoon, as a scarred and grizzled old veteran bent to kiss his chosen mare on the muzzle, Mara gave the first carefree smile she had shown in weeks. "The men are certainly becoming used to the horses. Not a few of their sweethearts have been complaining that they spend more time in the stables than they do in their rightful beds."

Hokanu grinned and slipped his hand around her slender middle. "Are you making such complaint, wife?"

Mara turned in his arms, and caught Justin staring with guilelessly wide blue eyes. The look reminded her poignantly of his father, before he made a rude symbol with his hands that he certainly had not learned from his nurses. "You're going to make a baby tonight," he said, proud of his deduction, and not at all nonplussed when the nearest of his nurses gave his cheek an open-handed slap.

"Impertinent boy! How dare you speak to your mother so? And wherever you learned that finger sign, you'll be whipped if you try it again."

With a red-faced bow to master and mistress, the maid hustled a protesting Justin off to bed.

"But the sun's still up," his voice pealed back in protest. "How can I
go to sleep when I can still see outside?"

The pair disappeared around the stair that led down the hill, Justin's
hair catching the lowering light like flame.

"By the gods, he's growing up," Hokanu said fondly. "We're going to
have to find him an arms tutor soon. His ciphers and writing are plainly
not enough to keep him from spying on the servants."

"He wasn't." Mara's hands tightened around her husband's trim
middle, appreciative of the muscles that his hours in the saddle kept
firm. "He sneaks out to the barracks, or the slave quarters, every
chance he gets. And listens intently when the men boast of their feats
with ladies of the Reed Life or serving girls. He is his father's son when it
comes to staring at the women, and something he said to my maid
Kesha this morning made her blush like a maiden, which she's
not."

Her head tilted sideways, and she regarded her husband through her
lashes. "He's a randy, rude little boy who had better be married off
young, lest he sow Acoma bastards like hwaet, and have half the fathers of
girls in the Nations after him with swords."

Hokanu chuckled. "Of all the problems you might have with him, that
one worries me least."

Mara's eyes widened. "He's barely seven!"

"High time he had a little brother, then," Hokanu said. "Another
little demon to look after, to keep his mind off bigger trouble."

"You're a randy, rude little boy," Mara retaliated, and with a quick,
breathless laugh slipped out of his arms. She raced off down the hill with
her robe half-undone in abandon.

Hokanu gathered himself in surprise and followed. Delight, more than
exertion, caused his face to flush. His Lady had not been playful for
entirely too long, since the poisoning. As he knew she desired, he ran
easily, and did not extend his long, athletic stride to overtake her until
she had reached the glen by the lakeshore.

The summer was fully upon them. Though dry, the grasses still retained a trace of green. The stinging insects of the early season had
dispersed, and the shrill of night callers had not yet died for the season.
The air was syrupy warm. Hokanu caught his wife in a flying tackle, and
both of them tumbled to the earth, breathless, disheveled, and utterly
departed from solemnity.

Mara said, "My Lord and consort, we seem to have a problem between us, that being a shortage of heirs."

His fingers were already loosening the rest of the ties on her underrobe. "Lujan's sentries patrol the lakeshore after dark."

Her smile came back to him, a flash of white in the dusk. "Then we have no time to lose, on several counts."

"That," Hokanu said gaily, "is hardly a problem." After that, neither of them had the attention to spare for talk.

The much-longed-for, and overly disputed, heir to the Shinzawai must have been conceived on that night, either there under the open sky, or later, amid scented cushions, after a late-night cup of sā wine shared in their private chambers. Six weeks later, Mara was sure. She knew the signs, and though she woke feeling miserable, Hokanu could hear her singing in the mornings. His smile was bittersweet. What he knew, and she did not, was that this child to come would be her last, the miracle that was all the healers of Hantukama's priesthood had been able to bestow upon her.

Until he overheard a speculative argument between the kitchen scullions and the bastard child of one of the household factors, it never occurred to him that the babe, when it came, might be female. He let the matter lie, and took no notice of the bets that were being laid in the barracks over the forthcoming child's unknown sex.

That this, Mara's last child, who was to be heir to his family name and fortune, might not be a son quite simply did not bear thinking about.

The pregnancy that had begun in such carefree abandon did not continue in the same vein—not since the poisoning, and not since the attempts on the lives of Acoma allies. Lujan tripled his patrols and personally inspected the checkpoints in the passes. The prayer gate over the river entrance to the lake was never without watchers in its towers, and a company of warriors was always armed and at the ready. But autumn came, and the needra culls were driven to market, and commerce went on without interruption. Even the silk caravans suffered no raid, which was not usual, and did nothing to set anyone at ease. Jican spent hours mumbling over armloads of tally slates. Not even the surplus of profits seemed to please him.

"Nature is often most bountiful before the severest of storms," he grumbled pessimistically when Mara complained that his pacing was making her neck ache. Weighed down by her swollen middle, she could hardly walk the floor with him, to follow his rendering of accounts.

"It's too quiet by far," said the little hadonra, dropping like an arrow-shot bird to the cushions before the mistress's writing desk. "I don't like it, and I don't believe that Jiro is sitting by innocently, up to his nose in old scrolls."

In fact, Arakasi's agents had sent word. Jiro was not idle, but had been hiring engineers and joiners to build strange-looking machinery in what had been his father's marshaling yard. That the equipment was intended for siege and sapping was probable, and by dint of suggestively placed gossip, old Frasai of the Tonmargu had been convinced by Lord Hoppara of the Xacatecas to spend imperial funds. Workers had been taken on to repair the cracks in the walls of Kentosani, and in the Emperor's inner citadel, caused by the earthquake set loose by the renegade magician Milamber when he had wreaked havoc at the Imperial Games years past.

As autumn dragged on, and the wet season threatened, Mara found herself as restless as her hadonra, and unable to do so much as pace. Her only respite came upon Justin's eighth birthday, when Hokanu presented him with his first real sword, not a mock weapon used by children. He had received the well-made small blade with solemnity and resisted the impulse to rush around swinging it at everything in sight. If Keyoke had instructed him on the proper behavior, such forbearance was lacking the next morning, when Justin charged with bared blade down the hillside to his lesson from his arms tutor.

Mara saw her son from the terrace, wishing she could go watch Justin take his instruction. But her healers would not let her stir from her cushions, and her husband, who usually was indulgent when she became stubborn, would not relent. The heir that she carried must not be risked. To ease her confinement, anything she requested was sent for.

Gifts from other nobles arrived as her time approached, some lavish, others minor tokens, the minimum tradition demanded. An expensive but undeniably ugly vase was Jiro's gift to the expectant Servant of the Empire. Amused to sardonic humor, she ordered it given to her servants so they might use it to carry out night soils from the house.

But her most welcome gift of all were the rare books delivered in chests that smelled of mildew and dust. Isashani had sent them, instead of the more usual lacquered boxes or exotic songbirds. Upon reading the inscription on the gift card, Mara had laughed. Beneath the makeup, and the feminine airs, there was no limit to Isashani's shrewdness. It was her son, Hoppara, who sent a traditional if astonishingly extravagant arrangement of sweet flowers.

Surrounded by painted vases, Mara breathed in the perfume of cut kekali blossoms and tried not to think of Kevin the barbarian, who had first taught her what it was to be a woman in the dusk of a garden, years past. A frown on her face that had nothing to do with the lighting, she studied a treatise on weapons and campaigns of war. Her frown deepened as she considered the likelihood that Jiro had also studied this very text. From there her thoughts wandered. Arakasi's messages arrived irregularly since she had charged him with his mission to acquire the Hamoi Tong's records. She had not seen him in months, and missed his quick wit and his unfailing appreciation of odd gossip. Closing the book, she tried to imagine his location. Perhaps he sat in some distant inn, disguised as a needra driver, or a sailor. Or he might be lunching late with a merchant in some distant city. She refused to consider that he could very well be dead.

Arakasi at that moment lay on his side amid a tangle of silk sheets, and ran light, expert fingers down the thigh of a nubile girl. That she was by binding contract another man's property, and that he risked his very life to seduce her, was not at the forefront of his thoughts. He had come in through the window. The absent master's bedchambers in the midafternoon were the last place any servant or guardsman bent on protecting the virtue of a slave concubine would expect to find her with a lover.

The girl was bored enough to be excited by the adventure, and young enough to believe herself immune to misfortune. Her latest master was old, and fat, and his prowess had flagged with age. Arakasi posed a different sort of challenge. It was she who was jaded, having been trained for pleasure and bed sport since the age of six. Whether or not he could successfully excite her was the sum of the issue at hand.

For Mara's Spy Master, the stakes that he dallied to win were a great deal higher.

In the half-light shed by closed screens, the air smelled heavy with incense and the girl's perfume. The sheets had been treated with herbs that in some circles were considered aphrodisiacs. Arakasi, who had read texts on medicine, knew the belief was a myth. The elderly master had wealth enough not to care if his money had been wasted. The miasma of scents was powerfully cloying, causing Arakasi to regret that the screens must stay closed. Almost, he would rather have endured the stinking loincloth and apron he had bought from the dyers in Sulan-Qu, which he used for disguise when he did not want well-bred passersby examining his face too closely. The reek at least would have kept him alert. As it was, he had to fight not to fall fatally asleep.

The girl shifted. Sheets slid away from her body with a hiss of silk on skin. She was magnificent, outlined in afternoon light, her hair in heavy honey-colored curls on the pillows. Slant eyes the color of jade fixed on Arakasi. "I never said I had a sister."

She referred to a comment some minutes old. The Spy Master's fingers slipped past her hip, dipped down, and continued stroking. Her magnificent eyes drooped half-closed, and her hands spasmed on the silk like a cat's paws, kneading.

The velvet-soft voice of Arakasi said, "I know from the merchant who sold your contract."

She stiffened under his touch, spoiling ten minutes of his careful ministrations. She had had men enough that she did not care. "That was not a prudent remark."

Insult did not enter into the question; that she was in truth little better than a very expensive prostitute was not the issue. Who had been the sister's buyer: that was dangerous knowledge, and the dealer who had made the transaction would hardly be so free, or so foolhardy, that he would tell. Arakasi stroked aside honey-gold locks, and cradled the back of the girl's neck. "I am not a prudent man, Kamlio."

Her eyes widened and her lips shaped a wicked smile. "You are not." Then her expression turned thoughtful. "You are a strange man." Breathing deeply, she feigned a pout. "Sometimes I think you are a noble, playing the part of a poor merchant." She fixed him with a steady gaze. "Your eyes are older than your appearance." When a lingering moment passed, and he gave no answer, she said, "You are not very forthcoming." Then she licked her lips suggestively. "Neither are you amusing. So. Amuse me. I am someone else's toy. Why should I risk disgrace to become yours?"

As Arakasi drew breath to reply, Kamlio raised a finger and stopped his lips. Her nails were dusted with gilt, costliest of cosmetics. "Don't say you'll buy me my freedom for love. That would be trite."

Arakasi blessed the rosy flesh of her fingertips with a kiss. Then, very gently, he removed her hand so he could speak. His expression was faintly offended. "It would not be trite. It would be true." Mara had set no limits on his expenses, ever, and for stakes so high as access to the tong's most guarded chieftain, she would hardly stint his needs.

The girl in his arms went icy with distrust. To free her from the seven-year contract signed and sold to her aged master would be worth the cost of a town house; but to buy out her worth, and the expense of her training and upbringing, from the merchant of the pleasure house who had invested in her—that would be as much as a small estate. Her contracts would be sold, and sold again, until she was faded to the point where even her skills between the sheets would be spurned. "You were never so rich." Even her voice was contemptuous. "And if the master who employs you is so wealthy, then I risk my very life to be speaking to you."

Arakasi bent his head and kissed her neck. His hands did not tighten against her tenseness; she could at any moment draw away, a nuance she understood, and in appreciation of the subtlety, she kept still. Few men treated her as though she had a will of her own, or feelings. This one was rare. And his hands were very schooled. She heard the note of sincerity in his voice as he added, "But I work for no master."

His tone conveyed the nuance. His mistress, then, would have little use for an expensive courtesan. The offer of freedom might be genuine, if he had access to the money.

Arakasi's hands recovered lost ground, and Kamlio quivered. He was more than rare: he was gifted. She settled a little, her flank melting into the curve of his body.

As though the footsteps of servants did not come and go in the corridor, separated by only a screen, Arakasi's touch drifted down the girl's golden flesh. She leaned into him. Pleasure came rarely enough to her, who was a thing bought and sold to meet the needs of others. Discovery might earn her a beating; her partner would wind up dishonorably dead on a rope end. He was either exceptionally brave, or else careless unto insanity. Through skin that had been caressed and cajoled into unwonted sensitivity, the girl could feel the unhurried beat of his heart.

"This mistress," Kamlio murmured languidly. "She means so very much to you?"

"Just at this moment I was not thinking of her," Arakasi said, but it was not his words that convinced as his lips met hers with a tenderness akin to worship. The kiss blurred all doubts and, soon after, all thoughts. The filtered sunlight through the windows blended with a red-golden haze behind her eyes, as passion was drawn out of her and savored like fine wine.

At last, gasping and drenched with the fine sweat of lovemaking, Kamlio forgot herself and clung to the lean form of the man as she exploded into relief. She laughed and she wept, and somewhere between amazement and exhaustion, she whispered the location of the sister sold away in far Ontoset.

Despite his mysterious background, it did not occur to Kamlio that her partner might be no more than a consummate actor until she rolled over.

The light touch that cradled her body was no more than the fold of warm sheets. She flung back damp hair, her beautiful eyes narrowed and furious to find the window opened, and himself gone, even to the clothes he had worn.

She opened her lips to call out, in a pique that would see him caught and executed, never mind his clever hands and lying promises. But on the moment the air filled her lungs, the latch on the screen tripped up.

Arakasi must have heard the heavy tread of her elderly master, returned early from his meeting with his hadonra. Stoop-shouldered, palsied, grey-haired, he shuffled into her chamber. His milky eyes blinked at the twisted sheets, and his dry, chill hands reached out and stroked her skin, heated still, and damp from a surfeit of passion.

"My dear, are you ill?" he said in his old man's voice.

"Bad dreams," she said, sulky, but trained to instinct to use the mood to increase her allure. "I dozed in the afternoon heat, and had nightmares, nothing more." Grateful that her deft, dark-haired lover had made clean his escape, Kamlio sighed and bent her skills upon her decrepit master, who was harder, it sometimes seemed, to please than she was.

Outside the window, screened from sight by a veiling of vines and unkempt akasi, Arakasi listened intently to the sounds that issued from the bedchamber. In relief, and an uncharacteristic anger, he silently donned his clothing. He had lied only once: never had he ceased thinking of his mistress. Over the years since he had sworn to Acoma service, Mara had become the linchpin of his life.

But the girl, half-spoiled, fully hardened to the resentment of a whore brought up to the Reed Life, had touched him. His care for her had been real, and that by itself was disturbing. Arakasi shook off the memory of Kamlio's long, fine hair and her jewel-clear eyes. He had work to do, before her freedom from usage could be arranged. For the information she had delivered in the naïve belief that she had disclosed only a family secret was the possible location of the harem of the Hamoi Tong's Obajan. The tenuous link she had managed to retain with her sister, used to exchange erratic communication, held far more peril than she knew.

It had taken months for Arakasi to trace a rumor that a girl of unusual beauty, a sister to another, had been purchased by a certain trader, one whom Arakasi had suspected as a Hamoi Tong agent. He was now dead, a necessary by-product of Arakasi's identifying him, but his purchase of so expensive a courtesan led Arakasi to the near certainty that she must belong to the Obajan, or one of his closest lieutenants.

And the fact she had been sent to Ontoset made peculiar sense; it was safer for the tong to have its seat so distant from where it was contacted, a minor shrine outside the Temple of Turakamu. Arakasi himself had many agents who suspected he was based in Jamar or Yankora, because that was where all their messages originated.

Arakasi had resisted the temptation to leave at once for Ontoset and had spent valuable weeks in Kentosani seeking out the girl's sister.

The Spy Master had studied his prey for weeks before making himself known to her. Turning away Kamlio's questions with vague references, he led her to believe him the son of some powerful noble, fallen to low estate because of a romantic adventure.

As he repeatedly risked shameful death to see her, at last Kamlio had welcomed him to her bed.

Without her, Arakasi might have searched a lifetime and never obtained a clue to what he sought by Mara's command. As he sat, still as stone, awaiting the dusk and the chance to steal away, he pondered how much he owed to a girl who had been raised up to be no more than a bed toy. He knew he should leave this woman and never see her again, but something in him had been touched. Now he confronted a new fear: that he might entreat Mara to intercede and buy the girl's contract, and that, once free, Kamlio might laugh at his genuine care for her.

For a man brought up by women of the Reed Life, understanding of her contempt came all too easily. Veiled by the bushes, suffering insect bites and muscle cramps from his pose of forced stillness, Arakasi sighed. He closed his eyes, but could not escape the sounds of Kamlio's marathon efforts in the bedchamber to gratify the lechery of a man too old to perform. Arakasi endured a wait that passed painfully slowly. Once he was sure the old master was asleep, he silently made his departure. But with him came vivid memories, and the uncomfortable, unwanted awareness that he had come to care for Kamlio. His feelings for her were folly; any emotional ties to those not of the Acoma made him vulnerable. And he knew that if he was vulnerable, so then was Lady Mara.

The messenger hesitated after he made his bow. Breathless still from his run through the hills bordering the estate, he might have been taking an ordinary pause to recover his wind; except that his hands were tense, and the eyes he raised to Hokanu were dark with pity.

The Shinzawai heir was not a man to shy from misfortune. Campaigns in the field had taught him that setbacks must be faced at once, and overcome, lest enemies gain opening and triumph. "The news is bad," he said quickly. "Tell me."

Still mute, and with a second bow made out of sympathy, the messenger drew a scroll out of a carry tube fashioned of bone strips laced together with cord. The instant Hokanu saw the red dye that edged the parchment, he knew: the word was a death, and even as he accepted the document and cracked the seal, he guessed the name inside would be his father's.

The timing could not be worse, he thought in that stunned, disbelieving interval before grief struck his mind like a fist. His father, gone. The man who had understood him as no other; who had adopted him when his blood sire had been called into the Assembly of Magicians, and who had raised him with all the love any son could require.

There would be no more midnight talks over hwaet beer, or jokes about hangovers in the mornings. There would be no more scholarly arguments, or reprimands, or shared elation over victories. The grandchild soon to be born to Mara would never meet his grandfather.

Fighting sudden tears, Hokanu found himself mechanically dismissing the messenger. Jican appeared, as if spell-called, and quietly dealt with the matter of refreshments and disposition of the bone token that couriers received in acknowledgment of completion of their missions. The hadonra finished with necessities, and turned back to his mistress's husband, expectant. Hokanu had not moved, except to crush the red-bordered scroll between his fist.

"The news was bad," Jican surmised in commiseration.

"My father," Hokanu said tightly. "He died in his sleep, in no pain, of natural causes." He shut his eyes a moment, opened them, and added, "Our enemies will be gloating, nonetheless."

Jican fingered the tassels on his sash, diffident, careworn, and silent. He had met Kamatsu of the Shinzawai; he knew the Lord's hadonra well. The most enduring tribute he could think to mention was not the usual one, or the most elegant. He spoke anyway. "He is a man who will be missed by his servants, young master. He was well loved."

Hokanu raised eyes dark with hurt. "My father was like that." He sighed. "He abused no man and no beast. His heart was great. Like Mara, he was able to see past tradition with fairness. Because of him, I am all that I am."

Jican allowed the silence to stretch unbroken, while outside the window the footsteps of a sentry passed by. Then he suggested, very gently, "Mara is in the work shed with the toy maker."

The new-made Lord of Shinzawai nodded. He went to seek his wife with a weight on his elegant shoulders that the news he carried made fearful. More than ever, the heir his Lady carried was important. For while Hokanu had cousins aplenty, and even a bastard nephew or three, none of them had grown up schooled to his foster father's breadth of vision. Not a one of them had the perception and the clarity of thought to fill the shoes of the man who had been the Emperor Ichindar's right hand.

The ambience of the work shed was an amalgam of dust, warmth shed into dimness by the sunlit tiles of the roof, and the aromatic scents of wood shavings, resins, and the pungency of needra glue. The corners were murky with shelves of scrap cloth, baskets of feathers, and an orderly arrangement of woodworker's tools, among which was a priceless metal knife, imported from the barbarian world, and with which Mara had bought the undying admiration and services of Orcato, toy maker, genius, and dissembler, with a penchant for lewd jokes and drink. Mara overlooked his coarseness, his tendency to forget her femininity and speak with her as if she were an equal, and his stink, which was always of unwashed sweat and the tecca seeds with which he spiced his food. When Hokanu entered, Lady and artisan were engaged with bent heads over a waist-high contraption of wood, around which were arrayed an army of painted toy soldiers.

"There," said Orcato in his tremulous old-man's voice that also held childish enthusiasm. "If you'd pull that string and release that lever, there, mistress, we'll know if we've wasted our time."

His sarcasm was belied by the unholy gleam of joy in his eyes; disheveled, hot, and heavily pregnant, Mara bent a face marred by a smear of dust across one cheek. She gave an unladylike whoop and yanked a tasseled cord.

The contrivance on the floor responded with a click, a whap, and a violent whipping of cord, timber, and wicker. What Hokanu recognized as a replica of an engine designed to hurl rocks over the walls of a besieged city did not perform its intended office. Instead, its throwing arm spun in an arc, discharging its missiles amid the neat ranks of its allies. Toy soldiers scattered and bounced through the dusty air, and rocks cracked in rebound off the walls. Hokanu ducked the ricochets and winced at the Lady's unfettered yell of delight.

Orcato the toy maker cackled with pleasure and from a pocket beneath his needra-hide apron produced a flask. "A toast to the Gods of Prank and Mischief?" He offered the Lady a swig, and froze, seeing Hokanu in the doorway.

"We've done it, my Lord," he announced, blithe as a boy in his excitement. "Found a way to turn Jiro's penchant for engines back upon his own troops." He paused, drank deeply, and cackled again, then offered his dripping flask to the master.

It was Mara who noticed the stiffness of Hokanu's face. "What has happened?" she asked, her sudden concern as jarring as a shout. She maneuvered her swollen belly around the toy engine, stepping upon the scattered ranks of soldiers.

Stung on top of grief by the sudden draining of joy from her face, Hokanu struggled for words.

"Dear gods," Mara murmured, reaching him, and awkwardly seeking his embrace. "It's your father, isn't it?" She tugged him to her, the unborn bulk of their child pressed between. He could feel her tremble and knew her sorrow was real. Everywhere, his father had been loved. He heard his voice recite woodenly, "He died naturally. In no pain. In his bed."

The toy maker handed over his flask. Hokanu accepted, and swallowed without much noticing what brew it contained. The sting of it freed his voice, and his thoughts began sluggishly to function. "There will be a state funeral. I must be present." Too much was he aware of his pregnant wife's vulnerability and the heir that now must not be risked. As he felt her drawing breath, he shook his head and said quickly, "No. You will not go. I will not expose you or our unborn child to our enemies."

She moved, on the point of protest.

Hokanu shook her gently, uncaring that the noxious spirits slopped from the flask with the gesture, staining the shoulder of her robe. "No. Kamatsu would understand, my love. He would do as I must, and implore you to go and visit your adoptive family, whom you have sorely neglected of late. You will travel to Kentosani and pay your respects to your Emperor Ichindar. He has lost a staunch defender in my father. It is seemly that you be there to temper his grief."

She relaxed against him; and he read in that her understanding, and her gratitude. She would not argue with him, although he knew by the way she hid her face in his sleeve that she wept for him, and for the fact that the ugliness of politics must see her parted from his side in his hour of bereavement.

"My Lady," he said softly, and buried his own face in her hair.

Behind him, across a floor littered with the fallen effigies of Jiro's army, the toy maker slipped soundlessly out.

12. Warning

The crowd shouted.

Acoma soldiers escorting their mistress fought to keep even ranks against the relentless press of bodies, all calling out in awe and appreciation of the Lady who was Servant of the Empire, and all straining with outstretched arms to gain even a touch of the curtains that shrouded her litter. Legend held that the touch of a Servant could bestow good fortune. Since the Lady herself was not within reach, her soldiers had learned that the commoners would settle for her clothing, or, barring that, for the curtains of her litter. After one time caught off guard, when Mara had gone out with what had seemed a suitable escort before the title had been bestowed by the Emperor, and arriving at an appointment across the city with both her robes and her litter hangings in soiled disarray, her officers had learned better.

Now Mara did not venture forth in public with fewer than an escort of fifty. Today, Lujan decided in a sweat, even fifty were barely sufficient. The folk loved their Good Servant to the point where they would risk crushed toes, bruises, and even a blow from a spear butt to get close to her. The worst, the most unnerving aspect of her popularity, was that the masses took no offense at the soldiers' roughness in holding them back. They shoved willingly into abuse that came near to serious injury, cheering and crying Mara's name.

Muffled in a plain robe, and out of sight beyond heavy curtains that trapped the heat uncomfortably, Mara lay with closed eyes on her cushions, her hands cradled upon her swollen middle. She could barely smell the temple incense that was particular to the Holy City, and carried so many memories. The perfume of the flowering trees reached her not at all, nor the musical calls of the vendors. She could only endure the jostle of the masses, and hear their deep-throated shouts. Wistfully she recalled the days of her youth, when, as a novice of Lashima's temple, she had walked these very streets on bare feet. She tried not to think of another later time, when a tall, red-haired barbarian had strode by the side of her litter, filling her ears with impertinent comments, and her eyes with his smile.

In the suffocating darkness behind drapes dyed red in deference to the Death God and the passing of Hokanu's father, she pondered instead upon her husband, gone alone to attend the state funeral, to face enemies and plotting, and to determine which of his father's friends would stand by him, now that he assumed the mantle of House Shinzawai. Heirless, he would become scrutinized by the merchants who sold courtesan contracts; he would be flirted with and flattered by unmarried younger daughters who sought to elevate their status by the chance to bear a powerful man's bastard.

She wished, thinking of her husband, that their leavetaking had not needed to be so hasty. But her birthing time was very near, and with the passing of a Lord so high in the imperial power structure, more than House Shinzawai must be secured through the change. The death of Kamatsu left vacant a prominent post in the Emperor's council, and political machinations would follow until that power had been redistributed into other hands.

More than her personal safety required Mara to visit the Emperor's family. And although the palace Imperial Whites would guard her young son, Justin, with all of the vigilance they showed to the Light of Heaven's own children, she worried.

For since the abolishment of the Warlord's office, with the High Council Hall filled only with echoes of the past, the palace had become the center of all intrigues. Arakasi had agents there; they would keep watch to scent out plots. But her life would be more confined, more chained to ceremony, and bereft of the day-to-day challenges of commerce she enjoyed while at home. Although Jican was more than trustworthy to handle trade matters in her absence, that fact did not console. Beneath lay the true apprehension: she did not wish to lie in childbirth in a strange bed, in the absence of Hokanu's loving protection. Were the child to come due before she could return home, her time in Kentosani must of necessity be prolonged, until the young infant was able to withstand the rigors of travel.

Mara's fingers tightened over her damp robes, as if to stifle the unborn child's healthy kicks. She was visited by an indefinable dread of the forces at work against them all, Acoma, Shinzawai, and the Emperor, that would neither wait nor rest while the babes who were in line to inherit spent the necessary years growing up.

The litter swooped down, and came to rest with barely a jar. Mara pushed herself upright as the curtains were parted, letting in a dazzle of light off sun-washed marble. She had reached the palace, and so deep was her preoccupation that only now did she notice that the din of the crowd had become distanced; the commons shouted and called still, but from outside the wood and gilt gateway that led into the Imperial Quarter of the City.

"My Lady?" questioned Saric. The Acoma First Adviser offered his hand to raise her. Incomo was not along on this trip, but had accompanied Hokanu to help assess the machinations of the guests that would descend upon the Shinzawai estates for the funeral. Though still in his thirties, Saric had learned much since he had left soldiers' ranks to take office with the Acoma. Mara had hesitated long before formally bestowing the office, and for a while had considered Incomo for the position, as he had served in that role with the Minwanabi. But in the end she had trusted his predecessor's first judgment: despite her constant scolding of him, Nacoya, Mara's previous First Adviser, thought highly of his nimble wit and quick apprehension. Saric was proving a good choice. Mara looked up, measuring the hazel eyes of the man, who looked steadily back, a smile very like his cousin Lujan's upon his lips.

"What are you thinking, my Lady?" he asked as he raised her from her litter. A gleam in his eyes belied the innocence of the question, and seeing that his mistress observed as much, he chuckled under his breath. Like Lujan, he often dared informality close to insolence.

Dryly, inspecting his well-made but otherwise plain traveling robe, she said, "I'm thinking we need to work upon your perceptions of formal garb."

"I have been too busy since gaining my office to find time for tailors, my Lady. I'll see to formal garb at once." Then he grinned. "I doubt the old grandmother's ceremonial regalia would fit me yet."

Meaning he had not an aged stoop to his shoulders, nor nearly enough grey hair. Touched by a pang for old Nacoya that held more of memory than grief, Mara said, "You have a free, loose tongue to speak of your responsibilities, when as far as I can see, you have already lost charge of my heir."

"Justin?" With a startled raise of eyebrows, Saric half turned. The boy was indeed gone from his side, when he had been there just a half-instant sooner. Saric hid an impulse to swear behind a stony expression. He ought to have anticipated the boy's restlessness, after the tantrum that had erupted earlier, when Justin had been forced to ride in a litter, rather than his preferred seat of conveyance: perched upon Lujan's broad shoulders at the head of the procession. That in the open streets, jammed with hordes of people out to admire the Good Servant, a boy left exposed offered a tempting target for enemy assassins did not signify to his childish penchant for adventure.

A fast glance around the marble courtyard, with its beautiful trees festooned with flowering vines, showed several archways the boy might have dashed through to hide.

"Well," said Mara regretfully, "he's unlikely to get himself killed in the palace, surrounded by two thousand Imperial Whites." She did not need to add that he was sure to get himself neck-deep into other mischief. And with the Emperor himself come out to greet her, to order soldiers out searching before completing the proper formalities of welcome would be an insult.

She straightened her sash, raised her chin, and stepped forward, prepared to make her bow before the Light of Heaven.

Ichindar himself offered his hand to help her back to her feet before her gravid form caused her awkwardness. His touch was warm, if every bone in his hand could be felt. Mara smiled, and gazed into his face, which was lined early by care. Although still in his prime, Ichindar bore the weight of his mantle and the mark of his responsibility. He had grown stooped since she had seen him last, and his eyes seemed larger, for his face had thinned. Never a warrior, he relied on the cut and richness of his robes to lend his figure the necessary majesty of his office. Today he seemed drowned in a diamond sparkle of cloth interwoven with priceless silver threadwork. His hair lay limp under a massive, golden-plumed headdress, and at throat, wrist, and waist he wore shining gold. His eyes were warm and bright as he studied her in turn, and gave her the imperial greeting.

Then, formalities dispensed with, he freed her wrists and removed his massive headdress. A servant ran forward, bowed to earth, and accepted its weight in silence. Ichindar, ninety-one times Emperor of Tsuranuanni, raked hands that sparkled with rings through honey-brown hair and grinned. "I've missed you, Lady. It has been long since you have brought us your company." His tone rang genuine, although it was no secret that he preferred male company. Driven by the need for an heir, he shared his nights with an endless succession of wives and consorts, all chosen for beauty and their prospects of bearing children rather than for wit.

But Mara he had named Servant of the Empire for her service in securing his power upon the golden throne. She had brought stability to the Empire at large through her help in abolishment of the Warlord's office, contention for which had dragged the Nations to the brink of civil war far too many times.

Although the course charted since was still unsteady, and although the traditionalist faction won itself more supporters daily, Ichindar counted Lady Mara a powerful ally and, more, a friend; her coming brought him rare joy. He studied her closely, saw her surreptitious glances toward the archways, and laughed. "Your son ran off just a moment ago with my eldest daughter, Jihilia. He's in the fruit gardens with her, probably in a tree picking green jomach. Shall we go there and slap sticky hands before both of them give themselves bellyaches?"

Mara's face softened. "Bellyaches would be the least of it," she confessed. "If I know my boy, there are probably sentries under dishonorable bombardment."

But by the time Mara had extricated herself from her train of servants and baggage, and the Emperor's personal staff had rearranged itself around her presence, a high, boyish shout of rage echoed over the sunlit serenity of the courtyard. As one, Mara and Ichindar hurried their steps, outdistancing their escort through the leftward arch.

They rushed down a path lined with bushes and beds of rare flowers, and reached the garden courtyard in time to hear a splash. The boy, Justin, stood on the marble rim of a fish pool, his hands on his hips, and his chest puffed out like a jigabird cock's. At his feet, dragged back by a sodden mess of white-and-gold robes, the girl sat in the water, her blond hair plastered to her head, and expensive makeup dribbled in smears down her furious face.

Mara's face assumed its sternest maternal expression, while the Emperor choked back laughter. But before either could intervene in what was about to develop into a wrestling match, a third figure raced into the fray, trailing robes as expensive as the girl's, but redolent with exotic perfumes. She also was blond, and radiantly beautiful, despite her hand-wringing protestations and an evident uncertainty about the more forceful aspects of parenthood.

"Oh!" she cried. "Oh! Miserable boy, what have you done to my jewel?"

Justin turned red-faced upon her, and said glibly and clearly over Jehilia's shouting, "She slugged me in the face, did your jewel."

"Oh!" cried the woman. "She would not have! My jewel!"

At this point, Mara strode forward, grabbed Justin by the arm, and hauled him off his perch on the pool rim. "So you tripped her, is that it?"

She received for her answer an insolent grin, and a flash of blue eyes amid a sun-freckled face. Her open-handed slap across the boy's cheeks ended the smile, and although his eye showed the beginnings of a purple bruise, Mara gave him no quarter. "You will give the Princess your hand, help her out of the fish pool, and apologize."

As the boy opened his mouth for protest, she shook him briskly. "Do this now, Justin. You have sullied Acoma honor and must make amends."

The offended Jehilia dragged herself to her feet. Fish darted in agitated swirls around her ankles as, glowering with temper, she prepared to be indulged.

"Oh, my precious, get out of that water," wailed the woman, whose resemblance identified her as Lady Tamara, Ichindar's first wife, and mother to the girl. "You could take ill, standing about soaking wet!"

Jehilia scowled, her rose-and-gilt complexion flushed crimson. She stared at Justin's extended hand as though it were a viper, while her father—Emperor of all Tsuranuanni and Light of Heaven—looked on in helpless amusement. He was better at ruling between warring Lords than at managing disputes between his offspring and those of his adopted family.

Mara assessed the impasse, and crisply admonished the girl. "Take Justin's hand, Princess. It is the only right thing to do, since you shamed his pride by striking him. It is cowardly to strike a man, since he will not hit a female in return. If Justin tripped you, you earned your ducking first, and I'd say you must learn manners from the misfortune. Act like a grown lady, or else I'll see your nurses thrash you both like the children you most certainly are."

"Oh! My darling should never be thrashed!" cried the mother of the Emperor's eldest. "Were anyone to try, I should faint."

At this, Ichindar turned hazel eyes bright with irony upon the Lady of the Acoma. "My life is made miserable by a surfeit of frail women. The children cannot be thrashed, or they will faint."

Mara laughed. "Thrash the children as they deserve, and let the ladies swoon all they wish. It might serve to harden them."

"Oh!" The Lady paled. As angry now as her daughter, she retorted, "Our Light of Heaven would not dare! He is a gentle man, and his wives all adore him."

Ichindar's mouth curved with faint distaste. Plainly, he would withdraw rather than endure further disharmony. Women confounded him, Mara knew. Saddened that he seemed so browbeaten, and also given insight into how it must feel to have been forced into matrimonial duty at the age of twelve, with a different wife or concubine sent to share the imperial bed each and every month thereafter, she again intervened.

Justin completed his apology to Jehilia. He spoke his words without sullenness or rancor, as quick to forgive as his barbarian father. When he completed his bow, Mara caught the girl's icy fingers and bundled her firmly toward her distraught and angry mother. "Jehilia," said the Lady of the Acoma, "take Lady Tamara inside and see her in care of a good maid. Then change your clothes, and come visit me in my garden court. I will show you, as my brother showed me, what to do when importunate boys try to trip you."

Jehilia's fury dissolved into delighted surprise. "You know how to wrestle, Good Servant?"

Mara laughed. "I'll teach you, and if Justin agrees to keep you clear of fish pools, he will help."

At her side, the heir to the Acoma mantle gave a whoop of contentment, and Jehilia, no less restrained, shouted like a warrior. Then she spun in a whirl of wet hair and chivvied her distraught and protesting mother from the garden, while Ichindar stared after in astonishment.

He turned toward Mara with a look of mystified respect. "I should command your presence more often, to marshal the conduct of my harem."

Mara's smile died. "Great gods, no. Do you know nothing of women? The best way to foment dissension among them is to give them into the power of another female. I'd find myself marshal of a nasty, robe-tearing rebellion, my Lord Emperor. And the only problem I can see between your august self and your harem is that they outnumber you, five hundred and thirty-seven to one."

The Emperor of all Tsuranuanni laughed. "True enough. I am the most jigahen-pecked husband in all of the Nations. If the ladies were not all so beautiful, I might find it easier to chastise them."

Mara made a sound through her nose. "According to my Force Commander, who cuts a swath through the maidens in his leave time, the prettier the face, the greater the need for chastisement."

"Perhaps," Ichindar allowed, a trace of wistfulness in his voice. "If I knew them better, I might be more inclined. Only those who bear me a child remain, you must remember. Of those five hundred . . . however many wives and consorts, I've spoken to only seven on more than a handful of occasions." His troubled tone was not lost on Mara. Palace walls were no protection from the gossip of the streets: even the Light of Heaven had heard the whispers of his lack of manly power in fathering a son. Though almost twenty years a husband, he had but seven children, all girls, the eldest only two years older than Justin. Ichindar gestured toward the coolness of the foyer. "Refreshments await, my Lady Mara. In your condition, it would be insult to keep you on your feet in the sun for an instant longer."

A haze of smoke from the funeral rites hung heavy upon the air. The acrid scent of ash stung Hokanu's nostrils where he stood, elbow braced on the rail of a gallery that overlooked a courtyard filled with guests. After the opulent gardens of the Acoma estate and the imperial residence, the Shinzawai garden looked tiny. Guests moved along the crowded narrow paths, speaking in low voices, partaking of light refreshments provided by servants at every turn. With Kamatsu's rank and honor, many had come who had no clan or family ties with him, straining the hospitality of the house.

The ceremony to honor the Shinzawai departed had been rushed, owing to the heat; the body of the patriarch had been kept waiting only until the arrival of the heir. Many of the guests had reached the estates ahead of him; those more polite or less brazenly curious had waited to come until after Hokanu was in residence.

Late afternoon sunlight slanted through the smoke that coiled still from the fire. The recitation of Kamatsu's honors had been long, lasting well past noon. Now the ashes were yet too hot to scrape into the ceremonial urn Hokanu would carry to the sacred contemplation grove that sheltered the family natami. The air smelled of citrus and cloves and almonds, to sweeten the stench of death, and with other, rarer scents, of the ladies' perfumes and the sweet oils used to sleek the hair of the dandies. Now and again the breeze would part the smoke, and the scents of the flowers bundled in the crockery pots throughout the dooryard won out. Fainter was the ink-like pungence of the dyes in the crimson death hangings. Sometimes there came the redolence of cooked meats, new bread, and cakes. The kitchen staff were busy.

Hokanu lounged in his red robes, his eyes half-closed; he could have been a man lost in daydreams, except for the fist clenched white against the balustrade. Below him, conversations centered on political topics. Two subjects predominated: the eligibility of the bachelors who vied for the ten-year-old princess Jehilia's hand; and which Lord was most likely to be appointed by the Light of Heaven to take up the staff of office left vacant by Kamatsu's death.

The avaricious carrion eaters might have waited until the old man's ashes were cold, Hokanu thought with resentment.

A step sounded upon the worn plank floor behind him. His back tautened in expectation of another servant who would address him as ''my Lord''; but the title was not forthcoming. Touched by vague dread, Hokanu half turned, his hand closed in reflex over the heirloom metal sword he wore to honor the day, and with which he had cut the red cords around his father's wrists, in the ceremony to free the spirit into the halls of Turakamu.

But he faced no assassin. A man of medium stature awaited him, robed anonymously in dark fabric.

Hokanu released the silk-wrapped hilt of the weapon with guilty speed. ''I'm sorry. Great One, I heard no chime to warn of your presence.''

''I did not come by arcane means,'' said the magician in his deep, familiar voice. He pushed back his hood, and sunlight flooded over features that were lined and, today, looked almost bitter. The line of his cheek and brow bore a marked resemblance to Hokanu; and if the mystery in them had been less, the eyes would have been almost identical. The Great One, whose name was Fumita, crossed the space to the gallery rail and gave Hokanu a formal embrace.

By blood, the two were father and son; but according to the strictures of the Assembly, ties of blood could not matter.

Cautious of the weariness in the older man's face, Hokanu whispered, ''You should not be here.'' Conflicting emotions, barely contained, raged within the warrior. His father had come late to his powers, a rare but not unheard-of event. As a man in his prime, he had left his wife and young son to don the black robe. Hokanu's early memories of Fumita were few, but vivid: the roughness of his cheek in the evening as a young boy threw his arms around his father's neck, the smell of sweat as he removed the armor worn in the soldiers' yard. The younger brother of the Lord of the Shinzawai, Fumita had been marked as the future Shinzawai Force Commander until the day when the magicians had taken him away. Hokanu remembered with pain how his mother had never laughed again.

Fumita's peaked brows twitched, a frown suppressed. ''A Great One may go anywhere, at any time.'' And the dead man was his brother; power had separated them, and mystery had kept them apart. Of the wife who had given up name and rank to enter a convent, the magician never spoke. He looked into the features of the son he could no longer acknowledge, and his silken robe that the breezes fluttered without effort seemed to drag at his stiffened shoulders.

He did not speak.

Hokanu, whose gifts of perception at times skirted the edge of arcane talent, spoke for him. ''If I intend to endorse my father's policies, and stand at the hand of the Emperor, I must announce my intentions plainly, and soon. Then the enemies who might otherwise ally against the Light of Heaven must show themselves to me, as his shield.'' He gave a short, humorless laugh. ''As if it matters. If I stand down, and let the honor of the imperial chancellorship be awarded to a rival house, the enemies will strike next at my wife, who carries the heir to our name.''

Coarse laughter lifted over the buzz of general conversation. A servant passed the screen that led to the gallery; he saw the young Lord in conference there with a magician, bowed, and silently left. Preternaturally sensitive to the scents, his surroundings, and the grief for his adoptive father that left every nerve end raw, Hokanu heard a cousin call out loudly in argument. By the slurred consonants, Devacai had wasted no time in sampling the wines. Small need to speculate what would happen to Shinzawai honor and fortunes were that distant branch of the family to inherit.

Somewhere deep in the estate house, a maid giggled, and an infant cried. Life went on. And by the intentness of Fumita's gaze, he had not come just to honor the funeral pyre of a departed brother.

''It isn't pleasant, I see, but you have something to tell?'' Hokanu said, his throat made tight with the effort it took to find the courage to broach the subject first.

Fumita looked troubled, a dire sign. Even before his donning the black robe, he was normally master of his expression, which had made him a wicked opponent at cards. He twisted his thumbs in his cord belt, and sat, perched awkwardly on a flower urn. Blossoms crushed beneath his weight, lending the thick scent of greens to the sultry, smoke-tinged air. ''I bring you warning, consort of the Good Servant.''

The choice of title told much. Hokanu longed to sit also, but sap stains on his mourning robes might be interpreted as a sign of weakness, as if he had forgotten himself, or been overcome with prostration. He stood, his feet hurting with the strain. ''The Assembly is troubled over my wife?'' he prompted.

The silence stretched out, broken by the voices of the guests, raised now, as the wine heated their conversations. At length, not looking at Hokanu, but at the boards, as if they might harbor unseen flaws, Fumita spoke carefully. ''Heed these things. First, the Assembly is as any other body of men when trying to forge an agreement. They argue, they deliberate, they splinter into factions. No one wishes to be first to suggest the ill luck of compromising the life of a Servant of the Empire.''

Hokanu sucked a fast breath. ''They know about Mara's toy maker.''

"And Jiro's ventures in experimental engineering." Fumita looked up, piercingly. "There is little in the Nations my kind do not know. If they equivocate, it is because they cannot agree upon any one course of action. But provocation of any sort will unite them. Fear that."

The smokes and the scents seemed cloying enough to drown in. Hokanu held the Great One's gaze, and behind stiff features read anguish. "I hear. What else?"

Fumita blinked. "You will recall that a former member of the Assembly, the barbarian Great One Milamber, once visited great destruction upon the Imperial Games."

Hokanu nodded. He had not been present, but Mara had, and Lujan. Their descriptions of the event were the stuff of nightmares, and nobody who had seen the tumbled stone, the scorched timbers where fires had fallen from the sky, and the riven buildings from the inner precinct to the dockside quarter where earthquakes had shaken the Holy City had forgotten.

"No Great One has the powers of Milamber. Most have far less. Some are more scholars than spell crafters." Fumita fell silent, his eyes expectant.

Hokanu caught the cue, and added the telling surmise. "Some are argumentative, petty, and perhaps too embroiled in self-importance to act decisively?"

"If it comes to trouble," Fumita said slowly, "you were the one who said this. Never I." Very softly, he added, "The best you can hope for is a delay of the felling blow. Those who wish an end to these changes in tradition are growing stronger. Forcing debate will buy time, but none of us who would aid you may stay the hand of another." He fixed his former son with a gaze that held unvoiced feelings. "No matter what, I cannot protect you."

Hokanu nodded.

"Say farewell to my brother Kamatsu in my stead," the magician finished. "He was joy and strength and wisdom, and his memory remains my inspiration. Rule wisely and well. He often told me he was proud of you." He withdrew a small metal object from his robe and thumbed a switch.

A low-pitched, unnatural buzz sawed across the murmur of conversation, and Hokanu was left alone on the gallery above a courtyard that seethed with relations and guests; among them were enemies, seeking weakness to exploit, or strengths, for the means to undermine. Such was the way of the Game of the Council. Only the newest Lord of the

Shinzawai thought, as he gazed through the haze at their finery, that never before had the stakes been so high. This time the prize, the bone of contention, was the Empire of Tsuranuanni itself.

The last, most private rite for the departed Shinzawai Patriarch was completed at dusk, as a low ground mist settled over the contemplation glade. The new Ruling Lord lingered in the sanctity of his family's sacred grove, soothed by the deepening shadows, and by the chance to be alone.

The shadows spilled long and purple between the fruit-laden trees of autumn. Hokanu chose a stone bench and sat down, but the heat still oppressed. No breeze came to cool him, and ash from the burning drifted still in the air, describing shafts through the foliage where the sun struck through. Hokanu fingered the raveled edges of the garment he had rent for Kamatsu's ceremonial farewell. His hands closed, hard, bunching the fabric. He had an estate filled with guests that he should be thinking of; it felt selfish to steal a moment of peace for himself.

But the stillness of the contemplation glade, and the lazy drone of the insects that fed upon windfall fruit, allowed him space to think. Fumita's warning had not been only for Mara, her consort perceived. Hokanu's brows drew together. The magician's spare words had been for the Shinzawai, and the son who now wore the Lord's mantle. When he had said, "I cannot protect you," the "you" was not plural but singular.

For if, as Lord of the Shinzawai, Hokanu chose aggression against the Anasati on Mara's behalf, the Assembly of Magicians would have no choice but to act—because he was Mara's consort; not her Ruling Lord, but half Acoma in heart, if not in name. He was not Servant of the Empire. He did not have Mara's rank and honors as his shield.

No, the core of Fumita's warning had not been for his Lady. It had been for himself, a caution against trying the patience of an assembly divided in opinion over issues that had no precedents.

Hokanu understood with a flash of cold sweat that he must at all costs keep the Shinzawai clear of the feud with Lord Jiro. He saw, with the family's talent for perception, just what Fumita had left unsaid. That he was now Lord of one of the most powerful houses in the Empire and, while not officially Clan Warchief, would inherit the leadership of Clan Kanazawai at the next council. If, through ties of marriage, Shinzawai and Acoma forces were seen to unite in common cause, leading Clan Kanazawai and Clan Hadama, no counterforce in the Nations could stop them. The fragmented Assembly would end their contention, forced by most desperate circumstance to act.

That reason must never be given, or Acoma and Shinzawai would both be ground down into the dust, never to rise, never to recover. Hokanu had seen the death of two hundred warriors, followed by the annihilation of an honored house, all at the hands of *one* magician. Hundreds of them, united, no army in the Empire could oppose.

Hokanu arose to leave. The sacred grove of Shinzawai no longer seemed a haven of peace, and the sweat on his skin gave him chills. The place at his side where Mara might have stood felt colder and emptier still.

13. Twist

Arakasi waited.

Below him, the sentry moved silently, upon feet clad in padded stockings designed for stealth. He wore the traditional black short robe and trousers of the Hamoi Tong assassins, and his head covering masked all but his eyes. Across his back a short bow was slung, and at his belt a hip quiver of arrows and a variety of hand weapons were hooked within easy reach. He moved beneath the tree where the Spy Master perched, barely breathing, and vanished into the dusk like a shade of the dead. Arakasi counted in his mind, his numbers a complex formula he had devised over years, that fixed an exact passage of time, independent of breathing, heart rate, or any other condition that might influence the count. Practice with sand-filled hourglasses had perfected his system to a fine point. When he reached the number that signified ten seconds, his searching eyes caught a movement at the far end of the trail. He knew satisfaction heady as triumph. The second sentry had arrived exactly as anticipated.

The most perilous task he had ever undertaken was off to an auspicious start. Arakasi held no illusions that such luck would long continue; he was one man alone, and in a position where even the favor of heaven could not safeguard a man's life. Arakasi lay motionless on a tree branch in the garden of the Hamoi Tong's Obajan. Below him paced a guard who would kill him without hesitation. Like his predecessor, this new sentry scouted grass, paths, and bushes for the telltale signs of an intruder. The Spy Master had left no tracks; yet he sweated. The guards were uncannily thorough. The second assassin moved along his beat. Counting for a specific interval, Arakasi judged his moment, then noiselessly lowered himself from tree to ground. Taking care to step only on the flat, ornamental stones between flower beds, he scurried off to a small depression within a drainage ditch where he had secreted his few belongings. There, behind a masking of khadi brush, just beyond the limit of the Hamoi Tong sentries' line of patrol, he breathed deeply and settled taut nerves.

At the edge of the woods a hundred paces west, his own backup man waited, knife already in hand to answer unwelcome discovery. Arakasi lifted a stripped branch and used gestures to indicate that the patrol was moving according to schedule. The garden he sought to infiltrate was protected by eighteen assassins, all alert, cautious sentries, but human enough to be fallible. The guard pattern they followed was complex and at first appearance seemingly random. But few observers had Arakasi's icy patience, or his keen fascination with mathematics. He had thought nothing of the days spent crouched in dirt, bitten by insects, and lashed by sun and rain. What mattered was that he had unraveled their measure, and worked up formulas to predict their routes.

His backup man wore the garb of a Lashiki bowman—a mercenary guard from the northern province. As with Arakasi, his outer trappings came no closer to his true identity than any of a dozen guises he had worn and then shed over the years. Nor was his real name Sabota. Arakasi never pressed him on this foible; his true origin was his own affair, for he had proven himself a reliable courier countless times over. Of all the agents near Ontoset the Acoma Spy Master could call upon, Sabota was the most trustworthy. And Arakasi had to give this man a mission as critical to the Lady's survival as his own.

A month's beard masked the Spy Master's face. He appeared more like a beggar than anything else, from the weeks spent in the countryside. Yet had there been a watcher close enough to see his eyes as he began a second, more complex signal with the stick, he could never have been mistaken for other than what he was: a supremely dangerous man about to embark upon a mission he did not expect to survive.

At the treeline, the man called Sabota studied the Spy Master's message. His memory was impeccable. He nodded once and left without a glance backward.

Crouched behind a thin screen of thorn, Arakasi closed his eyes. He did not pray. He substituted hope. For Sabota took with him instructions to the second-in-command of the Acoma spy network, a man Mara had never met whom Arakasi had designated his replacement should he fail to return from this endeavor.

The stakes were now set. If a countermessage was not sent within a specified number of days, a new Spy Master would present himself to Lady Mara. Every detail on the tong that Arakasi had managed to uncover would be passed along, and plans would begin afresh to seek the destruction of the Hamoi Obajan and counter the infiltrations attempted by Chumaka of the Anasati.

Arakasi closed his eyes. His head ached from tension, which was not normal. Life to him had always been a bloodless, calculated dance, with danger his dispassionate partner. It bothered him to think he might have held Sabota with him longer than necessary: he had discerned the key to the patrols two days ago. The waiting he had done since had not been for precaution; in fact, it had only increased the risk that the tong might alter its habits to foil just the sort of study he had finished. Arakasi rubbed his temples. Unused to self-conflict, he drew a series of breaths to calm himself.

Arakasi had been driven by an abiding loyalty to Mara since his long-sought vengeance against the Minwanabi had been completed by the Acoma. Concerns for his Lady's safety haunted him now, for if he died in this insane task, a man of even lesser gifts would be left to undertake his post. After the attempt to infiltrate the City of the Magicians had been abandoned, signs of tampering had surfaced since the agents in Jamar had returned to active status. This could only be the work of Chumaka of the Anasati. Through sleepless nights watching the tong's patrols, Arakasi had worried on the timing. With the net compromised, who knew how deeply, this was a frightening moment to contemplate handing over the reins. Arakasi gave himself a mental jab of reproach. Were he to die, what did his life matter? Never before had he wasted himself with worries that had no bearing on circumstances outside his control.

It was past time to be moving. Pushing aside another maddening incon-gruity, a memory of his hands sliding through the honey-gold hair of a courtesan he should have forgotten, he forced his thoughts to track the immediate. The next lull in the patrols was upon him. If he was to act tonight, he must not tarry, for by every indication gleaned through weeks of observation, the high, painted litter that had arrived at the estate house that afternoon had carried the long-absent master.

The Obajan of the Hamoi Tong was once again in residence at his pleasure retreat.

Arakasi wormed out of the ditch, pressed through the low bushes, and raced, bent over, down a garden path. He threw himself belly down in the shadow of a low tile wall, aware, now, that he was irrevocably commit-ted. There were no more gaps in the patrols along the perimeter, and would not be, until daylight made it impossible to cross without being observed from one of the guard posts set in wooden balconies that jutted from the house's peaks.

The wait under the wall would last an hour. To use the time, Arakasi reviewed all of his preparations, turning over each success and frustration that had marked his mission to its current moment.

It had been a painstaking trail, which had begun with the tracking of the honey-haired courtesan's sister. The slave trader who had brokered the girls had been easy enough to find, but at the market where Kamlio's sibling should have been turned over to her tong purchaser, all traces of her vanished.

The work then had been hampered by its proximity to Ontoset, where the new network begun to replace the one disrupted by the silk warehouse mishap was still in its building stages. Weeks of following false leads had yielded the conclusion that girls selected for the tong never reached the Ontoset marketplace.

Arakasi had backtracked along the route, and from a drunken driver's chance remark had learned that slave wagons bearing girls of unusual beauty were on rare occasions diverted into the rolling foothills to the north of the city. More weeks had been spent scouting out that area, to follow and map each footpath, game trail, and swamp in the wide lands north of Ontoset. Sabota and three other agents had done this, living off the surrounding land like bandits, stealing jigabirds or vegetables from farmers, fishing the brooks, even eating berries and nuts. One had been killed as he attempted to purchase grain in a village miles to the northwest—which had been a loss that yielded knowledge, for it marked that settlement as subject to the tong's control, where strangers were not welcomed. The ''farmer'' who had done the killing had taken the Acoma agent from behind with a knife; an expert in his own right with dagger work, Arakasi had examined the corpse fished out of the river. The murder was the work of a trained assassin. Arakasi had lain in the loft of a mill downstream, listening to gossip: the villagers who had observed the death never commented, but continued with their daily affairs as if nothing untoward had occurred.

No one had caught wind of the Spy Master's presence; no one had noticed the trail he had erased when he left. He reviewed again the checks he had run in Ontoset, counting the farm carts that entered, and noting what color dust filmed their wheels as they presented themselves at the guard gate. He had not been followed, for a certainty. More weeks had been spent in a roadside ditch, living off dried cakes and fruit. Months after the murder of his agent, Arakasi had traced three carts from that village. Back in Ontoset, he had worn a drover's robes and gone out for hard nights of drinking. Carts came and went, until finally one of those he had been seeking pulled in. A trip outside the tap with three swaying, singing companions: he had leaned on that wagon to piss, and with a knife concealed in his other hand had notched the hardened leather that bound the cartwheel's rim.

Sabota, watching at the roadside, had waited more days for rain. Then at last, that distinctively marked wheel's track had led to the location of the tong's pleasure palace.

Arakasi knew his work was good. No one should have connected his drunken binge in the tavern with another poor, traveling laborer walking between harvests with his head drooping in the heat. Still, he sweated. The man he sought to take was the most secretive individual in the Empire, and by far the best guarded. There were Lords who had died for merely beholding the Obajan's face.

Tasaio of the Minwanabi had been the singular exception, and the bribes he had paid in metal were the stuff of legend, if a man did not know he had purloined illicit contraband during his years of war service across the rift.

The break in the patrol would come soon. Arakasi chewed a strip of dried meat, though his appetite had fled. Food was for survival now; or else this would be the last meal of his life.

He swallowed the last of his stores and lay flat upon damp soil. Eyes closed again, he tuned his senses to the night, hearing every sound and insect, and smelling the moisture-laden air. Any change would find him instantly at the ready. His timing required absolute concentration. He waited, sweating harder. His thoughts sought to wander, marred by some new, formless apprehension he could not name.

That anomaly troubled him sorely, but could not be examined, for the moment had come. The crunch of sandals crossed the gravel path just the other side of the wall; ten seconds, twenty seconds, thirty: Arakasi flowed through the night like a phantom.

Over the wall in a vault, he crossed the garden, leaping over the paths and keeping to slate borders of the flower beds that his step not disturb the raked gravel. Light flickered through the trees. Arakasi dove belly down and scraped under the arch of an ornamental bridge. The water in the little stream was high at this time of year, its trickle hiding his splashing. He barely had enough headroom under the center beam to keep his face clear of the surface. The sound of current over a rock underneath masked his fast breathing as he froze, his heartbeat racing. Up the path came a group of men. Four were wearing the black of assassins, white sashes proclaiming them to be of honored rank. Two more moved through the garden, flanking the party as guards. Of the pair they protected, one was thin, clad in silk woven in the hamoi-flower pattern, his eyes roving back and forth in nervous review. But it was to the other man that Arakasi's attention was drawn.

This one was massively built, his wide girth carrying not one ounce of fat. He wore a flowing brown robe, the hood thrown back to reveal the face that would never be uncovered away from home. The man who might earlier have posed as itinerant priest or monk proudly displayed the long topknot and fall of hair that proclaimed him of supreme rank. His shaved scalp bore the complex red tattoos that adorned only an Obajan.

In the darkness under the bridge, as footsteps thumped and creaked across the boards above, pressed tight between the structure and damp mud, Arakasi grinned to know his work had not been wasted. He was within striking distance of the ruler of the Hamoi Tong.

But now was no time to strike. The flanking guards were beating the bushes on either side of the path. The abnormally high water made the cranny under the bridge too small to shelter a full-sized man without backing up the flow. And indeed, no ordinary skulker could have wedged himself clear of the streamlet by bracing his elbows on the side beams. Arakasi ignored his aching muscles. Now there were twenty-four assassins in residence at the estate. He held back elation. Even a chance gleam of light on his teeth could betray him. Eighteen or twenty-four assassins, he was sticking his head into the mouth of a harulth and daring the most dangerous predator in Kelewan to bite down.

The Obajan's party passed, probably on its way to enjoy the evening in the covered gazebo near the wall. Arakasi had the night left yet to wait. At the last hour before sunrise, he would attempt to enter the estate house. For there was only one way he had determined to infiltrate this nest of murderers, and after that, he grimly acknowledged, he had no safe way out.

As deep night at last began to fade, Arakasi trembled with fatigue. Lying now half in the water, he thanked Chochocan, the Good God, that the guard patrols had not changed their routine with the Obajan in residence. He forced himself to gorge his belly with water. The single most desperate act of his life lay ahead, as he prepared to gain entry to the estate house. The next sentry arrived on schedule. Arakasi peered out from under the bridge. As the guard reached the limit of his vision, the Spy Master slithered silently into the open. Heavy dewfall would mask the drips that scattered from his wet clothing. He moved fast, knowing that he must maintain an equal distance between two men intent on killing anyone they found. If the one ahead paused to scratch an itch or the one behind walked slightly faster than normal, Arakasi might die before he knew he had been discovered.

The Spy Master resisted the temptation to hurry. Few situations demanded such precise control. Scrambling as quietly as possible, he moved sideways, forearms, knees, and toes alone touching the ground. The toll on his already depleted strength was tremendous.

After two hundred feet of progress, Arakasi collapsed to the ground. He made himself dizzy choking back his gasps for air, but forced his ears to listen for any indication that he had been seen. No alarm was sounded. He studied the sky. The predawn grey was brightening now. From experience he knew that sentries had the most difficult time seeing at dawn and dusk, when all was reduced to blurred shadows.

Footfalls passed. The guard who had been to his rear passed within a yard of his position. But the sentry had his attention directed toward the outer wall, not upon the ground to the left of his feet. And it was a shadow in the grass beside the main house that Arakasi had become, his breath stopped, and his hands braced to move.

The sentry paused. Arakasi counted, dripping sweat. On a certain number, the guard moved on. At once Arakasi leaped to his feet, removed a cord from his belt, and threw its weighted end upward over a tree branch that arched toward the house between the balconies that housed more guards. Exposed on three sides, he had only seconds before the next patrol appeared around the corner. Luck must be his mistress here. Arakasi hurled himself upward, staying close to the thick trunk to avoid any rustling of leaves. He threw himself prone on the branch and reeled in his cord hand over hand.

His observations were now useless. He had had no way to penetrate the life inside the house, and so had no knowledge beyond an estimated floor plan gained by watching the goings and comings of the servants.

Arakasi heard voices and knew the house staff awakened. Soon cooks and body servants would be about their duties and he had to be in place.

Arakasi pulled himself along the limb. He had to be careful. This was a takai tree, grown for its lush fruit; the branches of bearing trees were weak and tended to break when more weight was added. The foliage was thin and provided little cover as he shinnied under the beams of a guard balcony. The need to keep quiet knotted his muscles and made his suppressed breath like fire in his chest.

Houses in Kelewan were usually constructed with a breathing space between the inner ceiling and the roof to let the heat under the eaves escape. This house should be no different, but a grating of wood might have been added to increase security. No clear safe haven remained to him, and he was too far inside the estate to turn back with any chance of safety. The sky might be lightening to silver, but the gloom under the rafters was complete. Arakasi groped into the shadow.

The way inside he had hoped to find did exist, but as he had suspected, thin slats of wood barred his way into the crawl space under the tiled roof above and the plaster ceiling of the rooms below. Arakasi drew one of his rare metal throwing knives. The steel could endure the punishment of prying the slats out at their pegged ends, where a Tsurani blade of laminated hide would have snapped. Arakasi worked quickly. He garnered scrapes and splinters as he wormed his way through the small opening, then used the grease of his own sweat to ease the pegs back without squeaking. He allowed himself a moment of silent exultation. He had done the impossible. Although cramped in a space too small for comfort, he was inside the building.

He rested while the guard changed in the platforms outside. Then he groped his way across the beams until he located the rooftree. He settled in to wait, the day before him to spy out the arrangement of the rooms unseen beneath.

Arakasi lay supine, listening closely to the dulcet tones of women's voices below him. His success now depended on the chance that the Obajan would be visiting his women, for the Spy Master doubted he could survive another day of sweating in the airless space beneath the roof.

The coarse-cut wood of dusty rafters bit into his thighs and arms, and chafed him through the light cloth of his robe. He endured, flexing one limb at a time to relieve cramps from impaired circulation. The air had grown stifling as the sun heated the roof tiles. Although he had gone without sleep for nearly two days, he fiercely resisted the need to rest. To fall victim to the body's needs in this place was to die. Should he doze, he might roll off the narrow crossbeam and come crashing through the thin plaster ceiling below him. With grim humor he also considered how the sound of his exhausted snores might lead the vigilant guards to his hiding place. Now, ready with his steel in darkness, his cheek and hands tickled by the aimless wanderings of crawling insects, he felt a heady mix of exhilaration and regret: exhilaration that he had won so close without discovery; regret that so many tasks remained undone.

Below him, cracks in the plaster admitted an orange glow of light. Servants had lit the lamps, which meant that night had fallen outside. He could hear the silvery laughter of women; among them now and again sounded a voice that reminded him of another girl, and an afternoon entanglement in silken sheets. Arakasi shifted, irked at himself. Kamlio was on his mind far too much: the feel of her rich hair under his hands, and her creamy skin, and her kisses; the very memory of her made him sweat with longing. Yet what haunted his mind, over and over, was no simple coupling of flesh. He dreamed of her deep eyes, the intelligence in them alternately dulled by boredom and made cunning by abuse. Her manner seemed hard, but it was a cynicism that roofed over a chasm of pain. He knew, as surely as his hands and his body had pleased her, that given time, he could reach the sweet nature hidden like treasure within her.

If he survived this evening's endeavors, he would buy her freedom, maybe show her the headier joys of a free life. If she would have him; if, after a lifetime of pandering to the whims of many masters, she did not find men distasteful . . . Arakasi's lip curled in self-contempt in the dark. He dreamed! He dreamed like a lovesick boy! Had life not taught him never to give credence to the unpredictable desires of the heart?

He smothered an impulse to curse.

It was irony, of the blackest and bitterest sort, that the mission that had caused him to know her might itself bring her to ultimate harm. With stark logic, in the stifling heat under the rooftree, he knew: he would require a miracle of the gods to emerge from his mission alive. The odds now favored his getting the strike at the Obajan he had planned for. But even should his blow prove deadly, evading the best of the tong's assassins —and after them, the vengeful wrath of the Tiranjan, Obajan's successor —was an impossible expectation.

Arakasi shivered from fatigue and tension. He changed grip on a knife handle gone strangely sweat-slick with doubt. How could one enchantress of a courtesan have tempted him to place her well-being above the will of Mara, his sworn mistress, whose life he loved above his own? Yet Kamlio had. For Mara, the Obajan of the Hamoi Tong would die. But if the Spy Master who undertook the deed escaped the consequences alive, he recognized that a small, secretive part of himself must remain his own. His care for the courtesan, which might or might not be love—and could easily be rooted in foolish pity—begged to be explored. The self-respect recovered with the destruction of House Minwanabi demanded this: that he hear his own needs as a man, and reconcile them with the duties that daily led him into danger.

A thousand times, he might have died nameless, in the guise of beggar, itinerant priest, sailor, fortune-teller, spice merchant, costermonger, messenger. And a thousand times he faced those risks without hesitation, for he had stared into the abyss and did not fear death. But now, when he needed hindrance the least, he found that it suddenly mattered. If death took him, he wanted his ashes honored on Acoma lands, and the pretty, sullen-eyed courtesan crying his name by his pyre. Now he found himself shackled by sentiment when, at any cost, his identity must remain secret.

The continuance of the Acoma, whose beloved Lady had restored him to honor, and perhaps even the Empire itself depended upon flawless self-restraint. Arakasi had lived such a disjointed existence that love had but once before fettered him, and then more through loyalty to the woman who had restored his pride and honor. And though he adored Mara, she did not trouble his dreams. Arakasi cherished her as a priest loved his goddess. But Kamlio had touched a piece of him that had been hidden from all others. Especially himself, he rued silently.

The laughter of the women subsided. Arakasi tensed, jerked from reminiscence by a tread that grated as it crossed the floor. The sound indicated studded leather sandals, and the weight of a large man. A female called out a welcome, and bare, perfumed feet lisped over tile; cushions and refreshments were being brought for the master's comfort, Arakasi surmised. He shifted position infinitesimally, his grip on his knife hot and dry.

The closeness of his attic perch seemed suddenly, unendurably stifling. He fought the instinct to gasp for more air, to move, to act prematurely; he willed himself against pain to force each muscle to relax and hold position. The mingled scents of perfumes wafted through the heated air, admitted through the gaps between plaster and beams. Presently Arakasi heard the clink of fine crystal, as serving girls brought refreshment to their master, and later, a vielle player who accompanied a singer for his entertainment. He smelled sweet oils, then, and heard the deep-pitched sighs of contentment of a man being attended by skilled masseurs. The Spy Master's own abused body obliged him by trying to cramp.

Patience, he reminded himself inwardly.

Later still, a light tread betrayed a towel girl's departure, her step shortened by her hamper of soiled linens. His eyes half-closed, Arakasi pictured the tableau in the chamber below his rafter perch. The musician had slowed his rhythms, and the singer abandoned lyrics, her voice sliding into a languorous humming. The crystal jug that held the spiced sā wine chimed as it was set on its polished stone tray—nearly empty now, Arakasi judged by the ring of the glass. Wax candles had burned low. The faint light that escaped through the tiny cracks in the ceiling had taken on the warmer tone cast by an oil lamp. He heard the sigh of fine fabric as it fell away, and the master arose with a creak of knees. His sigh was huge as he stretched.

For the first time since his entry into his pleasure harem, the Obajan of the Hamoi Tong spoke. ''Jeisa.'' He paused after the name, his eyes perhaps glittering with lust. ''Alamena, Tori.'' He waited, cruelly drawing out an interval of palpable tension, while the other, unsummoned women arrayed at his feet waited to know whether they would be chosen or spurned, their disappointment or their joy at their appointed turn of fate carefully hidden.

The Obajan sighed again. "Kamini," he finished. "The rest of my flowers are dismissed."

Arakasi blinked to clear the sting of what he hoped was sweat. Not Kamini; the gods were not kind tonight. Kamini he wished far away from the master's bedchamber through this hour, for she was sister to Kamlio, the girl who haunted the Spy Master's dreams.

Fiercely Arakasi wrenched his thoughts from the image of Kamlio's face. Daydream and grow careless, and he would die here.

A screen swished closed in the chamber below; presently another slid open, and Arakasi heard the chirps of evening insects over the hiss of the oil lamp. The attic had not cooled; the roof tiles held the day's heat yet, though the sun had long set, and the night was old enough for dew. The musician and the singer subsided to the barest whisper of a melody, over which Arakasi could hear the slither of silken sheets, and the muffled giggle of a girl. He waited, still as a predator, listening avidly for his prey's contented sighs to become the quickened breaths of passion, and waited yet as a girl began to moan in the throes of pleasure . . . or what seemed like pleasure. Arakasi banished thoughts of another girl, who had been taught since childhood to feign all the subtleties of joy. . . .

Arakasi reproached himself silently. He had sweated too much, and dehydration was making him perilously light-headed. He forced concentration, every muscle corded with tension. The knife in his hand felt like an extension of his living flesh as the Obajan, entwined in hot girls and damp silk, opened his mouth and cried out in the fulfillment of his release.

In that instant, the Spy Master shoved off, plunging downward through warm air. He struck the plaster ceiling and broke through, in a shower of fragments, and chips, and dust. His eyes, long used to the dark, saw clearly in the lamplight the humped mass of entangled forms on the mat below as he fell. He chose the uppermost, the most massive, and angled his knife accordingly.

He had but one instant to pray that the only time the Obajan of the Hamoi Tong would be more than a hand's reach from his weapons and guards would be in nakedness, in the act of coupling.

Then he crashed atop the sweating mass of the Obajan and his women, and sheathed priceless steel in flesh. Arakasi felt his blade turned by sinew and bone. He had missed a killing blow.

The Obajan was huge, but none of his bulk was fat. His groan of pleasure became a shout of pain and alarm. But Arakasi was thrown off his prey like a fish tossed from a bait boat. His heel caught on a woman's leg and he fell. Besides being strong, the master of assassins was fast. His hand shot out to a pile of weapons beside the bed. Three darts smacked into silken sheets, even as Arakasi rolled away. A girl screamed in pain and fear.

The oil lamp went out. A vielle fell with a crash, and the singer broke off, screaming. Feet pounded in the corridor, while Arakasi shoved free of entangling bedclothes and threw off a girl who clawed his shoulder with her nails. His second knife slid into his hand as if it had life and breath and a desire to match his need. He flicked his wrist, and released, and the blade flew true, into the Obajan's neck.

The master of the Hamoi Tong bellowed again, enraged. But the blade kissed the artery, and blood fountained. He raised his hand to staunch the flow, and all but lost his thumb on the keen edge still exposed. Against the pale square of the door screen, Arakasi saw the man's shoulders quiver in the stress of ebbing life. His scalp lock fell loose over his back as he crashed to his knees, and his chest wet with the fast flow of blood.

Arakasi twisted around, flinging girls and sheets one way and another in the darkness. He rolled, tossed a cushion in the direction of pursuing footsteps. Someone tripped and hit with a fleshy smack against the tile. Mistaking him for the assailant, four incoming guards sprang and bore the unfortunate man down. His protests masked Arakasi's movements as, hand to the wall, the Spy Master scuttled to the far side of the chamber.

He had just enough starlight to see by. Careful to keep any chance gleam of steel from betraying his position, Arakasi drew another knife from his belt loop. He threw, and one of the guards went down, clutching his belly, and howling. His noise distracted the rest, allowing Arakasi to draw more knives and dispatch the four guards who entered from the outer hall. They died, one after another, between the screaming of the pleasure women and the cries of the wounded sentry on the floor. The Obajan lay in the sheets, motionless in death.

Arakasi slipped through the screen and ducked out of sight around the lintel. He dared not wait to see if any of the girls had seen him go, nor if they had the wits to make outcry. With a leap driven by adrenaline, he sprang up and caught the corner beam of the roof. Dangling by his hands, he pulled himself into the shadows under the eaves, his last blade gripped between his teeth.

He was barely established in his hiding place when feet pounded into the room from the direction of the adjoining hallway.

"Outside!" shouted one of the assassins. "The man who killed our master fled into the garden!"

Desperate, Arakasi clawed a fragment of shingle from the gutter. With an underhand toss he pitched the bit of tile into a flower bed. The sharp-eared sentry who bolted through the door dashed headlong into the bushes, hacking the vegetation with his sword. Arakasi could have brushed the man's head with his fingertips as the man passed below.

More assassins rushed out. "Where is he?"

The swordsman paused in his slashing. "I heard movement."

"Quickly!" called the second guard. "Bring torches! The killer makes his escape while we delay!"

They fanned outward, combing the garden, while men with lights converged to aid in the search. Arakasi slung himself off the roof. A moving shadow in darkness, he sidestepped and ducked into an adjoining screen, back inside the house where the pursuers had not yet thought to check.

More men exploded from the bedroom. They met the first man, returning. "He must have gone over the wall. Patrol the perimeter, quickly, before he gets away!"

Shouts of inquiry issued from inside the harem. News of the Obajan's death roused the servants, some of whom gave way to panic. The tong was swift and merciless in retribution, and in a house this well guarded, the members would suspect that whoever killed their master must have an inside accomplice. The entire staff might be put to death to ensure elimination of any traitors. The more intelligent servants understood their best course of action was to flee. Fear alone bound these wretches to service with this murderous brotherhood; most preferred to chance an uncertain future than face dishonorable death.

Arakasi could only hope that the confusion caused by dozens of terrified servants would lend him opening, for while a saner man might seek escape, his mission was yet incomplete. For Mara's sake, he must return to the Obajan's study and steal the record journal of the tong.

Stillness had fallen over the adjacent bedchamber. Arakasi risked that the guards had left their dead master in the heat of the search. He reentered the screen he had broken earlier and stepped into a scene of carnage.

Blood splattered everything within ten feet of the bed. Beside the bulk of the slain master, a pair of naked girls remained, starlight limning their forms faintly silver. One of them stared at him, silent. With crazed, repetitive motions, she sought to wipe blood from skin smeared hope-

lessly scarlet. The other writhed in the sheets, moaning. Struck down by
a poisoned dart, she was unable to rise. With grim purpose, Arakasi
recovered two metal knives, one from the neck of the Obajan and another
from the stomach of a guard who lay sprawled at his master's feet.

Arakasi stepped past the foot of the bed, his glance passing over the
wounded courtesan. He stopped, his attention unwillingly arrested. The
girl's hair pooled like spilled oil in the moonlight, pale gold and glisten-
ing. Her face was upturned, exposed to the flicker of torchlight spilling in
from the garden. Like a wound to the heart, he saw that her features were
the exact same as her sister's.

They were twins.

Logic could not stay the lurch of Arakasi's heart. In moonlight, her
slim hands worrying at the dart that pierced her breast, she could not be
distinguished from the girl he had touched and bedded. Jolted by a pain of
the spirit that threatened to choke his breath, Arakasi fought to recapture
his icy, analytical nature. He was Acoma Spy Master, on a mission for the
Servant of the Empire. He must keep his wits and locate the Obajan's
scrolls.

But when he most needed steady nerves, his objectivity forsook him.
Before one dying courtesan, his own survival suddenly seemed as meaningless as trying to capture sunlight with bare hands.

Arakasi's intellect screamed that he must keep faith with Mara, while
his heart drove him to his knees beside the stricken girl. Time and
circumstance were blurred. He could no longer separate which was the
courtesan who had bound him to her, and which the twin sister. In the
dark, in the moonlight, in the aching loss of the moment, their identities
seemed to merge. Against every instinct of self-preservation, Arakasi
gathered her body into his arms. He cradled her, wide-eyed and motionless, until she quivered, gasped, and, after what seemed an eternity,
finally ceased breathing.

Arakasi felt as if he had been beaten. His nails had gouged his palms,
and his teeth had drawn blood. The salt-rich taste on his tongue and the
death stink that pervaded his nostrils pushed him to nausea. He barely
noticed the living woman who muttered amid bloodstained sheets. His
mind recorded but did not comprehend her babble. Arakasi snatched a
tearing breath and forced himself to unlock his rigid limbs. His heart
seemed frozen as the dead girl slipped from his grasp. By rote, he reacted
to a sound behind him, turned, and whipped out a knife. His throw was
almost true. The servant who sought entry was a castrate who served the
harem returned to look after his charges. The knife caught him a glancing

slash across the neck. He gagged and slammed into the door post. Fast Arakasi had always been; but tonight his limbs were clumsy as he stumbled across the dropped girl. His feet caught in soggy sheets and hooked upon cushions. He struck the castrate with a wrestler's move in the middle, and knocked him sideways. The dying man's strength was uncanny. Arakasi's hands sought a grip, and slipped. He dug his fingers into the wound and, by the spray of blood on his face, knew he had torn his enemy's artery. Using his knuckles to stop his victim from crying out, he received a bite to the bone.

Had the dead Obajan's guards not been sweeping the outer grounds for an assassin who by rights should be fleeing for his life, the struggle would have brought notice. As it was, hanging onto a dying man who careened into wall hangings and crashed against chests and tables, Arakasi felt a sense of the unreal. The castrate took a long time to bleed to death. When he at last fell limp, Arakasi reeled out of the room.

He had never seen the inside of the house. What sense of direction he had garnered during his wait under the rooftree now deserted him as he sought the journal that was the heart of the tong. Such a book recorded each contract and its disposition, in a cipher known only to the Obajan. Intermediaries were told nothing beyond the name of the victims directed to die.

The tong's records were the inheritance of the Tiranjan, who must take over rulership for the leader just assassinated. The journal would not be unprotected, and even before the commotion of the search died down, the Obajan's flower-robed adviser would be sending the Tiranjan to collect it.

Arakasi heard distant voices and a scream. His time in the house was now limited to less than a handful of minutes, and his mind remained muddled by the memory of a girl's tormented death. He whipped himself to review his past surmises, made through the hot hours of waiting under the rooftree. This was the pleasure palace. The Obajan was on sabbatical. The record book that was never beyond his reach would be here, in a place set aside for it. The door screen with the stoutest construction must be the strong room where the tong's scrolls would be kept.

Arakasi flitted down the corridor, keeping to the shadows as much as possible. He doused lanterns where he dared, shivering and starting at every distant noise. He rounded a corner and all but collided with a man whose back was turned. The chink of steel as he drew his last knife caused the man to whirl. He was a warrior, assigned to guard a locked door. Arakasi launched himself forward and sliced the tendons in the man's wrist, even as his foe reached down to draw his sword. The Spy Master felt no pain himself as he chopped bitten, bleeding fingers into the guard's windpipe, and rammed him with a crash against the wood.

Someone shouted at the noise.

Out of time, Arakasi bashed his enemy through the panel. The guard resisted, eyes widened in soul-deep terror. As he overbalanced backward into the confines of the strong room, the hand that still functioned scrabbled in desperation at the wall.

Then he went down. Tripwires mired his ankles, and darts were released from the walls. The floor where he struck dropped down with a grinding sound, and stakes of sharpened, resin-hardened wood erupted through pierced patterns in the tiles, impaling his twitching remains.

Arakasi paid his victim's death throes no mind. Clued by the man's last living act, he surveyed the wall, and found a niche between the murals. He recognized the hole for what it was, an opening for a locking pin that would disable the mechanical traps inside the room. He jammed his knife into the gap and rushed ahead.

Chills chased across his skin. He could hear running feet in the corridors, converging upon his position. Ahead of him, lit by a single lamp, stood a tall desk-like structure with a heavy book resting on the top. He leaped over the corpse of the guard, his thoughts racing.

If the door had been trapped, so the desk must be also. It followed that a thief who survived the defenses to get this far must be gifted, and a master of intricate mechanisms. Therefore, Arakasi chose the unpredictable tactic: he would make his attempt by force.

Arakasi swallowed the metallic taste of panic. He grasped the heavy ceramic lamp stand, bent down, and bashed through the inlaid paneling at the bottom of the desk. He looked up to locate and disarm the maze of fine threads and levers that would set off the snare were the book to be lifted, and beneath them found something else.

A tightly rolled scroll lay beneath the trip mechanism. He pulled it from its resting place and glanced at it. The outer parchment was written over in cipher and tied off with ribbons marked with the flower of the Hamoi Tong. The book on the desktop was a fake, set up in plain view as a trap. In his hand he held the true accounts of the tong.

The cries of alarm were now closer. Arakasi thrust the scroll into his robe and hurried to the doorway. He yanked his knife from the hole and ran, away from the voices that converged around the corner from behind.

He made blind haste, shaken to fresh fear by his success. As much as he had planned, as carefully as he had arranged his safeguards, he had never anticipated surviving beyond the moment of the Obajan's death. Now the stakes were redoubled; for without the journal scroll, the Tiranjan could not assume leadership of the clan. Contracts would go unfulfilled, and the Hamoi assassins would lose honor. In effect, Arakasi held the murderous brotherhood's natami in his hands. Without it, the tong would lose credibility and eventually drift away like smoke.

Shouting erupted in the corridor Arakasi had just vacated. The broken doorway was discovered, and screams followed, as guards rushed inside and fell to the traps reset when he had removed the dagger used as locking pin. Pursuit was immediate, as the survivors scattered searching through the house. Arakasi barely slipped out the window ahead of one hard on his trail.

A stinging in his shoulder marked a hit by an assassin's dart. It would be poisoned, surely, yet he had no choice but to ignore it. The antidotes he had brought on the chance he might get hit lay with his stores, hidden outside the perimeter. He rushed across the garden, leaped into a tree, and flung himself over the first wall. Poised for a moment, he heard darts and the heavier rattle of arrows flying through the branches above his head.

He looked frantically for opportunity. A panicked party of servants hurried past. Attempting to steal from the estate, they hugged the wall in silence as they sought a clear avenue to freedom.

Arakasi insinuated himself into their midst, causing one woman to scream and a man to throw himself on his knees and beg mercy. The Spy Master's black clothing had caused them to mistake him for an assassin, he realized with near-hysterical glee. Drawing a deep breath, Arakasi screamed, "The servants have murdered the Obajan! Kill them all!" His ragged shout sent the menials scattering in all directions, and he sprinted as they did, toward the outer wall. Let the tong trackers pick out his spoor from this confusion, he thought as he skinned his palms leaping over.

At the edge of physical and mental exhaustion, he made his way to a sheltered place he had selected against the faint chance he would complete his mission. There he had hidden his antidotes, and a cache of drugs that would force him to continued alertness and energy, until safety or death greeted him. He would pay a terrible price for their use, and weeks of rest would be needed, but survival would be worth the price. He dosed himself quickly and stripped off his bloodied clothing. He left them under a large rock. From another of his vials, he poured a pungent liquid that caused his eyes to water. It was the essence of a slu-leeth, a large swamp creature that other beasts found repellent. No dog known would track one, and indeed, exposure to its musk would ruin the animal's sense of smell for days. As he rubbed the stinking ointment on his skin, the sting in his shoulder reminded him he still had a dart in his flesh. He drew the barbed shaft out and slipped on a fresh shirt. The bitten knuckles he could do nothing for, and he cursed at the certainty that the hand would swell and infect.

He could do nothing more but trust that the antidote he had swallowed would counteract the poison. He had made a fair guess at those required, a legacy of the knowledge gained from his inspection of Korbargh's shelves.

Arakasi began to lope through the night, sandal-clad feet slapping steadily over the rocky trail that led to safety. Now as he coursed through dew-drenched grasses, memories of Korbargh's end, and another death, made him acknowledge the changes in himself. Never again could he take such measures against a man, not for Mara, not for duty, not for honor. Not since he had held a dying courtesan and confused her, for a moment, with another girl. Irrevocably, he had perceived his own heart. If Korbargh's antidotes and the poison in his body were not a match . . . Arakasi was fatalistic—until another memory surfaced: the mad girl in the Obajan's chamber. Her tearful hysterics replayed in his mind, her mumbling resolved with frightening clarity. She had said, *"He knows Kamini!"*

Kamini who was but one half of a pair of twins, one belonging to an impotent old man, and the other dead with the Obajan. Arakasi began to run then, out of breath and hurting before he started. For the first time ever, he prayed with fervor to the gods of Kelewan, begging Sibi, who was Death, not to call him to her brother Turakamu's halls. He needed luck, or a miracle, most likely both. For his lapse into distraction back in the Obajan's chamber was sending death to Kamlio's door. He had left the mad girl alive, and still babbling, and a search was on for an assassin. The Obajan's guards who remained alive might not cover every cranny of the estate grounds in the dark. But come daylight, when the Tiranjan arrived to direct the aftermath, a more methodical hunt would begin. The courtesan would be questioned.

Arakasi recognized a second ugly truth: because of Kamlio he could be made to talk should he be taken. He choked back anguish. The only way to save the twin that he loved was through Mara; and the only way to protect his Lady was through the girl, who knew he had worked for a powerful mistress with great wealth. There were few such Ruling Ladies in the Empire. The tong would redouble their attacks upon Mara. Where once the tong struck for honor, now they would attack for survival. Arakasi would be only minutes ahead of the assassins in his race to reach Kamlio. If he could find one of his new operatives in Ontoset he might pass along his precious burden, but he had no moment to delay. From the instant the fact came to light that the Obajan's murderer had recognized Kamini, the brotherhood would investigate, working back along the trail from the estate to the slave broker, to the surviving twin. They would leave corpses after their inquiries. If their agents in Kentosani received word before he could recover Kamlio . . .

Sweating, Arakasi increased his pace, through fields and gardens, and over the beaten earth of a game trail that led in the direction of the main thoroughfare. Ah, if he could have one of Hokanu's accursed horses, now . . .

Even in his affirmation of service to Lady Mara, he also moved as he must, to meet his own need. Arakasi became filled by a strange exhilaration, as if only now had it registered that he was alive. His insane assault upon the Obajan had succeeded, and he held the tong's records in his possession. That victory made him giddy. The jarring of the road under his feet, the sting of splinters in his skin, the burning of each labored breath, were all sensations to be cherished. Part of his mind recognized the effects of the drugs he had taken, but he also knew this preternatural awareness arose from his discovery of the true stakes at risk for him.

As he hurried through the night, he analytically examined this epiphany. As son of a woman of the Reed Life, he had never regarded love between man and woman as any sort of mystery. He had lived, always, by his wits, his perception, and his skills derived from level-headed study of his fellow human beings. He had seen Mara's involvement with the barbarian, Kevin, and been intrigued. He had attributed the fire in his mistress's eyes when the man had been present to a female's need to romanticize relationships. Why else go through the encumbrance and the bother of childbearing, he had coldly rationalized.

Now, running as if his heart would burst, his throat congested with unshed tears, he thought of a honey-haired girl, still living, and her dead identical twin sister. He saw, as he bashed through dew-drenched branches and stumbled with startling carelessness into the open moonlight on the road, that he had been wrong. Stupidly, pitifully wrong.

Half a lifetime he had lived, and almost missed the significance of the magic that poets called love. He skidded to a stop, and glanced in both directions to locate the litter prearranged to wait for him.

He pondered, as he gasped for breath, whether if he survived to spare the other, living girl from the tong's vengeance as this night's work was traced back to her—he wondered if the cynical nature born of crushed dreams, would ever permit her to teach him what he now most wished to know. He ached to see whether the emptiness he had discovered within himself could ever be fulfilled.

He spun around and, in the empty road, realized a second thing, as fearful as any other in this night of reckoning: this was the last mission he could undertake in the belief there would not be personal consequences. For irrevocably, he had lost the detachment that had set him apart from his fellows, and had given rise to the ice-clear objective vision that had made him a genius in his craft.

A need had wakened in him that changed him from what he was; no longer could he look upon others through his lens of unfeeling indifference. No longer could he mimic their ways, and assume any identity at will. The pale-haired courtesan had forever changed that.

A night bird sang, somewhere off in the wood. The foliage overhung the thoroughfare, dimming moonlight, and the fine-grained scattering of stars. Left in drifting mist, with an empty roadway and no clue, not even a flag of dust to determine which way the litter might be waiting, Arakasi chose a direction at random. Tortured to wry observation, he considered whether his opponent at the game of intrigue, Chumaka of the Anasati, had also possessed that flaw of human nature, and lived in the absence of love. Or if he had not, would Arakasi's newfound vulnerabilities leave him open to attack by a man that already had an uncanny penchant for spycraft, and who was Mara's implacable enemy?

Arakasi agonized, as the sound of night creatures seemed to mock him. Feeling more anguish in minutes than he had known all the years of his life, the exhausted, frightened, yet exultant Spy Master hurried on, toward a future and a goal more fearful than any he put behind him.

14. Revelation

The fog lifted.

Arakasi walked through the river quarter of Jamar in bone-numbing fatigue. Although he had shed all signs of pursuit nights past, he dared not stop for rest. The tong was behind him somewhere, following him like hounds on a game trail. They would lose him in this city, among ten thousand strangers, only to turn to their other lead—the clue that led to Kamini's sister. He had only a matter of days before they found Kamlio.

With Mara still in residence at the Imperial Palace, he would forfeit what precious lead time he had gained. The fastest commercial litter, with two extra crews of runners, had carried him from Ontoset to Jamar in a week. He could not sleep through the jouncing ride, but his drug-depleted body had fallen into a stupor for the few hours a day the bearers required to rest.

Now, six days after he had killed the Obajan, he had paid off the exhausted crew of litter bearers by the entrance to Jamar's main market, then lost himself amid the workers who set up the merchants' stalls and laid out the day's wares. Jamar was the busiest trading port in the Empire and the dockside quarter formed a small community on its own, where seagoing ships met rivercraft. Arakasi found a beggar boy sitting before a brothel, closed at this early hour of morning. He held up a shell worth a hundred centis, more wealth than the boy would beg in a year. "What is the fastest way upriver?"

The boy sprang to his feet and with gestures indicated he had no voice. Arakasi motioned for the boy to show him. Darting through the early morning crowd that collected by the sausage seller's shack, the boy led him upriver to a pier where a half-dozen small craft were tied up. There in plain view of a stout riverman, the boy pantomimed that this was where Arakasi wished to be. The Spy Master gave him the shell.

The transaction was not lost upon the riverman, who until that moment had counted the filthy man another beggar. Seeing that shell, he reassessed his evaluation and smiled broadly. "You seek quick passage upriver, sir?"

Arakasi said, "I need to reach Kentosani in haste."

The man's chubby face showed pride. "I own the swiftest craft in the city, good sir." He pointed toward the river, indicating a low, trim messenger boat, with a tiny cabin, moored some distance from the pier. "I call her *River Mistress*. Four banks for eight oarsmen, and full sail." Arakasi assessed her lines and efficient lateen sail. She might not be quite as good as her master's boast, but he would lose any time he might save in looking for one that might be marginally faster.

"She appears worthy," Arakasi said neutrally. "Are the rowers aboard?"

The captain said, "Indeed. We are waiting for a merchant from Pesh, who desires transport to Sulan-Qu. He has the cabin, sir, but if you are willing to ride on deck, you may take over the accommodations from Sulan-Qu to Kentosani. The price would normally be five hundred centis, but as you are sharing the boat halfway, I'll take three hundred."

Arakasi reached into a hidden pocket in his sleeve and withdrew a slug of silver the size of his thumb. At the glint of metal, more wealth than any riverman might expect to see in one place, the captain's eyes widened. "I will have the cabin," Arakasi said firmly. "And we leave now. The merchant from Pesh can make other arrangements."

Whatever ethical protestations might have been made died in the captain's mouth. Offered incalculable riches, he all but fell over backward in his hurry to escort Arakasi to the dinghy that bobbed at the bottom of the pier. Down the ladder they went and the captain rowed as if ten thousand demons pursued him, lest the merchant appear and honor demand the captain return for him.

Arakasi boarded while the captain tied the dinghy to the mooring and cast off the *River Mistress*. The green hull was sloppily painted, but there was no rot nor other signs of slack care. The captain might be a frugal man, but he kept his boat worthy.

The rowers and tillerman were given their orders and the captain escorted Arakasi to the tiny cabin as the *River Mistress* swung around into the current and began making her way upriver.

Little more than a low shack amidships, between the rowers and the tiller, there was enough room for two people to sleep inside. Two small ports on either side admitted light, and a small oil-burning lamp would provide light at night. The cabin was dark and musty, a faint stale smell of old lamp oil mixed with the lingering perfume of its previous passenger.

The ports had faded silk curtains and the cushions showed wear at their edges, and were well used, but Arakasi had endured worse on many occasions.

Arakasi said, "This will do. Now, one thing I demand: no one is to disturb me. Anyone who enters the cabin before we reach Kentosani will die. Is that clear?"

Arakasi was not the first strange passenger the boat owner had encountered, and given the price he paid, there were no objections to the conditions of the rental.

Arakasi sat and closed the small doors, then removed the bundle he carried inside his robe. The tong's journal had never been out of touch of his skin from the moment he had fled the Obajan's estate. Now, as he had his first chance to scan the pages, he began his study of the encoded entries. But the strange characters blurred before his eyes. With his head bent over yellowed parchment, he fell into exhausted sleep.

When he next regained consciousness, a glance through a porthole showed that they were halfway to the Holy City. He had slept for two days and a night. Snacking from a basket of fruits presumably left for the merchant from Pesh, he began to unravel the tong's cipher. It was a clever code, but not beyond Arakasi's gifts to solve, given that he had nothing else to do for three more days. He saw four columns, and surmised that each entry was comprised of four pieces of information: the date of the contract, the price agreed upon, the name of the target, and the name of the person buying the contract. Next to all but the last few were checkmarks.

Arakasi scanned backward through the records until he found another entry without a checkmark. He assumed this to be the name Mara of the Acoma, and the person paying the price, Desio of the Minwanabi. Another missing checkmark, farther back in the record would be Mara's name again, with Desio's father Jingu beside it. Comparison of the characters revealed that the code was a complex substitution, using a key that was modified with each use.

For hours Arakasi studied the pages, attempting one solution, then another, discarding a third. But after a day and a half of work, he began to identify the pattern of change.

By the time he reached Kentosani, he had translated the journal, and reviewed its entirety several times. He secured pen and paper from the captain, and made a key for Mara, not trusting to transcribe the text lest the journal fall into other hands. But he did mark one entry he had disclosed in some distress, for its ramifications demanded his Lady's attention.

When the boat reached the Holy City, Arakasi leaped from deck to pier before the owner had fully tied up the craft, disappearing into the press of the crowd without a word. He paused only long enough to acquire suitable clothing, and made his way to the palace. There he sent word, enduring the torment of waiting with the Imperial Guards as his message made its way from servant to servant, at last reaching Lady Mara. Had he more wits or time, he might have devised a disguise to approach her more directly. But the scroll he carried was too important, and he couldn't risk being killed as an assassin by the Imperial Whites.

When at last he was escorted into Mara's presence, in her private garden, she smiled, though her gravid condition prevented her from rising to greet him.

An afternoon breeze blew, whipping dust across the stones between the planters, as the Spy Master arrived before Mara and bowed.

With emotion that belied his usual dry manner, Arakasi said, ''Lady, the task is done.''

Mara did not miss the change in her Spy Master. Her eyes widened, and she motioned for the servants to leave, then indicated that her Spy Master should sit beside her upon the bench.

Arakasi obeyed and handed his mistress a bundle, wrapped in silk. She opened it and saw the scroll with its red ribbons and hamoi-flower stamping.

Mara said, ''The tong is destroyed?''

Arakasi's voice reflected unprecedented weariness. ''Nearly. There is a small matter left to resolve.''

Mara glanced at the cipher, saw the key, and put the journal aside for later study. ''Arakasi, what is wrong?''

The Spy Master found words difficult. ''I discovered . . . something about myself . . . on this journey, mistress.'' He took a deep breath. ''I may not be the man I once was . . . no, I *am* not the man I once was.''

Mara resisted the impulse to look into his eyes. She did not try to read his doubts, but waited for him to continue.

''Mistress, at the time when we are most challenged, by the Assembly and by Jiro of the Anasati . . . I am not sure I am equal to the tasks before us.''

Mara touched his hand in gentle affection. ''Arakasi, I have always admired your resourcefulness and the amusement I took whenever you would appear mysteriously, in this garb or that.'' She regarded him with seriousness underneath her light warmth. "But for each curious garb there was a story, a mission in which you endured danger and pain."

Arakasi said, "A girl died."

Mara said, "Who was she?"

"The sister to another." He hesitated, painfully unsure of himself.

"She is important to you, this other girl?"

Arakasi stared at the green sky above the garden, inwardly recalling a face that seemed to shift from that of a taunting courtesan to a dying, frightened girl's. "I don't know. I have never known anyone like her."

Mara was silent a moment. "I have said that I admired you the most among those in my service." Her eyes looked into his. "But of my closest officers, you have always seemed the least in need of affection."

Arakasi sighed. "In truth, my Lady, I also thought myself without that need. Now I wonder."

"You feel that the Spy Master of the Acoma cannot afford friendships?"

Arakasi emphatically shook his head. "No, he cannot, which leaves us with a problem."

"How much of a problem?" she asked.

Arakasi rose, as if giving rein to restlessness might ease his turmoil. "The only man I would trust to have the skill to keep you safe in my place is, unfortunately, the one who is trying to destroy you."

Mara looked up at him, a spark of humor in her eyes. "Chumaka of the Anasati?"

Arakasi nodded. "I must continue to seek out his agents and destroy them."

"What of this unfinished matter of the tong?"

Arakasi saw at a glance that she would have all the tale, so he told her of his trip to the south that had led to the death of the Obajan. He mentioned the risk the courtesan Kamlio posed to them. "As long as the tong holds out any hope of regaining their journal, its assassins will torture and kill anyone they suspect of having information. Only after their honor is compromised publicly will they begin to wither and die.

"That scroll is the only means they have of ascertaining who they are contracted to kill. Once it is learned that the journal has been stolen, any man may claim the tong owes him a death, and they have no way to prove him a liar. More, it is their natami, and its absence shows that Turakamu no longer looks upon their efforts with favor."

Arakasi tucked his fingers in his sash. He paused as if choosing words, then said, "Once you have reviewed the records to your satisfaction, I will insure that every rumor monger in the Holy City is aware of the theft. As word spreads, the tong will disburse like smoke."

Mara once again was not diverted from the underlying issue. "This courtesan. She's the one who has . . . caused such a change in you?"

Arakasi's eyes betrayed confusion. "Perhaps. Or perhaps she is but a symptom of it. Either way, she is . . . a danger to your safety. Out of prudence, she should be . . . silenced."

Mara observed her Spy Master's posture and manner, then made a judgment. "Go and save her from the tong," she ordered. "Silence her by bringing her under Acoma protection."

"It will require a great deal of money, mistress." His voicing a practical concern barely hid his relief and embarrassment.

"More than you have asked for before?" she said with mock alarm. Arakasi had been her most expensive retainer over the years, and the lavish provisions she had allowed him had earned her many a scolding from Jican.

"This is not something I do on behalf of the Acoma," he revealed, an implied plea that somehow won past his iron control. He was not the sure servant, but a suppliant. Only once before had Mara seen him like this, when he had thought himself a failure and begged her permission to take his own life with the sword. She arose and gripped his hand tightly. "If you do this for yourself, you act also for the Acoma. That is my will. Jican is inside. He will provide whatever funds you need."

Arakasi started to speak, but found no words. So he simply bowed and said, "Mistress."

She watched him depart, and as he entered her apartment in the palace, she beckoned to a servant hovering in the doorway. She needed a cool, soothing drink. As the maid came to attend her, Mara pondered upon the consequences of countermanding Arakasi's judgment. She took a risk, encouraging him to spare the courtesan. Then, she thought with a bitterness left over from past losses, what would the future bring for any of them if she made no allowance for matters of the heart?

Light shone through the dome. It caught like fire on the golden throne, and cast triangular dapples across the pyramidal dais. Twenty levels down, it warmed the marble floors and flashed on the rail where the supplicants came and knelt for audience with the Light of Heaven. Despite the small slave boys swishing plumed fans, the Emperor's throne room was airless. Officials sweltered under their finery, and the younger of the two present, Lord Hoppara, sat still. It was too hot even to fidget. The elderly Lord

Frasai reclined upon his cushion, now and again nodding under his ceremonial helm, as if he fought off sleep.

The five priests in attendance murmured, and tended their censers,
adding the reek of incense to the already stifling atmosphere.

On the golden throne, weighed down beneath layers of fine mantles,
and the massive plumed crown of the Empire, Ichindar looked too worn
and thin for a man in his late thirties. The day had been fraught with tense
decisions, and the session was not over. Once weekly, the Emperor held a
Day of Appeals, when, from dawn to sunset, he was available to his
people. He must sit in his chair of state, and give judgments for as long as
supplicants should appear, until the hour of sundown, when the priests
sang their evening invocations. Once, when a Warlord had held office
over the council, the Day of Appeals had been ceremonial. Beggars, low
priests, commoners with petty grievances—these had gathered to hear
the wisdom of a ruler who shared mystery with their gods. Ichindar often
had napped in his chair, while the priests acted as his voice, dispensing
alms or advice as their gods allowed in righteousness.

Since then the nature of the Day of Appeals had changed. The supplicants who came to beg audience were often nobles, and many times
enemies, seeking to weaken, extort, or break the imperial rule over the
Nations. Now, Ichindar sat rigid on the golden throne and played the
deadly Game of the Council, in words, in judgments, in the knowledge
that the stakes were often his own supremacy. Sundown always found him
exhausted, and many days he could not be trusted to recall the name of
the consort selected that week to share his bed.

Today he dared not bend his head more than a fraction, lest the weight
of his crown of state bow his neck. He flicked fingernails dusted with gilt
toward the woman who sat on the white-and-gold cushion at his feet.

"Lady, you should not be here, but resting in the cool gardens by the
singing fountains."

Heavily pregnant, and tired enough that her skin looked transparent,
Mara dredged up a smile. "If you try to command me, I'll spoil your
image of authority by refusing to leave."

Ichindar muffled a chuckle behind one wing of his pearl-crusted collar.
"You would, too, you insufferably willful woman. When I named you
Servant of the Empire, I created a monster."

Mara's smile vanished as she inclined her head toward the floor below,
where the next supplicant approached and made his bow. Her eyes turned
hard as precious metal, and the hand on her lap fan clenched white.

Ichindar followed her glance, and muttered what might have been a profanity under his breath. One of the priests twitched around in annoy-ance, then quickly faced front as the voice of the Emperor rang out through the domed chamber of audience.

"Lord Jiro of the Anasati, know that you have the ear of the gods through our ear. Heaven will hear your plea, and we will answer. Rise. You have leave to speak."

The slight snap to the consonants warned of Ichindar's irritation. His hazel eyes were chilly as he watched the Anasati Lord straighten up from his obeisance and stand at the rail, his avid, scholar's gaze trained intently upon the golden throne, and also the woman who sat before it, at the Emperor's feet. Jiro bowed. Although he observed the forms of courtesy, his graceful delivery somehow managed to mock.

"The imperial dais holds company today," he opened. "Good day, Lady of the Acoma, Servant of the Empire." His lips thinned in what a friend might have construed for a smile. An enemy knew better.

Mara felt a chill chase across her skin. Never before had a pregnancy made her feel helpless; now, under Jiro's predatory regard, she felt her clumsy heaviness, and that unnerved her. Still, she did not lose control and allow herself to be baited.

Ichindar's voice cracked across the interval that followed, as Acoma Lady and Anasati Lord matched stares. Slender and worn as the Emperor was, his authority was real, a palpable air of force even in that enormous chamber. "If you have come to us as supplicant, Lord Jiro, you will not waste our time in idle social chat."

Ever the smooth courtier, Jiro waved aside the reprimand with a flash of gold; he wore metal rings, his one affectation to flaunt his wealth. The rest of his attire was plain. "But my Sovereign," he protested in gentle familiarity, "I do come as supplicant. And my reason, I must admit, is a social one."

Mara resisted an urge to shift uneasily on her cushion. What could Jiro have on his mind? His informal tone was itself an insult to the Light of Heaven, but not one that could be noted without setting shame upon Ichindar's dignity. To react to Jiro's presumption was to give weight to him as a man. No one who sat on a god's throne could acknowledge so petty a slight.

The Light of Heaven maintained a frosty silence through the minute that Jiro stood with his brows suggestively raised. The subject under discussion would have to be pursued by the Anasati, were it to continue.

Jiro tilted his head, as if he only then recalled his true purpose. His face very subtly leered, and one eyelid drooped suggestively toward a wink. "I came because I have heard many rumors concerning your daughter Jehilia's famed beauty. I ask a boon, my Sovereign: that you share your joy in her with your people. I ask to be presented to her."

Mara reined back a burst of fury. Jehilia was but a girl, barely ten, and not yet come into her womanhood. She was not a woman of the Reed Life, to be gawked at by men who were not relatives! She was certainly too young for courtship, or even for the suggestion that she should be entertaining suitors. Jiro's subtleties were twisted and deep, that he should come here and dare such a thought in public. The ramifications were endless, not least the implied slight to the Light of Heaven's manhood. Without sons, he must secure the imperial line through his daughter's marriage, but how presumptuous the Anasati Lord was to imply credence of the gossip of the streets, that the Emperor would have no son, and that the ninety-second crowned head of the Nations would be the man who won Jehilia's hand.

But angry words could not be spoken; Mara clamped her teeth, aware of Ichindar's advisers standing red-faced with fury to the sides. Made sensitive to her own vulnerability, she was mindful that the three priests on the pyramid dais were affronted, but powerless to intervene. Lord Hoppara had taken a stranglehold on the place at his sash where a sword should hang, were weapons not forbidden in the presence of his Emperor. As father of the girl, Ichindar sat stone-still. The jewels on his mantle were frozen sparks, as if he had restrained himself from breathing.

For a long, tense interval, nothing stirred in the grand audience hall.

With unprecedented audacity, Jiro ventured a lazy-voiced addendum to his petition. "I have done some interesting reading recently. You do know, my Sovereign, that before your reign, seven imperial daughters were presented on or before their tenth birthday. I can tell you names, if you like."

Mara knew this was a second slap against a man whose office had once revolved around memorization of his family pedigree and other issues of religious context that had nothing to do with rulership. Ichindar would know of those seven girls, if not the mitigating circumstances of history that had forced their public presentation before puberty. And his office was much more, now, than religious ceremony alone.

The sun shone hot on the topaz and marble floors, and the Imperial Guards stood like statues. Then, with icy deliberation, Ichindar set his clenched fists on the arms of the golden throne. Anger stiffened his face like a cameo against the mantling weight of his collars. Yet his voice was controlled to its usual regal pitch when he deigned to give answer.

"My Lord of the Anasati," he said, precise consonants echoing off the high dome overhead, "it would please us better to present to you our son, when the gods choose to bless us with an heir. As to our daughter Jehilia, if the Lord of the Anasati enjoys paying heed to the gossip of her nurses, who boast that every infant they dote upon is blessed with extraordinary beauty, then we grant permission for a portrait to be made by one of the artists we patronize, and to be sent to the Anasati estates. This is our will."

The traditional phrase rang into silence. Ichindar was not the figurehead his forbears had been but an Emperor fighting to retain his authority. Mara sat back, limp with relief; his handling of Jiro's aggression had been exemplary. A portrait of a child! Ichindar had neatly taken the blade out of the dilemma. But, sadly, the greater issue remained. Jiro had dared to be first to voice the thought that Jehilia would become a husband's path to the golden throne. She would not remain a pretty royal child for much longer, but would become a hotly contested prize in the Great Game. Once a girl torn wholesale from the Goddess Lashima's order into the throes of the Empire's bloody politics, Mara felt her heart go out to the child.

Ichindar's hold upon the reins of rulership would slip on the day his eldest daughter married. Unless he could conceive a male heir, the traditionalists would use Jehilia as a powerful means to undermine him, especially if her husband was a well-placed, powerful noble.

On the floor below, at the supplicants' rail, Jiro crossed both arms over his breast in the time-honored imperial salute. He bowed before the Emperor's honor guard, and arose, smiling. "I thank my Sovereign Lord. A portrait of Jehilia to hang upon my chamber wall would be very pleasing indeed."

The dig was petty; Jiro had not quite dared to say "bedchamber wall," Mara noted with vindictiveness. But that he had stooped to so mean a comment in public hearing demonstrated his contempt for the man who sat upon the golden throne. And Mara realized, with a stab of intuition, that Jiro would not have been quite so vicious had she not been present. The taunt to Ichindar had been intended to goad her as well.

"I fear this day I have not been a benefit to you," she murmured as the great doors boomed closed behind the Lord of the Anasati.

Ichindar started to reach out to her in sympathy, recalled his formal audience, and restrained himself before an adviser needed to step forth and intervene. "My Lady, you are wrong," he murmured back. His hair clung to his forehead, too damp with perspiration to be stirred by the fan boys' efforts, and his fists had not loosened on his throne arms. "Had you not been present, strong as rock at my feet, I surely would have lost my poise!" He ended with a viciousness he had kept back from the enemy who had angered him. "It is a very unscrupulous man who will stoop to attack through a father's love for his child."

Mara said nothing. She had known many such unscrupulous men. Her memory turned poignantly to two murdered children, a boy and a girl both under five years of age—the children of the late Minwanabi Lord— who died as a direct result of her actions. Her hand rested upon the mound of her belly, over the swell of her unborn child. She clenched her teeth in resolve. She had lost a son, and another child by Hokanu she had never had the chance to know. Again she swore that the deaths of all of the young ones must not be for nothing. She would die and the Acoma name be as dust before the wrath of the Assembly of Magicians before she let Jiro reinstate the Warlord's office, and bring back the unconscionable bloody conflicts that had comprised the Game of the Council in the name of honor.

Now that the first steps toward change had been taken, she was determined not to give back old ground.

Her eyes and Ichindar's met, as if the thought had been spoken aloud between them. Then the doors opened, and the imperial herald announced the next supplicant.

It seemed a long time until sundown.

Hokanu stripped off his sweaty leather riding gloves. "Where is she?" he demanded of the white-clad personage that stood blocking the doorway.

But the immensely fat servant did not budge. His gleaming, moon-round face went stiff with displeasure at the Shinzawai Lord's poor etiquette, in showing such unseemly haste. The imperial hadonra was a man attentive to nuance, and he ran the vast complex of the Emperor's private apartments in the palace with unflinching, cold-hearted proficiency. Moths did not infest the imperial closets, the servants went about their duties like oiled clockwork, and anxious husbands did not disrupt the hadonra's morning round of inspection with commands better suited to the battlefield.

Fixed squarely in the vestibule's entryway, the huge man folded meaty forearms. "You may not pass at this time, my Lord."

Hokanu restrained himself from a pointedly nasty comment. "My wife, I was told, went into labor two days ago. I have been riding on horseback at speed from my estates beyond Silmani since then, and have not slept. I will know if my wife is safe and well, and whether my heir was born whole, if you will kindly let me pass through to her apartment.''

The imperial hadonra curled his lip. The redolence of the barbaric creatures that permeated Hokanu's presence was an offense. No matter how powerful the Lord, no matter that he was a staunch supporter of the Light of Heaven, he stank of his horseflesh, and he should have bathed before making an appearance in these hallways. ''You may not pass,'' said the servant, unperturbed. ''The Emperor has commanded a performance of sobatu for this morning.'' He referred to a form of classic opera, in the grand high style, of which only ten had been composed. Then, as if Hokanu were not educated, and the son of a preeminent house, the servant added, ''The Imperial Shalotobaku Troupe are using the chambers beyond for their dressing, and as I need not remind you, none may lay eyes upon them but the Emperor's immediate family.''

Hokanu bit back his irritation. Too hurried and too proud to argue over nuances of genealogy with a servant when he had yet to know the status of his family, he held himself rigid lest he reach out of rage for his sword and resort to threats. ''Then, good and faithful servant, you will do your duty by the Emperor's players and show me another way around the wing that they are using.''

The hadonra dug in his toes, and jerked his larded chin up another notch. ''I may not leave, my Lord. It is my duty to watch this doorway, and see that no one passes who is not of the royal blood.''

The comment was more than an anxious father's patience could stand. Hokanu bowed at the waist as if in accord with the hadonra's pompous adherence to etiquette. Then, without warning, he charged forward. His leanly muscled shoulder drove hard into the fat servant's belly. There was an explosion of air, and a grunt. Then the imperial hadonra folded like a fish and dropped, deprived of wind to give voice to his outrage.

Hokanu was beyond hearing in any case, having broken into a run the instant he gained access to the vestibule. Two nights and a day spent on horseback had not stiffened him to the point where he could not command his body. He dashed through a bustle of men in bright costumes, some wearing the provocative robes of courtesans, and all without exception painted with layers of gaudy makeup. He leaped over the humped back of a saganjan, the beast out of legend that past Tsurani heroes fought; the masked head turned to watch him go, while an inattentive midsection was jerked into an ungainly trip. The player dressed as the forelimbs twisted to stop disaster, while the belly section behind him stepped in the opposite direction. The concoction staggered, and a moment later the whole length went down in a muddle of kicking legs, and curses muffled under scales sewn of fabric and leather.

Unmindful that he had downed a dragon, Hokanu forged ahead, through a gaggle of girl vocalists wearing little but feathers. Plumage unmoored by his passage drifted in flurries in his wake. He ducked a wooden sword tied with streamers, and sidestepped lacquer-masked kara-gabuge, which reached out dwarf hands and tried to trip him.

He cursed, and avoided stepping upon what looked like one of the imperial daughters, sucking her knuckles, and staring at the surrounding panoply with huge, three-year-old eyes. She spotted Hokanu, remembered him for the man who had amused her with stories of monsters, and obligingly shouted his name.

Some mornings, Hokanu concluded, the God of Tricks had a man's measure, and no act of appeasement could bring respite, one bad moment leading to the next without letup. He was going to have to pay a stiff fee to compensate the honor of the imperial hadonra; not to mention whatever extortionate worth could be set upon the bruised dignity of a saganjan. He was red from embarrassment, and stinking of sweat as well as horse, by the time he left the chaos of the opera troupe behind and gained access to the corridor that led to his Lady's quarters within the imperial palace.

Outside the ornately carved screen that led to the women's chambers he met Misa, Mara's personal maid. Unable to contain his anxiety, he blurted, "How is she?"

The maid gave him back a brilliant smile. "Oh, my Lord! You will be proud. They are both doing well, and she is beautiful."

"Of course she is beautiful," Hokanu said, stupid with relief and loosened nerves. "I married her, didn't I?"

And he never thought to pause or question Misa's explosion of giggles as he hurried on, into a chamber filled with sunlight and breeze, and with the gentle song of a fountain in the gardens outside. There he felt his unwashed state most sorely, as he skidded to a stop on the waxed floor in the longed-for presence of his wife.

She sat on embroidered cushions, her newly slender body robed loosely in white. Her hair was unbound, her head bent, and a smile of rapture curved her lips as she raised her face and saw her husband restored to her. And yes, another white-wrapped bundle kicked in her arms, with dark eyes like hers, and rosebud lips, and swaddling ties of Shinzawai blue: his own blood heir by the Lady he loved.

"My Lord," said Mara in delight. "Welcome back. Let me present to you your daughter and your heir, whom I would call Kasuma after your brother.''

Hokanu's excited step forward checked in mid-stride. ''Kasuma,'' he said, sharper than he intended, but surprise made him clumsy. ''But that's a girl's—'' He stumbled to a stop, comprehending. ''A girl?''

Mara nodded, her eyes dancing with happiness. ''Here.'' She raised the little bundle, which made a sound of contentment. ''Take her, and let her know her father.''

Stunned, he stared unmoving at the infant. ''A daughter.'' The words would not sink in. He could only stand in mute shock, caught in outrage that the gods should be so cruel, that Mara be allowed only one child, and that he should be deprived of the son he needed to continue the greatness of his house.

Mara saw his confusion, and her smile died. The babe in her arms waved in abandon, making her difficult to support in an extended position; yet still Hokanu made no move to accept her warm weight in his arms. ''What's wrong?'' Mara asked, distress creeping into her voice. She was still weary from childbirth, and unable to fully master her poise. ''Do you think she is ugly? Her face will be less red and wrinkled in a few more days.''

Helpless, cut by his wife's growing distress, and by his own hard knot of rage that fate should be so unkind, Hokanu shook his head. ''She is not ugly, my beloved Lady. I have seen newborns before.''

Still holding the baby out toward the father, Mara stiffened with the beginnings of outrage. Baffled by her husband's distance, she flared, ''Then this one displeases you, my Lord?''

''Oh, gods,'' Hokanu burst out, annoyed with himself for losing all vestige of tact, but unable to rein back his disappointment. ''She is very lovely, Mara, but I wish she could have been a son! I need a strong heir so very badly.''

Now Mara's eyes flashed hurt, which slowly turned to anger. She withdrew her upraised arms, clutched little Kasuma to her breast, and stiffened in regal affront. Coldly she asked, ''Do you imply that a woman cannot assume the mantle of a great house, and make the name of her ancestors prosper? Do you think House Acoma could have been led to greater glories by a man? How dare you, Hokanu! How dare you presume that our daughter should become any less than I have! She is not deformed or stupid! She will have our guidance in her upbringing! She will embody Shinzawai honor, no less, and she does not need to be any swaggering boy child to find her way to the greatness that is her destiny!''

Hokanu raised opened hands. He sat down heavily on a handy cushion, confused, tired, and heartsick with disappointment that he lacked the ability to convey. He wanted what he had lost in Ayaki and Justin: the comradeship of showing a boy the warrior's path and a ruler's perceptions and guile. He needed the heart bond he had lost with his brother, gone to the barbarian world; and the man's love he had known for his father, lately departed to Turakamu's halls. He could never have back those ties to family, but he had yearned to pass on their heritage after him to a son. "You don't understand," he said softly.

"What don't I understand!" Mara cried back. She was very near to weeping. "Here is your daughter, from my body. What more do you need in an heir?"

"There," said Hokanu. "Mara, please, I have been thoughtless. Of course I can love Kasuma." He responded to the hurt behind his wife's anger and reached out in comfort.

"Don't touch me!" Mara burst out, flinching away. "Touch your little girl, and bid her welcome."

Hokanu shut his eyes. Inwardly he berated himself that his normally sharp perception should have deserted him in this most critical of moments. Better the saganjan had fallen on him, or the imperial hadonra had prevailed, than to have burst into Mara's chambers and made such a botch of his greeting. He reached out, gathered the infant from his wife's stiff arms, and cradled her. His heart did warm to Kasuma's energetic thrashing. The little pink lips puckered, and the eyes opened to show him bright jet jewels in a wrinkled red face. She was delightful, and beautiful, and indeed his heir; but she could not reverse his disappointment that she had not been born a boy.

Hokanu considered his alternatives, since Mara could have no more issue. He could take a mistress, or a courtesan, and get a son for the Shinzawai. But the thought of another woman in his bed made him ache in fierce rejection. No, he did not wish to have women about for breeding. Most Lords would not blink at that choice, but Hokanu found the thought repugnant.

He looked up to find Mara weeping. "My wife," he said softly, "you have given me a perfect child. I had no right to be clumsy and spoil what should have been a joyous moment."

Mara choked back a sob. After weeks in the Imperial Palace, attending the Emperor's councils and standing as his right-hand adviser, she was aware of the factions that sought to undermine the authority of the golden throne. She felt the tides of politics churning to upset new change, and to bring back the older, bloodier order of the Warlord's office. Like a blade against her neck, she sensed how near the Nations were to outright civil conflict. Now more than at any other time, they needed to present a solid front to the factions that favored traditionalist rule.

"Kasuma is part of the new order," she said to Hokanu. "She must carry the torch after us, and she will have Justin as her brother. She will lead armies, if she must, just as he will strive to maintain peace without force of arms that will be needful to build a better future."

Hokanu shared that dream. "I know that, beloved. I agree."

But he could not entirely shut off his grief, and his disappointment that his dreams would not be shaped by a boy who could share his love of rough sports.

Mara sensed the half-truth behind his tone. She hardened, visibly as she took her child back, her hands stroking the blanket that covered little Kasuma. The fact that Hokanu could not embrace the concept of his firstborn as heir was not a thing she could readily forgive, unaware as she was that the priest of Hantukama had imparted the fact that she would have no other children.

That bit of information Hokanu kept to himself, although he knew that to break his silence would bring Mara's immediate understanding. Looking at her, realizing that her cheeks were hollow, and her face aged with worry after her stay within the Imperial Palace, he decided that the slight estrangement in their relationship would repair itself, over time; but the grief that knowledge of her barrenness would impart might never leave her, life long. Let her cling to hope, he decided, his gaze upon her and his newborn daughter grown fond, but distant. "We will all manage," he mused, unaware he was thinking aloud. Then, mindful of the Great One Fumita's warning, he added, "Thank the gods, though, that the Shinzawai have no cause against Jiro of the Anasati. That would make a complication that none of us could afford."

Mara was looking at him strangely. Her preoccupation with her infant was eclipsed by an unpleasant recollection, Hokanu saw as he looked across the sunny chamber, and fully interpreted her expression. "What is it, my love?" he asked.

Her former hurt was not forgotten, but only placed in abeyance, for she answered sharply. "Ill news. Arakasi completed his mission against the Obajan of the Hamoi Tong, and he brought that."

She inclined her head toward the journal that lay upon a side table. Hokanu moved to inspect it. The writing was in a heavy black hand, and the words appeared to be in cipher. Hokanu was on the point of inquiring where the journal had come from, and what was its significance, when he noticed the water mark on the parchment that showed in slight relief where the sunlight struck it. The configuration of the pattern shaped the flower of the Hamoi Tong, and the scroll, with its ugly inked lines, could only be the record roll of purchased assassinations.

Aware still, and piercingly, of his wife's gaze upon him, the Lord of the Shinzawai said, "What is it?"

Mara took a deep breath. "Beloved, I am sorry. Your father had enemies, many of them. His death was not due to old age, or natural causes, but to an obscure poison delivered by a needle dart while he slept. Your father's death was executed by a tong assassin, paid for by Jiro of the Anasati."

Hokanu's expression went wooden, the flesh over his skull taut as a drumhead with shock. "No," he murmured in disbelief, yet aware of the truth of Mara's statement. He considered Fumita's warning at the funeral in a fresh light, and knew that his blood father, a magician, had somehow known of the tong's intervention in the natural order. Grief pierced him afresh, that Kamatsu's days had been shortened, that a wise and perceptive old man had been stolen away from his last days under sunlight.

It was outrage! An insult to honor! A Kanazawai Lord had been sent prematurely to the halls of the Red God, and warning or not, Assembly or not, Jiro of the Anasati must answer for the offense. Family honor and clan honor demanded a death to right the balance.

"Where is Arakasi?" Hokanu said harshly. "I would speak to him."

Mara shook her head sadly. "He delivered the scroll and broke the cipher, so that we could read its secrets. Then he requested a leave from duty, a matter of personal honor." Mara did not mention the sum of money he had requested of her, or that the reason involved a young woman. "His coup against the Obajan was a brave and risky deed. He did well to survive. I granted his request." She frowned slightly, recalling the interview, and her thought then that he would never have asked her a boon at so precarious a time had the confusion in his heart not been compelling. "He will report back to us when he can," Mara concluded. None had been more aware than the Spy Master of the explosive potential of the contents of the tong's record scroll. More than Kamatsu's death had been listed; and there were other assassinations as yet incomplete on the rolls, alongside the monetary payments made by the Lords who wished rivals or enemies dead.

Assassination in any form was a dishonor, both to the victim and, if the truth were found out, to the family who paid for the deed. The scroll recovered by Arakasi contained enough sensitive information to plunge the Empire into a chaos of feuding families, all vengeance bent, as Hokanu was.

But that Kamatsu should have died by an assassin's dart was an outrage she could not let pass. Her words were hard as barbarian iron as she said, "My husband, we have no choice. A way must be found to evade the Assembly's edict and bring down Lord Jiro of the Anasati."

"For Ayaki's sake also," Hokanu broke in. Never would he forget the sight of the boy's dying, with the huge black gelding broken with him.

"No." Mara's word held gentle regret. "For Ayaki we have already paid." And, tears in her eyes, she told Hokanu of the Obajan's personal feud with House Acoma, brought about by a forgery of Arakasi's that had caused five Minwanabi servants to be put to death, to end a past threat of enemy spying. "The tong took offense at the Acoma," she finished. "It acted on its own initiative to end my line, operating beyond the scope of the contract agreed to with Tasaio of the Minwanabi." Her last sentence came bitterly. "They failed. The Obajan is dead, fittingly, by Arakasi's own hand."

Hokanu stared at her, hard as flint with her motherhood forgotten in the face of dark thoughts and bloody politics. Kasuma fretted at the lack of attention, her face screwed up in the beginnings of a loud cry. "My wife," he said, saddened, and angered, and frustrated by the injustices of life, "let us go home."

His heart went out to her as her eyes turned to him, liquid with unshed tears. "Yes," she said. "Let us go home."

But it was not of the beautiful lakeside estate that she thought as she said the word, but of the wide pastureland estate where she had grown from childhood. Suddenly, strongly, irresistibly, she wished to return to the lands of her family. She wanted familiar surroundings, and the memories of her own father's love, and a time before she had first tasted the heady wine of power and rule. Maybe on the land of her birth she could come to terms with the heartache and her fears for the futures of both House Acoma and House Shinzawai.

15. Secrets

Mara sighed.

Hot, tired, and discouraged after her journey to the original Acoma estates, she found relief from the noon sun in the cho-ja tunnels, a nearly forgotten haven. Her marriage to Hokanu and the close-knit rapport shared between them had come to replace her need for such solace. But before that, in her early years as Ruling Lady, the spice-scented dimness of the underground passageways, with their scurrying workers, had provided a sense of protection when seemingly insurmountable dangers had oppressed her on all sides.

Yet her perils then had been from the plots of human foes. Overwhelming as her straits had seemed, unpleasant as her first marriage to an Anasati son had been at the time, she could not have imagined the trials that would beset her this day. Physical abuses had been replaced by wounds of the spirit, a betrayal by the only man who truly understood her heart. Whatever underhanded injury Jiro of the Anasati might contrive in the future, her true enemies were the magicians, who might on a whim annihilate the Acoma name, even to memory of its existence. And it was their edicts that sheltered Jiro as he plotted.

Kamatsu's murder had left a hard knot of rage in Mara's chest. Fears that must never be spoken of for Tsurani and house pride caused a constant grinding of teeth. Mara had felt this way before as she faced enemies, but never over so long a period, and never for stakes so high. All that she loved was in jeopardy. Since Ayaki's loss, stress had become familiar to the point where she had forgotten what it was to sleep and dream without nightmares.

The subterranean dimness shielded her. Isolated within her own silence, but not alone, she relaxed as her litter moved deeper into the familiar tunnels of the hive. Her bearers jostled past the bustling cho-ja, surrounded by the high-pitched commands of soldiers, and the clashing ring of chitinous forearms as patrol leaders slapped their midsection in salute to her retinue. Knowing her surcease was only temporary, Mara surrendered to the illusion of relief. For a space, she felt restored to past days when her responsibilities and her heartaches had been few. Her inner barriers loosened and moisture gathered in her eyes. She bit her lip, but did not blot away her tears. In the cho-ja hive, scantily lit by the violet-blue glow of light globes, her weakness would pass unnoticed. The worry, the frustration, the daily ache of her helplessness to redress the wrongs done her family by the Anasati, combined to oppress her. She could deny her emotions no longer. The death of two children, the break in rapport with her husband and closest confidant, threatened to overwhelm her.

The years when Mara had grown in confidence and ability to control any situation seemed empty. Her emergence to dominance in the time-honored Game of the Council became a false achievement, the edict of the Assembly at a stroke preventing the established ways of avenging wrongs against honor. Politics and intrigues had taken a turn down non-traditional paths. The advantage that Mara had always enjoyed, a willingness to break with convention, was now lost to her, as every Ruling Lord in the Empire scrambled to contrive new means to dominate ancient rivals.

The old ways had all been upset.

Even the destruction of the Hamoi Tong, and the clear knowledge of where Jiro's true culpability lay, brought little relief. For although one menace to the Acoma had been ended, the Great Ones yet prevented her from avenging a deep insult to honor.

Mara's return trip by river barge to the homelands of her ancestors had been a stopgap effort to set hurt and confusion at bay because, in truth, she had no sane place to seek solutions to the dilemmas that beset her.

Mara closed her eyes, rocked by the slight sway as her bearers wended their way downward into the tunnels. The air here was warmer, thick with the alien scents of the hive. Light globes were spaced at wider intervals, and the throngs of scurrying workers thinned. The tramp of humans' sandals became more prevalent than the click of chitinous claws. Mara knew her retinue must be nearing the Queen's cavern. But the route was no longer entirely familiar. Since her last visit, walls and arches that had been roughly hewn were now polished smooth, or carved and overhung with richly dyed hangings. If the arrangement of colors and tassels was unusual to human eyes, the effect was prosperous. The differences here seemed strangely at odds with impressions like untouched memory. But for the silver hair beginning to show at her temples, Mara might have been revisiting her girlhood. The house where she had played as a child, where she had first married and given birth, and acquired her taste for power, had initially appeared the same—until she remembered with a hollow stab to her stomach that silence ruled where once a young son had run roistering through the corridors.

She had felt a pang of loneliness. Ayaki was not the only loved one lost to her. The all too familiar surroundings brought heartache along with solace. By the gods, how she longed to see her red-haired barbarian, Kevin of Zūn, who had taught her the meaning of love and womanhood in the kekali gardens here; and Nacoya, her onetime nurse and First Adviser, whose scolding and sage advice had more often than not averted disaster. Another trail of tears seeped from Mara's eyes. Although Kevin had often infuriated her with his headstrong, mannerless ways, and Nacoya's fussy proprieties had sometimes been a hindrance, she missed them both. The understanding she had shared with Hokanu, which had grown to replace those lost relationships, had seemed a bastion of infallibility, until now. A shadow lay between them since his misgivings over the birth of his daughter. Still angry with him, Mara rubbed her cheeks on her fine silk cuffs. The fabric would water-stain, but she did not care! It had taken the near obliteration of her line to make Hokanu see her need to name Justin as Acoma heir. That she had needed to suffer the loss of their firstborn infant to convince him had caused less pain than this!

Now Hokanu's incomprehensible reluctance to accept Kasuma as Shinzawai firstborn was building another wall between them. A son, and only a son, would satisfy him, so it seemed. As if she could not bear a boy child in the future, Mara raged bitterly; or as if he were not free to exercise his right as Ruling Lord to lie with a dozen concubines to give him issue. No, the message behind his behavior was hurtfully clear: what he could accept in his wife he found unimaginable in a daughter, that a woman could be worthy of ruling a great house.

As she had so many times in the past when disheartened by despair, Mara had entered the cho-ja tunnels seeking an alien perspective, a different point of view that could give rise to new ideas.

A light touch roused Mara from reminiscence; Lujan nodded ahead, reminding that her retinue had reached the chamber of the Queen.

As her litter was borne through the final arch, with its squatting rows of sentries so still they might have been polished black statues, Mara composed herself. Entering the huge cavern, she used an old, silent meditation chant to shed her smoldering resentment. When at last her bearers lowered her down before the grand dais, she had recovered her proper decorum.

The cho-ja Queen dominated the chamber, her bulk supported by a massive pedestal of earth. Mara remembered how tiny the Queen had been when they had first met, far away in the hive where she had been hatched. The delicate creature had matured, coming to her full growth within the first year of her accouchement at the Acoma estate. Now she bulked many times the size of her attendants, dwarfing even the largest of her warriors, with just her upper torso and head retaining their original size. Workers scurried around her mammoth body, keeping her clean and comfortable, as she produced the eggs that provided the different classes of cho-ja: warriors, workers specialized in any of a dozen different crafts, and, should the hive became prosperous to the point of overcrowding, a new queen.

Mara gave a bow of the head, as was proper between equals.

"Greetings, Lady of the Acoma, Servant of the Empire," said the Queen, her high-pitched tones clear over the bustle of workers in the gallery.

"Honors to your hive, Queen," answered Mara as Lujan provided a hand to guide her to the cushions waiting for her. The rapidity of cho-ja communication was still a mystery to Mara; somehow the Queen always seemed to know in advance of her arrival, and as much could be determined, the hive ruler seemed to enjoy these visits. Mara had ceased trying to understand the cho-ja in human terms; living with an outworld barbarian had taught her that persistently seeing through Tsurani eyes kept her blind to refreshing insights.

While Lujan oversaw the placement and disposition of her honor guard, her servants laid out sweets and Midkemian tea for her refreshment, and also to share with cho-ja factors. Against Jican's pessimistic predictions after the poisoning by the false Midkemian trader, Mara had developed a fondness for the pungent drink. Never one to waste an opportunity, she had overcome her personal misfortune and had cornered the market in tea, coffee, and chocolate.

Once the banalities of tea-tasting and trade were concluded, the Queen tilted her head in what Mara had come to interpret as inquiry. "What cause brings you to us, Lady Mara? The delicacies you have brought as samples could as easily have been sent by runner."

Mara floundered for a reply. Her hesitation was unusual enough that Lujan broke his warrior's formality to glance askance to ascertain nothing was amiss. Made aware by his lapse that her quiet might be misinterpreted as duplicity, Mara chose honesty, though she risked appearing foolish. "I had no set purpose, beyond a need for your wisdom."

The Queen was silent. Around her the attendants scurried on about their tasks. The guard warriors remained squatting in immobility, but Mara knew how swiftly they could move upon command. Uneasy lest she transgress some alien point of etiquette, she resisted an impulse to follow up with excuses. If she should cause offense, and then show weakness before cho-ja strength, she might never escape these tunnels alive.

As though the Queen sensed her guest's discomfort, she said, "Many of your concepts are unknowable to us, Lady of the Acoma. This you name 'wisdom' is such a thing. Your human tonalities indicate an idea handed down from a past generation to a mind of less life experience. Forgive me, I do not wish to imply that our kind are in any way superior to yours, but our consciousness is not isolated. The hive mind we share by your terms would span millennia. To us your perspective is fleeting, tied as it is to the duration of one human life. Insomuch as we cho-ja can share a thing outside our understanding, we shall seek to give our aid."

Here the Queen folded her tiny, vestigial forelimbs, to indicate patience and an attitude of waiting.

Mara stared unseeing into the dregs of her tea. She was aware that a cho-ja's individuality was never separated from the hive mind; personal autonomy played no part in their culture, and only centuries of interaction between species had allowed the insectoids to conceptualize any sense of a human identity apart and alone from the whole. Individuality, to hive thought, held puzzling and conflicting ironies. The concept of foolishness, of someone acting against his own best interests or those of his family, seemed an insanity of irredeemable proportions to cho-ja perspective. And without foolishness, Mara thought wryly, the process of human learning could hold no meaning; the abstract term "wisdom" became too ephemeral for the hive mind to grasp.

Mara frowned, and tried afresh. "In my brief experience, your counsel and that of other humans has taught me I live in a small world. Until recently, I thought I had some control over that world." She need not repeat Ayaki's fate; or any other event. Word of the Assembly's intervention between herself and the Anasati had spread to the most remote province of the Nations, and although the cho-ja might not understand all the nuances of human affairs, they held an astute recollection of events.

Perhaps the hive mind sensed that the interdiction of the Assembly lay at the root of Mara's inquiries; certainly something warned them off. While the Queen customarily sat massive and unmoving, for the first time in Mara's experience the attendants around her went from frenetic motion to utter stillness. All activity in that vast hall ceased, though no apparent order called for silence.

Mara's uneasiness coalesced into fear.

The Queen had long ago revealed that cho-ja alliances were sold as commodities. Mara had paid lavish sums for the loyalty of the hives on both her estates. She shivered at the thought that the Great Ones' influence might extend even here, and that in words or inference she might call down their chastisement. A spell-wrought earthquake even a fraction as violent as the one that had shaken the Holy City when the Black Robe Milamber had unleashed his might would utterly devastate these tunnels. Arches and vaults would crumble into dust, and tons of black earth would fall. . . . Aware how her hands trembled, Mara thrust them into her sleeves. She must not think! Only act. And in truth, the Queen had not spoken to indicate which way hive allegiance might lie.

All that could be done was wait.

The silence became eerie in its intensity. In time, Mara's hyper-extended senses detected a faint buzzing, high-pitched as the beat of insect wings. She wondered whether this sound might signal some sort of wide-ranging communication, then decided it indeed must, since the Queen spoke with the authority of one who had reached a decision. "Mara of the Acoma, you made a point which, if I venture to presume, your kind might call wise. You observed that you live in a small world. You would do well to redefine the boundaries of that world, and look to other worlds that coexist with your own."

Mara chewed her lip, thinking fast. Behind the stilted, careful etiquette of the cho-ja Queen's phrasing she sensed reluctance. Alert for hidden opportunity, Mara pressed for more information. "What sort of worlds should I examine?"

The workers remained frozen in postures of repose as the Queen said, "This world of Kelewan, firstly. You have visited with us often, something no noble of your people has ever done. Even at the dawn of the Nations, when our two races forged the treaty that still binds, no Tsurani Lord tried this."

Mara raised her eyebrows. No scroll of history she had seen ever mentioned any formal agreement between cho-ja and human. Relations between Tsurani and cho-ja were dictated by tradition, she had assumed, as were all other facets of her life and culture. And yet the Nations extended back into antiquity; as the Queen so tactfully reminded, human memory was brief. "I have never heard of this treaty you speak of. Could you tell me more?"

The Queen's massive bulk held so motionless, she might have been a monument in black lacquer. "That is forbidden."

Astonished, Mara forgot the unearthly quiet and the frozen attitudes of the breeding workers. Her words echoed as she blurted, "Forbidden? By whom?"

"That is forbidden."

Shocked back to caution by the Queen's whipcrack inflection, Mara analyzed. If she had been rude, she had not yet been ordered from the royal chamber. Though Lujan's hands had whitened in alarm on his spear haft, the warriors of the Queen stayed crouched at rest. Pressed by curiosity and need to aggressive risks, Mara chanced that the Queen's reticence might stem from some outside source. As best she had determined, the cho-ja had no religion, no devotion to or belief in gods and forces beyond an earthly nature. If the prohibition were not from heaven, what remained? Tradition? Mara rejected that idea; the cho-ja were mercenary in their interactions, by human standards. Their consistency was due more to hive consensus than to habit. A covenant of secrecy seemed unlikely, since the hive consciousness disallowed the very concept: privacy was only possible between individual minds.

Choosing her way carefully, Mara ventured, "What of the cho-ja, my Queen? What is the history of your race?"

The Queen clicked her front claws in response to some unknowable impulse. Except for the fact that her attendants stayed locked in place, her tone might have been conversational. "We come from the Beginning, like any race, growing and gaining knowledge. There was a time, ages gone, when we lived simply. We were one of many intelligences that sought our place on a rich world and who strove at the time that man first came—"

"The Golden Bridge?" Mara interjected, trying to tie into what she knew of her own people's origins.

"So our history tells us," said the Queen. "Cho-ja eyes did not witness the arrival, but one day there were no men, and the next day a nation of refugees was encamped upon the shore near the place you name the City of the Plains."

Barely able to hide excitement, Mara asked, "You have tales from before the Golden Bridge?"

"Tales?" The Queen twitched a forelimb, as if in deprecation. "Your word translates to imply exaggeration, or embellishment based upon imperfect recollection. Please take no injury at my bluntness, but our kind need not dramatize for posterity. We remember."

Mara felt her heart race. "Do you tell me that you have that record in the hive mind?" she said, probing carefully because she sensed something momentous was at issue here. "Or that you actually have recall, as if you saw with your ancestors' eyes?"

''We are of one mind, and one people.'' At no discernible signal from the Queen, the breeding attendants surged back to their customary frenetic industry. ''What is experienced by one is shared by all, save when one dies in isolation, far from others.''

Relieved to be restored to a less sensitive subject, Mara considered the implications. She had long known that messages seemed to reach other hives with unbelievable speed; but in her wildest imaginings, she had not conceived that such communication might be simultaneous. ''You can . . . speak with the voice of one who was there . . . ?'' Her mind fought to encompass the immensity of a consciousness that held complete recall of the past.

The Queen clicked her mandibles, amused. ''We were there, Mara. As you humans might frame the concept, I was there . . . not this body, of course, or this mind, but . . . we were there. What my forbears saw I know as they knew.''

Mara signaled a servant to fill her teacup, forgetting that the water by now was cold. Lujan suppressed a grin at her absorption. While not so nimble of wit as his mistress, he had watched her turn obscure knowledge into advantage in the political arena too many times to discount her fancies as whim. As no man's fool, he, too, could imagine the profound impact of the Queen's revelation. Whatever one cho-ja saw was remembered by all cho-ja, obviously over centuries. Intrigued, he observed as Mara turned the discussion once more onto sensitive ground.

''What of the cho-ja, since the coming of man?''

The attendants kept up their ministrations as the Queen said, ''We were first among many, though not so numerous as now. We were forced to contest with other races, the Thūn, the Nummongnum, the Cha-desh, the Sunn.'' Of those names, Mara knew only the Thūn. She resisted the temptation to sidetrack in pursuit of details. If she survived to find means to secure her safety from the magicians, she would have years and leisure to pursue her fascination.

As if the Queen sensed her guest's bent, or perhaps from other, more sensitive reasons, the facts she revealed remained general. ''Our warriors are bred to protect; cho-ja is never set against cho-ja, save in times of starvation when one hive may contest with another so that only the most vigorous line will continue. A hive challenge for survival is performed without hatred; killing is not our preferred nature. But against other races we made war, for they have a different sense of their place in the worlds. Much hive life perished needlessly, for beings came among us who were terrible beyond intelligent law, who slew for more than food or protection. They make war for the love of slaughter, it seems to us then and now. They seize land they do not need, and start battles to award themselves an essence of thought we cannot comprehend, called honor.''

The blood drained from Mara's face. ''Tsurani.''

''Humans,'' the Queen amended in gentle sadness. ''You we see as different, Lady Mara, but the hive mind knows well: no other race upon this world you call Kelewan could match your people for viciousness. For men will fight without reason. As your Empire grew over the years, we cho-ja strove to see all issues between us resolved, yet again and again humans would come, seeking this thing or that, this right or that. And when we refused to grant unreasonable terms, bloodshed would follow. Many times we quit the contest, thinking the issue settled, only to be assaulted yet again for reasons that had no logic. In the end, we yielded.''

Mara tapped her fingers on her cup, watching ripples flick across her chilled drink. ''You were forced to treaty?''

The chamber's occupants snapped to total stillness, and the Queen's ringing tone went icy. ''That is forbidden.''

Mara's eyes widened. ''You are forbidden to speak by us?''

''That is forbidden.''

Now convinced she had not offended, but that the Queen must be bound by some term the cho-ja could not or had sworn not to violate, Mara let her thoughts leap ahead. ''Who holds the power to silence you —the Assembly? The Emperor?''

''That is forbidden.''

Mara unclenched her aching hand before she broke the fine porcelain cup. ''Forgive my curiosity. I shall seek that answer elsewhere.'' Trembling in apprehension and frustration, Mara tried a new thrust. ''What other worlds should I know?''

The tension in the chamber did not relent. Mara held her breath while the Queen kept silent, the subliminal buzzing again ringing down the tunnels. Eventually she clicked her mandibles and spoke. ''There are but two things I may tell you without violating my trust. First, there are those who, for their own purpose, seek to oppose you, against whom you must find protection. Hear well, for we know: there will come a day when you must defend your Acoma against powers considered supreme.''

Mara released a pent breath, her stomach suddenly queasy. She set down her teacup before her fingers, nerveless, dropped it. The only powers considered supreme in Tsuranuanni were the will of heaven, and the Assembly of Magicians. Since cho-ja adhered to no religion, the Queen's reference could not be more fearfully plain. The Acoma must prevail against the Great Ones!

While Mara struggled to stay poised, the Queen continued, "Perhaps, Lady, you might ask yourself: if other worlds exist, where are they?"

Mara struggled to reason past unknowable dangers that loomed deep as an abyss before her. "Do you mean Midkemia beyond the rift?"

"You may cross there through the portal fashioned by the Great Ones, but where is Midkemia within the cosmos?"

Mara straightened in astonishment. The last word was one she did not understand. Every Tsurani meaning that she knew of translated to mean "arch of the sky," or "star field." Did the cho-ja Queen imply that Midkemia was placed in the sky with the gods? But the concept was absurd, even laughable! Yet Mara had learned better than to make light of the beliefs of other cultures. A long-past war in the deserts of Tsubar had taught her so, as well as many a frustrating argument with her barbarian lover, Kevin. Though she tactfully kept her own counsel, her dubious surprise must have showed to the keener perception of the cho-ja.

"Would it challenge you less to think that worlds exist in multitudes, many no farther from here than you can walk in your lifetime?" the Queen inquired. Her attendants had awakened again from immobility, and were once more scuttling to and fro through the curtained-off alcove that housed the egg chambers.

Thrown completely off balance, Mara strove to find sense in the Queen's words. This was no mystery created by alien thought patterns; in human terms, the Queen almost seemed to be leading her in ka-ta-go, a guessing game played between Tsurani children, where hints and suggestions led two rivals in a race to name whatever object, or animal, or plant their opposing teams might choose. Mara decided she was being deliberately led around the subject the Queen had been forbidden to speak of. After deep consideration, she said, "I could walk many places beyond this Empire's borders before my time came to die."

"Yes." The Queen's mandibles shifted in parody of a human smile. "You could do so, certainly."

Encouragement, if not direct confirmation; Mara's excitement grew. "The Thuril!"

The Queen stayed carefully noncommittal. "There are others. Consider the boundaries of your nations."

Convinced now that the information she sought had been proscribed, Mara leaned eagerly forward. "Beyond . . ." Of course! How naïve she must seem! Like most Tsurani, she considered all nations to lie under sway of the Empire, save the lost lands to the south and the Thuril to the east. Softly she asked, "Are there folk who live to the east of the Thuril Confederation?"

Instantly the Queen said, "They are called the Chadana."

Barely able to contain her excitement, Mara whispered, "Human?"

"They are like unto you and the Thuril, my Lady."

Mara glanced at Lujan, who looked as astonished as she felt. How provincial her people were, to count themselves and their Empire the center of all the worlds. Tsurani philosophy could more readily accept humans living on another world across a rift than on other continents in Kelewan. "What lies beyond the lands of the Chadana?"

"An expanse of vast waters," the Queen replied. "They are salt, like the Sea of Blood, and are the home of the egu."

Mara had never seen one of the egu, the gigantic serpents that inhabited the depths of the oceans, but she had sailed, and had heard deckhands describe fighting off the creatures' depredations with lances tipped with fire. "Are there lands across those oceans?"

"Many nations, Lady," the cho-ja Queen allowed. "As many as the lands beyond the sea to our west."

Amazed to the point where he forgot protocol, Lujan risked a question. "Why do our people not know of these?"

Quickly Mara nodded in allowance of his impertinence. "Why?"

"That is forbidden."

Mara's thoughts crashed together. What was forbidden? Not the knowledge of the other nations beyond Tsuranuanni, or the Queen could not have given even these sparse facts. Did those foreigners across the seas have knowledge that the Black Robes deemed threatening? Mara repressed a shiver. Such thoughts were too perilous to voice aloud, even here. She and the massive cho-ja Queen regarded each other through a silence made tense with frustration. If only their two species could speak plainly, so much might be understood! Still, the unstated implications piqued driving curiosity. Mara felt enlivened with fresh hope. For while the powers of the Assembly might yet prove to be omnipotent, and her family's name become forgotten to time, still she had been made aware of a larger world beyond the Empire. She could journey across the borders in search of new knowledge, and perhaps find an answer to her quandary. Suddenly awakened to the hours she had spent in the caverns underground, Mara longed to depart. If she intended to leave the Empire on a quest, subterfuge would be needed, as well as supplies and careful planning. Her enemies, particularly Jiro, must not get wind of her departure. And as she reviewed practicalities, it occurred to her that areas of her own culture remained for her to explore. She could start with the temples, whose priestly initiates were schooled in powerful mysteries; and there were also the practitioners of magic of the lesser path, adepts and sometimes charlatans, who had not merited study in the City of the Magicians.

Anxious to get started, Mara prepared to end her audience with the Queen. "My Queen, the Goddess of Fate must have guided me here, for I have been given a fresh start on my difficulties."

The Queen waved a forelimb. "We are pleased. Though we yet think it odd you should journey so many miles downriver when we were so close at hand."

Mara raised her eyebrows. "Then the mind of the hives is also one? I could address you by speaking to the Queen of the hive upon the lands where I now dwell?"

"Always."

Hopeful of a way to maintain communication wherever her journeys might lead her, Mara said, "If I were to leave the Empire, would I be able to consult you if I sought out the cho-ja in some distant nation?"

"That is forbidden."

Mara straightened, tantalized again to the edge of discovery. "One question, if you may answer. Why do you treat with me and others, we who were your conquerors?"

The Queen hesitated. Fearful that at last she had transgressed prudence, Mara dared not so much as breathe. Then, with the continued activities of the breeding attendants, she reassessed: the Queen was less angered than weighing words. For a while, Mara expected to hear that this answer, also, was forbidden.

But the Queen relented, her head tipped slightly back, and her words stern. "We are not a conquered people, Lady of the Acoma."

"The treaty?" A far step from understanding, Mara sighed in vexation.

The Queen strove valiantly to clarify. "Even a captive nation may bargain."

Mara rose from her cushions, so that the servants she had signaled to pack up the tea utensils could go about their duties without disturbing her. "Why do you tell me these things, Queen?"

Black, multifaceted eyes fixed upon Mara, unknowable as the alien thoughts behind them. Then the cho-ja ruler spoke in what seemed almost wistful reminiscence. "Before I merged with the hive mind, a young Queen recalls a human girl who was kind and who said she was beautiful. Of all your nation, you alone come to us with the intent to create harmony. You bargain like others, but you are more . . . you are what I believe you humans would call a friend. If the burden that has oppressed my kind throughout this nation is ever to change . . . we will need friends with bold minds such as yours.''

So the "treaty" was not an accord, after all, but a forced acknowledgment of terms! Mara sucked in her breath. She dared not press for more, not when the Queen had waved her Force Commander forward to usher her from the breeding chamber. The discussion was being brought to a close.

Uncertain what the protocols might be for formal acknowledgment of friendship between races, Mara settled for the bow that denoted an alliance between houses, adding personal words of her own. "You have always been a friend to me. I would accord your people the same considerations as I would any house within my clan."

After the cho-ja Queen had nodded her own form of acknowledgment and awarded the Acoma retinue her gracious leave to depart, Lujan offered his Lady assistance into her litter. Gone was the lackluster quiet that had marked her sojourn back in her childhood home. Now Mara's eyes shone. Her movements were eager as she gestured to her bearer slaves to take up the poles of her litter. The Force Commander donned his plumed helm and marched at her side from the breeding chamber.

Companion of many years, commander of her armies, and onetime bandit, Lujan could not help but grin. Here went a mistress he would die for, without hesitation, not just for the honor and duty due any Ruling Lady, but for love and pride as well. Despite the overwhelming threat posed by the Assembly of Magicians, Mara showed the indefatigable spirit that had captured his heart from the start. For where a tired woman of middle years had entered these warrens, a Lady vigorous with renewed confidence, at the height of her power, would emerge. Against all probability, Mara had defied the limits of her circumstance: she had found a clear focus and a hope where none had existed, to find reprieve from difficulties that her culture believed unassailable.

Many were the Tsurani Ruling Lords who would have fallen upon their swords in despair at the breach of honor the Acoma Lady had been forced by the Great Ones to swallow. Her late enemy Tasaio of the Minwanabi, once the most powerful man in the Nations, had committed suicide rather than endure beyond shame. It was not cowardice but her own indomitable will that bound Mara to life.

The Assembly, Lujan decided in a moment of unabashed cockiness, had better look after its interests. Though how his diminutive Lady might find a way to face down powers of magic on a scale as vast as that commanded by the Black Robes, only the gods might know.

* * *

Afternoon sunlight fell through the screens and striped the parquet floor, and the akasi vines beside the garden walk scented the air of the room that had served Mara as study in the original Acoma estate house. The cho-ja–made clock still chimed softly on the hour; mellowed now by layers of wax was the patch of flooring by the screen that had been sanded and refinished since the day her first husband had stomped indoors wearing studded battle sandals in the aftermath of a sarcat hunt. Older memories crowded behind: of Lord Sezu setting the family chop to documents, while her brother, Lanokota, scrawled pictures in chalk on the floor by their father's feet. Mara recalled rubbing at the scribbled figures, her fat little-girl's palms a smudged and dusty white. The smell of chalk filled her nostrils now, even as in those bygone days of her girlhood. But the baby by her knee was Kasuma; and the boy who scrawled pictures only he understood onto sanded wood, a fiery redhead of a barbarian father. Hers were the hands that set the Acoma chop in the ink to seal the last letter of the day. A bin of ribboned parchments beside her writing desk awaited the arrival of the messenger runner, who would see them taken to the guild for swift delivery.

Mara set aside the heavy chop and mentally reviewed her instructions for Jican, Incomo, and Keyoke, back at the lakeside estate. They would keep her affairs running smoothly through what might become a prolonged absence. Irrilandi, her second Force Leader, was currently off with the Shinzawai, supporting Hokanu as he consolidated his control as Ruling Lord. There had been minor attempts by enemies, and one or two ruptures of alliances caused by pressure from traditionalist factions. Hokanu had not yet sent formal reply to the Emperor's request that he assume his father's imperial post. In his letter to Mara he had explained that his delay was a ploy designed to draw an unfriendly rival into the open.

He had written: *"My father's First Adviser Dogondi is a treasure—fiendishly clever, and a humorist. He likes to humble our foes by making them seem ridiculous. As he said to me the other day, 'Kill a man, and you cede him honor in the eyes of the gods. Laugh at him, and you shame him.'"*

Mara gave a half-smile in reminiscence of this truth. Then her pleasure faded as she considered the rest of her husband's missive. Although he was under much stress, and subject daily to criticism from several jealous cousins, he still might have asked in more depth after the health of his daughter. That Mara proposed a long and possibly dangerous journey while the child still needed a wet nurse did not seem to trouble him.

But then, in all fairness, Hokanu was not a man to harp upon his worries. He might be sick inside with concern, but not wanting to burden her. Mara might disguise her journey as a pilgrimage all she wished, and her traditionalist enemies might be fooled. The Anasati might swallow the ruse for several months before Jiro's First Adviser discovered the truth, but the Assembly of Magicians would quickly sift through subterfuge if they perceived any reason to question her motives. Mara shut her eyes and rubbed damp hair back from her brow. She put aside the nightmare memory of the fiery rain that had beset the Imperial Arena when Milamber had manifested his arcane anger.

If the Black Robes chose to stop her, all would be lost in one wrenching, brutal instant. She must not give them cause to suspect, and that meant weeks of careful planning.

Again Mara tried to thrust the horror of Milamber's destruction of the Imperial Games from her thoughts. The barbarian Black Robe had been unruly, even stubborn, she had heard. The Assembly itself had exiled him, after his acts, which had crossed the Order of Heaven by causing slaves to be freed. A thought occurred that perhaps this Milamber viewed life in the same quirky fashion her lover Kevin had . . . that life meant more than honor, and that religion did not rule the lives of men but instead offered guidance. Mara frowned. If Milamber had been considered a renegade by his fellows, might he not be a source of inspiration in her present dilemma?

Acting with headstrong impulse, Mara clapped her hands. The boy appointed by the servants as her runner slave appeared at the door, a tow-headed youngster scarcely ten years of age. He had been promoted from the post of herdboy to that of house slave, and still felt awkward wearing livery. Mara saw that he trembled in awe as he made his bow.

She took pity, though shy boys her sons were not, and she had better experience bullying young warriors into line than drawing a quiet one out. "Kalizo," she said. "Come here."

The boy scrambled back to his feet, all knees and wide eyes. He came to her, tripping awkwardly on the edge of the carpet. His sandals were new, the soles not yet softened with wear.

Mara fished a cho-ja—made candy from the vase by her desk. She tossed it into the air, and smiled as the boy shed his clumsiness and caught it. "Kalizo, can you tell me when the next silk shipment is bound for the City of the Plains, for export into Midkemia?"

"Next week, Lady." The boy had a lisp, made more pronounced by his mouthful of hard candy.

Mara debated a moment, then reached for her pen with shaking fingers. "I have a letter to go with the factor," she instructed. "Fetch him here, for I would have words with him."

"At once, Lady." The boy bowed, spun, and departed with a speed that justified his appointment to his new position. Mara bit her lip as he raced out past the screen. Then she hastily sealed her brief missive, which was addressed to Milamber, Magician, Kingdom of the Isles, Midkemia. As she set the wax and inked the Acoma chop, she wondered whether with the seal upon the letter she was inviting her own doom.

Then the silk factor arrived, escorted by Kalizo. Her misgivings fled before the need to give the man instructions that caused him to tremble. His evident nerves made little Kasuma fussy, and Mara had to call for the child's nurse. Justin tossed aside his chalk with a loud announcement that he was hungry. Straight and lithe, where Ayaki had been stocky, he sprang to his feet and challenged Kalizo to a race to the kitchens. Mara nodded dismissal to the runner slave, who shouted and grinned, not at all abashed at the prospect of a contest. As the two boys bolted off at top speed, Mara half expected to hear a squawk of protest from old Nacoya . . . but those days were gone forever.

Left alone with her thoughts as the sun dipped in the west, Mara called a servant to open the screens. Years had passed since she had seen the shatra birds fly at sundown over Acoma lands. Considered the lucky symbol of her house, the creatures were a source of delight to Mara, as they greeted the night like a ritual with a celebration of flight and song. As her eyes followed the dance patterns of birds against gold-edged clouds, Mara thought more on her husband. He had not taken any concubines, nor had he made further issue of his disappointment at Kasuma's gender. Mara supposed the matter was left dormant deliberately. Hokanu's sole reference had involved the promise of a deep talk upon her return to the estates. A boat, he had said, with only themselves inside and a tray of light supper and sā wine, on calm waters; no slaves, no servants, only a lantern and himself at the oars. That he left the matter unexplored in his writing spoke volumes about his discomfort. Mara rested her chin in her hands and sighed. Whatever he had to say, it would be months before she had the liberty to meet with her husband, on water or dry land. For all had been done to prepare for her departure on her quest to seek protection against the Assembly. All that held her now was a final consultation with Arakasi, who was due to report back at any time.

Much later, when the study room was lamplit, and the stars pricked the sky where the shatra birds had flown, Mara was disturbed in her reading by the door servant, who brought word that a shabby itinerant poet had arrived to beg the Lady's indulgence.

Mara looked up from her scroll in mild interest. "You did not send him on to the kitchen,'' she stated. ''This poet, did he say he had verses for me in so-mu-ta rhyming?''

The door servant frowned, the academic reference beyond his education to fathom. ''Indeed, my Lady. He insisted that would mean something to you.'' His face creased with misgiving. ''I should have sent him off. He is very ragged.''

Mara's expression warmed to a smile. ''Very ragged, unbathed, and perhaps with a woman in tow?''

The servant's eyes widened. ''You know him?''

''I do.'' Mara rolled up her scroll, taut with anticipation. ''Have him shown in.''

The door servant bowed, still mystified. ''Your will, Lady.''

Presently the poet and his woman were brought into Mara's private study. Arakasi wore a mantle that looked as if it were fashioned out of moth-eaten blankets, sewn over at the cuffs and hemmed with tawdry fringes torn off a floor carpet. His companion was muffled under a patched, sun-faded robe that had once been adorned with shell sequins. Most had been ripped off with wear, leaving a sad collection of hanging threads. Her feet were filthy, and her sandals in tatters.

Mara, with one swift glance, clapped for attendants. ''Wash water. Towels, soap, and something from my clothes chest that is pretty and clean.'' She peered under the concubine's hood, and glimpsed a shining sweep of hair so heavy and thick it looked as if spun from red-bee honey. ''Make the color green,'' she suggested to the maid. Then she smiled at Arakasi. ''How large a supper tray do you wish? As always, you appear famished.'' She raised a finger as her Spy Master drew breath to speak. ''The verses can wait until after you are both refreshed.''

Arakasi offered a performer's bow and raked back the hood of his mantle. In the lamplight, he looked exhausted, bruised in spirit, and held together by sheer nerves. Mara was taken aback. Then the concubine slipped off her overrobe, and the Lady of the Acoma watched Arakasi look at her, and understood all.

''You must be Kamlio,'' she greeted. ''I bid you welcome.''

The girl started to sink into the deep bow that denoted lowly station. Mara fractionally shook her head, and, fast as reflex, Arakasi cupped the girl's elbow, stopping her obeisance by dint of her slight recoil from his touch.

As though her gesture had not implied rejection, Arakasi addressed her quietly. ''The mistress has bought your freedom, not your service. Your contract is your own, to tear up or resell, as you please.'' His deft hands smoothed back the hood of her underrobe, baring a face of breathtaking beauty, and pale eyes bright as sparks with resentment.

Mara stifled an urge to recoil, so much did the manner of this girl remind her of another, a courtesan and a spy named Teani, who had once tried to kill her. "Gods," she whispered below her breath. "Gods take pity." Her expression was for Arakasi, and the tortured girl he had rescued from usage.

Kamlio spoke, her low, modulated voice perfectly tempered in hate. "I would hear such a promise from the Lady whose centis have bought me."

Mara thrust aside her anger at the impertinence. "You may trust my servant, Arakasi, as myself in this matter. Kamlio, I, too, owe him my life. I chose to accept that gift from him with joy. He may have found you, child. But never forget: it was I who bought you from bondage. You are not brought here as a reward for his service." The lamplight glittered off the girl's eyes as she tensed. Mara sighed softly and continued. "You are your own woman, Kamlio. Because of you, I have a son and a daughter who may survive and achieve their inheritance. My gratitude is unconditional. You may leave Arakasi, leave these estates, and go your own way at this moment. I will provide you with enough wealth to establish yourself, in business, as a trader, or simply to live in modest comfort for the rest of your life. Or you may use the gift as a dowry, should you seek a husband. However, should you wish to take service, I would be pleased to have you stay."

The faint hiss of the oil lamps filled the stillness that followed. Kamlio's fingers clenched and unclenched on the ragged cloth of her gown. She did not smile, or settle, or relax, but stayed poised, like a creature caught and cornered. Mara forced herself to meet that hostile, gemstone gaze. "What is your desire, Kamlio?"

Plainly the girl distrusted kindness. Her eyes shone too bright, and her manner posed a defiant challenge as she said, "Good Servant, great Lady, I'd prefer to be alone. I do not wish a pretty robe but an ugly one. I do not want the eyes of men upon me. I want a sleeping mat and a room to myself."

"As you ask, you shall have," Mara allowed. She sent for her personal maid, Misa, who had been many years in Acoma service, and ordered Kamlio shown to a guest chamber and made comfortable. When the girl had gone, and the servant who entered with wash basins and towels had allowed Arakasi to refresh himself, she gestured her Spy Master to the nearest comfortable cushion.

He sank into his seat as if his knees gave out. His eyes were sunken, almost haunted, and his mouth twisted crooked with irony. Softly he said, "Thank you, Lady."

Mara looked upon him with pity. "She means that much to you?"

The Spy Master steepled his hands under his chin, an old habit he had when attempting a difficult explanation. "She has changed me. When I look at her, I see my mother, sometimes. When she speaks, she reminds me of my sister. Both of them could be vicious, at the moments they hurt the most." He paused, then added, "She blames me for the death of her sister. Quite justly, I fear."

Quietly Mara gestured to the servant who waited at the door with the food tray. As the man entered with his burden in deferential silence, she regarded the Spy Master whom she had known for years, but whose life remained a mystery to her. After the man had served them, Mara motioned for him to leave. When she and Arakasi were alone, Mara said, "You never mentioned any of your family to me before."

Arakasi's gaze flicked up, sharply defensive. "There was little of worth to mention. My mother was a woman of the Reed Life, disease-ridden, run-down, and finally dead from her trade. My sister followed in her footsteps. She died at eighteen, at the hand of a violent client."

"I am sorry," Mara murmured, and meant it. She should have guessed, since Arakasi set such store by his house allegiance, that he had been born to an honorless family. "How did you come to take service with the Tuscai?"

Arakasi made a self-deprecating gesture. "There was a warrior who frequented our brothel. He lay often with my mother. I was just three, and was impressed by his loud voice, and the sword he carried with a jewel set in the grip. Sometimes he gave me candy, and ruffled my hair, and sent me on errands. I took them very seriously, only later coming to realize that he was just more tactful than most, sending me out of the way so he could take his paid woman without a foolish boy underfoot. At the time, I decided he was my father."

Mara did not prompt, but waited, while Arakasi picked a stray thread from a rip in his mantle. After a moment, he continued of his own accord. "When my mother died, and the soldier came to bed another girl, I climbed out a window and followed him to his barracks. He was a Strike Leader for the Tuscai. His wife was a cook. She fed me, behind his back. I lived mostly on the streets, lurking around hostels and guild halls, keeping my ears open. I sold information to the Lord of the Tuscai's hadonra, and over the years became invaluable to him. When I alerted the Lord of the Tuscai to a plot against his life at the hands of the Minwanabi, he allowed me to swear to his service."

Quietly, Mara wondered how much of the spy net had already been in place when Arakasi had sworn to the Tuscai natami. Probably most of the area around the Tuscai estates, for an honorless street boy to have caught the notice of a hidebound traditional Ruling Lord. It awed her, to learn how far her Spy Master had risen from such humble beginnings. Now there was the girl, Kamlio, whose fate had entangled itself with his in ways she did not want. As the servant poured sā wine and departed, Mara handed Arakasi a glass.

"Drink," she urged. "You need it." In fact, he looked wretched, and worn thinner than she had ever seen him.

The Spy Master returned her regard levelly, his lip curled in distaste. He disliked drinking: alcohol dulled his reactions. "Lady," he said in a voice that was rust and velvet, "I am not at all what I was."

"Drink! That is a command!" Mara snapped back. "You are human, and have a heart that can bleed, even if you only discovered that fact recently. And I say you are wrong. You are more than you were. The change that has happened is for the best."

"Not if you wish me to continue in my post as Spy Master." The admission itself seemed to shake him. Arakasi reached out, took a goblet from the tray, and downed it in one violent draught. "What would you know of best or worse?" he challenged.

"Everything." Her tone reproached. "I had Kevin and lost him. I had the perfect husband who understood my heart, until one foolish misunderstanding has set him at a distance. I had two children who are dead."

Shamed, Arakasi wrapped his long, expressive fingers around his glass. He said nothing, only stared at the rug. For a while the lamplight revealed his rigid effort to keep his breathing steady. "I had hoped the example of you and Hokanu might open her eyes to a new life." He shrugged fractionally, a self-conscious hitch of his shoulders. "You have both been my teachers, Lady."

Mara regarded the man who sat hunched and tight before her. His competence at times had humbled her, until now, when she realized how much of his achievements had been rooted in pleasureless, calculating logic. "Arakasi, set her free. Let her find herself." As his eyes swept up to meet hers, beseeching, she found she needed sā wine herself. She reached out for a goblet, tasted its bittersweet edge. "Think, most cunning of my servants. You were never resentful because you did not love. Kamlio can hate, she can feel bitterness, because she can be hurt. Her basic nature is a caring one, or why should she defend herself so savagely?"

His gaze dropped. "I pray to the gods you are right."

"I am right." Mara's conviction rang across the room's familiar dimness. But no truth could ensure the outcome. Whether Kamlio could outgrow her past and survive without scars, only time would tell.

Arakasi sat like a man tortured, twisting the fine-stemmed crystal around and around in his hands. It occurred to Mara, watching him, that he had lost his piercing insight. She spoke kindly in reassurance. "Your little lady will not leave these estates. She will stay, and serve here. That much I know."

"Or else she would have left at once?" Arakasi released an edged laugh. "How can you be sure?"

"She would not have accepted my hospitality." Mara smiled. "She has pride like fire." She speculated, "In my years I have come to judge human nature quickly. You are a fitting match for her."

He relaxed a little at that, setting the goblet on the polished floor, empty, and helping himself to a plate of fruit, cheese, and bread. In a fast change of subject, he said, "I received your message, Lady. I can guess why you called me." He mashed the bread together over a thick wedge of cheese, his feelings for the concubine certainly not set in abeyance. But his voice showed none of his conflict as he added, "I can already assure you. The City of the Magicians is impregnable. Send anyone there to attempt entry, and you will call down the Assembly's wrath upon you. We have attempted seven times to find entrance; four men are dead, the other three unaccounted for, and I number them also dead. None can be traced to us, but even so, another attempt may cause us to fall."

"I supposed as much." Mara watched him eat with an inner surge of relief. The day Arakasi ignored his appetite brought cause for major worry. While he chewed, she related her findings in the hive of the cho-ja, and then told of her plans to leave for the Thuril Confederation.

Arakasi gave back a dry grin. "I did not think you seriously intended a pilgrimage."

Mara's brows arched. "I am devout. Did I not once plan to vow service to Lashima's temple?"

A spark of irony touched her Spy Master's eyes. "That," he allowed, "was long before you met one red-haired Midkemian barbarian."

Mara colored deeply. "True." She laughed. Arakasi had always stimulated her wit. The heart he had kept hidden all these years was proving a delight to her. "I'll need you to hide my trail with subterfuge. Also, I want you to comb the imperial archives for history texts that might show us what circumstances led to our mysterious treaty with the cho-ja."

She looked across the low table and realized Arakasi had ceased eating.

The bread had fallen into crumbs between his fingers, and his eyes looked deep as pits. Gently she asked, "What's wrong? Are you afraid to leave the girl?"

"No." The Spy Master knuckled back his tangled dark hair. The poet's braid at his temple had slipped half-undone, the violet ribbon that tied it frayed at the ends, and sun-faded. "I am no longer the best man for the job, my Lady. My heart is no longer ruthless."

"Was it ever?" Mara countered.

Arakasi looked at her, open and pained as he had been but once in her presence, and that the time he believed he had failed her and caused old Nacoya's death. "Yes, Lady. Yes, it was. Once, I would have let Kamlio die at the hands of the tong without conscience. I have increased risk to you by returning for her. It took some persuasion and significant funds to extricate her from her existing term of employment. The transaction was far too public for my taste."

Mara considered the weight of his admission. She stared a moment at her wineglass, barely touched, and warm now in the soft evening air. "The Acoma have no one else to send," she said finally, and hid from him the cost of that confidence. She had Justin and Kasuma to think of; if, as Fumita had hinted, her being Servant of the Empire had been all that stayed the Assembly from annihilating her, she had to find the children protection, or they would be helpless, good for nothing but to be puppets of the Black Robes' whim, after she was gone.

"Arakasi, let me tell you something the cho-ja Queen implied to me. What if, all along, it was not tradition that has held this Empire static all these thousands of years? What if our people strove for growth and change, but were kept from it? What if the great Game of the Council, our bloody, violent heritage of honor, was not ordained by the gods but was used as a contrivance to keep us in our place?"

Arakasi's left eyebrow quirked. "You claim to be devout," he said in a low voice. "You know, beloved Lady, that what you say is heresy."

"I suggest instead," Mara said, "that our Great Ones have done more than keep the imperial peace. If I rightly understood what the cho-ja Queen tried to impart, the Assembly has held our whole culture stagnant. The Black Robes are the ones who barred us from change—not the gods, not tradition, and not our code of honor. That is why they intervened between the Acoma and the Anasati. For I have created too much change, I hold too much influence with the Emperor, and, as Servant, I am too much a talisman of the people's luck. If what I think is correct, the magicians are not just hoping I will break their prohibition on making war upon Jiro; they are depending upon it. Some may even be contriving to bring it about. They are awaiting any excuse to step in and annihilate me.''

A breeze through the screen caused the lamp to flicker, making Arakasi seem a shadow cut from stillness. ''Hokanu will never let go of honor and allow his father's murder to pass unavenged.''

''Precisely,'' Mara almost whispered. ''That would be expecting too much, even for a man raised by the progressive thinker that his foster father was. His blood father, Fumita, as much as warned him at Kamatzu's funeral. I believe, as does Hokanu, that the Assembly knew of Jiro's contact with the Tong assassins. They did not act to stop him. Deliberately. It is me and my line they want dead. And sooner or later, fate will provide them with a reason.''

The wick brightened. As the darkness shrank back, Arakasi sat staring at his emptied wineglass, his eyes fathomless as obsidian. ''And so you need me to sort through the Imperial Archives, and to cover your absence when you journey outside the Empire in search of answers.'' His fingers tapped an agitated tattoo on the floor as he continued to think aloud. ''You ask this of me, not for the Acoma or the Shinzawai, but for the people of the Nations whose cause you have adopted for your own.''

''You understand.'' Mara reached out for the carafe and refilled both of their goblets. ''I do what I do for more than my name and ancestors. Because I hold hope that slaves may one day be allowed to go free, and that boys such as you were, and girls like Kamlio, may have the chance to earn honor through their merits.''

''A large task. I salute you, Lady.'' Arakasi tossed back his wine. He regarded her, his bearing still bleak, but his expression one of admiration. ''Once I said I wished to follow in the wake of your path to greatness. I was arrogant, and cold, and fascinated as a man who prides himself on solving puzzles. Now I wish nothing beyond a house with warmth, and a woman to smile at who does not know the secret of joy. To my sorrow, I have learned. It is not a lesson to benefit a Spy Master who must act only for reason.''

Mara returned the smile that softened the sharpened angles that trials and years had lent to her face. ''Then when we have found our means to defeat the Great Ones, we shall have to appoint you to a new post.''

Arakasi released a cracked laugh. ''What post? I have tried them all. Which shall I choose, when all of them suited me no better than a suit of borrowed clothing?''

''When the time comes, you will know,'' Mara assured him. But the words were a banality. Arakasi looked like an unmoored boat that spun untended in a current. She worried for him, and for the jaded, bitter girl who slept in the Acoma guest suite.

Arakasi set aside his glass. A moth spun in crazed circles around the oil lamp, sending shadows swooping and arrowing through the light. He felt as giddy. The time had come for him to take his leave. The food tray held only crumbs, and a crushed crust of bread. His eyes stayed deep as he concluded, "I will undertake what you ask, for I see that you comprehend the price. But this once, I would dare to ask a boon from you."

Mara raised her wineglass and drank to his health in return. "You have always had from me whatever you have needed, without question. That has not changed."

Her Spy Master looked up at her, for the first time she could remember showing nerves and uncertainty. "Take Kamlio with you to Thuril. Even the chance of a passing trader glimpsing her and remarking on her beauty in Sulan-Qu might bring the tong in search. By the time you return, the tong should have begun to wither."

Mara's smile returned like the sun. "I was going to suggest that very course." The hidebound tenets of Tsurani culture had deprived the courtesan of hope; Kamlio had been born as a pleasure toy for men to waste as they pleased. If she was going to come to her senses, if she was to escape becoming the twisted, tormented creature that Teani had been, she must rediscover the stifled personality she had been trained since childhood to hide. The chance might come to her more quickly if she experienced a strange culture, and customs outside her experience.

Arakasi bowed deep in gratitude. "Gods bless you, mistress." He looked as if he would say nothing more, but wound up by blurting, "Take care of her. The Acoma are my life, but she is my heart." Then he arose to his feet, his poet's braid falling the rest of the way undone. He yanked off the violet ribbon as if it had offended him, and made his way silently through the screen.

Mara stared after him long after he had disappeared into the darkened hallway. Before her, the moth spun in one last, suicidal circle, and flared up as it passed through the flame.

"Gods pity them," Mara murmured to the empty chamber. Whether her words were for the courtesan and the Spy Master who loved her, or whether she referred also to her husband, who was being made to dance to the tune of the Assembly, was unclear.

16. Countermoves

The game ended.

Chumaka set down his shāh piece with a click, and a deep-chested sigh of satisfaction. "Checkmate, master." The raw dawn light only emphasized his bright-eyed alertness.

Perfectly groomed also, Jiro was once again chagrined to prove his servants' gossip, that his First Adviser's wit remained sharp, even before daybreak and breakfast. The Lord of the Anasati regarded the captured pieces clustered to one side of the game board. "You're filled with life this morning," he observed. "More so than usual, if I may speak my mind."

Chumaka rubbed his hands together. "Mara's spy net has become active again. I knew it was just a matter of waiting her out! Whoever her man in charge may be, he has just made a misstep. He thought to outlast me in this waiting game, but after years of dormancy, at last he has moved!"

Jiro stroked his chin to hide a smile. "There are few servants like you, who can bear to abandon years of work on the basis of mere suspicion."

The Anasati First Adviser warmed to the praise. He slipped off his heavily embroidered morning robe, and adjusted the thinner silk garment underneath to ascertain it hung without wrinkles on his narrow chest. On a plaintive note he added, "You invited me to your suite for breakfast. Do I have to beat you at a second round of shāh before we can eat, my Lord?" His nervous, nail-bitten fingers reached to reset the board out of habit.

Jiro laughed. "You old tigindi," he accused, comparing his adviser to a foxlike predator renowned for cleverness. "You'd rather play games than eat."

"Perhaps." Chumaka looked up, his eyes bright.

Jiro signaled another game by inclining his head. "What's on your scheming mind, anyway?"

Chumaka slid the last piece into place and gestured for his master to take the first move. "It's what Mara has in mind," he corrected.

Knowing better than to interrupt with questions, Jiro advanced a pawn. Chumaka's countermove was immediate. Forced to a brisk contemplation of strategy, Jiro wished he could match his opponent's penchant for following simultaneous topics as his adviser defined his comment.

"Later this week, your master engineer will be in Ontoset hiring carpenters and craftsmen to build war engines after the prototypes you have had re-created from the ancient texts."

Jiro looked up from the game board, not at all intrigued. His siege weapons were his most coveted plan, a secret kept even from his closest allies, or so he believed. He did not like the topic bandied about casually, and his tone showed controlled irritation. "Mara can't have heard anything about our prototypes in the charcoal burners' sheds—"

"In the forests north of Ontoset," Chumaka filled in, at his most irksome when he finished sentences out of sheer impatience. "Yes. She has known for quite some time." Chumaka waved at the shāh board. "It's your move, master."

Jiro advanced his priest to a new square with a flick of one finger. A flush stained his cheekbones, and his eyes narrowed as he demanded, "How did she hear? Why didn't you tell me our security was compromised sooner?"

"Patience, my Lord." Chumaka moved his empress onto the front line. "I tell you, always, when the timing is to your advantage."

Very near open anger, Jiro forced self-control. Chumaka's cleverness at times could be excessive: as if the man could not resist playing the game within his master's household. But what Chumaka lacked in humility he more than made up for in innovative service. The Anasati Lord pitched his pent-up fury against the shāh board, and waited, icily quiet, for his impertinent adviser to qualify.

Chumaka smiled with the glee a child might show at discovering an insect could evade his goading through flight. "My Lord, it is good to see you have mastered the art of patience. We have allowed Mara's machinations against us to come to flower, the better to spoil her design. She has conceived a cunning plan to infiltrate your craftsmen at the construction site with a few of her own. Once there, they would work very handily to be sure your great siege engines have design flaws. We then use them in battle, or so the Mistress of the Acoma hopes, and the mechanisms will misfire and cause damage to our own troops, or at the least simply not function, leaving you with some very expensive kindling wood outside the walls of the city."

Startled into inadvertent admiration, Jiro raised his eyebrows. "Mara came up with such a plot?"

"A master toy maker in her employ." Chumaka moved another shāh piece and placed Jiro's priest in jeopardy. "It's quite an amusing plan, really."

Frowning, inconvenienced by the game, but unwilling to concede himself outmatched on both fronts, the Anasati Lord considered his next move with thinned lips. His First Adviser's tendency to keep secrets bordered on disrespect. But Jiro held back from criticism. His weakness at shāh was his desire for fast conclusions. He needed Chumaka's love of intricate plotting, which was content to spin webs and set traps against enemies long years in advance. Jiro chose to save his priest from attack; today his mood was prudent. "What move did you have in mind, First Adviser?"

Chumaka gave back a reptilian smile. "Why, to steal Mara's gambit from her. I have a list of her infiltrators' names. We can arrange to have them hired on, bring them deep into Anasati territory, and then have them disappear."

"Kill them?" Jiro's distaste for crude measures diverted his attention, and he had to force himself to keep pace with Chumaka's next move.

The First Adviser advanced another pawn, setting two of his master's pieces under threat. "I'd like to take the infiltrators quietly." He spoke as he did when contented, low-pitched, as a cat might purr. "Not kill them. They may have useful information for us. I'd like to know just how Mara's toy maker planned to sabotage our siege equipment, for one thing; I'm sure the modifications would be very clever to elude the notice of those overseeing construction. That's more idle curiosity than anything else.

"But far more important, if we can force one man to talk, and learn their method for passing information as well, we can send back false signals through the Acoma spy net. The Lady will not know her plot has been spoiled until the actual day we take the field against the Emperor. When our engines assault the walls of the Imperial Precinct, she will expect them to fail and cause us chaos, and she will have her forces arrayed to take advantage of that situation." With an almost sensual glee at the possibility of reversing Mara's plot, Chumaka said, "Instead, our new equipment will function flawlessly, and the Acoma will find themselves upon the field, *outside* the walls, while we are already securing our position within."

Jiro sacrificed his fortress, and tipped his head to concede his First Adviser his argument. "I will leave you to oversee the arrangements." Extracting information by force from a captive was not a detail he relished thinking about. He did not have a weak stomach; torture simply did not interest him. The treatises he had read told as much as he cared to know on the topic. "And as far as Ichindar is concerned, I thought we'd agreed I should goad a traditionalist fanatic into assassinating him rather than take him head on with an army." Almost spitefully, Jiro finished, "The Black Robes seem to dislike the idea of a civil war."

"Of course; nothing is more destructive to any society." Chumaka advanced another piece and looked up to accept the satchel of new correspondence brought in by his assistant. "But as we discussed, even a dead Emperor will have supporters. They will hole up behind walls with his heir. If you, as the nations' savior, step in and divert chaos by restoring the office of Warlord, you must also seize Jehilia as your power base. Even without Mara and Hokanu's resistance, you will need to break the city's defenses to get to the Imperial First Daughter . . . before someone else does."

But for the gleam that wakened in his eyes from review of future hopes, Jiro seemed absorbed in the shāh game. Chumaka turned from the board and riffled through the rolled dispatches. He selected one, squinted to be sure it had not been tampered with, then split the seal. He scanned the lines, not needing to pause to interpret the cipher. "Interesting," he mused to himself. Idly, he wondered how irritated his master was likely to become when he learned of the ex-Minwanabi warriors that Chumaka maintained in secrecy in a remote northern province.

If they became useful in arranging Mara's downfall, Chumaka decided, he would receive a citation for them. How he wished he belonged to a household that did not have touchy internal politics! Or a master of such heated pride. As Jiro completed his next move, Chumaka flicked his empress to a new square. He speculated whether a woman's rule would follow the same fashion as a man's; was Chumaka's Spy Master counterpart in the Acoma household permitted a free hand with his work? Only exceptional brilliance could keep such a network intact past the fall of House Tuscai. And Mara's willingness to take masterless men into service had shown the falsehood of counting such without honor. Certainly those who had labored as spies for the Lord of the Tuscai seemed even more diligent on behalf of the Acoma.

Or had the creature who directed them been Lord Sezu's man all along? Chumaka judged not, since Mara's father had dealt straightforwardly in council and on the battlefield. The Anasati First Adviser stroked his chin, peripherally aware of his master's expletives over the shāh board as he saw his attack plan threatened. He set aside the dispatch and reached for the next, the contents of which caused him to snap off his cushions with a thoroughly uncharacteristic oath.

Diverted from his straits on the shāh board, Jiro raised his eyes in languid inquiry. "What passes?"

"The devil!" Chumaka gestured with the parchment scroll, which appeared to contain random squiggles. "I've miscalculated, maybe; underestimated him, almost certainly."

"Who?" Piqued, Jiro pushed the board out of harm's way as his adviser began pacing. "Do we have a problem? A setback?"

Chumaka looked askance, his eyes deep as still pools. "Maybe. The Obajan of the Hamoi Tong has been assassinated. In his pleasure harem."

Jiro gave a small shrug. "So what?"

"So what!" Chumaka curbed his agitated movement. Seeing Jiro's darkening expression at his sharp tone, he said, "Master, the Obajan was one of the best-guarded men under heaven, and he has been stabbed to death. What's more, his killer escaped. Clean. Very professional work." Chumaka consulted his scroll more closely. In dawning astonishment, he added, "It says here that the tong brotherhood have disbanded. They are now masterless men: grey warriors."

It pointed to one possible conclusion. "That can only mean their records were lost?" Jiro's voice was forced and level. The contents of the tong's accounts could dishonor his house several times over, not least for the latest cash outlay, to buy an attempt on old Frasai of the Tonmargu, who lent his ear to Hoppara of the Xacatecas too often when he wanted advice on policy decisions. As long as Frasai remained alive, Kamatsu's death would serve traditionalist causes very little. Hokanu would stand in his father's post soon enough, but his tie to Mara and the Acoma would hamper him against any move made by Jiro's allies only when Frasai's vote of support was eradicated. If the Imperial Overlord fell, the Imperial Chancellor would find his powers in the Emperor's council crippled at a stroke. But Jiro needed Frasai's death to be caused in discreet fashion; killing one's own clansman, especially one's own Clan Warchief, was an extreme act even by Tsurani standards.

Chumaka responded, bemused with thought. "The secret accounts were stolen, or so every rumormonger in the Holy City now reports. I wonder if Mara has the tong's records?" She must, he deduced. If an ally had access to such sensitive secrets, Anasati agents would have been informed; a foe would simply turn the information to immediate advantage, unless . . . the only enemy the Anasati had that was under constraints not to initiate conflict was the Acoma/Shinzawai faction that centered on Mara. Chumaka stroked his chin, the shāh game utterly forgotten. What if he had miscalculated? What if the Acoma Spy Master was a better player than he? What if a trap yawned under Anasati affairs, just waiting for a misstep to snap shut?

"You're worried," Jiro observed, in his best tone of false boredom.

Observing that his master was hiding extreme displeasure, Chumaka did his best to wave the matter away. "I am careful," he allowed, self-aware enough to know that his worst nightmares seldom resolved in daily life. His active imagination helped make him master of his job. In his eagerness to close with his Acoma opponent, he could easily have been drawn into carelessness. He must pull back, wait, and watch, like a patient hunter. The trainees of Mara's toy maker must be taken with utmost caution.

Then, as if a sixth sense reminded him that he had been still too long, and that his master's restless intellect was on the verge of expressing annoyance, Chumaka smiled brightly. "Shall we eat? Or shall we finish our game, which you are very close to losing?"

Jiro glared at the arrangement of the players on the game board. He made a deprecating gesture that turned into a clap to summon servants. "Two defeats on an empty stomach are more than any master should face before daybreak." He must have followed that observation with thought of the dead Obajan, for he looked nettled enough to eat floor pegs. "Damn her," he murmured in a voice he thought too quiet for his First Adviser to overhear. "If not for the Assembly's protection, I'd see her shamed and begging."

The gardener blotted his brow. Leaning in apparent idleness on his rake handle, he surveyed the surrounding flower beds under the afternoon sunlight. The blooms were the brilliance of rainbows, no dried seedpods or wilted petals left shriveling in the heat to mar their freshness. The soil was level, and weed-free as it had been since the hour the worker had started. Each shrub was trimmed to provide beauty at an economy of space. The retired imperial officer assigned to this household used his apartment infrequently. Since he valued peace and silence, his gardens had been arranged to set the bustle of the Holy City at a distance. Half blind from cataracts, he tended to forget the faces of his gardeners. Hence his lovely, private little garden across from the city library offered the perfect rendezvous point for a Spy Master who desired clandestine exchanges of information bought through a bribe to one of the archivist's copyists.

Arakasi spat on his palms as any diligent gardener might do, and again took up his rake. His sun-browned hands looked as if he had practiced such labors life-long as he scratched parallel rows in dry soil. Except for his eyes, which kept covert surveillance on the entrance to the archives across the thoroughfare, he assumed his role to perfection.

In this he was even more meticulous in his caution than usual. After the change in outlook triggered by Kamlio, he distrusted his reactions. He no longer held confidence in his ability to act with his former speed. As he raked, he worried; would emotion make him hesitate? He no longer saw people, even enemies, as ciphers on a game board. His personal conscience, as opposed to his duty as a servant, posed a conflict he feared to put to the test.

Since his thwarted attempts to infiltrate an agent into the City of the Magicians, he understood that any inquiry into old texts on arcane subject matter, or probing into proscribed eras of history, might draw notice. Also, the libraries were Jiro's passion, and Anasati spies comprised half the staff. Since the Imperial Archives were rarely visited except by students of history, most of them initiates at one temple or another, any stranger sent in as agent would cause inquiry. Since Ichindar's ascension to absolute rule, the Day of Appeals had become the place to air disputes over obscure points of law. The High Council no longer sent couriers to peruse the stacks of fading parchments for clarification on the fine points of tradition under debate by merchants or guilds.

Arakasi had been hard pressed to find a student initiate whose loyalty was not already compromised. In the end, he had needed to call in a favor from the acolytes of the Red God, who felt they owed Lady Mara their favor. As the Spy Master raked, and darted surreptitious glances at the carved doorways across the thoroughfare from the garden gate, he felt disquiet over how useless his established operation had become. He dared not try calling upon his resident agents in the palace, since by now Arakasi assumed they were all under Chumaka's surveillance. Enough signs had arisen to indicate that the palace branch of his network was compromised. So Arakasi had sent in an otherwise harmless student, to lead Chumaka's agents off the trail. The Acoma Spy Master knew the enemy would not be misled for long.

Two priests of Turakamu, and a student acolyte bearing sealed requests from the High Temple, had all recovered texts on the subjects Arakasi had requested. His nights had been spent by candlelight, reading lines in faded ink. Each dawn he had sent coded messages to Mara at the old Acoma estate, narrowing down the possibilities: the time of the conflict that had resulted in the secret treaty with the cho-ja could have been tied to a civil disruption eighteen hundred years earlier, two centuries after the founding of the Empire, or to another period four hundred years afterward, when no war was mentioned, but a review of family pedigrees showed inheritances passing to first and second cousins, and an inordinate number of underage heirs. If a plague was responsible for such breaks in otherwise established dynasties, the texts of the time held no reference to such.

The tax rolls of those times had also shown increases in levied funds; treasury ledgers held strange gaps, blank lines, for entries showing how such wealth had been spent. Now Arakasi waited to receive the list of imperial commissions for the two periods under examination. If the Emperor's seneschal had paid sums to guild artists to paint battle scenes, or sculptors to design commemorative victory arches, surely there would have been a war. Temple records could then be followed up for prayer-gate donations sent in by wealthy widows who wished the spirits of husbands departed on the battlefield to be kindly judged by the gods. Arakasi frowned over his raking. If he could establish proof of a war, he could root through family records, and perhaps in the private sector ferret out facts, or entries in the diaries of dead rulers, telling of a conflict that might have been excised from the public record.

Mara had been circumspect in her instructions, most likely out of deference to her Spy Master's misgivings over continued pursuit of his trade. She had no illusions: she knew, as he did, that his tie to Kamlio left him vulnerable. But spare his heart and his talents, and the Acoma would fall to the greater, more sinister design of the Assembly of Magicians. For more and more, the fact emerged: the Black Robes prevented change. They had allowed Ichindar's ascension because it suited them to balk Tasaio of the Minwanabi; but sooner or later they were going to support the traditionalist view and a resurgence of the Warlord's office, forcing Ichindar once more to a role of religious ceremony.

Resisting an urge to wipe his sweating forehead, Arakasi scraped his rake through the earth in an inward storm of resentment. His studies of the records showed by omission, in subtle twists and turns, just how the Great Ones had directed the Empire to stagnation. It did not take a historian to ferret out the unexplained holes in the fabric of Tsurani history.

Like a weaver worrying a tangle of threads, picking apart one knot at a time, Arakasi followed from one cryptic reference to another to map out a report conspicuous by its absence. His pulse quickened as it never had, throughout his hunt for the Obajan of the Hamoi Tong. All objectivity was displaced by recognition that he was involved in the greatest match of his life; for while he ached to restore the feelings of the girl who had captured his affection, he must aid his mistress to challenge the mightiest body the Empire had ever known: the Assembly of Magicians.

Arakasi shied away from contemplation of the future. He saw each day as risk. He knew, as Mara did, that he could no longer continue as her Spy Master, in the unlikely event that her house could stand against the Assembly's will and survive. Adjusting the sash that bound his smock, and brushing the weapon belt beneath that held his hidden knives, he regarded the swept walkways and the rows of fragrant flower beds. If fate should destroy the Acoma, or if when he resigned his post Mara should have no honorable position to offer him within her household, he had his laborer's skills to fall back on, he thought on a note of black humor. Inspecting his hands, thick with dark soil that hid the calluses of a dozen trades, he considered there were less-worthy pursuits than tending growing things.

Killing was certainly one of them. His decoding of the tong's record scrolls had nearly made him ill at their dispassionate listing of generation after generation of death and cruelties. Mara had been right to use him as her own, ruthless instrument, to destroy the Hamoi Brotherhood at their root.

But her rightness did not make Arakasi any more able to forgive himself for such usage. Where Tsurani ways admitted only honor won for his mistress, his interaction with Kevin the barbarian had tainted his thoughts; Mara's own forgiveness of his very human failure in the bleached heat of a kekali garden had shocked the first cracks in his outlook. The bastions of his isolation had crumbled since, until now, naked of self-deceit, he saw.

He had trained himself to be set as a weapon against others of his own kind. Kevin was right; the cho-ja were right; Mara and Hokanu were right to desire change in the stagnation of old ways. Although unconditional consent had been the way between master and servant for all of the Empire's long history, Arakasi had seen the evils of such thinking mirrored in Kamlio's hardened eyes. His awakened vision showed him guilt.

"I am not what I was," he had said to his mistress in their meeting after his successful assassination of the Obajan. It had been less a statement than a baring of his spirit to her view. He sighed, profoundly saddened that, through the hours he had spent gardening in the past, he had never paused to appreciate the results of his labors. Now, he saw the neat rows of young blossoms with changed perspective. Feeling a strange tightness in his chest, the Spy Master considered that the lowly gardener might be closer to finding balance upon the Wheel of Life; certainly it was pleasant to imagine a life in constant harmony with the universe.

Arakasi rubbed his hands and returned to work. His awakened awareness, here, became a liability. Despite the apparent tranquillity surrounding him, destruction was very close.

The day waned. Reddened sunlight fell through the pillared entrance to the garden. An elderly hawker pushed his cart along the street outside, his singsong patois offering bundled tanzi bark to the wives of the free workers headed homeward from the temples to the dockside quarter. Shabby, just one step higher than slaves, such families burned tanzi to sweeten the air and mask the stinks of the fisheries on the riverfront side of town. Incense wafted from the Square of the Twenty Gods, where the priests threw open the massive doors of the temples. Sundown rites drew the aristocracy out to worship, when the streets were cooler and the merchants departed; the first lacquered litters of the nobles swept by, interspersed with the rumble of the empty costermongers' wagons, returning to the farmlands after the day's market.

The hour just before sundown was a time when all classes of people mingled in the streets; when couriers removed their headbands and guild badges and walked home to their wives and supper, whistling. Arakasi fetched his wheeled barrow and began to gather up his hoe, rake, and trowels. He watched the arched doorway of the library keenly, anticipating the distractions of the hour to cover the emergence of his errand boy; workers were wearied from their labors and thinking of the evening meal, while the curtains of the nobles' litters would be drawn closed, to sequester them from the gaping of commoners.

The moment the youth appeared, Arakasi would leave the garden, pushing his barrow, and the scribe would pass him but for a brief moment, close enough to deposit his report among the tools.

Arakasi heard the sound first as a distortion upon the air, almost dismissed amid the rumble of a wine broker's dray that ground over the cobbles beyond the gate. Then instinct had him ducking down behind his wheelbarrow before the vehicle passed, and his ears identified the disturbance for what it was: the bone-aching, arcane buzzing that preceded the appearance of a Great One.

An icy sweat drenched the back of his neck. Had they come for him? Traced his presence to a ploy of Lady Mara's? Habit alone held Arakasi to his cover, that of a sunburned gardener putting up his tools at the end of his day's labor. His heart raced and his hands shook like those of a man with the palsy. He had known fear in his life, many times; but never before had it held any power over him. It had never, until Kamlio, breached the guarded inner core of his heart.

The pair of Black Robes appeared an eyeblink later. The unnerving buzz died away, leaving a silence no longer filled with the drone of foraging bees. The sounds of the street seemed strangely removed, as if the world began and ended at the marble pillars that flanked the garden gates.

Arakasi did not have to feign awe as he threw himself down behind the wheelbarrow, his face pressed against the dusty furrows his own rake had scribed in the earth.

The Great Ones took no heed of him. As though he were no more alive than a carved statue, they moved down the garden path toward the gateway and stopped under the shadow of the arch. Their eyes stayed trained intently on the library's front stair across the street. Their backs were turned; from Arakasi's vantage, their feet were shod incongruously in velvet shoes better suited for carpeted indoor floors. They ignored the common gardener crouched behind them as if he were but another feature of the surroundings, not a person able to overhear them.

One dark, hooded head bent close to that of his comrade. "He should be along any moment now. The scrying showed he would cross the street and head in this direction."

The magician so addressed returned a barely perceptible nod.

Arakasi felt little relief when he realized that the Black Robes had not come for him. Still trembling, nearly paralyzed with fear, he dared a peek outward. Above the tines of the rake, framed between the enigmatic black forms of the magicians standing under the arch, he saw his messenger at last emerge from the library, a laden satchel slung from a strap across his shoulder.

"There!" The Great One who had spoken pointed at the young figure of the scribe as he moved at a normal pace down the steps. "There he is."

A nod of the second hooded head answered, and in an unusually deep voice. "As you guessed, his satchel carries scrolls."

"Subject?" The first magician's voice was curt.

His fellow closed his eyes, placed one hand against his forehead, and gestured in the air with the other. His passes perhaps described a spell, or a symbol, or some incomprehensible ritual of power. The Spy Master felt his flesh prickle, as the tingle of magic visited him.

The low voice rumbled as the magician said, "It's a list. The imperial requisitions for funds for the arts. Victory arches, commemorative statues, memorials . . ." A pause while the two Black Robes seemed to ponder this. Then the cold-voiced one said, "The time period of these lists is sensitive to our interests. Very."

Arakasi clenched his hands in his plain worker's smock, fearful that the drum roll of his heartbeat could be heard over the stillness of the garden.

A lady's litter passed, hurried along by bearer slaves adorned with silk headcloths. Delayed by the traffic, the scribe paused on the other side of the street. Traces of a woman's perfume twined over the scents of blooming flowers and the earthier odor of needra soil left by animal-drawn conveyances. The Black Robes whispered, craning their necks to regain sight of Arakasi's messenger, who, all unsuspecting, now crossed the teeming main thoroughfare with the jaunty stride of a boy who anticipates a reward in centis to spend at the taverns.

"Certainly he should be questioned," said the magician with the cold voice. "It's unlikely the boy is conducting such research on his own. We must detain him and find out whether anyone might have hired or forced him to ferret out such facts."

The other Great One murmured agreement.

Arakasi felt a jolt of near panic. If the scribe were forced to talk, his cover would instantly become forfeit. And even before Kamlio, even without his awakened sense of vulnerability, the Spy Master understood he would have no chance of keeping secrets through an interrogation by those able to read thoughts. Mara's hand would be revealed, instantly and inescapably, and the continuance of the Acoma be put in jeopardy.

He must act.

Cold under his worker's smock, Arakasi felt the metal of his throwing knives. Propped upon one forearm, he groped to loosen his sash. His hands felt sweat-slick and numb as he reached under his robe and grasped the ebony handles of two blades: one for the hapless scribe, the second for himself. He must kill an innocent man in cold blood, and immediately cut his own throat. After that he must hope the Red God would take him before the magicians could bind his wal to his body and force him to speak in betrayal.

The Black Robes had stepped together, obscuring Arakasi's view of the street. Fear bound his chest like a rope. The blade in his trembling hand, poised to throw, felt like a dead thing, a splinter. His belly was on fire with nausea. Almost, he hoped the worst might happen: that the magicians would not move, and that the scribe would step in through the arches to his garden rendezvous, unknowing.

But if that happened, if he did not get a clear view and a moment in which to kill, Mara would be destroyed.

"He comes," murmured the first magician. The pair moved apart, deeper into the shadows. Like still, hooded statues, on either side of the gateway arch, they waited for the man who wove across the busy thoroughfare.

The press momentarily thinned. A cake seller walked by, trailing the scent of cinnamon. Two boys ran, chasing each other and shouting, while a puppy gamboled in and out between their legs. The scribe dodged around a portly water seller, his expression preoccupied, and his ink-stained fingers taut on the flap of his satchel.

He stepped into the shaded walkway before the garden gate.

Arakasi fought back revulsion. He had killed, many times. Never had he reacted like this. Mortality had held no meaning to his stone-hard heart, and he had felt no weakening rush of empathy for his victim. His will faltered, even as he cocked his arm to throw.

Sunlight flashed silver on the knife blade, drawing the scribe's notice. His eyes widened, even as the Great Ones stepped into view, clearly intending to intercept him.

Arakasi bit his lip. He must act! He measured distance, aimed, and battled to banish his inner sickness.

"Halt," the leftmost magician commanded in his ringing, metallic voice.

The scribe did as bidden, paralyzed with terror.

"We would question you," said the second magician, his voice a gritty bass.

In a state of trembling pallor, the scribe said, "Your will, Great Ones."

Gripping the wheelbarrow as though his fingers might punch through weathered wood, Arakasi forced his clamor of feelings to stillness. Murder must have shown in his eyes as he rose to one knee to throw, for the scribe staggered back, panic written plain on his face. He saw certain death in Arakasi's hand, and in a knife blade flashing downward into the beginning of a throw.

He broke and spun. His satchel banged against his hip as he dodged in desperation back into the crowded street, running as though his heart might burst.

The deep-voiced magician stiffened in surprise. The other shouted, outraged, "He defies us!"

The Black Robe nearest the gate raised his hands. A crash like thunder shocked the air, rattling the tools in the wheelbarrow, and flattening the flowers in a suddenly scything breeze. Arakasi was thrown flat against the earth. He shoved his blades under his prostrate body and hid his face behind his hands, while blast after blast shook the garden, accompanied by flashes like lightning. Screams erupted in the street, and sounds of fleeing footsteps and the bawl of terrified needra. A carter snapped his goad to whip up a laden wagon, and the puppy that had been frolicking with the beggar boys began yelping. Shivering uncontrollably, Arakasi peered between his fingers.

Except for the passersby who ran helter-skelter away from the garden entry, the street looked little different; the setting sun still cast red light across the library stair, and temple incense wafted upon the air. Except that its sweet odor now mingled with a scent of charred meat, and a pitiful smoking lump lay on the cobbles, unrecognizable as anything human. Nearby, untouched by the blast, rested a spilled satchel of scrolls that turned and rolled, their ends flapping in the dying eddies of wind.

"Why would the fool have run?" ruminated the magician with the low voice. To his companion, he added, "You should have not been so quick to burn him to a cinder, Tapek. Now we have no idea who employed him. This time you've indulged your temper at the cost of information."

The other Great One defended his act in disgust. "There are only two possible suspects, the Acoma or the Anasati. No one else has a motive to send for inquiry into the archives. And it is unthinkable that any lesser man should defy us, and be allowed to disobey." He turned from the gate, his downturned mouth clearly visible beneath his hood. His gaze flicked over the wheelbarrow, and the gardener's tools, and settled, ice-hard, upon the prostrate figure of Arakasi.

Mara's Spy Master felt the touch of that stare like a spear thrust in the back. He could not stop trembling, nor did he dare to move. With the breath stopped in his throat, he held his pose of submission.

The magician stepped closer. Velvet-shod feet stopped bare inches from his face. Mingled with the dust and the wet green scent of broken flowers, Arakasi could smell the pungency of ozone.

"Did you know that man?" demanded the Great One.

Incapable of speech, Arakasi shook his head.

The second Black Robe moved up to join his companion. "He could be lying. We must be sure," he said, his voice a thunder of doom in Arakasi's ears. He stepped nearer.

Arakasi sensed motion, as if the magician made a pass with his hands.

"Who was that man?" came the deep voice of the mage. "Answer!"

The honed edge of spellcraft cut through the Spy Master's mind. Trapped by undeniable power, he felt his lungs expel air, and his lips and tongue forced to speech. "He was but a scribe," he heard himself say. "His name was unknown to me."

Arakasi closed his eyes in fear. Sadness at never seeing Kamlio again clashed against his most vivid memory of that afternoon they had shared in physical love, her languid smile and hard eyes trapping his heart forever.

Across his jumble of recollection, the voice of a Great One said, "His mind is chaos. He thinks we shall kill him and . . . he longs to see a woman." Harsh laughter escaped the magician. "The fool dreams of a beautiful young courtesan he once knew. His only thought is to see her once more before he dies."

Arakasi felt the compulsion born of magic dispel from his mind and body, even as the other Black Robe said, "A guilty man would be thinking of his master or escape." That Arakasi remained too stunned to move lent credibility to Tapek's conclusion. "No, he is not our man. The scribe's contact fled, no doubt. This witless old gardener knows nothing." His manner shifted toward irritation. "You were correct to chide me. Still, we now know someone seeks forbidden knowledge. We must return to the Assembly."

The pair stepped away.

His sweat-drenched body coated with clinging dust, Arakasi lay still. His ears recorded the sharp buzzing sound, and the inrush of air as the Great Ones departed. But it was dusk before his strength returned. He rose shakily to his feet and stood for a long time with his weight braced against his wheelbarrow.

Outside the gates, in the street, Imperial Whites were directing slaves to clear away the remains of the scribe. A drudge hovered to one side with a bucket and brush, to scrub the charred mark from the cobblestones. Around his tableau the fine, sequined litters of the nobles carved a wide berth. The ragged street boys that gathered to stare at anything unusual were tonight nowhere in evidence.

Arakasi sat on the edge of his wheelbarrow and listened to the rasp of night insects, while the afterglow faded from the sky. The moon spread copper light over the wilting heads of shorn blossoms. He did not need to see the scrolls that the scribe had died to bring him. The presence of the Great Ones confirmed the truth behind his hunches concerning the histories. Soon he would have to slip away and make a report to Lady Mara.

Worse was the inward uncertainty born during the heat of his peril. Even now he could not determine whether he actually could have fulfilled his duty. Even now he did not know if he would have followed through and thrown the knife.

Mara, Arakasi thought to himself, *Lady. I have become a liability to your cause.*

But in the cool night, no answer came. He could do no more than his best, for his Lady had no one else who could approach the measure of his skills. And as well as he knew her, Arakasi believed that if his mistress were to face him now, there would be no reproach in her eyes.

She understood his conflicts. The gift of that, in a ruling mistress, almost moved him to tears. As he shifted to his feet and raised the dew-wet handles of the wheelbarrow, Arakasi wondered whether his Lady's compassion would be great enough to break through Kamlio's bitterness. Almost he laughed at his thought, in terrible, edged self-reproach. How very near the Assembly had come to learning everything about his Lady's plot to thwart their decree. Long before Kamlio might find herself, all of them might be dead, charred and smoking like the corpse in the street, and with as little warning.

17. Advice

Mara sat quietly, her daughter a warm weight clasped against her shoulder. Fat, baby hands tangled in her hair, reaching for the carved bead earrings she wore. Kasuma was enchanted by anything red, and if she could close her hand around whatever object held her fancy, she would determinedly try to stuff it into her mouth. The Lady of the Acoma rescued her jewelry from the tiny Shinzawai heir by sliding her downward and bouncing her on her knee. The child's coo of delight mingled with Justin's shouts that drifted in through the screen. The boy continued to study a warrior's skills, and under Lujan's unforgiving tutelage was swinging a practice sword at a pell. Impatient as his barbarian father, the boy insistently cried to his teacher that wooden posts were stupid, that he should be permitted to strike at something that could move. Like the jigabirds he had been punished for harassing yesterday, Mara thought with a half-smile. The cooks would as soon be quit of Justin's pranks.

The Lady savored the moment. Since her parting from Hokanu, rare intervals like these brought the only happiness she knew.

Kasuma gave her a wet smile. Mara touched the baby's nose, intentionally slowing her movement to allow the little hands that thrashed to catch her bracelets and make them chime. Today, along with her everyday jade, she wore the priceless copper wristband once given her by Chipino of the Xacatecas, expressly to please her child. Kasuma's glee warmed her. Is this how my mother would have felt, wondered the Lady of the Acoma, looking down into my face? How different the course of her life might have been had her mother lived. Would she have stayed on and vowed service in Lashima's temple, while Lady Oskiro became Ruling Lady of the Acoma? Would her mother have ruled as Isashani had, through gentle female wiles? Or would desperation have driven her to try dangerous innovations?

Mara sighed. This endless circling of supposition served nothing. All that she knew of her mother was a painted portrait Lord Sezu had commissioned before the Lady's untimely death in childbirth.

From the yard outside, Lujan's voice called in reprimand, and the whack of Justin's practice strokes resumed at a steadier rhythm. Mara could not hear the clack of a wooden sword without being reminded of Ayaki. While Justin looked nothing like her departed firstborn, there came the odd moment when a glance, a turn of the head, or boyish laughter would call his older brother to mind. Ayaki would have passed his manhood ceremony, Mara realized. That many years had gone by. He would have been fitted for battle armor, not the pretty ceremonial regalia given to young boys—she twisted her thoughts away from useless dreaming. Aware of Kasuma's fingers picking at her bracelets, Mara had to force herself not to brood upon the other child by Hokanu, the one taken before birth by the Hamoi Tong.

In another hour, her two remaining children would be gone, sent on the road with a trusted retinue to the Imperial Household in Kentosani. They would be safer there until Hokanu won free of his Shinzawai obligations and was able to return home to the lakeside estate.

Mara shut her eyes. Tomorrow would see her off on her own journey, one that would begin in familiar territory, but that could lead her far beyond the familiar. She took this last interval to savor her little daughter. The gods only knew how long she might be away. The years of Ayaki's growing that she had missed while away on war campaign in Dustari hurt her the worst, in retrospect. Now that the boy was gone, she resented the years that politics had forced her from his side.

Worst, most poignantly, she did not want Kasuma growing up with no memory of her mother beyond a painted image.

A soft baby foot thumped her in the chin. Mara smiled, opened her eyes, and sighed to see the wet nurse return to collect her daughter. The day was passing too quickly. The large woman bowed, brisk in the face of her duty. Plainly she did not enjoy being witness to a mother's parting from her child.

"It's all right," Mara reassured her. "I know there are things to pack, and Kasuma should have a chance to nap before she is bundled off in a litter with her brother. Justin won't let her sleep, he'll be so busy brandishing his stick sword at make-believe robbers through the litter curtains."

The nurse's sternness softened. "My Lady, your little ones will both be well and happy. You must not worry."

"Don't let the Emperor spoil them," Mara warned, hugging Kasuma so tightly the baby wailed in protest. "He's terrible with children, always giving them sweets, or jewels that the babies only end up putting in their mouths. He'll cause one of the poor things to choke one day, unless one of his silly wives finds nerve enough to teach him what's safe for an infant.''

"Don't worry," the nurse admonished once again. Personally, she thought it was greed that kept the imperial mothers from restraining their consort's generosity. She held out huge, warm hands and accepted Kasuma from her mother. The child cried harder, reaching chubby fingers toward the retreating clink of the bracelets.

"Shhh. There, little blossom," crooned the nurse. "Give your mother a smile to take with her on the road."

That moment, while Mara fought a sadness that pressed her near to tears, a single chime cut the air. In the courtyard, the clack of Justin's practice stopped abruptly. By his howl of annoyance, Mara presumed Lujan had reached out and caught the stick in mid-swing. Her eyes locked with those of the nurse, sick with hidden fear. "Go," she said. "Quickly. Buy what you need on the road, if you must, but head straight for the litter. Lujan will bring Justin, and assemble an escort and bearers, if it is not already too late."

The nurse gave a quick, scared bow, Kasuma's cries muffled against her shoulder. Then she bolted for the door. As well as her mistress, she knew: the chime that had sounded heralded the coming of a Great One.

Mara shook off paralysis. Heart pounding in apprehension, she shoved away the wrenching grief that she had not been able to say farewell to her son. Although logic insisted that if the Great Ones chose to act against her, the boy would be no better off on the road, a mother's instinct would not be denied: to send the children away from pending trouble as fast and as far as possible. She wrenched her eyes from the empty doorway where the nurse had disappeared with her daughter, and clapped for her runner slave. "Summon my adviser. Quickly." She started to ask also for her maid, to bring a fresh robe and a comb to repair the tangles left by Kasuma, but stopped herself.

The rare metal she wore on her wrist was sufficient to impress, and she doubted her nerves could withstand even the minute of stillness required to have a maid tidy her hair.

Barely able to master her dread, Mara left the comfort of the garden outside her quarters. She hastened down dim hallways, the waxed wooden floors sounding strangely hollow under her tread, after the stone she had grown accustomed to in the lakeside manor to the north.

Every estate house had a room with a pattern inset into the floor, which provided a place for the magicians of the Assembly to arrive by arcane means. While the decor of such chambers varied from plain to ostentatious, the summoning symbol was unique to each. Mara stepped through the low doorway into the five-sided room. She took her place just outside the mosaic in green-and-white tile that depicted the shatra bird that was her family symbol. A stiff nod was the best she could manage to acknowledge the presence of Saric and Chubariz, the hadonra appointed by Jican to manage her ancestral estates. At the sound of the chime, both had presented themselves, as was appropriate to a Great One's appearance. A moment later, Lujan arrived, breathing hard, his gaze fixed, and his grip taut on his sword.

A second chime sounded, signaling the moment of arrival. A crack of displaced air ruffled Mara's loose hair and twisted the plumes of Lujan's formal helm. Mara clenched her jaw and forced her eyes straight ahead.

In the center of the pattern stood a bearded man in brown robes. He wore no ornaments. His garments were not of silk but of woven wool, clasped at the waist with a leather belt and a brass buckle of barbarian design. He wore boots, not sandals, and in the close heat of the windowless chamber, a flush touched his pale skin.

Saric and Lujan both hesitated, halfway into their bows. They had expected a man in black, a Great One of the Assembly. No magician they had heard of wore other than the traditional jet robe, and certainly none sported a beard.

Mara bent in obeisance, prolonging the motion to allow for furious thought. The City of the Magicians might lie to the north of Ontoset, but the climate was not cold enough to freeze. Only one reason could account for the dress of her caller: he was not Tsurani-born. Her impulsive note sent across the rift the month before must have attracted an answer. Before her stood the barbarian magician Milamber, whose powers unleashed in wrath had once freed slaves and devastated the Imperial Games.

Mara's fear did not lessen at her deduction. This Midkemian's beliefs were unknown to her. She had witnessed the violence of his acts, which had culminated in exile from the Assembly that had given him his early training. His loyalties and his volatile temperament might still be theirs; his swift and direct arrival after her vague overture was disconcerting, when Mara had anticipated no reply more elaborate than a letter.

Although Milamber would not be here on direct business of the Assembly, there was no guarantee he would not react in the interest of his Tsurani counterparts. Events between the worlds since his disgrace had caused him to work in league with them. Mara arose from her bow.

"Great One," she opened in the steadiest voice she could manage, "you honor my house."

The dark eyes that met Mara's seemed to hold veiled amusement. "I am no Great One, Lady Mara. Just call me Pug."

Mara's brow creased. "Did I mistake? Is your name not Milamber?"

Busily studying the unfurnished, wood-paneled room, Pug answered with an informality that typified most Midkemians. "It was. But I prefer to be known by the name given me in my homeland."

"Very well, Pug." Mara introduced her First Adviser and her Force Commander. Then, left at a loss as to how she should behave, and unwilling to be first to broach deeper matters, she said, "May I offer you refreshments?"

Pug's attention swung back, disconcertingly intense. But the hands that had raised such fearful powers of destruction in Kentosani remained still at his sides. He did nothing more than nod his head.

Mara led the way down the wooden stair, through the dim inner corridors, to the great hall. Saric, Lujan, and her hadonra followed at a respectful distance, their eyes alive with curiosity and awe. The Acoma First Adviser had heard his cousin's account of the destruction at the Imperial Games many times over hwaet beer. Lujan moved on his toes with alertness, aware that he dared not so much as think of handling his weapons before a man of such power; Saric sized up the barbarian magician, wrinkling his nose at the strange musty odors of birch smoke and tallow that clung to the man's clothing. Pug was a man of normal height for a Tsurani, which made him short by the standards of his homeland. He looked unassuming, except for his eyes, which were deep in mystery and terrifying for their power.

As the party entered through the wide doors leading to the great hall, Pug said, "A pity you are not at your usual abode, my Lady Mara. I had heard of the great hall of the Minwanabi when I lived within the Empire. The descriptions of the architecture fascinated me." In an almost amiable tone, he elaborated, "You know I also built my estate upon the property of a fallen family. Near Ontoset, the former home of the Tuscai." Mara glanced at her guest. There was nothing friendly about his eyes, which looked deeply into hers. If he was indicating he knew something of her household, her Force Commander, First Adviser, and Spy Master all having served the Tuscai, he showed only a pleasant façade. Always moving, Pug's glance roved over the room where Mara's Acoma ancestors had held court. Typical of most Tsurani halls, it was open on two sides, screens leading to a shaded portico. The ceiling was vaulted beam, roofed over with wood and tile, and the floors, waxed parquet that showed the wear of generations.

"Impressive," he added, in reference to the war standards strung in rows from the rafters. "Your family is among the oldest in the Empire, I understand." He smiled, and years dropped away from his face. "I assume you've changed the decor since taking possession of your other abode? The late Lord Tasaio's tastes were said to be execrable."

His bantering tone set Mara at ease. Though she suspected that was his purpose, and was loath to put down her guard, she was grateful to let taut nerves loosen. "Indeed. My late enemy liked his cushions in leather and fur, and his tables inlaid with bone. There were more swords and shields decorating the walls than Jican inventoried in the Minwanabi armory, and the only silk we found was in the battle streamers and war trappings. The guest rooms looked like an officers' barracks. But how do you know so much of my dead enemies?"

Pug laughed with such openness that it was impossible not to share in his mirth. "Hochopepa. The old gossip officiated at Tasaio's ritual suicide, and if you recall, he is quite portly. His letters to me held complaint that there was no seat in Tasaio's household that was not hard, upholstered with wooden tacks, and narrow across the cushions as if made for a man in battle trim."

Mara smiled. "Kevin of Zūn often told me that the most subdued art here would be counted 'garish' in your land. One might argue that tastes are a function of perspective." The Lady of the Acoma waved her guest toward the circle of cushions that lined the dais where the ruler in residence held court. "So I have learned over the years, yet so often it is easy to forget."

Pug deferred to her, allowing Lujan to see her seated first. As a Great One, he would have been entitled to be shown that honor. But up close, he was unassuming as a commoner. Mara found it difficult to equate this affable man with the figure of towering pride and power that had single-handedly ruined a former Warlord. But it took more than appearances to settle her adviser and her Force Commander. Saric and Lujan waited until the magician had made himself comfortable before they sat themselves. Her more retiring hadonra looked as if he were on trial for a capital crime.

Servants hurried in with trays, offering meat and cheeses and fresh fruits. Others brought hot water and an assortment of beverages. Pug helped himself to a plate with sliced jomach, and before Mara's trained staff could offer, poured himself what he must have presumed would be chocha. He sipped, and the half-moons of his eyes visible over his cup widened in surprise. "Tea!"

Mara fussed in worry. "Did you wish something else? My cook can have chocha brewed shortly, if that is your wish, Great One."

Pug held up his hand. "No, tea is fine. I'm startled to find it here." Then his eyes narrowed as he added, "Though by all reports, little to do with the Lady of the Acoma should be surprising."

Infused with sudden uneasiness, particularly that he should be acquainted with her affairs across the rift, Mara drew breath to demur. "Great One—"

Pug interrupted. "Please. I renounced that title when it was offered, at the time the Assembly asked to reinstate me." At Saric's startled lift of the brows, the Midkemian magician nodded. "Yes. They retracted my order of exile, after the conflict with the Enemy that came to threaten both our worlds. I am now also a Prince, by adoption into the royal family. But I prefer Pug, magician of Stardock, to any other title." He helped himself to more tea, then loosened his wool collar to ease himself in Kelewan's warmer climate. "How is Hokanu? I have not seen him since"—a frown knitted his brows—"since just after the battle of Sethanon."

Mara sighed, hiding sadness as she nibbled a piece of fruit from the tray. "He is well, but contending with some unpleasant rivalries among his cousins since he inherited his father's title."

Regret played across Pug's expression as he set down his cup. The jomach lay untasted beneath his hands, which were fine-skinned, the nails impeccably manicured. "Kamatsu was one of the finest men this land has known. He will be missed. In many ways, I owe him for much of what I am today." Then as if uncomfortable with dark thoughts, Pug grinned. "Has Hokanu developed the same passion for horses that consumes his brother?"

Mara shook her head. "He enjoys them, but not nearly so much as Kasumi did." Quietly, sadly, she added, "Or Ayaki."

Pug focused on the reference with the open, barbarian sympathy that in Kevin had so often been disconcerting. "The death of your son was a tragedy, Mara. I have a boy close to his age. He is so bursting with life—" He broke off, fingering his sleeves in discomfort. "You have been very brave, to endure such a loss without becoming callous or uncaring."

It was uncanny how much this barbarian magician knew of her affairs and her heart. Mara flashed a glance at Saric, who appeared on the verge of comment. She signaled her wish to speak first, before courage forsook her entirely.

"Pug," she opened, the familiar address coming awkwardly, "I sent you that message out of desperation."

Pug folded his hands in his cuffs and regarded her, utterly still. "Perhaps it would be wise to start from the beginning."

His eyes were old, as if he had beheld vistas wider than the human mind should encompass, and griefs more terrible than the loss of a single child. For an instant, Mara glimpsed past his mystery to the powers that coiled within this man whose manner seemed as easy as a chatty cousin's. She recalled the black-robed figure that had single-handedly destroyed the Imperial Arena, a gigantic stone edifice that had taken decades to build. Hundreds had died and thousands been injured in a fearful explosion of power, all because Milamber, this magician, had objected to the brutality of human combat as a display. Despite his everyday appearance and warm manner, he was a mage of unknowable dimension. Mara shivered sharply, feeling like a girl before the awareness of leashed might that this man seemed to hide so adroitly.

And yet it must equally be recognized that, alone, Pug had flown in the face of tradition, and had earned himself exile for deeds the Assembly could not countenance. If the Acoma were to gain protection, he was a potential key to knowledge.

Mara chose to risk all. She dismissed Lujan and her advisers, and when she was alone with the barbarian magician, she spoke freely. She began with the year the death of her father and brother forced her to assume control of her house, and recounted the triumphs and defeats that had followed. She spoke without pause, neglecting her tea and the food on the tray for a long time, finally ending with her confrontation with the Anasati that had brought intervention by the Assembly.

Pug interrupted with a question. From that point forward, he asked often for clarification of a thought or enumeration of a detail, or probed her to learn the motive behind an action. Mara was impressed at the quality of his memory, for he often sought more information on something mentioned more than a half hour prior. When Mara mentioned Arakasi's latest findings concerning the lapses of continuity in ancient documents in the Imperial Archives, Pug's questions became yet more pointed.

"Why did you wish my help in these matters?" he asked at last, his tone deceptively mild.

Mara knew nothing would suffice but total honesty. "It has become apparent that the Assembly might oppose me, not to keep peace, but to arrest change within the Empire. Great Ones have been reining the nations back from growth for more than a thousand years, if my advisers' and my Spy Master's assessments are correct.'' Although she might be judged and destroyed for the boldness of her accusation, Mara shed her uncertainties. If she backed away from this chance to gain knowledge, the Acoma were lost anyway. She forced herself to frame in clear words what had become a lifetime dedication since Ayaki's death. ''Your Midkemian ways have shown how the time-honored traditions we Tsurani most revere become destructive when they result in stagnation. We have become a cruel people, since the Golden Bridge. Merit has been replaced by elaborate codes of honor, and by a rigid caste system. I would see change, and an end to merciless politics for personal honor. I would see our Lords become accountable for their actions, and our slaves set free. But I suspect the Assembly would prevent even the Light of Heaven from enacting such shifts in policy.''

Mara looked up to find Pug staring into his empty teacup. Late sunlight slashed the wooden floors, and the cheeses had half melted on the food tray. Hours had passed, all unnoticed. Ruefully Mara realized that the Midkemian magician's questioning had not only caused her to reveal more than she had planned, but also had crystallized her thinking, ordered her mind, and delineated exactly which problems lay ahead of her. More in awe of the barbarian magician than before, since she had not noticed his molding of her thoughts, Mara clenched her hands together. In a fever of anxiety, she awaited his terrible judgment, or the gift of his understanding.

For a while nothing moved in the great hall but the war banners stirred by the breeze. At last Pug broke his silence. ''Much in what you say puts me in mind of things I have felt . . . things I have done.''

Nervously Mara said, ''I don't follow.''

Pug smiled. ''Let us simplify by saying that the Assembly is filled with disagreement. From without, the society of magicians might seem a monolithic entity, a body that occasionally intervenes in the affairs of the Empire but habitually keeps itself separate.'' He gestured widely as folk from his culture were wont to do. ''That is far from the case. Each Great One may act as he sees fit, upon any occasion, for his training is predicated upon serving the Empire.''

Mara nodded.

Pug's gaze caught hers, dark with an irony that might have been amusement had the topic been less grave. ''However, there are times when two magicians may have radically different views of how best to serve. On rare occasions, disagreements give rise to conflict.''

Mara dared a supposition. ''Then some of the Great Ones may not sanction the intervention in my war against the Anasati?''

"They would be the minority," Pug allowed. Perhaps his own memories of exile from the Assembly came to mind, for he seemed to weigh Mara's eagerness. "I am also sure that others argued that your death would solve the matter quickly." Deliberately careful in his wording, he neither confirmed nor denied her speculations concerning the Assembly's hold over the Empire's development; in bald fact, he had told her little that Fumita had not already hinted to Hokanu at Kamatsu's death rites.

Mara restrained her frustration as Pug rose, plainly with intent to end the interview. Desperate not to lose her hope of aid, she blurted, "I wrote you on the chance you might know how I may defend myself against the Assembly if the need arises."

"I thought as much." Suddenly hard as barbarian iron, Pug laced his hands together under his wide sleeves and regarded her as she, too, rose to her feet. "Walk with me to the pattern."

Mara waved back the servants who closed in to collect the food tray, and the two warriors who moved from their positions by the outer door, to accompany her as escort. Aware that Pug could depart from any place in her house, she surmised that his request stemmed from a wish for privacy. As she led him from the great hall into the dimmer inner corridor, Pug drew her to his side with a touch upon her arm. "Why should you have concern for your safety, Mara of the Acoma?" Softly he added, "If you were a good child who ceased troubling your parents, you would have nothing to fear by way of punishment."

In better times, Mara might have smiled at the image. "The last agent I sent into the Imperial Archives to research significant financial discrepancies in certain historical periods was destroyed outright by the Assembly."

As if Pug had been born knowing the halls of a strange house, he turned up the steps toward the pattern room. "Knowledge can be a dangerous thing, Mara of the Acoma."

He did not ask which years her agent had inquired into, or what findings he had unearthed; his silence on those points only underscored Mara's fears. She stepped into the pattern room at the magician's side. Pug turned and closed the door. She did not see the pass he made with his hands, but she felt as if a cold wind blew across her, and she knew that a spell had been invoked. Pug straightened, his expression grave. "For a few minutes, no one, not even the most gifted of my former brethren, can hear what you say."

Mara's face drained of color. "Great Ones could listen to what passed in my great hall?"

Pug smiled in quick reassurance. "Most likely it never occurred to any of them to try—it's considered a breach of proper behavior. Though I can't guarantee that much for Hochopepa if the matter is weighty enough. He's a bit of a snoop." The last was said with affection, and Mara realized that the portly magician must have been one of Pug's friends and supporters, after the upheaval in the Imperial Arena. As much as any Black Robe could be, this Hochopepa might be sympathetic to the Acoma cause.

Pug's next question caught her back from speculative thought. "Mara, you realize that the changes you work for will turn the Empire upon its collective ear?"

Tired to her bones from the strain, Mara leaned back against the wood-paneled walls and regarded the shatra bird symbol inset into the floor. "Should we continue as we have, and be ruled by men who murder children, and let good people become beaten down and ruined by servitude when their talents and efforts deserve better? Jiro of the Anasati and the faction he leads would see petty power struggles take precedence over all else. It is heresy for me to say so, but I can no longer believe that the gods endorse such waste."

Pug made a deprecating gesture. "Then why concern the Assembly? Have an assassin dispose of Jiro. You certainly have wealth enough to buy his death."

The ordinary callousness of his statement at last disarmed her. Mara forgot he was a magician, forgot his terrible powers, forgot all but her own bitter anguish. "Gods, don't speak to me of assassins! I destroyed the Hamoi Tong because it was too readily available as a weapon for grasping Ruling Lords to further their own selfish causes. The Acoma have never dealt with assassins! I will see my line dead and lost to memory before I begin such practice. Seven times have I been marked for death. Three times the lives of my loved ones have been sent to Turakamu's halls by the tong in my place. I have lost two sons and the mother of my heart to its bloody hands." Then, reawakened to awareness of whom she addressed, she finished, "There is more to this than my hatred of assassins. Jiro's death might settle honor, but that ends nothing, solves nothing. The Assembly would still seek to ruin my house. Because Ichindar, and Hokanu, and I myself, as Servant of the Empire, all seek to replace what is missing from our lives."

"Missing?" Pug prompted as he folded his arms across his chest.

"Within us. Within the Empire."

"Go on."

Mara looked deep into Pug's eyes. "Do you know Kevin of Zūn?"

Pug nodded. "Not well. I first met him here—"

"When?" Disrupted utterly from her train of thought, Mara's eyes widened in disbelief. "You never called upon me. Surely I would have remembered such a momentous event!"

Pug regarded her with bitter humor. "I was of a somewhat lower station at that time, being one of Master Hokanu's slaves. Kevin and I exchanged only a few words. But I have seen him once since his return to the Prince's court in Krondor, in a reception for the Border Barons."

Mara repressed a wild leap of the heart. In a tight whisper she asked, "Is he well?" Her eyes pleaded.

Pug nodded, aware of the deeper emotions behind that simple question. In answer to a need her pride would never acknowledge, he volunteered, "Kevin has made a name for himself in the service of Prince Arutha. Third sons of minor nobles need to find their way by their wits. From what I have heard and seen, he does well, indeed. He serves in the north of the Kingdom, with Baron Highcastle, and has advanced in rank several times, I believe."

Mara's voice fell and her eyes lowered as she softly said, "Has he wed?"

"I do not know, I'm sorry to say. Stardock is far from court, and detailed news does not always reach us." When Mara raised her gaze, Pug observed, "Though I'm unsure which answer would please you most, yes or no."

Mara loosed a rueful laugh. "I do not know either."

Golden light seeped under the door as a servant lit lamps in the hallway; dusk lent purple shadows to the closed confines of the pattern room. Suddenly reawakened to the passage of time, Pug said briskly, "I must go." He forestalled Mara's second attempt to delay him, saying, "I have no gift for you of magic or wisdom, Lady. I am not of the Assembly, but even still, the oaths I swore when I was admitted to its brotherhood bind my mind, if not my heart. Even with my powers, some training is difficult to disobey. I cannot aid you in your struggle. But I can offer this: you are wise to seek counsel outside the Empire, for you will find few allies within."

Mara's eyes narrowed as she realized that he knew of her secret preparations to journey over the borders; but how he had found out, or what made him able to read beyond what she had taken pains to conceal as a pilgrimage, she could not guess. "So it's true the cho-ja may not aid me."

Pug's face split into a grin. He moved away from her side, almost boyish in his delight. "You are further along in unraveling the great mystery than I would have thought." His expression returned to a neutral mask as he finished, "Those within the Empire who might wish to be your allies are prevented. No, you must seek outside the Nations."

"Where?" Mara pressed. "The Kingdom of the Isles?" But at once she knew the lead she suggested was a false hope. Already she spoke with the most powerful man from beyond the rift.

Pug stretched his arms out, letting the sleeves of his brown robe fall away. Obliquely he said, "Did you know my wife was Thuril? Interesting place, the Highlands. You should visit them sometime. Give my regards to your husband."

With no further word, he raised his hands above his head and vanished. The inrush of air into the space he had occupied filled the silence, while the chamber dimmed into the darkness of coming night.

Mara sighed and opened the door. Blinking against the sudden dazzle of lamplight, she saw Saric and Lujan awaiting her. To her adviser and her officer she said, "Nothing has changed. We begin our pilgrimage tomorrow."

Saric's eyes lit with excitement. After a glance to be sure no servants lurked within earshot, he whispered, "We go beyond Lepala?"

Mara bit back an answering smile, careful not to show more enthusiasm than a pious journey might warrant; though she, too, was excited and curious at the prospect of crossing the borders into unknown lands. "By fastest ship. But we must visit the temples before we travel east. If we are to gain by our visit to Thuril, we must be circumspect in our departure."

The preparations left to be made before dawn demanded attention, and Lujan and Saric took leave of their mistress to attend them. As they departed, alike in their movements as only blood kin could be, Mara looked after them and sighed. The house seemed empty and quiet without the children. Regretting she had lost her chance to bid them a proper farewell, she moved in the direction of the stair, and her study, where the servants would be bringing her evening meal. First light would not come soon enough to soothe her unsettled nerves. Now that her path was clear, she was anxious to be away.

She could not surmise what lay in store for her across the border in the lands of a people who had been enemies of the Empire through years of wars and skirmishes. The treaty that bound the current peace was an uneasy one; the highlanders of the confederation were quick to offend and belligerent by nature. But the most powerful magician of two worlds had circumspectly encouraged her exploration. If nothing else, Mara sensed that he, alone of any, fully understood the stakes. More, he knew the terrible scope of the perils she needed to surmount.

As she moved past bowing servants, toward the comfort of her quarters, she wondered what Pug's appraisal of her chances at success might have been. Then she had second thoughts, and decided she was wise not to have asked. If the barbarian magician had answered at all, his words would surely have taken the heart from her.

The priest shouted. Echoes reverberated off the massive vaults of the temple ceiling, which towered above carved wooden pillars and buttresses. The assembled circle of red-robed acolytes answered in ritual chant, and a rare metal chime sounded to signal the ending of the morning ceremony. Mara waited quietly in shadow at the rear of the chamber, her honor guard surrounding her, and her First Adviser at her side. Saric looked absorbed in thoughts far removed from religion. His fingers tapped a tattoo on the corcara-shell bosses on his belt, and his hair looked rumpled, as if he had raked his fingers through his bangs in impatience. While none of her warriors disclosed any sign of discomfort, their stiff postures indicated that they were less able to turn their minds to other matters while in the Red God's sacred precinct. Most of them offered inward prayers to the Deities of Luck and Fortune that their final meeting with the Death God would be long in coming.

And in truth, Mara thought, the Temple of Turakamu was not a place designed for comfort. An ancient altar, once the site of human sacrifice— and still such, rumor ran—squatted on the raised platform at the chamber's center. Stone benches surrounded the site, worn by the feet of many worshippers, and grooved with drains that led to recessed basins at the feet of statues that were centuries old, their surfaces smoothed and stained by the touch of generations of hands. The walls behind their niches were painted with human skeletons, demons, and demigods with multiple legs and arms. The figures writhed or danced in postures of ecstasy; despite their grotesque aspect, they reminded Mara of other icons and paintings that adorned the House of Fruitfulness, one of the many shrines of Lashima, visited by women who prayed for conception. Yet while Turakamu's temple depicted no sexual overtones, there was a sybaritic quality to the murals, as if those hideous intertwined figures were celebrating, not suffering.

Awaiting her audience, Mara considered that while the Red God's priests were frightening, in conversation they insisted that as all people meet their end at the feet of Turakamu, death was a fate, not to avoid, but rather to be accepted with understanding.

The circle of acolytes reformed into a double column, wreathed in the twining smokes of incense. Mara saw the caped figure at the head of the procession pause to address a supplicant who begged the god's mercy for one recently departed. A writ crusted with seals changed hands; most likely a draft from the family offering a generous contribution to the temple if its bequest was answered. As the paintings farthest from the sacrificial altar showed, humans with beatific expressions bowed before the Red God's throne to hear divine decision concerning rebirth into life, their next station on the Wheel designated by the balance of their debts against honor. The recently departed, it was believed, could be enhanced in the eyes of the Red God through prayer, and while the poor came on foot to make obeisance and light cheap clay lamps, the rich came in litters bearing lavish sums for private temple rites.

Mara wondered whether such practices influenced Turakamu, or were the encouragement of earthly priests who desired rubies for their mantles, and comforts for their refectories and sleeping cells. Certainly the massive gold tripods that supported the lamps by the altar amounted to the wealth of a kingdom. Although each temple of the Twenty Gods had costly trappings, few were as sumptuously appointed as even the smallest ones dedicated to Turakamu.

A voice roused Mara from reverie. "Good Servant, you honor us." The procession of acolytes had reached the rear door and was filing slowly out, but the High Priest in attendance had stepped out of the column and approached the Acoma retinue. Under his paint and his feathered cape, he was a man of medium stature, aging, but bright of eye. Up close, it was apparent he had been taken aback, and his nervous hands moved up and down the bone wand with its skull bosses that he had flourished during the rites. "I knew you were going on pilgrimage, Lady Mara, but I had presumed you would visit the great shrine in the Holy City, not our humbler abode in Sulan-Qu. Certainly I did not prepare for the honor of a personal visit."

Mara bowed slightly to the High Priest of Turakamu. "I've no wish to stand upon ceremony. And in truth, my trip here is for reasons other than plain devotion. Rather, I have need of your counsel."

The High Priest's brows rose in surprise and disappeared under the chin of the skull mask he wore, perched on the crown of his head now that the ceremony was ended. He was not stripped nude and stained in red body paint, as was customary for rites performed outside sacred ground. But his hair was braided with relics that looked like bits of dismembered birds, and the accoutrements visible beneath his cape of scarlet feathers seemed even less inviting. As if aware that his formal dress was not conducive to interviews, he passed his wand to the boy acolyte who waited in his shadow, and doffed his robe. The cross-belts on which his relics hung were of ancient design, and two other attendants rushed forward and removed them from his shoulders with reverent care. They bore the regalia off, chanting, to its place in locked closets hidden away in a warren of passageways.

Left in a simple loincloth, his eyes still striped with paint from the ceremony, the priest seemed suddenly younger. "Come," he invited Mara. "Let us retire to more comfortable surroundings. Your honor guard may come along, or they may await your pleasure in the garden inside the gates. It is shady there, and a water boy will answer their needs for refreshment."

Mara waved Lujan and Saric to her side, and indicated that the rest of her retinue might retire. None of the warriors looked relieved, but their steps were animated as they wheeled in formation and headed for the doorway to the outer garden. Men in martial professions were never comfortable with Turakamu's followers. Superstition held that a soldier who spent too much time in devotion to the Red God risked attracting that deity's favor; and those whom Turakamu came to love would be taken in their youth from the battlefield.

The High Priest led the way through a small side doorway into a dim corridor. "When not in formal guise, I am called Father Jadaha, Good Servant."

Half smiling at his formality, the Lady replied, "Mara will do, Father."

She was ushered into austere quarters with walls of unadorned paneling, and unpainted screens. The prayer mats were dyed red, for the glory of the god, but those used for sitting were woven of natural fiber. Mara was shown to the plumpest of a poor lot of cushions, threadbare with use, but clean. She allowed Lujan to seat her, and offered a hasty inward prayer for Turakamu's forgiveness. Her thoughts in the temple had been wrong; plainly, the Sulan-Qu priests used the moneys given by petitioning families only to adorn those chambers dedicated to their god.

Once Lujan and Saric had placed themselves at their mistress's side, the High Priest sent his servant for refreshments. A body servant with a bad scar and one eye saw to the removal of his ceremonial paint and brought him a white robe with red borders. Then, over a tray of chocha and small cakes, the High Priest addressed his visitor. "Mara, what service may the Temple of Turakamu offer you?"

"I am not certain, Father Jadaha." Mara helped herself to a square of sweet cake out of politeness. While Saric poured her chocha, she added, "I seek knowledge."

The priest returned a gesture of blessing. "What poor resources we have are yours."

Mara let her surprise show, for his quick acceptance was unexpected. "You are very generous, Father. But I humbly submit, you might wish to hear of my needs before you make sweeping promises."

The High Priest smiled. His one-eyed servant retired with evident respect, and given a view of a face cleansed of paint, Mara saw that the chief devotee of the Death God was a pleasant older man. Slender and fit, he had a scribe's beautiful hands, and his eyes sparkled with intelligence. "What should I fear in making promises, Lady Mara? You have shown your mettle in your great service to the Empire. I doubt your motives now are selfish at heart; not after the behavior you demonstrated after the demise of House Minwanabi. More than generous, your actions were . . . unprecedented. Not only did you observe correct forms in removing the prayer gate Desio erected in dedication to your death, you selflessly made sure that no dishonor was implied to the temple in asking the prayer gate to be relocated off your lands. It is we priests who are in your debt, for your part in ending the tyranny of the High Council. Once again, our guidance is allowed proper influence over the course of daily life." The priest gestured ruefully and helped himself to a huge slice of cake. "Changes in the power structure happen slowly. Those Ruling Lords who resist our influence are close-knit in their opposition. Still, we are making progress."

Mara now recalled the words of the delegate from Turakamu's temple who had officiated at the relocation of Desio's prayer gate. At the time, overwhelming emotions had caused her to dismiss the priest's remarks as ingratiating flattery. Only years later, did she appreciate his sincerity. The discovery of support in a place she had not expected bolstered her courage. "I need to inquire about the nature of magic."

The High Priest froze with his cup of chocha halfway to his lips. He blinked once, his thoughts distant. Then, as if the Lady's request had been commonplace, he resumed sipping his drink. He allowed the beverage to linger on his palate before he swallowed, perhaps because he wished to buy time for consideration, or, as Saric's wicked insight might infer, to forestall an unseemly fit of choking.

Whatever his priestly motive, his manner was calm when he set down his cup. "What would you know of magic?"

Doggedly Mara pursued the topic, though it was dangerous. "Why are such powers considered the sole province of the Assembly? For I have seen priests who could wield them."

The High Priest regarded the small, determined woman who was ac-knowledged to be the second most influential figure in the Empire after the Light of Heaven. His eyes held unfathomable shadows, and a coldness not there the moment before. "The sanctions imposed by the Assembly upon your dispute with Jiro of the Anasati are well-known, Mara. If you are seeking to arm yourself against the Black Robes, you embark on a ruinous course." He did not use the honorific "Great Ones" and that nuance was not lost upon Mara and her advisers. As with the cho-ja, was it possible the temple hierarchies felt less than enamored of the magicians?

"Why should you assume that I plot against the Assembly?" Mara asked with impolitic bluntness.

Father Jadaha seemed unperturbed by her directness. "My Lady, ser-vice to Turakamu leads my kind to know the darker side of human nature. Men long in power do not care to be shown their vulnerabilities. Few demonstrate wisdom when confronted by change and self-recognition. Sadly, many react in defense of positions that have lost their meaning, simply because they fear to see their security undermined, even for growth, even for the betterment of their lives. They resist change simply because it is outside the comfort they know. You represent luck and hope and good fortune to the folk of these nations. You have been their cham-pion, unwittingly or not, because you opposed tyranny and cruelty when you brought about the abolishment of the Warlord's office. You have successfully questioned the long-standing power structure that rules this land. That must be interpreted as challenge, whether you will such or not. You have grown to great heights, and those who see you as their rival have felt your shadow fall across them. Two powers such as the Assembly and the Servant of the Empire cannot exist without conflict. Thousands of years in the past, the Black Robes perhaps earned their place outside the law. But now they interpret their omnipotence as their gods-given right, their sacred honor, if you will. You represent change; and they, the very fabric of tradition. They must defeat you to maintain their ascendence. This is the nature of Tsurani life."

Father Jadaha glanced through the screen, cracked open to admit the outside air. The snap of a carter's whip drifted in from the street, overlaid by the cry of a fish monger selling that morning's catch. As if the intrusive sounds of ordinary life set mortal bounds to his thinking, the priest sighed. "Once we who swore service to the gods held influence and great reach, Mara of the Acoma. Once we were able to encourage our rulers for the betterment of all men, or at least use our influence to curb excessive greed and evil." He fell silent, his lips thinned with what may have been bitterness. Then he said, "There is nothing I can offer that will help you against the Assembly. But I have a small gift for your journey."

Mara repressed apprehension. "Journey?" Had her subterfuge been so transparent that even this High Priest in Sulan-Qu saw through the purpose of her pilgrimage? Stiff-faced, silent, and reminded by a touch from Saric that she must not tip her hand through an assumption, Mara watched the priest arise and cross to an ancient wooden chest.

"To find what you seek you must travel far, Mara of the Acoma." He unlocked the catch and raised the lid. "I believe you already know that." His incongruously graceful hands rummaged through the contents of the chest. Mara caught a glimpse of parchments, and the ribboned edges of seals, through a puff of disturbed dust. The priest muffled a sneeze in his sleeve. "Your pardon." He flapped an ancient treatise to clear the air, then resumed his train of thought. "The gossipmongers on the streets say you carry enough baggage to return to the sandy wastes of the Lost Lands. Anyone with a shell centi can buy that fact from them."

Mara smiled. She found it difficult to reconcile the priest who had officiated at the morning rites to the most feared god on Kelewan with a man who might buy gossip on the street. Ruefully she said, "I had hoped to imply that we carried great tribute to offer the temples where I will pause to pay my respects to the Twenty Gods. In truth, though, you are right. My pilgrimage will lead me to board ship and travel downriver to Jamar."

The High Priest straightened from the chest, a smear of dust on his nose and a twinkle in his eyes. He held an ancient parchment, cracked and flocked with age. "I would be a poor counselor for the afflicted if I could not read through subterfuge. But we priests do not see through the eyes of rulers. It is our business to interpret with an eye to understanding." He offered the document to Mara. "Read this. It might yield you some insights."

Sensitive to the finality in his tone, Mara handed the parchment to Saric to store in his satchel. She pushed aside her cake plate and rose. "Thank you, Father."

The priest held her eyes as Lujan and Saric moved in response to her intention to depart. "Do you seek answers in the Lost Land, Mara?"

Wise enough to know when not to be circumspect, Mara said, "No. We leave from Jamar for Lepala."

As if the topic she addressed held nothing more momentous than small talk, the priest waved away a small insect that alit upon the rim of the cake plate; then his hands folded comfortably in his sleeves. "This is good, daughter of my god. The shamans of the desert are . . . unreliable. Many of them treat with dark powers."

Saric could not restrain a small exclamation at this. The Priest responded with a chuckle. "Your First Adviser seems surprised."

Mara nodded her permission, and Saric made hasty apology. "Excuse my apparent disrespect, Father, but most would consider . . . your master a . . . dark power."

The High Priest's face crinkled with silent laughter. "Believe me, that misapprehension often has its advantages! But death is just another side of the mystery of the Wheel of Life. Without its portal into Turakamu's halls, wherein all spirit finds renewal, our current existence would be a mindless endeavor lacking soul." The High Priest moved to usher Mara's party from his quarters, but he continued speaking. "Our magic, as you would call it, is no unnatural power." He pointed his finger at the insect that circled over the cake platter. A sharp, almost subliminal shadow seemed to cross the air and the creature plummeted to the floor. "We use this aspect of nature sparingly, to ease the suffering of those who are near their end, yet unable to release their own hold upon flesh. The spirit of life is strong, sometimes mindlessly so."

"Such could be a powerful weapon," observed Lujan in a voice deeper than usual. Mara realized that, though he hid it well, he was as apprehensive of Turakamu's servants as any one of his warriors.

The Priest shrugged. "Never that." With no more ado, he pointed his finger at Lujan's breast. The Acoma Force Commander made a visible effort to keep from flinching, and sweat sprang along the band of his plumed helm.

Nothing happened.

Even Mara realized her heart had raced in fear as the Priest added quietly, "It was not your time to meet the Red God, Force Commander. Mine are the powers of my god. I could not send you to his halls on my own authority."

Saric, to whom all of life was a puzzle to be solved, was first to overcome his apprehension. "But the insect . . . ?"

"This was its time." The priest almost sounded weary. "To make a point, I expect."

Sobered, Mara bade the priest thanks for his advice and good wishes. She and her party were shown from the temple by the one-eyed servant. At the base of the marble stair, they were rejoined by her honor guard. Mara stepped into her litter, lost in thought. She did not at once give the command to her bearers to rise, and in that interval, a ragged street urchin raced from a side alley and crashed squarely into Lujan.

The Force Commander swore under his breath. He righted the youngster, crinkled his nose at the smell of unwashed clothes, then abruptly became expressionless.

Mara stifled her amusement. Under the noise of another street hawker, this one peddling cheap silk scarves and perfumes suitable for women of the Reed Life, she whispered, "Another of Arakasi's messengers?"

Saric pricked up, while Lujan stuffed the note he had palmed into his belt, under pretense of wiping his hands. "Vermin," he said loudly after the fleeing child. Dropping his voice so only Mara and Saric could hear, he added, "Where does the man find such filthy creatures to do his bidding?"

Mara was unwilling to disclose that her Spy Master had once been such a luckless boy, and that his use of them as his message bearers might be twofold: they would not be marked by other men's spies because they were of little account, and they could not read. Since Arakasi had met Kamlio, Mara additionally suspected that pity entered in, since her Spy Master might wish to justify spending the centis to allow those less fortunate youngsters a chance to buy themselves a meal they need not steal. In a noncommittal voice she said, "Did he find one?"

Saric gave her a stern look. Aware that she referred to a magician of the lesser path, which Arakasi had set out to find since the misfortune that had ended his search through the archives, the First Adviser snapped Mara's curtains closed. He said in his most infuriating tone of familiarity, "The sooner we move out to find a tavern for your nap, the quicker you will find out."

"We will call on the man after dark," Mara whispered through the cloth.

Saric and Lujan exchanged glances of fond exasperation. Their mistress seemed giddy as a girl. Plainly, she found the challenge of her pending inquiries into the forbidden exhilarating after long months of frustration. As the bearers raised the litter, Saric and the Acoma Force Commander fell into step together.

"Was she like this when you left for the campaign in the desert?" the First Adviser murmured to his cousin.

"Not then." Lujan pushed back his helm with a smile. "But Keyoke told me about the wild march cross-country into the territory of the Inrodaka to win the alliance of the cho-ja Queen. By his account, then she was worse."

"Gods save us," Saric said, making a sign to avert misfortune. But his eyes were laughing, and his stride, like his cousin's, was springy with excitement.

"Your curiosity will kill us all one day," Lujan murmured. "It's a damned lucky thing for my recruits that you gave up your warrior's sword for the mantle of an adviser."

Then the honor guard and litter bearers set off for the tavern where Mara would reside while in Sulan-Qu.

18. Evasion

The door flap stirred.

Jamel, the lesser-path magician, started at the sound, his sweaty hand gripped tight to the knife he held to his breast. He had only seconds to act, he knew. His body would take a while to relinquish life after he fell upon his blade. Apprehension for the agony he would suffer made the little man hesitate. He shifted his wet fingers, biting his lower lip. He must summon courage! The Black Robes had spells to command the wal to remain enfleshed. If he was not before the Red God's divine judgment seat by the time the magicians arrived, his torments at their hands would be worse than painful death.

For he had defied them, blatantly, in speaking with Lady Mara of the Acoma. The magicians had been direct in their orders concerning the Good Servant. She was not to be told anything of magic, even should she come with bribes in hand to inquire.

Feeling the pouch of metal centis against his skin, Jamel repressed a sour laugh. He would never have the chance to spend them! Much as he might wish for the time to give them into the hands of the street girl down the way who was his friend, fate would not allow him even the grace of generosity. He had chosen his path. Too late, now, to wish words unsaid and resolves undone.

One last time, Jamel ran his gaze around the cluttered hovel that had been his home. Here he had made many marvels to delight the children of the rich; but how much different his life might have been if his powers had not been confined to the fashioning of toys! Hungry for the knowledge he had been denied, thirsty for the testing of limits that he had never been permitted to attempt, Jamel loosed a bitter sigh.

"Gods go with you, Lady Servant," he said fearfully. "And may the curse of Zurgauli, God of Ill Luck, permanently visit the Assembly." So saying, he threw himself down onto the floor before the cushions where Lady Mara's officer had sat.

The knife against his heart bit deep, and his agony, at the end, was brief.

* * *

Blood soaked into the dry earth of the floor; the ragged edges of torn cushions showed seeping crescents of scarlet where the warm, wet flow had been dammed, then absorbed, by the fabric. Jamal's quivering, clenched fingers fell lax, and his opened eyes shone motionless in the glow of the brazier's coals. The next instant, a stir of air swept the chamber, fanning the curled ash of the parchment that had contained notes to Mara before it burned. The calley-bird feathers in the urn by the clothes chest streamed in the disturbance, and the bells of an unsold child's toy chimed their priceless song into the stillness. Outside, in the dark of the night, the mongrel dog still howled.

Then over the rush of air came a faint buzzing, and the hovel of a sudden was not empty. Next to the cooling corpse of Jamel appeared two black-robed figures, both of them thin as misers, though one was old, and one young.

Shimone pushed back his hood, his jutting nose outlined in red by the dying coals of the brazier. He glanced around the hovel, taking swift inventory of every item amid the clutter; he paused, and sniffed thoughtfully. His slippers were damp, and the puddle he stood in was warm. The corpse might have been just another item of bric-a-brac for all the reaction he gave. His deep eyes flashed as he glanced to his companion. "Too late," he said.

Tapek shoved Jamel's body with his toe, and his thin lips turned down in disdain. "By only seconds." He spat the words like a curse. "If the wretch had not found his nerve for just a minute longer . . ."

Shimone shrugged. His thinning silver hair caught light like a cock's comb as he roved the width of the hovel, tracking sticky footprints as he examined the shelves, the bins of faded scrolls, and the battered chests with more care. "She was here. That is enough." He reached out one finger and jingled the doll with her priceless headdress of metal bells. "And anyway, the wretch is dead. He saved us the bother, really."

Tapek's heavy, cinnamon-colored brows gathered into a frown. "Is it enough?" He stepped over the unfortunate Jamel and blocked his companion's restless pacing. "What did the dead man tell her? That's the issue! We know Jamel broke his obedience. He could have said anything before he drove that knife through his heart!"

The slight hiss of the coals was now the only sound in the night. The dog had stopped barking. Even the far-off rumble from the dockside ceased. The commonplace noises of Sulan-Qu had quieted for an instant, as if the city held its breath.

Shimone reached out a finger like a twig and touched Tapek on the breast. He moved his hand. No spell arose, but as if it had, the younger magician stood aside. As Shimone moved past to continue his examination of Jamel's belongings, he said, "You want to know what she asked? See, then. But I think we waste our time. She knows, now, what she knows. That cannot be changed, but only acted upon."

Tapek rolled his shoulders, clearing his wrists from his sleeves. His eyes, pale as oil, threw back the hot light like a fanatic's. "Indeed we will act. But it is proof of Mara's defiance of our edicts that will move the likes of Hochopepa off his enormous arse. We need consensus within the Assembly, and he and his faction work to prevent that."

"Hocho is not a procrastinator," Shimone defended, his voice made faint by the fact that he had stooped to peer into the dusty cranny under a shelf.

"Well," Tapek said hastily, for he was not deaf to subtle chastisement, "what lesser-path mage would *not* speak to Mara? She is revered by commoners. They would give her anything she asked, just to win grace in the eyes of the gods. If she corrupted Jamel, what more proof would Hochopepa and you need to condemn her to death?"

Shimone straightened, absently dusting blood and dirt from his sleeve cuffs. "Jamel was hardly such a fool. You will see."

"I will see!" Insistently Tapek raised his hands. He flashed a last glare at his colleague, whose behavior had been difficult, if not obstructive. While a long-time friend of Hochopepa's, Shimone had always seemed reasonable. "*You* will see," Tapek added. Then he began to murmur the incantation to summon back in spectral form the actions of the immediate past.

Cold seemed to weave through the close atmosphere of the hovel, though the air itself remained still. Shimone stopped his inquisitive poking through the objects on the shelves. He thoughtfully bent and closed the eyes of the corpse. Then, bright in movement as a bird, he stood back against the wall with folded arms to observe the result of Tapek's spell.

The younger magician's incantation drew to a sibilant close. His raised hands held steady as if to focus his will and powers. Light glowed beyond the brazier that was not cast by fire or coal. It brightened to an icy silver-blue, then spread into a hazy translucence that slowly sharpened in outline to show the form of Jamel seated, his face turned expectantly toward the door flap. Moments later, visitors entered: Mara and her two officers. Conversation began between the parties, eerily soundless. Shimone seemed as attentive to the noises outside, in the poor quarter, as to the unfolding of Tapek's truth spell.

Lipreading showed the contents of the discussion to be petty: Mara's concern centered on the estrangement of her husband, which had begun months back at the birth of her daughter. An innocent enough tableau; except that Jamel began, most irritatingly for the magicians assigned to this inquiry, to fuss and toy with a length of silk. Conveniently often, it seemed, the cloth obscured sight of his mouth. By the ripple of the silk caused by his breath, it was evident that he hid speech. But no spell of past recall could recover the sound of his words. The imprint of light striking objects in the room could be summoned back into coherent form, to be read for many days after, but sound was too fragile to endure more than seconds.

Tapek swore. Fixed as a relli, he watched as Jamel arose and conducted Mara toward the wall. There they turned their backs to the room, and to appearances, the lesser-path mage proceeded in all seriousness to instruct the Lady in just the sort of fakery—passes in the air with his hands, motions that meant nothing but were intended to impress the ignorant folk who came calling to buy this or that change in their miserable lives— that demeaned the reputation of magicians as a whole, and that Tapek scorned. His hands shook with anger as he maintained the forces that drove his spell, and he said acidly, "The Lady seems remarkably stupid, all of a sudden. Is this the fourth repetition of this rubbish, or the fifth?"

To his fury, Shimone appeared to be laughing—not outright, that was never his way, but his deep eyes seemed dancing with light. "I warned you, Tapek. Jamel was not an idiot. And no, the Lady is certainly not stupid."

The veiled disapproval in his colleague's tone renewed Tapek's frustration. Still, out of determination and pique he endured the specters' charades, until Jamel finished tracing meaningless symbols and resorted to scribbling on a parchment, hunched over it to conceal the writing. Since the spell only recalled the imprint of past events as if the observer were standing in the room, no matter where Tapek moved, Jamel's writing could not be read. Tapek glared at the brazier, only to realize that Shimone had spied the ashes of the burned parchment already, probably soon after their entry into Jamel's abode.

"Indeed," observed the older magician in answer to Tapek's thought, "the words were lost before we ever arrived."

Tapek released his spell the instant that Mara received the carefully folded parchment and took her leave. Unmindful of blood-wet earth or sodden cushions, Tapek stamped in leashed temper around the brazier, every inch of him tense. "Gods, but if only I could stand where that wall is, and recast my truth spell, I'd learn much, for you could see by their stances that the Lady and our dead man spoke openly when facing the shelves!''

Shimone, ever the realist, shrugged. ''We're wasting time.''

Tapek rounded on his colleague, who stood now like an elderly Lord impatiently suffering the slowness of an inept servant. ''Mara!'' Tapek exclaimed. ''We shall ask her!''

As if released from thought into action, Shimone stalked toward the door. He twitched aside the flap of hide and stepped through into the hardly less cloying stink of the alley, saying, ''I wondered when you'd finally think of that.''

Leaving the corpse of Jamel where it lay, Tapek barged through on the heels of his companion. His red brows jutted in a thunderous frown. If he had dared to speak freely upon the subject, he would have accused Shimone of obstructing him. The old mage was a companion of Hocho-pepa, and the two of them often championed strange causes. Together, had they not defended Milamber after that disastrous scene at the Imperial Games? It mattered little to Tapek that Milamber had later proven his worth to the Empire by warning the Emperor and the Assembly of the danger the Enemy posed. His feelings regarding Elgohar, the magician who had imprisoned Hochopepa and tortured Milamber, were mixed; Elgohar had been mad, of course, but he had done as he had thought best for the Empire. But Milamber had destroyed him, and along with his other outrages, had demonstrated the risks brought by radical departures from tradition. Tapek was convinced Mara's recent actions were, if not proof, then a strong indication that she plotted to defy the Assembly. And that was an affront to tradition that made the pale magician tremble with ire.

Deep in outraged speculation, Tapek all but ran into Shimone, who had stopped in the street and to all appearance was listening to the wind.

''Which way are you going to look?'' Shimone inquired.

Tapek's scowl deepened. It demeaned him to act the part of underling, but if he did not summon another spell to recall the past, and left that bit of business to Shimone, plainly the old fellow would meander through the process and contrive to waste half of the night!

There followed several frustrating hours, while Tapek, worn by the effort of sustaining the spell, conjured the phantom image of Mara and her two officers. These, her First Adviser and another wearing the plumes of Acoma Force Commander, escorted their Lady on a meandering ramble through the back streets of the poor quarter. Their path circled, even doubled back! Tapek fumed. Dogged as the possessed, he followed. And was forced to wait, while the Lady paid a business call upon a cloth merchant. Money changed hands. A package, sealed and wrapped, was handed to her adviser. Then the parade began afresh. At last the Lady returned to the square where her attendants and escort awaited. She got in her litter. To his annoyance, Tapek realized that the town watch called out the hour of three o'clock! Even fat old Hochopepa, he decided, would have wasted less time than the confounded Servant of the Empire.

The spectral image of Lujan paused, reached up to adjust his helm. The set of the feathers seemed not to suit him, and he twisted them this way and that, his wrist obscuring his face while he gave elaborate instructions to the Strike Leader in command of his mistress's honor guard. Then, at long last, the ghostly, ice-pale replica of the litter rose in the grip of its spectral bearers. The cortege floated on across the darkened streets of Sulan-Qu, with Lujan and the First Adviser taking the wrapped package upon an unspecified errand, their lips moving in a crossfire exchange of doggerel whose content was obscene.

Shimone, in his maddening, obtuse way, was chuckling over the humor, which was straight from the gutter. He almost seemed reluctant to pursue Mara's litter, which, thought Tapek, steaming, was what they had been sent from the city to do in the first place!

Several times Tapek had to refocus his concentration, as he pursued the phantom image. On the wide boulevards, the surrounding buildings and the busy streets gave back muddled images overlaid with hundreds of others. It took great energy of the mind to track the chosen party. Only because the few people still about in the early hours before dawn immediately gave way to the Black Robe, could Tapek keep the illusion of Mara's litter in sight. And she was taking the most damnable rambling course. Tapek was nearly exhausted when the spell led at last to the steps of the Temple of Turakamu. There, the phantom figures and the litter they carried merged outlines as past converged with present and Mara's slaves lowered their burden to the ground. Tapek waved his hands and dispersed his spell. The blue glow faded, showing Mara's litter parked on the pavement, empty. He blinked, to dispel the fatigue that slowed the adjustment of his vision.

Mara's guard and servants were gone, presumably to take their ease in some tavern while their mistress attended to business within. The stars overhead had begun to pale with false dawn, and Tapek was in a sore mood from stubbing his toes on the cobbles. He scared the wits out of the slave who was sweeping the Red God's front stair, and sent the wretch scurrying for the High Priest. A Great One was free to move as he chose, but even magicians observed tradition. By tradition, magicians never entered a temple without permission.

Shimone was silent throughout.

Thankfully, the wait was brief. The High Priest of the Death God was robed, still, from his visit with Mara. "How may I serve you, Great Ones?" His bow was formal, precise in degree of deference for one of his exalted rank.

Tapek reined back his annoyance. "We seek the Lady Mara for questioning."

The priest straightened up with an expression of consternation. "That is regrettable, Great One. The Lady arrived here not long ago, troubled in spirit over personal matters. She took counsel from me, but was not consoled. By her wish, she retired into the inner sanctum of Turakamu's temple. She has gone into seclusion, Great Ones, for meditation and peace. It is to be hoped that my god will inspire her to overcome her difficulties."

Tapek felt enraged enough to yank out his hair, but settled for tossing his hood back from his head. "How long will she be? We shall wait."

The priest trembled, perhaps with apprehension, though his eyes seemed supremely untroubled as he replied, "I am sorry. I much doubt Lady Mara will be coming out this night, nor any night in the near future. She left instructions with her bearers to remove her litter to her Sulan-Qu estate in the morning, for she would stay in seclusion for some time. Weeks at the least, perhaps months."

"Months!" Tapek shifted from foot to foot, then directed a glare at the priest. "Months!" he exclaimed again, his voice echoing down the empty square. The Black Robe continued his tirade with venom. "I hardly believe that so contrary a woman as Lady Mara would be concerned for her spiritual state at this advanced hour!"

The priest tugged his robes around himself as if gathering his divinely bestowed dignity. "Great One, a mortal may be concerned for the state of her soul at any time," he corrected gently, then folded his hands in a beatific attitude.

Tapek surged forward as though he would storm up the stair and violate the peace of the temple precinct. But Shimone shot out a hand and restrained him.

"Think," said the older magician, his tone snapping. "The sanctity of the temples extends back thousands of years. Why break such a time-honored tradition as sanctuary, Tapek? Mara must come out sometime. And if she does not, our ends are met, not so?"

The fire-haired magician looked as if he had bitten into sour fruit. "You and Hochopepa and Fumita are fools, to seek to protect her!" he said in a furious whisper that only his colleague might hear. "She is dangerous!"

"As dangerous as a public confrontation between the Assembly and the temples?" asked Shimone, his voice menacing.

Tapek seemed to cool slightly. "You are right. She is not worth making into a public issue."

Shimone nodded, silent, but satisfied. A faint buzzing had begun upon the air, and by the time the priest realized the confrontation was over, the two Black Robes had vanished in an inrush of breeze and the lingering echo of Tapek's anger.

The clack of the capstan on the decks of the trader ship *Coalteca* slowed and stopped with a jar against wood as the heavy, leather-wrapped stone anchor thudded home against the cathead. The captain bellowed orders for the sailors in the rigging to loose the brails. The squeal of halyards followed, as yardarms lifted, and brightly painted canvas bellied to the sea wind. Confined belowdecks, Mara paced across the tiny stern cabin. Against her every wish and instinct, to be in the open as the vessel set sail, her concealment was necessary. Still, after weeks denied fresh air and sunlight, Mara chafed. She flashed a glance at her Force Commander, whose normally weathered face also had grown pale during their journey through the cho-ja tunnels from the city of Sulan-Qu to the remote, peninsular port of Kolth.

Mara had never journeyed through the southernmost reaches of Hokani Province. But she had heard secondhand descriptions from Jican, and balked curiosity left her irritable. How she would have loved to have stolen aboveground, even in the dead of night, to view the City of the Plains! The great rift that led to Midkemia was located there, where Kevin had been sent back to his homeland, as well as the mansion-like stone guild halls that were the hub of southern imperial commerce.

But the Assembly's anger was not to be risked for frivolous whims. Luck and Lujan's ingenuity had left a false trail that ended with the Lady of the Acoma in apparent seclusion in Turakamu's temple in Sulan-Qu. If the Black Robes were even to suspect they had been deceived, if one lowly beggar on the street chanced to recognize her as Servant of the Empire, her life and the lives of her family could immediately become forfeit. And so Mara had done the unthinkable, by the mores of Tsurani aristocracy: she had donned the robes of a slave woman, and left Sulan-

Qu in the company of Lujan and Saric, both wearing the unmarked armor of mercenaries. The farmers and merchants who were abroad before dawn had assumed she was a battle prize. They had not thought to question her slave's grey, but stared openly at her slim figure and lustrous hair. A few had called ribald comments, to which Lujan, with strength of imagination, had responded in kind. His shocking coarseness, had hidden that Saric at first had been unable to shed tradition for an act, and had stiffened at the insults to her person.

A message left with an agent of Arakasi's network had brought quick action. When Mara and her two officers had reached the cho-ja hive on her estates, she was joined by ten hand-picked warriors in armor without house markings, and another, a dock worker she had never seen before, who spoke Thuril as his birth tongue. With them came Kamlio, clad again in the rags in which Arakasi had delivered her, and made sullen by the prospect of traveling underground with the insectoids, who terrified her.

The journey south had been trying. Weary from nerves and confinement, and the alien experience of being stared at as chattel, Mara threw herself down in the cushioned alcove she had once shared with Kevin on a long-past journey to Tsubar. In these familiar quarters, the loss of him stung deep, as if their parting had happened yesterday. Almost she regretted her purchase of the *Coalteca;* why had she not had the sense to let go of sentiment and buy some other blue-water trader?

Yet the *Coalteca* had been available; she had acted without consulting Jican. The ship was lucky, she felt; her triumph with Lord Xacatecas in Dustari still held the admiration of the Nations, and now that she had such dire forces as Jiro and the Assembly arrayed against her, she needed every reassurance to bolster her, even those rooted in superstition.

Kevin might have laughed at her irrationality. Impatient with herself for dwelling in the past when all the future lay in jeopardy, Mara turned from memories of her barbarian lover, only to find herself worrying for Hokanu.

Her husband did not know where she was, and must not, for safety's sake, receive even clandestine word until she was deep into Thuril territory. Sharply Mara regretted that she had had small opportunity to speak with him since their unhappy meeting after Kasuma's birth. Now, more than anything, she longed to confide in Hokanu, to receive his steady understanding and his apt insights. She worried for him, as he contended with relations who sought to move up in the family hierarchy. Contentions inevitably arose after the deaths of strong Ruling Lords, when others who saw themselves as rivals to the heir emerged to assuage their ambitions. Mara sighed. She hoped, if Hokanu chose to accept the staff of office offered him by Ichindar, that he would visit their children in the imperial court. Kasuma should not grow older without knowing the love of a father, and Justin certainly was more of a handful than any of the imperial servants had backbone enough to handle. Again Mara sighed, wondering if she would return from Thuril with aid against the fearsome might of magic, only to be bested by two little ones who had turned into spoiled brats.

''You're thinking that maybe this whole voyage was a mistaken endeavor?'' observed a quiet voice by the companionway.

Mara looked up, surprised to find Saric standing in the doorway to her cabin. The creaking sounds of the working ship had masked her adviser's approach, and the plain robe he wore made him blend into shadow.

Mara smiled wanly. ''I'm thinking we could have done without Kamlio's sullenness,'' she said, not wishing to divulge her true thoughts.

Saric returned the mercurial, triangular grin that showed when his mood was mischievous. ''Certainly, from that one's complaints over sleeping arrangements, one would have thought she was the great Lady and you the browbeaten servant.''

Mara laughed. ''Have I been so dour?''

Her adviser folded himself onto a sea chest with neat grace. ''Have you felt so dour?'' he asked.

''Yes.'' Suddenly aware that her heart had lifted with the motion of the ship's sailing, Mara raked the pins out of her hair and let it unfold down her back. She gestured around the dim cabin, with its brightly woven cushions and its beaded curtains, bought from a desert trader, that clacked and rattled with each heel of the ship. ''I am tired of close walls and secrecy.'' She did not add that she was nervous. To go into a foreign land, bearing none of the grand trappings of her rank, and with only ten soldiers and a guide who had been born a beast herd! This was not at all the same as her past trip into Dustari, when she had moved in the company of her own loyal army, with her command tent, and all of her accustomed comforts at hand.

Saric gave her a wry look. ''You are wishing you had given in to risk, and bought another litter in Kolth.'' The sparkle in his eye indicated he had more to say. Mara withheld comment, until her First Adviser raked back his straight-cut bangs and added, ''Lujan did try the markets, you know. He found a used litter, an immense black lacquered affair all set with river stones and fringes.''

A storyteller's pause developed.

"Go on," Mara prompted, skillfully distracted from ill temper. "Why did our brave Force Commander not buy the monstrosity?"

Saric's smile widened with deviltry. "No bearers in the slave market had enough meat on their bones to lift the damned thing, and we'd not have enough hands free for swords if your honor guard was left to take the burden. Besides, Lujan said, if you and Arakasi's courtesan were mewed up in that thing together for more than an hour, you'd wind up fighting like tseeshas."

Mara's jaw dropped at his allusion to the catlike creature known for combativeness between females. "Lujan said that?"

Saric said nothing, which gave her an inkling. "Lujan said no such thing!" she cried back in indignation. "Are you trying to brew up mischief again, and see your cousin disgraced?"

Saric had the honesty to look sheepish.

"Out!" his mistress cried. "Leave me, and send in Kamlio. If she doesn't want a bath, I most certainly do, before we've passed so far beyond shore that the seas become too rough for a basin."

"As my Lady wishes," Saric said, smoothly arising for his bow. As he stepped out, not at all shamefaced, his Lady realized that he had accomplished his objective; her downcast mood had lightened. She might have missed the City of the Plains, and the excitement of embarkation from Kolth; but she was headed for territory no Acoma in her memory had ever trodden.

All of the mountains of Thuril lay before her, and her heart leaped in anticipation of unknown adventure.

Later, bathed and scented, if plainly clothed, Mara stood in the bow of the *Coalteca,* watching the splash and tumble of foam and the leaping play of the iridescent jalor fish. She laughed in delight at the flash of their scales in the sunset, oblivious to the piercing regard of Kamlio.

"What do you see that is amusing in these desolate waters?" the onetime courtesan asked sourly. Deliberately, it seemed, she omitted the honorific of "Lady," as if daring Mara to take umbrage.

"I see beauty," Mara replied as if the question had not stemmed from bitterness. "I see life. Our moments of peace between contentions are to be cherished. This I have learned since I came to be Ruling Lady."

Lujan approached from amidships, his plumeless helm taking on a cobalt gleam from the deepening sky overhead. He bowed to Mara and said, "We make good speed, mistress."

Mara raised her eyebrows. "Have you become a sailor, Force Commander?"

Lujan smiled, his expression less devious than Saric's, but every bit as jaunty. Mara was struck afresh that this was a moment to be treasured.

"No," her officer admitted, "but the captain said as much." Removing his helm with a grimace, for it did not fit as well as the more elaborate one he had left behind in Sulan-Qu, he raked his fingers through damp hair and breathed deeply of the sea air.

Disregarding Kamlio's uninterested presence at her side, Mara observed, "This voyage brings back memories."

Lujan peered up the height of the foremast, to the gaudy spread of canvas that netted the last golden sunlight. "I miss the barbarian, too, mistress. Even if he did spend half the last voyage with his face buried in a basin."

Mara couldn't resist laughing. "Hard-hearted soldier," she accused. "One day a storm will get the better of your stomach, and then you will stop thinking sea sickness is funny."

"Gods," Lujan said with bitten pungency, "don't wish such a fate upon me with my cousin aboard. He would cook me soup with fish scales in it as a remedy, and then tell all of my favorite reed girls what I looked like with green skin." As Kamlio stiffened in silent antagonism, Lujan turned toward her the charming grin that lured half the prostitutes in the province to lean dangerously far over their gallery railings to call to him. "No offense, lovely flower, but my girls all adore their jobs. They don't begrudge me their favors, and I don't treat them as property. I am not the merchant who bought and molded you for bed sport, and neither am I one of the masters who used you. Hear wisdom, and stop looking for those others in the face of every man you chance to meet."

Kamlio looked as though she might spit venom. Then she shook back her pale gold hair, gathered her tawdry, patchwork robe, and swept away in stiff-backed silence. She did not turn her head a hair at the whispered comments and admiring looks of the sailors, but hustled down the companionway into the mate's cabin she had been given for her quarters.

"Don't say it," Mara murmured quietly, as she sensed the epithet her Force Commander was about to utter under his breath. "You would certainly antagonize her less if you ceased calling her 'lovely flower.' "

Lujan looked pained. "But she is one. If she were to tear her face and become scarred, her body would still make a man itch and sweat." Then he reddened at his frankness of speech, as if only then recalling that the person he so addressed was female, and his mistress.

Mara touched his arm in reassurance. "I am not offended that you speak intimately with me, Lujan. You have become like the brother I have lost, since the hour you took service in that distant glen.''

Lujan jammed his helm back over untidy hair. ''I know you, Lady, as I know my own heart. But that Kamlio confounds me. I don't know what Arakasi sees in her.''

''He sees himself,'' the Lady replied. ''He sees things he recalls from his past, and wishes to spare her the pain he once suffered. That is a powerful attraction.'' She stared off into the gloom, wondering if that was also the reason she ached so sorely from her strained relations with Hokanu. Silently she pondered whether Lujan, as another man, might understand the reason for her husband's cold reaction to the birth of his daughter. Were Lujan a brother, and not her Force Commander, she might have asked him. But here, in public on a ship's deck, traditions and appearance prevented her.

The falling dark spread around them like a curtain of privacy. Mara studied her Force Commander's face in the gathering twilight. He had new lines, and the beginnings of white at his temples, since she had taken him from his life as a grey warrior. Without her noticing until now, she saw that his face had begun to weather with the hours he spent drilling troops. More and more, his complexion was growing as leathery as Keyoke's. *We are growing older,* Mara thought sadly. *And what have we to show for our days and our labors?* Her children were no more secure than she had been from their enemies; and if Hokanu had been less skilled at command, he might have had to shed his own family's blood to keep his pack of cousins at bay.

Mara sighed, knowing that if her brother had survived to inherit, instead of she, the Minwanabi would very likely have succeeded to the Warlordship, and the precarious changes won by the shift in power to the Emperor would never have happened at all. Sometimes Lujan's teasing humor recalled Lanokota. But her brother had been barely into his manhood, just testing himself against the challenges of life, when she lost him. This man at her side was fully come into his power and maturity as a warrior. The hardness ingrained through his outlaw years had never entirely left Lujan, despite the fervor of his loyalty, and the affection he had won from his predecessor, Keyoke. Struck that such a fine man should have sons, Mara said impulsively, ''You ought to marry, you know.''

Lujan set his back to the rail and grinned at her. ''I have thought, recently, that it might be time to have a son or daughter.''

Made sensitive by what had happened between Arakasi and Kamlio, Mara wondered suddenly if he did have a love, but perhaps one that was not freely his to ask. ''Have you a woman in mind?''

Laughing, regarding her fondly, Lujan said, "I am down to fewer than a dozen."

Aware that she had been mildly baited, Mara said, "You will always be a rogue! Find an understanding woman, else she will take you to task for your flirting ways, Lujan."

"She would scold me anyway," the Force Commander admitted. "I have this terrible habit, you see, of wearing my weapons while in bed."

He was only halfway joking; events through the years since she had come to power as Ruling Lady had caused all her warriors to take on a battle-ready alertness. There had simply been too many attacks, from too many unseen sources. Now, worst of all, no sword in the Nations could save her. Mara lost her inclination toward humor. She stared ahead, toward the horizon, and wondered if she would find what she desperately needed to ensure Acoma survival on that distant, unseen shore.

The lookout cried from the crosstree, "Land ahead!"

Mara rushed to the rail, her cheeks flushed in the morning breeze. Even Kamlio, who moved nowhere with enthusiasm, followed. Off *Coalteca*'s eastern forequarter lay the faintest hump of indigo, the first shoreline anyone on board had glimpsed through the days of a brisk but uneventful passage.

"Honshoni," said Lujan. "They say the red-bee honey from those hills is sweeter than any in the Empire."

Lepala also was famous for silks and exotic dyes, and the beautifully patterned weaving such luxuries encouraged. Mara sighed, longing to pause and explore the wharf markets of the south. Xula, Lepala, and Rujije were places of enchanting tales of spired buildings and scarlet-railed galleries. Lords of Lepala were said to keep rare fish in pools, and harems numbering in the hundreds. Homes there had pierced shutters to shade from the sun and break the force of the sea winds, and gardens with huge, hot-climate flowers which bloomed only at dusk, but which filled the evening air with exotic fragrances until night's chill caused them to close up again. The streets were paved in a stone that shone like gold when damp. The sailors' gossip made the vendors' stalls and bordellos seem exotic. They spoke of drinks of prodigious potency, inns filled with colorful caged birds, and eating establishments where customers were cooled by pretty girls and boys with large feather fans. But *Coalteca* would not make port in any of these busy cities of commerce until Mara's party had been safely seen ashore in a secluded, uninhabited cove far inside the bay between Honshoni and Sweto. Only a few fishing villages dotted the north and south shorelines.

The Thuril Confederacy claimed the eastern edge of the bay, its only access to deep water; and since the magicians of the Assembly were apt to appear and disappear at whim anywhere within imperial borders, Mara had agreed with her advisers that she must not risk any unnecessary landfall. *Coalteca*'s legitimate cargo would be offloaded on her return trip north, and if the Black Robes or any lurking Anasati spy should come to suspect the deviation in her normal sailing course, the Lady would already be away, deep into foreign territory and, if the gods were kind, beyond reach.

The landing, when it happened a few days later, was in as bleak a site as anything Mara might have dreamed in nightmare. The beachhead where the longboat delivered her was deserted, a gray-blue crescent of flinty, sea-smoothed shale alive with the scything forms of birds. As Lujan lifted her over the thwart and carried her ashore, white and indigo shorebirds circled overhead. Their cries echoed mournfully above the wind and the crash of breakers. Dust blew across the rugged hills beyond, scrub-covered and forlorn, and high above these, turning grey-blue with distance, rose the tables of the Highlands, bordered at the horizon by mountains whose peaks were lost in brooding masses of cloud. The slate-backed spine of the range had proven a fortress impregnable for the Tsurani who had attempted to make war upon Thuril. Time and again the Empire forces had invaded these inhospitable lands, only to be harried back through the foothills by the fierce, naked swordsmen with their dyed skins and their barbarous war cries.

Short, soft-spoken, and wrinkled like the skin of a dried fruit, the guide paused before her and said in his stilted accent, "Lady, it were best you command your people to stand out of plain sight."

"I will need to give them a reason," Mara responded. "They are honorable warriors, and would take it ill if they were told they must sneak about like thieves, particularly where there is not so much as a dwelling, even a fisherman's shack."

The guide licked the gap where two of his front teeth were missing. He shifted from foot to foot, obviously uncomfortable, then bobbed in a quick bow. "Lady, the peace between the Empire and Thuril is uneasy. Only formal envoys and licensed traders cross the border, and only at designated checkpoints. Were your people to be seen within two days' walk of these shores, or anywhere near the imperial border, you would be taken as spies." Whatever the Thuril did to punish spies, by his tautness of expression it was not pleasant.

Knowing that her own people took captured Thuril for the games in the Imperial Arena, Mara no longer argued the need for secrecy. She beckoned Lujan over to her and murmured in his ear, ''Force Commander, we will sorely need the knowledge you gained as a grey warrior to keep our presence here secret until we have made our way far inland.''

Beneath the straggle of hair that escaped the brim of his helm, Lujan gave her a wild smile. ''Ah, Lady, the last of my guileful ways will be known to you! When you learn how well honorable warriors can be made to skulk, will you ever trust them again to guard your valuables?''

''They may have my valuables with all my blessing, if the purpose of our mission is successfully accomplished,'' Mara replied, too grim for humor, and recognizing the first taste of the hardships to come on these strange shores.

There followed several days that put Mara in mind of her race cross-country before her first marriage, to win the alliance of the cho-ja Queen. Then as now, she had slept with minimal shelter on hard ground, amid a small retinue of warriors. Parts of that trip she had traveled on foot, the trail being too rough for her litter. Then, too, there had been urgency, as her party crossed the estates of enemy Lords in the deeps of the night.

But in Kelewan there had been dense forest, almost jungle, to hide in. Low-lying mists had concealed her party at dawn and dusk, and provisions had been carried by her bearers.

In Thuril the stony soil grew only sparse bushes and grass, providing scant cover. At times she had to hike in gullies, chilled by the winds of these higher altitudes, her thin sandals soaked from standing amid peaty clumps of moss. Her ankles became scratched from the sharp-stemmed sedges, and her hands calloused from using a walking stick to keep her balance. Once they passed a village, skulking through pastures on their bellies under the moon. Dogs barked at them, but sleeping herdboys did not rouse.

Mara grew accustomed to the taste of tough game brought down by the bows of her warriors. She developed aches in muscles she never knew she possessed, from long hours and miles on her feet. In a strange way, she reveled in the freedom, and in the deep, cloud-scattered bowl of the sky. But her warmest pleasure was watching Kamlio.

The girl let her long hair twist and tangle, uncared for by maids for the first time in her life. She stopped tightening her lips and looking white when the warriors spoke to her; the few who approached her had been rebuffed, and unlike other men she had known until Arakasi, they left her alone as she asked. She went by herself to wash in the icy streams, and shyly began to offer her help at the fireside, where it became plain that she had a knack for cooking. She also asked Lujan to teach her self-defense with a knife. These lessons commenced in the half-dark, each night, where Kamlio's dulcet tones sharpened in a fishwife's cursing as she missed her throw and tried again.

Lujan took her shrewish mood in stride. "Really," he said, one evening when she seemed to be having a particularly difficult time, "you should ask Arakasi to show you knife work. He is a master, and knows the best way to use the wrist."

Kamlio spun in such fury that the Force Commander grabbed her hand just behind the bare blade of her weapon, unsure she would not sink her knife in him.

"Gods!" Kamlio cried, venomously offended. "It was that one I sought to defend myself from!"

She tore away and flounced off into the dark. Lujan watched her go, clicking his tongue in reproof. "Woman, against our Spy Master, nobody wins at knives." As she vanished, he added softly, "You need nothing of defense against him. If you chose to carve out Arakasi's heart, I believe he would stand still and let you."

Much later, in the depths of that moonless night, Mara awoke to hear the girl sobbing. Softly she said, "You need never see Arakasi again, Kamlio, and that is the problem, is it not?"

The former courtesan said nothing, but her sobs eventually wore themselves out in sleep.

The next morning dawned cloudy and chill. Kamlio returned red-cheeked from gathering wood, her eyes red-rimmed as well. "He killed my sister!" she spat at the Lady of the Acoma, as if in continuation of the words shared in the night.

"He killed the Obajan of the Hamoi Tong, on my orders," Mara corrected. "The Obajan's own darts killed your sister."

Kamlio threw down her armload of wood onto Lujan's fledgling fire, sending up a cloud of sparks and smoke.

The herder who was their guide cursed in Thuril. "Foolish girl! Your pique could cost us our lives!"

Lujan reacted first, ripping off the cloak he wore over his armor. He cast it over the tiny fire, then leaped and grabbed the water bucket nearby, dousing the cloth before it could flare up. Dull wisps of steam seeped from the folds, amid the stink of burnt querdidra wool. "Up," he snapped to his subofficer. "Break camp. No breakfast, and we march at once. That smoke could have been seen, and for our Lady's sake we must take no chances."

The little herdsman threw the Acoma Force Commander a grateful glance for his good sense, and within minutes, Mara's party was back on the trail, hugging gullies and what cover the meager landscape could offer.

Four days later, the guide deemed it safe to travel more openly. He accepted coin from Mara, and dared descend into a narrow, smoke-filled vale to buy supplies from a village market. The imperial centis were suspect, but they had value, and the country folk in their simple needs did not care to question the origin of the currency or those who spent it. Mara suspected she was not the first Tsurani the guide had brought this way. Smuggling between the Empire and Thuril was risky, but highly profitable. It seemed a reasonable vocation for a man of mixed heritage who could pass in both cultures.

The herdsman returned with two hide bags of provisions, jerked meat, and a cloak of hill weave to replace the one Lujan had damaged in the campfire. The burdens came back into camp lashed to the back of a small grey beast, horselike in shape, but with long ears, and a tail like a paint-brush.

"Donkey," the herdsman guide replied, in answer to Mara's curious question. His burred accent accepted the word awkwardly, but Mara recognized its origin as Midkemian. The presence of an animal that could only have come from the other side of the rift, through the Empire, made it clear smuggling was a major trade of this region. "Less ornery than querdidra, Lady, and sturdy enough for you to ride."

At this Mara raised her eyebrows. "Me? Ride that? But it's barely as big as a newborn needra calf!"

"Walk, then," the herdsman said, in less than respectful tones. "But the shale in the heights could twist your ankles, and your warriors would quickly tire if they had to carry you." For Kamlio he had bought boots with stout soles, laced up the front, and topped with fur. Mara eyed the ugly footwear with distaste, and the donkey with trepidation. Then, with a sigh, she surrendered. "I'll ride," she said. "Show Lujan how to help me to mount."

The herdsman bobbed another of his fast bows that Mara swore were his way of hiding amusement.

"Don't feel apprehensive," Lujan teased as he arrived at her elbow to help her astride. "Think how I felt on that day in the desert when I had to mount a cho-ja. They're slipperier, for one thing, and I was panicked I would fall off and land on my own sword."

"That was Kevin's idea, not mine," Mara said in her own defense, then steeled herself as her Force Commander lifted her strongly and set her down like a feather in the dyed leather hill saddle strapped to the beast's back.

The animal was small, Mara tried to reassure herself, and the ground no more than a cloth yard away. If she fell, the worst she could get would be bruises, small price to pay if she could find protection from the Black Robes in these strange, barren hills. And in fact, the gait of the donkey was not so hard, it being short of stride and its feet marvelously sure as it plodded along.

Mara found her perch upon the creature's back less than comfortable, but she hid her soreness with Tsurani implacability as her party wound ever higher into the forbidding hills. In the afternoon, when she dismounted and the beast was led off to water, she confided to Lujan that had she known what sort of creatures donkeys were, she would never have permitted their importation. "Small horse indeed," she had snorted as she settled stiffly on the ground to share a meal of hard bread and sour cheese.

Lujan only grinned. "They are most reliable, I am told. Already the man who sells them across the borders in Honshoni is seeking another herd, for they far outshine the querdidra as beasts of burden."

With this, Mara was forced to agree, despite her aching posterior. She had endured the company of the foul-smelling, evil-tempered querdidra as she had transversed the mountains of Tsubar on campaign against the raiders of the desert. But as the donkey raised its stringy tail to dump manure, she kept her opinion silent. If it was a superior creature to the temperamental, six-legged native pack beast, it certainly was no cleaner in its habits.

Suddenly the herdsman who was their guide spun around, his crust of bread forgotten in his hand. Facing the wind, his eyes narrowed, he scanned the bleak, scrub-covered hills as if he could read their rock and vegetation like a scroll page. "We are being watched," he said in a low voice to Lujan. "I suspected as much since we left that village."

The Force Commander pointedly kept chewing his food. As if there were no immediate peril, he asked, "Should we arm ourselves?"

The herdsman faced around in shock. "Not if you wish to live. No. Keep on. Act as if nothing were wrong. And if anyone approaches, make no threatening move, no matter what is said or done to provoke you. Insure no hothead among your men speaks or draws his sword."

Lujan gave back an even smile that only Mara could read as a false show of humor. "Have some cheese," he invited the herdsman.

But no one had any stomach for eating, and within a short time the company regrouped and started to move on. They had gone barely a dozen paces when a shout rent the air. A man with black braids and a great, billowing cloak of the same dull green-grey as the soil leaped directly above the lead guard onto a large rock that overlooked the narrow trail.

Lujan held up his hand as Mara's guards tensed. But none of his warriors forgot their orders not to draw weapons, despite their surprise. The Thuril highlander had appeared as if from nowhere. Dressed in his native kilt and double crossbelts hung with two swords and several knives, he called out, "Why do you invade the land of Thuril, Tsurani?" His thick accent made his demand nearly unintelligible, and his tone was unmistakably belligerent.

Mara kicked the little donkey, to overcome its reluctance to move forward again. Before it could stride out, the little herdsman sprang to its bridle to restrain it. He replied to the challenge, prompted by the custom of the land. "I am Iayapa, warrior," he said in the Thuril tongue. "I speak for the Lady of the Acoma, who has come on a mission of peace."

The man leaped down from the rock, his cloak billowing and his kilt flipping up to bare an expanse of muscled thigh. The cross-garters of his sandals were tasseled below the knee, and his weapon harness chinked with stone talismans. Up close, it could be seen that his head was shaved, save for a round patch at the crown, where his braids had been allowed to grow since childhood. They tumbled as long as his waist as he landed, their ends also tied with talismans.

Into his mistress's ear, Lujan said softly, "He is not dressed for war, Lady."

Mara nodded. She had read that the Thuril shed their clothing when fighting, going nude but for their battle harness, feathered helms, shields, and weapons, for they took pride that their manhood was not shriveled by fear and ensured their enemies knew this.

The man swaggered toward Mara, who was now slightly ahead of the others, as the donkey sidled nervously. Mara sawed at the reins, frantically and silently reminding herself to act as if nothing were wrong.

The highlander said something in his coarse dialect and grabbed the donkey's bridle. He breathed into its nose, and for some strange reason the creature quieted. The man then rattled his knuckles through his talismans, and stepped around the donkey's head. Coming face to face with Mara, he leaned forward until his nose missed touching hers by a hair's width.

Iayapa called, "Good Servant, make no move. He tests your mettle."

Mara held her breath and forced herself not to close her eyes. Peripherally, she was aware of her uneasy men, their hands itching to draw weapons; and of Kamlio, who had forgotten her distaste for men and had crowded close to the nearest warrior in fear. But the Acoma discipline held. Her warriors kept still, and when Mara refused to lower her gaze or pull away, the highlander released a great, garlic-scented breath and withdrew. He grunted, allowing that her courage was sufficient. "Who speaks for you, woman?"

Before Iayapa could stop her, Mara spoke. "I lead here."

The man bared white, even teeth in an expression that was no smile. Browned by strong sun, his face wrinkled in contempt. "You have sand, woman! I'll allow you that, but lead these men? You are female." To Lujan, who was nearest, the highlander rephrased his question. "You! I do not answer a woman's tongue, and I would know: what brings you to come with warriors into our lands? Do you seek war!" This last seemed to be a joke, for he burst out in raucous laughter.

Mara waved Lujan to silence, and as though the brawny man did not stand at her donkey's shoulder, addressed her herdsman guide. "This highlander seems amused. Does he think our presence funny, or does he intend slight to our honor?"

But whether he followed his own advice, or was simply cowed to silence, Iayapa said nothing.

Mara frowned, forced to rely upon her own judgment. By Tsurani accounts, the Thuril were bloodthirsty warriors, quick to attack, savage in fighting. But the opinions of an invading army were suspect, Mara felt. The only other Thuril she had observed had been captives sent into the arena. These men had proven themselves to be assertive, independent and courageous. They had suffered beating by Tsurani overseers rather than fight as a spectacle for their captors' amusement.

Mara addressed the man again. "I seek your chieftain."

Much as if an insect had spoken aloud, the highlander looked surprised, "You seek our chieftain?" He stroked his chin as if thinking. "What cause have you to disturb him? He already has a woman to warm his nights!"

Mara bridled, but held back her temper in time. She gestured to stay Lujan, who was poised to rush forward to answer the insult. Mara forced herself to calm study of this brash highlander. In truth, he appeared young, barely more than twenty-five years of age. By Tsurani custom, he was just old enough to inherit. And like those of a boy given first responsibility, perhaps his manners were all swagger, to make himself seem important in a larger world. "I do not speak to boys. Take me to your chieftain now, or I will ask that you be punished for your rudeness when I seek him out myself.''

The man stepped away, in a mock show of intimidation. ''My Lady! But of course.''

He spun on his heel in a swirl of cloak and kilt, and set two fingers to his lips. His whistle pierced the air, causing Mara's warriors to start.

''Draw no swords,'' she commanded in a low voice to Lujan.

Her Force Commander gave a hard look to his men, willing them to hold fast, even as, in a scrabble of rocks and gravel, more than a score of men sprang into view around their position. All were heavily armed, from bows, spears, and swords to bristling rows of throwing knives; not a few of the fiercest and largest carried double-headed axes. Mara's small guard was outnumbered three to one, and if it came to a fight, the trail where they stood would become a slaughter ground.

Prepared for death, Lujan murmured, ''They may not have been looking for trouble, but they are ready should it find them.''

The highlander on the trail glanced to his circle of supporters. He grinned wickedly. ''You heard the female! She thinks to command our chieftain to have me beaten for rudeness!'' Rough laughter greeted this statement, punctuated by the hiss of swords being drawn.

Mara swallowed hard. Aware that she must either fight or stand down, before her men were killed out of hand and she and Kamlio were taken for gods only knew what fate, she forced her dry tongue to shape speech. ''I said we came on a mission of peace! To prove this, my men will disarm.''

At Lujan's incredulous glance, she added, ''Do so!''

Obedient to a man, her Tsurani guard loosened their sword belts. The clatter of weapon sheaths striking hard stone seemed pathetically swallowed by the wide expanse of sky.

The young warrior's grin became predatory. He reached up, jerked off the hide tie that secured his braid, and snapped it taut between his hands. ''Bind them,'' he rapped out. He looked at Lujan as he added, ''You are Tsurani! Enemies of my people. We shall see whom my chief shall order beaten!''

Mara closed her eyes as the ring of the Thuril rushed in upon her defenseless party, but she did not react soon enough to miss the lecherous looks the nearer men shot toward Kamlio. Her ears still heard their comments, in a strange language, but derisive in tone. Gods protect us, she thought, what fate have I commanded for my people? For by every tenet of honor, and every belief of the religion she was born to, she should have seen all her warriors dead to a man, and herself killed, before she consented to surrender.

"You did right, great Lady," Iayapa said urgently. But as rough hands dragged Mara from her perch on the donkey, and greasy leather thongs creased her wrists, she was not reassured. More than Acoma shame was at stake here, she reminded herself as her warriors endured in silence as they, too, were trussed hand and foot. Honor, pride, even peace, would mean nothing if the Assembly was not challenged in its omnipotence.

But as she and her people were pushed and prodded and jeered at like slaves, she was not sure she would not rather be dead.

19. Captive

Mara fell.

The highlander who had shoved her into the line of march laughed as she landed on her knees on rough stones. He caught her arm, jerked her painfully back to her feet, and pushed her ahead again. She stumbled into Saric, who stood firm to support her, his horrified outrage barely kept under control.

"My mistress should at least be permitted to ride on the donkey," he protested, knowing by his Lady's grim expression that she would not speak out of pride. He bit off each word as if it were a curse.

"Be silent, Tsurani dog! The beast will be put to better use!" The highlander who appeared to be in charge beckoned and gave instructions to an underling.

Mara held her chin high, trying not to look at Lujan's bleeding face. He had refused to raise his wrists to be bound, and although he had not fought, it had taken coarse handling to force his hands behind his back to lash them. His eyes were dark with rage as he saw to what "better use" their small beast of burden would be put: Kamlio had caught the fancy of these barbarous Thuril. Her beauty was considered a prize, and it was she, not Mara, who was to ride.

When Saric again dared to protest, he was struck in the face and shouted at in broken Tsurani. "The dark-haired woman is nearer the end of her childbearing years. She is of little value."

Mara endured this additional shame, her cheeks burning. But as her kilted captors organized her party for the march, she ached inside with uncertainty. She had no clue what these Thuril might do with her and her men. But after what she knew of Tsurani treatment of highlander captives, she expected her fate would hardly be pleasant.

The Thuril hurried their prisoners upward into the highlands. Mara slipped and stumbled on the slick shale and splashed through knee-deep becks that tumbled out of the heights. Her wet sandal straps stretched, and her soles wore to blisters. She bit her lip, holding back tears of discomfort. If she flagged, one of the highlanders would shove her on with an elbow, or the flat of his sword or ax. Her back bore unaccustomed bruises. Was this misery what Kevin and others of his countrymen might have felt while being driven in coffles to the Tsurani slave market? Mara had thought she understood when she had decided that slavery was a wrong against humanity. Now she gained firsthand insight into the suffering and the fear such unfortunate folk must feel, subject to the whim of others. And while her plight was perilous, she was still a free woman and would be again, if she survived, but what must it be to know that there is never a hope of escape? Kevin's deeply personal anger on the subject no longer mystified her.

Kamlio sat on the donkey. The former courtesan's face was pale, but her expression was impassive, a proper Tsurani's. But as the girl glanced her way more than once, Mara saw terror and concern behind her mask. Something in Kamlio had begun to awaken if she felt concern for the mistress who tripped and pressed forward on foot by the donkey's tail.

The lowland hills became craggy as the day wore on, and the Thuril pressed their captives ever higher into the plateau country. Through the discomforts of sweat and exhaustion, Mara reminded herself of the higher purposes that had caused her unconditional surrender. But moral abstractions seemed to take on less importance as thirst dried her throat and her legs began to tremble with the exertion of a forced march. Again she tried to stiffen flagging resolve: she must discover the secret behind what the cho-ja and the lesser magician had named "the Forbidden." A puzzle lay before her in this hostile land, all the more maddening in that the solution lay outside Tsurani experience. Mara had no hint of what to expect when and if she should gain the ear of someone in authority. She did not even know the Thuril language, far less what questions to ask. How arrogant she had been when she had boarded the *Coalteca* in the belief that she might journey to these alien shores and, through talk and force of personality, make a sufficient impression to be heard in courtesy by her people's enemies! Born to power, never in her life deprived of the privileges of her rank, Mara perceived how foolish her presumptions had been. As exalted Servant of the Empire, revered by her people, she had never once considered that foreigners might act differently. The lessons she had learned from Kevin of Zūn should have warned of the differences between peoples. Would the gods ever forgive her stupidity?

Fear preyed increasingly on her mind as her captors drove her without rest through a high pass in the hills. The donkey plodded ahead, oblivious to human concerns and content to be what the gods had made it, a beast of burden. No less a burden do I carry, thought Mara, tripping again and feeling the wrench in her tied wrists as she fought to keep her balance. Lost in miserable thought, she did not note Saric's and Lujan's tortured looks of worry.

The fate of more than her family rested upon her strength. Captivity taught her a painful lesson: no man or woman should live at the whim of another. But that was the only way to describe the wretched lives of Tsurani common folk. Their fate, and that of the lowest slaves, depended upon her as much as the fate of nobles. But reform in Tsuranuanni could not be begun, until the Assembly's omnipotence was broken.

Bitter possibilities surfaced to harry Mara's brave resolve: that Kasuma might be her last child, that separation from Hokanu might last for the rest of her life, that she must leave unsettled his reluctance to name a daughter as his heir. Kevin's contrary nature had well taught her that loving a man did not guarantee peace with him; no time in her life had been more sorrowful for her, and few more regretted, than the moment the imperial decree had forced her to send the barbarian away. She feared that Hokanu might lose her in as abrupt a manner, leaving unsaid all that meant the most between them. Mara swallowed, fighting despair. If she could not reason with these Thuril, if they traded or sold her into bondage, then if Hokanu was to have a son, another woman must bear his child for him. That thought caused worse pain than any physical discomfort.

Only belatedly did Mara realize that their march had slowed. Her captors paused in a vale between hills purpled with the shadows of late afternoon. Down the slopes ran a company of younger Thuril warriors. In a swirl of cloaks, brandishing weapons, they laughed boisterously. A jubilant rendezvous engulfed the party who shepherded the smaller band of prisoners. The newcomers viewed Kamlio with raised brows and hoots of appreciation. They fingered Mara's plain robe, loudly talking, until the Lady grew annoyed at being stared at.

"What do they say?" she demanded sharply of Iayapa, who stood with his head hanging. He shrank still further at Mara's imperious address.

"Lady," admitted the herdsman, "these are rough men." Derisive shouts arose at his deferential manner, and someone said in gruff and broken Tsurani, "We should call that one Answers-to-Women, eh?"

Whoops and laughter arose, nearly drowning Mara's furious inquiries and Iayapa's desperate appeal: "Lady, do not ask me to translate." Behind her, one of the young men was gripping his crotch and rolling his eyes as if in pleasure. His companions found the remarks he uttered hilarious, for they clapped each other's shoulders and chuckled.

Iayapa said over their din, "You would be offended, great Lady."

"Tell me!" Mara demanded as Saric and Lujan shuffled closer and took their accustomed positions at her sides to shield her from the taunts of the foreigners.

"Lady, I mean no disrespect." Had his hands been free, Iayapa would have prostrated himself. Bound helpless, he could only look strained. "You order me. The first one, the fellow with the green cloak, he asked our guide if he had taken you yet."

Mara said nothing, but nodded.

Iayapa sweated, despite the cool highland air. "The one who guides us says he is waiting for us to reach the village, for you are bony and he needs many cushions and furs." Almost blushing, he blurted the rest. "The third one who grabbed himself says that a man has answered to you. That might mean you are a witch. Does the one who guides us not take a risk, should he attempt to touch you, that you might rip off his . . . manhood and feed it to him. The others think this is very funny indeed."

Mara wrenched in annoyance at the thongs that tied her wrists. How could she answer such lewdness with dignity, bound as she was like livestock? She considered for a moment, glancing at Lujan and Saric. Both men looked fit to murder, but they were as helpless as she. Yet nothing under heaven would cause her to endure such abuse from strangers without even token resistance! Left only her tongue, Mara raised the most scathing shout she could muster. These crude barbarians might not understand Tsurani, but by Turakamu, they could comprehend her intent by her tone.

"You!" she snapped out, jerking her head in the direction of the highlander leader who had taken them. "What is your name!"

The crag-nosed man at the head of the troop stiffened, and, almost before thought, turned toward her. The younger man beside him left off clutching his crotch and stared at his elder in astonishment. He said something, to which his leader made a gesture of incomprehension. Instead, he addressed Iayapa in his own language, and the others laughed.

Mara did not wait for translation. "This swaggering fool with no more brains than the beast who carries my serving girl now claims he cannot understand me." Her consonants sharpened with malice. "Even after he exchanged words in Tsurani down the trail from here?"

Several of the highlanders turned at this, some revealing surprise. So! Mara thought. There are others who can speak our tongue, albeit badly. She must make the most of this.

Mara played along with the embarrassed highlander's charade and addressed Iayapa alone. "Tell this buffoon, who forgets words as well as his mother forgot the name of his father, exactly what I say.'' Mara paused, then added into shocked silence, ''Tell him he is a rude little boy. When we reach his village I shall ask that his chieftain beat him for inexcusable manners toward a guest. Inform him further that should I seek company for my bed, it would be with a man, not a child still longing for his mother's shriveled breast, and more, that should he touch me, I will laugh when his manhood fails to rise. He is as ignorant as a needra, and smells worse. He is uglier than my most disreputable dog and worth less —for my dog can hunt and has less vermin. Tell him his very existence brings shame upon his already honorless ancestors.''

Suddenly inexplicably gleeful, Iayapa translated. Before he had finished the first sentence, the eyes of every Thuril warrior fixed upon the Lady of the Acoma. By the time the translation of her tirade was completed, their stony stillness frightened her. Her heart banged in her chest. They might easily kill her. Any Tsurani Lord so addressed by a captive would have had her strung up by her neck and kicking. But fate could hardly hold worse than to be dragged into slavery, Mara felt. Whether or not these men would hang her in total dishonor, she showed them nothing but the face of haughty contempt.

Then the mood broke. All but the target of Mara's insults exploded into knee-slapping peals of mirth. ''The shrew has a tongue for words, did you hear?'' someone cried to the insulted man in accented Tsurani. This confirmed that he spoke the language well enough to realize what had been said of him before Iayapa's translation. Several of his companions were laughing so hard they had to sit down, lest their knees buckle. The warrior Mara had berated studied her, then as color rose into his cheeks, he nodded once.

Lujan pressed closer to Mara's side as another of the Thuril warriors shouted, waving his bow at Mara in salutation. Made aware by the man's grin that she was not going to be summarily executed, Mara said, ''What did he say?''

Iayapa shrugged. ''That you know how to insult like a man. It is something of an art among the Thuril, mistress. As I learned well at my mother's knee, they can be a most irritating people.''

In time the pandemonium subsided. The younger troop banded together and took their leave to resume duty, some still chuckling as they took the outbound trail. Mara's captors, including their red-faced leader, hustled their Tsurani charges around the next bend toward home. Late sunlight slashed across a meadow. Beyond the open ground lay a wooden walled town of steeply peaked roofs. Curls of smoke rose from stone chimneys, and the spears of sentries could be seen on the wall walks. The town's position guarded another trail that wound into the hills.

The highlander warriors quickened the pace, in a hurry to bring in their captive prizes.

"Strange," murmured Saric, his indefatigable curiosity still evident despite the rigor of their march and the uncertain fate awaiting him. Unlike any Tsurani, these Thuril seemed indifferent to chatter between their prisoners. "While this grass offers good grazing for livestock, it is not eaten short, but only cut across by the paths of the flocks and herders."

At this comment, the Thuril leader glanced over his shoulder, his lip half-curled in contempt. In blatant contradiction of his earlier claim of ignorance of the Tsurani tongue, he said in a mangled accent, "You should be glad to have an escort through this meadow, Tsurani dog. Without us to show you which path to tread, you would be lost. For this ground is still trapped from the last visit your kind made to our hills!"

Lujan answered thoughtfully, "You mean your folk still maintain fortifications from the last war?"

"But the fighting ceased more than a decade ago," Saric objected.

Lujan confided softly to his cousin, "Long memories." Behind his insouciant tones lay foreboding. That the Thuril kept their village guarded with lethal deadfalls after so much time revealed a resentment that would complicate any overtures toward negotiation; as soldier, Lujan had heard the tales told by veterans of the ill-conceived invasion into Thuril. A man was better dead than taken prisoner, to be turned over alive to the vengeful treatment of highlander women.

But he concealed his fears from Mara as they were herded past the deadly meadow, and on, over a wooden bridge that spanned a moat, fed by a swift-running river. The water rushed over rock snags and whirled in black eddies through pools too swift for a swimmer to cross. As Lujan's eyes measured the possibility of escape across the current, the leader of the highlanders noticed.

He waved a leather-gauntleted arm at the rock pools. "Many Tsurani warriors drowned there, sword captain! More broke their necks on the stone, trying in vain to build a rope bridge." He shrugged, and his grin returned. "Your commanders are not stupid men, just stubborn. In time, they threw platforms across there"—his cloak fringes danced as he pointed to a ledge by the lowered bridge—"and there." He indicated another outcrop farther down. Then, as if warriors from the past still screamed battle cries into the dusk-grey air, he glanced up at the looming wall of the palisade. "It was a near thing."

Mara had pushed through her fatigue to follow the conversation. "You must have been a very small boy in those times. How do you remember?"

Distracted by vivid recall, the highlander leader forgot that he answered a woman. "I was up on the battlement, bringing water to my father and uncles. I helped carry the dead and wounded." His face twisted into long-nurtured bitterness. "I remember."

He jabbed Lujan forward with a blow and led across the bridge. The looming shadow of the gateway cut off all view of sky and fortifications. The leader answered to a challenge from an unseen sentry, then hustled the Tsurani captives through. Lujan took note of the log battlements, faced on the outside with smooth boards, but left unfinished inside, with bark and stubs of branches still left on the trunks, as if the defense works had been erected in haste. "It must have been a fierce battle."

The leader laughed. "Not that fierce, Tsurani. We were up in the hills by the time the third attack came and your soldiers seized the palisades. Our leaders aren't stupid, either. If your people wanted the village so much, we would let you have it. Taking a place is one thing; holding it is another." With a sneer of contempt, he added, "We wouldn't let you have the hills, Tsurani." He waved broadly toward the peaks that notched the sky above the wall. "There is our true home. In these valleys, we might built halls and houses to meet, and trade, and celebrate, but our families are raised in the high country. That is where your soldiers died, Tsurani, as we attacked your foragers and patrols. Hundreds perished in our raids, until your kind tired of the Highlands and went home."

By now past the fortifications, and into the avenue of commerce, the party of prisoners attracted notice. Women beating their laundry clean with stones in a wide public basin paused in their work to point and stare. Urchins in colored plaids screamed and ran to look, or stared wide-eyed from behind mothers who carried cloth-wrapped loaves of bread from the baker's. Some of the dirtier, wilder children capered about the bound strangers, shouting; afraid some might fling stones, Lujan jerked his head at his warriors, who jostled closely around their mistress to give what protection they could.

But no hostilities were offered, beyond glares from middle aged women, who perhaps had lost sons or husbands to imperial warriors in battle. The donkey bearing Kamlio caused the most furor, as children swooped close with excited chatter. The highlanders fended them off with mock gruffness. Still the little ones shouted. "It has only four legs!"

"Why doesn't it fall down?" cried another about the age of Ayaki before he died.

The soldier who led the beast took the din in good stride, giving the children outrageous answers that made them squeal and scream with laughter.

After a studied silence, Mara observed, "If these noisy barbarians intended to kill us, surely the mothers would not let their little ones mingle, but would be hustling them away home."

Lujan crowded nearer to his mistress. "Gods grant you are right, my Lady." But his thoughts remained apprehensive. He could see the covetous glances Kamlio attracted from the men who passed on the street. The women who bundled up their washing looked sharp-faced and unfriendly, and a groom carrying a water pannikin spat in their direction in contempt. The Thuril were a fierce race, the veterans who had returned alive from fighting in these hills had insisted. The young were toughened at the knees of mothers who were awarded as battle prizes, or carried off by force in raids.

As the highlanders brought their captives to a halt in the square, it could be seen that the entire village consisted of a ring of buildings built against the wall, leaving an openair market at the center, with portable tent stalls for traders, and palings of thorny stake to enclose livestock. Mara's party was driven into the largest of these pens, while onlookers laughed and called out in derision. Iayapa refused to answer Saric's requests for translation, and Mara herself was too weary to care. She longed only for a patch of clean ground to sit down; the dirt she trod was thick with droppings left from its animal occupants. She envied Kamlio her seat on the donkey, until she looked over at the younger girl and realized by her pinched pallor that she probably had sores from sitting so long in the saddle. The men did not let her down, but tied her mount to a pole by the gate, then leaned on folded arms against the posts, and murmured in appreciation of her loose golden hair and her beauty.

Furious that so little care had been taken for even their most basic human needs, Mara shouldered past her officers. At the gate, where, the highlanders clustered, she demanded in a loud voice, "What are you going to do with my people?" Trembling with anger that was fueled the more by fear, she tossed her head to shake tangled hair from her eyes. "My warriors require food and water, and a decent place to rest! Is this the hospitality you show to strangers who come on a mission of peace? A slave's bonds, and a livestock pen? Shame to you, carriers of vermin who were spawned in the dirt like pigs!" Here she borrowed the Midkemian word for a beast whose habits were considered reprehensible.

The foreign word seemed to upset the Thuril, who scowled as their leader stamped forward. Red with anger or maybe embarrassment, he shouted to Lujan, "Silence the woman, if you wish her to live."

The Acoma Force Commander glowered back. He said in a voice that could easily be heard on a battlefield, "She is my mistress. I take my orders from her. If you have the wits not to make water in your bedding at night, you would do the same."

The leader of the highlanders roared in fury at this insult. He might have drawn his sword and charged forward, but one of his companions caught him back. Words were exchanged in Thuril. Lujan could only stand in dumb but dignified incomprehension as the irate leader allowed himself to be placated. The highlander muttered something short and guttural to the spokesman who had restrained him. At length, he loosed a huge guffaw that cut off as silence. The men around him snapped into attentiveness.

"That must be their chieftain," Saric murmured. He had moved up to Mara's shoulder, unnoticed until he had spoken. Mara noted that their escort all looked toward a cloaked man who had emerged down the wooden stair of the most imposing building that edged the square. Street children scattered from his path as he crossed the open expanse, and the women carrying their loads of damp wash homeward averted their faces in deference.

The newcomer was old and hunched, but he moved with a sureness that could still negotiate the roughest trail. Mara estimated his age to be about sixty years. Tokens of corcara carved by Tsurani hands were woven into his braid, no doubt worn as battle trophies. Mara repressed a shiver as the elder neared enough for her to make out that the buttons on his cloak front were fashioned of polished bone. The tales were true, then, that Thuril believed that an artifact taken from a dead foe would lend them strength in life. Her finger bones could as easily wind up as an ornament in some warrior's attire.

The highlander chief paused to share words with the squad captain who had charge of the prisoners. He pointed to the golden-haired courtesan and the donkey, said something else, and smiled. The squad leader saluted, plainly excused from duty. By his look of self-satisfaction, he would now be going home to his wife.

Mara seemed worn and disheartened, and driven by sympathy for her, Saric shouted, "Aren't you going to introduce us?"

The highlander officer froze between strides. His men and his chieftain looked on in bright-eyed interest, as the man considered whether he should reply to the hail of a prisoner. Then, in burred accent, he called back, "Introduce yourself, Tsurani! Your woman seems capable enough with her tongue!"

Another of the highlander warriors offered with malicious amusement,

"Our captain is Antaha, guideman of the Loso. I give you his name so that when you appeal to our chieftain to have him beaten, he will know whom to seek out."

This interruption was greeted by uproarious laughter, shared by the old chief, and even the street children and the women by the washing well. Irked past restraint by these strange, annoying people, Mara again pressed to the fore.

To the chieftain, who chuckled and slapped his knees, she called imperiously, "I am Mara, Ruling Lady of the Acoma, and I have come to the Thuril Confederacy on a mission of peace."

The chief lost his mirth as if slapped. Shocked to silent anger, he regrouped. "A woman standing in querdidra droppings comes claiming to be someone of rank and an emissary of peace?"

Mara looked whitely furious. Aware that she neared her breaking point, and that to insult this chieftain in public would earn her certain reprisal, Lujan turned desperately to Saric. "We must act, even if only to distract her."

But the young First Adviser stepped forward without seeming to hear. As Mara opened her mouth to speak, Saric broke protocol and shouted down her voice with his own. "Chief among the Thuril," he cried, "you are a fool, who offers our Lady of the Acoma no better hospitality than a livestock pen! You speak of Mara, Servant of the Empire, and a member of the Emperor Ichindar's royal family!"

The chieftain jerked up his square chin. "She?" If his word seemed filled with contempt, Saric's statement was not entirely wasted. The elderly man did not add any derogatory comment, but summarily waved Antaha back to duty. This time, the chief's words were rapid and commanding, and Iayapa, under pressure from Saric, translated.

"He says that if Antaha should bring animals into camp, then he must look after them: feed them, water them, and give them bedding. Not too much, though, for straw is scarce, and the gods do not love waste. The girl on the donkey is to be sheltered in a hut. Her beauty is great, and should be treasured for the man who will win rights to claim her to wife." Iayapa looked troubled, for at this, Mara's eyes seemed to bore into him with the hardness of flint.

But her command held no personal resentment as she said, "Finish."

Iayapa nodded and bleakly licked his lips. "The chief of this village says also that he has heard of the Servant of the Empire, who is family to the Tsurani Emperor. He adds that Ichindar is ruled by women, and that he, a born highlander, will not deign to speak with a woman of any claim to royal lineage on the open street. But because of the existing treaty between Tsuranuanni and the Confederacy, neither is he free to authorize his village men to claim Mara as spoils.''

Hoots of disappointment ran through the squad of highlanders who had escorted the Lady's party in. Two of the more impudent ones made obscene gestures.

Then the chieftain turned toward the captives in the pen and addressed Mara's Force Commander in Tsurani that was accentless, learned during former wars. ''If you have a need that is not met, Antaha is charged responsible. Tomorrow he will gather an escort of twenty warriors, and take you and your females on to the high chief at Darabaldi. Judgment, if such is called for, will be dealt by the council there.''

Saric looked thunderous, but he listened when Iayapa touched his arm in entreaty. ''First Adviser, do not provoke these men or their chieftain any further. They are not a people in love with arguments over points of etiquette. They mete out deaths very swiftly, and do not regret. Morning could have found all of us lying here with cut throats, or worse. To be sent to Darabaldi rather than parceled out among those who captured us is, in fact, a great concession.''

Saric regarded the dung that crusted his sandals, and exchanged a disgusted glance with Lujan, whose fingers seemed lost without a sword to hand in his scabbard. ''Cousin,'' the Acoma adviser said gravely, ''if this is a great concession, dare we even speculate what a small one might have been?''

The strain told, but could not entirely vanquish the spirit of Mara's Force Commander. He broke his Tsurani façade of impassivity and stifled a deep chuckle. ''Gods, man, you'll be speculating on points of philosophy in the smoke of your funeral pyre, I know it.'' Then, as one, he and the First Adviser turned to tend their mistress, who to their experienced eyes looked small and disheartened and alone, though her back was straight, and her face as imperious as always.

She was watching an enterprising group of highlanders taking charge of Kamlio and the donkey. ''Do you think they will harm her?'' she demanded of Iayapa, and to the ears of those closest to her, anxiety colored her tone.

The onetime herdsman shook his head. ''There are never enough women of childbearing age in this harsh land, and Kamlio is beautiful, which makes her doubly valuable. But the chieftain of this tribe must grant his approval before any man could bargain for her as a wife. Lacking his consent, she may be admired, but not bedded. All the unmarried warriors know that to trouble her now would forfeit any chance to ask for her as a mate. Since many single men in the Highlands die without ever winning wives, even so small a chance to claim a woman is not to be risked.''

Mara swallowed. ''Do they have no courtesans in this land?''

Iayapa looked offended. ''Only a few, in Darabaldi. Not many women choose that life, with no honor to their tribe. The young men may go to them once or twice a year, but that gives no comfort during long winter nights.''

Over the little herdsman's head, Lujan and Saric exchanged glances. ''Funny place, this,'' Saric muttered, again glancing sourly at the dung-littered ground upon which, it appeared, they must all wait out the night. These Thuril thought nothing of stealing a girl or a woman from her home in a bloody raid. Even the most repressed Tsurani wife had the right to be heard in public by her Lord. ''Barbaric indeed!'' Saric muttered. Then he shivered as a cold wind cut down off the heights. He glanced at his diminutive Lady, and admired the grit that enabled her to keep her dignity. That she should be bound, and handled, and treated no better than a slave by total strangers, made him furious enough to kill.

As if she read his thoughts, she turned to him that sweet smile which never failed to inspire loyalty and pride. ''I will manage, Saric. Just keep that warrior cousin of yours from losing his temper over things that do not matter. For this''—she raised her hands, still tied with rawhide strips —''and this''—she scuffed her foot at the soiled ground—''are unimportant. The Assembly of Magicians would do worse. If I can speak to the Thuril High Chief at Darabaldi, that is all that must concern us.''

Then, as the gloom deepened, and tallow candles shed an orange glow behind the oiled-hide windows that fronted the square, she bent her head and appeared to be meditating as the priestesses of Lashima's temple had taught her during a girlhood that now seemed far in the past.

Warmed by Saric and Lujan, pressed close, and protected from the cold and filthy ground by the cloak her Force Commander had insisted upon lending her, Mara awakened to a touch on her shoulder. The sleep of total exhaustion left her slowly. She blinked, stirred, and opened her eyes to darkness broken by a thin glow cast from the few windows still lighted across the square.

''What is it?'' Her body was stiff, and aching with every bruise and sore she had gotten in the day's long march.

''One comes,'' Saric whispered, and then she, too, saw the cresset that weaved across the square.

The cloaked figure who carried it was a woman. She bobbed her head, but did not speak, to the sentry who guarded the pen. A token changed hands, a flash of carved shell reflected briefly by flame light.

Then, with a rich laugh, the sentry admitted her. She stepped into the livestock compound, her lantern held high over her hooded head. She scanned the rows of Mara's warriors, roused from their rest, and banded together in wary defensiveness.

"Lady of the Acoma?" Her voice was gruff and rich, not that of a young woman, but one that had seen many years of life and laughter. "My Lord has relented, and says you may shelter for the night with your servant, in the hut with the unmarried women."

"Dare you trust her?" Saric said in his Lady's ear. "This could be a ploy to separate you."

"Well I know it," Mara whispered back. Then, loudly enough to be heard, she said, "If your intentions are honest, cut my bonds."

The Thuril woman stepped closer with the torch, lighting a path for herself between Mara's warriors. "But of course, Lady Mara." She reached inside her cloak with her free hand and removed a dagger.

Mara felt Lujan flinch taut against her at the sight of the bared blade. But with his hands tied, he could do little to defend her.

He watched in sick anxiety as the highland woman reached down and deftly cut the rawhide that bound the Lady's hands.

Mara rubbed her wrists, forcing her face not to reflect her discomfort as the circulation returned to her cramped fingers. "Free my officers and my men also," she demanded imperiously.

The woman stepped back, sheathing the knife at her belt. "I may not, Lady Mara."

"Then I do not come," the Lady of the Acoma said icily in return.

The cloaked woman shrugged, indifferent. "Stay out here, then. But your servant girl has need of you. She will not stop shaking."

Fury flowed through Mara. "Has Kamlio been hurt?"

Pride held the highland woman silent; and from the dark outside the ring of torchlight, Iayapa said, "Good Servant, you offer insult. This is the chieftain's wife come to offer you better hospitality, and to imply harm to your serving girl is to give affront to all in this tribe. Her gesture of kindness is genuine, and I advise you to accept."

Mara drew in an icy breath. It was all very well to allow these barbarians their own honor—but what of her own! To leave her warriors here in this dung pit shamed her as their Lady.

Saric felt her uncertainty through the contact of her body with his.

"Lady," he said in a low voice, "I think you must trust her. We gave up our option to fight already. As prisoners, what can we do but chance the consequences of that earlier decision?"

At heart, Mara knew her adviser was correct. But the part of her that was born and raised Tsurani refused to yield so easily to such honorless practicality.

Lujan elbowed her gently in the ribs. "My Lady, do not worry for your warriors. They will sleep in this querdidra pen as an honor in your service, and if any complain of it, I will see him whipped as a man in need of toughening! I have brought my best soldiers as your guard into this land. Each of them had to prove himself to be here, and I expect them all to die on command if need be." He paused, and added wryly, "To lie in a little dung is a lot less painful than a trip at a sword's point to Turakamu's halls."

"True," Mara agreed, too sore and heartsick to raise a laugh at his attempted humor. To the torch-bearing woman she said, "I will come." Stiffly she clawed her way to her feet. Her blistered soles stung as she stepped forward, and with an exclamation of sympathy, the chieftain's wife reached and steadied her. Slowly Mara limped across the pen toward the gate that the sentries held open.

One of them commented in Thuril as she and the chief's wife passed. The highland woman did not turn at his noise, but instead said something back in contempt. "Men!" she confided to Mara in fluent Tsurani. "A pity it is that their brains are not as quick as their organs to rise when the occasion warrants cleverness."

Surprised enough to have smiled, had she felt less miserable, Mara gave in to curiosity. "Is it true your people take their women to wife by stealing them from their families in a raid?"

The cloaked figure by her side turned her head, and Mara received the impression of a visage lined by hardship and amusement. "But of course," said the Thuril chief's wife. Her tone was half laughter, and half blistering scorn. "Would *you* lie with a man who had not proven himself a skillful warrior, a man to make his enemies afraid, and a handy provider?"

Mara's eyebrows arose. Tsurani girls, after all, sought the same qualities in a husband, even if they held different rites of courtship. The Lady of the Acoma had never thought to view a custom she had presumed barbarous in such a light. But in an alien way, this woman's words made sense.

"Call me Ukata," the chief's wife said warmly. "And if I am sorry for anything, it is that it took me this long to drum sense into my silly husband's head, to allow you reprieve from the cold!''

"I have much to learn of your Thuril ways," Mara admitted. "By the talk of your warriors and your chief, I would have thought that women held little influence in this land.''

Ukata grunted as she assisted Mara up the low wooden step of the centermost house in the square, a long, beamed hall with a thatched roof. The smoke from the chimney smelled of aromatic bark, and strange fertility symbols were scratched into the doorposts. "What men claim and what they actually are make different tales, as you must know at your age!''

Mara held her silence. She had been blessed with a husband who heard her as an equal, and a barbarian lover who had shown her the meaning of her womanhood; but she was not unfamiliar with the lot of others whose men held dominance over them. The most unfortunate were like Kamlio, helpless to gain influence over decisions that affected them; the best were formidable manipulators, like Lady Isashani of the Xacatecas. Men regarded her as the supreme example of the Tsurani wife, and yet neither Lord nor ally nor enemy had ever gotten the better of her.

Ukata raised the wooden latch and pushed open the door with a creak of hinges. Gold light washed out into the night, along with sweet smoke from the bark that burned in the stone fireplace. Mara followed the chief's wife inside.

"Here," said a kindly female voice, "take off those soiled sandals."

Mara was stiff and slow to bend; hands pressed her into a wooden chair. There, accustomed as she was to cushions, she perched awkwardly while a girl with russet braids removed her footwear. The soft, woven carpet on the floor felt luxurious to her chilled toes. Weary enough to fall asleep where she sat, Mara fought to stay alert. She could learn a great deal about the Thuril people if these women were interested in talk. But listening to the burred accents, and seeing shy smiles among the unmarried maidens whose home she would share, Mara realized she lacked Isashani's finesse when it came to gatherings among women. More at home with the politics of a clan meeting and the seat of rulership, the Lady of the Acoma rubbed one blistered ankle and strove for the inspiration to cope.

She needed a translator. The unmarried girls at a glance all appeared to be under sixteen years of age, too young to have lived at the time of the last war and to have learned any Tsurani. Mara looked through the lamplit ring of faces until she located Ukata's grey head; as she suspected, the chief's wife seemed to be extricating herself for departure.

"Wait, Lady Ukata," Mara called, giving the address her own people would award a woman of noble rank. "I have not properly thanked you for my rescue from the livestock pen, nor have I had the chance to tell your people why I am here."

"Thanks are not necessary, Lady Mara," Ukata replied, turning back. The youngest girl of the company gave way to allow their elder a clear path, until she stood before Mara's chair. "Our people are not the barbarians that you Tsurani suppose. As a woman who has borne children and seen them die in battle, I understand why our men still hold your kind in hatred. As to why you are here, you may tell that to our high chief at Darabaldi."

"If I am allowed to be heard," Mara responded with a snap of acerbity. "Your men, you must admit, have short attention spans."

Ukata laughed. "You will be heard." She patted the Tsurani Lady's hand, her touch calloused but gentle. "I know the High Chief's wife. She is Mirana, and we were raised in the same village, before the raid in which she was taken to wife. She is tough as old rock, and garrulous enough to break the will of any man, even that meat-brains who is her husband. She will see that you are heard, or insult his manhood before his warriors until his sex parts wither from shame."

Mara listened with startled surprise. "You seem very calm when you speak of the raids that take you from home and family," she observed. "And do your husbands not beat you for saying uncomplimentary things of them?"

A flurry of questions from the young girls, and many cries of "Da? Da?" followed Mara's statement. Ukata gave in and translated. This raised a round of giggles, which quieted as the chief's wife spoke again. "Raids to win wives are . . . formal . . . a custom in these lands, Lady Mara. They stem from a time when women were even more scarce than now, and a husband established his standing by the age when he successfully stole a wife. Nowadays women are carried off without bloodshed. There is much shouting and pursuit, with terrible oaths and threats of retribution, but it is all for show. Once that was not so—the raids in past times were bloody and men died. Now a husband earns his accolades by how far afield he goes to bring home a mate, and how vigorously she was defended by her village. This house for unmarried girls lies deepest inside our defenses. But also, you will note, only girls of an age and an inclination to have a mate come to live here."

Mara regarded the ring of young faces, smooth and unmarked yet by life. "You mean that all of you here *want* to be taken by strangers?"

At their look of blank incomprehension Ukata answered in their stead. "These youngsters watch the lads who visit the village, who spy in turn on the girls." With a smile she said, "If they deem a boy is lacking in grace, the girl will scream with conviction, instead of the mock shouts of fear, and the suitor so rejected will be chased away by the fathers of the village. But few young girls would wish to be left when the warriors come naked to raid. To be overlooked is to be considered ugly or blemished. If a girl is not stolen by a raider, the only way she may win a husband is to wait until two suitors come for the same girl, then throw herself on the back of the one who failed, and ride him home without being pushed off!"

Mara shook her head, mystified by such a strange custom. She had much to learn if she was to gain understanding enough to negotiate for help from these foreigners.

Ukata added, "It is late, and you will be starting out early in the morning. I suggest you allow the girls to show you to a sleeping mat, and that you rest through the night."

"I thank you, Lady Ukata." Mara inclined her head in respect and permitted herself to be led into a small, curtained cubicle that served as sleeping quarters for Thuril girls. The floor was lined with furs, and the small oil lamp left burning showed a drift of yellow hair scattered amid the bedding. Kamlio lay there already, curled motionless on her side. Her fair skin showed no bruises. Relieved that Arakasi's pretty courtesan had taken no harm, Mara gestured to the Thuril girl who lingered that her needs were met. Then, she gratefully slipped off her soiled robe. Clad in her thin silk underrobe, she crawled under the furs, and reached up to extinguish the lamp.

"Lady?" Kamlio's eyes were open, watching. She had not been asleep at all, but only shamming. "Lady Mara, what will happen to us?"

Leaving the lamp alight, Mara snuggled the furs around her chin and studied the girl who regarded her with eyes like luminous jewels. No wonder Arakasi had been overtaken by desire! Kamlio was appealing enough to bewitch any man, with her creamy skin and fine, fair coloring. As badly as the Lady of the Acoma wished to offer reassurance, she knew better than to lie. If her Spy Master had been thawed into discovery of emotion by the allure of this courtesan, what might the Thuril with their tradition of taking women by raiding do to keep her? "I don't know, Kamlio." Mara's uncertainty showed through despite her best efforts.

The ex-courtesan's delicate fingers tightened over the bed furs. "I don't want to stay among these people." For the first time when dealing with her personal wishes, her gaze did not shy away when she spoke.

"What would you do, then?" Mara seized upon the vulnerability that their straits as prisoners had created. "You are too intelligent to remain in my service as a maid, Kamlio, and too uneducated to assume a post of more responsibility. What would you like to do?"

Kamlio's green eyes flashed. "I can learn. Others have risen to rank in your service who were not born to it." She bit her full lip and after a moment, some of the tension seemed to leave her, as if she let down some inner barrier by expressing ambition. "Arakasi," she said uncertainly. "Why did he insist upon asking you to buy my freedom? Why did you grant his request, if not to leave me to him?"

Mara briefly shut her eyes. She was too tired for this! One wrong word, one insufficient answer, and she risked all that her Spy Master hoped for happiness. Honesty was her best course, but how to choose the best phrases? Beaten down by a headache and by pain in every muscle— stiff from the day's forced march—the Lady of the Acoma found that in fact Isashani's tact was beyond her. The bluntness she had learned from Kevin of Zūn must suffice. "You remind him of his family, who also were born to a life that did not suit them, and who also never learned how to love."

Kamlio's gaze widened. "What family? He told me that you were all of his family and all of his honor."

Mara accepted the burden of that statement. "I may have become so. But Arakasi was born masterless to a woman of the Reed Life. He never knew the name of his father, and he saw his only sister killed by a lustful man."

The courtesan absorbed this news in silence. Watching, fearful that she might have said too much, but unable to stop short, Mara added, "He wants your freedom from the past, Kamlio. I know him well enough to vow to you this: he would ask you for nothing more than you would give him freely."

"You love your husband that way," Kamlio said, in her words a cutting edge of accusation, as if she distrusted the existence of such relations between a man and a woman.

"I do." Mara waited, wishing she could lay her head down and close her eyes, to lose this and all other problems in the oblivion of sleep.

But Kamlio's need prevented that. She picked nervously at the furs, and in an abrupt change of subject, said, "Lady, do not leave me here, among these Thuril! I beg you. If I were forced to become the wife of such a foreigner, I would never find out who I am, what sort of life would please me. I think I would never understand the meaning of the freedom you have given me.''

"Have no fear, Kamlio," Mara said, losing her battle against her overwhelming exhaustion. "If I leave this land at all, I will bring all of my people out with me."

As if she could trust this reassurance with her life, Kamlio reached out and snuffed the light. After that, Mara could only suppose that the girl shared no more words in confidence, for the Lady of the Acoma slept without dreams in the close, herb-scented cubicle.

When morning came, Lady Mara and her servant woman found themselves well treated to a warm bath in the women's quarters, followed by a breakfast of fresh breads and querdidra cheese. Kamlio appeared pale but composed. Yet Mara noted a fragility to her manner that she believed stemmed from worry rather than bitterness. Outside the hut, a great commotion of shouting and laughter issued from the vicinity of the village square, but Mara could not make out the cause through the blurry, translucent windows of oiled hide. When she inquired, the young women who were her hostesses gave her blank stares. Without Ukata present to translate, little else could be done but endure through the simple meal in politeness until an escort of highlander warriors arrived at the door and demanded that the two Tsurani women come out.

Kamlio whitened. Mara touched her hand in reassurance, then raised her chin high and stepped outside.

A wagon waited by the low stair beyond the door. It had high sides woven of withe, and was drawn by two querdidra and the recalcitrant donkey. Its grey hide was flecked with spittle from the six-legged beasts' spite, and in vain it tried to kick at the traces to retaliate. The querdidra blinked their absurdly long lashes and wrinkled their lips as if laughing.

Tied to the wagon were Mara's warriors. They did not smell of the dung that had been their last night's camp, but were clean, if drenched. Lujan, as he saw his Lady descend the stair, looked flushed with some inward satisfaction, and Saric was stifling a smile. Startled by her warriors' neat appearance, Mara looked further and realized that the Thuril highlanders who swaggered about on guard detail were eyeing her captive retinue with what seemed a newfound respect.

Suspect though she might that somehow the pandemonium she had heard through the walls of the house might be connected, she had no chance to inquire. The Thuril warriors closed around, and she and Kamlio were bundled up over the wagon's crude backboard into a bed lined with straw. The withe rose up on either side, too tightly woven for Mara to see out. The warriors lashed the tailgate firmly closed. Captives still, the women felt the jolt as the drover leaped up and gathered the reins, and then the creak of withe and wheels as he slapped his team with his goad and hastened them forward.

The donkey and the querdidra pulled badly together. The wagon swayed and jolted over ruts, and the straw smelled of livestock, taken, as it was, from some goodman's byre. Kamlio looked so sick with fear that Mara bade her lie down in the straw. She offered the girl her overrobe, for the wind cut down off the heights in chilly gusts. ''I will not see you abandoned, Kamlio,'' she assured. ''You did not come here to become some rough Thuril's wife.''

Then, too restless to sit still, Mara leaned against the withe on the side nearest to Lujan and demanded to know how her warriors had gotten their soaking.

As before, the Thuril guard set over them did not care whether their captives talked. Lujan was permitted to step close to the painted spokes of the wheel and answer his mistress all he liked.

''We complained that we did not care to march into their capital smelling of dung,'' the Acoma Force Commander said, his voice deep with choked-back amusement. ''So they allowed us to go under guard to bathe in the river.'' Now a chuckle escaped Lujan's control. ''Of course, our armor and clothing were soiled, so we stripped to clean that also. This caused a great commotion among the highlanders. Iayapa said it was because they do not go naked except to battle. There was much pointing and shouting. Then someone called out in bad Tsurani that we were no sport for insults, being unable to understand the rasping grunts these folk call a language.'' Here Lujan paused.

Mara leaned her cheek against the creaking withe. ''Go on.''

Lujan cleared his throat. Plainly, he was still having difficulty suppressing amusement. ''Saric took up that challenge, shouting to Iayapa to translate everything, no matter how ugly the words were, or how obscene.'' The wagon jolted over a particularly bad rut, and Lujan broke off his narrative, presumably to jump across. ''Well, the words got very personal indeed. We were told by these Thuril how we got all of our battle scars. If they are to be believed, the women of the Reed Life in our land are practiced at putting our best soldiers to rout with their fingernails. Or our sisters all lie with dogs and jigabirds, and we scratched each other with our nails all vying to have the best view.''

Here Lujan broke off again, this time grimly. Mara gripped the withe tightly enough to whiten her knuckles. The insults Lujan had mentioned were shame enough to a man's honor to require vengeance, and the Lady doubted her Force Commander had repeated the worst slander. Hoarsely, for she was sorrowful and angry that she had brought such brave warriors to such a disgraceful pass, she said, "This must have been terrible to endure."

"Not so terrible." A toughness like barbarian iron entered Lujan's voice. "I and the others, we took example from Papewaio, Lady."

Mara closed her eyes in remembered pain for brave Pape—who had saved her life many times over, and come as a consequence to wear the black rag of a condemned man for her sake, and then equally for her sake, to forgo the death by his own blade that he had earned, and to live on, his dark headcloth symbolic of a triumph that only his Lady and those who knew him might understand. Lastly, he had died to save her life, in an attack by a Minwanabi enemy. Mara bit her lip, jostled from her remembrance by the sway and jolt of the wagon. She hoped that these warriors, the finest and best of her honor guard, would not suffer the same untimely end. Old Keyoke, her Adviser for War, had taught her well that death in battle on strange soil was not, as old custom held, the best end a warrior could earn.

"Go on," she said, hiding the tears in her voice from Lujan.

Almost, she could imagine her Force Commander's shrug. "Lady, there is nothing more to tell. Your warriors agreed not to take umbrage at empty words from the Thuril. And the highlanders seemed surprised by this. They called down and asked why we did not bother to defend our honor. And Vanamani called right back that we were *your* honor, Lady. We would hear no word that was not spoken from your lips, or the lips of an enemy. At that point Saric broke in and added that the Thuril were not enemies, but foreigners, and that the words of such were empty as the howl of wind over stones." Lujan delivered his last sentence in wry amusement. "You know, the highlanders stopped slanging us then. Our loyalty impressed them, I think, that we would not be baited, even when under command of a woman who was out of sight and a captive as we were. Iayapa said that many Tsurani in the times of the wars were taunted to take foolish charges, and so were killed off by highlanders hidden in the rocks."

"Lujan," Mara said, her voice tremulous with gratitude despite her wish to seem impassive, "all of your men are to be commended for their valor. Tell them I said so, as you can." For each and every one of them had stood firm beyond the call of duty, beyond the tenets of Tsurani culture that held honor above even life. Each of these men had given over their personal honor into her hands. Mara studied her palms, red-marked from her grip on the withe. She prayed to her gods that she would prove worthy of such trust, and not get them all sold into slavery that would be the nadir of dishonor.

20. Council

The hours dragged.

Confined to the wicker wagon, exposed to buffeting winds and the sun that appeared and disappeared between the clouds that brooded over the highlands, Mara strove to keep her patience. But the uncertainty, and the boisterous shouts of the Thuril escort warriors, wore at her nerves. To pass the time, she asked Iayapa to describe the lands they were crossing. He had little to tell. There were no villages, only a few isolated hamlets clinging to rocky hillsides, surrounded by scrub grazed thin by the herds. Over the purple hills at the horizon larger mountains loomed, rock-crowned where they were not covered by cloud. Darabaldi, the city of the high council of chieftains, was said to lie in the foothills of the great range. When Mara asked Iayapa to inquire on the length of their journey, she received in return only laughter and ribald comments. Driven at last to useless exasperation, she turned to teaching Kamlio the calming techniques of meditation she had learned as a temple novice.

Gods knew, the poor girl might need all the solace she could learn to give herself, before their fates were determined at the hands of these people, Mara thought.

The highlanders paused only to eat sausage, sour querdidra cheese, and bread, washed down with a light, sour beer that was surprisingly refreshing with the meal. These breaks were enlivened by loud boasts and sometimes wagers, when warriors would contest at arm wrestling.

Darkness fell, and fog settled in cold layers over the land. The donkey grew too tired to kick at the querdidra that shared its traces, even if the six-legged beasts still curled their lips at it and spat. Mara curled close to Kamlio for warmth. Perhaps for a while she slept.

The stars formed a brilliance of pinpoint patterns overhead when she roused to the barking of many dogs. Herd dogs, Iayapa identified, not the larger, heavier breed of hound used for hunting. By the smoke on the air, and the pungent smell of confined livestock, rotting garbage, and curing hides, Mara presumed their party approached a village or larger habitation.

"Darabaldi," she received in gruff-voiced reply when she inquired. But when she pressed for information concerning when she might speak with the council of chieftains, her escort returned only coarse comment. "What does it matter, woman, or are you eager to learn what man will buy you? Maybe you worry that he will be old and have no manhood left in him to rise?"

To this outrageous statement, Saric ventured a rough term in the Thuril's own language, perhaps learned by the bathing pool that morning. The highlanders were not offended in the least, but laughed back and, grudgingly, appeared to allow her First Adviser some respect.

Torchlight spilled across the wagon. Mara looked up at a tall gatehouse topped by fat-soaked cressets that gave off greasy smoke. From battlements of stone and log, and Thuril warriors in drab plaids called down challenge to the approaching party.

Antaha shouted back, then launched into rapid-fire speech accompanied by gesticulations, some of which were crude. From the evident amusement of the sentries, and their glances in her direction, Mara presumed their captor gave account of her capture. The bathing scene by the river was apparently not omitted, for the sentries elbowed one another in the ribs and hooted at Lujan and Saric.

Then the guards and their Tsurani captives were waved on through, and the wagon jerked forward with a bray from the donkey and shrill squeals from the querdidra. "Well," Mara commented to Kamlio, "everyone in town will know we are here, by the fanfare of our draft beasts."

More than ever she wished that the withes were low enough to allow her a view, but changed her mind a moment later at a pattering sound that might have been thrown stones, or dried dung, striking the sides of the cart. Shouts in Thuril blended with the screech of children caught at mischief, and the barrage stopped. Looming over the top of the withes, Mara saw two-storied stone buildings, and signboards painted in dull colors swinging in the wind. The galleries and sills of the windows all had carved totem posts, and peaked gable roofs that looked strange to Tsurani eyes. The eaves were also carved in what looked like runes or writing, beneath roofs of weathered thatch. Windows seemed to be shuttered and barred, except for ones stuffed with plump-cheeked women who called out and made obscene gestures of welcome.

"Whores," Kamlio judged in edged bitterness. Mara could see her unspoken fear that such a garret might become her future home.

Mara bit her lip. She knew that Kamlio was far more likely to become the woman of a chieftain's son, but she could not stop herself from wondering: if her Spy Master were to find himself masterless again, would he swear service to the Shinzawai, as Hokanu must surely request, or would he remain a free agent, and come to these hostile hills, searching a succession of Thuril towns for the girl who had stolen his heart? Given a wager, Mara would have guessed he would come searching for Kamlio.

The wagon jounced over what might have been a stretch of cobbles or stone paving, then lurched to a halt. The withe tailgate was opened by a blond highlander who grinned to show missing teeth, and Mara and Kamlio were beckoned to step down. Beyond the Thuril guard and onlookers who clustered around, a long house backed up to the village wall; to Mara's quick glance, it seemed a small fortress. The bossed wood doors of the structure stood open, but the entrance was hung with cloths woven of animal wool into patterns of squares and lines. Before Mara could observe more, a Thuril warrior shoved her toward the blanket flap. Kamlio, Saric, Lujan, and Iayapa were singled out to follow.

Mara marveled at the softness of the fabric she brushed past. Then, the others clustered at her heels, she was inside, blinking at the sting of smoky air in a windowless room.

The gloom was pierced by the reddish gleam of banked embers, kept more for cooking than for warmth in close air that was pungent with wool, boiled stew, and pent humanity. Upon an upraised settle before that immense stone hearth, an old woman sat cleaning querdidra wool on a card of bone nails. Little more than a silhouette on the floor below, an older man crouched cross-legged on a woven withe stool. As Mara's eyes adjusted, she saw he had grey hair. His mouth was deep-cut and sullen, framed by a long mustache that hung down his pouched jaw. The ends flashed with colored beads that rattled as he lifted his chin.

Iayapa spoke quickly in a hushed voice to Saric, who in turn murmured, "This one wears the face hair of a chieftain. By the talismans of rank dangling from it, he could be the high chief himself."

Mara smothered her surprise. She had expected a great personage, not an ordinary-seeming fellow in an unadorned green kilt. The bowl he ate from was crude wood, his spoon a battered implement of corcara shell. Taken aback by his lack of ceremonial trappings, the Lady of the Acoma almost missed noticing the other men, seated as they were in shadow, in a semicircle, their conversation fallen to a hush at the entrance of her party.

For an interval, the incoming Thuril and their captives regarded those seated, who stared back silently, unmindful of the meal they had been eating scarcely a moment before.

Astonishingly, it was the old woman who stopped her carding and broke the silence first. "You might ask them what they want."

The man with the chief's mustache spun in his seat, jabbing in her direction with his spoon. Gravy flew in spatters from the bowl and struck with a hiss into the coals. "Shut up, old hag! I don't need you telling me what to do!"

As Mara again raised her brows, startled by both the lack of propriety or any sort of formal ceremony, the chief of the Thuril spun back. His beads and his mustache whipped outward with a clatter as he jerked his chin at Saric, who was closest. "What do you want, Tsurani?"

When Saric wished, he could be masterful at misleading expressions. The half-light thrown off by the coals showed him stone-still, as if the Tsurani high chief had addressed the empty air.

Mara took her adviser's cue and stepped forward. Into silence, she said crisply, "I have come to your land seeking information."

The Thuril chief stiffened as if slapped. His eyes jerked to the Lady who stood before him, then flinched away. He seemed to stare over her head, and so could not miss the wide grins of Antaha and the other warrior escorts.

"You stand there and allow a woman captive to speak out of turn," he roared in a battlefield bellow.

Not the least nonplussed, although his ears stung from the shout, Saric pushed forward. Despite his bound hands, he executed a creditable bow. "Antaha does so, worthy chief, because the Lady is Mara of the Acoma, Servant of the Empire, and family to the Emperor of all Tsuranuanni."

The chief stroked his mustache, twirling the beads at the ends. "Is she so?" His pause extended through a clatter of wooden plates and spoons as his cronies all set down their meals. "If this woman is indeed the Good Servant, where are her banners? Her army? Her great and illustrious command tent?" A sneer developed in the chief's deep baritone. "I have seen how Tsurani nobles travel in foreign territory! They carry half their possessions along with them, like merchants! I say you lie, outlander. Or why is she"—he made a derogatory gesture toward Mara—"attended by so few guards? We are enemy countries, after all."

At this, the old woman by the settle tossed down her carding, her face crinkled in disgust. "Why don't you ask her yourself? She said she came seeking information. It must be very important to her."

"Shut your great cave of a mouth, old woman!" Explosive in his indignation, the chief jabbed a hand that still clutched a crust of bread at Mara's party, not at all willing to address the Lady directly. "We are not the barbarians you Tsurani suppose, you know."

Mara's composure snapped. "Are you not?" How she wished she could speak the Thuril language. As it was, her own must suffice. "And do you call bedding my honor guard down in a livestock pen *civilized?* In my land, not even slaves live so meanly!"

Taken aback, and embarrassed by stifled chuckles from Antaha and his warriors, the chief cleared his throat. "You were asking me about information . . ." His eyes narrowed. "Enemy, by what right do you come here making demands?"

But before Mara could answer this, Iayapa thrust between her and Saric, bristling with purpose. "But Lady Mara did not come here as our enemy. Her warriors disarmed at her command, and not once did they call back in insult, though the villagers and the guards at the Loso did their best to revile them."

"He speaks truth," Mara cut in, unwilling to accede to the silly Thuril custom that a man should not acknowledge public speech from a female. As if in admiration of her spunk, the old woman by the settle smiled. Mara continued, "Now as to the information I seek . . . ?" She left her question hanging.

While the chieftain looked uncertain, the old woman thumped him from behind with her toe. "She is waiting for you to tell her who you are, you wool-brained fool."

Turning to glare at the woman, who could only be his wife to escape punishment for such liberties, the chieftain shouted, "I know that, woman!" He twisted back to Mara, sucking himself up straight in self-importance. "Yes, it must be important information—"

"Your name," the old woman prodded calmly.

Still unmindful of his morsel of bread, the chieftain shook his fists. "Shut up, woman! How many times must I tell you to keep silent in the lodge hall? Plague me again, and I'll beat your fat backside with a thorn switch!" The woman ignored the threat and took up her neglected carding.

The chieftain puffed up his chest, which only displayed to plain view the gravy stains of varied ages on his vest. "My name is Hotaba. I am chieftain of the Five Tribes of the Malapia, and, for this season, high chief of the council here in Darabaldi." Pointing at the man sitting farthest from him, also wearing a warrior's scalp lock and mustache, he said, "This is Brazado, chieftain of the Four Tribes of the Suwaka." Then pointing at the last man, who wore no mustache, he said, "This is Hidoka, his son." His eyes shifted past Mara's shoulder to fix upon Saric, as he finished, "My own son, Antaha—"

Acerbically Mara cut in, "We've met."

Now the high chief crashed his fists to his knees in anger. Crumbs flew as his crust broke to bits under the blow, and his brows lowered into a fearsome frown. Mara resisted a shaky urge to step backward; she had gone too far, in her boldness, and this time these Thuril would retaliate for her interruption.

But the old woman on the hearth cleared her throat loudly.

Hotaba's glare shifted in her direction, then vanished as he shrugged in resignation. "That loud-mouthed interfering female is Mirana, my wife." As if in afterthought, he added, "If she were not so good at cooking and sweeping, I'd have had her cut up for dog meat years ago."

Antaha said, "The chief at Loso thought it best to send these captives directly to you rather than await the next trading caravan, Father."

The chieftain tapped his mustache, to a clink of beads. "Little need for guards these days, eh? What with the Tsurani being meek like little gachagas." Mara recognized the term and knew it was unflattering even before the worried glance Iayapa shot toward Lujan and Saric. But after what they had endured at the river pool that morning, both showed indifference to being compared to grain-stealing rodents.

While the high chief was still waiting for reaction to his derogatory comment, Mirana interjected, "You still haven't asked Lady Mara what she wishes to know."

Hotaba sprang to his feet, looking for all the world as if he were about to commit murder. "Will you shut up, woman! You continue to speak in council! I should have you stewed and thrown to the carrion birds, and raid for myself a young, obedient, *silent* wife!"

The other Thuril men in the long hut seemed as unconcerned by the threat as Mirana did. Her hands never broke rhythm in their work, and only her foot tapped as if in pent back impatience. As if Hotaba saw her quiet as a warning, he took a breath, and through clenched teeth said to Mara, "What do you wish to know, Tsurani?"

Mara glanced at Lujan and Saric, both of whom impassively observed the exchanges. Her adviser gave back a slight shrug. He could hardly guide her through this negotiation. By Tsurani standards, the Thuril were rude and unruly, given to theatrical displays of emotion, and utterly uncouth. The past day and a half in their presence had only further mystified them about what constituted an unforgivable outrage. No slight of language seemed to faze these folk; the worst insults seemed but jokes to them. Honest courtesy was the safest approach, Mara determined. "Hotaba, I need to speak with one of your magicians."

Hotaba's puffed cheeks went flat. His ruddy color subsided, and he seemed to notice the mashed mess of crumbs in his fist for the first time. "A magician?"

As plainly as Mara could read a foreigner's expression, he seemed flabbergasted. She pressed ahead. "There are things I need to know that only a magician who is not part of the Assembly within our Empire can tell me. I have come to the Thuril Confederation because I was given to understand that answers may be found in your nation."

Hotaba's expression of surprise dissolved and turned shrewd. He was not anxious to attend to the subject she had broached, Mara saw, as his bright eyes darted back and forth, studying her companions. She edged sideways, trying to shield the girl who cowered behind her, but Kamlio's windblown drift of pale hair was conspicuous even in shadow. Worse, Antaha saw the direction of his father's gaze, and snatched the opening to gain favor. He pushed forward, dragging Kamlio ahead by her arm until she stood at the fore.

"Father, behold. We have a prize of these Tsurani."

Mara stifled white-hot outrage, both for Kamlio's shrinking discomfort, and for the brusque sweeping aside of the subject she had risked all to broach. Yet from the lust that flashed in the old chieftain's eyes, she saw that she dared not take umbrage lest she force a display of male pride.

Low-pitched whistles of admiration erupted from the other council members. All stared at the courtesan with hungry, appreciative eyes, and not even Mirana's sour glare could dim the interest of her husband. Hotaba let his gaze wander over Kamlio's ripe curves like a man about to be served a delicacy. He licked his lips. "Nice," he murmured to Antaha. "Exceptionally so." He inclined his head to his son. "Remove her robe. Let us see what delectable fruit it hides."

Mara stiffened. "Hotaba, you may tell your son that neither I nor my servingwoman Kamlio are to be considered his prizes. We are not your property, Thuril chief! Kamlio's flesh is her own, as her service is mine, to do with as I bid. And I do not bed her with strangers."

Hotaba started as if slapped from a dream. He looked at Mara, assessing. Then his sour, loose mouth tightened into a smile of malice. "You are in no position to make demands, woman."

Mara disregarded the statement. As if her officers did not stand bound like slaves at her shoulder, and as if she did not stand disheveled and entirely without the ceremonial state due a great Tsurani Lady, she let the fury of the moment stiffen her spine.

Her composure made an impression, if not the best. Hotaba's smile widened. Even Mirana stopped her carding, as a charged and dangerous stillness gripped the airless room. "Lady," the high chief announced in edged sarcasm, "I will offer you a bargain: the information you seek, against the person of your yellow-haired maid. A more than fair trade, I deem. The woman is of inestimable value, as rare in her beauty as practitioners of honest magic are among your kind. Surely the knowledge you came to find is worth the flesh of one servant, when upon your estates in the Empire you command many thousands of souls?"

Mara closed her eyes against sickness, and her teeth against a sharp desire to shout useless imprecations. Her mouth felt dry as ashes. Who was she, to barter Kamlio's life and happiness away, even for the good of her family? Though, as Ruling Lady, Mara held that right within Empire law, still, she had to force speech.

"No." She at least sounded decisive, if her mind seethed with doubts. Gods, what honorless being had she become, to set the life of one difficult servant before the well-being and survival of her house, her husband, and her children! What was one wretched courtesan before all of her honor, all of her loved ones, and, ultimately, the power base of Ichindar himself? Yet where once she would have commanded a servant or slave to do as these Thuril bid, today, when all depended upon her one word, she could not demand that sacrifice.

Into that charged stillness, while the men were too stunned to react, and Saric fought back an expression of outright astonishment and dismay, Mirana spoke. As if matters of household were of more account than lives and fates, she announced, "I'm done with my carding."

But her hands were shaking as she set wool and tools back in the basket by her knee, Mara saw. Hotaba merely turned and nodded once to his wife. The old woman rose, furled her shoulders in layers of fringed shawls, and motioned for Mara to follow her.

The Lady of the Acoma hesitated. She thought to insist that she should stay with her officers and people to oversee their disposition, as their ruler. But Mirana gave a slight shake of her head, as if she could guess Mara's thoughts.

Saric received hasty words of counsel from Iayapa, and he bent with whispered advice. "Go, my Lady. This culture is not as ours, and your point has been made. You will perhaps hurt the cause you came for if you stay to argue your point. Iayapa agrees that Mirana knows her husband well. Follow her lead, he thinks, and I concur."

Mara flashed a last, haughty glance at Hotaba, making him aware that she acted for her own reasons, and not those of any Thuril. Then, stiff-backed, she joined Mirana on her way to the door.

When Lujan stirred to follow, Mara gave back a gesture to keep him in place. None of them were safe here, among these barbarians; and, weaponless, there was very little that any warrior could do to protect his mistress before the highlanders overpowered him. Mirana seemed to understand this, for she raised her voice one last time.

"Stay here with my husband and lie about how fierce you are in battle and bed, soldier. I shall not keep your mistress long."

To Mara she added, "Your serving girl will not be touched, rest assured, until this matter is settled." Then, with surprising strength, Mirana clamped down on Mara's arm and hustled her outside.

The colder air hit the women's faces with a sharpness that reddened the skin. Mirana moved at a brisk pace, forcing Mara away from the long hut with no chance for change of mind. She ducked down an alleyway where bakers finished their day's work, by the smell, and a small dog devoured crusts from the hand of a girl with plaited hair. Reminded of her own daughter, who might never grow old enough to own a pet, Mara stumbled.

Mirana jerked her forward. "None of that," she said in sharply accented Tsurani. "You were strong enough to leave your homeland, to challenge the Assembly, and come here. Do not fall victim to self-pity now."

Mara's chin snapped up. Startled, she said, "What is my fate to you?"

"Very little," Mirana said matter-of-factly. Her dark eyes fixed on the Lady of the Acoma, watching for some sort of reaction. Mara gave none. After a moment, the chieftain's wife added, "Very little, if you were like other Tsurani we had known. But you are not. Hotaba ascertained as much, when he offered you the bargain for your servant girl."

Mara's chin went up another notch. "She is not mine to offer, even for the chance of rescue from the perils that threaten my family. I gave her a choice, and she remains with me of her free will. She is not a slave. . . ."

Mirana gave a shrug, which set her fringes swinging and tangling in the cold, sharp breeze. "Indeed, by our laws also, she is not yours to bargain. But the Lords in your land do as they will with the lives of their servants, slaves, and children, daily, and think the gods gave them the right."

"They believe so," Mara said carefully.

"And you?" Mirana's question came sharp as the stroke of a querdidra quirt.

"I do not know what I believe," Mara admitted, frowning. "Except that as Servant of the Empire I once set my nationhood above my own blood. Now I can no longer count my own blood above that of any other man. Kamlio is with me because of a pledge I gave to another to shield her as he would. My honor is no less than that of the man who entrusted her safety to me. There is honor that is mindless obedience to tradition, and there is honor that is . . . more.''

Mirana's regard grew piercing. ''You are different,'' she mused as much to herself as to Mara. ''Pray to your gods that such difference will be enough to win your freedom. You will have my support. But never forget that in Thuril, the men will talk more freely, and give more favors, when women are not present. Ours is a harsh land, and the man who shows himself as too soft will not keep the wife he has raided.''

''Another man would steal his woman away?'' Mara asked in surprise.

Mirana's withered lips cracked into an unabashed grin. ''Perhaps. Or worse, his woman would leave his house and hearth, and stuff his blankets with snow for his folly.''

In spite of her worries, Mara laughed. ''You do that here?''

''Oh, yes.'' Mirana observed that her guest was chilled. She slipped off one of her shawls and wrapped it around the Acoma Lady's shoulders; it smelled of woodsmoke and, more faintly, of unbleached fleece. ''Let us visit my favorite bread shop, where the sweet rolls will be hot and fresh-baked at this hour. I will tell you what else we do here, besides pretending to take the jigabird crowing of our men very seriously.''

Where the atmosphere in the council house had been stifling, the air in the bread shop held the sharp, dry warmth of the ovens, comforting in the damper climate of the highlands. Mara sat down awkwardly on the hand-hewn wooden chair. The stone floors in these chillier hills did not make Tsurani cushions practical. Shifting from one seat bone to the other to try to find a position of comfort, Mara resigned herself to another evening filled with light social chat. Like the chieftain's wife in Loso, Mirana seemed content to hold conversation to light matters, while the council of the town's elders went on without her. ''Men can be such children, don't you think?''

Mara forced a polite smile. ''Your husband seems an angry child, then.''

Mirana laughed, settling on the chair opposite a wooden table whose surface was grooved where shop patrons had sliced into fresh loaves over a chat with friends. Shedding several layers of shawls, and revealing white hair tied with braided cords of wool, Mirana sighed her indulgence. ''Hotaba? He's a windbag, but I love him. He's been threatening to beat me to silence for forty-two years, almost since the day he hoisted me onto his shoulder and raced over the hills to escape my father and brothers. He hasn't laid a hand on me in anger yet. We are a people for great threats and insults, Mara. Boasting is an art here, and a well-fashioned insult will earn the slighted man's admiration rather than scorn.''

Here she paused, while a young boy in a spun wool smock paused by the table with a tray. Mirana switched languages to order hot sweet bread and mulled cider. Then, after a glance at Mara's dark-circled eyes, she asked also for wine. The boy accepted three pierced wooden tokens from Mirana's hand, and scurried off, head turned over his shoulder when he thought the chief's wife might not be looking, so he could stare at Mara's outland clothing.

Mirana filled the interval with small talk, while the boy came back with food and drink, and Mara made a pretense of eating. Nerves kept her from hunger, though the coarse brown bread smelled wonderful, and the drink was not the sour vintage that Tsurani veterans of the Thuril wars claimed these hillfolk produced.

Outside the streets deepened into darkness as a cortege of young girls passed by chattering, overseen by young men, servants or maybe brothers, who carried smoking torches to light their way. Behind the shop's crude tables, the baker's boy scraped out the ovens, and the coals beneath greyed over with films of ash.

Warmed by the wine, but with her hands in a cold sweat with worry, Mara chafed. While she exchanged inane social chat, where was Kamlio? What would happen to Saric, Lujan, and her warriors? Worse, did Hokanu even have a clue where she had gone, since the day she had left the Acoma estates for a visit to Turakamu's temple? Her departure then seemed a dream, so far removed did affairs of the Empire seem from this place with its loud-voiced, boastful men, and cloudy uplands.

''Why did you come here looking for practitioners of magic?'' Mirana demanded with a sudden, disconcerting directness.

Mara started, almost dropping the crockery mug that held the dregs of her drink. The small talk, she suddenly sensed, had been but an excuse to bide time. She had no reason left to withhold the truth. ''I have learned over the years that the Assembly of Magicians keeps a stranglehold over the Empire's culture. Our traditions maintain injustices that I would see changed. Although the magicians have set restraint over House Acoma because of a feud with House Anasati, the sanctions are not held fairly over both sides. Anasati has been allowed to set assassins on allies of my people; sadly, my husband's father has been killed. The Great Ones' edict against Acoma vengeance is proven now to be pretense, an excuse to obscure the true issue. I will bring change, against the Assembly's wishes, and for that, I find myself and my children endangered."

"So these lofty aims are really simply the needs of survival?"

Mara looked hard at the old woman, realizing that here was as sharp a mind as Lady Isashani's. "Perhaps. I like to think that I would have pursued the proper course for my people's best interests even if my own house and loved ones were not at risk—"

"You turned outside your lands to Thuril," Mirana broke in. "Why?"

Mara turned the near-empty mug between nervous fingers. "The cho-ja gave me riddles that pointed to the East. A lesser-path magician who had a bitter heart toward the Assembly pleaded that I search here for answers. I came to Thuril because my line will die if I do not find answers, and because I have seen too much misery in the name of politics and the Game of the Council—many I have loved are in the Red God's halls because of our lust for power. Injustice and murder in the name of honor will not cease if the Assembly is allowed to overrule the Emperor and reinstate the Warlord's office."

Mirana seemed to ponder this, her eyes on the crumb-littered table and her hands quietly folded. At length she reached some inner decision. "You shall be heard."

Mara was given no time to puzzle over how Mirana might influence the men's council. Neither did she see any sign exchanged, or sent, but the next minute the flap door to the bread shop swept open, admitting a gust of icy air. Three of the oil lamps that lit the empty bread shop extinguished in the blast.

An ancient highlander in a heavy cloak entered. Backlit by the remaining lamp, the newcomer's features were only faintly discernible by the rose glow of the oven's dying embers. Multiple layers of woollen robes smelled of querdidra, and the ears just visible beneath the hood were hung with disks of corcara shell that twisted and flashed at each step. Of the face, Mara could see little but wizened skin under the hood's enveloping shadow.

"Stand," Mirana whispered urgently. "Show respect, for come to hear you is the Kaliane."

Mara raised eyebrows at the unknown foreign word.

"Kaliane is the traditional name for the strongest among those versed in the mysteries," Mirana explained to ease her confusion.

The cloaked figure stepped closer, and a sparkle and flash showed the mage's mantle to be bordered in costly, rare sequins of silver. The patterns seemed to form runes, or maybe totems of a more complex sort than adorned the doorposts of the houses. Mara bowed with the same respect she might show to a Great One come to visit her estate.

The Thuril magician did not acknowledge with any gesture beyond raising one withered hand to claw back the voluminous hood. Mara saw revealed a shock of silver hair, looped into braids like Mirana's, but knotted in ritual bindings. Beneath this crownlike arrangement was the aged face of a crone.

A woman! Forgetting manners, the Lady of the Acoma gasped. ''Your assembly of magicians allows females?''

The ancient woman tossed her head with a click of her heavy earrings, her manner dangerously vexed. ''We have nothing like your Assembly in this land, thank the gods, Mara of the Acoma.''

Two townswomen appeared at the bread-shop door, to complete a late errand. On the point of entering, they spied the cloaked enchantress, bobbed a hasty obeisance, and backed out into the street in silence. A young man on their heels also turned and hurried away. The hide flap slapped shut, but the room felt drained of warmth.

''Forgive me,'' Mara murmured, almost stammering. ''Lady Kaliane, I am sorry, but I never guessed—''

''I have no title. You may address me as the Kaliane,'' the crone snapped back, seating herself with a swish of robes. She arranged her long sleeves, folded tiny hands, and suddenly looked very human and sad. ''I know that your Empire's Assembly''—she all but spit the word—''kills all girls who are discovered to have the talent. My predecessor in this office was a refugee from Lash Province who barely escaped with her life. Her three sisters were not so fortunate.''

Faintly ill from nerves and wine that did not sit well with worry, Mara bit her lip. ''I was told such by a magician of the lesser path who hated the Assembly. But in my heart I could not force myself to believe it.''

The Kaliane's pale eyes were deep as she locked her gaze with Mara's. ''Believe it, for it is true.''

Shaken, and infused with fresh fear for the loved ones left behind, Mara locked her teeth to keep from shaking. Though the Kaliane was slight, and bundled up like an aged grandmother in layers against the draft, her presence radiated a power sharper than the bite of any mountain frost. Aware that her every word would be weighed in judgment, Mara spoke before the last of her courage ebbed away. ''I was told the Assembly fears you. Why?''

''Truth,'' the Kaliane rapped back. She loosed a cracked cackle that inspired chills. "In your Empire, slaves are mistreated, and told it is the will of your gods. Your Lords contend and kill for honor, but what do they accomplish? Not glory. Not the favor of heaven, no. They lose sons, engage in war, even fall upon their swords, and for nothing, Lady Mara. They have been duped. Their vaunted honor is naught but the shackle that keeps the power of the nations fragmented. While house contends against house in the Game of the Council, the Assembly is left free rein. Its power is vast, but it is not without limit, nor has it always been so strong."

Touched by hope in the light of such a frank admission, Mara said, "Then you might help me?"

At this the Kaliane's face became a mask of inscrutable wrinkles. "Help you? This has yet to be determined. You must accompany me upon a short journey."

Afraid to leave Lujan, Saric, and, worst of all, Kamlio in the hands of highlander captors without her, Mara knew a stab of dread. "Where would we go?"

"There are things you must see. A council of my peers must hear your reasons and your history, and question you." Then, as if sensing the source of Mara's discomfort directly, the Kaliane softened her unequivocal demand. "We shall be gone no longer than the time it takes two women to talk, lest your warriors become fearful for you, and try something stupid in desperation."

"I am in your hands, then," Mara said, her resolve forced over the indecision in her heart. Tsurani in upbringing, and not yet so immersed in desire for change that she could discount all the codes of her people's honor as false, still she could not escape the awareness that she would not be offered another chance. She embraced the Kaliane's option in desperation, but was unprepared for how swiftly her acquiescence would be followed up. The Thuril crone reached across the narrow table, took Mara's wrist in dry, sure fingers, and spoke a word.

Mara heard only the first sibilant syllable. A rushing in her ears drowned the rest, fierce as the buffet of a sea gale. The floor dropped away from her feet, as did the chair she perched upon. The shadowy walls of the bread shop also vanished, replaced for an eye's blink by an expanse of a howling grey void.

Time froze. The air went icy and thin. Mara might have shamed her ancestors and cried out in terror for her life, but the passage through the void ended suddenly, leaving only an impression.

Restored jarringly to firm soil, she found herself standing in a plaza lit by cho-ja globes. Her wrist was still clasped by the Kaliane's hand, which was steady, whereas her own shook like storm-blown reeds. Where Tsurani cities were built upon level ground, the buildings here had been carved in tiers into the steep granite face of the hills. On the valley floor, the open square that surrounded Mara was circled by terraces, each level fronted by doorways, windows, and shops. Her eyes lifted to follow the lines of columns, buttresses, and arches, arrayed in breathtaking artistry against the backdrop of night. Totems supported galleries with wood and stone railings, some carved into dragons or the great serpents of sea and sky that figured prominently in Thuril myth. Spires and domes speared upward against starry skies, or pierced through lamplit streamers of mist. Mara caught her breath in delight at a beauty her Tsurani-bred mind could not have imagined. Never had she expected such a city in these barren uplands! The streets were peopled with highlanders in plain kilts and trousers. Most young warriors went bare-chested, despite the evening chill, but a few sported brightly woven shirts. Women wore long skirts and loose-fitting overblouses, the youthful ones offering glimpses of slender arm or rounded bosom to draw admiring glances from passing young men.

"What is this place?" Mara murmured, drawing in a deep breath of incense, and staring upon wonders like a farm yokel on her first trip into town.

"Dorales," said the Kaliane. "You are the first Tsurani to see this city, perhaps." More ominously, she added, "You could be the last, as well."

The enchantress's quaint phrasing caused Mara a shiver. She felt as if she were dreaming, so alien was this place, and so vast; like a vision too beautiful to be real. The slender spires, the thousands of brightly lit windows and doorways, the leering totems, and the press and jostle of street life—all lent a feeling of precariousness, as if at any moment she might be swept unconsenting into nightmare. Amazement and uneasiness would have held the Lady frozen in place had the Kaliane not tugged her forward with the same brusque impatience a mother might show a reluctant child.

"Come! The circle of elders expects you, and there is no wisdom gained by making them wait."

Mara stumbled numbly forward. "You say I am expected? How?"

But the Kaliane had little patience for what to her ears were aimless questions. She towed Mara through the crowd, drawing much attention in the process. Bystanders stared and pointed, and not a few spat in contempt. Tsurani pride caused the Lady of the Acoma to ignore such insults as beneath her dignity, but she was left in no doubt that these people considered her an unforgiven enemy. Dreadful, creeping doubt plagued her, that imperial Lords should in contemptuous ignorance have dared call the Thuril barbarians; this city with its marvels of engineering most emphatically proved otherwise.

Curious even through shame, Mara asked, "Why did my people never hear of this place?"

The Kaliane hustled her past a painted wagon pulled by two sour-tempered querdidra, and driven by a wizened man wearing a cloak of patchwork colors. He carried a strange musical instrument, and passersby tossed him coins, or called out cheerful encouragement for him to play. He gave them back colorfully pungent imprecations, his red cheeks dimpled with a smile.

"Those of your people who would hear of this place, your Assembly would kill to keep silent," the Kaliane replied tartly. "The towers you behold, and all of the carving of the rock, were done by means of magic. Were you to be permitted entry to the City of the Magicians in Tsuranuanni, you might see such wonders. But in your land, the Great Ones keep the marvels their power can create to themselves."

Mara frowned, silent. She thought of Milamber, and his reluctance to speak of his experience as a member of the Assembly. After witnessing the fearful powers he had unleashed in the Imperial Arena, she was struck by conclusion that the oaths that bound him to the Assembly must have been fearfully strong, to force one of his stature to keep silence. She knew nothing of the characters of the magicians, but from Hokanu she had come to understand that Fumita was not a greedy man. Powerful, yes, and steeped in mystery, but not one to place selfishness above the common good of the nations.

As if the Kaliane held uncanny means to read Mara's thoughts, she shrugged under her heavy cloak. "Who knows why the magicians of your land are so secretive? Not all of them are bad men. Most are simply scholars who wish only to pursue the mysteries of their craft. Perhaps they first formed their brotherhood to ward off some threat, or to suppress the wild, dangerous magic of renegade magicians who refused to be trained to control, or who used their powers for ill. The gods alone might say. But if there were good and cogent reasons for such a course of action in the past, time has seen them corrupted. That thousands of daughters have been murdered to suppress their talents is utterly inexcusable by Thuril law."

Touched by an unpleasant possibility, Mara asked, "Am I being held on trial for the injustices of all Tsuranuanni?"

The Kaliane bobbed her head and fixed her with a glance that itself inspired dread. ''In part, Lady Mara. If you wish our help against the Assembly, you must convince us. If we act, it will not be for Acoma survival, nor for your personal gain, nor even to make the Empire a fairer nation. For to us the honor of your ancestors, and even the lives of your children, are as meaningless as dust in the wind.''

Mara might have slammed to a stop at once, for what was more innocent than the lives of her baby daughter and her son? But the crone's grip bound her like fetters and dragged her inexorably toward the looming arch of an imposing, many-tiered building. ''What does move your people, if not the lives of the young?'' Despite all effort, Mara's dismay showed through.

The Kaliane's reply stayed as impersonal as the grind of waves on the beach. ''If we mourn, it is for the loss of the mages who died with their talents untried. With each one of them, irrevocable knowledge was lost. And if we despair, it is for the cho-ja, masters beyond our finest initiates of mystery, that in your land are disbarred from the magic that is the glory of their race.''

''The Forbidden!'' Spurred to excitement, Mara forgot for a moment to fear. ''Was it arcane power that the cho-ja Queen meant when she spoke of the Forbidden?''

Lost in shadow as she stepped under the massively carved arch, the Kaliane answered obliquely. ''That, Lady Mara, is the secret you must unlock if you are to survive in your contention against the Great Ones. But first you must convince the Elder Circle of Thuril of your worthiness. We will hear and judge. Choose your words carefully, for once you have seen this place, the perils you face are redoubled.''

Beyond lay a maze of corridors, vaulted like tunnels, and lit with rows of cho-ja globes. The floors were marble. The artistry of the fluted pillars took Mara's breath away: not even the Emperor's palace held stonework polished to such a lustrous shine. The people who congregated in antechambers and doorways wore beaded costumes, headdresses of feathers, and some the plain kilts of servants. Others in white robes the Kaliane named acolytes of the craft. All without exception bowed to her passage, and Mara felt their stares upon her back like the touch of heated coals. There was magic here, a weight of power upon the air that made even echoes seem oppressive. Fervently Mara wished herself home, surrounded by familiar walls, and by customs she understood.

The Kaliane guided her into a wider hall that led into an echoing antechamber. Thousands of tiers of candles lit the expanse, burning Mara's eyes with intense light. Beyond lay a yet more immense room, surrounded by pillared galleries carved and pierced in arrays of intricate patterns. There dozens of robed figures crowded landings that circled the room, rising six levels high. Ladders, and successions of narrow, spiral stairs provided access to the topmost floors.

"This is our archive," the Kaliane explained. "Here we house all of our knowledge, and copies of all writings upon the subject of our craft. It serves also as our meeting hall, on those occasions when the magicians of Thuril gather together, which is as close as our kind come to being organized. We have no fellowship such as your Assembly, and keep no formal officers beyond the Kaliane, who is empowered only to act as spokeswoman."

Mara was led through a gap in a railing on the lowest level. Her elbows brushed against walls inlaid with corcara shell and ebony in spiraling patterns that made her uneasy. The newel posts were carved totems, beaked, clawed, and fierce of expression. The creatures were scaled, or winged in feathers, and their eyes were cut with the predatory slant of a snake's.

The Kaliane ushered Mara across an intimidating expanse of bare floor. There were no furnishings, not even patterns, beyond a circle that lay at the center. Its perimeter seemed to be marked out in golden light, unmistakably the effect of some spell. Aware of the levels above, now crowding with robed forms who all faced her way, the Lady of the Acoma felt like an object of sacrifice before the ritual that would seal her final fate.

"There." The Kaliane pointed at the magical circle. "Step in and stand, if you have courage enough to be judged. But be warned, Lady Mara, Servant of the Empire. Lies and deceit are impossible for any who cross that line."

Mara tossed back her hair, fallen loose over her shoulders in the absence of the accustomed attention of her maids. "I do not fear truth," she said boldly.

The Kaliane released her restraining grip. "So be it," she said, a look near to pity in her eyes.

Mara moved toward the line without trepidation. She did not fear truth, in the moment she raised her foot to step across the bar of yellow light. Yet in that instant she felt pierced by a force that negated all of her will, and by the time her foot struck the flooring on the inward side of the spell, every vestige of her self-confidence was torn from her.

Halfway across the line, she could not retreat. The part of her body that lay within the spell circle was frozen in place as if shackled. She had no choice but raise her other leg and enter fully, though to do so now terrified her beyond thought.

Helplessness acquired new meaning. Her ears heard no sound, and her eyes saw nothing but the shimmering golden web of force. She was physically unable to move, or sit, or clasp her arms close about her chest to quell the thump of her fast-beating heart. Slavery itself seemed a freedom, before the magic that ringed her into confinement; her very thoughts were held prisoner. Mara fought despair, even as someone high up in the galleries called down a question.

The Kaliane repeated the query in the Tsurani language. "Lady of the Acoma, you have come here asking for power. You claim you will use it to defend, to aid the common good. Show us how you came to hold this belief."

Mara tried to draw breath to answer, and found she could not. Her body would not answer her desire; magic held her from speech. Panic drove her to anger. How could she defend her intentions if the spell prevented her from speaking? The next moment she discovered that her thoughts had also escaped her control. Her mind seemed to overturn, then to spin like a pinwheel toy made for a child's amusement. Memories sifted past her inward eye, and she was no longer in the chamber of the magicians in Dorales, within any magical circle. She was seated in her study in the old Acoma estates, arguing hotly with Kevin the barbarian.

The illusion of his presence was so real that the tiny part of Mara's mind that retained separate self-awareness longed to take shelter in his arms. In dawning trepidation, she realized the intent of the Thuril truth spell: that she would not be permitted to answer any inquiries verbally.

These mages would ask, and take their answers directly from her experience. She would be given no chance to justify, to reconcile the outcome of any event with explanations. These magicians would observe her actions as they happened, and then judge. She was in fact put on trial, her only defense the acts that comprised her past life.

Mara realized this much in the instant before the spell claimed her wholly, and she *was* in the study on that long-past day with Kevin, facing him in heated anger as he cried, "You push me about like a chess . . . shāh pawn! Here! There! Now here again, because it suits you, but never one word of why, and never one second of warning! I've done as you've bid—not for love of you, but to save the lives of my countrymen."

Then Mara herself replying, in red-faced exasperation: "But I gave you promotion to slave master and allowed you charge of your Midkemian companions. You used your authority to see them comfortable. I see they have been eating jigabird and needra steak and fresh fruits and vegetables along with their thyza mush."

On the memory played, as real as the moment it happened, even to its ending in a flushed entanglement of passion. Mara knew a wrenching moment of disorientation as, one encounter after another, her relationship with Kevin unfolded, each day bittersweet with joys and frustrations, and difficult lessons. Forced to see again in retrospect, she recognized her own narrow-minded arrogance; how miraculous it was that Kevin the slave had seen anything in her apparent hard-heartedness to love and nurture at all! The days unreeled in staggering jumps as the magicians manipulated her recall. Again she endured the horrors as wave after wave of assassins were repulsed from her town apartments on the Night of the Bloody Swords. Again she stood on a butana-whipped hilltop and exchanged words with Tasaio of the Minwanabi. She saw the Emperor Ichindar break the staff of the Warlord's power, her assumption of the title Servant of the Empire.

Again she saw Ayaki die.

There followed another question, mercifully, and the scene changed to the fragrant noon heat of a kekali garden where Arakasi abased himself before her, begging leave to take his own life. Again she shared the scented, dry evening air in Lord Chipino's command tent on campaign against the desert men in Tsubar.

Time whirled, turned, backtracked; and scene overlaid scene. Sometimes she was sent back into childhood, or to the silent halls of meditation in Lashima's temple. Other times she suffered the brutality of her first husband. Again she faced his grieving father, over the wrapped bundle of a grandson, now dead also, by equally treacherous means.

Wrenchingly, she shared afresh her relationship with Hokanu, and his uncannily accurate understanding. Through the eyes of the Thuril magicians, she came to realize that his rare perceptions were in fact an unfledged aspect of talent. A near miss of fate might have seen him a member of the Assembly, rather than as husband at her side. How much poorer her life would have been without him, she realized. A part of her heart ached for the distance grown between them, and between the manipulations of the truth spell, she vowed she would remedy the misunderstanding that lingered since Kasuma's birth.

Lastly, Mara saw herself in Hotaba's long house, delivering a flat refusal to trade her servant Kamlio for freedom to pursue her business in Thuril. A probe like a needle pierced her, but found only sincerity in her heart.

The spell's reel of memories lagged for a stretch, and words leaked through, spoken by she knew not whom. They were in Thuril but understanding of their meaning came to her.

Said one voice, ''She is indeed different from other Tsurani: to see honor in a slave, and to recognize the rights to freedom of a servant, even above her blood family.''

And the Kaliane, replying: ''I believed so, or I would not have brought her.''

Upon the heels of that first thought came, ''Yet do we concern ourselves with Tsurani well-being?''

Another voice of the mind answered, ''Justly governed neighbors are to be desired, and perhaps . . .''

Yet another mind spoke. ''But there is an opportunity to put right the great wrong . . .''

More words that seemed to blur together; someone mentioned risk, and someone else spoke of the cho-ja empire.

Mara's hearing faded. She felt suddenly weak in the knees. And then the golden ring of light that held her imprisoned melted away, and she felt herself collapse.

The Kaliane's strong hands caught her. ''Lady, it is over.''

Weak as a baby, and shamed to discover she had been crying in the throes of the spell, Mara fought to recover from the shambles of her composure. ''Have I convinced you?''

''No. That will be argued through the night,'' the Kaliane admitted. ''Word of our decision will reach you at dawn. For now I will return you to Mirana, who will see you are given a chance to rest.''

''I would prefer to wait here,'' Mara protested, but she lacked the will to resist. Strength left her, and she knew no more beyond darkness like the night between stars.

21. Decision

Mara awakened.

It was dark; she breathed in the scent of burning beech logs, and the mustier odor of querdidra wool. There were wooden rafters over her head, faintly picked out of shadow by the weak red light from the hearth. Blankets covered her. They constricted her limbs as she rolled over, puzzled as to her whereabouts.

Her head ached. Memory of events returned slowly, and then in a rush, as she saw the basket of carding Mirana had carried from the long house and the council with her Thuril husband. Now Mara remembered the excursion to the bread shop, and the dreamlike visit to Dorales in the company of the Kaliane. Suddenly stifled by the dark warmth and the blankets, she pushed herself erect.

"Lady?" ventured an uncertain voice from the shadows.

Mara turned, to see Kamlio's oval face, alert and watchful with concern. "I am all right, little flower," she murmured back, unthinkingly using Lujan's nickname.

This time Kamlio did not flinch at the diminutive. Instead she shed her own bedclothes, and prostrated herself in abject abasement against the sanded boards of the floor.

Mara was not flattered but disturbed, though servants and slaves had made such gestures to her lifelong. Such was the Tsurani way, to give total loyalty to please one's master. However, after the experience in the golden spell circle, the tradition left Mara sickened. "Get up, Kamlio. Please."

The girl did not move, but her shoulders spasmed under her river of pale hair. "Lady," she said miserably, "why did you set me before your very family? Why? I am not worth so much, surely, that you could not trade me to these Thuril to keep your children safe."

Mara sighed, bent her tired back, and caught Kamlio's outstretched wrists. She tugged, ineffectively because she was left weak from the truth spell. "Kamlio, please, arise. My concern for my children is paramount, truly, but the life of another free individual is not mine to bargain with, even for my loved ones' survival. You have not taken my honor for your own; you are not obligated to House Acoma.''

Kamlio allowed herself to be coaxed upright. Swathed in a night robe borrowed from the Thuril that was overlarge for her slender curves, she crouched on the edge of her cot. Her eyes were deep as pits in the dimness. Mara saw they sat in what must be Mirana's sewing room, by the loom frame tucked in one corner, and crates of cloths strewn about. She was still trying to reorient her nerves from the trauma of reliving the past brought on by the truthespell when the ex-courtesan spoke.

''Arakasi,'' Kamlio said in halting and pitiful certainty. ''You did this for him.''

Weary to the bone, but compassionate, Mara shook her head. ''I did nothing of the sort for Arakasi—though he has sacrificed again and again for my family.''

Kamlio did not look convinced. Mara twisted a fold of blanket around her shoulders, and perched on the edge of her own cot, facing the girl. ''You are not in any way indebted to my Spy Master.'' The Lady of the Acoma gestured emphatically. ''I'll repeat this if I must until you are old and deaf, or until you see fit to believe me.''

Silence followed Mara's stab at humor. The coals in the hearth hissed against the whistle of wind around the eaves. In the Thuril uplands, the breezes played endlessly, dying out only at dawn. The hour of the night could not be determined, but the fact that in Dorales the magicians and the Kaliane yet debated upon their decision played upon Mara's nerves. She focused upon Kamlio's troubles to stave off her own worries.

''Arakasi,'' the ex-courtesan repeated, a frown marring her forehead. ''Whatever does he see in me? He is clever enough, surely, to win any woman to his bed.''

Mara considered carefully. ''I can only offer conjecture,'' she ventured at length. ''But I believe he sees his salvation in you. A healing, if you will, for certain of life's disappointments. And I equally suppose that he wishes to give you in return what he could not give his own family: happiness, security, and a love neither bought nor bargained for.''

''You found such a love with Hokanu,'' Kamlio observed, her tone spiked with accusation.

Mara forced herself not to feel ruffled. ''Partly. In Hokanu I found near-perfect understanding. He has been my spirit's companion. In another man I found the love that I believe one such as you might discover in Arakasi. As to any other woman sharing our Spy Master's bed, I avow not—I honestly do not know his appetites and passions—but he is not a man who shares his feelings or his affections easily. Arakasi offers you a very solemn trust, and would never have done so, as reticent as he is wont to be, if he did not first believe you worthy.''

''You sound as though you admire him,'' said Kamlio.

''I do.'' Mara paused in recognition of this truth. ''For a man of formidable cleverness, who lived his life as a grand game of strategy, I would guess it took great courage to take the step to acknowledge compassion. Though one who knew always where he stood, able to second-guess most of the moves of his fellows, Arakasi now is like a sailor adrift upon an unknown sea. He must draw his own chart to see his way back to familiar harbor. He has thrown away competence for self-discovery. For one such as he, it must be as frightening an undertaking as any he could imagine. But I have never seen him run from a challenge, even those that other men would consider impossible.'' Looking for a moment into the girl's eyes, Mara added, ''These words make a poor substitute for the experience of knowing the man himself.''

Kamlio digested this information slowly. Her small hands worried at her robe, twisting the fabric into wrinkles. ''I cannot love him,'' she admitted, the words wrung from her as cruelly by circumstance as she herself treated the hapless cloth, ''nor any man, I think. His hands once gave me pleasure, true enough, but bed sport for me is an empty pastime.'' Her eyes seemed unfocused in distant memory. ''I grew to hate the hour of sundown, when my master would come to me.'' She paused, then added bitterly, ''There were times when I felt like a performing dog. Fetch this robe. Rub this place. Turn this way.'' Looking again to Mara, she said, ''There is nothing of feeling or love in knowing a man's body, Lady, for one such as me.'' She lowered her eyes. ''I confess, the real attraction in taking a younger lover was in the danger. Arakasi brought me to pleasure, Lady, because he risked death to do so.'' Moisture gathered in her eyes. ''Gods, Lady, do you see what a twisted thing I've become? There were whole months when I considered suicide, except that I felt too low, too honorless, to sully a blade with my blood.''

Tsurani pride, Mara thought. She longed to reach out and reassure the tortured girl; except that to Kamlio, touch of any sort upon her body was divorced from emotional contact. Though words alone seemed cold, Mara had no other comfort to offer. ''Arakasi understands this far better than you think.'' She waited a moment for this to sink in.

Thoughtfully, Kamlio nodded. ''It is true that he did not once try to touch me since the hour he bought my freedom. Since you told me he was a reedwoman's son, I realize why. But at the time, I was too furious over the death of my sister to notice.''

Mara took this for encouragement. "If you cannot love him, be his friend instead. He has a lively intellect, and piercing wit."

Kamlio looked up, her eyes sparkling with held-back tears. "He would settle for so little from me?"

"Try him." Mara smiled. "Love doesn't demand; it accepts. It has taken me my life to learn this." Lowering her voice, she added, "And the gift of two exceptional men." Looking at Kamlio directly, she took on a conspiratorial tone. "I have seen nothing, and no man living, who was capable of shaking Arakasi's nerve. The challenge of your friendship might teach him some much needed humility."

Kamlio flung back her glorious hair, her expression turned impish. "Are you implying I could get back at him for his presumption where I am concerned?"

"I am thinking you could learn from each other," Mara finished. Then she glanced around the room. "But that depends upon us returning from these highlands alive."

Kamlio's brief happiness drained away. "They could force you to trade me."

Mara's insistence came back whip-crack sharp. "No. I am a Lady, and Tsurani. I stand by my word. Your life is not mine to bargain away. Either I win my requests upon my own merits, or I face whatever fate the gods intend. If it comes to your continued captivity, Kamlio, hear now that I give you my blessing to take your own life by the blade or to escape into freedom as you can; you are a free woman. Let there be no question that your blood or your desires are any less honorable than Lujan's, or Saric's, or those of any other warrior of my honor guard." Suddenly overwhelmed by how tired she was, Mara stifled a yawn behind her blankets. "But I do not think things will come to that. The later events of my evening cause me to surmise that Hotaba's offer was a test. My test. If I won any concessions, we will not know until the morning. Sleep now, Kamlio. For the rest of this night, we can only wait patiently on the outcome."

Daybreak, and the silence as the winds stilled, found both Lady and courtesan sleeping. Mara lay curled in a tangle of black hair, the blankets twined tightly around her shoulders from restless dreams. She started upright on a sharp intake of breath at the touch of Mirana's hand.

"Lady, arise and dress quickly," softly urged the chieftain's wife. "The Kaliane has returned to announce the decision made in Dorales."

Mara threw herself out of the cot and gasped at the chill in the air. The hearthfire had gone out during the night. While she pulled on her ice-cold robes, Mirana rebuilt the blaze with kindling, so that Kamlio might wake up in better comfort. The crack in the shutter showed grey. Clouds or mist obscured the sunrise, and Mara felt stiff in her joints.

There were silver hairs caught in her comb as she finished making herself tidy. Her heart beat too fast in apprehension, and her thoughts circled again and again back to home, and the children, and Hokanu. Would she ever regain the chance to repair her marriage? Gods, she prayed, let me not die on foreign soil. Let Kamlio return home for Arakasi.

For the first time where the girl was concerned, Mara saw hope in the doomed tie to her Spy Master. Thuril captivity had shaken the child from bitter cynicism, made her reexamine her self-worth and those bits of her life that were now her own to control.

"Hurry," Mirana urged quietly, so as not to wake Kamlio. "The Kaliane is not known for patience."

Mara laced her cold feet into her sandals, the leather worn thin now, and stretched out from wetness and sliding on the shale of the mountain paths. One of the toes was frayed out. Who in the Empire would recognize her for the Good Servant, with her face unpainted, and her robes as plain as a pot girl's? Rising and walking out the door to meet the Kaliane without even token appearance of her rank took a shameful amount of courage.

Mara strove without success to feign unconcern. But her palms were sweating and her hands trembled, and she had to be grateful to the horrid, clammy mist for hiding the moisture in her eyes.

Her memories brought back within the golden circle troubled her more than she cared to admit. Were Kevin here, he would have commented in atrocious humor, even in so tense a moment. Mara missed his irreverent sense of mistiming that chiding had never managed to correct. Long before she was ready, she found herself chivvied by Mirana into the wide main square, where the tatterdemalion person of Hotaba awaited, along with a figure hunched under layers of robes whose person emanated presence more awesome than the Emperor's.

Mara swallowed her pride and bowed low. "I await the Kaliane's decision," she murmured.

Old, clawed hands tugged her erect. "Lady, stand upright. Here obeisance is an insult." The Kaliane regarded the Acoma Lady with a stare as piercing as the bit of glass Jican used to magnify questionable guild seals to check their authenticity. "Lady Mara," said the enchantress in her dry crone's voice, "our decision has been made. We have decided to support your cause in this way: you will be granted permission to journey, along with the one of your company that you designate. You will be shown through the high passes, to the gates of Chakaha, the cho-ja city wherein dwell their masters of magic.''

Mara's eyes widened. The Forbidden! she thought to herself. If cho-ja could breed mages, and the ''treaty'' with the Assembly forbade them to practice within the borders of Tsuranuanni, much of the cho-ja Queen's reticence was explained. Her excitement mounted.

The Kaliane seemed to sense this, for her next words were stern. ''Lady Mara, know that the cause of the Tsurani people is not our cause. Thuril made war only when our lands were invaded. We do not hold it to be our duty to concern ourselves with the politics of an enemy nation. However, the cho-ja may see their part differently. Their people within Tsurani borders are a captive nation. You will be given your chance to be heard by them, and to win their alliance if you may. But be warned: the cho-ja hive will view you as an enemy. Our people can conduct you in safety to the hive's borders and no farther. We cannot act as your spokesman. Neither can we intervene to spare you if the cho-ja receive you with enmity. Understand me clearly: you could die for your good intentions.''

This was an uncertain step forward, Mara assessed in the split second that followed, but a step nonetheless. Clearly she said, ''I have no choice. I must go. I will take Lujan, my Force Commander, and in his absence, my adviser Saric will captain my honor guard.''

The Kaliane's eyes flickered with what might have been guarded admiration, or maybe pity. ''You have courage,'' she admitted, and then sighed. ''You also do not know what you face. But very well. Be assured that your servants and warriors will be shown the hospitality of guests until your fate is known. If you return, they will be restored to you. If you die, they will bear your remains back to your homeland. So say I, the Kaliane.''

Mara inclined her head to seal her agreement that these arrangements were satisfactory.

''Well,'' Mirana snapped from the sidelines, ''husband, are you going to stand there gaping in disappointment because you could not wrest away the gold-haired lass for our son, or are you going to go to the soldiers' compound and roust out Force Commander Lujan?''

''Shut up, old woman! The peace of the dawn is sacred, and you profane life itself with your noise.'' He squared his shoulders and glared, until the Kaliane cast him a glance of disapproval. Then he hurried off at a shuffling, comical run on the errand as his wife had bidden him.

As he vanished, the Kaliane gathered her robes against the streaming mist. To Mara she said, "You will leave as soon as supplies can be gathered for your journey. You will go on foot, as the uplands are too rough for other conveyance." She paused, as if assessing some inward thought, then added, "Gittania, one of our acolytes, will act as your guide through the passes. May the gods smile upon your efforts, Lady Mara. It is no easy task you have set for yourself, for the cho-ja are a fierce race with a memory that does not readily allow forgiveness."

An hour later, following a hot meal, Mara and her one-man delegation were ready to set off. A small crowd of noisy children and idle house matrons, headed by Hotaba and his council, gathered to see them off. They were joined by the acolyte Gittania, who proved to be a slight, mousy-haired girl who looked lost in the voluminous folds of the cloak of her order, a knee-length garment woven in blinding patterns of red upon white. She had flushed cheeks, a sharp nose, and an irrepressible smile. Where the sober, broken colors of Thuril plaids tended to blend with the landscape, Gittania's garb would mark her like a target.

Lujan was quick to comment upon this. "Perhaps," he philosophized in rare reflection, "she wears her gaudiness like those birds or berries that are poison, a warning that her magical powers bring retribution to any who might attack her."

Although he spoke quietly, the acolyte heard him. "Actually not, warrior. We who take vows as apprentices are marked apart because we wish to be seen. For the years of our learning, we are bound to serve any man or woman who needs assistance. The cloaks serve as badges of recognition, that we may be easily found."

Huddled against the streaming mist, Mara asked, "How many years do your kind apprentice to the masters?"

Gittania gave back a rueful grin. "Some, up to twenty-five years. Others never reach passage, and wear the white and scarlet for life. The youngest master on record held apprenticeship for seventeen years. He was a prodigy. His accomplishment has stood unbettered for a thousand years."

"The requirements of your peers are tasking indeed," Lujan observed. Since war was a young man's trade, he could hardly contemplate the patience it must take to spend half a lifetime in study.

Yet Gittania did not seem resentful of such arduous standards. "A master wields great power, and with it, tremendous responsibility. His years as an acolyte teach temperance, patience, and, above all, humility, and provide time to develop wisdom. When one has tended sick babies at the bequest of every herder mother in the fells, one learns in time that the small things count for as much as, or perhaps more than, the great affairs of rulership and politics.'' Here the girl paused for a saucy, side-long grin. ''At least, of this my elders assure me. My years are too few yet to understand the significance of a baby's rash in all the great turnings of the universe.''

Tired as she was, Mara laughed. Gittania's outgoing honesty was a pleasant change after Kamlio's difficult moods and sullen bitterness. Although the Lady had fears enough concerning the outcome of her forth-coming encounter with the Thuril cho-ja, she looked forward to the journey as a time to settle her worn nerves, and to contemplate how she would handle her audience with a strange cho-ja Queen. Gittania's blithe humor would certainly be a balm to ease the strain.

The Kaliane had silently observed the conversation, while the bundles of food and waterskins were made ready on the back of a querdidra. ''The cho-ja are secretive, untrusting,'' she confided in last minute counsel. ''Once this was not so. Their masters and ours mingled freely, exchanging ideas and knowledge. In fact, much of our foundational training as mages derives from cho-ja philosophies. But the war centuries ago between cho-ja and Tsuranuanni taught the creatures that men with power can be treacherous. Since then the hives have been reticent, and contact reluctant to nonexistent.'' She moved to stand before Mara, and said, ''I do not know what you will face, Good Servant. But I warn you one last time: Tsurani are anathema to these cho-ja. They do not forgive what has happened to their counterpart hives across the border, and they may well hold you accountable as if you had been the very one who forced the treaty upon them.''

At Mara's expression of surprise, the Kaliane reacted sternly. ''Believe me, Lady Mara. Cho-ja *do not forget,* and to them good does not tolerate the presence of repression or evil. Right-thinking men, they would say, would have dissolved the so-called treaty that forbids Tsurani cho-ja their rights to magic. Each day that passes without such remission keeps the crime fresh; to them the insult of centuries past is as one committed this moment. In the hives of Thuril, you might find no ally against your Assembly, but only a swift death.''

Sobering the words might be, but Mara was not deterred. ''Not to go is to embrace defeat.'' With a nod to Lujan and a wave to Gittania to indicate her readiness, she faced the town gates.

From behind, Kamlio watched her mistress's departure with wide eyes. Mara had captured her admiration. Had the Lady looked back, she might have seen the ex-courtesan's lips move in a vow that, should any of the Acoma party survive to return to the Acoma estates, she would give the Lady what she so plainly hoped: an attempt to be friends with Arakasi. Kamlio bowed her head as Mara became lost to view and Lujan's plumes disappeared in the mists. She swore her oath, humbled that the fears that seemed overwhelming to her had little substance when compared with the dangers that Mara strode to meet with straight back and raised chin, and no sign at all of trepidation.

The journey through the Thuril high pass proved an arduous trail. After one day's travel, the terrain steepened; gorse-covered highlands reared up into rocky outcrops scoured clean of moss by wind. The sun seemed always scudded over by clouds, and the valleys, swathed in streamers of mists that twined over the courses of becks and streams. Mara managed the stony footing with difficulty, helped over the rougher patches by Lujan's steadying hand. Her sandals became scuffed on the shale, and she had no breath to spare for talk.

Gittania seemed as untroubled by the territory as the querdidra billy they brought to carry their supplies and bedding. She chattered almost constantly. From her comments as they passed by this valley or that, which sheltered its little village or cluster of herders' hamlets, Mara learned more about Thuril life. The highlanders were a fierce race, wedded inseparably to their independence, but contrary to the opinion held by most Tsurani, they were not warlike.

"Oh, our young men play at battle," Gittania allowed, leaning during a rest break upon the tall herder's staff she used to steady her walking. Lujan also guessed she knew how to use it as a weapon, if it did not also serve as a staff for magic. But that assumption was shattered when Gittania accidentally broke the wood and, without ceremony, bought another stick from a man who trained herd dogs. Now her fingers ran up and down, stripping off the rough bark that might give blisters. "But raids, fighting, these are things young men do to gain the skills to steal their wives. A few boastful ones venture into imperial lands. Most do not return. If they are caught, and fight, they have broken the treaty and are outlaws." Her face darkened as she said the last.

Mara recalled the captives condemned to die as sport for Tsurani nobles in the arena, and was shamed. Did any of the games masters who staged such atrocities have a clue that the men they sent out to duel were just boys who might have first committed no worse a mistake than a prank? Had any imperial warrior or official ever troubled to question the ones who strayed across the border, naked and painted as if for war? Sadly, she thought not.

Gittania seemed not to notice the Lady's melancholy contemplation. She gestured with her staff over the scrub-covered valley, dotted, here and there, with the querdidra herds bred for cheese and wool. "Mostly we are a nation of traders and herdsmen. Our soil is largely too poor to farm, and our strongest industry is weaving. The dyes, of course, are very costly, imported as they are from your warmer lowlands, and from Tsubar."

Gittania chided herself for her rambling talk, and urged Mara and Lujan to set off once again. The pace she set was brisk. Days were shorter in the uplands, where the high crowns of the hills pushed the sunsets earlier. The place where at last they made camp was in a hollow between two rock-crowned knolls. A stream gushed from a spring there, and short, wind-stunted trees offered shelter.

"Wrap well in your blankets," Gittania urged as she and Mara scoured the dinner utensils clean in the icy water. "Nights get cold in these highlands. Even in summer, there can be an occasional frost."

Morning saw leaves and grass etched in a silvery patina of ice crystals. Mara marveled at their intricate patterns, and admired the fragile beauty as a chance ray of sun fired the edges like gilt. Barren this land might be, but it had a wild grace all its own.

The trail steepened. More and more, Lujan had to assist Mara in the climb, as his studded battle sandals gained better purchase than hers, which were soled in plain leather. The roof of the clouds seemed close enough to touch, and the querdidra herds thinned, forage being too sparse to sustain them. Here the splash and tumble of spring-fed streams formed the sole sound, beyond the whip and moan of the wind.

The pass itself was a winding ledge that snaked between steep, slate faces that glistened black where water seeped from the earth. Mara gulped deep breaths of the thin air, and commented on the strange, sharp smell that seemed to ride the gusts.

"Snow," Gittania explained, her cheeks nipped red by the chill, and her smile the warmer by contrast. She tugged her scarlet-and-white sleeves down over her hands for comfort, and added, "Were the clouds thinner, you might see ice on the peaks. Not a sight you Tsurani are accustomed to, I'll warrant."

Mara shook her head, too breathless to speak. Hardier than she, Lujan said, "There are glaciers in the great range we call the High Wall. Wealthy lords in the northern provinces are said to post runners into the hills to gather rare ice for their drinks. But for myself, I have never seen water harden from the cold.''

''It is a magic of nature,'' Gittania allowed and, seeing Mara's distress, called for another short rest.

The passes fell behind, and the trail descended. On this side of the mountains, the lands were less arid, and the plantlife thorny and leaved in silver grey. By Gittania's explanation, more rain fell here. ''The clouds will thin before long, and then we will be able to see the cho-ja city of Chakaha in the distance.''

No querdidra herds grazed these slopes, the vegetation being too thorny to be edible, but a few families eked out a living by harvesting plant fibers to twist into rope. ''A hard living,'' Gittania allowed. ''The cordage is among the best available for strength and longevity, but this valley is a long, difficult distance from the seaside markets. Carts cannot cross the pass, so all of the haulage must be done by packbeast, or on the backs of strong men.''

It occurred to Mara that the surer-legged cho-ja might handle such a burden over the rugged trails with an ease unmatched by any human, but she was too unsure of what relationship the Thuril hives might share with humans to offer any such suggestion. And then the thought left her mind, for the trail crooked and dipped down, and the clouds thinned and parted to reveal the valley below, spread out like a tapestry beneath a high, pale green Tsurani sky.

''Oh!'' Mara exclaimed, utterly forgetful of protocol. For the sight that greeted her and Lujan was a wonder more overwhelming than even the intricate beauty she had witnessed in Dorales.

The mountains fell away, thorny growth and stony washes descending into a lush, tropical valley. The breezes carried the scent of jungle vines, exotic flowers, and rich earth. Frond trees raised fanlike crowns skyward, and beyond them, more delicate than the gold filigree wrought by the most skilled of the Emperor's jewelers, arose the cho-ja hives.

''Chakaha,'' said Gittania. ''This is the cho-ja's crystal city.''

As if spun from glass, fingerlike spirals rose from pastel domes that sparkled in all colors, like gems in a crown. Rose, aquamarine, and amethyst arches of impossible delicacy spanned the gaps between. Shiny black cho-ja workers, looking like strings of obsidian beads in the distance, scampered across these narrow catwalks. Mara feasted her eyes upon the gossamer, sparkling architecture, and was further astounded. In the air above, winged cho-ja flew. They were not the jet black she was accustomed to, but bronze and blue, with accenting stripes of maroon. ''They are so beautiful!'' she breathed. ''Our Queens in Tsurannuanni birth only black cho-ja. The only color I ever saw was the shade of an immature Queen, and she darkened like the rest with her maturity.''

Gittania sighed. ''Cho-ja magicians are always brilliantly marked. You have none in the Empire because they are forbidden there. To our sorrow, Good Servant, and your everlasting loss. They are wise in their power.''

Mara did not immediately answer, entranced as she was with Chakaha. The glass spires were backed by a blue range of mountains whose tops sparkled white against the sky.

''Ice!'' Lujan surmised. ''There is ice on those peaks. Ah, but I wish Papewaio were here to see this wonder! And Keyoke. The old man will never believe what we saw when we return home to tell him.''

''If you return home,'' Gittania said in uncharacteristic acerbity. She made a shrug of apology to Mara. ''Lady, I may go no farther. You must follow the trail into the valley from here, and seek your way to Chakaha on your own. There will be sentries. They will intercept you long before you reach the crystal gates. Gods go with you, and may they allow you audience with their Queen.'' The acolyte fell awkwardly silent as she reached into her mantle and pulled out a small object, oblong in shape, and heavily dark as obsidian. ''This is a reading stone,'' she explained. ''It carries a record of the memories the Kaliane's council called from you within the golden truth circle. It shows why we granted you passage through our lands, and gives our advice to the hives of Chakaha. The cho-ja magicians can interpret its contents, if they choose.'' She pressed the object into Mara's hands with fingers that were cold with nerves. ''Lady, I hope the memories recorded in the stone will help. The Kaliane spoke of some of them. They form an eloquent testimony on behalf of your cause. Your danger will be in establishing contact, for these cho-ja can kill swiftly.''

''Thank you.'' Mara turned the stone over in her grasp, then tucked it into her robe. Glad that her Force Commander's weapons had been returned, for she disliked the notion of walking unarmed into a potentially hostile camp, Mara took her leave of Gittania. ''Please give your Kaliane my thanks also. With the grace of the gods, and good luck, we will meet again.''

So saying, she nodded to Lujan, and stepped off toward the lush lowland valley where the city of Chakaha awaited. Neither she nor her handsome Force Commander looked back, Gittania saw. That saddened her, because over their three-day march, she had come to like the Good Servant, whose curiosity held so much compassion for others, and whose hope was to change the course of Tsurannuanni's future.

* * *

The trail descended sharply, over stones that were loose underfoot. Lujan steadied his Lady's elbow, and though his touch was sure, Mara still felt the precariousness of their position. Each step forward carried her farther into the unknown.

Brought up in the crowded sprawl of the Acoma estates, accustomed to the throngs of Tsurani cities, and to the presence of servants, slaves, and the numerous officers that made up the households of the noble-born, she could not recall a time in her life when she had been so alone. Her meditation cell in the temple of Lashima had been isolated from others only by the thickness of a wall, and during the most solitary of her evening contemplations at home, a single word would bring servants or warriors instantly to attend upon her needs.

Here there was only the wild sweep of fog-shrouded stone slopes behind, and the jungle ahead, with its indigenous population of cho-ja, whose culture was other than the safe, treaty-bound commerce she knew with the insectoids upon her estates.

Never in her life had she felt herself so small and the world she trod so large. It took all of her will not to turn back, to call after Gittania, and ask to be guided back to Thuril territories, which now did not seem strange or threatening, but simply and understandably human. But back in the Thuril village awaited the rest of her honor guard, and Kamlio, dependent upon her efforts; and linked to them, her family and children and all of the lives upon three sprawling estates answerable to Shinzawai and Acoma. She must not let them down, must secure them haven against the wrath of the magicians to come. Mara faced resolutely forward, and resorted to conversation.

"Lujan, tell me: when you were left the life of a grey warrior, and had no hope for a life of honor, how did you cope?"

Lujan's helm tipped, as he looked askance at her. In his eyes she saw that he, too, sensed the immensity and emptiness of the landscape surrounding them, and that he was Tsurani enough to be uneasy as well with the solitude. How much we have grown to understand each other, Mara thought; how the difficulties of this life have woven our efforts together into a relationship that is special, and cherished. Then his reply stopped her introspection.

"Lady, when a man has lost everything that his peers and fellows consider to be important, when he lives a life that is meaningless by the tenets of his upbringing, then all that is left is his dreams. I was very stubborn. I held to my dreams. And one day I awoke to find that my existence was not all misery. I realized that I could still laugh. I could still feel. Feasting on wild game could still ease my belly, and a tumble with a kind woman could still make my blood race and my spirits soar. An honorless man might suffer in the future when Turakamu took his spirit, and the Wheel of Life ground his fate into dust. But day to day? Honor does not add to joy.'' Here the man who had led the Acoma armies for close to two decades gave an uncomfortable shrug. ''Lady, I was a leader of thieves, brigands, and unfortunates. We as a band might not have had the great honor that house colors may give a man. But we did not live without creed.''

Here Mara could see that her Force Commander was embarrassed to silence. Aware that his discomfort stemmed from an issue that was central to the man himself, and aware, too, that more than curiosity prompted her, she urged gently, ''Tell me. Certainly you realize that I do not hold to traditions for their own sake.''

Lujan gave a small laugh. ''We are alike in that more than you know, my Lady. All right. The men that I led swore a covenant with me. Outcasts though we were, and cast off by the gods, that did not make us less than men. We formed what might be called our own house, swore loyalty to ourselves, and added that what befell one would be shared by all. And so you see, Mara, when you came and were willing to embrace us all in honorable service, we could not have accepted save as a whole. When Pape devised his clever ruse to find distant kinship so that we might be called to Acoma service, had one man been refused, we all would have turned away.''

Mara looked at her Force Commander in surprise, and by the sheepish look in his weathered face, deduced further. ''This covenant you speak of, it still exists.'' She did not ask, but stated.

Lujan cleared his throat. ''It does. But when we swore you our loyalty by the Acoma natami, we added a coda, that our wishes, needs, and honor came second after yours. But within your loyal army there is still a band of us who feel a special kinship to one another, one we cannot share with your other soldiers, no matter how honorable they may be. It is a badge of honor unique to us, as was Papewaio's black band of condemnation his own peculiar accolade.''

''Remarkable.'' Mara fell silent, her eyes downcast as if she negotiated a particularly hazardous step, but the footing was less rocky now, the trail of beaten soil bordered by the first fronds and greenery that edged the jungle. The glass towers of Chakaha had disappeared with the loss of altitude, eclipsed by the dense, high crowns of tropical trees. Their danger was not lessened but increased, and yet Mara spared a moment from worry to ponder what her Force Commander had revealed: that he was a leader born, and that his loyalty was rare and deep; that even after advancement to a high post, he had kept his word with the ruffians turned soldiers that he had once commanded. It was noteworthy, Mara thought, that the man at her side had an inborn sense of himself and his personal responsibilities that ran deeper than in most Lords who ruled in the nations. All this, Lujan had done, without fanfare, without recognition, without even the knowledge of his Lady, until now.

Mara glanced aside at him, and saw his face had resumed the mask of Tsurani inscrutability appropriate to a warrior in house service. She was glad the opportunity had arisen to learn what had passed between them. All that remained to be asked of the gods was the opportunity to ensure that such special qualities and talents that Lujan had revealed might be brought to full flower. If they survived, Mara decided, this was a man who deserved rewards above and beyond the ordinary recognition for exemplary service.

Then her thought was interrupted by a rustle in the undergrowth. The first of the high trees lay ahead, their trunks ancient and wide enough that five men with linked hands would have difficulty girdling their circumference. As their deep shade fell chillingly over Mara and Lujan, a ring of cho-ja sentinels arose seemingly out of nowhere, silent, shiny-black, and naked but for their natal armor of polished chitin. Bladed forearms were turned outward at an aggressive angle.

Lujan jerked Mara to a stop. His second, instinctive movement to thrust her behind him and away from the danger and then to draw his sword was checked, as he saw that they were surrounded. These cho-ja wore none of the humanlike accoutrements of rank that their counterparts in the Nations affected, and they moved in uncanny silence.

For a moment, the two human invaders and the insectoid sentinels stood motionless.

Mara was first to break the tableau, giving the full bow an envoy might use to greet a foreign delegation. "We come in peace."

Her words were punctuated by a snap as in unison the sentinels raised forearms to guard position. One among them advanced a half-step, its face plates unreadable. These cho-ja of Chakaha made no effort to mimic human expressions, and the result left Mara uneasy. These foreign insectoids might attack and butcher them both where they stood, and not even Lujan's fast eye might detect the signal that started the slaughter.

"We come in peace," she repeated, this time unable to keep the tremble from her voice.

For a drawn-out moment, nothing moved. Over the drone of insects in the jungle, Mara thought she detected the high-pitched buzzing she had earlier experienced in the chamber of the Queen who inhabited her home estate. But the sound ended before she could be certain.

Then the one who had stepped ahead, and who might be classified as their Strike Leader, spoke out. "You are from the Empire, human. Peace to your kind is but a prelude to treachery. You are trespassers. Turn and go, and live."

Mara sucked in a shaky breath. "Lujan," she said in a tone she hoped sounded convincing, "disarm yourself. Show that we mean no harm by surrendering your blade to these whom we would call friends."

Her Force Commander raised his arm to follow her order, although she could see by his tension that he disliked the idea of giving up what small defense he might offer her.

But before he could set hand to sword grip, he heard the snap, snap as the cho-ja left guard position and angled their weight forward to charge. Their spokesman said, "Touch your sword, man, and you both die."

To this, Lujan jerked up his chin in a flushed blaze of anger. "Kill us, then!" he half-shouted. "But I say that if you do so, when my intent is to surrender, you are cowards all. With my sword, or without it, at your first charge we are dead." Here he glanced at Mara, asking unspoken permission.

His mistress returned a stiff nod. "Disarm," she repeated. "Show that we are friends. If attack follows, then our mission is wasted effort anyway, for the Lady of the Acoma and the Servant of the Empire does not treat with a race of murderers."

Slowly, deliberately, Lujan reached for his sword. Mara watched, running with sweat, as his hand touched, then closed over the weapon hilt.

The cho-ja did not move. Perhaps above the drone of the insects, their buzzing communication gave them discourse with their Queen, but Mara could not tell. Her ears were numbed by nerves and the fast, loud pound of her heart.

"I will draw and set my sword upon the ground," Lujan said tightly. He kept his movements careful, and seemed outwardly confident, but Mara could see the drops of perspiration sliding down his jawline beneath his helm as, ever so slowly, he drew the sword from the scabbard, took hold of the blade with bare left hand so that his intent not to fight could not possibly be mistaken, and placed the weapon point toward himself upon the earth.

Mara saw the cho-ja shift their weight forward as one, a movement she had seen before. In another second they would charge, despite her pleading for peace. As loud as she could make them, she mimicked the sounds of greetings she had learned from the hive Queen upon her estates, a poor human attempt at the clicks and snaps made by the cho-ja throat.

Instantly the cho-ja stood like statues, frozen a heartbeat away from murder. Yet when Lujan's sword rested upon the ground, and he straightened, defenseless, their postures did not ease.

Neither did the leader of their party speak out. Instead, a great gust of air arose, lashing Mara's hair into disarray, and causing Lujan to squint through watering eyes. Down through the canopy of jungle descended a cho-ja form, leanly streamlined and brilliantly striped. It possessed an unearthly beauty that was somehow almost dangerous, and above neatly folded limbs its seemingly delicate weight was suspended upon crystalline wings that beat up a storm of wind.

A cho-ja magician had come!

Mara drew breath to exclaim in involuntary delight, but her throat gave voice to no sound. The air around her seemed to shimmer suddenly, and the forms of the cho-ja advance guard shattered into patternless color. Her feet lost contact with the ground, and Lujan's presence became lost to her. There were no trees, no jungle, no sky; nothing at all could her senses detect that was familiar, but a chaos of whirling light.

She found her voice, and her cry became one of terror. "What are you doing to us?"

A reply boomed back from nowhere, echoing in her mind. "Enemies who surrender become prisoners," the voice admonished.

And then all of Mara's perception drowned in a great tide of darkness.

22. Challenge

Mara awoke.

Her last memory of open air, and lush jungle, and a patrol of cho-ja sentinels did not mesh with her present surroundings: a narrow, hexagonal chamber of windowless, featureless walls. The floor was of polished stone, the ceiling fashioned of a mirrorlike substance that threw back the light of the single cho-ja globe that drifted unsupported at the chamber's center.

Mara raised herself on her elbows, then her knees, and discovered that Lujan stood behind her, awake, and visibly battling against a restless bout of nerves.

"Where are we?" asked the Lady of the Acoma. "Do you know?"

Her Force Commander spun to face her, pale with anger only barely held in check. "I don't. The where hardly matters, though, because we are being held as enemies of the city-state of Chakaha."

"Enemies?" Mara accepted Lujan's hand to help her rise; she noticed his scabbard was empty, which partially explained his edginess. "We were brought here by means of magic, then?"

Lujan raked back sweat-damp hair, then from habit tightened the strap that secured his helm. "Magic must have conveyed us from the glen. And only magic can secure our release. If you look around, you will see there is no door."

Mara quickly checked. The walls arose sheer and smooth, unbroken by any sort of portal. At a loss to account for the freshness of the air, the Lady deduced that the chamber must be entirely wrought of cho-ja spellcraft.

The conclusion made her tremble.

She was no longer dealing with humans, who might by their nature share some empathy. Cold with foreboding, Mara knew she and Lujan had become embroiled in the unknowns of the hive mind. More than ever, she was confronted by the incomprehensibility of an alien species whose "memory" and "experience" spanned millennia, and whose framework of reason would be judged only by collective prosperity and survival.

Worse, unlike the hive she had conversed with inside the Empire's borders, these free, foreign cho-ja had never been forced to coexist with
humanity except on terms they chose. There would not be even the
imperfect understanding she shared with the Queen with whom she exchanged companionship over the years.

Lujan sensed his Lady's despair. "We are not without hope, my Lady.
These are civilized creatures who hold us captive. They must be disin-
clined to kill out of hand, or we would have died on the trail."

Mara sighed, and did not voice her following thought: that if they were
adjudged enemies, it was not for their individual deeds, but for the
actions of all Tsurani over every age of history. The past records of
sincere treaties broken by bloody betrayals were too numerous to count,
and within Mara's lifetime, the tenets of the Game of the Council had
many times caused sons to kill fathers, and clansmen to rend clansmen.
Her own hands were far from clean.

Her first husband's ritual suicide had been manipulated by her; so even
if the hive mind were to measure her by the acts she alone had authored,
contradiction would be found in abundance—between the vows she had
sworn in marriage, and the hatred she had held in her heart for Jiro's
brother; and in her betrayal of Kevin, the barbarian she loved, then sent
away against his will, ignorant she carried his child. It occurred to her, as
she bit her lip to keep back tears born of shame, that it was not the cho-ja
way to learn by mistakes, for all of the errors made by ancestors were
available to living memory. They were a race for whom the past did not
fade. Forgiveness for them would not be the ever renewable resource it
was for humankind—grudges might be kept for millennia.

"Lujan?" The echo of Mara's voice in that confined chamber was
hollow with fear. "Whatever should become of us in the end, we must
find a way to be heard!"

Her Force Commander spun in a frustrated circle. "What is left to do
for you, Lady, but to pound on these walls with my fists?"

Mara heard the desperation he tried to mask behind bravado. His
distress sobered her; ever since leaving the *Coalteca,* nothing of Lujan's
training as a warrior had served him. He had held no army to command.
The day the Thuril first arose in ambush upon the trail, she had forbidden
him to defend her. At Loso, he had suffered insults that he would have
spilled blood over rather than endure. He had been humiliated, driven in
bonds like a slave, against every instinct of his upbringing. Out of his
depth, separated from his warrior companions, he must find his circumstances incomprehensibly bleak.

Lujan had humor, and cleverness, and courage; but he owned none of Arakasi's detached fascination with the unknown. Sobered to acknowledge the demands she had placed on her Force Commander's loyal spirit, Mara touched his wrist. "Bide patiently, Lujan. For either we are near to our end, or our goal is just within reach."

Striking to the core of her thoughts, Lujan replied, "I feel most worthless, my Lady. You would have done better to bring Arakasi, or to have kept Saric at your side."

Mara attempted humor. "What? Endure Saric's questions, even when the gods themselves impose silence? And Arakasi? Lujan, do you suppose that he could have watched Kamlio led away without flying weaponless in the face of armed guards? Unless, of course, she had clawed him to ribbons on the *Coalteca* before we even saw landfall. No, I do not think I would wish either Saric or Arakasi with me at this time. The gods work as they will. I must trust that fate brought you here for a reason."

The last line was false conviction. In truth, Mara knew only foreboding. Still, her effort had coaxed a quirk of a smile from her officer. His fingers had ceased drumming against his empty scabbard. "Lady," he allowed wryly, "let us pray you are right."

Tedious hours passed, with no daylight in sight to reveal the passage of day to night, and no interruption or sound to break the monotony. Lujan paced the tiny chamber, while Mara sat and unsuccessfully tried to meditate. Tranquil thought evaded her, torn through again and again by longing for her children and husband. She fretted, afraid she would never again have the chance to make peace with Hokanu. Irrational worries gnawed at her: that if she failed to return home, he would marry and beget sons, and little Kasuma might never inherit the legacy that was her due. That Justin might be killed before manhood, and that the Acoma line would fail. That Jiro, with the backing of the Assembly, would topple Ichindar's new order, and the golden throne of the Emperor become relegated to a seat for a slave to religious ceremony. The Warlord's office would be restored, and the Game of the Council resume with all its internecine feuding and bloodshed. Lastly, the cho-ja of the Nations would forever remain bound to subservience through unjust treaty.

Mara's eyes snapped open. A thought occurred, and her heartbeat accelerated. These cho-ja might not be moved by a Tsurani, a sworn enemy—but would they turn their backs upon their fellows in captivity within the Empire? She must make them understand that she, as the only opponent of the Assembly with the rank and influence to threaten them, offered the cho-ja within Tsuranuanni their first hope of change.

"We must find a way to be heard!" Mara muttered, and she joined in step with Lujan's pacing.

More hours passed. Hunger began to trouble them, along with the urgency of bodily needs too long denied.

To this last, Lujan remarked wryly. "Our captors might at least have equipped our cell with a latrine. If they leave me no better choice, I shall have to shame my upbringing and empty my bladder upon their floor."

Yet before that point of crisis could arise, a flash of intense white light smote the eyes of the Lady and her officer. Blinking against temporary blindness, Mara realized that the walls that held them appeared to have dissolved. She had discerned no moment of disorientation, nor heard any whisper of sound; and yet whatever spell of release had been keyed, she found herself no longer confined. Had their prison been an elaborate illusion, she wondered. Daylight fell through a high, transparent dome tinted soft purple. She and Lujan stood at the center of a patterned floor, the tiles fashioned of glass, or precious stones, and laid with a breathtaking artistry. The mosaics Mara had seen in the hall of Tsuranuanni's Emperor seemed clumsy as a child's scrawls by comparison. The beauty might have held her staring in wordless admiration, but a double-file escort of cho-ja warriors prodded her forward.

Frantically, she glanced around for Lujan. He was not with her! She had been mesmerized by the floor, and if he had been led away, she had not seen where. Another prod from her escort sent her stumbling ahead. Leading the column of warriors, she saw a cho-ja with yellow markings on its thorax. By the tools hung in the satchel at its belt, it appeared to be a scribe; and it followed on the heels of another figure of towering height that trailed what Mara had at first presumed to be some sort of gossamer mantle. More careful inspection revealed wings, overlaid in elaborate folds as a lady's train might be. They slid with the faintest of rustles over the polished floor, emitting sparkles of light that danced and died in the air. By the sense of power that chased prickles over her skin, Mara understood she beheld a cho-ja magician up close.

Awe held her tongue-tied. The creature was tall! Built with slender, stilt-like limbs, it moved with a grace that recalled to her Kevin's long-ago description of the elves that inhabited his world of Midkemia. But this alien being owned more than beauty. Its sleek, wide head was crowned with antennae that at times gave off a glow. Its foreclaws were ringed with precious metal, silver and copper and iron. What from a distance had looked like striped markings were actually more intricate, a maze of thread-fine lines that almost seemed to have meaning, like temple runes, or text beyond the ken of human perception. Curiosity warred with Mara's fear, until only uncertainty for her fate held her silent. Upon her rested the future of the Empire and, as had those predecessors named Servant by past Emperors, she felt that responsibility weigh upon her.

She was ushered down a passageway, and through an outer door that let onto a catwalk of dizzying height. It crossed in an arch between two spires, affording a dramatic view of the glass city, its surrounding jungle, and the teeth of the mountain ranges that hemmed the valley around. Mara saw more of the cho-ja magicians in flight over the city's towers, before her escort of warriors hastened her ahead. She was urged across the catwalk, which had no railings but was surfaced with a strange, almost tacky substance for secure footing. The pillared entry at the far end opened into another wide, domed chamber.

Here more cho-ja squatted in a semicircle, these marked similarly to the one she had guessed to be a scribe. Their colors were baffling, accustomed as she was to the unadorned black of the creatures in her own land. She was led into the center of their congress, and there the tall magician swept around and fixed ruby eyes upon her. "Tsurani-human, who are you?"

Mara took a deep breath and forced her voice to sound firm. "I am Mara, Lady of the Acoma and Servant of the Empire. I come to you to plead for—"

"Tsurani-human," the magician interrupted in a sonorous boom. "These before you are the judges that have already convicted you. You are not brought here to plead, as your fate has already been determined."

Mara went rigid as if struck a blow. "Convicted! Of what crime?"

"The crime of your nature. Of being what you are. The actions of your ancestors were your testimony."

"I am to die for what my ancestors did ages past?"

The cho-ja magician ignored the question. "Before your sentence is read, and for the sake of Tsuranuanni, the human-hive-home that birthed you, our custom holds that you shall be granted the right of testament, that your kind not be deprived of such wisdom you choose to impart. You are granted the hours until nightfall to speak. Our scribes will record what you say, and their writings will be sent back to your hive-home in the hands of the Thuril traders."

Mara regarded the patterned features of the cho-ja magician, and rage took her. Like Lujan, she desperately needed to attend to the functions of her body. She could not think with a full bladder, and she could not accept what the magician's short speech had implied, that she was just one member of a hive, and that her permanent absence held no more consequence than knowledge gained or lost.

The ruby depths of the magician's gaze showed no quarter. Argument would be futile, she knew. The bluster that had won her through to audience with the Thuril council would here gain her nothing. Humbled by the feeling that this civilization made her Empire's achievements seem less than the efforts of a human babe to make order in a sandbox, she repressed her desire to shout in frustration at her fate. In the eyes of this race of beings, she was an infant: a dangerous, murderous infant, but a child nonetheless. Well then, she would indulge the curiosity that plagued her! Perhaps there would be inspiration to be gained. Pressed by a white heat of impulse, Mara put aside her concern for her family and country. She gave in to the instincts of a child.

"I have no great legacy of wisdom," she announced in a bold voice. "Instead of giving knowledge, I would ask: in my birth-lands, there is a treaty that holds the cho-ja nation captive. In my land, to speak of it or to impart knowledge of the war that gave rise to its making is forbidden. If the memory of this great battle and the terms of its peacemaking are recalled in Chakaha, I wish to be told of these events. I would ask to know the truth of the past that has condemned me."

A buzzing murmur arose among the tribunal, a sibilance that grew into a cacophony that set Mara's teeth on edge. The cho-ja guard squatted behind her, motionless as though they might hold their position until the end of time. The scribe that stood by the magician twitched once, then shifted its stance as though with uncertainty. The magician itself did not stir, until, suddenly, it raised its wings. Gossamer folds unfurled with a gusty hiss of air, and snapped taut with a crack that silenced the chamber immediately. Mara stared like a peasant shown wonders, noting that the wings connected somehow to the forelimbs and hind limbs of the creature, almost like webbing, but vast as sails. The forelimbs were many-jointed, and extended high overhead until they nearly touched the roof of the dome.

The magician turned on its stilt-like legs. Its now heated gaze swept the stilled tribunal, and as it turned full around, it glared again down at Mara. "You are a curious being," it said.

Mara bowed, though her knees threatened to give out on her. "Yes, Great One."

The cho-ja magician hissed a high-pitched breath of air. "Assign me not the title your kind awards to those perpetrators of treachery, your Assembly."

"Lord, then," Mara rang back. "I offer my humble respect, for the oppression of the Assembly has been mine to suffer also."

A twitter from those assembled arose at this, then stilled. The magician's glare seemed to sear through Mara's skin and touch the core of her thoughts. Swept by a sense of violation, and a moment that rang like fever, or the pain of contact with flame, she cringed and choked back a scream. Then the sensation passed, leaving dizziness. She fought to keep her balance and stay upright.

When her senses cleared, the cho-ja magician was speaking rapidly to the tribunal. "She speaks truth." Its tone had turned musical, perhaps resulting from surprise. "This Tsurani has no knowledge of the doings of her ancestors! How can this be?"

Mara mustered the tatters of her dignity and answered for herself. "Because my kind have no hive mind, no collective memory. We know only that which we experience, or are taught by others, within the span of the days of our lives. Libraries preserve our past history, and these are mere records, subject to the ravages of time, and the limitations set upon them by those factions who set down their contents. Our memories are imperfect. We have no . . ." Then she intoned the click-chuck that the Queen on her land had used to indicate the hive consciousness.

"Silence, Tsurani!" The magician furled its great wings, with a sigh of air currents and a sparkle of light that arose from no visible source. "We are not children. Humans have no hive mind, this we know. The concept is awkward, a thing that ill fits our thought processes. We understand you use libraries and teachers to convey your hive-nations wisdom through the generations."

Mara seized upon what appeared to be a moment of neutrality. "One of your kind once told me that the hive mind of the cho-ja resides with the Queens. What one Queen knows, all experience. But I ask, what happens if a Queen is to die with no successor? What becomes of her workers and her males, and all the individuals that make up hive society?"

The magician clicked its mandibles. "Her subjects have no mind," it allowed. "Should mishap kill a Queen, her rirari, those of her chosen breeding attendants, will behead her survivors out of mercy, for, mindless, they would rove aimlessly and die." It stated this without guilt, the concept of murder being different than that for a human.

"Then," Mara surmised boldly, "they would not forage for food, or sustain themselves to survive?"

"They could not." Metal flashed as the magician made a curt gesture with its forelimb. "They have no purpose beyond the hive. I am no different. The Queen who bred me is all of my guiding directive. I am her eyes, her hands, if you will, and her ears. I am her instrument, even as this tribunal is her arm of judgment. Part of me is conscious, and I may act in independence if it is of benefit to the hive, but all that I am, all that I know, will remain with the hive when this body no longer functions.''

''Well, I offer that we humans are not like cho-ja subjects. Even as do your Queens, we each have our own mind, our own purpose, our own directive for survival. Kill our rulers and Lords, and we will each go on with our affairs. Leave but one child alive, or one man, and he will live out his days according to his own wishes.''

The cho-ja magician seemed bemused. ''We have thought for generations that the Tsurani hive is insane; if it must answer to teeming millions of minds, we know why!''

''That is individuality,'' Mara said. ''I have little of importance to offer the Tsurani nation, as one person. Instead, I repeat my request to know the actions of the ancestors that have caused your tribunal to condemn me without hearing.''

The scribe-like creature at the magician's side peered at Mara and for the first time spoke. ''The telling might take until nightfall, which is all of the time you are allotted.''

''So it must be,'' Mara said, steadier now that she had been able at least to open conversation with these alien cho-ja. Of more immediate concern were the bodily needs that had been denied, and how much longer she must be forced to put them off.

But the cho-ja, after all, were not entirely insensitive. The magician's scribe spoke again. ''Your will shall be granted, along with whatever comforts you may require to keep your ease through the hour of sundown.''

Mara inclined her head in thanks, and then bowed. When she arose, the magician cho-ja had departed, without sound, without ceremony, as if it had melted away into air. The scribe-type cho-ja remained, directing a sudden influx of unmarked workers who were dispatched to attend Mara's needs.

Later, refreshed and fed from a lavish tray of fruits, breads, and cheeses, Mara reclined on fine cushions while, still before the tribunal, she was given the services of a cho-ja orator whose task was to fill in for her those gaps in Empire history that were forbidden within the borders of the Nations.

Relieved of discomforts, Mara waved for the cho-ja orator to begin recitation. While the afternoon spilled purple shadows through the pillared windows, and the sky above the crystal dome deepened toward sundown, she shared a tale of great sorrow, of hives burned by hideous, crackling bolts of magic, and thousands upon thousands of cho-ja subjects mercilessly beheaded by the rirari of slaughtered Queens. She heard tell of atrocities, of eggs stolen, and cho-ja magicians put to useless torture.

Cho-ja in those times had been ill prepared for the realities of an arcanely waged war. They had magic with which to build marvels, magic to adorn nature with the beauty of intelligent artifice, and magic to bring fortune and favorable weather. In such peaceful arts, the insectoid mages held the accumulated wisdom of centuries, and the oldest among them had carapaces whorled and stippled with the patterns of a million spells.

Here Mara dared an interruption. "Do you mean that the markings on your mages are badges of experience?"

The orator bobbed its head. "Indeed, Lady. Over time they become so. Each spell that they master becomes inscribed in colors upon their bodies, and the greater their powers, the more complex are their markings."

The orator went on to emphasize that the cho-ja mages from the era of the Golden Bridge held no spells for warlike violence. They could cast beneficial wards to protect, but these were no match for the aggressive magic of the Assembly. The wars involving magic were not battles but massacres. The treaty that bound the cho-ja of the Nations to subservience had been submitted and sworn into being entirely out of need to survive.

"The terms are harsh," the orator finished on a note that might have been sorrow. "No mages are to be hatched within Tsuranuanni. Cho-ja there are forbidden to wear the markings that show age or rank, but must be colored black in adult life, even as your Tsurani slaves who are human are restricted to garments of grey. Commerce with cho-ja outside your borders is not allowed, exchange of information, news, or magical lore being specifically forbidden. It is our suspicion, if not the sad truth, that the Queens within your nations have been forced to excise from hive memory all record and means of cho-ja magic. Were you Tsurani all to perish, and the Assembly's edict become obsolete, it is doubtful if an Empire-bred Queen could still create the egg to hatch out a mage. And so the sky-cities of our kind are forgotten, reduced by human decree to damp warrens beneath the earth. Our proud brethren are forced to become grubbers in soil, with their arts of spell-building forever lost."

By now the sky beyond the arch had darkened under twilight. The tribunal, who had heretofore sat in perfect stillness, arose, while the orator in obedience to some unspoken signal fell silent. A cho-ja sentinel at Mara's back prodded her up from her cushions, and the magician's scribe tilted its head her way in a manner that suggested regret. "Lady, your time of last testament is now ended, and the moment for your sentencing is come. If you have any last bequest, you are urged to state it now."

"Last bequest?" Wine and sweet fruit had dulled the edges of Mara's apprehension, and the familiarity shared with the orator throughout the afternoon made her bold. "What do you mean by this?"

The magician's scribe shifted its weight and became implacably still. The tallest of the tribunal cho-ja delivered her answer. "Your sentence, Lady Mara of Tsuranuanni. After your last testament is given, it will be formally read that you are to be executed at tomorrow's dawn."

"Executed!" A jolt of adrenaline and fear caused Mara to square her shoulders, and ire lit her eyes. She abandoned protocol. "What are your kind, if not barbarians, to condemn an envoy unheard?" The tribunal members twitched, and the sentinel cho-ja angled forward aggressively, but Mara was already frightened witless and she did not take any note. "It was a Queen of your own kind who sent me here to treat with you. She held hope for those cho-ja who are a captive nation within our Empire's borders, and she saw in me the chance to rectify the human misdeeds of the past. Would you execute me out of hand, when I am the opponent of the Assembly, come here to ask aid against their tyranny?"

The tribunal regarded her with identical sets of gem-hard eyes, unmoved. "Lady," rang their spokesman, "state your last bequest if you have one."

Mara closed her eyes. Were all of her efforts to end here, with her life? Had she been Servant of the Empire, wife to a fine Lord, Ruling Lady of the Acoma, and adviser to the Emperor only to die in shame on foreign soil? She repressed a violent shiver, and stayed the hands that itched to scrub the sweat of outright terror from her brow. She had nothing left to her at this moment beyond the dignity of her people. Her honor she no longer believed in, after hearing of what her forebears had done on the battlefield against a peaceful civilization. And so her voice rang oddly steady as she said, "Here is my last bequest: that you take this." She held up the magical token given her by Gittania, which should have been her testimony to these hostile aliens. She forced herself to press on. "That you take this record, and incorporate it into your hive memory along with the details of my 'execution,' so that all of your kind to come will recall that humankind are not alone in the perpetration of atrocity. If my husband and my children—indeed, if my family that serves as my hive must lose me in retribution for the treaty of the Assembly, then at least my heart's intentions must survive in the hive mind of my killers.''

A buzz of noise met her statement. Mara yielded to reckless, icy resolve. ''This is my last bequest! Honor it as my death wish, or may the gods curse your kind unto the ending of time for perpetrating the very injustices you deplore in us!''

''Silence!'' The command rocked the chamber, reverberating off the crystal dome with force enough to deafen. Cringing from the sheer volume of the sound, Mara took a second to realize that the command did not arise from the tribunal but came instead from a cho-ja magician that had materialized out of nowhere at the chamber's center. Its wings were deployed to full extension, and its markings were complex enough to lose the eye in dizziness. It stalked toward Mara, hard turquoise eyes like the ice that sheathed the distant mountains. When it halted before the Lady, its stance was menacing.

''Give me your token,'' it demanded.

Mara offered the object, certain she could not have done otherwise even had she been of a mind to resist. There was magecraft in the cho-ja's tone that compelled response from her flesh.

The cho-ja mage scooped up the token with a touch that barely grazed her skin. Ready with an appeal she had no chance to deliver, Mara was startled by a blinding flash. Light enveloped her, densely implacable as suffocation, and when her senses recovered from the shock of spellcraft, the domed chamber of the tribunal was gone, swept away as though it had never been. She found herself returned to the hexagonal cell, windowless and doorless as before, but now the stone floor was scattered with colored cushions and a pair of Tsurani-style sleeping mats. On the nearest of these crouched Lujan, his head resting in his hands, and his mien one of total despair.

At his Lady's arrival he started to his feet and gave a warrior's obeisance. His bearing might be correct to the last detail, but hopelessness lingered still in his eyes.

''You have heard what is to become of us?'' he asked of Mara. There was a whipsnap of fury in his tone.

The Lady sighed, too discouraged to speak, and unwilling to believe that she had come all this distance to be summarily consigned to an unjust fate.

''Did they ask your last bequest before they read your sentence?'' Lujan asked Mara.

Numbly she nodded; and between hopelessness and grief, she thought of one small detail that offered comfort: the cho-ja of Chakaha had not read her sentence. Somehow the token and the disruption caused by the reappearance of the cho-ja mage had interrupted the formal proceedings.

Unwilling to read hope into that small anomaly, Mara made conversation. "What did you ask for, as your last bequest?"

Lujan gave back an ironic smile. As if nothing were wrong, he offered his hand and helped Mara down to a more comfortable seat amid the cushions. "I did not ask," he allowed. "I demanded. As is a warrior's right when condemned by the state for crimes committed by his master, I claimed death by single combat."

Mara raised her eyebrows, too sober to be amused, but wildly seizing upon the implications of this development. Right of death by combat was a Tsurani custom! Why should these Chakaha cho-ja honor such a tradition? "Did the tribunal that judged you grant your bequest?"

Lujan's crooked grin told her as much, before he answered, "At least I shall have the opportunity to chop at some chitin before they have my head."

Mara stifled an inopportune rise of hysterical giggles at his vehemence. "Who have the Chakaha cho-ja selected as their champion?"

Lujan shrugged. "Does it matter? Their warriors all look the same, and the hive mind most likely ensures that they are of equal ability. The only satisfaction I may have is that I will be chopped to pieces in combat before their headsman gets his chance to cut my neck." He loosed a bitter laugh. "Once I would have considered such a death in your service to be a warrior's honor, and the paeans that would have greeted me upon my entrance to Turakamu's halls would have been the only reward I desired." He fell silent, as if in deep thought.

Mara ventured conclusion of his statement for him. "But your concept of honor has changed. Now a warrior's death seems meaningless beside the opportunities offered by life."

Lujan turned a tortured glance to his Lady. "I could not have summed up so neatly, but yes. Kevin of Zūn opened my eyes to both principles and yearnings that the Tsurani way can never answer. I have seen you dare to challenge the course of our entire culture, as no male ruler might have done, for fear of ridicule by his peers. We are changed, Lady, and the Empire is poised on the brink of change with us." He glanced around, as if to savor what life was left to him. "I care not for my own life; who have I to mourn after me who will not soon follow me into death when we fail?" He shook his head. "It is the frustration of losing any opportunity to somehow . . . pass along what we have learned, that these insights will not perish with us.''

Mara spoke insistently to cover her own pang of fear. ''Hokanu will be left, and our children, to carry on after us. They will somehow rediscover what we have, and find a way to act without blundering into this cho-ja trap.'' She let out a long sigh. Looking at her old companion, she said, ''My largest regret, most strangely, is that of a wife and a woman. I'm everlastingly sorry that I cannot return to make peace with Hokanu. He was always the soul of sensitivity and reason before: something of importance must have prompted his behavior toward Kasuma. I maligned him unfairly, I think, by accusing him of a prejudice his nature would not allow. Now it's too late to matter. I must die with the question unasked that could restore our understanding. Why, when I could easily bear another child that is male, did Hokanu act so aggrieved when he learned that his firstborn was a daughter?''

Her eyes sought Lujan's in appeal. ''Force Commander, you are a man who understands the game between sexes well, or so I have been informed through kitchen gossip. The scullions never tire of describing the serving girls and ladies of the Reed Life who languish for your company.'' She gave a wry smile. ''Indeed, if they are to be believed, there are droves of such women. How is it that a husband as wise as Hokanu should not be gladdened by the birth of a healthy, unblemished daughter?''

Lujan's demeanor softened, very near to pity. ''Lady, did Hokanu never tell you?''

''Tell me what?'' Mara demanded sharply. ''I was harsh with my husband, and bitterly outspoken. So deeply did I believe his behavior was in the wrong, I drove him from me. But now I regret my hard-heartedness. Maybe Kamlio taught me to listen more carefully. For like these cho-ja of the Thuril territories, I condemned my husband without ever asking his testimony.''

Lujan stood a moment looking at her. Then, as if reaching some decision, he folded to his knees before her. ''Gods forgive me,'' he murmured softly, ''it is not my right to break confidence between a Lord and his wife. But tomorrow we will die, and I have always been your loyal officer. Lady Mara, I would not have you pass this life without the understanding you desire. Hokanu was stricken with a grief, but he would never have spoken of its cause, even had you returned and begged to hear. But I know what sorrow afflicted him. I was in the chamber when the healer of Hantukama informed your husband of what he, in his kindness, swore he would never reveal to you: that after the poisoning by the tong that cost you your unborn babe, you should bear but one more child. Kasuma was your last issue. Hokanu kept the secret because he wished you to hold the hope of another pregnancy. His daughter is a joy to him, never doubt, and his consecrated heir for the Shinzawai mantle. But he knows, and is saddened, that you will never give him the son he longs for in his heart.''

Mara sat stunned. Her voice came out small. ''I am barren? And he knew?'' The full import of Hokanu's courageous resolve struck her, sharp as the most stinging thorn. He had been raised motherless and his blood father had been taken beyond reach by the Assembly of Magicians; Hokanu's whole world had been one of male camaraderie, with his uncle, who became his foster father, and his cousin, who became a brother. This was the root of his longing for a son.

But he was also a man of rare sensitivity and appreciation for the company of intellectual minds; where another Lord with less heart would have taken on courtesans as his gods-given male right, Hokanu had loved her for her mind. His craving for equality in companionship had become realized in marriage to a woman with whom he could share the most inspirational of his ideas. He spurned the usage of concubines, the company of women of the Reed Life, the pleasures to be found with bought creatures like Kamlio.

Now Mara understood how he had been faced with a choice abhorrent to him: to take another woman to his bed, one that meant nothing beyond her capacity to conceive and breed, or to go without a son—to forgo the fraternity he had shared with his adoptive father, his brother, and Justin, whom he had given back to Mara for the sake of Acoma continuance.

''Gods,'' Mara all but wept. ''How stone-hearted I have been!''

Instantly Lujan was beside her, his strong arm supporting her shoulder. Mara sagged against him. ''Lady,'' he murmured in her ear, ''you of all women are not insensitive. Hokanu understands why you reacted as you did.''

Lujan held her as a brother might, in undemanding companionship, as she ran through all the details to the half-painful, half-hopeful conclusion that if she died here, her beloved Hokanu would have Kasuma for his heir, and freedom to take another wife to bear him the son he longed for. Mara clung to that thought. At last, to escape her own woes, she said, ''What of you, Lujan? Surely you do not contemplate the leaving of this life without regrets?''

Lujan's fingers stroked her shoulder with a rough tenderness. ''I do have one.''

Mara turned her head and saw that he seemed to be studying the woven patterns of the cushions. She did not press for his confidence, and after a moment he gave a wry shrug.

"Lady, it is strange how life shows us our follies. Always I have enjoyed the favors of many women, but never held the desire to marry and be content with one." Lujan stared fixedly, self-conscious, but oddly freed from embarrassment by the fact that with the dawn, he must face an ending of life, an ending of dreams. The nearness of his accounting with Turakamu lent them both the solace of honesty. "Always, I told myself, my roving ways were the result of my admiration for you." Here his eyes flashed toward her in a glance of truthful adoration. "Lady, there was much about you for a man to appreciate, and a toughness that made other women seem . . . if not lacking, then at least smaller of stature." He made a tight gesture of frustration at the inadequacy of words. "Lady, our journey into Thuril has taught me to know myself too well, I think, for ease of mind."

Mara raised her eyebrows. "Lujan, you have never been less than the exemplary warrior. Keyoke overcame his distrust of grey warriors to choose you above others to fill his former post as Force Commander. In these late years I believe that you have come to hold as much of a place in his heart as Papawaio did."

"Now, there is a tribute." Lujan's lips quirked toward a smile, and then hardened. "But I have been less than honest with myself, now that my spirit lies near to its reckoning. I am sorry, this night, that I never found any woman to share my hearth and home."

Mara regarded the bent head of her Force Commander. Recognizing that in some manner Lujan wished to unburden himself, very gently she said, "What kept you from starting a family and raising children?"

"I outlived my master of the Tuscai," he admitted with a tightness in his throat. "The misery of a grey warrior cannot be described, for his life is outside society. I was a young man, strong, and skilled in arms. And yet there were moments when I very nearly did not survive. How would a child or a woman fare, were they to be left houseless? I saw the wives and children of my fellow warriors driven away as slaves, forever to wear grey and answer to the needs of a master who cared little for their comfort." Lujan's voice sank almost to a whisper. "I see now that I was afraid that someday those children would be mine, and my woman become some other man's to use as he chose."

Now Lujan looked his mistress squarely in the face. There was an unnerving depth to his eyes, and a ring to his voice as he added, "How much simpler it was to admire you from afar, Lady, and guard your life with my own, than to live the possibility of the nightmare that even yet wakens me sweating from my sleep.''

Mara reached out and touched his hands, then kneaded them until they relaxed their furious grip. ''Neither you nor any unborn child of yours will ever in this turn of the Wheel go masterless,'' she said softly. ''For I very much doubt that either of us will escape this prison with our lives.''

Now Lujan did smile, a strange serenity to his bearing that Mara had never seen. ''It has been my pride to serve you, Lady Mara. But if we do live past tomorrow's dawn, I ask a boon of you, that you command me to find a wife and marry! For I think that with the magicians as your enemy, such straits as these might easily be repeated, and if I am to die in your service, I should prefer not to face the Death God with the same regret in my spirit a second time!''

Mara regarded him with a smile of deep affection. ''Lujan, knowing you as I do, I doubt I shall have to command you to do what is clearly in your heart to do. But, we must win past tomorrow's dawn.'' Crossing her arms as if to ward off cold, she said, ''We must sleep, brave Lujan. For tomorrow will come.''

23. Contest

Sleep was impossible.

Since her strangely intimate exchange of confidences with Lujan, Mara felt no urge to converse. The Acoma Force Commander had shown no inclination to sleep and settled cross-legged on his mat. The cho-ja had confiscated his armor along with his sword. Left the padded underrobe designed to protect his skin from chafing, he looked both undressed and vulnerable. Battle scars normally concealed by his raiment were exposed, and although he was as fastidious as any Tsurani officer, his last opportunity for a bath had been in an icy river current while enduring Thuril jibes. His clothing was greyed with dirt, and his hair spiked up into whorls from long hours under his helm. Muscled as he was, he seemed somehow diminished without his trappings and officer's plumes.

Looking at him, Mara was forced to recognize his human side, his maleness that would never know fatherhood, and the incongruously tender comfort he had given with hands better accustomed to the grip of a killing sword. As if his coming fate held no consequence, he meditated peacefully, his soldier's discipline forcing worries aside to husband strength against demands of battle.

Mara, despite every training of the mind garnered in the temple of Lashima, was left without such solace. This time her mind found no ease in ritual; if she was not feeling regret for loved ones who had been lost, she felt rage against an intolerant fate that condemned her to failure in protecting those still alive. Try as she might, her thoughts could not be forced to subside toward anything approaching tranquillity.

The ignominy of imprisonment without any way to contact her captors left her galled. The magical chamber effectively sealed the condemned away from all other living beings. Sourly Mara wondered whether even gods could hear prayer in such a place. And with no windows, nor even the sounds of outside activity, the minutes dragged. Darkness itself would have carried a blessing of change, but the cho-ja globe drifted always, its light stark and constant.

The dawn would come, inevitably.

And yet for all the creeping agony of waiting, daybreak caught Mara unprepared. Her racing, trapped thoughts still circled, repeatedly reviewing events and questioning whether this action, or that word, or that decision differently handled might have won them alliance and freedom. Her futile pondering left her with a crushing headache. With the flashing magical whirl of light that signaled the dissolution of their prison, Mara felt tired, and depressed.

A double-file guard of cho-ja marched forward to take custody of the condemned. Mara retained enough presence of mind to rise and cross to where Lujan waited, awake and already on his feet.

She took his dry hands into her own clammy ones. Then she regarded his expressionless face and intoned the ritual words, "Warrior, you have served in highest honor. You have leave from your mistress to claim what death you choose. Fight well. Fight bravely. Go singing to the halls of Turakamu."

Lujan sank into a bow. His return courtesy seemed to exhaust the patience of their captors, for Cho-ja guards advanced and hauled him to his feet. Mara also was grasped and tugged away as a herder might drive a needra calf to slaughter. She lost sight of Lujan as the bodies of cho-ja warriors closed around her. They allowed her no chance for protest, but set her on the march through the maze of hallways that riddled the city of Chakaha.

She raised her chin high, though pride seemed meaningless. The cho-ja of these lands were not impressed by honor, or courage, nor did they have any care for human dignity. She presumed that very soon she would be greeting the spirits of her ancestors; but not as she had always expected. Here, now, the most glowing of her Tsurani attainments and even her illustrious title of Servant of the Empire seemed empty. Now she would have traded all for a last glimpse of her children, or one tender embrace from her husband.

Kevin had been more right than ever she knew. Honor was only a glorified word for emptiness, and no sane replacement for the promise of continued life. Why had it taken until now for her to fully understand what prompted the opposition of the Assembly? And if help to break their stagnating hold upon Tsuranuanni could not be found here, and these Thuril cho-ja would make no alliance, where would Hokanu seek for resources to end the tyranny the magicians so jealously guarded? If there were answers, they must remain a mystery. The cho-ja guard were indifferent as beings of stone. They moved briskly through the corridors, and across two catwalks that sparkled like glass. Mara regarded the clear sky, never so green and fresh before now. She smelled the fragrance of rich earth and jungle greenery, threaded through with the perfumes of tropical flowers; and on the breeze she drew in the scent of ice carried on the winds from the mountain peaks. She drank in these pleasures of life, and also the beauty of Chakaha's tracery of towers. She walked, bathed in colored arrows of light caused by sunbeams that shone through the towers, and her spirit shrank from the senseless end to come, the giving up of all hope, and the end of all dreams.

Too soon, the cho-ja guard escorted her into the translucent purple dome where the tribunal had judged her the day before. Now there were no officials present, not even scribes. The chamber was occupied by the spindly presence of a single cho-ja mage. It stood in a domed alcove. Upon the marble floor at its feet was a scarlet line that described a perfect circle.

Mara recognized the figure's significance. Set to a diameter of twelve paces, with a simple symbol scribed at east and west, where two warriors would stand confronting each other, she beheld the Circle of Death, traditionally drawn within the Empire for time out of mind. Here would two warriors battle until one lost his life in the ancient rite of challenge that Lujan had chosen in place of honorless execution.

Mara bit her lip to hide an unseemly apprehension. She had once stood to witness a husband's ritual suicide with less trepidation in her heart. For then she had regretted the waste of a young man whose own family's neglect had left him open for her exploitation. That indeed had been the first moment when the Game of the Council had shown itself to be less than a rigid code of honor and more a license to indulge any excuse to exploit another human's faults. Now honor itself seemed empty.

Mara beheld Lujan, standing between the cho-ja guards on the opposite side of the room. She knew him well enough to read his stance, and she saw, with a terrible pang, that the human warrior who would take up his weapons to die no longer subscribed to the beliefs he had been raised in. He valued the esteem he might gain in the Red God's halls far less than the lost chance to marry and rear children.

To Mara, Lujan's challenge to combat was a tragic and meaningless gesture. The honor he might win for his shade was like the fool's gold that Midkemian swindlers foisted upon the unsuspecting merchant. And yet the charade would be played through to its senseless conclusion.

Lujan was both more and less than the grey warrior she had rescued from masterless oblivion in the mountains. Guilt for her own responsibility in that change closed her throat. She had difficulty breathing, far less holding herself expressionless and erect as a noble Tsurani Lady must while in public.

The cho-ja mage waved a forelimb, and an attendant scurried into view, bearing Lujan's confiscated weapons and the plain, unmarked armor he had worn into Thuril. Not without disrespect, it crouched and deposited the gear at the warrior's feet.

"Our hive has no knowledge of the manner of usage of these protections," intoned the cho-ja mage, which Mara interpreted as an apology that the worker could not offer Lujan the courtesy of helping him arm.

On impulse, she stepped forward. "I will assist my Force Commander."

Her words echoed across the dome. But unlike in a gathering of humans, no cho-ja present turned its head. Only the mage twitched a forelimb to permit Mara to cross to Lujan's side. She bent and selected one of his grieves from the floor, then flashed a glance at his face. By the slight arch to his brows, she saw he was surprised at her gesture, but also secretly pleased. She gave him a surreptitious half-smile, then bent to lace on the first of his accoutrements. She did not speak. He would understand by her unprecedented behavior how highly he was regarded by her.

And in truth, the handling of armor was not unknown to her. She had girded on Hokanu's sword many times, and before him, her first Lord Buntokapi's; and as a child, she had played at adult behavior with her brother, Lanokota, when he had carried his wooden practice sword to workouts with Keyoke.

Lujan gave her a nod to indicate that she had the lacings right—tight enough to bind, but not so much that they would restrict his movement. She finished with the heavy, laminate sword that had more than once stopped enemies at her door. When the last buckle of the sword belt was clasped, she arose and touched Lujan's hand in farewell. "May the gods ride your blade," she murmured, which was the ritual phrase one warrior might say to another who sallied forth, expecting to die.

Lujan touched her hair, and tucked a drifting strand back behind her ear. The familiarity might have been an impertinence, had Lujan not come to hold the place of her dead brother in her heart. "Lady, feel no sorrow. Had I the choices of my youth to make over, I would live them all again." His mouth quirked with a ghost of his old insolence. "Well, maybe not quite all. There were the instances of an unwise wager or two, and then the fat madam of that brothel whom I once insulted. . . ."

The cho-ja mage rapped a hind limb upon the paving with a sound like the crack of a mallet. "The time appointed for the combat is at hand!" it intoned, and at no other discernible signal, one of the cho-ja guard advanced to the edge of the circle.

It waited there, its bladed forelimbs shining in the soft light under the dome.

Lujan flashed Mara his most insouciant grin, then sobered, his mien as taut as any time he had waited poised for battle. Without a look back, or any sign of regret, he walked to the circle and took his place on the side opposite his cho-ja opponent.

Mara felt alone and vulnerable. Uneasily she noticed that her cho-ja guard had closed the space she had crossed; they now stood arrayed at her back, as if prepared to block her retreat, or any other desperate move she might attempt. Her knees shook. It embarrassed her that even that small weakness showed.

She was Acoma! She would not flee her fate, nor would she demean Lujan by shirking her place at the circle's edge. Still, when the cho-ja mage intoned the procedure, that at its signal both Lujan and the cho-ja warrior appointed to face him should cross within the line and commence the contest, the Lady fought back an overpowering wish to close her eyes, to shut from view the petty striving that was all Lujan might claim for his epitaph.

Lujan gripped his sword. His hand was firm, and his sinews did not quiver from apprehension. Nervousness seemed to have fled him, and indeed, to Mara's eyes he seemed more assured than before other forays in the past. This battle was to be his last, and that knowledge eased him. Here, on the edge of the circle of challenge, there were no unknowns to worry over: the outcome of this fight would be the same whether he fought well or not, whether he won or he lost. He would not leave the circle alive. To wish events had been otherwise was a waste of his strength, and a lessening of the courage he had been born and raised to exhibit. According to the creed of the Tsurani warrior, he had let no one down. He had served his mistress well and fully; he had never turned his back on any foe. By all that he had been taught to believe, his death by the blade here was a fitting thing, the culmination of honor that was more sacred to the gods than life itself.

Quiet in his readiness, Lujan inspected his sword edge one last time for flaws. There were none. He had drawn it for nothing but sharpening since departure from Tsuranuanni.

Then all considerations were ended as the cho-ja mage spoke out.

"Hear me, combatants. Once the line of the circle is crossed, the ward of its making will activate. To step over the line again, either from within, or if another should try to intervene from without, will bring death. The terms of battle shall be according to Tsurani tradition: either the condemned shall die in combat inside the circle, or if he proves the victor, he shall be permitted to choose the hand of his executioner. I, mage of the city-state of Chakaha, stand as the witness that these proceedings require."

Lujan gave the cho-ja mage a crisp salute. The cho-ja warrior he was to fight gave no acquiescence at all beyond a change in stance, from a position of rest to the angled crouch that signaled its readiness to charge. Beads of reflected light glanced off the knife-sharp edges of its forelimbs, and its eyes sparkled inhumanly. If pity and regret were part of the hive mind, such emotion was not reserved for the fighting arm of its society. The cho-ja warrior held but one directive: to do battle and to kill. In Tsurani conflicts, Lujan had seen companies of the creatures turn a battlefield into a butchery, for unless the weather was cold, the speed and reflexes of a human warrior were inferior. At best, he judged by the humid air that wafted through this chamber, he might get in a few parries before his body was diced up. His passage to Turakamu would be quick and almost painless.

His mouth tipped into a ghost of a crooked grin. If he was lucky, he would be drinking hwaet beer with his old friend Papawaio in Turakamu's halls before sundown.

"Cross the line and commence on my signal," intoned the cho-ja mage; and it stamped its hind limb against the floor with a sound like the chime of a gong.

Lujan's levity faded. He sprang into the circle, barely aware of the red flare of heat at his back that spelled the activation of the death ward. The cho-ja warrior came on with all of the speed he had anticipated, and he barely completed three steps before his guarding blade clashed into chitin. Against this foe, his peril was doubled, for cho-ja possessed two forearms with which to sally and chop at him. He, with his longer blade, had the better reach; and that humans were more naturally inclined to two-legged stance meant he could sometimes snatch the advantage of height as well.

But the cho-ja was superbly armored. Only a lunge with the point or the most hefty of two-handed chops could wreak any damage through chitin. Their joints were their sole point of vulnerability, yet too often their speed precluded tactics. Lujan parried and parried again. His footwork stayed light to deflect the cho-ja's double-sided attack. He squinted, circled, and spun his blade in the tight-knit forms proven over time to best defend against a cho-ja opponent. Blade clashed with chitin as he tested: the creatures usually had preferred sides. The right limb might tend more to guard, while the left was cultivated for attack. Sword and bladed forelimbs whirled in deadly dance. Lujan became aware of a stickiness to his grip; exertion had set him sweating. Inwardly he cursed. Once the leather wrappings of his sword hilt became saturated, they would loosen. His hold might slip, making his blade work sloppy. And against a cho-ja adversary, even the slightest change of angle must be fatal. The strength behind their blows was such that a direct hit on the outer curve of a laminate Tsurani sword could shatter its cutting edge.

Lujan beat back another attack, snapped straight as the guard limb of the cho-ja effected a stroke that would have severed him at the knees. His leap back saved him from harm, but a burning sensation in his heel as he landed warned how near to the edge of the ward circle his evasive maneuver had carried him. He feinted, used a disengage that Kevin the barbarian had taught him, and was nearly fatally surprised when his stroke rasped across chitin and snicked the edge of a leg joint.

The cho-ja warrior hissed and clattered back, its claws stiffened with alarm.

And Lujan was nearly taken in the neck by its return stroke, so unprepared for his small success that he had dangerously overextended. He half turned on reflex and caught a glancing slice in the shoulder that peeled through armor and grazed enough flesh to sting cruelly. The parry he barely brought up to deflect the guard limb jarred him down to his sandals.

It took the spinning leap of an acrobat to escape from being cornered. He ducked away from the milling whirl of the cho-ja's attack, desperately aware of his peril. He needed to catch his breath. The fight would give him no chance. As his toughened hide blade crashed together with chitin again, he used his bracer to deflect the guard blade, while the attack blade whistled for his throat. He lunged, trusting impetus to carry him inside the arc of the cho-ja's main thrust. He hit its jointed forelimb on the unbladed inside of the elbow and it folded, its sharpened side deflected harmlessly against the back plate of his armor.

The blow still had force enough to wind him. Lujan danced back a half-step, to bring his blade back in play, while the cho-ja warrior huffed in astonishment. Lujan followed with the classic riposte, and his curved sword stabbed in at the juncture where a mid-limb joined its thorax. The cho-ja scrabbled back, wounded. Its mid-leg was no longer neatly folded, but dragged, limp at its side. Caught in wonderment that his attack had gone through, Lujan felt the dawn of revelation: these cho-ja were inexperienced at fighting humans! They were well enough schooled to combat the ancient forms of Tsurani swordsmanship that they had faced in ages past. But the shut down of information across the borders must have prohibited any experience with the innovations that had followed the Tsurani treaty. The newest refinements of bladework introduced by the wars with Midkemia, and styled on their barbarian way of fencing, had never been encountered by the hives outside the Empire. Chakaha's warriors held to the old ways, and despite their superior speed, despite their double-bladed style, a Tsurani human held an advantage: his newer techniques were not predictable, and Lujan had drilled against cho-ja warriors in the past.

Thought during battle slowed the warrior; Lujan took a cut to his calf and another to his forearm behind his left-hand bracer. Despite his wounds, he realized that the cho-ja was holding back. Perhaps it was the tiniest bit hesitant because of Lujan's unorthodox attack patterns, because either one of its blows could as easily have lopped off a limb. Something had caused it not to follow through with its full strength and capability.

Lujan paid special heed to his footwork, which was paramount to the Midkemian style. He slapped the cho-ja's next stroke aside as he might have dispatched a practice stick, then tried another disengage. To his gratification, the cho-ja retreated, proving his theory that it did not understand Midkemian fencing tactics.

Lujan grinned in a wild, adrenaline-sharpened exultation. He had crossed practice sticks with Kevin the barbarian many times and, better than most of his peers, had mastered the foreign technique. More suited though it was to a straight sword than to the broader blade his own culture favored, there were forms a Tsurani swordsman could execute with good effect. The cho-ja was now disadvantaged and uncertain, and for the first instant since Lujan had claimed his right to challenge, he entertained the hope of victory.

He feinted, lunged, and felt his next stroke connect. Grinning wider, he saw a spurt of the milky liquid that served the cho-ja as bodily fluid. His opponent dropped briefly to its unwounded mid-limb as it counterattacked; but four-legged posture was sure sign of a cho-ja prepared to retreat. Lujan lunged for his opening, a clear stroke to his foe's neck segment. Never mind that its dying follow-through would take him in the heart. His would be the victory, his the first lethal strike. He would gain the time-honored Tsurani reward of death in battle by an enemy's blade.

Yet even as his trained body responded and on ingrained reflex began the stroke that would end all contention, his mind shied away.

What was such a death, if not futile?

Had he learned nothing in his years of service to Mara? Would killing this cho-ja, against whom he had no quarrel, achieve one single bit of good toward her goal?

It would not, he saw in a rush of cheated anger. Nothing would be served, except to confirm Tsurani ways in the hive mind of the cho-ja of Chakaha.

What is my life or my death worth, Lujan thought, trapped in a split second between motion. To become the victorious warrior, no, to kill his opponent out of hand, would serve no living thing: not Mara, not this hive, and not the captive nation of cho-ja within Tsurani borders.

Gods, he raged in a moment of lacerating inner anguish: I cannot live by the warrior's code alone; and neither can I die by it.

His hand followed the heresy of his thoughts. Lujan pulled his stroke.

The move was awkwardly timed of necessity, and it cost him. He gained another slash in the thigh, this one deep enough to cripple.

Back he stumbled, hopping on his good leg. His cho-ja opponent sensed his weakening resolve. It reared up. A whirling forelimb sliced down from above, and Lujan deflected the cut, barely. His forehead was laid open to the bone, and as blood ran down his face and blinded his eye, he was aware of Mara's stifled outcry.

He stumbled back. The cho-ja pursued. He felt hot pavement beneath his heel, and knew relief: he had reached the outermost edge of the circle. If he crossed over, he would die.

He would perish anyway, but perhaps not entirely for nothing. His end could still make a point. Even as his opponent scuttled to finish him, he parried furiously, and cried out to the looming figure of the cho-ja mage who stood yet in judgment over him.

"I did not come here to kill! You cho-ja of Chakaha are not the enemies of my mistress, Lady Mara." Chitin rang against his blade as, desperate to be heard, he parried again. "I will not fight any longer against a being she would have for a friend." He parried again, lunged to drive his opponent momentarily back, and in that half-second of respite, threw down his sword in disgust. On his good leg, he spun, turning his back to the killing stroke.

Before him glowed the scarlet line of the circle. He was grateful, in that arrested moment of time, that he had got his positioning right: the cho-ja warrior could not cross in front of him without violating the wardspell, and so dying. If it killed, it must use the coward's stroke, the murderer's cut, and butcher him from behind.

He drew a shuddering breath, eyes raised to the cho-ja mage. "Strike my back, who would be your friend and ally, and see your unjust execution done."

Lujan heard the whistle of the air parted by the cho-ja warrior's bladed forearm. He braced himself, prepared for the bone-rending finish to its descent. The end was foregone conclusion. At this point in time, a man with a sword could not curb inertia and snatch back the stroke as it fell.

But the reflexes of a cho-ja were not human.

The blade stopped, soundless and motionnless, a hairsbreadth from Lujan's neck.

The cho-ja mage reared back, its sail-like wings upraised as if in alarm. "What is this?" it rang out in what plainly served as astonishment. "You break the tradition of the Tsurani. You are a warrior, and yet you give up your honor?"

Shivering now in the aftermath of nerves and adrenaline, Lujan managed a steady answer. "What is tradition but habit?" He shrugged stiffly, feeling the sting of his wounds. "Habits, as any man may tell you, can be changed. And as any Tsurani will tell, there is no honor in killing an ally."

Blood dribbled into his left eye, obscuring his vision. He could not see to tell whether Mara approved of his gesture. A moment later, it did not matter, for the blood left his head in a rush. His wounded leg gave way, and he fainted and fell with a grinding crash of armor to the floor. The red circle died in a fizzle of sparks, and the great domed chamber went hushed.

Lujan wakened to a sharp tingle of pain. He gasped, opened his eyes, and saw the head of a cho-ja bent within inches of his own. He lay on what felt like a couch. Pointy, claw-like appendages gripped the wounds in his forearm and thigh, and by the prick of what felt like a needle, he realized he was being sewn up by a cho-ja worker physician.

While the medicinal skills of the creatures were exemplary, and they did neat, careful work, they had spent little time in the art of practicing upon humans. Lujan stifled a second grimace of discomfort, and judged that their knowledge was decidedly lacking in the area of anesthetics. Even on the field, he would have been given spirits to dull his awareness of the pain.

So it was that he took a moment to notice the secondary, more pleasant sensation of small, warm fingers gripping the hand of his unwounded arm.

He turned his head. "Mara?"

Her smile met him. She was close to weeping, he saw, but with joy, not sorrow. "What happened, Lady?"

Belatedly, he realized they were no longer in the domed chamber of judgment, nor restored to confinement, but were installed in a beautifully appointed chamber high up in the tower. A window behind Mara showed sky and clouds, and left the Lady awash in bright sunlight. She squeezed his hand in near to girlish excitement, though in truth, this trial had aged her. The gray shot through her dark hair had grown more pronounced, and her eyes showed deep crow's-feet from prolonged exposure to the weather. And yet, never before had her face seemed more beautiful; maturity had given her depths and mysteries impossible to the trackless face of youth.

"Lujan, you have won for the Acoma highest honor," she said quickly. "By your act in the circle, you proved to these cho-ja of Chakaha that Tsurani tradition is not the all-consuming way of life they believed it to be. For ages they have seen Tsurani demonstrate a lie. They understood all I said, even knowing through their magic that I believed in my convictions, but their own past taught that such displays of peaceful ways were but preludes to more violence and betrayal."

She took a deep breath of relief. "You have won us reprieve, through your courage and innovation. Your actions lived as one with my words and convinced them that perhaps we are different from our ancestors. The cho-ja mage in attendance was astonished by your act, and was convinced to review the memory stone left to us by Gittania. On it were records of my meeting with the hive Queen on the old Acoma estates, and her entreaty made an impression."

"Our sentences are rescinded? We're to go free?" Lujan gasped out, as he could when the cho-ja physician paused in its labors.

"Better than that." Mara's eyes glowed with pride. "We are to be given safe passage through Thuril to our ship, and with us when we return to Tsuranuanni will travel two cho-ja mages. The city-state of Chakaha has decided it will aid us, in the hope that the liberation of the Tsurani cho-ja may be accomplished by the Emperor. I have pledged to use my office to intercede; I am almost certain that once I explain to Ichindar the truths we have learned, he cannot say no."

"Gods!" Lujan exclaimed. "Everything we could have asked for has been granted." He was so excited he forgot his hurts and attempted to move.

At this, the cho-ja physician said, "Lady Mara, this warrior's wounds are severe. Excite him not, for he must rest for several weeks if his leg is to heal as it should.'' Black, faceted eyes swiveled toward Lujan. ''Or would the estimable Force Commander prefer to limp?''

Lujan felt suddenly flooded with strength, and he laughed. ''I can be patient while my body repairs itself. But not so patient that I can stay in bed for weeks on end!''

He rolled his head on the pillow, warmed afresh by Mara's smile. ''Rest you easy,'' his mistress commanded. ''Never mind the delay. Word will be sent back to Hokanu by way of the Thuril settlements, and from thence, with the traders overseas. For we have time now, Lujan. And while your wounds are knitting, I shall prevail upon our host hive to show us wonders.''

24. Homecoming

The barge left the shore.

Mara leaned on the rail and drew a deep breath of the warm breeze. The familiar smell of dank earth, fresh lake water, wet planking, and the slight taint of sweat from the slaves who manned the oars made her shiver. Home! In scarcely another hour, she would reach the estates. She savored the heat of the sun on her flesh.

This was the first glimpse of sky and daylight she had had since a stealthy night debarkation from *Coalteca,* and weeks of underground travel across the Empire by cho-ja tunnels. For the cho-ja mages had confirmed what heretofore had been her surmise: that the Assembly of Magicians could not spy through the dark earth. What transpired in the cho-ja tunnels lay beyond their ability to scry, a difficult concession at the time of the treaty. And so her band of picked warriors, her servant Kamlio, and the two Chakaha cho-ja had thus proceeded to reenter the Empire in secret.

This they had accomplished with neither permission nor help from the local cho-ja who dwelt there, lest harboring the Chakaha mages in any fashion void the terms of the treaty. The mages' presence was shunned with scrupulous precision, so that none of the Empire cho-ja could claim to have seen them pass or to have known of their existence. Mara's request that all cho-ja vacate the tunnels before her until after she had passed had been accepted without question by the Tsurani cho-ja Queens. They might suspect, but they could answer truthfully they had no knowledge of what Mara attempted.

As a result of near-total isolation, Mara felt distressingly uninformed. Only a few scraps of news were given her by those cho-ja workers she encountered while waiting for the answer from the local Queen that she might pass through the hives unobserved; the only important information was that a Great One yet maintained surveillance over the entrance of the Red God's temple in Sulan-Qu, waiting for her to break her seclusion.

That might have been amusing, had it not revealed her danger. Even after the passage of months, that any member of the Assembly, however minor, still should deem such a watch to be necessary meant her next few actions must be well plotted and executed without flaw; she felt in her bones that only her unique rank was keeping her alive, for certainly some members of the Assembly must be at the end of their patience.

Mara had dared not pause to establish contact with Arakasi's network of agents along the way. The pace she had set to reach the Empire's heartland had been relentless. As she had not cared to risk her own exposure, or to compromise the hives that gave her shelter, she had no way to determine how Jiro might have spent the months of her absence. She did not even know if her husband had successfully dealt with his dissident cousins and clan rivals who had ambition to upset his inheritance. Mara had learned only moments before from workers on the docks that Hokanu had returned to their lakeside estates, and that the Lady Isashani had teasingly tried to pair him off with a concubine who had in some way failed to please one of her dead husband's many bastards. Hokanu had sent a charming refusal. Although in such social gossip Mara could find no implication of threat, she asked out of caution for the foreign mages to stay closeted within an unused chamber in the hive nearest to the estate. With them she left two warriors to attend their needs, and these bound strictly to secrecy. They would emerge to forage only at night, and would not divulge their duties to any of the Acoma patrols or local cho-ja. Mara gave the soldiers a paper affixed with her personal chop as Servant of the Empire, instructing anyone that the two soldiers should be permitted to go their way without question. Such precaution would give no protection from her adversaries, but it would prevent friends or allies from blundering into her secret.

Mara leaned into the breeze and faintly smiled. She had much to tell Hokanu! The wonders she had seen during Lujan's convalescence in Chakaha defied rational description, from the exotic flowers the cho-ja workers cultivated that bloomed in combinations of colors not seen anywhere else, to the rare liquors distilled from red-bee honey and other elixirs that they traded with their eastern human neighbors. Within her baggage she had brought medicines, some made of molds, others extracted from seeds or rare mineral springs, that her healers would call miraculous in their curative properties. She had watched the heated forging done in the glass works where they created everything from vases to cutlery to building stone that shone in clear colors like gems.

She had watched apprentice mages master their first spells, and seen the fine scrollwork of patterns appear on their unmarked carapaces. She had watched the most ancient of the mages, who was lined in a maze of colors, at his work. He had shown her visions of the far past, and one, misty with a haze of unresolved probability, that showed the future as yet unformed. It had looked much like dyes awash in a fishbowl, but sparkling with flecks like golden metal. "If that is my future," Mara had said laughingly, "I shall perhaps die a very wealthy woman."

The cho-ja mage had said nothing in return, but for a moment his shiny azure eyes had looked sad.

Mara could not contain her high spirits. She watched a flock of march birds take flight over the reed beds, and remembered the models that had flown like birds in Chakaha, and other living, untamed birds beguiled to sing in counterpoint. She had seen animals grow fur in colors as brilliant as exotic silk. Cho-ja magic held ways for stone to be spun into fibers and woven, and ways for water to be fashioned into braided cable that flowed uphill. Between times she had been feasted with exotic foods and dishes seasoned with spices that were as intoxicating as wine. There existed enough trade possibilities in Chakaha to tempt Jican to commit sacrilege, and with excitement akin to any schoolgirl's, Mara longed for her perilous quandary with the Assembly to be resolved, so that she could resume more peaceful pursuits. Her problems were not yet ended; in her high spirits she could not help but feel that things must work out in her favor.

That mood of frivolous excitement had over-ruled Saric's more sober advice to remain in the cho-ja tunnels until close to her estate house. Mara was so homesick for the sights and smells of Tsuranuanni that she brought her company above ground near the lakeshore, and then commandeered a barge from her own Acoma tradesmen to finish her journey by water.

A shadow fell over her. Musing cut short, Mara looked up. Lujan had crossed the deck and paused at her side. His inspection of her honor guard was complete, and if the armor they wore was unmarked in house colors, their lacquer accoutrements sparkled. Lujan had decked his helm with officer's plumes of Acoma green. He moved yet with a limp, but his wound had healed cleanly under the ministrations of the cho-ja physicians. In time, he would recover fully. At present, his eyes glinted with mischief, and by that Mara knew his excitement equaled her own.

"Lady," he greeted, with a salute. "Your men are ready for their homecoming." The corners of his mouth bent wryly upward. "Do you suppose we'll give the dock sentries a fright? We've been gone for so long, they might see our colorless armor and think us all spirits returned from the dead."

Mara laughed. "In a way we are." A second figure approached and paused on her other side. Sunlight glowed on a mantle of cho-ja silk, patterned by the Chakaha mages with an intricacy that might be the envy of any of the Emperor's wives. Mara saw a fall of gold hair beneath the hood, and her heart warmed. "Kamlio," she greeted. "You look extraordinarily pretty."

In fact, this was the first time Mara or any of the warriors who had ventured off into Thuril territory had seen the girl dress other than plainly.

Kamlio lowered her eyelashes in shy silence. But the building embarrassment caused by Lujan's stare of admiration a moment later gave rise to her reluctant explanation. "After our experiences with the Thuril, I learned to trust my Lady's word—that I will not be married off or given to any man I do not choose." She gave a self-conscious shrug that set the colored fringes on her garment flying free in the wind. "There is no need, here on your estate, to hide in tattered clothes." She sniffed, perhaps with disdain, perhaps with relief. Lujan received a flickering glance that hinted at temper. "Our men do not steal their wives by raiding, and if the Spy Master Arakasi chances to be at the docks, I would not wish him to think me ungrateful for the raised station bestowed upon me."

"Oho!" Lujan laughed. "You have come far, little flower, that you speak his name without spitting!"

Kamlio tossed back her hood and gave the Force Commander a sultry pout that might have been prelude to a slap. At least Lujan thought it might, for he raised his hand in mock fear to ward off the result of womanly fury.

But Mara interceded, stepping between her officer and the former courtesan. "Behave, you two. Or else the dock sentries will not mistake you for ghosts, but for miscreants fit to be sent off for punishment. Doubtless there are enough dirty latrines in the barracks to keep you both cleaning for a week."

When Lujan gave no insolent reply to this threat, Mara raised her eyebrows and looked to see what was amiss. She found his levity banished, and his expression as stern as any he might wear in the moment before charging into battle, as his eyes turned to the distant shoreline. "Lady," he said in a tone grim as granite, "something is wrong."

Mara followed his gaze, her heartbeat accelerated by sudden fear. Across a narrowing strip of water lay the landing, and the stone walls and peaked cornices of the estate house. At first glance, all seemed tranquil. A trader barge much like the one her party rode upon lay warped to the bollards. Bales and boxes lay piled on the dock from the offloading, presided over by a tally clerk and two stalwart male slaves. Recruits in half-armor were dashing from the practice field, as if they had just finished sparring. Smoke rose in a spiral from the kitchen chimneys, and a gardener raked fallen leaves off a walkway between courtyard gardens. "What?" Mara asked impatiently, but the answer became obvious as the sun caught and flashed on a sparkle of gold. The anomaly drew her eye, and she saw the imperial runner who raced away down the lane leading from the great house.

Mara's unease crystallized into dread, for such messengers rarely brought good news. No longer did the sweetness of the breeze offer comfort, or the beauty of the green hillsides lift the heart.

"Bargeman!" she cracked out. "Get us to shore with all speed!"

A string of orders answered her command, and the rowers bent over their looms in double time. The clumsy trader barge bored ahead, spray flying in sheets from its blunt bow. Mara restrained an urge to pace in rank impatience. She was paying for her brash impulse now. Had she listened to Saric's more prudent suggestion and continued underground to the hive entrance nearest to the estate, she might already be getting information from a runner sent to meet her. Now she was powerless to do other than watch and wait, while every possible scenario of disaster played through her imagination. Kamlio looked terrified, and Lujan sweated in feverish anticipation, lest the troops he should rightly be commanding be called to the field without his knowing why. He might be wielding his sword all too soon, Mara thought. Judging by the furious activity on the docks, it was plain that no time could be spared to allow his scars the restful recovery they required.

Already drums boomed from the estate house, the heavy, deep-noted ones that signaled a marshaling of the garrison. "It will be war," Lujan surmised, an edge to his words. "The rhythm is short, patterned in threes. That code spells a call for total mobilization, and Irrilandi would never stir his old shanks so fast for less than serious trouble."

"Keyoke must have shared in that decision," Mara thought aloud. "Even before he was appointed Adviser for War, he was not an officer to take extreme measures without reason. If Jiro's hands are presumably still tied by the Assembly, what could have happened? Is it possible some hothead has called upon Clan Honor, or worse, that House Shinzawai might be under attack?"

Lujan stroked his sword grip, as miserable with taut nerves as she.

"We cannot know, Lady, but I cannot shake off the hunch that what we see is the beginning of something worse."

Mara turned her back to the rail. She found her adviser Saric looking on, and at her tight-lipped silence, he offered, "Should I shake up the barge master to force more speed from the rowers?"

Her face as pitiless as fine marble, the Lady of the Acoma nodded. "Do so."

The barge was commodiously built to carry cargo, and its lines took unkindly to speed. The increase as the oar slaves applied themselves to extremity was negligible; the bows seemed only to carve up more spray, and the roil of the oar strokes raise deeper eddies. Mara saw the bodies of the rowers run with sweat before many minutes had passed. Activities on the docks at the landing intensified, even as she steeled herself to look.

The bales and boxes that only minutes before lay spread out for tallying were now trodden by a massing wedge of warriors. The trader barge had been cut loose half-unladen, and the tally keeper set on board in frantic arm-waving dismay. He sprang shouting into the stern as a shove from a plumed officer carried his craft from the dock. Two brawny stevedore slaves were all he had left to man the craft to safe anchorage, and his cries of outrage flew across the water like the yips of fisher birds, soon lost in the boom of the drums. Like the massing warriors, Mara had little concern for the fate of the clerk and the barge. The length of the shoreside warehouses, great double doors had opened along the waterline, revealing the wooden rails of the launching ways for the craft stored in the dry sheds. Slaves swarmed in the shadows inside. Out of the dimness deployed the Acoma war boats, long double-hulled craft steadied with outriggers, and planked across their lean length with archer platforms. More slaves rowed these toward the landing, where company after company of bowmen boarded. As each boat was filled, it pushed off into the lake, with the outriggers lowered, like a water bird's great wings dipping to touch the water. Before the outriggers were fully lashed into place, archers had taken position along the narrow firing platform along the top of each pontoon.

Lujan ticked numbers off on his fingers. After counting a dozen boats, and noting the banners that flew at the prow and stern of each, he knew which companies had been called to action. His conclusion was chilling. "This is a complete defensive deployment, mistress. An attack must be in the offing."

Mara's apprehension burned away in a surge of fierce anger. She had not crossed the sea and treated with barbarians and nearly lost her life in

Chakaha to see all fall to ruin upon her return. She had sent Hokanu word that she was on her way back to the Empire; but detailed communication was too dangerous, an invitation to enemies to set an ambush should it fall into wrong hands. And when the need of secrecy was past, for her own selfish pleasure she had held out at the moment of reunion in the hope of giving her loved ones a joyful surprise. But there would be no celebration upon her return. Setting aside both her anticipation and disappointment, she hardened her manner and turned to Saric. "Break out the Acoma standard and let my personal pendant fly beneath. It is time to make our presence known. Let us pray there is one sentry not racing to put on war armor who can carry word of our arrival to Hokanu that his Lady is back on Acoma soil!"

The honor guard on the trader barge's decks raised cheers at her brave words, and directly the green banner with its shatra bird symbol was run up the pole at the stern. No sooner did it unfurl upon the breeze than an answering cry arose from the shore. One of the tiny figures on the dockside pointed, and there followed a great shout from the army gathered and engaged in boarding. The noise settled into a chant, and Mara heard her name called over and over, along with the title bestowed upon her by the Emperor, Servant of the Empire! Servant of the Empire! Her concern nearly gave way to tears, that her people could raise such a commotion of affection at her return, with dire trouble afoot.

The barge master shouted himself hoarse with frantic orders, and slowly his craft was poled into the gap that opened in haste at the jammed dockside to receive Mara's landing. A figure in scarred blue armor hurried out from the press. Beneath the crested helm that denoted the Lord of Shinzawai, the Lady saw Hokanu's face, concern and gladness struggling to burst through proper Tsurani reserve.

That her husband wore his scarred, sun-faded battle armor, and not the decorative ceremonial gear reserved for state occasions, was sign enough that bloodshed was imminent, for Lords did not march with their troops for any but a major engagement. Yet after close to a half year of absence, and the months and agonies of misunderstanding, Mara paid that detail little heed. She could not pause for formal greeting, but ran forward the instant the gangplank spanned the gap from rail to dock. She rushed like a girl ahead of her officers and threw herself headlong into her husband's arms.

As if she had performed no breach in proper manners, Hokanu gathered her close. "Gods bless your return," he whispered into her hair.

"Hokanu," Mara replied, her cheek pressed to the unyielding curve of his breastplate, "how I have missed you!" And then the worries of the moment marred their reunion, killing their fleeting surge of joy as she recalled the absence of her little ones. "Husband! What passes? Where are the children?"

Hokanu set her back at arm's length, his dark, worried eyes seeming to drink in the sight of her face. She was so thin and sunburned and vital! His longing to ask the most simple question after her health was painful to read on his face. But the smothered panic behind her question demanded answer. Urgency warred with Hokanu's native tact, and in the end he settled for bluntness. "Justin and Kasuma are safe as yet. They are still in the Imperial Palace, but ill news has come." He took a quick breath, as much to brace himself as to allow her a moment to prepare. "My love, the Light of Heaven has been murdered."

Mara rocked back as if physically pushed off balance, but Hokanu's fast grip prevented her from falling backward into the lake. Shock drained the blood from her face. Of all the calamities she had imagined might happen in her absence, and after all of the perils she had escaped to bring back the Chakaha mages, the death of the Emperor was the last event she could have anticipated. From somewhere she summoned enough presence of mind to ask, "How?"

Hokanu gave an unhappy shake of his head. "The news just came. Apparently an Omechan cousin attended a small imperial dinner yesterday. His name was Lojawa, and before thirty witnesses, he stabbed Ichindar in the neck with a poisoned table knife. The vial of poison must have been hidden in the hem of his robes. A healing priest was brought within minutes, but help came too late." Quietly, almost kindly, Hokanu finished, "The poison was very fast."

Mara shivered, stunned. This atrocity seemed impossible! That the slender, dignified man who had sat on the golden throne, hag-ridden with worries, and driven nearly to distraction by the quarreling of his many wives, should never again hold audience in his grand hall! Mara mourned. No more would she offer counsel in the lamplit privacy of his apartments, or enjoy the man's gentle and dry wit. He had been a serious man, deeply concerned for his people, and often careless of his health under the crushing burdens of rulership. Mara's delight had been to try to make him laugh, and sometimes the gods had allowed her some success, giving his sense of humor free reign. Ichindar had never been the figurehead for her that he had been for the multitudes he had ruled. For all of his grand state, and all of the pomp that his office demanded—that he should always seem the image of god on earth to the Nations—he had been a friend. His loss was overwhelming and the world was poorer. Had he not seized courage and opportunity and sacrificed his own happiness for the burden of absolute rule, none of the dreams that Mara had journeyed to Thuril to save would ever have grown beyond idle fantasy.

The Lady of the Acoma felt old, too shaken to look beyond the horizons of personal loss. And yet the bite of Hokanu's fingers on her shoulders reminded her that she must. This tragedy would bring terrible repercussions, and if their combined household of Acoma and Shinzawai were not to sink in the backlash, she had to renew her grasp on current politics.

She fixed first on the name Hokanu had mentioned, that of a total stranger. "Lojawa?" Dismay cracked her Tsurani façade. "I don't know him. You say he is Omechan?" In desperation, she appealed to her husband, whose advisers were versed in recent events, and presumably had offered some theories. "What possible motivation could have driven an Omechan to such an act? Of all the great families that might vie to restore the Warlord's office, the Omechan stand the furthest from claiming the power of the white and gold. Six other houses would see their own candidate enthroned before the Omechan. . . ."

"The news just came," Hokanu repeated, at a loss himself. He gestured to a waiting Strike Leader to continue directing troops into the boats. Over the stamp of hobnailed battle sandals across the dock, he added, "Incomo hasn't had time to make sense of the details yet."

"No, not a Warlord's office," Saric broke in, too fired by a sudden insight to observe proper protocol.

Mara's eyes swung and locked with his, but she whispered, "No. You are right. Not a Warlord's office." Her face went from pale to deathly white. "The golden throne itself is now the prize!"

The stooped, grey-haired figure who elbowed his way through the press to Hokanu's side overheard. Incomo looked rumpled, red-eyed, and more shriveled with age than Mara recalled. The cares of the moment made him querulously shrill. "But there is no imperial son."

Saric spoke fast in correction. "Whoever takes the hand of Ichindar's eldest daughter, Jihilia, becomes the ninety-second Emperor of Tsuranuanni! A girl barely twelve years old is now heir to the throne. Any of a hundred royal cousins who might bring a war host to storm the walls of the Imperial Palace could try to claim her in marriage."

"Jiro!" Mara cried. "This stroke is brilliant! Why else should he be studying and building siege engines in secret all these years! This is the plot he must have been working on all along." It meant that her children were not just unsafe, but in jeopardy of their lives, for if the Anasati were to break into the Imperial Palace with their armies, any child with both enemies and a tie to the imperial line would be at risk.

Interpreting her appalled silence, Saric burst out, "Gods, Justin!"

Mara choked back panic at her adviser's cruel understanding. Even her highest honor now worked against her: as Servant of the Empire, she had been formally adopted into Ichindar's family. By law and tradition, her boy was legitimately of the blood royal. Not only were her issue subject to royal privilege, but Justin could arguably be a claimant to the throne as a royal nephew, and Ichindar's *closest* male relation.

Jiro would delight in arranging the demise of Justin and Kasuma as a normal action in his feud with the Acoma, but with the throne as a goal, he would be doubly implacable in seeing Justin dead. Nor would any other candidate for Jehilia's hand be inclined toward mercy where a rival heir might be concerned. Justin was but a boy, and fatal "accidents" could easily happen in time of war.

Mara reined back a terrible urge to shriek curses at the gods for this ugliest twist of fate. She had the Assembly to contend with all along, but counted on its edict to hold Jiro at bay until they were neutralized; but this tragic assassination had placed the lives of her children once again in the moil of politics—and had set them down at the heart of the conflict!

Hokanu's eyes betrayed his realization of the peril, and a half-stunned Incomo voiced their worst fears aloud: "Both Acoma and Shinzawai could be rendered heirless at one stroke."

Awakened to remembrance that such momentous matters must not be discussed among troops on the docks, Mara responded to Hokanu's urging and made her way through the surging ranks of warriors toward the great house. In a flat tone of foreboding, she said, "I see you have mobilized our home garrison already. For the sake of our children, we must also send runners to our allies and vassals and command them to make ready for war."

Hokanu steered her across the threshold with hands that by some miracle did not tremble. He did not pause to object that such a call to arms must certainly draw reaction from the Assembly, but in a stony voice said, "Incomo, see to this. Send our fastest messengers, and ones who are loyal enough to give their lives in this service." To Mara he added, "In your absence, I have set up relays of messengers to pass between here and the Shinzawai estates. Arakasi helped, though he did not approve of the project. It was done in haste, and requires much man-power, but precaution was needed to see our dispatches through without delays. My cousin Devacai has caused difficulties enough that he might as well be acting as one of Jiro's allies.''

As Incomo hurried off, his spindly legs pumping beneath the flapping hem of his adviser's robe, Mara waved for Lujan and Saric to stay and give counsel. Spotting Kamlio looking lost as she trailed in their wake, Mara indicated that the girl should follow also.

Then her mind returned to the trouble at hand as Hokanu added, ''Our supporters will be brought to the field in swift order. For a while we may be able to hide some of our troops under the banners of our allies, but that won't suffice for long. Gods smile on our cause, and send chaos and dust to confuse the eyes of the Great Ones! It will be a relief to see an end to this inactivity at last!'' His eyes narrowed. ''The Anasati have too long avoided Shinzawai revenge for ordering my father's assassination.'' Then, he paused, and spun Mara into the longer embrace he had withheld in the public view of the docks. ''My dear, what a terrible homecoming. You left on your journey to Thuril to avert the ugliness of war, and now you return to find that the Game of the Council is causing bloodshed once again.'' He gazed down at her face and waited, tactfully not inquiring about the success of her mission.

Mara caught the drift of his unspoken questions, among them a wonderment that she no longer seemed to hold his mishandling of Kasuma's birth against him. Her near-brush with death had reordered her priorities. As if all the world had not thrust pending disaster upon their combined house, she murmured answer to the matter that lay closest to her heart. ''I have been told of a certain fact you should have revealed to me, and at once.'' Her lips curved in a sad little smile. ''I know I can have no more children. Let that not be an impediment to your begetting the son you desire.''

Hokanu's brows arose in protest, first, that she seemed to receive such news with equanimity, and second, because the greater significance of her journey had been ignored by her. But before he could speak, Mara added, ''Husband, I have been shown wonders. But we must speak of them later and in private.'' She stroked his cheek, and kissed him, and then, still loving the sight of him, she demanded without averting her eyes, ''Has Arakasi sent any messages?''

''A dozen since you have left, but nothing since yesterday. Not yet, anyway.'' Hokanu's hands firmed around her waist, as if he feared she might draw away as the exigencies of Ruling Lady stole her attention.

To Saric, Mara commanded, ''Send word through the network that I want Arakasi back here as soon as possible.''

Mara turned to see Kamlio standing with a look both fearful and determined. Whatever she had said to Mara, in the distant mountains of Thuril, about dealing with the Spy Master, now vanished with the realization that he would soon be here. The former courtesan saw Mara's eyes upon her, and she threw herself prone on the floor in the lowliest obeisance of a slave. "Lady, I will not displease you."

"Then do not distress Arakasi at this time," the Lady replied. "For all of our lives may come to depend upon him. Rise." Kamlio obeyed and Mara said more kindly, "Go and refresh yourself. Gods know, we have endured a harsh journey, and there will be little enough time to rest in the days to come." As the girl crept away, Mara said briskly to Lujan, "Help Irrilandi finish deploying our warriors, and when they are away to their mustering point—" Here she paused and asked of her husband, "Which mustering point did you designate?"

Hokanu gave her a half-smile in which anxiety outweighed amusement. "We gather on the riverbanks at the edge of the estate, on the assumption that Jiro will float his main army down the Gagajin. The Assembly cannot fault us for defying any edict if we maneuver within our own borders. Under clan colors, Shinzawai forces will march toward Kentosani from the north, and a mixed garrison of Tuscalora and Acoma forces split off from your estate near Sulan-Qu will march by road to intercept any companies of traditionalist allies, or Anasati troops that take the slow route overland."

Mara speculated, "Jiro would have prepared for this day."

Lujan expanded her thought. "The siege engines? Do you think he has them hidden in the forests south of the Holy City?"

"South or north," said Hokanu. "Arakasi reports that the location of the Anasati engineers is a closely kept secret. Several of the messages he sent in your absence mention their being dismantled and shipped via circuitous routes to points unknown. He also wrote that the saboteurs we sent in with the toy maker's plans have reported back only once. By the code, we can assume all is well, and that they are in place with the siege engines. But their location has been effectively guarded."

"I would have hidden troops away also, were I in Jiro's place," Mara mused, then finished her last orders to Lujan before dismissal. "I want conference with you and Irrilandi before the last boat leaves the docks. We do not know any of Jiro's plan of deployment?" She read the negative on Hokanu's face, and knew that they shared the same thoughts that Arakasi's fears might be realized, and that Chumaka's spy network had evolved to surpass the Acoma's. How else could such massive engines be moved without observation? Mara went on, "We can only guess, and design our campaign to match all contingencies."

While the Acoma Force Commander saluted and hurried out, Hokanu looked upon his wife in fond exasperation. "My brave commander of armies, do you think we have been idle during your absence?" And he drew her through the archway into the scriptorium, where cushions were clustered for a council meeting, and a sand table now replaced the copy desks. There, shaped of clay, was a replica of Szetac Province, complete with the arrays of pins and markers that a tactician would use to represent companies of warriors in the field.

Mara glanced over it. Her body took on a rigid set, and her face became stamped with purpose. "What I see is a defensive deployment."

Her gaze traveled from the sand table and lingered on Saric, her last adviser still present. She ended with an entreaty directed toward her husband. "What we sought to prevent, an all-powerful Warlord, has brought us to a worse pass: there is no High Council to ratify the girl Jehilia's blood right of ascension to the throne as Empress. Unless the Assembly itself intervenes, Justin is caught between the jaws of a coup as a legal claimant; as such, he is a dead puppet, or a sharp weapon that any dissident contingent can use as an excuse to rip this land asunder in civil war. Bereft of the council, we cannot appoint a regent to bind the government to stability until the rational solution of marriage can reinstate a new Emperor of the line. Even if we had enough loyal supporters in the Imperial Precinct to seize control and reconvene the council, we would have deadlock and bickering and murder to make the Night of the Bloody Swords look like a practice match between companies of green recruits. The violence would continue until one house emerged strong enough to force support to favor his cause."

Saric looked grim. "Which cause, mistress? After Ichindar's boldness in seizing absolute rule, what Lord's ambition would be sated with the restoration of the Warlord's title?"

"You do see." Mara's words were crisp. "A ratification will not happen. Even with all of our backing, can you imagine a girl of twelve ruling? With Ichindar's pampered First Wife as regent? If Lord Kamatsu were still alive as Imperial Chancellor, perhaps, with our resolve, we might see a woman where now there is a girl. But if I read your comments aright, Hokanu, Kanazawai Clan support has fragmented under pressure from your rivals and discontented cousins. You hold the office, but not yet the unified clan that your father had forged. Possibly Hoppara of the Xacatecas would stand forth as our ally, but Frasai of the Tonmargu is still Imperial

Overlord. Feeble old man that he is, he still commands Hoppara's office, and as clan brother to Jiro, if chaos breaks loose I doubt he can hold out for a stalwart and independent course. No, a new council could not stem the bloodshed now. Instead, the first Lord who can take control of the palace will force the priests to place Jehilia upon the throne, then take her to wife and see himself anointed Emperor.''

Saric concluded, as always, with another question. "You believe that Jiro was behind the Omechan assassination of the Emperor?"

But his words went unheard. Hokanu was staring into the deep eyes of his wife in something close to outright horror. He said very quietly, his voice edged with menace, or a note of great pain, "You are not thinking of defenses, Lady. You will not be calling out our troops to join with the Imperial Whites against the storm that must soon beset Kentosani?"

"No," Mara admitted into an icy quiet. "I will not. If I get to the Holy City first, I mean to attack."

"Justin?" Saric's voice held a high note of awe. "You would set your son on the throne as Jehilia's husband?"

Mara spun around fast as a cornered beast. "And why not?" Her whole body quivered with stressed nerves. "He is a lawful contender for the divine office of Emperor." Then, into the shocked stillness that followed, she cried out in heart-wrung appeal, "Don't you see? Don't any of you see at all? He's just a little boy, and it's the only possible way to save his life!"

Saric's mind had always been nimble. He was the first to sort the ramifications, and see past Mara's wounding fear. To a stiff-faced Hokanu, he added with no trace of his customary tact, "She's right. Justin alive would pose a threat to any outside faction who took the girl and forced wedlock. No matter how strong the self-styled Emperor's army, he would draw his enemies to the throne with him. No point of law would be overlooked, and Mara's popularity as Servant must force recognition of Justin's adoptive blood tie. Dissidents would seize upon Justin's cause as a rallying cry, whether we willed it or no. Others might be willing to kill us all to win the opportunity to put the boy on the throne as their puppet."

"Civil war." Mara sighed, sounding wrung to her very core. "If Jiro or any other Lord gains the crown, we would have no Emperor, no revered Light of Heaven, but only a more glorified Warlord. It would be a merging of the worst of both offices, when we would hope to wed the best."

Hokanu moved suddenly. He caught her shoulders, turned her face into his chest in time to conceal her dissolution into tears, then stroked her in sad gentleness. "Lady, never fear to lose my support. Never fear that."

Muffled into his warmth, Mara said, "Then you don't disapprove?"

Hokanu smoothed back the hair torn loose from her headdress in the fever of their earlier embrace. His face looked suddenly lined with care and no small foreboding. "I cannot pretend to love the idea, Lady of my heart. But you are right. Justin will make a wise ruler, once he reaches maturity. And until then, as his guardians, we can continue to reject the atrocities of the Game of the Council and enforce a new stability in the Nations. The people must all bow before his and Jehilia's combined claim, and the gods know, the unfortunate girl deserves a mate close to her own age and inclinations. She would indeed be miserable as a puppet, wed to a man viciously driven by ambition, as Jiro is."

Then, as if sensing that Ayaki's loss lay very near to the surface of his wife's thoughts, and that with this chilling threat to Justin her need for solace at this moment must outweigh all other matters, Hokanu lifted his Lady bodily in his arms. He cradled her tenderly against the breastplate of armor and bore her out of the scriptorium. As he turned down the corridor in the direction of their bedchamber, he called to Saric over his shoulder, "If you have brought back from Thuril some means to stay the hand of the Assembly of Magicians, pray to the gods it will work. For unless I am totally mistaken, it must soon be Jiro of the Anasati we face across the field of war."

Once in the privacy of the master suite, Mara pushed impatiently against Hokanu's cradling embrace. "So much to do, and so little time!"

Ignoring her struggles, Hokanu bent and laid her down on the sumptuous cushions of their sleeping mat, and only his fighter's reflexes permitted him the necessary speed to catch her wrists as she immediately tried to shove herself erect. "Lady, we are not caught unprepared. Arakasi has kept us well informed, Keyoke is a craftier strategist than you or I, and Saric will waste no time in giving them word that Justin's claim must of necessity be pressed." As Mara's eyes bored furiously up into his, he gave her an ungentle shake. "Take an hour! Your people will all be the better for being left free of distraction. Let your Force Commander consult with Irrilandi and Keyoke and do his job! Then when he has had time to assemble his ideas, we can hold council, and forge the wisest course between us."

Mara looked again as if she might crumble. "You're not worried for your Shinzawai holdings in the north, or your cousin Devacai's meddling?''

"No." Hokanu was bedrock-firm. "I inherited Dogondi for Shinzawai First Adviser, remember? My father relied on him for years, particularly when he was absent from home as Imperial Chancellor. Dogondi's as crafty as any man alive, and with our new messenger relay in place, he will hear of your need for aid in Justin's cause before sundown tomorrow. Incomo and he have worked together like old cronies. Trust the efficiency of your good officers, Lady. My own servants you have won over shamelessly. Not one who wears Shinzawai blue would do less than give their lives for you, but not if you throw your uninformed opinion into their works just now.''

Another more violent tremor coursed through Mara's body. "How have I done without you all these months?'' she marveled in a voice shaved thin by jangled nerves. "Of course you are right."

Hokanu felt her relax. When he judged it safe, he released her from restraint and waved for a maid to remove her travel clothing. As the woman set about her ministrations, he soon found he could not resist joining in the unwrapping. As the Lady's overrobe came off, and the ties to the underrobe were loosened, he played his hands along the smooth warmth of her flesh. "A bitter homecoming,'' he mused.

"Not the one I would have chosen, husband. I have missed you."

The maid attendant might as well have been invisible.

Hokanu smiled. "And I you." He reached to unbuckle the fastenings of his breastplate, then lost his concentration at even so simple a task as the maid let Mara's inner robe fall away. The sight of his Lady, even tired and dusty from the road, with her hair tumbling loose from its pins, took Hokanu's breath away. She noticed his bemusement and at last managed a smile. Putting her hands over his, she began to work the leather straps through the buckles until he laid his lips upon hers and kissed her. After that, neither noticed as the maid took over the task of his undressing, then bowed to master and mistress and softly stole from the room.

Later, when the couple lay replete with their lovemaking, Hokanu ran his finger gently along the line of Mara's cheek. The light through the screen silvered the streaks of age starting to grow in her black hair, and her skin showed weathering from the harsher sun of the southern lands. Even as he caressed her, she stirred and murmured again, "There is so much to do, and little time."

Mara pushed herself up onto her elbow, a restlessness to her manner that now could not be denied.

Hokanu loosened his embrace, knowing he could not hold her. A war waited to be fought, in open repudiation of the Assembly's disapproval; young Justin's life depended upon the outcome.

Yet as Mara did arise, and clapped for her maid to return to attire her in battle dress, her husband stared after her with a terrible, gnawing poignancy. Hereafter, nothing between them would be the same. Either Jiro would sit on the golden throne, and Mara and all he loved would be destroyed; or they would perish in their attempt to make Justin Emperor; or perhaps most painful of all, Lady Mara would become ruler of Tsuranuanni. Still he simply had no choice; for his own daughter's sake he must add his knowledge of war and trust that the legendary luck of the Good Servant would keep both them and their children alive. He pushed away from the mat, reached Mara in one stride, and while she had one arm helplessly caught in the process of her robing, took her face in his hands and gently, lovingly kissed her. Then he said, "Take time for a bath. I will go ahead of you and take counsel with Lujan and Irrilandi."

Mara returned the kiss, and flashed him a brilliant smile. "No bath would ease me so much as one we could share."

Hokanu let that cheer him, but as he slipped into his discarded clothes and hurried to the council of war, he could not help but recognize that whether they would survive or fall in this full-scale conflict, inevitably their lives would embrace change. He could not shake the foreboding that the events must force distance between him and the Lady he held most dear.

25. Assembly

Chumaka smiled.

He briskly rubbed his hands together as a man might do to warm them, but the day outside his window was hot. What the Anasati First Adviser reacted to was a chill of deep excitement. "At last, at last," he muttered. He swooped amid his clutter of papers and correspondence to grab what looked to be a nondescript notation of tally marks on a creased scrap of paper. But the markings hid a complex code, and the imbedded message was precisely the one that Chumaka had prodded and plotted and cajoled to bring about.

Ignoring the raised eyebrows and questioning manner of his clerk, Chumaka hurried out to seek his master.

Jiro preferred to pass midday in indolence. He never took a siesta, nor, like so many Ruling Lords, did he amuse himself through the heat in lascivious play with concubines. Jiro's tastes were ascetic. He considered the chatter of women distracting, so much so that on a whim he had once ordered all of his female cousins consigned to chaste service in the temples. Chumaka chuckled at the memory. The girls would have no sons to become rivals, which made the master's short-tempered arbitration a wiser move than he knew. Jiro instinctively preferred privacy. At this hour he would be found at his bath, or else reading in the cool, breezy portico that connected the library with the scribes' copy chamber.

Chumaka paused at the junction of two inner corridors, dimly lit since no lamps burned in the heat, and faintly scented with the wax and oil used to treat the wood floors. His thin nostrils twitched.

"Not the baths, today," he muttered, for he could smell no trace of scent borne on the air by the passage of Jiro's bath slaves. The master was fastidious to the point of fussiness. He liked his food spiced to briskness to keep his breath sweet, and favored perfumes in his wash water.

The old, drooping ulo trees that edged the portico outside the library cooled the air even in the most sultry summer weather. Jiro sat on a stone bench, a scroll in his hand, and more heaped haphazardly around his feet. A deaf-mute slave attended him, ready at the twitch of his master's finger to attend to the slightest need. But Jiro's needs were notably few. Beyond the occasional request for a cold drink, he often sat at his reading until midafternoon, when he would meet with his hadonra to discuss estate finances, or arrange for a recital of poetry, or walk in the pretty gardens designed by his great-grandmother, which it had been his pleasure to see replanted and restored.

Immersed in his reading, Jiro did not immediately respond to the rapid tap of Chumaka's sandals against the terra-cotta tile of the portico. When he did notice the sound, he looked up as if at an intrusion, his brows pulled down in vexation, and his manner stiff with restraint.

His expression changed at once to resignation. Chumaka was the most difficult of his servants to dismiss without the fuss of enforcing his rank as Ruling Lord. Somehow Jiro felt it demeaning to deliver bald-faced demands; they were crude, and he prided himself on subtlety, a vanity that Chumaka was well versed in the art of exploiting.

"What is it?" Jiro sighed, then checked his bored exhalation, realizing that his First Adviser was showing the unabashed toothy smile he reserved for felicitous news. The Lord of the Anasati brightened also. "It is Mara," he second-guessed. "She has arrived home to find herself disadvantaged, I hope?"

Chumaka waved his coded note. "Indeed, master, and more. I have just received word directly from our spy implanted in Hokanu's messenger service. We have precise descriptions of how she plans to deploy her troops." Here the Anasati First Adviser's manner dampened, as he recalled how difficult it had been to break the private cipher of Hokanu's correspondence.

As if sensing that a lecture on such subtleties might be forthcoming, Jiro pressed the discussion ahead. "And?"

"And?" Chumaka for a moment looked vague as his train of thought recentered. But his eyes never once lost their sharpness, and his mind worked impressively fast. "And our ruse worked."

Jiro reined back a frown. Always, Chumaka seemed to expect him to follow the vaguest of references without any accompanying explanation. "Which ruse do you speak of?"

"Why, the one concerning the engineers of the siege engines and the toy maker's plans. Lady Mara believes we were duped into hiring her false workers. She has arranged for no attack on our forces that are positioned to storm Kentosani." Here Chumaka gave a wave of dismissal, "Oh, she's cozened her husband to call out the Shinzawai troops from the north. They will attack our northern flank, she believes, while we are in disarray and still struggling to recoup from the deaths she expects will happen in the mishap that results from the first firing of our battle rams and ballistas.''

''They won't fail,'' Jiro mused, his narrow face softening at last. ''They will shatter those ancient fortifications and our men will already be inside.'' He gave a short bark of laughter. ''The Shinzawai troops will arrive only to do homage to a new Emperor!''

''And to bury their boy heir,'' Chumaka added in a low voice. Again he rubbed his hands together. ''Justin, now. Should we say he was killed by fallen masonry, or that he was mistaken for a servant boy and given over to the slave master as spoils? There are many unpleasant ways for a boy to perish in the slave pens.''

Jiro's lips thinned in disapproval, and his eyes narrowed. He was not comfortable with practices he considered brutal or purposely crude— after a childhood spent being bullied by his younger brother Buntokapi, he had no patience in that respect. ''I want it done quickly and cleanly, without unnecessary pain; a 'miscast' spear should do well enough,'' he snapped. Then his tone turned thoughtful. ''Mara, though. If the living body of the Servant of the Empire were to fall into the hands of our troops, she would be another matter.''

Now it was Chumaka's turn to shy from the discussion. Tsurani enough to arrange for men to be tortured or killed when matters made such measures necessary, still he did not relish the idea of causing pain for the Servant of the Empire. The look in Jiro's eyes whenever he contemplated the Lady Mara inevitably gave him an inward urge to shiver.

''I shall arrange to send your Force Commander, Omelo, this latest news of Acoma and Shinzawai deployment, with your leave, my master.''

Jiro gave a languid gesture of acquiescence, his thoughts still focused upon revenge.

Barely waiting for this signal of approval, Chumaka backed off, bowing, his spirits reviving almost at once. Before Jiro had retrieved his scroll and returned to reading, the Anasati First Adviser was hurrying off, muttering ideas and plans half under his breath.

''Those Minwanabi warriors who did not swear service at the time of Mara's ascension to the title of Good Servant, now . . .'' he mused. A wicked gleam flashed in his eyes. ''Yes. Yes. I think the time is appropriate to call them in from that frontier garrison and add their ranks to the confusion of our enemies.''

Chumaka hastened his step, loudly whistling now that he was out of his master's earshot. ''Gods,'' he broke off his tune to whisper, ''what would life be without politics?''

* * *

The Empire mourned. On the announcement of Ichindar's death, the gates to the Imperial Precinct had boomed shut, and the traditional red banners of mourning had unfurled from the walls. The land roads and the waterways of the Gagajin had come alive with messengers. The rare metal gongs and chimes in each of the temples of the Twenty Higher Gods then rang in homage at the passing of Ichindar, ninety-one strokes, one for each generation of his line. The city would stay closed to trade for the traditional twenty days of mourning, and all merchant shops and stalls not essential for the maintenance of life had their doors sealed with red bunting.

Inside Kentosani, the streets were subdued, the hawking cries of food sellers and water brokers stilled; and the chanting of the priests in prayer for the holy departed rang out in the mourning quiet. By tradition, conversation was forbidden in the streets, and even the city's licensed beggars had to seek alms in pantomime. The Red God Turakamu had silenced the Voice of Heaven on Earth, and while Ichindar's embalmed body lay in state amid a circle of lit candles and chanting priests, the Holy City also observed its silence of respect and sorrow.

On the twenty-first day, the Light of Heaven would be placed atop his funeral pyre, and the chosen successor anointed by the priests of the Higher and Lesser Gods would ascend the golden throne as the ashes cooled.

And in anticipation of that day, plots seethed and armies massed. The Assembly was not oblivious to the restlessness of humanity.

Outside the city gates, anchored along the riverside, or cramming the dockside of Silmani and Sulan-Qu, rested the trader barges caught outside the gates by the observance of the Emperor's mourning. Prices for rental of warehouse space soared to a premium as merchants vied to secure shelter for perishable goods caught in transit, or for valuables too choice to be left on boats under insufficient guard. The less fortunate factors bid for space in private cellars and attics, and the least fortunate lost their wares to the rising tides of war.

Clans gathered and house companies armed. The roads became clouded with late summer dust raised by thousands of tramping feet. The rivers became jammed with flotillas of barges and war craft, and all oared or poled transport were engaged to ferry warriors. The merchants suffered, as trade goods were tossed wholesale into the river to make way for human cargo, and shortages in the cities ensued as provender was bought up by the cartload from the costermongers who many times sold out their produce before it could arrive at the city markets. Bartering by the roadside was often conducted at spearpoint. The farmers suffered. The rich complained of high prices; the merchants, of desperate shortfalls; while the poorest went hungry and mobbed the streets in unrest.

The Ruling Lords who might have lent patrols to quell the masses and restore order were busied elsewhere, sending their warriors to support this faction or that, or using the upset of routine to stage raids against enemies whose garrisons were pared down for field battle. Riots threatened in the poor quarter, while profiteers grew fat on inflated prices.

The Empire's various factions armed and banded together into vast war hosts, and yet for all of the house colors that sent troops to converge upon Kentosani, the banners of three prominent houses were conspicuous by their absence: Acoma green, Shinzawai blue, and Anasati red and yellow.

In a high tower in the City of the Magicians, closeted within a study cluttered with books and scrolls and dominated by a dented hard-fired clay samovar of foreign craft and origin, the Great One Shimone sat with bony fingers laced around a teacup. He had developed a fondness for the Midkemian delicacy in its myriad varieties, and servants kept the brazier under the samovar hot day and night. The cushions the Black Robe perched on were as thin as his ascetic tastes. Before him rested a low three-legged table whose top was inlaid with a seeing crystal, through which danced the images of mustering war hosts. It showed brief glimpses of Mara and Hokanu in conference with advisers, followed by a view of Jiro gesticulating to make some point with a stiff-lipped Omechan Lord who looked reluctant.

Shimone sighed. His fingers tapped an agitated rhythm on his tepid cup.

But it was Fumita, sitting almost invisibly in the shadows opposite, who voiced the obvious thought. "They fool nobody, least of all us. Each waits for the other to move, so that when we appear, they can say with clear conscience, 'We were but defending ourselves.' "

Neither magician belabored the sad, self-evident conclusion: that despite their personal endorsement of Mara's radical ideas, the Assembly's prevailing sentiment ran against her. Acoma and Anasati had sounded the horns of war. Whether or not Mara and Jiro officially unfurled their standards, whether or not they had formally announced their intentions and petitioned the priest of the War God to smash the Stone Seal on the Temple of Jastur, all but the splinter factions in some way took their lead from Anasati and Acoma. The Assembly of Magicians would unavoidably be forced to take action. In the strained silence that followed between

Fumita and Shimone, a buzzing sound could be heard beyond the door. This was followed by a heavy thump and a fast tread, and the wooden latch tripped up.

"Hochopepa," Shimone said, his deep eyes seeming lazily half-closed. He set down his cup, flicked his hand, and the vistas in the seeing crystal muddied and faded away.

Fumita arose. "Hocho in a hurry can only mean that enough of our number have gathered for a quorum," he surmised. "We had best join him in the great hall."

The door to Shimone's private chamber creaked open, and a red-faced Hochopepa shoved through, his large girth hampered by the clutter. "You'd better make haste. One hothead down there in council just proposed to blast half the population of Szetac Province to cinders."

Fumita clicked his tongue. "No discrimination was made between spear-carrying warriors and peasant families driven to flee the path of the armies?"

Hochopepa sucked in fat cheeks. "None." He backed, wheezing out of the doorway, beckoning for his companions to follow. "And for worse news, the point you just made was the only argument that stayed the vote. Otherwise some fool would be down there right this moment turning everything in sight to smoking char!" He turned down the hall without waiting to see if the others followed.

At this, Fumita was through the doorway hard on the stout mage's heels. "Well, I think we have the imagination between us to trump up a few more objections and slow them down a while longer." He glanced over his shoulder to admonish Shimone, who could seem as reluctant to move quickly as to use words. "It can't be helped, my friend. This time you are going to have to talk as much as the rest of us to help the cause along."

The ascetic mage's eyes snapped open to show a spark of affront. "Talk is quite different an expenditure of energy from empty chatter!"

As the thin magician's glare swiveled toward the portly leader of the party, it was Hochopepa's turn to look offended. Yet before he could find something heated to say in his own defense, Fumita hustled him ahead. "Save your energy," he said, hiding a grin behind solemnity. "What inspiration we have we'd better muster for the council chamber. They are probably quarreling like Midkemian monkeys down there, and here we go rushing in to make it worse."

Without further discussion, the three hurried down the corridor to the entrance to the Great Hall.

* * *

The debate Mara's supporters hastened to join continued for days. Many times in the course of the Empire's history arguments had divided the Assembly, but none before had raged so long and so hotly. Stray winds ripped through the great chamber that served as meeting hall in the City of the Magicians, as more and more members gathered. The high, tiered galleries were nearly filled to capacity, an event only equaled in recent times by the occasion of the debate of Milamber's exile and the abolition of the office of Warlord. The only absentees were Great Ones in their dotage. The air grew stuffy with the crowding, and since no meeting of the Assembly ever adjourned without a final decision, the proceedings dragged on day and night.

Yet another dawn seeped grey through the high windows of the dome, silvering the lacquer floor tiles and revealing weariness in every face present. It lit in drab colors the only activity: in the middle of the vast chamber, a stout magician paced back and forth, declaiming.

Fatigue etched Hochopepa's face. He waved one stout arm, and grated on in a voice made hoarse by hours of nonstop oratory, "And I urge every one of you to consider: great changes have begun that will not be undone!" He raised his other arm, and clapped his palms together to emphasize his point, and several of the elderly Black Robes started in their seats, roused from dozing. "We cannot simply wave our hand and have the Empire return to the old ways! The days of the Warlordship are finished!"

Shouts of disagreement sought to interrupt his argument. "Armies are marching while we deliberate," cried Motecha, among the more outspoken of the Great Ones who disapproved of the late Ichindar's policies.

On the floor, the stout magician held up his hand for silence, actually grateful for the momentary respite. His throat was scratched raw from speaking. "I know!" He waited for stillness to settle and went on. "We have been defied. So I have heard many of you repeat over and over"—he glanced around the room, aware of a change that rippled like the movement of the tide through his audience—"and over and over." Even the more staid members of the council were now shifting in their seats. Their backsides were numb from sitting, and no longer were they content to settle back and politely listen. More than just the impatient had started to cry out interruptions, and not a few were standing belligerently on their feet. Hochopepa admitted to himself that he would have to yield the floor at last, and hope Fumita or the wily Teloro could find a strategy to draw the discussion out further.

"We are not gods, my brothers," Hochopepa summed up. "We are powerful, yes, but still merely men. For us to intervene rashly with force, from pique or fear of the unknown, would but increase the chance of lasting damage being visited upon the Nations. I caution all that no matter how inflamed passions may be, the effect of our act will be lingering. When emotions at last cool, shall we regret having done that which even we cannot undo?'' He ended his speech with a slow lowering of his arms, and an even slower shuffle across the floor. The heaviness in him as he sank into his seat was not feigned; he had successfully tied up the floor for two and a half days.

The current spokesman for the Assembly returned onto the floor, blinking as if a bit bemused. ''We thank Hochopepa for his wisdom.''

While the huge chamber echoed with the rising buzz of conversation and dozens of Black Robes vied to speak next, Fumita leaned across Shimone and whispered to his wilted companion, ''Well done, Hocho!''

Drily Shimone interjected, ''Perhaps for the next few days we will be blessed with a less loquacious companion when we gather over our wine.''

Spokesman Hodiku said, ''We shall hear Motecha!''

The short, hook-nosed elder, whose two cousins had once been known as the Warlord's Pets, arose from his seat. Motecha moved with spry steps across the floor, and spun with a flutter of robes. His sharp, narrow-set eyes passed over the assembly briefly, and he said, ''While it has been interesting in no sparse measure to hear our brother Hochopepa recount the history of events, in great detail, this does nothing to change fact. Two armies are even now jockeying to engage in combat. Skirmishes have already occurred between them, and only those of us who are fools do not see through the sham of masking their house colors behind the banners of clan cousins or allies! Mara of the Acoma has defied our edict. Even as we speak, her warriors march and engage in illicit warfare!''

''Why name her ahead of Jiro of the Anasati?'' the impulsive Sevean called back.

Teloro seized the opportunity of the interruption to add fuel to the argument. ''You call the actions of these armies defiance. I urge remembrance upon us all: the Light of Heaven has been murdered! It must be contested, Motecha, that circumstances have forced a call to arms. Lord Hokanu of the Shinzawai would naturally defend the royal family. Mara was Ichindar's staunchest supporter. Jiro, I submit, builds siege engines and hires engineers to plot for his own ambition, not to stabilize the Empire.''

Motecha folded his arms, emphasizing his round-shouldered posture.

"Was it circumstance that led both Jiro of the Anasati and Mara of the Acoma and her consort to order their armies into the field? Neither of their home estates was threatened! Is this conflict in truth inevitable? Did the supposed 'Good of the Empire' 'force' Mara to order the secondary garrison from her natal estate to prevent Anasati forces and allies from their use of the public roads to Sulan-Qu?"

"Come now!" cracked Shimone. He had an authoritative voice, when he chose to raise it, and now his stillness held pent-up ire. "How do you know it was Mara who instigated the attack, Motecha? I heard of no battle, but only a skirmish that ended with a drawing of lines. Do we whimper civil war when there has been little but a calling of names and an exchange of insults and some sporadic bowfire?"

Teloro expounded a second point. "I would have you note: The banner at the fore of the lines near Sulan-Qu was not Acoma, but that of Lord Jidu of the Tuscalora. He may be Mara's vassal, but his estate lies directly in the path of Jiro's march. The Lord of the Tuscalora could legitimately be defending his lands from invasion."

Motecha narrowed his gaze. "Our colleague Tapek went to the field and observed, Teloro. I may not be the student of history that your friend Hochopepa is, but I can certainly hear the difference between a defensive position and an army launching an assault!"

"And Jiro's collection of siege engines in the forests outside *Kentosani* are for defense?" Shimone cried back, but his point was drowned by the hubbub of other voices.

The Spokesman shouted for order. "Colleagues! The business at hand requires order."

Motecha shrugged his robe straight like a jigacock puffing its feathers. He stabbed a finger at the galleries. "Arrows have been fired between a vassal of Mara's and Anasati warriors masquerading under the banner of Clan Ionani. Are we going to sit about arguing until our edict is defied a second time? Tapek reports that troops have felled trees for buttresses to give their archers better cover."

Clearing his throat, Hochopepa croaked hoarsely, "Well then, Tapek could have ordered a stop to the shooting." This brought laughter and an upwelling of derogatory comments. "Or was it the fact that stray arrows show little regard for the majesty of a Black Robe that gave our friend Tapek pause?"

At this, Tapek sprang to his feet, his red hair brilliant against the black robes behind. He shouted, "We already told Mara to stop once! Has she so swiftly forgotten the troop of warriors we destroyed as an example upon the field?"

"Motecha has the floor," objected the Spokesman. "You will stay seated unless you are formally given leave to lead the discussion, friend Tapek."

The red-haired magician subsided to his seat, muttering to the contingent of young friends who sat with him.

Motecha resumed his point. "I submit that Jiro of the Anasati has made no move in aggression. His siege engines may surround the walls of Kentosani, but they do not fire! And they may never do so, if Mara is prevented from linking up with her support inside the Imperial Precinct."

"What support? Do you imply that Mara has been party to treachery?" called Shimone. "That she had no hand in the Omechan plot to kill Ichindar has been documented!"

Again the Assembly erupted into disorder. For several minutes Spokesman Hodiku had to hold up his hands to restore quiet. The muttering subsided reluctantly, with Sevean caught still gesticulating as he expounded some point to a colleague. He lowered his voice, looking sheepish.

Hochopepa mopped sweat from his brow. "It begins to look as if I did not need to spend my voice in speechmaking." He chuckled under his breath. "Our opponents are doing a fair job of tangling the issue by themselves."

"Not for much longer, I fear," Shimone said ominously.

Motecha added further accusations, more outspoken than any of his predecessors'. "I say Mara of the Acoma is the culprit! Her disregard, no, her contempt of tradition is well documented. How she came to wear the honored title of Servant of the Empire is for others to conjecture. But I suggest that she and the late Emperor had an . . . understanding. It is Mara's son, Justin, she would raise as pretender to the golden throne, and I endorse Jiro's right to defend against this unconscionable show of Acoma ambition!"

"That ends it," Fumita said gloomily. "Sooner or later, the adoptive privilege of Mara's children had to be raised. Someone had to drag the boy into the quarrel."

There was true sadness in his tone, perhaps in his personal remembrance of the son he had renounced upon his call to join the Assembly. Yet whatever else he might have added became drowned in a wave of shouting. Magicians sprang to their feet, and several seemed to glow with the light of inner anger. Through the tumult, Spokesman Hodiku waved his staff, and when he was ignored, gave over the floor to a young mage named Akani.

That many a seasoned elder had been passed over in favor of a Black Robe barely out of his apprenticeship effected an immediate and resounding silence.

Akani kept command of it with the voice of a powerful orator. "Assumption of facts not in evidence," he summed up crisply. "We know nothing of any plotting by Mara of the Acoma. We cannot deny she has lost her firstborn son. Justin is her sole heir. If she were party to a plot to raise him to the Emperor's station, she would hardly have set such intrigue in motion while she was absent from the court. Only a fool would leave the boy to fend for himself through a change in succession without Acoma or Shinzawai defenders. Justin is housed with Ichindar's children, in the imperial nursery, which I remind you was quarantined upon his death for twenty days of mourning! A child's life could be lost to a thousand mishaps in such a span of time. If Acoma troops march, they do so to spare their future Lord. Companions, I suggest," Akani finished tartly, "that we not be swayed by *speculation* and *street gossip* in the making of our decisions."

Shimone raised his grey furred eyebrows as the young magician continued a reasoned, dispassionate argument. "Good choice of argument. The boy thinks like an imperial court litigator."

Hochopepa chuckled. "Akani studied for that post before his magical powers forced him to be recognized as a Black Robe. Why do you think I called in a favor to ask Hodiku to choose him when the discussion swung toward violence? Jiro's supporters, like our outspoken Tapek, must not be permitted to stampede us into acting rashly."

And yet even Akani's skills as litigator could not keep the floor tied up for long. Feelings ran hot, and by now even those Black Robes who had been neutral to the contention were clamoring for decision, if only to bring the long, tiresome session to an end.

Pressure from all sides erupted to draw the proceedings to a close. Akani had exhausted his eloquence, and in fairness to his earlier ruling, the Spokesman Hodiku had to yield the floor to allow Tapek his say.

"Trouble now," Shimone said flatly.

Hochopepa's brow wrinkled, and Fumita became statue-still.

Tapek wasted no time in convincing oratory. "It is fact, companions, that the Assembly acted as a body once before and ordered Mara not to attack Jiro. For the Good of the Empire, I demand her life be forfeit!"

Hochopepa shot to his feet, astonishingly fast for one of his girth. "I dissent."

Tapek spun on his heel to face the stout magician. "What mortal in all our long history has ever been allowed to live after defying our edict?"

"I can count several," Hochopepa shot back, "but I doubt that would settle the issue." The stout magician's voice was stripped down to gravel. Now he abandoned flowery, long-winded phrases. "Let us not act impulsively. We can kill Mara at our leisure, should we so decide. But this moment we have more pressing problems to consider."

"He's going to force a vote," Fumita murmured worriedly to Shimone. "That could precipitate disaster."

Shimone's brows seemed frozen into a glower as he replied, "Let him. Disaster is inevitable anyway."

Hochopepa moved down the aisle. Clown-like in his bulk, red-faced and smiling with good nature, he did not seem at all contentious, and such jovial posture in the face of tense proceedings lent him liberty, if only for comic relief. Spokesman Hodiku did not reprimand him as he wandered out onto the floor and began to pace in step with Tapek. His naturally short stride was forced to extend to ridiculous length to match the taller magician. Hochopepa's fat jiggled under his robe, and his cheeks puffed with exertion. He capped his ridiculous appearance by waving a pudgy hand just under Tapek's nose in vehement gesticulation.

As Tapek sucked back his chin to avoid being stabbed by a fingernail, Hochopepa said, "I suggest we try other expedients before *we obliterate the Servant of the Empire.*" Several members of the Assembly winced at such bald reiteration, and Hochopepa boldly seized the advantage to drive home his point. "Before we commit an act never before done in the history of our Nations—to destroy a holder of the *most honorable title a citizen may obtain*—let us consider."

"We have considered—" Tapek interjected, stopping dead.

Hochopepa kept walking and with apparent clumsiness seemed to slam into his younger colleague, knocking him off balance. Tapek was compelled to stumble ahead, or fall flat. Flustered and caught at a loss for words, he was swept on as Hochopepa continued his monologue.

"We should stop the bloodshed first, then order Mara and Jiro to the Holy City. There they can be held while we judge this issue in a less muddled fashion. Shall we vote?"

The Spokesman called, "A question is on the floor."

"I hold the floor!" Tapek objected.

Hochopepa at that moment trod heavily upon the redhead's slippered toe. Tapek's mouth opened. His cheeks turned white, then burned bright red. He rounded angrily upon Hochopepa, who stood with his full weight bearing down as if oblivious. And while Tapek was distracted by discomfort, Hodiku pressed on with the proceedings.

"Now, it's been a long and boring session," Hochopepa whispered to

Tapek. "Why don't we both sit down and regain our composure before the very serious matter of casting our vote?"

Tapek growled between clenched teeth. He knew it was now too late to disrupt protocol and countermand the call for a formal vote. As Hochopepa raised his bulk off Tapek's toe, the offended magician had little choice but to limp off, grumbling, to rejoin his cadre of young bloods. The Spokesman raised his hand. "Hear the options, yea or nay. Shall we order the fighting halted and Mara and Jiro to the Holy City for accounting before our body?"

Each magician in that vast chamber held up one hand. Light sprang from their upraised palms, blue indicating agreement, white abstention, and red disagreement. The blue glow clearly dominated, and the Spokesman said, "The issue is settled. Let the Assembly adjourn for food and rest and gather again at a later date to decide who should be sent to deliver word of our summons to the parties, Mara of the Acoma and Jiro of the Anasati."

"Brilliant!" exclaimed Shimone, seemingly oblivious to the black looks shot in his direction by Tapek and Motecha. All around them, magicians were rising stiffly to their feet, sighing in anticipation of a meal and a long rest. The session had stretched out to the point where it might take days to recapture the enthusiasm to gather another quorum and see an official spokesman appointed. And when a matter had been formally voted to resolution by the full Assembly, individuals like Tapek were denied their option of independent action. Shimone's ascetically thin lips stretched in a way that suggested a smile. "Personally, I think I could sleep for at least a week."

"You won't," Fumita accused. "You'll be snuggled up with a bottle of wine and hunched over your scrying crystal, just like the rest of us."

Hochopepa sighed deeply and said, "We have narrowly averted what would have been perhaps the most destructive action in all of our long history." He glanced around to ascertain that no bystanders were paying undue attention, then whispered, "And we have won a few days' grace. I pray that Mara has some clever plan in play that I don't see, or that her voyage into Thuril won her some protection that she can deploy quickly. If not, and we lose her, we fall back into the atrocities of the Game of the Council for another span of ages. . . ."

Fumita was blunter. "Chaos."

Hochopepa stiffened his spine. "I feel the need for something wet and soothing for my throat."

Shimone's deep eyes sparkled. "I have some of that Keshian wine you love so much stashed away in my quarters."

Hochopepa's brow puckered in abject surprise. "I didn't know you had dealings with Midkemian traders!"

"I don't." Shimone sniffed in reproof. "There's a shop near the docks in the Holy City that always seems to stock a supply. My servant doesn't ask how the proprietor came by such without imperial tax stamps on each bottle, and who would argue with what seems a reasonable price . . . ?"

As the three magicians made their way out of the vast assembly hall, their conversation turned toward the commonplace, as if light words and camaraderie might somehow stave off the immensity of the crisis about to overwhelm their land and culture.

26. Battle

The camp burned.

Smoke swirled across the battlefield, acrid with the stench of burned hide and the fine-woven wool of cushions and hangings that customarily adorned the field tents of Tsurani Lords and officers. War dogs yapped and snarled, and a boy runner raced to find a healer to attend to a wounded officer. Mara blinked watering eyes and turned her back on the soldiers who picked through the ashes to gather up corpses and weapons. The raid at dawn had been a success. Another of Jiro's traditionalist allies had died in his command tent, while his officers and warriors had rolled out of their blankets in disarray. Lujan was unsurpassed at ambush and surprise raids; better than his counterparts who had never known the hardships of a grey warrior's existence, he knew how to take advantage of subterfuge and guile. Most of the fighting had involved minor allies and vassals of the Acoma and the Anasati; other clashes had happened between houses that had old blood debts to settle. And while the magicians would be swift to condemn a massed attack on a formal plain of war, smaller struggles such as these had so far passed unpunished.

Such forbearance could not long continue, Mara knew, as she turned wearily toward the small, unadorned shelter hastily thrown up on a space of ground unhacked by fighting. Lujan knew it, too; he threw himself into each skirmish with near-to-fanatical energy, as if he could not rest until one more enemy was dead.

Hot, tired, and rubbed raw by the unaccustomed weight of full armor, Mara passed through the flap into the shade of her personal quarters. Swirls of dust entered with her. She waved, and a maid scurried out of the dimness to unlace the straps of her battle sandals. The sumptuous comforts of the pavilion-sized Acoma command tent had stayed packed away at the estate, its substitute a simple tent borrowed from stores, that had previously served as shelter for needra herders. Since her trip to Thuril, Mara's view of certain Tsurani customs had soured; and anyway, the green-dyed command tent with its silken banners and trappings and tassels would only serve as announcement to the magicians of her whereabouts.

The herder's tent was hot. It filtered out the direct sun, and some of the noise, as officers called orders, and wounded men moaned in the throes of their pain. "Water," Mara requested. She raised a grimy hand and unfastened the chin strap of her helm.

"Great Lady, let me help." Kamlio hastened around the rude flap that divided the structure in half. Better schooled than the maid to answer the needs of men, the buckles of armor were familiar to her. Expertly she applied herself, and as the encumbering layers of lacquered platework were lifted from her mistress, Mara sighed in relief. "Bless you," she murmured, and nodded her thanks to the maid who handed her a cup of cool water. Never again would she take such service for granted.

Kamlio freed another buckle and noticed Mara's slight flinch. "Blisters, Lady?"

Mara gave a rueful nod. "Everywhere. I can't seem to grow calluses fast enough." The trappings of the Warchief of Clan Hadama were items she seldom wore, but now, more than ever, every badge of office and sign of rank must be displayed. She was on a field of war, commanding troops, and an alliance of forces not seen in modern history. They might march under the banners of a hundred minor houses, or be her own forces masked under the standard of her clan; but they numbered seventy thousand, fully half the might of the Empire. Their lives, if not their ultimate survival, were her responsibility.

This war has come too fast! she raged inwardly while Kamlio removed greaves and breastplate and finished with the straps of the braces. War hosts had gathered before she had been able to settle a single plan of action, nor even to arrange a consultation between Keyoke and the cho-ja mages from Chakaha. Ichindar's assassination had happened while she had all the necessary pieces for victory within her grasp, but before she had any chance to assess how best to use them.

Kamlio had just unfastened Mara's breastplate when footsteps sounded outside the tent. As the heavy, ornate helm with its bosses and plumes and cheek plates was lifted off, Mara closed her eyes in weariness. She pushed back the hair plastered in wet streaks to her forehead and neck. "Open the tent flap," she commanded her maid. "If that's Lujan, back already, I fear bad news."

The maid flipped back the needra hide that curtained the door, while Kamlio rummaged for refreshments and cups for water. The warriors had been on the field since daybreak, and whichever officer approached to report, he would be hungry and thirsty.

A shadow crossed the light, limned in a drift of smoke. Mara blinked stinging eyes and made out the plumes of her Force Commander as he saluted, fist over heart. Her expression must have shown apprehension, for his mouth split at once in a smile of reassurance, made the more vivid by the soot that darkened his face.

"Lady, the Zanwai and Sajaio are in full flight. The day is ours; if one can rejoice over winning a pitiful strip of ngaggi swamp, the ashes of some tents, and six mongrel war dogs that are inclined to tear the throat out of anything that moves—one of the casualties was their handler—then rejoice. The strike force that attempted to organize a retreat was quickly routed, mostly because the officer in charge had little more brains than House Sajaio's dogs."

Mara regarded a sky fouled grey with smoke, then spoke with bitterness. "How much longer are we going to have to remain here in defensive line to keep the Anasati forces pinned to the southeast of Sulan-Qu?" It irked her to know that Jiro had other forces hidden to the north. Any day she expected word that the Holy City was under siege. With the Shinzawai army under Hokanu in forced march, but still several days away from Silmani and the Gagajin, she had no choice but to rely on the toy maker's plans and the engineers she had sent to infiltrate Jiro's operation. She could only lie awake each night and pray that her carefully planned sabotage would work, and that when Jiro ordered his great engines to breach the walls, the mechanisms would misfire and create havoc.

The cho-ja mages could not help in this war. Their magic must be kept secret until the most desperate moment when the Assembly at last acted, for with rival factions massing to descend on Kentosani, full-scale conflict was only a matter of time. The rival armies could only face off for so long, abiding skirmishes and small encounters. Neither would be deterred by the dozen or so smaller armies that jockeyed for the most advantageous positions from which to pick over what bones the great houses might leave in their wake of destruction.

Mara motioned for the Force Commander to enter her quarters. "How long? Jiro must make a move soon, either to break our lines or to order his allies from the west in siege of the Holy City. How much longer can we hang back without jeopardizing support to Hokanu? If something goes wrong . . ." Her voice trailed off; she felt beaten down by the forced agony of waiting, fully armed and at the ready, yet unable to advance. If she ordered her main army to march on Kentosani, she left open a way for the Anasati forces to reach the river or the trade roads, or to attack her from the rear. As long as the Acoma forces held their lines, Jiro's Force Commander could not attack and break through to Sulan-Qu without inciting retribution from the Assembly.

But it pained her to hold firm, knowing that Ichindar's assassination was but the first step in a complex, linked plot. Jiro had not spent years building siege engines or paid lavish bribes and won alliances in the estates surrounding the Inrodaka for nothing. The threat to Justin would come from the west, she was sure, and were her enemies to break through the defenses of the Imperial Precinct before she could get there, her children would lose their lives. The Imperial Whites were good warriors, but with Ichindar dead, who would command their loyalty? Ichindar's First Wife could not even control her own daughter. The Imperial Force Commander would defend the Imperial Precinct, but without a clear authority from above, his men would be an unknown factor. They would fight, but would they defend with the same dedication and selflessness her own forces gave to her? Any warrior might be expected to falter, if the Lord ordering the assault upon the Imperial Precinct might be the next Emperor. Now, more than ever, Mara perceived the flaws in the Tsurani order of rule.

''Gods,'' she exclaimed in frustration, ''this campaign would be bloody but straightforward if we could plan without interference from the Assembly!''

Lujan considered his mistress's restlessness with concern, experienced as he was in the frailties of men kept too long at battle pitch with no fighting. His mistress was stretched near to breaking with tension. The padded robe she wore under her armor was wringing wet with sweat. She had been stubborn, and had overseen the action while standing directly in the sun. He kept his voice mild as he said, ''You should take every opportunity you can to sit down and rest, my Lady.'' As example, he pointedly removed his helm and sank cross-legged on the nearest cushion. ''Action could break out at a moment's notice, and little good you will be to your people if you are worn out or in a faint from the heat.'' He scratched his chin, unable to fully silence his own gnawing worry. ''Though it is certainly obvious to everyone that the magicians are conspicuous by their absence.''

''A bad sign,'' Mara allowed. ''Hokanu's guess is that they deliberate over a united ultimatum. If either Jiro or I engage our forces directly, they will act, be sure of that.'' She let the maid peel off her underrobe, and gestured for a dry replacement. ''I'll bathe later, when the smoke has settled and things have a chance of staying clean.''

Lujan rubbed at a bruised elbow, but broke off the motion as Kamlio handed him water. He drank deeply, his eyes turned toward the command map unrolled on the bare earth beside the table. Stones weighted the corners, and the middle held whorls and lines of colored tiles that displayed the disposition of every faction's forces up to the latest report. The spoiling impatience that ate at his Lady was shared by every man in the ranks. Action was needed, Lujan knew, to keep their wits sharp, and to prevent rash moves born of frustration. Even a small engagement would serve, focusing attention and discipline to keep the troops whetted to keenest edge. He considered the map in depth, then pulled his sword to use as a pointer. "It's clear that a group of neutrals has set up a defensive position along the eastern branch of the river Gagajin, between the fork north of the Great Swamp and the city of Jamar. They could march west and harry Jiro's flank, but more likely they'll be satisfied to wait and declare for the winner at the last."

Mara spoke around the efforts of the maid, who sponged and dried her face, then slipped on her clean robe. "What are you thinking? A diversion? If we could stir them up and make them move around, could we confuse things enough to hide an advance by a few of our companies?"

"Keyoke suggested we might take them captive, steal their armor and banners, then slip a company of our men north under their false identity." Lujan's mouth quirked in amusement. "Not at all honorable, Lady, but there are men of yours who are loyal enough not to care." His eyes held frank admiration for Mara's slim fitness, and for the blisters she bore without complaint. "But the question came down to what forces we could break away to start the skirmish that would not be obvious to our enemies."

"I could arrange that, I think," offered a velvet-toned voice. A shadow emerged out of the blown smoke, poised in the gap of the doorway. As always, Arakasi's appearance had been silent. Accustomed as Mara was to his unexpected arrivals, she barely masked her flinch. Kamlio, taken unawares, spilled the water crock over the map. Counters washed awry in the flood, and water pooled ominously in the hollow that represented Kentosani. Movement in the tent was arrested as Arakasi caught sight of her for the first time since she returned from Thuril; his eyes widened for an instant, showing depths that beseeched. Then he recovered cool control and his gaze flicked back to the map. Fast as reflex, he kept talking. "The spilled water has nicely summed up the situation we have building. Lady, did you get my reports?"

"Some of them." Mara touched Kamlio's hand, and urged her to leave, or sit down. "Let the maid take care of mopping up," she murmured kindly. Kamlio had never looked more like a gazen caught vulnerable under thin cover; and yet Thuril had changed her. She did not turn sullen and stiff, but gathered her courage and sat.

Arakasi took a quick breath, and his eyebrows twitched quizzically. Then, all business, he knelt by the table and laced his hands in plain view on top, as if, with other eyes watching, he dared himself to fidget or shake. He did not look tired, Mara judged, but simply harried, and he wore no disguise beyond a plain black robe edged with white. Although communications had passed between them since her return from the South, this was the first chance he had to make a personal appearance since the Emperor's assassination. "Lady, it is as we feared. The Inrodaka and their two vassals were in league with Jiro; their declarations of neutrality were feigned. The siege engines were hidden in the forests, and are now moving toward Kentosani."

"Where?" Lujan asked crisply.

Arakasi caught the drift of the Force Commander's concern. "Southwest of the Holy City." He summed up the worst. "There are traditionalists from Neshka Province involved as allies, and to the north, the Inrodaka have sent out flanking troops that will certainly harry Hokanu's march south. He has better numbers; he will not be stopped, but will suffer losses and be delayed."

"Allies from Neshka?" Mara said. "These we can fight." To Lujan, she asked, "Could the garrison from my estate by Sulan-Qu march to the west and intercept?"

Arakasi interrupted, uncharacteristically blunt. "The troops are too close to Kentosani already. You could only harry the rear guard, and maybe force them to turn a few companies to engage us. That would thin out the forces left for the siege, but not stop them."

"And the lands of your birthright would be left stripped too thin to be defended effectively," Lujan added. He frowned in furious thought. "Your original bargain with the cho-ja queen gives you two companies of warriors. They would be adequate to repulse any independent force who tried looting or raiding, but not Jiro's army if he chooses to concentrate Anasati effort in that direction."

"The magicians forbid such a move," Mara countered, leaning to one side to allow the maid to pass with towels to soak up the puddles on the tactical map. "My estates by Sulan-Qu should be sacrosanct." She tapped her fingers together in painful decision. "Kentosani must be our first concern. If Jiro wins the golden throne, all of our causes are lost. We have only the toy maker's plans to foil him. And if our plot there is successful, many of the enemy will die when the siege engines are set into play. That will make numbers of troops critical. Pare them down, and Jiro might not have enough men left to scale the walls before Hokanu can win through. No, the estates by Sulan-Qu must be risked. The unknown to be feared is the Assembly. What will the magicians do if we strip the Acoma lands by Sulan-Qu and engage these tradionalists from Neshka Province?''

"No man can know," Arakasi allowed. As if he were not aware of Kamlio watching his every move, he helped himself from the tray of refreshments brought in when Mara's maid finished with the cleanup. "But it is my guess that there the Lord of the Anasati may have outsmarted himself. He has taken best care that his supporters from Neshka appear to be acting on their own. If Jiro wins the throne, and the Assembly accuses him afterward of overly ambitious action, he has left himself a convenient appearance of noninvolvement. He can demur, and say that the alliance was formed out of popular opinion, and his bid for the imperial crown was not his doing at all, but one launched by traditionalists in his behalf as the most worthy candidate.'' Between bites of bread, the Spy Master added, "Mistress, your opposition to such a move might be encouraged by the Assembly as a natural balance of power.''

"The Sulan-Qu property might be sacrificed on such a supposition," Lujan warned. He stirred through sopped counters with his sword, to bare that section of the map.

Mara's exasperation showed as she said, "We are like two duelists who have been told that certain moves will cause the judge to strike the offender down, yet not told which moves they are.''

Arakasi set aside his crust to manipulate the pieces into fresh positions, and under his hands, an ominous clot of assorted colors fanned out toward Kentosani. "Jiro may command the more critical position for assault on the Imperial Precinct, but we are a larger force with more resources.''

Mara took up his unfinished thought. "We have deep support from Lord Hoppara of the Xacatecas, but he is mewed up in Kentosani. His office gives him no leave to act without an Emperor, save to defend, and Isashani in Ontoset can only send Xacatecas forces to him to catch up with events.'' Mara sighed. "Politically, we are disadvantaged. There are more who favor a return to the old Council than who stand with us. No, this will not be a drawn-out war. Either we win decisively, and early, or Jiro will gain a broader base of supporters.''

Lujan fingered his sword edge, as if annoyed by the nicks that had yet to be sharpened out following the morning's minor action. "You fear desertion and betrayal?''

"I do not fear them," answered Mara, "but should we falter, I expect them.'' As order was restored to the map, she chewed her lip, and decided. "We must threaten the siege, at any cost. The estates by Sulan-Qu must be risked. Lujan, how should we proceed?''

The Acoma Force Commander gathered up his sweat-damp helm. "We can ask our friend Lord Benshai of the Chekowara to begin moving northward toward your old estates, but keep him on the western bank of the river. Let Jiro wonder if he goes to reinforce our garrison there, or if he will continue on to the Holy City."

Mara gave back a smile of fierce satisfaction. "Tempt him to commit even a fraction of his Anasati troops to hamper House Chekowara, and his hand will be tipped for the Assembly to read."

"Should Jiro move across the river to intercept him, Benshai will run like a frightened calley-bird," Arakasi said drily. "His house servants say behind his back that Benshai mumbles words of cowardice in his sleep."

Mara sighed. "If we're lucky, Jiro doesn't know that."

Now Arakasi spoke, an edge of frustration to his tone. "Jiro certainly knows. His adviser Chumaka might as well have his ear by the Lord of the Chekawara's fat mouth, listening to his every breath. My agents have proof that he kept Clan Hadama in disarray through the years he served as Clan Warchief. Despite his rich robes and stern-looking soldiers, he is all appearance and no substance. No, he might march resolutely up the river, but the first suggestion of an Anasati attack will send Benshai of the Chekowara running south. Jiro will know the moment your estates near Sulan-Qu are unguarded since half of Benshai's courtesans are Chumaka's spies."

An underlying vehemence in Arakasi's tone caused Kamlio to straighten. Almost, she drew breath to address him, before a flush swept her cheeks. She glanced down in painful embarrassment.

Mara noticed, slightly ahead of Lujan. She touched her Force Commander's wrist beneath the table to still the discussion of weighty matters, and force the cross-current of tension between Spy Master and ex-courtesan to develop into reaction.

Arakasi spoke first, a ring like barbarian iron beneath his soft-spoken manner. "I don't like the Lord of the Chekowara's habits." His distaste was plain as he added, "Young girls who are spies are a specialty of Chumaka's. Mara was once nearly killed by such a one. Her name was Teani." He paused, his eyebrows tipped upward in inquiry. "If you want to know anything of my thoughts, on this or any other subject, you have only to ask. Only, please leave off staring at me as if I were a book scroll, or a puzzle, or some sort of talking pet."

Kamlio started to her feet, confusion on her face. "I don't think of you that way." She seemed breathless, as if she had been running. She started to bow, her mouth parted to ask Mara's leave to depart; but the bland expression on her mistress's face gave her no promise of quarter. She blinked, raised her chin, and looked at the Spy Master in wide-eyed vulnerability. ''I don't know what to ask you. I don't know what to think of you. But you frighten me to the depths of my heart, there is truth.'' Her soft almond eyes filled with tears. ''I am scared and I don't know why.''

For an instant the Spy Master and the girl confronted each other in tortured confusion. Lujan stayed riveted, his hand too tight on his sword.

After an unbearable second, Mara realized she must be the one to break the tension. ''Kamlio, you fear because at last you know what it is to have something to lose. Go now, and find cold water, and wash your face.'' As if the girl had been bound by invisible strings that had been cut, she bowed in grateful relief and hurried off around the curtain into privacy.

At the wounded look on Arakasi's face, Mara gave a youthful grin. ''You're winning,'' she whispered. ''The girl has let you see into her feelings.''

Arakasi let his wrists fall limp across his knees. Strained and transparent with hope, he said, ''You think so?''

Lujan burst into a broad laugh and gave the Spy Master a comradely clap on the shoulder. ''Man, take my word for it. Most of us endure this nonsense when we are still in boyhood, but your youth seems to have arrived later than most. Lady Mara's right. You'll have the lass in the blankets if only you're willing to show her a bit of you that needs her help.''

Arakasi sat with his brows peaked in comic puzzlement. ''What?''

''She has to see that you need her,'' Mara offered.

When the Spy Master's mystified expression failed to clear, Lujan said, ''Gods, she's never seen you make a mistake. You killed tong assassins, and lived; you made love in her master's bed, and if you sweated, it was in passion rather than fear. You touched her in ways few men could, I would wager, which means you were the first person alive who saw into her feelings. That frightened her because it meant that her beauty or her training failed, or that you were too smart to succumb to her allure. A man in her arms is not supposed to be left with the wits to think beyond his stiff organ. So she's scared. None of her skills will avail her where you are concerned. She can wear no mask for protection. She is offered a man who can understand her, but whose feelings she can't read in return. Bedroom pleasures she's bored with, because caring for a man is outside her experience. She'll have to be led and shown. But for that, she must lose her awe of you. Try tripping on a stone and falling at her feet one day, and see if she doesn't jump down beside you and start doctoring your skinned knees.''

Mara said, ''For a lout who takes advantage of women, you can be surprisingly insightful, Lujan.''

While the Force Commander grinned, Arakasi said, ''I'll think on it.''

''If you think even once with a woman, you're lost.'' Lujan grinned. ''At least, no one I know has ever fallen in love for logic.''

''Lujan's right,'' Mara encouraged, innately aware of the truth. Hokanu and she shared perfect understanding, a harmony of body and intellect. But with the headstrong, outspoken Kevin, who had argued with her, and sometimes made her scream in frustration, she had known passion that the years had not dimmed. For a moment her heart quickened at his memory—until a gust of smoky air swirled through the tent, reminding her of battle and the weight of today's problems that demanded immediate attention. ''Send for our Adviser for War,'' she said. ''We must make plans for every contingency and do one thing until matters come to a head: stay alive.''

The tent fell silent for a moment before anyone moved; wind carried the noise of an armed camp in the throes of what could all too soon become a great war, or else a circle of cinders at a stroke from the Great Ones of the Assembly.

The squall passed, and the drip of wet trees mingled with the shouts of officers directing their troops to set up camp. The armor worn by the warriors was without marking; and the tents they labored to set, drab brown. To casual observation, there was nothing to distinguish this company's encampment from thousands of others in key locations throughout the Empire; except that this one appeared to guard no crossroads, bridge or ford, or holding of significance. Miles removed from the possibility of a fight, this troop prepared to bed down in the trackless forests at four days' march to the northwest of Kentosani.

The discipline was no drill and far from slack as servants and rank-and-file warriors labored to drive tent pegs and set ridgepoles. On a slight rise, beneath a stand of sodden evergreens, one man paced in agitation, while a shorter, leaner figure swathed in an oiled wool cape hopped at his heels to keep up.

''How much longer must I wait?'' Jiro snapped in exasperation.

A servant crossed his path and bowed. Jiro stepped around; well accustomed to the master's dicey moods since the armies had marched, the servant pressed his face to wet leaf mold. "Your command tent shall be ready shortly, my Lord."

Jiro whirled, eyes narrowed in displeasure. "I wasn't speaking to you!" While the wretch so addressed abased himself headlong in the mud to atone for his master's displeasure, the Lord of the Anasati switched his glare to the First Adviser, who just then caught up to him. "I said, how much longer?"

Chumaka brushed a water drop off the end of his nose. He looked smug, despite wet clothes and the day's march through pathless wilderness. "Patience, Master. A wrong move now will spoil the planning we have labored for years to bring about."

"Don't talk circles around my question," Jiro said, in no temper to suffer his First Adviser's rhetoric. "I asked you how long? We cannot leave siege engines in place around Kentosani and keep them idle indefinitely. Every day that passes brings us risk: the Omechan Lord we have left in charge could grow restless, or pursue his ambitions on his own. And delay only allows the Shinzawai forces to march that much closer to the aid of the Imperial Guard. We dare not presume that the Assembly will not be spying on our actions. They could intervene, and forbid an attack at any time! What in the name of the gods, Chumaka, are we waiting for?"

If the Anasati First Adviser was surprised by this tirade, he did no more than stop in his tracks. His leathery features stayed expressionless, while Jiro kept pacing ahead. Six energetic steps later, the Lord finally noticed that the servant he had commanded to answer no longer flanked him. He restrained himself from snarling a curse. As always, Chumaka had allowed for every contingency. Either Jiro must acknowledge his fidgeting by walking back for his answer, or he must command his First Adviser to return to his side—and the distance between them was just wide enough that the master must raise his voice, showing all within earshot that he needed to assert himself to make a petty point.

Jiro might have shouted just to vent his spleen, but since he had an Omechan contingent as guest, he was forced to capitulate and stride back to Chumaka.

Annoyed as he was for other reasons, this personal setback left no rancor. In fact, Jiro admired his First Adviser's finesse. A Lord who displayed nerves and temper had no inherent dignity; and one who aspired to an Emperor's crown must learn to set insignificant irritations aside. Always the instructor, Chumaka was far too subtle to issue a reproach before warriors and servants that might reveal his master's poor self-control.

It was just such traits that would make Chumaka the ideal imperial adviser, Jiro mused with a curl to his lips that just missed being a smile. His mood now much improved, he regarded his adviser, whose habitual stoop was emphasized by the drag of his wet garments. "Why should we grant Mara more time to advance her interests? Your intelligence confirms that she intends to claim the golden throne for Justin."

Chumaka tapped his cheek with one finger, as though considering; but by the calculating glint in his eyes, Jiro knew he was under close observation. "Master," Chumaka said presently, "your command tent is prepared. I suggest we discuss this issue inside, in comfort and privacy."

Jiro laughed. "You are slipperier than a fresh-caught fish, Chumaka. Well then, we shall dry off and the servants shall heat us tea. But after that, no more roundabout talk! By the gods, I will have my answer from you. And after all these delays and excuses, it had better be revealing!"

Now Chumaka smiled. He bobbed a quick, self-deprecating bow. "Master, have I ever failed to match my actions to your desires?"

His temper changeable as the wind-blown clouds overhead, Jiro answered through clenched teeth, "Mara is still alive. Bring me her head, and then I will agree that you have not failed me."

Not the least discomfited by what another man might regard as a plain threat from the Lord of the Anasati, Chumaka said, "Indeed, master, that is what I am working myself to achieve."

"Hah!" Jiro moved through the gloomy woods toward the largest tent. "Don't try me, old man. You'd work yourself to the bone for the sheer love of intrigue."

Chumaka wrung out the hem of his dripping cloak and followed his master into the command tent. "My Lord, it is a fine point, but if I should do such a thing for its own sake, that would be vanity. The gods do not love such faults in a man. Therefore, I work for the glory of your cause, my Lord, and there the matter ends. I am ever your loyal servant."

Jiro ended the discussion with a deprecating wave. He preferred his philosophy out of books, which did not have Chumaka's irritating tendency to belabor every issue half to death.

The interior of the command tent was still in the process of being set up. One lantern had been lit, and servants bustled about unpacking cushions and hangings. From the outside, Jiro's quarters might appear plain, but inside, he insisted on his comforts, his fine silk tapestries, and two chests of book scrolls. Lately he had been reading up on obscure issues of law, imperial state functions, and precisely which ceremonies must be officiated by which priests of the Twenty Gods to make the crowning of an Emperor proper in the eyes of heaven.

The reading had been tedious, made worse because the lanterns attracted bugs and cast poor light. The Lord of the Anasati snapped his fingers, and a boy body servant jumped to attend him. "Remove my armor. See that all the leather straps are oiled, so they do not dry stiff." Jiro waited, statue-still, as he suffered the boy to undo the first buckles.

Although his high office allowed the attentions of a servant, Chumaka hated the pretension. He shucked his damp wool and found a seat. Jiro's silent, efficient house staff had just brought him a steaming pot of tea when a buzzing sound cut the air.

"A Great One comes!" he called in warning.

Jiro jerked free of his last bracer and spun around, while behind him, to a man, his serving staff fell prone upon the floor. As a gust fanned the tent, and the hangings rippled from their supporting poles, Chumaka set down the teapot and faded into the shadows toward the back of the tent.

The magician appeared in the center of the one rug that had been unrolled from its bundle. His fiery red hair trailed out from under his hood, and he seemed not to care that he trod over silk cushions as he approached the Lord of the Anasati. The eyes beneath his cowl were pale and sharp as they darted from side to side, and fixed at last on the Lord who waited with his armor heaped at his feet.

"My Lord of the Anasati," greeted Tapek of the Assembly of Magicians. "I am sent as delegate to command your presence in the Holy City. Troops have been deployed, and for the good of the Empire, the Assembly requires an accounting to avert the outbreak of open war."

Glad of the wet hair that concealed the fact that he was sweating, Lord Jiro raised his chin. He gave a perfectly deferent bow. "Your will, Great One. It shall not be the Anasati who break your edict. But I make so bold as to point out: if I go, who will see that Mara of the Acoma and her Shinzawai husband keep the edict against armed conflict?"

Tapek frowned. "That is not your business, Lord Jiro! Do not presume to question." Although the Great One was far from unsympathetic to the Anasati cause, he disliked the idea that any Lord dared to voice even token objection. But as Jiro bent his head in deference, Tapek relented. "The Lady Mara has been issued a like summons! She is also commanded to appear in Kentosani. As you are, she is given ten days' leave in which to do so! The day after the imperial mourning ends, you will both convene with members of the Assembly to state your cases."

Jiro thought rapidly and repressed a smile of satisfaction. Ten days' fast march would barely be sufficient to allow Mara to reach the Holy City. His position was closer, not with his main army to the south as all would suppose, but in this secret location near Kentosani in preparation for his planned siege. Mara would need to scramble to meet the Assembly's demand, while he would have days of leeway to seek advantage. To cover the bent of his thinking, the Anasati Lord said, "These are unstable times, Great One. Traveling the roads is not safe for any Lord, with every other ambitious noble stirring about with his army. Mara may have your sanction against attacking my personal train, but she has other supporters and sympathizers. Many friends of the late Emperor have political cause to see me dead for my leadership of the traditionalist faction."

"This is true." Tapek gave a magnanimous gesture. "You are permitted to travel with an honor guard to ensure your safety. When you reach the Holy City, you may take one hundred warriors within the walls. Since the Imperial Whites still enforce order inside the city, that number should be proof against assassins."

Jiro bowed deeply. "Your will, Great One." He held his deferential pose through the buzzing sound that signaled Tapek's departure. When he arose, he found Chumaka once again seated upon the cushions, dusting at the footprints left by the magician between sips of his tea. His manner was inscrutable, as if no great visitation had happened; except that a flush of unholy satisfaction colored the First Adviser's craggy face.

"Why are you so full of yourself?" Jiro demanded, half snatching the dry robe brought to him by his servant. The Lord stepped over his discarded armor and, checking to be sure no grit sullied his personal cushion, sank cross-legged across from his adviser.

Chumaka set down his cup, reached for the teapot, and calmly poured for his master. "Send your runner to fetch in the Omechan heir." The Anasati First Adviser handed his master the tea, then rubbed his hands together in bright-eyed anticipation. "Our plot ripens well, my Lord! In fact, all unknowing, the Assembly has helped it along!"

Jiro took the cup as if it were filled with foul-tasting medicine. "You equivocate again," he warned; but he knew better than to stall in sending his runner off on the errand Chumaka suggested.

As the messenger boy left, Jiro peered at his adviser over the rim of his teacup, then took a sip. "We will be inside the walls of Kentosani in four days with one hundred of my best fighting men," he allowed. "What else do you have brewing in that head of yours?"

"Great deeds, master." Chumaka raised a hand and ticked off points on his fingers. "We will leave this camp and set off for Kentosani, in strict compliance with the Great Ones' summons. Next, assuming Mara acts in compliance—that's safe, since if she doesn't, she's as good as dead by the hand of the Assembly, and we have won—anyway assuming she is no fool, while she is still many days' march to the south of Kentosani, we are inside the walls and covertly prepared for a raid on the Imperial Precinct.'' Chumaka grinned, and tapped his ring finger. ''The Omechan Force Commander, meantime, acts on his Lord's orders and begins the siege of the Holy City, as we have planned all along. But here is the change for the better, courtesy of the Assembly: you, my master, are innocent of this attack, being inside the walls. If the magicians protest the breaking of the imperial peace, you cannot be implicated. After all, you cannot be expected to answer for a popular move to set you on the throne. But alas for the Imperial Whites, the old walls prove weak indeed. They are breached, and a war host invades the streets.''

Chumaka's eyes sparkled. Less excitable, ever cynically cautious, Jiro set down his tea. ''Our allies under Omechan break into the Imperial Precinct,'' he responded. ''Mara's children suffer an unfortunate accident, and lo, the imperial mourning ends, and there is a new Emperor upon the golden throne by the time Lady Mara arrives in Kentosani, and his name is Jiro.''

Now Jiro's faintly underlying scorn surfaced to outright irritation. ''First Adviser, your ideas have several flaws, if I may point them out?''

Chumaka inclined his head, his enthusiasm like banked coals that at any moment might ignite a bonfire. ''Mara,'' he second-guessed. ''I have not accounted for the Acoma bitch that you want dead so badly.''

''Yes, Mara!'' Tired of his adviser's conversations, which at times seemed convoluted as his shāh tactics, Jiro vented his annoyance. ''What about her?''

''She will be dead.'' Chumaka let a dramatic pause develop as he shifted his haunches to allow a servant behind him to spread another carpet on the tent floor. Then he said, ''Do you think the Assembly would stay its hand if her troops were to attack your main army by Sulan-Qu?''

This time, Jiro caught his drift. ''The Great Ones will kill her for me!'' He leaned forward, almost slopping the tea on the table. ''But that's brilliant. You think we can goad her into attacking?''

Chumaka smiled in satisfaction and poured himself a second cup of tea. Through the dimness of the tent, his teeth gleamed. ''I know so,'' he allowed. ''Her children's lives are at stake, and she is a woman. She will risk all to defend her babies, depend on it. And unless she calls an attack, your troops in the South will break camp and march around her lines to support your newly established rule by controlling the lands outside the walls of Kentosani. This her clever Spy Master will tell her with absolute certainty, for it will be the truth.''

Bemused by the implications, Jiro mirrored his First Adviser's smile. ''The magicians will be busy chastising Mara, while I seize the golden throne. Of course, we may lose all of our Anasati army, but that will not ultimately matter. The Acoma will be obliterated, and I will be left with the highest honor in all the Empire. Five thousand Imperial Whites will answer to me then, and all Lords will bow to my will.''

The tent flap opened, interrupting Jiro's enraptured speculation. His face went expressionless at once as he turned to see who entered.

A young man ducked through the doorway, striding briskly. His armor, also, was unmarked, but his snub nose and flat cheeks identified him unmistakably as a scion of the Omechan. ''You called for me, Lord Jiro?'' he demanded in an arrogant alto.

The Lord of the Anasati arose, still slightly flushed with excitement. ''Yes, Kadamogi. You will return to your father at speed, and tell him the hour has come. Five days from now, he will attack Kentosani using the siege engines I have provided.''

Kadamogi bowed. ''I will tell him. Then you will hold to the vow you made for our support, my Lord of the Anasati—when the golden throne is yours, your first act as Emperor will be to restore the High Council, and to see an Omechan reclaim the white and gold as Warlord!''

Jiro's lip curled in barely suppressed distaste. ''I am hardly senile, to have forgotten my promise to your father so quickly.'' Then, as the young Omechan noble stiffened with the beginnings of affront, the Anasati Lord added placatingly, ''We waste time. Take my best litter, and my fastest bearers to see you on your errand. For myself, I must consult with my Force Commander to oversee disposition of my honor guard.''

''Honor guard?'' Kadamogi's heavy features darkened in confusion. ''Why should you need an honor guard?''

In a mercurial change of mood, Jiro laughed. ''I march also upon Kentosani, and by order of the Assembly. The Great Ones have summoned me there to offer an accounting concerning deployment of my troops!''

Kadamogi's face cleared as he gave back a deep-chested chuckle. ''That's rich. Very. And our plot to restore the High Council is nearly a foregone conclusion.''

Now Jiro gestured in animated anticipation. ''Indeed. The siege will be short, having help from the inside, and the supporters of the Good Servant will be set upon by the Assembly.'' Glee touched his tone as he finished, "The magicians will kill Mara for us. Servant of the Empire she may be, but she will die in magic flames, roasted like a haunch of meat!"

Kadamogi's fat lips stretched into a smile. "We should drink a glass of wine to that ending, before I leave, yes?"

"A fine idea!" Jiro clapped for his servants, and only noticed in passing that the cushions where Chumaka had sat were no longer occupied. The empty teacup on the table was gone also, leaving no sign that the First Adviser had been there at all.

That man is more devious than the God of Tricks himself, Jiro thought; and then the wine came, and he settled down to an evening of camaraderie with the heir to the Omechan mantle.

Outside the command tent, in the drizzle as evening fell, a shadowy form moved through the trees. Over one arm, Chumaka carried the oiled wool cape haste had not allowed him to don. As he walked briskly toward the tent that housed the Anasati messenger runners, he appeared to be counting on his fingers. But it was not sums he muttered in a monotone under his breath.

"Those leftover warriors who were of the Minwanabi, and who did not swear to Mara, now—yes, it is time for them to earn their keep, I think. A precaution, yes, just in case Mara slips through the grasp of the Assembly. She is clever. We cannot suppose we know all the details of her inner council. That time she supposedly spent in the temple in seclusion has yet to be adequately explained. How could she be there, then suddenly be upon her own estates . . . ?"

Chumaka hurried on, not tripping over roots or blundering into trees, though it was very dark, and the camp was strange. Preoccupied as he seemed, he stepped cleanly over guy lines and tent pegs, while he finished formulating his backup plan. "Yes, we must have sets of armor lacquered in Acoma green for these men, and have them insinuate themselves into the Lady's honor guard—at least, they will stay in hiding until the last minute, when the Lady is on the run, and then they will slip in among her warriors and slaughter her defenders. Posing as loyal Acoma, they can either capture her and turn her over to the Black Robes, or take their pleasure and kill her themselves, in revenge for the Minwanabi master whose line she obliterated. Yes . . . that would be the thing." Chumaka reached the compound where the messengers' tent was set. He startled a sentry as he stepped out of the gloom, and nearly received a sword thrust to the chest.

"Gods save us from our own men!" he exclaimed, bounding back and throwing up his bundled cloak to catch the blade. "It's Chumaka, you blind fool! Now find me a messenger who is fresh, and quickly, before I decide to report your incompetence to the master."

The soldier bobbed his head in fearful deference, for it was known that any who displeased the First Adviser came to unfortunate straits. He ducked into the messengers' tent, while behind him, in gently falling rain, Chumaka resumed his singsong musing.

27. Defiance

The palanquin jolted.

Mara snapped awake at the thump, disoriented by the close confines, until she remembered. She was not in her tent, but on the road, answering the summons by the Assembly to appear in the Holy City. For two days now she had been traveling at speed in her most ornate, formal palanquin, changing the thirty bearers required to lift the monstrous thing in shifts, and eating on the move. It was night; she knew not what hour.

Light breeze stirred the curtains, smelling of rain, as Keyoke, who sat across from her, leaned out. Although still muddled with the aftereffects of sleep, she could hear by the tone of her Adviser for War as he exchanged words with someone outside that a problem had arisen.

She pushed herself upright on her cushions. ''What passes, Keyoke?''

The old man ducked back inside the palanquin. By the light cast by the oil lamp hanging from a ring overhead, his face more than ever seemed chiseled from seamed granite.

''Trouble,'' Mara surmised.

Keyoke returned a curt nod. ''A messenger sent by Arakasi brings ill news.'' Then, well aware such detail was no afterthought, he added, ''The man met us on cho-ja back.''

Mara felt her heart thud in raw fear. ''Gods, what's gone wrong?''

The elderly campaign veteran knew best how to break the news cleanly. ''Jiro's location is at last made known. He was not with the Anasati troops, as we supposed. He is ahead of us, by now just over one day's march from Kentosani.''

Mara slumped back, crushed by the sudden ebb of hope. ''That leaves him five days in which to wreak mischief unopposed, since that doddering fool Lord Frasai saw fit to send Hoppara of the Xacatecas home after the Emperor's murder.''

''Mistress,'' Keyoke interrupted in worried tones, ''that's not all.''

Distracted by horrible images of possible death for her children, Mara forced herself to track the immediate issue. Seeing the grave expression on Keyoke's face, she surmised the worst: "Jiro's siege engines." Her tone was dulled by the scope of a disaster that seemed to widen by the second.

Keyoke gave back the clipped nod he used during battle councils. "The attack on the walls is poised to begin, and Arakasi has discovered that our efforts at sabotage have failed. The toy maker's plans we labored to implement were never set in place. Presumably, the engineers we sent were apprehended and put to death, and false reports of their success sent back through your network. Arakasi could say only that the assault against Kentosani's walls will occur without mishap, under Omechan colors. Once Jiro is safely inside the Imperial Precinct, his hands will seem clean. His coming bid for the Golden Throne could legitimately be justified as an attempt to restore the peace."

Mara bit her lip hard enough to hurt. "He's not in the Imperial Precinct yet?"

Keyoke's expression stayed wooden. "Not yet. But the messenger's news is not fresh, and much can have happened since he rushed south."

"We are not ready for this!" Mara burst out. "Gods, how could we be ready for this?" Her voice shook with despair. Ever since her return from Thuril, calamitous events seemed to be trampling over her with unrelenting speed. Fate was cruel, to thrust her into conflict unprepared, when she had the means to avert total ruin so nearly within her grasp. If only she had a peaceful interval in which to plan, and set to use the advantages she held in the presence of the Chakaha mages!

"Mistress?" Keyoke prompted gently.

Aware her silence had stretched too long, Mara made herself rally. "We are already lost, in all likelihood, but I cannot let go without a fight. If I fail to act, my children will soon be killed, and without them, my line ends with me." Forcing resolution in her voice, she added, "I would not see my faithful servants left in heaven's disfavor, without a mistress, as I go meekly to answer *Emperor* Jiro's justice."

"All would rather perish fighting in Acoma service than linger as grey warriors," Keyoke allowed.

Mara repressed a violent shiver. "Then we are agreed that the circumstances are extreme." She leaned forward and whipped back the curtains of the palanquin. "Lujan!" she called.

The Acoma Force Commander snapped her a salute, droplets flying from his plumes. "Your will, my Lady."

"Send the bearers off at a distance and order them to rest," Mara said crisply. "When they are settled out of earshot, deploy my honor guard in defensive circle around the palanquin. Then I would have Arakasi's messenger, the cho-ja who bore him, Saric, Incomo, and yourself report to me. We must hold council at once, and make immediate decisions."

Her orders were carried out with dispatch, despite the darkness and the rain. Mara spent the interval in furious thought, while Keyoke considerately tied back the curtains to allow her chosen advisers to gather around the palanquin. As the sides were opened to the night, the lantern light pooled on the cushions, fading with distance as it washed a ring of familiar faces. Beyond them, the dark was absolute.

Mara regarded each of her officers, from Keyoke, whom she had known since her girlhood, to Saric, promoted as a young man to his post of First Adviser, to Incomo, reprieved from an enemy prisoner's fate of death or slavery. All had given her miracles, in their time of service. Now she found herself forced to ask more, to demand, in fact, that some of them lay down their lives. There was no time for recriminations, no moment even to dwell upon sentiment. Expediency was paramount, and so she gave out what she expected might be her last commands to them in this life, her voice tersely emotionless. To allow her feelings to show was to invite emotional breakdown.

First she addressed the cho-ja, who was to her imperfectly educated eye an elderly worker. "First, and most important, your Queen has my thanks for the loan of your services."

The cho-ja worker inclined its head. "My services were purchased, Lady Mara."

"Your Queen has my gratitude in addition to monetary payment. Let her know if you have means." Mara paused, and heard the thin, high-pitched buzzing that signaled cho-ja communication. When the sound ceased, she asked, "Is it meet that I ask questions of you, good worker? And may I request of you another labor, without compromising your body's need of rest?"

Again the cho-ja inclined its head. "The night air is mild, Lady Mara. I have no need of rest unless it turns cold. State your needs."

Mara sighed in barely perceptible relief. One small obstruction less lay before her. "I require my Force Commander, Lujan, carried south at speed to rejoin my army near the city of Sulan-Qu. He must travel in utmost haste; my line's survival depends upon it."

"My service is yours," the cho-ja intoned. "I will bear your officer willingly."

"Should I survive, the Queen of your hive may demand debt of me," Mara said in sincere appreciation. "I would also ask that you give my adviser Saric clear instructions on the location of the cho-ja hive entrance nearest our present position.'' As the cho-ja worker inclined its head in acquiescence, Mara added, ''Saric, go with him. Learn where the hive is; select ten soldiers from my retinue who can move quickly; and also borrow for me a partial suit of armor that will let me pass as a warrior in the dark.''

Saric gave a hasty bow and left the circle. One face fewer, Mara thought; she swallowed hard. The next order she had to deliver became the more difficult. ''Lujan?''

Her Force Commander leaned forward, his hair raked in wet streaks at his temples, and his hand resting upon his sword. ''Pretty Lady, what is your desire?''

His tone was rakish. Mara suppressed a half-laugh, half-sob. ''I require the impossible, soldier.'' She forced a smile. ''Though, gods know, you already gave me as much in the challenge circle in Chakaha.''

Lujan gave a deprecating wave. His eyes also seemed too bright for the dimness of the lantern light. ''Say on, Lady. There is no need for hesitation between us—particularly after Chakaha.''

Mara suppressed a tremor of nerves. ''Force Commander, I require you to rejoin my army in the South. Should the Anasati forces attempt to break their lines and move anywhere, north, east or west, you will commit all of our companies and engage Lord Jiro's. Fight them to a standstill; keep them from joining their master in the Holy City. When the Black Robes arrive to chastise you, forestall their wrath in any manner that you can.'' Now she paused to gather the force of will to keep control. ''Lujan, I ask that you dedicate the lives of the Acoma warriors to the last man before you allow Lord Jiro's army to travel one step closer to Kentosani.''

Lujan slapped a hand over his heart in salute. ''Lady Mara, you have my solemn word. Either your army shall prevail, or I will wage such close war that the Black Robes must annihilate us all, Anasati and Acoma both.'' He bent his head in a swift bow and straightened. ''For your honor, my Lady.''

And then he, too, was swallowed up by the night. The Lady of the Acoma scrubbed her fingers over her face. She felt clammy, whether from mist or sweat she did not know. If Lujan survives this, and we should meet again, Mara vowed, I will give him a reward such as his dreams cannot encompass. But only if Justin sat the golden throne could any of them have a prayer of survival. Even should the Acoma prevail, Lujan might be beyond reward, for no one who defied the Assembly survived;

no one. Mara raised her chin and phrased the question that had to be asked. "Keyoke, ever faithful grandfather of my heart, do you see any other option?"

He looked at her, hard-bitten from his years on fields of battle. "I see none, daughter of my heart. To yield up to your enemy the life of your innocent son would save nothing. If Jiro ascends the golden throne, our lives and Acoma honor are as dust. What matter if the Assembly burns us to ashes first?" He smiled with the humor only soldiers facing death can muster. "Should we die with honor, we shall be known to history as the only house willing to challenge the Assembly. That is no mean accomplishment."

Mara fixed her gaze straight ahead. Alternatives did not exist. Now she must forge ahead, with the last order; the hardest of all to deliver. "Keyoke, Incomo." Her voice faltered. She jammed taut hands into her lap and willed herself to believe in a strength that was all false bravado. "From here our ways must part. You must go on with the palanquin and the honor guard. Keep on the road to Kentosani, and behave as if nothing untoward has occurred. This may seem a small service compared to the deed I have assigned to Lujan. But I say in deepest truth, your task may prove the most important. The Black Robes must not guess that my path has diverged until the latest possible instant. Your lives are precious to me, and to the continuance of House Acoma. But no Lady of my rank would journey to a meeting with magicians in the Holy City without her most valued senior staff. Your presence is essential to keep up proper appearances. On this the chance of saving Kasuma and Justin must depend."

"Mara-anni." Keyoke used the gentle diminutive of her childhood. "Set aside your fear. For myself, I am an old man. The friends who might remember my youth are mostly in Turakamu's halls, and if the gods are kind and grant my dearest wish, I would ask to meet the Red God many years ahead of you." Keyoke paused, then, almost as afterthought, he broke into a fond smile. "My Lady, I would have you know this. You have taught me the true meaning of a warrior's creed. Any man can die fighting enemies. But the real test of honor for a man is to live and learn to love himself. In my long life, I have accomplished many deeds. But it took your gift of an adviser's post to show me the meaning of my accomplishments." A suspect shining adorned Keyoke's eyes as he gave his Lady his final request. "Mistress, by your leave, I request permission to help Saric select the ten warriors who will accompany you in your flight to Kentosani."

Beyond words, Mara inclined her head, concealing her sudden tears as Keyoke delved among the cushions for his crutch, and arose. He swung himself off into the dark, erect as he had been in youth, and with the same dedication that had seen him through a lifetime of wars. When Mara at last found the courage to raise her head, he was gone from sight; but she heard his voice demanding the loan of a sword and helm from the spare supplies.

"Dammit," he said, borrowing a swear word from Midkemia when someone suggested he should ride in the palanquin in dignified comfort. "I shall go armed, and on my feet, and any man who dares to suggest otherwise can cross swords with me and earn himself a beating!"

Mara sniffed. Only two faces remained of her inner circle: Arakasi's messenger, who was a virtual stranger, and Incomo, whom she had scarcely come to know as well as the others who had worn Acoma colors longer. The fine-boned, stooped old adviser had seen service with two houses, and the obliteration of one master at Mara's hand. And yet he did not seem awkward as he faced the mistress he had sworn to serve. Though he was a tentative man, his voice was now unusually strong. "Lady Mara, know that I have come to love and respect you. I leave you with all that I can give: my counsel, poor though it is. I charge you, for the good of the Empire we both revere, to hold to your goals. Seize the golden throne ahead of Jiro, and know absolutely that you do right by this land and its people." He smiled shyly. "I, who once faithfully served your most bitter enemy, was given more honor and joy in your service than I could have imagined any man might know. When I served the Minwanabi, I did so for duty, and the honor of my house. Had Tasaio been defeated by any other ruler, I would have died a slave, so I know firsthand the value of your principles. The changes you labor for are just. Make Justin Emperor, and rule well and wisely. You have my devotion, and my everlasting gratitude."

Awkward of body as he was with emotions, Incomo arose. He gave a deep bow, and another shy smile, then hastened away to fill Saric's ears with last-minute advice, whether or not it was wanted.

Mara swallowed past a tightness in her throat. She regarded Arakasi's messenger, who seemed weary enough to fall asleep on the cushions without the bother of lying down first. "Can you tell me whether the news you brought has also been sent to my husband?" she asked gently, hating to disrupt his peace.

The man blinked and roused. "Mistress, Lord Hokanu will have heard ahead of you, since he was closer to Kentosani. Arakasi dispatched other couriers to carry word to the Shinzawai when the first in our relay was sent to you.''

Mara longed to know what Hokanu had done when the ugly news reached his ears. She might never learn; or she might live to regret the final knowledge. For whether or not she had made her husband's life forfeit by her orders to Lujan, which were in blatant disregard of the Assembly's edict, in her heart she suspected that her husband would never allow Jiro to reach the sanctuary of Kentosani. Revenge for his murdered father would not permit, and in addition, the life of his heir was at stake. Hokanu would serve his honor and attack, Mara thought, whether or not he had a prayer of success.

She regarded the exhausted messenger and delivered her last instruction, which she hoped would give him his best chance at life. ''You will leave this company,'' she commanded in an iron tone. Instantly the messenger was alert and listening closely to her commands. ''You will go at once, and you will swear to me that you will not stop until you have reached the next courier in your relay. You must send the following instructions to Arakasi: tell him to seek out his happiness. He will know where to find it, and if he demurs, tell him that is my injunction as his mistress, and his honor requires he obey.''

Fully awake now, the messenger bowed. If he found the message odd, he simply assumed it was but another clever code. ''Your will, my Lady.'' He arose and stepped off into the dark.

Alone in the palanquin, Mara released the curtain ties. The fine silk fell with a sigh of sound, affording her a rare moment of privacy as she buried her face in her hands. The reprieve she had won in Chakaha now seemed futile. Had she died there, the outcome would still be the same: her son's life sacrificed for Jiro's ambition. She wondered in self-pity whether fate might have treated her differently if, so many years past, she had not slighted Jiro by choosing Buntokapi for her husband.

Was this snarled, vicious political mess the gods' vengeance for her vanity? Was she being punished for her selfish, all-consuming drive to keep her family's name and honor, begun with the sacrifice of a man's life? She had wed Buntokapi only to see him die as a result of her scheming. Had he silently cursed the Acoma name, in the moment he had fallen on his sword? Mara felt a chill course through her flesh. Perhaps things were all foreordained, and her remaining children would die as Ayaki had, as pieces sacrificed in the Game of the Council.

Mara's shoulders spasmed as she choked back a sob. Over the years, each move of the Great Game drove the stakes higher. Now nothing less than an Emperor's throne would ensure the safety of her family. To protect her children, she must change the course of the Empire's history, and discard long centuries of tradition. She felt frail and vulnerable, and the feeling of beaten desperation would not leave her. Then her moment of soul searching ended; she had no further chance to ponder if she would survive to greet her children on this side of the Wheel of Life as Saric returned to the palanquin with an armload of borrowed armor.

"My Lady?" he queried softly. "We will need to make haste. The nearest cho-ja hive is a day and a half distant. If we are to have a prayer of reaching Kentosani in time enough to matter, we dare not delay for a second."

Her Adviser wore armor himself, Mara realized. Observant almost to a fault, he caught her glance of surprise as he knelt to help her arm. "I was a soldier once," he reminded. "I can be so again—I've not let my swordwork become entirely lax. That is all to our advantage. A small company of fast-marching warriors must perchance draw less notice when they are not accompanied by a man clad in robes of high office, don't you think?"

Saric's habit of speaking in questions did have the effect of drawing the mind away from insoluble problems. Forced to respond despite her worry, Mara conceded the wisdom of the disguise.

"Gods preserve us, we may need an extra sword before all is said and done." Saric expertly applied himself to the buckles of Mara's breastplate, while with false appearance of normality, the company's water boy made his rounds with his bucket and dipper, as he would through a natural pause for rest.

Lujan slid off the cho-ja, his body leaving streaks in the dust that caked its carapace. He staggered slightly from stiff muscles, and was caught and steadied by the fast reactions of the sentry standing guard outside the command tent. "Where is Force Leader Irrilandi?" the Acoma Force Commander croaked through his parched throat. "I bring orders from Lady Mara."

The Patrol Leader on day duty arrived breathless, having seen the cho-ja race in. After one glance at his exhausted commanding officer, he assisted Lujan to take a seat on a cushion in the shade. "Irrilandi is out with the scout patrol. There has been movement reported among Lord Jiro's troops. He went to see for himself," he summed up.

"Send our swiftest runner to fetch him back," Lujan commanded. Servants rousted from the command tent by the day sentry arrived with cool water and towels. Lujan accepted a drink, then waved them off to undertake the task of seeing the cho-ja who had carried him made comfortable. His voice stronger since the dust was washed from his throat, he added, "Whatever the creature requires, see that its needs are promptly met."

The servants bowed and backed off, to crowd around the tired cho-ja. Lujan knuckled the aching muscles of his thighs, speaking fast, and like a swirl in a deep current, the surrounding encampment heaved into motion in response.

While runners dashed off to convene a meeting of officers, and begin the process of a main muster, Lujan summoned the highest-ranking warrior at hand and directed at him a rapid-fire string of questions.

The officer's answers were direct, and as he used his sword to trace out the deployment of the enemy troops, Lujan also perceived the emerging pattern that had concerned Irrilandi.

"Jiro's troops have gathered to march," he summed up.

"You see that, too," the officer's worried eyes followed his Force Commander's hands, which had tightened fiercely on his sword hilt. "Though the gods alone know why the Anasati Lord would issue such a command. His war host can't attack our holdings or our force without invoking the wrath of the Black Robes."

Lujan looked up abruptly. "I have news. Jiro has started his bid to take the throne in Kentosani. Though cursed if I can figure how word traveled so swiftly from his position in the north to the Anasati Force Commander in the field."

The scout rubbed sweat from his face. "That I can answer. He has birds."

Lujan raised his eyebrows. "What?"

"Birds," the scout insisted. "Imported from Midkemia. They are trained to fly to a homing point, with a message scroll fastened to their leg. They are called pigeons. Our archers shot two of them down, but others got past."

"The messages were in cipher?" Lujan asked, then answered himself. "None of Arakasi's decoding patterns translated?"

The scout leader gave a nod indicating that the Anasati codes were still unbroken.

Lujan forced his aching body to obey his will, and stand, and walk. "Accompany me," he ordered the scout leader; to the duty officer he added, "When Irrilandi arrives, have him meet me in the command tent over the sand table."

The dimness inside the pavilion offered no relief; the rain had ended, and the sun beating down on its hide roof heated the air to steaming closeness. Lujan unstrapped his helm. He splashed the dregs of his water cup over his already sweat-drenched hair. Then, rubbing salty droplets from his eyelashes, he leaned on the rim of the sand table. "These are accurate?" he asked in reference to the rows of colored silk flags and troop markers.

"Updated this morning," the scout replied.

Silence fell. From outside, the commotion of warriors rushing to muster filtered through the tent walls and hangings; as fine a commander as any in the Empire, Lujan kept his ears tuned to their activities while his eyes roved the sand table in swift assessment.

"There," he announced presently, his dusty hands reaching and rearranging whole companies of markers at a sweep. "The Plain of Nashika. That is where we will take him."

The scout gasped in fear and turned pale. "We attack Lord Jiro? Force Commander, what of the Black Robes?"

Lujan never paused as he manipulated markers. "The Black Robes shall do as they will. But by our Lady's order, we attack. If we hesitate, or fail her, every man in this army will be masterless, grey warriors cursed by the gods."

The tent flap slapped back, admitting a swirl of dust and the long-striding figure of Force Leader Irrilandi. Lean and toughened as cured bark, the older man jerked off his gauntlets and positioned himself at the sand table opposite his superior officer. He wasted no word of greeting, but swept a glance that missed nothing across the changed deployment of markers. "We will attack, then," he surmised, his typically bitten-off speech animated by a lilt of pleasure. "Good. At first light, I presume?"

Lujan looked up, a hardness to him that his mistress had seen only once, and that in the moment before he had entered the challenge circle in Chakaha. "Not at first light," Lujan corrected. "Today, immediately after nightfall."

Irrilandi grinned voraciously. "Darkness will offer no cover. You won't deceive any Black Robes."

"No," Lujan agreed. "But we might have the satisfaction of spilling as much Anasati blood as we can before dawn comes. Let the Great Ones find out what's happened after they stir from their sleep and view the result of our night's activities."

Irrilandi studied the sand table. "Plain of Nashika? A good choice."

"Tactics?" Lujan queried back tersely. "I would have your opinion before we meet with our officers and commit to engagement."

Now Irrilandi gave back a chuckle. "Fight a wide, sprawling battle, one with many small forces and multiple vectors of attack. We have enough numbers, and gods know, we can field dozens upon dozens of messengers to ferry orders and information back and forth. No single arrow point of attack this time, with feints and false deployment; a swarm of arrow points striking at scores of places along the line!''

Lujan paused in puzzled assessment, then caught his Force Leader's drift. He threw back his head and laughed in admiration. ''You crafty old son of a harulth! That's the best advice I've heard in all my years of service. Create as much confusion as possible, so maybe we can steal time and inflict as much damage as possible!''

''If we're going to force the Assembly to incinerate us, let us take enough of the enemy into the halls of Turakamu to cause a great song of honor.'' Irrilandi looked up with a deadpan expression that could make Keyoke at his most unresponsive seem animated. ''Let's hope it works. Gods pity us, it's a flimsy enough countermeasure to stack against the aroused might of the magicians.''

The afternoon passed in flurried activity, mostly overseen by Force Leader Irrilandi as Lujan stole his last chance to catch up on sleep. Although the orders that were given amounted to a virtual death sentence, no man among Mara's thousands shirked his part. To die was Tsurani, and to meet the Red God in battle, the finest accolade of the warrior. If the Acoma name continued, and rose in prestige and power, the better were a man's chances of earning higher station on the next turn of the Wheel of Life.

It was ironic, Lujan thought as he rose and ate a hasty meal at sundown, that the very traditions and beliefs that lent these warriors incentive were the ones that Mara would change, should Justin survive to be the Nations' next Light of Heaven. Some of the officers knew of this twist of fate; if anything, they worked the harder. If a warrior had one recurrent nightmare, it was to waken one day and find himself still alive and taken captive by an enemy. Officers were traditionally killed, but an unusually cruel victor might keep them alive to toil as slaves with no possibility of reprieve. If Mara would discontinue the glory of bloody death in battle, she would equally eradicate the degradation of slavery that ground a man down regardless of his talents or his merit.

Sunset washed the sky gold and copper, then deepened into starlit night. Mara's warriors assumed their final formation at the edge of the Plain of Nashika under cover of darkness. The command to engage the enemy, when the moment came, was silent.

No horns sounded, drums beat no tattoos, and warriors did not shout their mistress's name or any other Acoma battle cry. The start of the greatest conflict of succession to be fought in Tsuranuanni began without the fanfares that traditionally accompanied a war.

The only warning that the massed army of the Anasati had was the thunderous pounding of thousands of feet as the Acoma forces charged. For once the Anasati were not served by Chumaka's superior intelligence; he had made the obvious conclusion: the Acoma war host must be positioning themselves for a dawn attack.

Then the night resounded with the crash of swords, and the cries of the fatally wounded. The fighting was vicious and without quarter. Within the first hour, the ground became churned to muck, watered red by the blood of the fallen. Lujan and Irrilandi took turns overseeing the action on a raised hillock, moving counters across the sand table under a pool of lantern light as messengers came and went with reports. Orders were dispatched and formations advanced, or retreated and drew the enemy into pockets. Ground was won and lost, and won back again at crippling cost in lives. The dusty floor beneath the table became littered with counters as Force Leader and Force Commander cast away colored pins to account for losses, which were ruinous, as though every man fought with berserk energy, the better to court the known death by the sword, rather than risk perishing in magic-born flames.

Each of Mara's two senior commanders rode out in turns on the cho-ja worker to bolster the morale of the troops, or to draw sword and lend an arm in the fighting to stiffen a line where needed.

The moon rose, bathing the struggle in copper-gold light. The fighting broke up into knots, where the lines were thin, with men shouting the names of Mara or Jiro to make their loyalties known. Armor colors became one in the dark, and friend was near impossible to distinguish from foe. Swords grew dark with blood, and a warrior had to rely upon his training to keep his stroke true; the eye could not track the speed of swordplay with every blade masked in gore.

Dawn came, dulled by a pall of fog and dust. The wide plain was littered with bodies, trampled by the contention of the living. Swords cracked under the stress of thrust and parry, and dead men's blades saw fresh action.

Lujan stood braced against the sand table, knuckling grit from his eyes. "They have lost more than we, but I'd guess that our dead number scarcely three hundred fewer than the Anasati." Aware of a stinging wrist, but not remembering the swordcut that had parted the skin, Lujan focused with an effort on the sand table. If the troops were pared down by losses, the fighting patterns had, if anything, grown more complex through the last hours.

To Irrilandi he concluded, "If the cho-ja is willing to undertake another errand, have it bear you to our western line. Pull off half a company and use it to relieve the pressure on companies under Strike Leader Kanaziro." He pointed to the center of the line, where the bloodiest fighting had taken place.

Irrilandi snapped off a salute and departed to speak with the cho-ja; after a few words, the creature scuttled away with the Force Leader on its back.

Lujan leaned tiredly against the sand table. He wondered where Mara was: whether she had reached the cho-ja tunnels in safety, or if not, whether the Black Robes would overtake her without his knowing. Justin could have inherited the Acoma mantle already, with none of the Acoma senior staff aware of a change in succession. The end might already have come, while on the Plain of Nashika men fought and died in futility.

Such thinking was poisonous, the product of stress and fatigue; Lujan forced himself to attend to the markers on the chart table, and to listen to yet another scout reporting in with word of still another change in the lines. Jiro's army had lost ground this time. Five minutes later, the hillock in question would be lost again, as it had been in turns through a seemingly endless night. Lujan realized by the shadow that pooled under his hand that the sun was now fully risen and climbing higher in the sky.

He felt a breeze against his neck, and almost as afterthought, realized that the buzzing noise in his ears was no natural effect of exertion on too little sleep. Turning, he saw three men in black robes materialize a few feet away.

The youngest stepped briskly forward, his thin, high-cheekboned face solemn. "Force Commander," he announced, "I seek your mistress."

Lujan sank into a bow, awe mixed with fear on his face. Clearing his throat of dust, he spoke the simple truth. "My mistress is absent."

The magician advanced. His feet were clad in slippers, Lujan noticed, laced in front, and soled in soft hide unsuited for outdoor wear. That stray fact caused him an inward shudder. This magician expected complete and immediate obedience, without any need to exert himself beyond walking a few steps.

Aware of his frantic heartbeat and his face dripping nervous sweat, Lujan forced himself to reason. These are powerful men, but only men, he reminded himself. He licked dry lips, recalling a judgment he had been forced to carry out as a grey warrior: he had needed to put a man to death for a crime against the camp company. His own sword arm had performed the execution, and he remembered clearly how difficult it had been to strike down the condemned. Lujan could only hope that even a Great One might hesitate before taking a life.

The Acoma Force Commander held still, though his muscles betrayed him and trembled; the urge to rise up and face threat or to give in to weakness and flee was torment.

The magician tapped one pointed, curled-back slipper toe. "Not here?" he said in acerbic reference to Mara. "At the moment of her triumph?"

Lujan held his chin to the earth and awkwardly offered a shrug. Knowing that each second stolen here might gain his mistress an infinitesimal improvement in her chance to survive, he spoke slowly. "The victory is not yet won, Great One." He paused, coughing slightly. The raspy sound lent credence to his need to stop and clear his throat once more. "And it is not my place to question my mistress, Great One. She alone would know what matters demand her presence elsewhere, and so she gave over command of this battle into my poor hands."

"Curse this rhetoric, Akani," snapped another voice. Lujan was aware of a second set of feet before his face, this pair wearing Midkemian-style boots studded with wooden nails. The redheaded magician, he identified, who was tallest of the three delegates, and obviously the one most inclined to inflamed thinking. "We waste time, I say. We know that Mara is bound north toward Kentosani in her litter, and a fool can see from this hilltop that a war is in progress, between Acoma and Anasati forces. We have been defied! Immediate punishment must follow."

The Black Robe addressed as Akani replied in more modulated tones. "Now, Tapek, calm down. We must not draw hasty conclusions. These forces are fighting, all too true, but since none of us saw the battle start, we do not know which side was the aggressor."

"That point is moot!" Tapek said through clenched teeth. "They fight, and our edict forbade armed conflict between the Acoma and the Anasati!"

After a short silence, through which glares were exchanged between the magicians, Akani once again addressed Lujan. "Tell me what passed here."

Lujan raised his head from the dirt just enough to squint through the dust that drifted in curtains upon the air. "The battle is close, Great One. The enemy holds a stronger position perhaps, but the Acoma have superior numbers. At times I think we shall prevail, while at other times I despair and compose prayers for the Red God."

"This warrior treats us like fools," Tapek objected to Akani. "He speaks in circles like a merchant trying to sell shoddy goods.'' One studded boot lifted and prodded Lujan in the shoulder. ''How did this battle begin, warrior? That's what we asked to determine.''

''For that, you must inquire of my mistress,'' Lujan insisted, casting himself prone with his forehead pressed to the earth. Although he skirted open defiance of the most powerful men in the Empire, he interpreted Tapek's question in the broadest way possible; Mara had never discussed the ancient roots of the rivalry between House Acoma and House Anasati after all; that sort of history was more in Saric's province. Keeping up his posture of loyal servant, Lujan prayed no magician would reformulate the question to ask who ordered the first attack.

Risking a peek upward, Lujan studied the Black Robes with the same eye he would apply to any new recruit: he dared to assess them as men, and determined that while Akani was intelligent, and certainly no fool, he was not predisposed to wish Mara or the Acoma forces harm. The red-head Tapek would take extreme action at little thought; he was the dangerous one. The third in the party seemed a bystander, watching the exchange as a factor might, who had little ambition and no stake in the outcome. He did not seem distressed.

Tapek nudged again with his boot. ''Force Commander?''

Aware he would be instantly dead if he replied directly to Tapek's query, Lujan tossed caution to the winds. He acted as if strain had upset his wits and disrupted his train of thought. In a tone of awed reverence, he said, ''Great One?''

Tapek's fair skin flushed. On the point of an explosion of temper, he was checked by a touch from Akani, who smoothly intervened. ''Force Commander Lujan, withdraw the Acoma forces and end this battle.''

Lujan's eyes widened. ''Great One?'' he repeated, as if the order astonished him.

Tapek shook off Akani's restraint and bellowed, ''You heard me! Order the Acoma forces to retreat, and end this battle!''

Lujan made a show of abject prostration. He prolonged his obeisance until just shy of the ridiculous, then said unctuously, ''Your will, Great One. Of course I will order a retreat.'' He paused, allowed his brow to furrow, then added, ''Would you permit me to arrange the retreat in a manner that will minimize harm to my warriors? If the object is to spare further bloodshed . . .''

Akani waved his hand. ''I would not see needless death. Arrange the withdrawal in any manner that pleases you.''

Lujan willed himself not to sigh in relief as he straightened as far as his knees. He beckoned to a nearby runner and said swiftly, "Orders to the Lord of the Tuscalora. Have him withdraw his soldiers to the south, then hold and support for those who shall be following him"—he flashed a glance at the Black Robes, and received a tiny nod from Akani, a fuming glare from Tapek, and vague intentness from the third in the magician's party—"to protect their retreat, you see," he ended in a rush.

The messenger was half petrified with fright. He took a moment to notice dismissal. As he hastened off, Lujan waved over another runner, and gave a long-winded set of instructions that involved two flanking maneuvers and what to an outside ear was impenetrable military jargon. As this messenger hastened off, he bowed again to the party of magicians. "May I offer you refreshment, Great Ones?"

"Some juice would cut the day's heat," the bystanding Black Robe agreed. "These robes are not comfortable in full sunlight."

While Tapek began to shift weight and tap his foot in irritation, Lujan clapped for servants and made a production of debating which wine should be sent, and what sort of camp rations were fit to be served to visitors of great rank. The wrangling threatened to go on for some time, until Tapek snapped that no delicacies were expected; plain jomach and water would serve the needs of his colleagues nicely.

"Dear me," Akani objected in a voice of lighthearted reason, "I personally thought the imported Midkemian wine sounded delightful."

"You stay and sip drinks with this half-wit who calls himself a Force Commander," Tapek nearly shouted. "Some of us have more important matters to attend to, and I think that in the interests of the council that delegated us as emissaries, one of us should observe to be certain that the warhosts on the battlefield are indeed breaking off the engagement."

Akani gave the younger magician a look of reprimand. "The Force Commander obeyed without question and ordered his troops to withdraw. Do you question his word of honor?"

"I need not," Tapek nearly snarled.

At this point the third magician, who had been staring vaguely off in the direction of the distantly moving armies, said, "Actually, Tapek may have a point. From a seer's vantage, I see no sign of any lessening of the struggle."

To Lujan's astonishment, Akani gave back a bland wave. "As I understand it, these things take time." Glancing keenly at the Acoma Force Commander, he stroked his chin. "Something about one vassal holding in support while another company retreats . . . was that it, Force Commander?"

Lujan smothered a start of revelation. Some of the awe left him as he realized: these were but men! They had factions just as did contending Ruling Lords in the Game of the Council. By all appearances, the Black Robe Akani was tactfully trying to aid Mara's cause without overt disregard of the Assembly's edict. Lujan stifled an unjustified countersurge of confidence and said, "Absolutely so, Great One. The Lord of the Tuscalora—"

"Oh, don't bore us with the details!" Tapek interjected. "Just tell us why Mara of the Acoma dared to believe she could order this attack and pass unscathed, when she has been expressly forbidden to do battle with Jiro of the Anasati by our order."

Lujan licked his lips, his nervousness unfeigned. "I cannot know that." The gritty dirt under his knees ground into his flesh, and the unaccustomed pose strained his back. Worse torture visited his mind. He could cause Mara's death through a wrong choice of words. By the gods, he was well trained to fight, but Saric's turn for statesmanship was no talent of his. He floundered, seeking a way around direct truth. "My orders from her were to prevent the army of the traditionalists from marching north toward Kentosani. As you have said, she is en route to the Holy City, also by order of the Assembly."

"Ah hah! So she is." Tapek folded his arms and stroked his sleeves in satisfaction. "Now we will hear the truth. What route has she taken to get there? No sly words! On pain of death, tell me directly." At this, Tapek raised one finger, and a blossom of flame flared up, searing the air with a hiss. "Now answer!"

Lujan arose to full height. If he was going to be killed, or spoil Mara's chances, he would do so as a man and a warrior, on his feet. "Your will, Great One. My Lady planned to travel by back roads, with her honor guard lest she encounter trouble."

The quietest magician of the three, Kerolo, said, "And if she were to encounter trouble?"

Lujan swallowed and found his throat paper-dry. He coughed and forced himself to find his voice, which now, at the last pass, was even and strong, as he willed it to be. "She would seek refuge in the nearest cho-ja hive."

The magicians Kerolo and Tapek exchanged disturbed glances and, as one, moved to activate their transport devices. A buzzing filled the air, slicing through the lessening cries of battle, and the distant clash of swords. Then a breeze parted the pall of dust, and the pair were gone, leaving Akani studying Lujan in clearly troubled silence. A moment passed. Lujan stayed stiffly correct as any recruit might while enduring the inspection of a senior officer. An understanding seemed to pass between the two men, different though their stations in life were. Akani's regard turned shrewd.

He said, "No more guile. Your mistress has, if not allies, then sympathetic ears in the Assembly, but even they will stand aside before open defiance. What cause has Mara to count upon cho-ja aid?"

Lujan shed any attempt at subterfuge. With this Black Robe, further ploys would earn short shrift. Still, afraid to reveal too much, he selected his words with extreme care. "She has long been friends with the cho-ja Queen upon her natal estates. She has over the years bought favors from the hive, many of them in the cause of Acoma defense."

Akani frowned, his expression the more terrifying for the fact it was understated. "The cho-ja beyond the borders of her estates willingly take up her cause?"

Lujan raised spread palms to the sky in the traditional Tsurani shrug. "That I cannot say, Great One. Only the Lady herself knows what bargains may or may not have been struck."

Akani's gaze turned piercing, seeming to turn the Force Commander's thoughts inside out and expose them to blinding light. Chills chased across Lujan's flesh, and he trembled. And then the sensation passed.

"You speak the truth," Akani allowed. "But be warned, the Assembly will get to the bottom of this issue. It sadly may prove that we might have to part company in our cause, Acoma Force Commander." With a nod that could have conferred respect, Akani activated his transportation device and departed in a blast of disturbed air.

Lujan reached out and caught the edge of the sand table to keep from folding at the knees. Mara, he thought in despair; what would become of her? For while Jiro's army would by the grace of the Assembly be forbidden to advance to Kentosani, the true foe was awakened. While Lujan had seen his Lady achieve the impossible before, and while he had boundless faith in her genius for improvising the unpredictable, even a Servant of the Empire could not long defy the Assembly and survive.

28. Retribution

The litter was heavy.

Eight bearers were needed to carry its weight of fine hardwoods, inlaid with corcara shell and bossed with rare studs of iron. If the costly silk hangings, heavily embroidered and fitted with fringes and tassels, were designed to dazzle any onlooker, the admission of light and air was forfeit to splendor. Since dawn had brightened enough to allow reading, Lord Jiro of the Anasati had commanded his servants to pull back the curtains and bundle them under leather ties.

The effect might not have been as elegant as when the drapes were lowered, but Jiro was unconcerned. There was no one of importance to notice.

The forest road that led south east toward Kentosani held no caravans or other nobles. Save for an occasional bonded messenger, it was empty of all but refugees, common folk fleeing the cities; food was scarce, and families in the poorest quarters were first to starve. These were ragged people, covered with sores, clothed in tatters. They cradled wailing infants or towed older children who stumbled and tripped, weak from malnutrition. Beloved grandparents were borne upon the backs of younger men. The countryside offered a slim chance of game to be caught or nuts and berries to be foraged.

Jiro paid such wretched folk no heed: their poverty was as the gods willed. The soldiers in his vanguard cleared the way for his retinue to pass, and except for the crying of the children, through the dust, they seemed little more than groveling shadows.

While his bearers sweated under the strain of forced march, the Anasati Lord sat at ease on piled cushions, with layer upon layer of scrolls lying opened across his knees. The heap was caught back from spilling over his ankles by the braced pommel of his sword, pinched between his armor-clad knees.

Long and lean as a hunting hound, First Adviser Chumaka kept pace at the litter's side. As toughened as any warrior, he seemed unfazed by exertion as he answered his master's questions, which were few and infrequent, and widely divergent in subject from the lengthy, tedious treatises on imperial law expounded in the scrolls.

"I don't trust the Shinzawai," Jiro snapped, seemingly without provocation. "His brother Kasumi spent years fighting on the barbarian world, as part of the Blue Wheel plot to undermine the Warlord, and the honorless, crafty ways of the Midkemians have also influenced Hokanu."

Chumaka bent an intent gaze upon his master and said nothing for a comfortless interval. And as if the man held power to read thoughts, Jiro knew: his First Adviser understood he was remembering Tasaio of the Minwanabi, a brilliant field general whose army had been humbled by Mara's through an unanticipated tactic brought about by advice from a Midkemian slave. That House Minwanabi no longer existed did not bear mention. Nervous fears needed no fanning for their spark to blossom into flame. Just short of reprimand, Chumaka said, "My Lord, all that the hands and the minds of men may achieve has been done to ensure your success. Now fate, luck, and the will of the gods must have their way. You will sit the golden throne, or not, as they allow."

Jiro leaned against his cushions, shifting in discomfort at the bite of his armor. Not a vain man, he well understood the power of appearance. As specific in his dress as any artist, he would have preferred a light silk robe in Anasati red with gaganjan flowers embroidered at the cuffs. But since Ichindar's assassination, no noble dared to travel the public roads unarmed. It further irked Jiro that Chumaka was right; just how right, the Lord was unwilling to repeat. He had heard every report; he had presided over council meetings. He knew what they told of the enemy's movements.

And the news held good.

Hokanu of the Shinzawai was still at least two days' march north of Kentosani, while the Lord of the Anasati's cortege would be through the grand gates by late afternoon, most certainly by sundown. Over and over, Jiro listed the reassurances to himself: he would reach the Holy City uncontested by Mara's allies; when the Shinzawai arrived, they would be exhausted; the magicians had been given insult by the Acoma when Mara's forces engaged the Anasati army to the south. The magicians had their full attention turned toward Mara, and were ignoring the Lord of the Anasati, who gave every semblance of perfect obedience to their commands.

Jiro's hands tightened over the book scrolls in his lap. Startled by a crackle of dry leaves, he cursed, annoyed that any distraction should cause him to mishandle old records. With frowning concentration, he straightened the crumple from aged, ink-faded hide; while yet again Chumaka seemed to interpret his private thoughts.

"You interpreted the message brought in by pigeon last evening," the First Adviser assured in what seemed casual comment. Jiro saw better. The man's shrewd eyes were locked on the road ahead, as if he could read past the dust kicked up by the feet of the advance company of the Anasati honor guard. The First Adviser might seem absorbed by the march, but in shrewd choice of words, he added, "Mara's Force Commander initiated an unprovoked attack. By now the Assembly will have acted. Think on that."

Jiro's lips twitched, just missing a smile. His imagination supplied detailed images of Mara roasted by magic. But every contemplated torment that might befall his enemy brought him no comfort. He wished to see the corpse of the woman who had spurned him spitted on steel; he longed to have the skulls of her children, ones she had deigned to have other men sire, broken like eggshells at his feet. He could tread on their brains, and be sure of his triumph. And yet: the luck of a Servant of the Empire was legendary, more than superstition. Mara's title bestowed a divine blessing no man might easily dismiss. More than once Jiro had presumed her days over, only to see her somehow triumph.

The worm of uneasiness continued to gnaw at him. All unnoticed, his hands clenched again over parchment. Brittle skin cracked, and bits of rare gilt flaked away and stuck to his sweating palms.

"You will not feel secure until you sit the golden throne," Chumaka summed up crisply. "When the priests of the Twenty Greater Gods all bow at your feet and endorse your right of succession, when the masses hail you in prostration as their Light of Heaven, then your nerves will cease clamoring."

Jiro heard, but could not help but scan the road ahead to the Holy City. Inwardly he repeated the logic that insisted he had an open path between himself and final victory. The Assembly would not hinder him, once Mara was dead. Indeed, they must endorse his cause, if only to avert the chaos and anarchy that had ravaged the peace of the Nations since Lojowa assassinated Ichindar. That Jiro had been behind that act no one suspected; the plot had been engineered covertly, over years of careful planning. Culpability could not be traced beyond the Omechan, and not even torture might wring out the truth. With the Warlordship promised to their line, they would be ill served to reveal the conspiracy. Jiro shifted thought. It did not unduly grieve him that the army bequeathed to him with the Anasati mantle must of necessity destroy itself to hold Mara's warriors in place and turn the Assembly's wrath against her. Their death would be honor, as it would serve to raise their Lord above all others in the Empire. Their spirits would be welcomed to the Red God's halls in triumph as Jiro's enemies were forced to acknowledge him supreme.

The Lord of the Anasati closed his eyes, suffused with anticipation. First to prostrate himself before the imperial seat would be Hoppara of the Xacatecas. That upstart puppy had tagged after Mara's skirts since the first, and his meddling mother had done nothing! For all her much vaunted appreciation of male ways, Isashani had never encouraged her firstborn to strike off on his own, as a man should. Because of the dowager Lady and her lap-hugging son, more than one plot to shame the Acoma had gone astray! Jiro sweated, remembering how many times Hoppara had stiffened the spine of old Frasai of the Tonmargu to the point where he had supported the interests of the late Emperor over those of his own Ionani Clan brothers!

Jiro's temper heated as he reviewed the list of slights. To him, forgiveness was weakness. He was not a man to forget where his plans had been crossed.

A frown marred his forehead as he considered which enemy he would humble next. If the magicians were magnanimous in their punishment of Mara's disobedience, Hokanu might also survive to kiss the floor before the dais of the Golden Throne.

Jiro stifled a chuckle. The unquestioned sovereignty Mara's supporters had labored to give Ichindar would fall to him, an Anasati, as legacy! He would wield such omnipotence well, oh yes; he would reinstate the High Council, and the Warlordship, and then preside over all, including the temples, in unprecedented primacy. His powers would be godlike, and there would be no woman born within the Empire who would not prostrate herself before his glory. He could fill his bed with whatever maiden he wished, and none would refuse his favors! That Mara of the Acoma once had spurned him would forever more cease to matter, for her line would be as dust. He, Jiro, ninety-two times Emperor, would be remembered as the man who had seen a Servant of the Empire shamed and brought down. His deed would stand as a memorial in the eyes of the gods: unprecedented, the perfect coup in the Game of the Council, for no Lord could dare a greater enemy than one beloved by the masses.

Someone shouted from the woods. Snapped out of reverie, Jiro straightened. Parchments and scroll cases cascaded around his feet. He forgot to pay heed, fixed as he was on the movement that erupted among his soldiers. "What passes?" he demanded in clipped tones, only to discover that Chumaka was no longer at the litter's side.

The man had an inconvenient independence about him. Jiro fumed as he spotted his First Adviser's greying head bent close to the plumed helm of Force Commander Omelo.

Jiro's annoyance lapsed as he read concern in the officer's expression. "What passes?" he demanded more loudly.

Omelo straightened into the bearing expected of a commander of armies. He strode to the litter, with Chumaka tagging bright-eyed at his heels. "One of our scouts found his partner, who had been detailed to investigate our flank."

Jiro's frown redoubled. "The man was shirking duty?"

Omelo's face shifted not a hairsbreadth. "No, Lord. The contrary. He was dead. Killed." Concise with bad news, he finished, "An arrow, in the back."

All but in breach of protocol, Chumaka broke in. "Had he been standing, or running?"

Omelo half spun, eyes narrowed. Always a stickler for protocol, he turned back to his master, and replied as if it had been Jiro who had addressed him. "My Lord, our man was shot down while running. The scout read the tracks." He gave a brisk salute, fist over heart, and a bow. "With my Lord's leave? We would be advised to array our warriors into a tighter formation. Whatever news our slain scout wished to convey back to you, someone did murder to silence him. And the arrow had an unmarked shaft."

"Bandits? Or some ally of the Acoma? You think there's danger?" Jiro fired back, then remembered himself. Delay of any sort might prove fatal; regaining his dignity, he waved his Force Commander to resume his duty and rounded on his First Adviser. Chumaka's face was never what one expected. Now he showed reflective interest, as if he were confronted by some delightful twist in a puzzle.

"You don't seem worried," Jiro observed, sarcastically dry.

"Fools worry." Chumaka gave a shrug. "The wise man strives for awareness. What will happen will happen, and worry will not serve, but anticipation might provide survival."

Through the bustle as his warriors closed ranks, Jiro studied the road. No refugees littered the verges. That in itself cried warning, since, like birds, they were timid creatures who were apt to fly from trouble. The way ahead stretched empty, sunlit under drifting scarves of dust. By contrast, the impenetrable shadow beneath the trees seemed like night. Forward, past a gentle curve, the road dipped, then crossed a glen where light and shade spread in dappled patches. Insects zipped through, flecked by light, but nothing warm-blooded made a sound. Jiro hushed his tone in nervousness. "I see nothing to beware of."

But still, some nameless uneasiness drove him to finger his sword hilt. Despite his smooth words, Chumaka also seemed tense.

Only a fool would not worry, Jiro avowed silently. He wrestled to hold back impatience. The stakes he bid to win were enormous, the highest in history. He could not expect to take the imperial seat unopposed. He loosened a damp hand from his weapon and tugged to loosen the thong around his neck that fastened a document bag beneath his armor. On the parchment, in concise words of state, were all the official points of law that must be included in his contract of marriage to Jehilia.

He stroked the leather like a talisman. There would be no mistakes made, no details omitted, once the gates of Kentosani were passed. No page had been left unread in the libraries; Chumaka and Jiro between them had perused every legal record on every dynasty that existed, and only the imperial chop, affixed by Ichindar's First Wife, Tomara, remained to be secured to seal into record Jiro's fitness as royal suitor. Ascension to the throne would perforce follow. No court litigator or house First Adviser, no legal mind in the Empire, could dispute the Anasati claim in the face of those documents. There might be other nobles with claims as good as Jiro's, but none better—once Justin of the Acoma lay dead—and none of those would dare challenge the Anasati right.

A shout caused Jiro to look toward the woodline. His hand whitened on his sword. Did something move, just beyond his vision? Jiro kicked his feet free of the book scrolls, striving to peer into the gloom of the deep forest. A faint thunder carried on the still air. The warriors shifted, crouched in their already strained state of readiness.

One of the older campaigners stiffened. "Force Commander," he ventured, "I know that sound."

Omelo said, "What is it?"

Jiro turned, to identify the man who had spoken as one of the survivors of the honor guard once sent with his brother to attend Ichindar's treaty delegation to the barbarian world of Midkemia; the peacemaking had ended in slaughter, with the blood of a thousand firstborn Tsurani soaking the field. Halesko of the Anasati had fallen in the first attack; only one of his honor guard survived to win back through the rift, carrying, with three other men, the unconscious body of the Emperor. In honor for saving the Light of Heaven, the man had been given a place in Jiro's bodyguard. He spoke now with urgency. "I heard this sound fighting the barbarians, Lord." As a rumbling closed in from the direction of the forest, he raised his voice. "The enemy is mounted! Horses! They ride horses!"

The next moment, chaos exploded from the trees.

A line of blue-clad warriors, each astride a four-legged barbarian beast, charged headlong toward the company. Omelo screamed commands; he had studied the reports of soldiers who had faced cavalry before upon Midkemia. Only one tactic had a prayer of success for warriors on foot. The warriors that accompanied their Lord were the flower of the Anasati forces. They obeyed without hesitation, spreading out to avoid being trampled, where men who had never experienced a charge might in error have stayed rooted and been run down. Jiro's bearers reversed in awkward fear and fell back, setting as many of his inner guard as possible to stand between their master and the onrushing Shinzawai cavalry.

Jiro swallowed back panic. The Shinzawai were not two days' distance from the Holy City, they were here! The beasts were fast! And heavy! Their hooves chewed up gouts of turf and shook the earth. The litter bearers faltered, uncertain in their step. Rocked ungently into a post, Jiro barely noticed. The horses came on in a wave, the lances of the riders gleaming in sunlight.

The foremost ranks of warriors met the charge. Brave, steady, determined, they never had a chance. The lances impaled them, screaming, or hooves scythed them down like hwaet. The most nimble managed to duck aside, only to perish on the swords of blue-armored riders. Only the veteran of the Midkemian wars won free. His swift stroke hamstrung a beast from behind, and it collapsed in a kicking heap. The rider rolled clear, cursing over his mount's strangely human-sounding scream. Sword met sword, the victor of the clash lost in the ocher rise of dust.

The second rank fared little better. One man stabbed a horse in the chest, before he was overrun. The riders spitted most of the defenders, but their lances were then useless, as those not broken or rammed human flesh were too long to counter foemen now inside their reach.

Jiro felt sweat trickle inside his armor. His teeth showed in a snarl of oaths. He could die here! And the waste of it: to go as Halesko had in the mess of battle! To perish by the sword, as any unread fool could, blinded by lust for honor! Jiro rejected such a death. He would see Mara humbled first!

He kicked clear of his cushions and sprang from his litter, vicious as a cornered sarcat.

Omelo was still on his feet, shouting orders. The initial rush of the charge was blunted, the following ranks in ragged order as the mounts of the Shinzawai swerved to avoid the fallen. Lances had taken one man in two. Now mounted swordsmen whirled in pirouette; as one with their hellish beasts, they skirmished with foot warriors who coughed in the dust. The Anasati warriors never flinched. They stood ground with valiant courage, and sliced at disadvantage against foes who battled higher than their heads.

Tsurani swordsmanship was weakest against blows from above. The best fell, their helms cloven, and their blood soaking the dry road.

And still the riders came on. They converged upon the litter and the close-ranked inner guard of Jiro's warriors. Last and most staunch in his defense, these screamed defiance. Even the most brash could see: they were not going to be enough.

Omelo shrieked a blasphemy. Chumaka seemed nowhere to be found. Swords whined through air; some slammed blade to blade in parries, and were deflected. Too many bit deep into red armor, spilling more precious red blood.

Hokanu's cavalry trampled on over the fallen. Another horse went down, thrashing, and a warrior too close was felled by a kick from flying hooves. Jiro swallowed a rolling surge of nausea. He raised his blade. War was not his strength; but fight he must, or die.

The cries of the mortally wounded set his teeth on edge. He braced for his first blow, dizzied and overwhelmed by the brutal reality of battle. Only family pride held him upright.

A horse reached his lines, and reared up, black against the hot sky as its hooves cut the air. Teeth flashed white in a face shadowed by a helm bearing Lord's plumes. Jiro knew: the rider was Hokanu.

The Lord of the Anasati looked up into eyes that held no pity: eyes that were dark as Kamatsu's, that stripped Jiro to his living spirit and knew him for a craven murderer.

In them, Jiro saw his end.

He met the first sword stroke evenly, as he had been taught. He managed to parry the second. A warrior was dying under his feet; he stepped on him, and almost tripped. Bile stung his throat. He had no strength. And Hokanu bore down, his mount sidling like a demon, his sword a slash in sunlight.

Jiro stumbled back. No! This was not happening! He, who had prided himself on reason, would be butchered wholesale by a sword! Numbed through his vitals with dread, he spun and ran.

Any concept of dishonor was driven from him by the horror of what thundered at his heels. Jiro's breath labored. His sinews screamed with exertion, all unnoticed. He must reach the woods. Cleverness could prevail over the sword, but only if he survived the next five minutes. He was the last of his father's sons. It was not shame, but only reason, to survive, whatever the cost, so that Mara, curse her name, should die ahead of him. Then the gods could do with him as they would.

The sound of fighting dwindled, punctuated by the jarring thud of hooves pounding dry ground. Jiro's breath rasped in his throat as he reached the trees and scrambled up a small stone outcropping to gain what he recognized as safety.

The breath of the horse no longer blew past his ears. It had stopped; the forest deterred it. Jiro blinked to clear his vision. Shadow seemed to blur his eyes, after the dazzle of noon. He flung himself, panting, against a tree bole.

"Turn and fight," snapped a voice, a half-pace from his heels.

He spun. Hokanu had dismounted. He waited, sword raised, faceless in shadow as any executioner.

Jiro bit back a whimper. He was betrayed! Chumaka had erred, and erred badly, and now this was the end. Red anger washed away panic. The Lord of the Anasati raised his weapon and charged.

Hokanu flicked Jiro's sword aside as if it were a toy. A veteran of war, he had a stroke of iron. Jiro felt blade meet blade in a vibrating shock of pain. The sting shocked his nerves, loosened his grip. His weapon flashed, spinning, from his grip. He did not hear the thrash of its fall into the undergrowth.

"Omelo!" he screamed in white panic. Somebody, anybody, even one warrior of his honor guard must be alive to heed his cry. He must be saved!

His wits stumbled to function. "Dishonor to you, who would kill an unarmed enemy."

Hokanu bared teeth in what was not a smile. "As my father was unarmed? Dead in his bed of a poisoned dart? I know the assassin was yours." Jiro began to deny it, and Hokanu shouted, "I have the tong's accounts!" The Lord of the Shinzawai looked like terror incarnate as he lowered his blade, then, with a turn of his wrist, slammed it point down into earth, leaving it vibrating as he released the hilt. "You are dirt, no— less than dirt, to whine of honor to me!"

He advanced.

Jiro crouched, prepared to wrestle. Good! he thought. Wits were going to triumph after all! He had convinced the honorable fool of a Shinzawai to take him on hand to hand! Though the Anasati Lord knew he was no champion wrestler, death would be slower than the downswing of a sword stroke. He had bought time, perhaps, for one of his honor guard to win through and save him.

Still playing for delay, Jiro stepped back. He was too slow. Hokanu was hunter-quick, and driven by revenge. Rough hands grabbed at Jiro's shoulders. He raised an arm to shove free, and felt his wrist caught and twisted. Pitiless strength forced it back and back, until bone and tendon quivered in protest.

Jiro hissed through his teeth. Tears blurred his eyes. The cruel hold only tightened. Blinking his vision clear, Jiro looked up. Hokanu loomed over above him, a sparkling shower of reflection on his helm from the partially blocked sun.

Jiro strove to speak. His mouth worked, but no intelligent words came forth. Never in his pampered adult life had he endured pain, and its kiss stole his reason.

As a man might handle a puppy, Hokanu jerked him up with one hand. His eyes were mad; he looked like a demon who would not be sated with only blood. His fingers were claws, tearing away Jiro's ornate helm with a snap that wrenched his neck.

Jiro's sweat ran to ice. He gasped in recognition.

And Hokanu, murderously, laughed. "Thought I would wrestle, did you? Fool! I set aside my blade because you do not deserve a warrior's honor; you who bought my father's assassination deserve a dog's death."

Jiro choked in a rattling breath. As he groped for a plea for mercy, Hokanu shook him. In a whisper near to a sob, only one thought found voice: "He was an old man."

"He was beloved," Hokanu blazed back. "He was my father. And your life defiles the world that he lived in."

Hokanu wrenched Jiro off his knees, shaking loose the pouch of documents. The Shinzawai Lord shifted one hand to seize the thong. Jiro jerked back, graceless in his terror. "You would not sully yourself with my death, if I am so wretched a creature."

"Wouldn't I?" The words were a snarl as the strap twisted tight. Jiro felt the bite of a strangler's garrote around his neck.

He thrashed and clawed. His nails broke on blue armor. Hokanu pulled the strap tighter. Jiro's throat closed. His head pounded. Spittle leaked from his working lips, and his eyes bulged. The dishonor of his death confronted him, and he twitched and kicked in frantic desperation as his face went scarlet.

Yet Hokanu was a battle-seasoned soldier who had never let his training lag. He bore down upon Jiro with a hate that knew no end, but drove his blood to fury as reasonless as the flood of sea tide. For their lost child and his dead father, Hokanu twisted the strap as Jiro's color deepened to dark red, purple, and then blue. He kept on until long after Jiro had fallen limp. Leather bit deep, through skin and trachea and flesh. Weeping, shivering in the release of reaction, Hokanu kept twisting, until a Shinzawai Strike Leader found his Lord over the fallen foe. It took strong hands to separate master from corpse.

Empty-handed, Hokanu subsided on his haunches in the leaf mold. He covered his face with bloodied fingers. "It is done, my father," he said in a voice hoarse with emotion. "And by my hand alone. The dog has been strangled."

The blue-plumed Strike Leader waited in patience. He had seen long years of service and knew his master well. Spying the document pouch that twisted around Jiro's throat, he removed its contents, assuming them to be something his master might wish to review when his wits returned.

After a moment Hokanu stopped shaking. He arose, still looking at his hands. His expression was blank. Then, as if the mess on his knuckles were nothing more than clean dirt, and the dead thing sprawled wretchedly in its red armor nothing more than killed game, he turned and walked away.

The Strike Leader strode after his Lord. To his companions who fought tight skirmishes in the roadway, he shouted, "Call to the field! Jiro of the Anasati is dead! The day is ours! Shinzawai!"

Like fire in a dry field, the word of Jiro's fall spread through the fray. Standing next to the overturned litter, Chumaka, too, heard the call: "The Anasati Lord is fallen! Jiro is slain!"

For a moment, the Anasati First Adviser regarded the spilled scrolls at his feet and thought about the other document Jiro had worn next to his skin. What would happen when that was found? He sighed. "Fool boy," Chumaka murmured. "Coward enough to run, but not to hide." Then he shrugged. Omelo was rising from his knees, a scalp cut running blood down his cheek. He looked ready enough to kill, as proud as ever save that something in his eyes had gone flat. He looked to the Anasati First Adviser and said, "What is left?"

Chumaka considered the broken remains of Jiro's honor guard, both the living and the dead. Out of one hundred, scarcely twenty were still standing. Honorable numbers against horses, he thought analytically. He resisted a strong wish to sit down; mourn he could not. He was no creature driven by love. Duty was duty, and his pride had been outwitting Anasati enemies; that, now, was ended. He glanced at the Shinzawai horsemen who were closing in, a ring of impenetrable flesh.

Chumaka hissed through his teeth. To the Force Commander he had known since earliest childhood he said, "Omelo, my friend, while I respect you as a soldier, you are a traditionalist. If you wish to fall upon your sword, I suggest you do so before we are disarmed. I urge you not to. For myself, I would order our survivors to put down their arms, and hope that Mara is as forgiving now as she has been in the past." Almost too softly to be heard, lest his hope shine too bright, he added, "And pray that she has some post left unfilled that we are suited for."

Omelo shouted orders for all swords to be put down. Then, as blade after blade fell from stunned fingers, and the beaten Anasati warriors watched with burning eyes, he regarded the seamed, enigmatic features of Chumaka. Neither man heard the noise as Shinzawai warriors invaded their ranks and made formal the Anasati surrender. Omelo licked dry lips. "You have such hopes?"

And both men knew: he did not refer to Mara's past record of clemency. The Lady upon whose mercy their lives, if not their freedom, henceforward must depend was one marked for death. If by the gods' miracle she could survive the Assembly's ire, there was still the last, most bitter cohort of Minwanabi warriors who had been armed in Acoma green and sent out. Their orders were Chumaka's, and as near to their hearts' desire as life and breath: to kill her by any means, and see Jiro's purpose complete.

Chumaka's eyes darted, then kindled as a gambler's might. "She is Servant of the Empire. With our help, she might survive the Assembly yet."

Omelo spat and turned his back. "No woman born owns such luck." His shoulders hunched as a needra bull's might, before the goad that lashed it into obedience. "For myself, you are correct: I am a traditionalist. These new things are not for one such as I. We all must die sometime, and better free than slave." He looked at the sky above, then said, "Today is a good day to greet the Red God."

Chumaka was not quite quick enough to avert his face before Omelo lunged forward and fell in final embrace against the blade of his own sword.

While the blood welled red out of the old campaigner's mouth, and the Shinzawai Lord hurried with a cry toward this, the last Anasati man to fall, Chumaka bent down, shaken at last. He rested a withered hand against Omelo's cheek, and heard the Force Commander's final whispered words.

"See my warriors safe, and free, if Mara lives. If she does not, tell them: I will meet them at . . . the door to . . . Turakamu's halls."

* * *

Thunder boomed in full sunlight. The reverberations slammed across clear sky and shook the forest trees to their roots. Two magicians manifested, hovering in midair like a pair of ancient gods. Black robes fluttered and snapped in the breeze of their passage as they skimmed above the wood, seeking.

The red-haired one used his mystic arts to rise yet higher. A speck like a circling hawk, he soared above the countryside, scanning the road that dipped and meandered through hills and glens on its northward course toward Kentosani. Tapek's magic might grant him the vantage and the vision to equal any bird of prey; yet the shadows still obscured, leaves and branches mantling the ground. He frowned, his curse flying with him on the wind. They were here, and he would find them.

The corner of his eye caught movement. He spun, easy in his flight as a mythical spirit of air, and studied. Brown flecks, all moving: a herd of speckled gatania—six-legged deer—not horses.

He resumed his course in peevish irritation, back, down the length of the road. And there it was: an upset litter lacquered red, and shiny in sunlight with interlaced whorls of corcara shell. Costly work, fit for only the highest-ranking Lord, and with curtains in the colors of the Anasati.

Tapek swooped downward, nearly diving like a raptor.

Less intent on the chase, still Kerolo was not caught off guard. He spotted his fellow mage's descent, and hastened his progress to overtake.

His lip curled in what seemed contempt, the red-haired mage pointed to a cloud of settling dust farther up the roadway. "There. Do you see?"

Kerolo took a studied look at the aftermath of tragedy that milled in the roadway: horses, lathered still from a charge. Warriors in Shinzawai blue, dismounted now, with the huddled remnants of Lord Jiro's honor guard held at swordpoint. Omelo dead inside the circle, sprawled on the blade of his own sword; Chumaka beside the fallen officer, shocked past cleverness for once. The Anasati First Adviser stooped low with his hands over his face, as near to tears as he had ever been since his boyhood.

"The Lord is not with his men," Tapek observed in his iciest tone. All the while, his eyes flicked up and down the road, taking stock of the fallen.

"He is not with his warriors," Kerolo said softly, almost sadly in comparison. "Nor would a commander as staunch as Omelo fall upon his own sword for no reason."

"Jiro's dead, you think?" Tapek returned, a wildness akin to joy lighting his restless eyes. Then he stiffened, as if he stood on firm earth. "Look. Under the trees."

More slowly, Kerolo responded. After a moment he, too, saw what lay beneath a small rise in the ground: not ten paces distant from Hokanu's abandoned sword, left standing upright in the earth, still clean.

Before Kerolo could sigh, or utter any word to express his wish that vengeance must continually run to bloodshed, Tapek snapped out, "He was strangled! In dishonor Lord Jiro died. We have been defied again!"

Kerolo gave a Tsurani shrug, regret in his mild expression. "We were too late to prevent killing. But none may dispute that Lord Hokanu deserved the traditional right of reprisal. It is known who was responsible for his father's assassination."

Tapek seemed not to hear. "This is Mara's doing. Her husband has ever clung to her hem. Does she believe we will permit this bloodshed just because her hands seem to be clean?"

Kerolo tucked his fingers in his voluminous cuffs, unconvinced. "That's supposition, particularly since the Assembly already must decide what action to take over her army's engagement on the Plain of Nashika."

"Decide?" Tapek's brows climbed in affront. "You cannot be thinking of reconvening the council! Our debate and delay have already cost the Empire one great house."

"Hardly that extremity." Kerolo's mildness assumed a fragile edge, like a sword blade ground too long at the whetstone. "There are cousins left who bear descent from the Anasati: a half-dozen young women consigned to the temple who have not yet taken binding vows of service."

Tapek was not to be placated. "What? Set power in the hands of yet another untried female? You amaze me! Either a hapless girl who will watch her inheritance destroyed before she is Ruling Lady for a year, or *another* Mara! That choice twenty years ago is precisely the same circumstance that spawned this difficulty in the first place."

"The Assembly will appoint an Anasati successor after we resolve the issue between the Shinzawai and the Acoma," Kerolo insisted. "We must go to the City of the Magicians. Now. This news should be heard promptly."

At this Tapek's eyes narrowed. "Fool! We can take her now, in her guilt!"

Kerolo kept to himself his suspicion of possible cho-ja collusion. He did not repeat his inward fear: that already Mara might have won herself a greater ally than any mortal Emperor. "Jiro is already dead," he argued gently. "What use undue haste now? There will be no further conflict. With Jiro dead, what need is there?"

Tapek almost shouted. "Do you think that Jiro was my reason for stringent opposition of Mara? She threatens *us,* you fool! She has greater ambitions than merely a rival's death.''

Unhappy at the reminder, Kerolo still strove for calm. ''I am neither blind nor always the slave of protocol. But I must insist, brother. With our edict still in force, even were Mara as bloody-minded as some other Lords of our acquaintance, none of the Anasati claimants may be hunted down. *We* must decide which of them is fittest to assume the Anasati mantle. Come; the matter is too weighty for us to act unilaterally. We must consult the wishes of our brethren.''

''They are idiots, or worse, accomplices!'' Tapek fumed back. He paced over air, spun, and whipped back to stab a finger at his companion. ''I will not stand idle through this crisis! I must act, for the Good of the Empire!''

Kerolo bowed in stiff-faced opposition to the invocation of the ritual phrase. ''My place is to inform the others.'' His hand dropped to his pocket, and his teleportation device buzzed like the whine of an angry insect.

''Fool!'' Tapek spat at the empty air, his word half whirled away by the suck of air left at his brother mage's departure.

Tapek looked down. Below, under cloudless noon, Anasati and Shinzawai completed the time-honored, paired dance of victor and vanquished.

Then, as if their actions were of no more consequence to him than the buildings and the battles of insects, they were abandoned to their own devices as he, too, reached for his device and departed.

29. Destruction

The air snapped.

Tapek materialized fifty feet up in the air in a new location, many miles to the south of Jiro's death site. The magician's expression was vexed. His hunt to pin down the location of Mara's litter promised difficulty, since she, unlike Jiro, had chosen her route for subterfuge. Her Force Commander had admitted as much, when he confessed her choice of back roads. Tapek shook a stray lock of hair from his eyes and gazed intently down on the landscape. Hwaet fields stretched below, gold turning dull brown, for the harvest was neglected. A dusty road wound parallel to a creek bed, quickly dry again, in keeping with the season. Nothing moved but a needra bull, pacing the confines of his pen. His herd boy lay under a tree, twitching off flies in the steamy heat. Since he had no reason to glance up, he failed to notice the magician hovering directly overhead.

To Tapek's outlook, the slave boy had as little consequence as the flies. The magician crossed his arms and drummed his fingers against his sleeves. A search by line of sight was not going to be effective: the territory where Mara was likely to be was simply too large. Urgency ate at him. Kerolo had left something of significance unsaid, the red-haired mage was convinced of it. Why else should anyone of his arcane abilities feel the need to rush like a child to report to the Assembly?

What was Mara plotting, that she should have dared give attack orders to her troops on the Plain of Nashika? Tapek licked his lips, brooding. The woman was devious. Even if Jiro's death was not her doing, but solely the province of Hokanu, still, someone representing the Assembly should seek her out, if only to make apprehending her easier when fat windbags like Hochopepa were finally forced to acknowledge her transgression. The Assembly would move from words to punitive action, Tapek had no doubt. Nothing else could come of the fact that their absolute authority had been compromised.

A spell of finding should suffice to track the Lady, Tapek resolved. His midair stance unnecessary for such a conjuring, he let himself settle slowly toward the ground. As his feet touched earth, the needra bull winded a snort of alarm, curled up his tail, and bolted. Its herd boy roused with a start. He saw the magician as he scrambled to his feet. With a cry of fear, he flattened himself in terrified obeisance, belly to the earth.

The needra bull thundered on toward the far fence, turned, and circled. Its hooves chewed up good grass. But in the fearful presence of a Black Robe, the slave feared to rise and calm it.

Which was proper, Tapek reasoned; the populace should feel nothing but awe toward those of his rank. Tapek ignored both boy and beast. Self-absorbed, he stood by the trembling slave and murmured an incantation.

He touched his palms together to close his gathered power, shut his eyes, and released. Tendrils of invisible force extended from his person. They emanated across the countryside, searching. Where they touched roads or back thoroughfares, even the most rudimentary trails used by farmers to cart produce from the fields, the magical sensors brightened. They turned and followed the byways. As invisible threads, they coursed even the smallest footpaths. Within minutes, Tapek stood at the center of an outflung array of magic strands. His probes became an extension of himself, an expanding net that was sensitized to detect the presence of movement. Like a spider in a web, he waited. A twitch at his nerves brought his attention to bear on a shaded lane where two servants loitered at love. The magician let that strand slip and turned his focus on others. Here passed a small band of grey warriors, hunting for an unguarded needra herd; hunger drove them into lands that normally were populated and defended. They were not the only such band; thieves had grown bold during the Empire-wide unrest. But Tapek stayed detached. These wretched folk at their lawlessness were no concern of his. He dismissed the grey warriors' presence, seeking another company; less predatory, perhaps, and better armed, but moving just as furtively. He identified two small honor guards belonging to minor nobles; these warriors were simply hurrying with their masters to shelter under the protection of stronger benefactors.

His probes twined across wooded lands and fields left untended. He crossed an expanse of dried thyza paddies, the dead shoots stuck up through cracked earth like serried ranks of brown quills. Birds pecked and squabbled over the heads of shriveled grain.

And yet the movements of scavengers were not all that disturbed this sector. Past the arid fields, under cover of a copse of ulo saplings, Tapek's snare sensed something else: a half-glimpsed flash of green armor, and the rapid tramp of feet. His lips twitched. Now, at last, he touched upon a larger force, all of one hundred strong. This was hers: his quarry.

Tapek focused his mind upon the site, and power defined its image. A dark-lacquered litter with shatra-bird hangings moved rapidly down a back road. The bearers were picked for strength and speed, and around them, in a sun-caught blaze of green armor, marched Mara's honor company of warriors. They were fighting fit, and armored as much for battle as for ceremony. What set them apart from all other retinues was the presence of a mantled adviser who wore a soldier's helm, and who swung along briskly on a crutch. The rich fall of his robes could not quite hide the fact that he had lost his left leg.

Keyoke, Tapek identified, his smile a flash of white teeth. No house in the Empire but Mara's kept a cripple in high office. The old man yet kept his pride, not letting his infirmity slow the pace. Yet his presence further indicated Mara's culpability, Tapek guessed. The venerable former Force Commander would not be set at risk in the field unless the Lady felt great need for reassurance. Quickly the magician concluded his surveillance. Another grey head was also in Mara's company: Incomo, a senior adviser whom the Lady had learned to value since her acquisition of his service from her vanquished Minwanabi enemies.

Incomo was never one to endorse outright innovation. Such was the allure of the Lady's charisma that even her onetime foes were moved to support her in conspiracy. Tapek felt a flicker of ire. That this mere woman thought that she could move outside the law, and even by implication lay claim to the rights reserved for the Assembly, was dangerous. Her actions made her anathema. The gods themselves must know outrage.

Tapek gauged the distance between himself and the fleeing retinue. His closed eyes twitched with tension as he collapsed his net of power. The single tendril that connected him with Mara's location he kept. A sudden fey giddiness passed through him as he shifted the balance of his powers and touched them to that strand. He disappeared from his vantage point by the pasture silently, leaving the stupefied slave still groveling, and the needra bull to settle its discord unattended.

The magician reappeared on a lane miles distant, under dappled shade, slightly to the rear of Mara's column.

His arrival was accomplished without fanfare. Still, his presence might have been expected, so swiftly did the rear ranks of Acoma soldiers stop short and whirl in place to face him. Their swords were ready, if not yet drawn, as if he, a Black Robe, presented the menace of a common bandit.

The moment passed when his dark cloth should have been recognized for what it represented: a magician's robe could never be mistaken for the rags worn by a masterless thief of the road. Despite this, Mara's warriors did not bow or ease their stance. The two advisers stood silent.

Here was impudence! Tapek fumed. The issue could no longer be disputed. Irked that the Assembly should yet be wasting itself with council and talk, Tapek hissed an involuntary breath in anger. Mara's entourage showed disrespect of the first order, to face him as if he could be threatened by weapons of war!

Their boldness must go no further, Tapek resolved.

He assumed a fearful mien.

Despite a curt order to hold from Keyoke, the servants and slaves who marched at the core of Mara's retinue scattered and fled through the ranks of her guard. The bearers who held the litter trembled visibly, but a woman's voice from behind the curtains stayed their panic. At some second, unseen signal, they started forward at a run, the litter swaying and rocking in time to their ungainly race.

Thunderstruck with astonishment, Tapek stood rooted. Obstinance was one thing; but this! That Mara's servants should dare to display anything other than instant obeisance in his presence was unthinkable!

Then the Strike Leader of Mara's honor guard shouted, "Come no closer, Great One."

Tapek shivered with affront. No one who was not a magician had raised his voice against him since he was a boy with talent yet undiscovered. Such insolence shocked the mage to fury after years of unquestioned obedience. Ready to spit with revulsion, or lash the very air with wild power, he shouted, "My words are as law, and your mistress has transgressed our edict! Stand away or die!"

The Acoma officer might be trembling, but his words held nothing of compliance. "Then we will perish defending our Lady and enter the halls of the Red God as honored Acoma warriors!" He snapped a signal to his men. As one body, the green-armored company fanned out, blocking the Black Robe's path.

The escaping litter gained ground. Keyoke exchanged a word with the officer. Tapek recognized Sujaura, one of the two Acoma Senior Force Leaders. The officer gave Keyoke a curt nod. A crutch saluted, signaling decision. Then Keyoke spun on his good leg, and half hopped, half swung after his retreating mistress.

Incensed by the inconceivable effrontery of this futile, armed resistance, to be faced by Tsurani with anything but abject servility, Tapek's anger manifested as pure power.

He raised his hands. Energy crackled and gathered around his fore-arms. It poised above his palms, brightening into a corona too fierce for human vision.

Mara's warriors might be dazzled blind, but they answered by drawing their swords. Tapek heard the hiss of blade leaving sheath even over the buzz of the arcane forces he gathered. His rage stopped thought. One with the surge of his magic, he knotted his killing fury into a concentrated ball. The magic coalesced within his hand to a rainbow play of colors that flashed and melded, heated to searing red.

''See what your mistress's folly has brought you!'' Tapek screamed as he hurled his bolt of power at the honor guard. The ball of searing light leaped out, expanding with a crackle that shook the earth. The warriors nearest to Tapek were overtaken, and violent, flaming death erupted among their ranks. Leaping like a thing alive, the spell-wrought flame sprang from man to man, and in an instant living flesh flared up as a torch. The fires brought agony without relief. Men screamed, though the intake of breath scorched their lungs, and sucked the spell into their bodies to ravage their inner tissues. No matter how brave and resolute, the stricken warriors crumpled to their knees, then writhed in mindless suffering on the ground. Green armor blackened and blistered. The tor-ment was hideous, beyond mortal endurance; except that the watching magician regarded them and did endure, stone-hearted. His red hair blew and tangled in drifts of smoke, and his nostrils pinched at the acrid stench of scorched hair and hide.

The spell was not recalled. Tapek let the minutes pass until the flames at last quenched, their fuel spent. No bone and sinew remained to be burned. Only skeletons were left; charred, smoking fingers clenched blackened weapons. Sparks still danced in the eye sockets of the skulls, as if life lingered yet inside, still feeling, still howling in silent torment. The mouths gaped, forever frozen into screams.

Tapek relished his satisfaction. Before him stood only the inner core of warriors, the last rank left alive to guard the road before the vanishing litter; and beyond these, their higher officers, Force Leader Sujanra and the adviser Incomo. All stood fast, confronting death as true soldiers of the Acoma; even the palsied old adviser.

Tapek stepped forward, stiff with disbelief. Drained beyond anger or amazement, and light-headed from the potency of his magic, he struggled to muster his wits. ''What is this? Are you blind? Fools? You saw what became of your companions!'' He gestured toward the ashes of what lately had been living men, and his voice rose to a shriek, magic-en-hanced. *''Why are you not on your bellies, crying mercy?''*

None of Mara's surviving honor guard moved. Her senior officers kept a grim façade and said nothing.

Tapek took another step ahead. The slowest of the fleeing slaves had fallen prone, overcome by the display of a Black Robe's unrestrained wrath. They lay in the ditches a dozen paces back from the roadside, weeping and shivering, their foreheads pressed to earth. Tapek ignored these as if they were faceless, of less import than winnowed grass underfoot. Wind blown cinders stung his eyes as he crossed the seared ranks of the dead. Blistered bits of armor and finger bones crunched under his feet. Closer he came, and closer still; Mara's retinue held fast.

Down the road, curtains flying awry, the green-lacquered litter bounced as its bearers raced with their burden. Keyoke had caught up to them, despite the encumbrance of his crutch.

Tapek regarded their futile flight with contempt as he addressed the warriors before him. "What does your loyalty matter in the end? Your mistress will never survive to escape."

The Lady's defenders refused speech. The plumes on Sujanra's helm twisted and quivered, yet that detail gave no satisfaction. The movement was no part of cowardice, but only the influence of the wind. The Force Leader's will was rock, his resolve unbending. Incomo stood like a priest in the holy ground of a temple, his face revealing an expression of profound acceptance.

Tapek gazed upon each of these warriors who had witnessed his wrath, and still could not be made to fear. One thing remained that might hurt them, might yet shatter their front of solidarity and defiance.

His anger burning again, Tapek gauged the distance between himself and the site where Mara's litter had retreated around a bend. He marked a lightning-torn tree. With a flexing of his will, his magic relocated him to that spot.

As the Black Robe appeared, Keyoke whirled and stopped. Braced on his crutch, he assumed guard stance between the mage and his mistress's litter.

"Tell your Lady's bearers to halt!" Tapek demanded.

"Let my Lady command her slaves as she will." Keyoke slipped his crutch from under his arm. He gripped it with both hands and twisted, releasing a hidden catch. The smoothed wood parted with the clean, clear hiss that signaled a blade being drawn from a scabbard concealed inside. His voice was not an old man's, but rang like that of a field general as he said, "Neither will I stand aside, unless my Lady so orders."

Tapek was beyond astonishment. He glared, but saw no yielding. Keyoke's face was weathered leather, scribed with too many lines and too many years of hard living to alter its set and show weakness. His eyes might not be so clear of late, but they burned with the surety of his self-worth. He had faced the worst a warrior could imagine, to survive and overcome the shame of living maimed. Death, his steady gaze seemed to say, held no secrets, but only final quiet rest.

"No need, old man," the magician snapped. He moved toward the thicket where the bearers had scurried, dragging Mara's litter to shelter.

Keyoke moved with surprising speed. The magician found himself targeted by the lunge of a sword's point, wielded by a cripple.

The speed of the attack confounded Tapek, and just barely, he dodged aside. "You dare!" he shouted.

For all that had gone before, that any man alive should attempt violence against him was beyond Tapek's imagination. Keyoke not only dared, he repeated the act. His sword whined down, snapping a rip in black cloth. Tapek hopped away, his movements less graceful than those of the one-legged swordsman as he barely escaped the deadly blow. The blade flicked, cut, and forced him back yet again. Harried almost off balance, Tapek could not summon concentration. To focus his will and access magic was impossible as he ducked and sidestepped and backed away from the old man's attack. "Stop! Stop at once!" cried the magician. Unaccustomed to physical exertion, it was all he could do not to pant.

Mockery tinged Keyoke's next feint. "What, you cannot outrun even me?"

Forced to teleport out of reach, Tapek reappeared, breathing hard. Tsurani enough to burn with shame for his retreat, and half choking in throttled rage, he drew himself up with as much majesty as he could muster. From a deep pit of black wrath, he summoned power. Magic gathered in him and made the air crackle with ozone. Blue energies discharged around him, as if he centered a small-scale lightning storm.

Still Keyoke admitted no fear. As he leaned on the blade he had carried in his crutch, his normally impassive mien gave way to a thin-edged scorn. He observed, "My mistress is right. Your kind are nothing but men, no wiser or nobler than other men." Seeing his words sting the magician, who now stood trembling, he added, "And fearful, childish men at that."

From behind, amid the standing handful of Acoma honor guard, a warrior snickered.

Tapek roared in mindless fury. His focused might unleashed. His hand fell in a cutting motion, and a shadowy shape swooped out of empty air. The apparition reared up, then towered, a darkness like a well of moonless night. It poised for only a heartbeat, then spun in a rush toward Keyoke.

On reflex, the old man raised his blade to parry. Fast as a more youthful man, he met the thing edge on. But his foe this time was nothing solid. His weapon passed unobstructed through inky darkness. He did not twist aside in attempted flight, even as the spell cut inside his guard. Because Keyoke met the spell unflinching, it struck him full in the chest.

Armor might have slowed it; the shimmering silk of his adviser's garb daunted the dark not at all. Its fell touch shriveled the fabric. After that, Keyoke's voluntary control was sundered. The proud old warrior who had dandled Mara in childhood stiffened. His fingers loosened. His sword fell from his hand as the shadow bit into him. His eyes lost their determination, widened in agony and terror.

And yet at the last, the fighter had the victory. His tired heart could not withstand the shock and the pain that a younger man would have endured; his spirit, its term long served, had in late years kept a light hold on life. Keyoke tottered, his chin tipped toward the sky as if in salute to his gods. Then he collapsed in a heap, his body as dead as the stones beneath him, and his face relaxed in peace.

Tapek's rage remained unquenched. He had wanted the old man to scream and beg, to howl in animal misery, that Mara, cowering in her litter, might know her beloved Advisor for War had suffered as a dog might, expressly at the whim of its master. Tapek cursed. Regret goaded his temper to new heights. He had wanted Mara dead before her old warrior's life flickered its last, so that Keyoke would see her sent to Turakamu before him, and die knowing his lifework was wasted. Consumed by white fury, the magician lunged after the litter, abandoned now by its bearers and sitting forlorn in the thicket. Tapek muttered incantations and snapped harsh spells out of air. He bit off his words and spiked each breath with gestures. His conjury raised a cluster of silvery disks that hovered, spinning, above his hands. Their edges were keener than knives, and the breeze carved by their passage gave off a dissonant hum. "Go!" the mage commanded.

The death discs whirled away faster than sight, and carved through the thicket. Their touch sucked life. Green plants and saplings withered, shriveled in a moment to dry twigs. No object held power to stop them; no barrier could slow their course. They crossed stone as if through shadow, and sliced through the litter curtains without rending a thread. As they converged inside, a woman's choked-off scream rang through the glade. Then came silence, unbroken by the rustle of songbirds.

Every wild creature had long since fled.

The warriors at Tapek's back remained. Whipped to outrage by the attack on their mistress's litter, their Strike Leader called them to charge.

Tapek loosed a maniacal laugh as he pivoted to face them. The swords in their hands looked foolish, and the battle lust in their faces the grimace of rank fools. The magician amplified his spell. He waved his hands, sending disk after disk spinning into the ranks that rushed him.

Men fell. They did not scream, having no moment to draw breath. One instant they lived and ran, shouting Acoma battle cries. The next second, cut by the mage's killer disks, they withered. Their legs folded, spilling them like stick figures onto dry earth. Tapek's fury remained in full flood. As if determined to scorch and kill everything in sight, he continued to hurl magic. Flash after flash left his hands shaped as spells of destruction. The air chimed and sang off the edges of his spinning projectiles long after the last of Mara's warriors had fallen dead, Incomo sprawled among them in a crumple of silk robes like some incongruous trodden flower.

Tapek's strength ebbed suddenly.

Exhausted, dizzy and fighting spinning vision, the magician had no choice but to pause and catch his breath. He did not gloat. Resentment still smoldered within him, that mere men had defied him. He did not regret their demise at his hand, but that he had been goaded into killing Mara too quickly. Her end had deserved to be painful and prolonged, for the trouble she had caused the Assembly.

Tapek shrugged his robe straight, then picked his way between carcasses toward what once had been a green thicket. A scattering of slaves and servants cowered whimpering, their faces pressed to earth. The death spells had winnowed their numbers, and what few were left were half-mad. Tapek stalked past and pushed through dry sticks and blackened branches toward the dead patch of earth surrounding the Acoma litter. Dried leaves and brittle twigs crumbled to dust at his passage.

Only the litter's bright lacquer was undimmed; spared the effects of life-draining magic, it seemed almost artificial in the brilliance of untrammeled sunlight. Tapek stepped ahead and swept aside the curtains with their embroidered blazon of shatra birds.

A lifeless woman reclined on the cushions, staring with eyes frozen wide in astonishment. Her limbs were clothed in the robes of a great Lady, but her features were not Mara's.

Tapek's curse rang out over the ruin in the roadway.

He had accomplished nothing but the execution of some maid wearing

Mara's robes. He had been duped! He, a mage of the Assembly, had been lulled by the presence of Keyoke and a handful of officers and soldiers into the belief that he had overtaken the Lady. Instead, she had counted a victory upon him, anticipating his hot temper. The soldiers had all known, before they died, that she had bested a Great One of the Assembly; as had the old man. Keyoke had played along with the ruse, no doubt to his fullest amusement before he died.

Tapek glared through the woods in frustration. Except for a cowering handful of slaves, his spells had cut down all life. Any in the Acoma retinue of high enough station to know the Lady's whereabouts were now slaughtered, and no satisfaction could be gained by questioning or torture of witless slaves.

Tapek found curses insufficient vindication. Neither could he subside and meekly swallow the irony of Mara's triumph. He snapped up his hand, creating a vortex of scintillating colors above his head. Faster and faster he whipped the energies, then, with a flick of a wrist, cast the deadly rainbow toward the woods. The energies struck the trees and undergrowth. Magic raised a crack and a shimmer that exploded in alien blue-white light. The singed air gave off a stench of cooked metal, and living matter was immolated. Where the slaves had been, there was nothing, not bones, not shadows, but only a scouring of uncanny spellcraft.

The coruscation dimmed, then flicked out. Sweat-drenched, Tapek stood panting. His eyes swept back and forth, examining the scope of his handiwork. Before his feet yawned a crater stripped of soil. The rock of the earth stood bare to view and above it, for yards in each direction, nothing crawled or flew. Revealed also were the Acoma servants who had managed to flee the farthest. No longer sheltered by brush or trees these lay writhing in the aftermath of the magic that had lashed them. Their faces and skin were blistered, blackened leather; their hands were seared fingerless. These few still twitched, dying in lingering agony that could find no voice even to scream.

"Splendid," said a voice out of air.

Tapek started, turned, and saw Akani, lately arrived from the City of the Magicians. He wore a shield spell against arcane attack, that sparkled like a bubble in the afternoon sun.

Too spent to offer greeting, Tapek sagged. His strength was at lowest ebb, but he took heart at the possibility of swift reinforcement. "Good. You are needed. I am exhausted. Find—"

Akani interrupted in annoyed acerbity. "I will do none of your bidding. In fact, I was sent to find you. Kerolo sent word that you were acting rashly.'' With cold eyes and a study for detail, Akani reviewed the ravaged countryside. ''I judge the case was understated. You've been played for a fool, Tapek. A child could be expected to react to taunts, but a full-trained mage of the Assembly? Your excesses speak ill of us all.''

Tapek's features turned thunderous. ''Do not mock me, Akani. Mara set a clever trap to defy us!''

The litigator turned magician said in contempt, ''No need. You do an exceptional job of aiding her cause by yourself.''

''What! I am no ally of hers!'' Tapek tottered forward, fiercely irked that his powers were spent.

Akani dispensed with his defenses, a subtle insult to emphasize the plain fact that his fellow mage was reduced to helpless fuming. With a regard to the last twitching bodies of Mara's servants, he said, ''You realize that if Lady Mara fled her litter in disguise, you have left not a face intact to tell.''

Tapek responded with pique. ''Then engage your strength to find her! Mine has been fully exhausted in this cause.''

''Wasted, more like. Nor will I act on this further.'' Akani advanced on his colleague. ''I was dispatched by the Assembly to fetch you back. You have acted without warrant on a matter that is *under discussion;* that is a shameful breach of our covenant, and matters are far graver than you know. You were exhorted to use prudence, yet you let your passions rule you. If the Good Servant is not already dead, you have destroyed the very officers we had at hand who might have revealed the extent of her plot against us.''

Tapek frowned. ''Plot? Against the Assembly? You mean she's done more than defy us?''

Akani sighed. His youthful face looked tired. Moved by his background in law to examine all sides of an issue, he admitted, ''We drove her to it. But yes, Lady Mara may have in mind to disrupt our treaty with the cho-ja.''

''She'd never dare!'' Tapek exploded, but the memory of Keyoke's brazen challenge contradicted that presumption. There was nothing that gods-accursed Acoma bitch would not try. Nothing.

''The Lords of the Nations never expected her to survive the might of the Minwanabi, let alone destroy them,'' Akani qualified dryly. ''Our kind have long been inured to struggle by dint of our exalted position. We have forgotten to guard against contention, and our past complacence brings us peril.''

Then, as he saw aggression kindle in his colleague's eyes, the ex-litigator added, ''Your part in this matter is finished, Tapek, by the Assembly's decree. Now come with me." Taking his teleportation device in hand, Akani activated it, then firmly gripped Tapek's shoulder. The two magicians vanished in an inrush of air that sucked eddies in the drifting smoke, and wafted fresh air over the last, jerking spasms of dying Acoma servants.

The Lady's boldness had saved her. Tapek, in his impromptu search, had never thought to look off the roads, in the deepest, thickest undergrowth. He perceived no deeper than Mara's outer trappings as a pampered noble Lady, and could never have imagined how profoundly her foray into Thuril had changed her. Besides her bold strike into rough country, the direction Mara had taken when she left her litter and main company was not northward toward Kentosani. Instead, she had cut due southwest, in direct line toward the nearest cho-ja tunnels.

She and the warriors with her traveled without rest through two nights. Now, near sundown of the second day, the Lady stumbled on her feet. Saric walked at her shoulder, his touch at her elbow holding her upright, though he was scarcely more able himself.

The one scout who still maintained alertness raised a hand. Only when Mara had been restrained gently to a stop did she realize the reason for his signal.

The birds in the high, dense canopy of ulo trees had stopped singing.

She motioned for her rear guard to halt and said, "What is it?"

Saric poised, listening. The Strike Leader on point quietly urged his warriors to search the treetops.

"Are we in danger from ambush?" Mara asked in a whisper.

The scout who had first given warning shook his head. "Hardly here. Even thieves would starve if they staked out this area of the forest. No traffic to keep them supplied." He cocked his head, and was fastest to note the approaching noise of armed men. "A patrol, I think, my Lady."

"None of ours," Saric concluded. He glanced at Strike Leader Azawari, who nodded, while the small band of hand-picked warriors drew swords. To the scout the Acoma adviser said urgently, "How far are we from the tunnel entrance?"

"A mile at best," came the answer; too far to run in this company's exhausted state, even if they were not to be harried from the rear.

Saric stepped before his Lady, who sweated under her layers of borrowed armor. She had carried the added weight well enough, but her skin was chafed raw from the unaccustomed motion of walking. Still, pluckily, she kept up appearances and reached for the sword at her side.

Saric clamped her hand in a freezing grip, his penchant for questions lost to urgency. "No. If we are attacked, you must flee and seek to hide. Save the sword for yourself, to fall on if need be, should you be taken. But to try to hold here would be folly." More kindly he added, "You have no training, mistress. The first stroke you met would cut you down."

Mara looked him sternly in the eyes. "If I must run, you will follow suit. Nacoya did not school you for your office only to see you wasted in armed combat."

Saric managed a half-flippant shrug. "A sword thrust would be kinder than a magician's spell." For he had no illusions. Their small, fast-moving party might have escaped notice from the Assembly, but not for long. Yet to remain beyond reach of arcane retribution, his Lady must live to find refuge in the cho-ja tunnels.

Mara noted her adviser's sharp silence; she tried not to think, as he did, of the Great Ones. To open her thoughts to such fears, she must surely collapse and weep: for Lujan and Irrilandi, perhaps dead with all of her armies; for Keyoke, Force Leader Sujanra, and Incomo, who were all that remained of her old guard, and who had been set out as bait with her litter, their lives her diversion, and their sacrifice her last hope for Justin.

Where Hokanu was, the gods only knew. That he also might be most hideously lost did not bear imagining. Worst of all, Mara shied off from the question that gnawed at the edges of her mind: that Justin might indeed survive to claim heirship to the golden throne, but at the cost of every other life that was beloved to her.

Mara bit her lip. Poised with Saric on the edge of flight, she firmed her will to keep from trembling.

The sounds of snapping twigs and marching men drew closer. Her party's trail was plain to read; they had taken no care to hide their tracks, since they had passed far enough from the road that their presence was unlikely to draw notice. Once in the deep wilds, speed had been deemed of the essence.

Or so her reduced council of officers had decided, and they paid for that misjudgment now.

Strike Leader Azawari sorted his options and chose. "Fan out," he murmured to his warriors. "Give them no solid rank to charge on. Let it be man to man, and confusing, to hide our Lady's escape for as long as we can."

Saric's fingers tightened over Mara's hand. "Come," he whispered in her ear. "Let us be off."

She resisted him, rooted and stubborn.

Then the rear rank scout straightened up and gave a glad shout.

"They're ours!" He laughed in stark relief and pointed to the glimpse of green armor that came and went between the trees.

Men who had begun to scatter pulled back into one main body. Swords slid into scabbards, and grins flashed in the deep-woods shadow. Somebody hammered someone else's armored shoulder, and words passed around of a wager. "Ten to one that old Keyoke prevailed, and sent us reinforcements!"

"Hush!" rapped their Strike Leader. "Form ranks and be quiet."

Azawari's sternness reminded: there was grave danger still. The new arrivals might only be bearers of bad news.

Now the ranks of the warriors appeared, striding briskly through the forest. They seemed fresh. Their armor was correct, if bearing scrapes in the high-gloss finish from forced march through close brush. Mara fought the need to sit down, to steal a moment of rest while her two forces exchanged tidings and regrouped.

Only Saric's iron grip kept her propped on blistered, aching feet. "Something's not right," he murmured. "That armor. The details are wrong."

Mara stiffened. Like him, she sharpened her gaze to search faces. Threat of peril prickled the hair on her neck. The men were all strange, and that distressed her. Too often, her people were not known by sight, since her armies had grown vast over the years.

It was Saric, first earmarked for his station because he never forgot a face, who hissed, "I know them. They were once Minwanabi."

The approaching force numbered thirty, and it closed in relentless formation. The Force Leader at the fore raised a hand in friendly salute, and called the Strike Leader with Mara by name.

Unobtrusive in her warrior's garb, Mara stared at Saric. Her face had paled. Even her lips were white. "Minwanabi!"

Saric nodded fractionally. "Renegades. These were ones that never swore to your natami. That dark-haired man with the scarred cheek: him I cannot mistake."

One soft-hearted moment of pity, Mara recalled, and now she had treachery in payment for the clemency that had prompted her to let these foemen go free. She had only a split second to judge her call; for these warriors in another five steps would be among her ranks, dangerous as adders were they turncoats.

It tore her inside, to think they might be loyal; but Saric's memory was impeccable. Keyoke and Lujan had sworn by it. She sucked in a shaky breath and snapped a nod to her First Adviser.

Saric raised the alarm, that her woman's voice might not give her away. "Enemies! Azawari, call the charge!"

The Strike Leader's order bellowed over chaos as the lead ranks of traitors discarded appearance, drew swords, and leaned into a fighting run.

Mara felt her arm half jerked from its socket as Saric spun her from the ranks, and behind him. "Go!" he half screamed; even under pressure his adviser's tendency to seek subterfuge remained. "Run and send word to the others!" he shouted, as if she were a younger soldier dispatched away as messenger.

The first swords clashed as the pair of green-armored companies closed in combat. Men grunted, cursed, or shouted the battle cries of the Acoma. They blinked sweat-stung eyes, and engaged, and prayed to their gods for the judgment to enable them to separate friend from foe.

For all were armored alike in Mara's green.

Strike Leader Azawari called encouragement, then reached and jerked Saric from the fray. Years of training made him sarcat-quick, and he interposed himself in the adviser's place, parrying the stroke of the foeman already engaged. "Guard our messenger," he snapped. "You know where he needs to be!"

Saric's features twisted in frustration. He had been a warrior before he was an adviser; he could be so once again. Where better the need? But the teaching of old Nacoya forced him to review all options. There was his Lady, running hard through the trees, tripping over roots in her ill-fitting armor. She was no swordsman. She should not be stripped of all protection, or counsel, and Saric's split-second knack for sound reason showed him the wisdom of Azawari's choice.

"Tear out the hearts of these dogs!" he grated hoarsely. "I'll see that our messenger reaches the main column. We'll be back before you have time to kill them all!"

Then he ran in a white heat of fury. Of course, no advance column existed. The guards who defended were all here, and outnumbered three to one. That his Lady had come this far, had traveled into perils in Thuril and sacrificed her most beloved servants, for this! A petty bit of treachery, no doubt the handiwork of the Anasati Lord. Such a plot could not—no, would not!—bring down the honored Servant of the Empire. She might risk all to preserve her children, but Saric understood this race was for higher stakes than the lives of a boy and girl, no matter how dear to him.

He raced ahead, no longer torn in his desires, but stung to greater effort by the outmatched struggles of his fellows. From behind came the rattle and crunch of swords striking armor. Screams sounded between grunts of human effort. The false soldiers chewed into the ranks of loyal Acoma with devastating steadiness. They were Minwanabi on a long-anticipated vengeance raid. They did not care how they fell.

Mara's men had more weighty matters on their mind as they strove to stem the enemy's rush. They did not do battle simply to preserve their Lady's honor. They killed when they could, harried when they could not, and painstakingly kept themselves alive to draw out the fight as long as possible.

Their fierceness did not pass unnoticed.

In bare minutes, one of the attackers recalled the messenger sent away to report. He shouted to his officer about the unlikely escort commanded by a Strike Leader who could ill spare the loss of any one available sword.

"Hah!" cried the Minwanabi officer in his stolen Acoma colors. Satisfaction thickened his tone. "You are no rear guard! Your Lady does not ride in a litter under better protection up ahead, eh?"

Azawari had no answer but the fury of swordplay. He slammed his blade down on the helm of a foeman, and stepped back as the enemy crumpled. "Find out," he invited grimly.

"Why should we?" Another Minwanabi dog was grinning. "Men!" he commanded. "Disengage and pursue that messenger!"

Saric heard the cry as he raced after Mara. He cursed, and slammed through an interlaced hammock of branches that his slighter mistress had slipped through. Shouts burst through the foliage at his back. False guardsmen now raced in chase at his heels. No Acoma could win free to stop them. Every loyal sword was already engaged, and the enemy's numbers were greater.

Saric blinked sweat from his eyes. "Go, go on," he urged Mara. It made him ache to see how she stumbled. Her endurance was steel that she should still be on her feet at all.

He must buy her time! For soon she must rest. If he slowed the rush of her pursuers, perhaps she could find a cranny to hide, at least until her true warriors could reduce the numbers against her.

Saric ran. He reached Mara's side, caught her elbow, and sent her in a flying boost over a fallen tree trunk. "Run!" he gasped. "Don't stop until you hear no sounds of pursuit. Then hide. Sneak on at nightfall."

She landed on her feet, staggered sideways, and fended off a branch, still running. Saric had spent his last moment to watch out for her. The pursuing Minwanabi were on him.

He whirled. Three swords came at him. He parried the one that mattered, and let the dead tree entangle the others. One Minwanabi stumbled back, gagging on blood, his chest pierced.

Saric jerked his blade clear, twisting to avoid a cut from the side. A branch bashed his ribs, the same that a moment ago had spared him. He raised his bloodied blade and lashed downward. Met by a solid parry, he let his momentum spend itself on the enemy sword, then snapped his elbow at an angle. His stroke sliced past the foe man's guard and killed him. To himself, the former officer turned adviser gasped, "Not so bad. Haven't lost too much."

The soldier left alive sought to dodge past, to extricate himself from the windfall's weave of branches and close upon the boyish form he now suspected must be Lady Mara. Saric lunged to intercept. A searing slash along the back of the adviser's left shoulder warned of his mistake. Another guard had rushed him. Pinned in place against the downed tree, Saric spun and lashed out, taking his attacker in the throat. The first soldier had by now won free, and passed by running hard. Saric muttered an irreverent prayer. His path was clear. He had only to keep on. Fatigue brought agony as he punished tired sinews into motion. He raced, moaning in his need for air. He overhauled the warrior in false colors, and slammed into him from the rear. Armor deflected his stroke. He found himself engaged, while yet another foe slipped past and around, running after Mara's fleeing form.

Saric fought, hampered by his useless shoulder. Blood ran down his arm and spattered the ground under his feet. His sandals slipped on slicked leaves. He could barely defend himself. Weakness seemed to travel in waves through his sinews. His enemy was grinning, a bad sign. In a moment his efforts would end in grief. Then a soldier called his name.

Saric stretched his lips in joyless recognition. Azawari still lived. As the Acoma Strike Leader raced to the adviser's relief, and more Minwanabi in false armor converged in a knot to prevent him, Saric managed a brief contact of eyes between strokes.

Each man knew his fate. Each smiled, welcoming the certainty, the final relief that mortal flesh could no longer deny. Saric was struck upon the side. The blow made him stagger, tearing a gasp from his throat. The Acoma Strike Leader faced three more opponents. He was shouting in what seemed defiant rage, but Saric recognized cold purpose behind his insults. "Come, Anasati puppets!" Azawari danced and brandished his sword. "You may tell your children you sent Azawari, Strike Leader to the Servant of the Empire, to the Red God's halls! If you live to have children! If they can admit to fathers who shame them by wearing honored colors not their own. Die for your insolence, Minwanabi dogs!"

But the warriors were not goaded into striking; instead, they measured their distance. The middle one leaped at Azawari, while the others dodged to each side, resuming the chase after Mara. Azawari flung sideways. The warrior who lunged at him missed his stroke, and the one who ran left screamed as a sword slid between his ribs. The one who dodged right checked his rush, uncertain. Azawari held no such hesitation. He flung himself after, not caring whether a sword whined between. He took a blow to the flank, but brought down the runner in a lunge.

Saric saw the green-plumed helm fall. He blinked back furious tears, aware that the gallant Strike Leader had bought Mara precious seconds, for the last of the treacherous trio had to stop his rush and stab his fallen body twice to ensure his death was certain.

The First Adviser raised his blade; too slow, for his muscles were spent. He missed the stroke. Pain slashed hot across his neck, and the brightness of the world seemed suddenly dull and distant. Saric tottered and fell. The last thing he knew before darkness swallowed his senses was the rich smell of moss and the sound of enemy soldiers leaving the site of bloody victory to pursue one last running form: Mara. Saric struggled to say a prayer for the Good Servant, but words would not come. He had no breath, and no more speech in him, after all. His final thought, as death took him, was of Nacoya, who had trained him. The indomitable harridan would be shrill when he met her in Turakamu's halls, and found him fallen to a warrior's honor despite her best efforts to raise him to higher station. More than eager to cross words with his touchy Acoma predecessor, for his mind was far from ready to quit the fight, Saric almost smiled.

30. Pursuit

ara ran.

Brush hooked her ankles, and her breath burned her throat. She fought her way forward, gasping. Long past the point where her body needed rest, she knew if she stopped, she was dead. Enemies pursued her relentlessly. As she ducked under branches, she caught glimpses of them: figures in green running after.

There was something profoundly evil in the sight of men wearing her house colors chasing behind with murderous purpose. Mara thrashed through a strand of creeper, driven by more than fear. That green armor had always represented those willing to die for her, willing to protect her at any cost, and enemies wearing Acoma colors brought her to the edge of despair.

How many had died of this last conjoined treachery of Minwanabi and Anasati? Saric and Azawari, two of her finest younger officers, ones she had determined to spare. The soldiers with her had been fit, tough men chosen for their dependability in an emergency. But with their eyes upon the Assembly of Magicians, who among them had guessed that the trap to overtake them so near to their goal would be so mundane, yet so murderous?

The cho-ja tunnels were just a short march distant.

Always a healthy woman, Mara was nevertheless not the girl she had been when she had assumed the Acoma mantle. The wrestling matches and foot races with her brother were thirty years behind her, and her breath tore now from her chest. She could not continue; yet she must.

The soldiers behind were closing on her. Encumbered by heavier armor, they had marched some distance before the encounter; the race for a time had been even. Now it was not. Mara's next step became a stumble. Her foemen neared. For tortuous minutes, the only sound she acknowledged was the pounding of sandal-clad feet upon the earth and her own labored breathing.

Mara could not speak for breath and for sorrow. There were two at her heels, one just a pace behind, and the other a bare half stride more, and coming hard. Almost she could sense the raised blade at her back. Any instant she expected the shock of the thrust, followed by pain and a spiraling fall into darkness.

To die by the blade was honor, she thought wildly. But she felt only black rage. All in life she had striven for would become wasted because of a warrior's narrow-minded hatred and revenge. She could do nothing; only punish her body forward in what might be the last step she took. So would a gazen die, nailed in flight by the mailed claws of the sarcat who hunted for meat.

The ground began to rise. Mara threw herself into the grade and tripped. She fell hard. A sword cut the air where her body had been, and a warrior gruffly cursed.

She rolled through dry leaves. Her armor hampered her, and the sword at her side she had not thought to toss away hooked on a root and trapped her.

She looked up to a dizzy impression of greenery and flecks of bright sky. Across these reared an enemy face in a nightmare of friendly colors. Mara saw the sword rise to slash down and take her. She had no breath to cry out, but could only fall back, thrashing, in a futile effort to escape.

The warrior who raced one pace behind reached the scene at that instant. His blade rose and fell a bit faster by a fraction, and the flesh he hewed down was the enemy's.

Sobbing in exhausted reaction, Mara did not realize until after the dying man slammed in a heap across her legs that not all green armor held traitors. One familiar face had survived, bleeding from a cut cheek. "Xanomu," she cried. "Bless the gods."

He heaved off the corpse, jerked her up, and shoved her stumbling away from him. "Go, mistress," he gasped out. His voice was cramped by pain, due to worse wounds in his body. "Find the cho-ja. I will delay your enemies."

Mara wanted to praise him, to let him know her gratitude for his valor. She could not catch her wind.

Xanomu saw her struggle. "My Lady, go! There are more coming, and only I to hold them."

Mara whirled, tears half blinding her. Xanomu's dream of seeing her safe to the cho-ja was false hope: the insectoids would not fight. They were bound by the Assembly's treaty, and surely by now they knew of her defiance of the Great Ones' edict.

She ran anyway. The alternative was to be butchered where she stood, as two hulking warriors smashed out of the undergrowth and sprang, with only Xanomu's failing strength to delay them.

The struggle was brief, barely a half-dozen sword strokes before the gurgling moan of a man cut through the neck. Xanomu had fallen, his life sold to gain his mistress a few more yards through the forest. The trees were thinning, Mara thought; or maybe her eyesight had begun to fail, dazzled by the beginnings of a faint.

She blinked away tears or maybe sweat, and darkness rose up like a black wall to swallow her.

She flung out a hand, as if to break a fall, and her fingernails scraped across chitin.

Cho-ja! She had reached the mound. Black bodies closed in on her, pressing her upright on all sides. Mara gasped, panting, a helpless prisoner. These were not warriors but workers, a tight-knit band of foragers who seemed to be headed back to their hive.

She knew better than to believe she was safe. Between gasps, she said, "You . . . are bound to obey . . . the Assembly's . . . edict! You must . . . not fight!"

The cho-ja ignored her. They could not do battle in any event, being workers unspecialized for combat. No weapons or tools were carried among them. But as they knotted tighter around Mara, and her pursuers sprinted out of the trees, she realized: the insectoids could not fight, but only die.

The lead warrior screamed to his companions, and in a rush, they charged. Swords flashed in late-day sunlight as they hewed down a worker marching in procession with its fellows.

It fell without sound, kicking and rolling in its pain. As if only now cognizant of their threat, the workers left living clashed together into a single body, with Mara wedged at their center. She was pressed too close to fall to the ground; neither could she shove her way against the current as the insectoids simultaneously thrust forward in a teeth-rattling sprint. Like flotsam caught in a current, she was carried along. She could not see for the dust and the clack of chitin-covered bodies. Turf ripped at her feet. She lost a sandal. Then the mound of the hive rose up, suddenly, and they descended into darkness.

The Minwanabi in false armor shouted and raced after them into the tunnel.

Mara gave up the distraction of thought. Borne along with the workers, and blind in a morass of familiar smells and sounds, she made no effort to analyze. Her eyes adjusted slowly, and she twisted her head to make sense of the commotion and clamoring behind her. For a long moment she did not identify the strange, scraping rattle of blades striking unprotected chitin.

Cho-ja bodies littered the tunnel floor, and still the false warriors came on. The cho-ja about Mara slackened pace with a jerk, and a high-pitched buzzing stung her ears.

The next instant, a dark tide eclipsed the last light from the entrance. She knew that cho-ja workers were inserting themselves in the path of flight and that the pursuing soldiers could do nothing to reach her unless they hacked themselves a path through living bodies.

Mara felt too pummeled with weariness to weep for grief or relief. Her mind was punished with the recognition that, even though this hive was under attack, its warrior defenders dared not risk a response for fear that the Assembly might charge its denizens with breaking the treaty. Although she knew that the cho-ja counted individual lives—workers in particular—as expendable at need, she knew regret that any such life should be sacrificed to save her.

The last faint daylight vanished, as the cho-ja rounded a corner. Mara was conducted in total darkness. Aware as she was since her trip to Chakaha in Thuril that cho-ja were by nature day creatures, she perceived strategy in the lack of illumination. Her escorting party of workers was leading her ever deeper into the hive, past countless twistings and turnings of the way. The Minwanabi were being lured into following. Doom awaited them. They would never come alive out of this maze. The cho-ja need not trouble themselves with killing. Humans who lost themselves in the tunnels beneath the earth would wander until they perished, wasted from thirst and hunger.

"Convey my thanks to your Queen," Mara murmured.

The worker cho-ja deigned not to reply. It might have been the treaty that held them silent, or it might have been sorrow for their fallen fellows. Mara felt the touch of their bodies against her, no longer crushing, but as tender as if she were cradled within a giant fist. It occurred to her belatedly that she had been caught up to the point of blindness by her personal concern for Justin. These cho-ja were doing her no favor but perhaps in their way lending her aid for the sake of their own cause, since she had brought back cho-ja mages for the purpose of defeating the Assembly.

These beings saw their freedom in her survival.

Mara realized that the slavelike workers might be forbidden to communicate. But the possibility existed that their Queen was not acting from strict neutrality but, in her covert way, an ally to Mara's human cause.

The workers were going somewhere quickly. They showed no sign of spacing their bodies apart to let her fall by the wayside. What if they had been sent on an "errand" that by design was meant to coincide with the direction she desired to go? Or worse, what if they went mindlessly on about their hive's purpose, and she was carried in a direction she did not care to go? Time, above all, was of the essence. Her children's survival depended upon swift action.

Mara gulped a breath. Her legs were spent. Even had she wanted to, she could not achieve so much as one step unassisted. Neither could she stay safely wedged between the carapaces of a dozen fast-moving bodies whose destination was unknown.

If she dared to presume, she might ask to ride.

The effrontery of that supposition might get her killed—should she slip while trying to climb on a moving cho-ja, encumbered as she was by her armor, the cho-ja continuing to ignore her as they trampled her fallen body.

Worker cho-ja had no concept of the Tsurani concept of dignity. Still, Mara could not bring herself to think of them as mere beasts of burden, and that bias, along with her recovering strength, kept her silent. She recalled Lujan's expression on that long-past day in Dustari when the slave Kevin had made the preposterous suggestion that had led her armies to victory on the backs of cho-ja warriors.

Tears flooded her eyes at the memory. Lujan had looked pale and sick as he stared at the broad, black body he was expected to mount. Yet he had done so, and gone on to win a great war.

Who was she, to risk such as he on the Plain of Nashika, and yet not dare the same heights?

Her heart faltered at the prospect. Yet she was lost if she did not find a way to unite the cho-ja in rebellion against their oppressors, and rejoin the Chakaha mages who waited in hiding in burrows back at her estates; her son and daughter would be dead, at the hand of the first rival claimant to the golden throne. If the pretender was not to be Jiro, there would be others equally merciless.

And the Assembly of Magicians would never while she breathed forgive her slight to their omnipotence.

There remained her last card left to play, the final desperate plan she had outlined during her last council before war had broken out. For that, she must reach the Queen of this hive and be received for audience.

She did not feel bold, and had to force courage. Her voice sounded shaky, when at last she summoned nerve to try speech. "Take me to your Queen," she requested.

The workers did not respond. "I must have words with your ruler," Mara insisted louder.

The workers did not answer, but they stopped. The sudden jolt into stillness all but spilled Mara from her feet. "I have to see your Queen," she cried, shouting now, and raising a storm of echoes.

Light bloomed down a side corridor. Mara turned that way and, over the humped carapaces of the worker party, saw an approaching band of warriors. These were Tsurani-bred cho-ja, helmed as men would be, with a Strike Leader wearing plumes at the fore. He reached the juncture of the tunnels and turned eyes like onyx upon the disheveled woman amid the workers. "I am Tax'ka. I have come to grant your request and conduct you to this hive's Queen."

Mara forgot weariness in a great wash of relief. As the workers parted to clear her way, she stepped forward, and came as near as a breath to howling frustration as her fickle knees gave way.

The cho-ja Strike Leader knelt. "You may ride," it intoned. "Our Queen is not minded to wait upon your weariness."

Mara was too tired to bridle at a remark that from a human would have been taken for insult. She struggled back to her feet and accepted a worker's assistance to help her mount on the Strike Leader's midsection. She settled astride, insecure upon the black and slippery carapace. Her sweating hands found no grip that seemed trustworthy, and the cho-ja in its silence seemed unwilling to spare concern for her human discomfort.

"Go," she said, resolved. "Take me to your Queen with all haste."

The cho-ja's stride as it surged forward was startling for its smoothness. Mara clung without further worry, leaning forward, so that she might grip tight to the warrior's chitinous neck. She had no clue how far the cavern of the Queen might lie from this outlying tunnel. Some hives were so vast she could be riding cho-ja back for hours to cross them. The spice-scented air of the tunnel fanned her face. Her sweat dried, and her breathing returned to normal.

She had leisure to notice smaller discomforts: the cramp of overtaxed muscles, and the maddening sting of blisters beneath her armor. The passages the Strike Leader and his company traversed were unlighted. Lacking any sense of vision, Mara was reduced to clinging blindly while her escort sped on its errand.

The journey was the strangest in her memory. The darkness was unrelenting, never giving way to the chiaroscuro of blacks and greys found in the stormiest night upon the surface. As she was jostled and jarred, Mara could only wait for vision to return. Yet every expectant moment was followed by another, until she had to clamp her teeth to stifle a rising scream.

At some point in the journey, Tax'ka inquired after her well-being. Mara gave back vague reassurance, though she felt none within; the rapid travel in utter darkness became a timeless voyage through contemplation. Fatigue and tension ruled her mind, providing sights where light and nature did not: imagined movements glimpsed at the edge of her vision caused her heart to pound and her breathing to become rapid and shallow. In time she shut her eyes, to make the darkness seem less menacing. The measure was a stopgap, and gave no sense of security. Each time she forgot herself and tried to see again, only blackness met her efforts. Her terror returned redoubled.

At last she sought calm in silent meditative chants.

An interminable interval later, a voice called her name.

Mara opened her eyes. She blinked at the surge of light, for not only were cho-ja globes glowing blue all about her, but oil lanterns burned hot-white with flame.

She awkwardly dismounted.

The Force Leader who had carried her saluted, and said, "At your command, mistress. Our ruler awaits."

Mara glanced across the cavern. Ahead of her rose a half-familiar shape, a dais fashioned of banked earth. The cho-ja Queen reclined upon it, the enormous mass of her body screened from view behind rich hangings. As Mara met the gaze of the being who towered above her, her knees did not tremble only from fatigue.

The cho-ja Queen watched with eyes like black ice as her human visitor arose from her bow. Before Mara could utter even the most basic polite greeting, the ruler spoke.

"We cannot help you, Lady Mara. You have by your actions set the Assembly of Magicians against you, and we are forbidden to aid any they call foe."

Mara forced her back straight. She removed her helm and raked back the damp coils of her hair. Letting the useless helmet hang by its strap from her hand, she nodded. She had no choice now but to take the boldest course she had ever dared attempt. "Lady Queen," she said as steadily as her state of nerves would allow, "I beg to differ. You must help me. The choice has been taken from you, for the terms of your treaty with the Assembly are already broken.''

Silence fell with the abruptness of a blow. The Queen reared back. ''You speak from ignorance, Lady Mara.''

Never more aware of her danger, Mara closed her eyes and swallowed. She struggled against an irrational instinct to flee: she was underground, very deep. To run would avail nothing. She was at these cho-ja's mercy, and if they could not be made to help her, all causes were lost.

Mara called back. ''Not as ignorant as you think.''

The Queen stayed neutral. She did not settle to recline on her dais. ''Speak on, Lady Mara.''

Mara chanced fate. ''Your treaty has been violated,'' she ventured. ''Not by your kind, good Queen. By me.'' The silence in the chamber was like deafness, it was so complete. Mara swallowed fear and resumed. ''I broke your treaty, which by any unbiased judgment was unfair. I went to Chakaha. I spoke with your kind, and saw them as they were meant to live, free, and aboveground. I presumed, good Queen. I made a judgment, for the good of your race as well as my own people. I dared to ask alliance, and when I returned to the Empire's shores, I brought with me two cho-ja mages sent to aid your cause.''

The hush became more profound at this news. Mara felt as if she raised her voice against a crushing weight of unspoken disapproval. ''These mages shelter in an unused burrow within the hive near my estates. The Assembly will not pause to distinguish whether your kind are innocent of their harboring. They will act as if all cho-ja are conspirators. Therefore the treaty is broken already, by my hand, for the betterment of this Empire, of which the cho-ja must now fight to reclaim their rightful free share.''

The heavy silence became prolonged; ''Have you anything more to say?'' The Queen's tone was like the ring of struck crystal.

For reply, Mara bowed deeply. ''My word to you is complete.''

The Queen expelled a hiss of air. She swayed back and forth once, twice, then subsided onto her dais. Her eyes glittered. ''Lady, still we cannot aid you.''

''What?'' The expostulation left Mara's lips before she could think. She remedied her lapse with another bow, this one low enough to be counted almost subservient. ''The treaty's terms are broken. Will you not rise to opportunity and bid to recover your freedom and reclaim your rightful destiny?''

The cho-ja Queen seemed sad as she gathered herself to answer.

"Lady, we cannot. Our word was given. The breaking of the treaty was your doing, your treachery. You do not truly know our ways. It is not possible for us to violate an oath."

Mara frowned. This interview was not proceeding as she had pictured. Driven by a raw fear, she said, "I don't understand."

"The breaking of promises is a human trait," the Queen stated without rebuke.

Still puzzled, Mara struggled for comprehension. "I know that your kind never forget a memory," she mused, attempting to unravel this impasse.

The Queen voluntarily qualified. "Our given word cannot be broken. That is why humans over the years continually had the better of us. Each war ended in a treaty that we were compelled by our nature to abide by. Humans have no such instinctive restraints. They break honor, and do not die of it. We recognize this odd behavior, but we cannot—"

"Die!" Mara interrupted in shock. "Do you mean that you cannot survive the breaking of a promise?"

The Queen inclined her head in affirmation. "Just so. Our given word is binding upon us, inextricably linked with the hive mind that itself is sanity and life. To us, a promise is as confining as walls and chains would be to a human—no, more. We cannot rebel against the tenets of our ancestors without calling madness upon the hive, a madness that brings death, for we would cease to feed, to breed, to defend ourselves. For us, to think is to act, and to act is to think. You have no words to embrace the concept."

Mara gave in to the weakness in her knees. She sat abruptly upon the bare earth, her armor creaking in the stillness. Her voice was small, as close as she had ever come to sounding mollified. "I didn't know."

The Queen said nothing to exonerate Mara. "That is a common response by humans who at last perceive their error. Yet it changes nothing. You did not swear to the terms of the Forbidden. You cannot break what does not bind you. Only the cho-ja or the Assembly can violate this ancient pact."

Mara cursed herself for pride and vanity. She had dared to think herself different from her fellow Ruling Lords; she had presumed to know her cho-ja friends, and had been guilty of an atrocity as great as any that her kind had perpetrated against the insectoid race in the past.

The Chakaha council had trusted her: wrongly, it would seem. She shrank from the association that eventually the mages she had cozened into coming to the Empire must know how poorly she had judged.

How many times had Ichindar, on his seat of power, suffered for his human follies when they had come to adversely affect the people he had been set by fate to rule? Mara felt diminished with shame. She had aspired to set her son on the golden throne; to save his life, she believed.

How little she had reckoned the ramifications at the time, to set a weight of responsibility not even she could encompass upon the untried shoulders of a boy.

Mara set her face in her hands, burdened with something worse than mere despair. She contemplated the finality of death, that she had stubbornly named a waste of resource; now she was no longer sure. The gist of her philosophy had altered under her, until no course of action felt sure.

"The magicians will seek reprisal against your kind," Mara ventured at last. She looked up humbly at the Queen. "What will you do?"

The massive insectoid regarded her with an expression no human could interpret. "Some of us will die," she replied with the implacable honesty of her kind. "This hive will very likely be first, since you were permitted an entry and an audience."

"Can you not flee?" Mara badly wanted to hear one word of hope or encouragement, that all was not lost for these creatures whose friendship had sustained her through a lifetime of trial and difficulty.

The Queen twitched a forelimb, perhaps in the cho-ja equivalent of a shrug. "I am already within the deepest chamber of this hive. It is not possible to move me anywhere else. Once our Queens mature enough to lay eggs, we lose our mobility. Here, at least, I will survive until the last. Your Great Ones may destroy my body, but the hive mind will preserve my memory, and the record of all that passes here. Another hive will protect our mind, and when a new Queen is spawned, the mind will renew with her."

Small comfort, Mara thought, not to be forgotten for eternity. She did not speak of the foreboding in her heart, that worse might happen: there might indeed be an end without memory for the cho-ja nation held captive in the Empire. Her brashness might have bought their permanent extermination. She recalled the trust she had won from the Chakaha council, and her need to weep became painful.

She was given no chance to dwell upon guilt or misgiving. The next instant the Queen cocked her head to one side as if listening.

A rapid-fire, high-pitched buzzing was exchanged between ruler and her servants. The communication ceased as if cut off. Workers and warriors departed, and the Queen tilted her head toward her human guest.

"What is it?" Mara asked, dreading to hear the answer.

"Great Ones have come," replied the Queen. "A delegation thirty strong has surrounded the entrance of my hive. They accuse us falsely of oath breaking, and they demand that your person be surrendered."

"I will go out to them," Mara said, the trembling in her knees redoubled. She wondered if she could force her sore body to stand. "I would cause your kind no more trouble."

The cho-ja Queen jerked a forelimb in an unmistakable gesture of negation. "You are not our prisoner. We have broken no oaths. It was you who brought mages over the borders, and there is no statute in the treaty that forbids us to give you audience. You may go. You may stay. Or the Black Robes may come and fetch you out. Neither option is any of our affair."

Mara's eyebrows rose in shock. She held her speech, striving to avoid any more errors of assumption. Carefully she weighed her next words. "If I choose not to surrender my person, you must know that the Assembly will misinterpret. They will believe in your complicity, and seek retribution."

The Queen seemed less serene than hard as polished obsidian. "They will believe wrongly, if what you postulate is accurate."

Mara swallowed. She felt as if the firmness of the earth might at any moment crumble beneath her feet. "Your people could be harmed by such a misunderstanding."

The Queen did not relent. "Then they would be harmed. That does not make the Black Robes' misjudgment any closer to the truth. We have kept to the terms of our treaty, as our kind must. If they, as humans, act in error, then the error is theirs, *as are the consequences.*"

Mara frowned, pondering upon the meaning that might lie beneath the Queen's words. The lady of the Acoma had skirted proscribed issues once before, seeking clues concerning the Forbidden. Now, unable to suppress the hope that sparked in her, she wondered whether these wily cho-ja in fact *sought* to provoke a misjudgment.

As she drew breath to give voice to this thought a sudden terror gripped her. The air in the chamber grew too thick, as if a great pressure wave rushed through the tunnels to crush her. Covering her ears as pain stabbed them, Mara gasped in shock. An explosion shook the earth, tossing her down. She struck earth on her side. A cry exploded from her, as the chamber around her became laced with lightning and fire.

Over the concussion of air struck to thunder, the Queen shrieked in agony and what may have been pure cho-ja rage.

"The magicians attack! Our hive is destroyed! The treaty that binds us is broken!" Then language was abandoned. The Queen's voice rose to painful dissonance as she buzzed her last communication to her kind.

Mara choked on burning air. Her eyes streamed tears, and her skin scorched in the beginnings of searing torment. Justin, she thought, Kasuma: I have failed you both—

Her eyes were blinded by a dazzling flash of light, then smothered in all-consuming darkness.

She screamed. The world she knew upended. No earth pressed against her body, and no sense of gravity bound her down. From heat, her flesh shriveled in the bite of a cold like frost.

And then there was only darkness that extended beyond eternity.

31. Kentosani

A wareness returned.

Mara blinked, her reemerging senses confused. She struggled to orient herself, but her consciousness refused to resolve more than the rudiments of cohesive impression. Her body reclined on what felt like cushions. Warm air surrounded her, and gentle illumination. She could make out nothing else, no solid detail of chamber or setting. The burning, agonizing nightmare of sorcery and destruction seemed banished as a nightmare would be upon waking.

"Where am I?" she murmured.

"Safe," said a voice. By its ringing, disembodied tone, Mara knew: a miracle had occurred. Spared the wrath of the Assembly by the narrowest margin, she must be in the presence of the cho-ja mages. In Chakaha, they had demonstrated their ability to move her from place to place by magic. So they must have done now, pulling her out of the ruins of the hive even as the Black Robes achieved its destruction. The knowledge that cho-ja had suffered strangely brought her no distress. Alarmed, Mara pushed herself upright.

Her concern immediately dissipated, slipped from her like water. She made out the shadowy forms of the cho-ja mages, crouched on either side of her. They had been busy in her absence. The burrow they inhabited was now adorned by furnishings created by their craft. The peace that Mara now experienced was also due to their influence. "You practice your arts already, spellcasters?"

One mage returned a gesture of reassurance, forearms turned so that the sharp edges were averted from chance accident. "Your aura was tinged with fear and anger. If I presumed to ease your mind, forgive me, but the time is now for clear-headedness, yes?"

Mara swallowed. "The hive was destroyed by the Assembly. I am sorry."

The second mage shifted with a rustle of wings. "Necessary sacrifice," it intoned in emotionless brevity. "The Queen's memory is preserved intact, and the unjust treaty has been broken at last. Cho-ja warriors are freed to march within the Empire. They will now support your cause, Servant of the Empire.''

Her cause! Mara felt cold at the words. She had wished to secure her children's safety, and to expunge stagnation and cruelty from her people's culture. But an entire cho-ja hive had just been sacrificed to save her, and now she was being called to fullest account for her pledge to the council in Chakaha. The Empire's Queens held out the expectation that she would go on to win freedom for their race.

''Yes,'' the cho-ja mage to her left intoned in response to her thought. ''The imperial seal with temple endorsements on a document that restores cho-ja to full citizenship should be sufficient to revoke the Assembly's unfair judgment.''

Mara gathered her inner strength. ''First, the Great Ones must be defeated,'' she warned. The prospect of outright confrontation with the magicians terrified her.

The mages inclined their heads in what seemed maddening serenity. ''The means are at hand. But time grows short.''

The speed at which events were overtaking the Lady of the Acoma carried its own weight of care. Mara fought off overwhelming despair. She had lost her advisers. Arakasi was gods alone knew where. Lujan's fate was unknown to her. The Acoma armies might now be ashes, and her husband could have been obliterated by the Assembly in the moment when they declared her its enemy. Jiro of the Anasati might already be in the Holy City, and her children dead. And even if by miracle the Imperial Precinct was still secure and under the protection of the Imperial Whites, there remained the armies of the Anasati and the Omechan poised outside the city walls.

Mara chided herself. Listing every possible ramification of misfortune served nothing, but would only cancel what slender advantage the Chakaha mages had won for her. She saw death at every turn, whether she acted or not. Better to fight, and take matters in hand as best she could. Whether Justin and Kasuma were well or not, or whether an Omechan or an Anasati pretender had already assumed the golden throne, she owed the cho-ja who had spared her an honorable best effort.

''I need information,'' she urged, rising immediately to her feet. Her whole body ached. She ignored its twinges, and briskly turned toward the Chakaha mages. ''Your aid will be necessary. Once I understand the array of the forces laid against us, I will need to reach the Holy City more swiftly than the wind.''

The Chakaha mages straightened from their crouch. They bowed to her and then flanked her. "Your will is as our command, Lady Mara," said one. "Ask us what you would know. We will engage our arts to show you."

Filled with trepidation for the losses she now had no choice but to count, Mara forced herself bear up. "My husband, Hokanu," she opened, the tremble in her voice scarcely controlled. "Where is he?"

"Close your eyes," bade the Chakaha mages.

Mara obeyed, foreboding in her heart. An energy tingled through her: magic. She beheld more than darkness behind her lids: caught by a sensation akin to dizziness, she saw Hokanu bending over a tactical map of the Holy City. He gestured to rows of white pins on the walls, his helm cradled in his hand, and his face worried. He looked as though he had not slept in a fortnight.

The sight of him was more than Mara could bear. "He is alive!" she cried, near tears in her relief. Her joy and thanksgiving to the gods for this turn of fortune left her weak. Then she set aside wonderment to consider the practical. The mages informed her that Hokanu and his company of swift cavalry had crossed the city gates ahead of the siege. The Shinzawai infantry companies still marched from the North, but they would be of no use as relief forces, Mara saw, as her cho-ja mages showed her Black Robes forbidding the ranks of blue-clad warriors access to the Holy City.

Mara had been declared enemy, and her allies were forbidden to give aid. Without orders to defy the Great Ones, Tsurani training came to the fore and Hokanu's warriors obeyed.

"The Imperial Whites," Mara mused. "They will defend. Who beside Hokanu might command them?"

For answer, she was given a second view of the chamber where the council discussed tactics. Mara identified the figures who clustered about the Shinzawai Lord whose dreams matched her own: Arakasi was present, quiet as a shadow, and looking grim. Near him was the Shinzawai First Adviser, Dogondi, his face implacable, as he conducted animated discussion with another that Mara recognized with a start for Chumaka, who was the Anasati First Adviser.

Unthinking, she questioned aloud. "What does Chumaka do here?"

For answer, the mages showed her more images: a glade in a forest where Hokanu twisted and twisted a leather thong, choking the life out of Jiro. The faded color and rippling quality of the vision identified the seeing as a past event. Mara saw Jiro go limp in Hokanu's grip. The Lord of the Anasati was dead!

And yet, based upon her husband's current activity, Kentosani suffered under siege. "Who directs the attack on the Holy City?" she demanded to know.

The scene behind her eyes spun and shifted focus. She beheld armies and wooden engines, and a Force Commander in Omechan colors. The outer walls had crumbled and been breached. The Imperial Precinct itself was under attack, and the plumes on the walls showed several factions defending: Imperial White, and another. In amazement Mara made out the purple and yellow of Xacatecas. "Hoppara is in Kentosani?"

"Sent by his mother, Isashani," one Chakaha mage intoned. "He whom you name Hoppara reached Kentosani ahead of the attack, and organized the Imperial Whites to defend. The Omechan Lord knows of Jiro's death, but he dreams of seizing the Anasati plot as his own. You still have a foe who wishes to rule upon the bodies of your children."

Mara bit her lip. Her own armies—if they had escaped destruction, and if the magicians had not already forbidden them movement—would be too far south to attack the force menacing the Imperial Precinct. Her other allies appeared to have fled, or were stalling elsewhere, fearful of transferring the aroused wrath of the Assembly against themselves.

Her dismay must have been evident. "Lady," one of the mages broke in. "You are not without an army. Every cho-ja warrior in the Nations is yours to command."

"How can they be?" Mara's tone was bleak. "The Queen of the hive that was sacrificed inferred that cho-ja can never break a promise. The warriors you offer to my cause are already sworn to answer to other ruling Lords. Your people have contracts of service that span generations."

The mages buzzed in what Mara had come to interpret as cho-ja laughter. "No longer," said one. "Close your eyes," the second directed. "Let us show you."

Infused with a growing wonderment, Mara did so. She beheld a dry field upon which the armies of two minor nobles engaged in battle. A fat young man in Ekamchi colors was exhorting one of his Strike Leaders. "But they can't quit the field," he shouted, his sword arm waving dangerously near the face of his senior adviser. The servant jumped back in vexation as his master ranted on. "These cho-ja owe me and my father their allegiance."

The Strike Leader shook his head, stiff-faced. "They say not, master."

"How!" The Ekamchi son reddened under his battle helm. "Their kind are as slaves! They never break an alliance!"

"They do now." The Strike Leader turned from his commander, and watched with stony eyes as rank after rank of cho-ja warriors disengaged from combat and marched in swift order from the field.

"This cannot be!" shrieked the Ekamchi son. He ran forward and planted himself in the path of the ranking cho-ja Strike Leader. "You are traitors," he accused. "You break oath."

The cho-ja officer returned a click that showed scorn. "Three thousand centis in metal and gems have been delivered to your father's treasury. Such was the price that bought our service. All past bargains and alliances are ended; all payments are refunded."

The Ekamchi boy spluttered, but as the cho-ja officer crouched into a posture that threatened attack, he was forced to give ground.

Mara opened her eyes, shaking with unbridled laughter. "What a surprise to most Ruling Lords that the cho-ja were something more, or perhaps less, than loyal mercenaries."

"Humans have much to learn concerning our kind," the Chakaha mages agreed tactfully. "Old ways have changed. Not even the Assembly could wring from our people another treaty like the one that endured in such misery through thousands of years. When the war of the mages was lost, our magic was not developed for defensive purposes. Be sure that such weakness has been remedied in those lands beyond the Empire."

Mara beheld the perilous glitter in the eyes of the Chakaha mages, and her blood ran cold in her body. Traditions were broken, and danger was in the wind, and now was her moment to seize advantage if she would, to secure the next age's peace. She mastered her inner trepidation and opened. "Messages must be sent, and actions taken to enforce Justin's claim to the golden throne before the Assembly can interfere. Here is what must be done."

Mara waited, suppressing the deep quiver of fear. Her hair was piled high on her head, elaborately looped and braided, and fixed with precious metal pins. Golden pins, she thought, and the arrogance of her presumption, to put on imperial gold, made her feel the more small and uncertain. And yet there could be no half measures, if the Empire as a Nation was to survive.

Her head swam with recollection of the orders she had given between her bath and her robing. She drew a deep breath. To the cho-ja Force Commander, who crouched at her elbow, she said, "Where are we exactly?"

Like his counterparts in free Chakaha, this warrior eschewed the trappings of human commanders. His jet-dark carapace had begun to show a faint turquoise stripe, perhaps a decoration, perhaps a mark of rank. Mara looked forward to the chance study of such distinctions, if the gods saw fit to grant her victory. Then she dismissed speculation as the warrior pointed upward and said, "Directly above is the imperial antechamber. The ones you requested should gather for a legal coronation ceremony already await inside the audience hall. All preparations are in order, and your people anticipate your arrival."

Mara braced herself. She waved away the maid called in from the Imperial Palace, who had edged between the ranks of the warriors for one last adjustment of her dress. The gown she wore could not possibly hang without wrinkles, taken as it had been from attic storage. It had belonged to the last dowager Empress, a larger woman than Mara, but it was the closest to Acoma green that could be found, so it would have to do. Hasty stitches had gathered in the waist, and pins nipped up the long hem. Mara felt encased in layers like a needle cushion. The heavy fabrics chafed the sores left from her armor, and rice powder could never conceal all the scrapes and scratches she had sustained in her flight through the forest.

Feeling every inch the hoyden bundled under a disguising mass of finery, she said, "When you cut through to the outside from this tunnel, the Black Robes will know something is afoot."

The mages inclined their heads. "We are prepared for them, as best we can be."

Mara took a grip on her nerve, which seemed by the minute to ebb. "Then send me Arakasi. I would confer with him before we start the final move."

It was still disconcerting to the Lady how swiftly the mages could translate her merest wish into command. She had no sooner finished speaking than her Spy Master was delivered into her presence, as disgruntled as anyone had ever observed him.

Arakasi arose from where he had been dumped by the spell, face down upon the earthen floor. Unlike the imperial maids who had been summoned earlier by magic to attend to Mara's robing, the Spy Master did not lose his wits. His raised brows settled into a frown that immediately smoothed as he glanced about and identified the presence of cho-ja. Next he fixed upon his mistress, who was almost unrecognizable in imperial robes of state.

Then he was on his knees, bowing. "My Lady." Where once his voice would have been expressionless, now there was a tremulous note of joy. "I am glad to see you well."

"Rise," Mara commanded. She came as near as her nervousness would allow to laughter. "Justin wears no crown as yet, and I am due no such obeisance. It is a custom I would see dispensed with, if our plans succeed as we hope." She peered through the gloom at the long-missed person of her Spy Master, and, abashed by the intentness of her scrutiny, Arakasi bent his head, chagrinned.

"You wear the clothes of a cleaning drudge!" Mara exclaimed.

Her Spy Master gave back a broad chuckle. "How better to spy upon one's superiors without drawing undue notice, my Lady?" His nose wrinkled. "Though I would prefer to attend Justin's wedding and coronation in garments that were not caked with scouring sand."

Both Lady and Spy Master quieted as the pressure of events forced sobriety. "The priests of all the orders are gathered," Arakasi affirmed. "Some may be a little shy of perfect in their robing, since a few were summoned directly from their beds. Once we had their honorable selves all present in the great audience hall, those who complained could not be permitted to leave. According to Chumaka's study of the law, Justin's claim could be disputed if even one High Priest failed to be in attendance. Getting the Sisterhood of Sibi to come was the most difficult task—not even the High Priest of Turakamu was willing to contact them."

"How did you manage?" Mara asked.

"Without alternative, I simply went into the temple myself. I was allowed to live long enough to tell them why I did what few men have dared." Arakasi smiled slightly at his memory. He was perhaps the only petitioner in centuries to enter the Temple of Sibi uninvited, and certainly the only one allowed to leave. "The temples support your cause at this time, since the alternative would set them the more firmly under the heel of the Assembly. But sentiments could change, if civil order is not swiftly restored. We'll get no second chance. Great Ones are out in force in the city. More than a dozen watch the entrances to the palace, as they are certain you'll somehow try to mask your arrival in the confusion."

Mara's frown was instinctive. "They've entered a city under threat of civil war, and done nothing to repress the Omechan siege?"

Arakasi looked grim. "Indeed not. My best impression is that they have forsaken their insistence on peace in favor of their own concerns." He looked hard at the diminutive woman who seemed half-smothered under the weight of her imperial overrobes. "I don't know what you've accomplished in the South, but I would hazard a guess, my Lady, that the Black Robes have learned to be afraid of you."

"Not of me," Mara corrected, embarrassed. "Of these." Her gesture encompassed the cho-ja mages who stood like sentinels to either side.

Arakasi regarded her alien companions, his eyes widening at the splendor of their many-colored wings. "I never knew your kind could be so beautiful," he said in awed reverence.

The Chakaha mages brushed aside the human praise without awkwardness. The left-hand one addressed Mara. "Good Servant, danger grows as we speak. Human warriors are entering the tunnels by the Great Ones' command, searching for word of your hiding."

"Where?" Mara demanded, the memory of the burned-out hive that she had so narrowly escaped all too recent a horror. "Has there been bloodshed?"

"Not yet," the second mage replied. "The warriors obey the restraint of the Assembly not to fight unless they meet opposition. And the cho-ja will not embrace conflict until they are confronted without alternative. For now, they abandon the hives that are invaded, leaving many empty galleries and tunnels to be searched in profitless darkness. The human armies make poor progress. This moment they concentrate their sweep to the south, near the estates of your birth. But the search will be widened, very soon. Your Great Ones are not fools."

"Then the hour is come," Mara said, startling all present with what seemed an indomitable strength. "We will go forward."

At her word, the cho-ja mages gave a signal. A task force of workers marched to the fore of the tunnel and began to burrow upward. Dirt pattered down, and then chunks of mortar and tile. Light pierced the gloom, yellow and clear, from the domed skylight over the imperial antechamber.

A cho-ja stuck his head through the opening. He buzzed back a brief communication, and the mage to Mara's left said, "The antechamber is clear of enemies. Your husband and son await." Then it paused, as if in hesitation. "Lady," it intoned, "we wish you luck and brave fortune. But move swiftly. Our spells cannot stay the Black Robes' attack indefinitely. You will have a short time to achieve all that you must, and then there will be chaos and a devastating backlash of thwarted energies. We wish you to know, if you fail, or if we fail you, that it was for this battle that we were sent from Chakaha. We are more than your defense, Good Servant; we are an embassy to bring in a new order."

Mara looked upward into the mages' alien visages, which reared above her with expressions no human alive could fully know. It did not escape her that both had unfurled their wings into fighting stance, as they prepared to stand down the might of a unified Assembly. Their courage moved her to tears. "Let it be known, good friends, that so long as I live, I will not fail you. We will triumph or die together."

She turned and faced forward at once, lest the fullness of her courage collapse under the weight of the dangers that threatened. Straight, stiff-backed under her gold-studded robes, the Servant of the Empire started forward toward the opening.

Mara made her way with unsteady steps over the fallen earth and the clumps of tile and mortar. Unobtrusively, Arakasi moved to steady her elbow. She flashed him a grateful smile, glad for his human touch after the company of so many cho-ja.

And then she was out, dazzled by late-day sunlight, and by the flash of a magnificence of gold armor.

She caught her breath. Red hair pushed out from beneath the helm of imperial gold; Justin's red hair, she realized with a great thump of her heart. He did not look like a boy anymore, armored in the finery of an Emperor. Mara shook to realize that this was the hour of his wedding.

She faltered in her step as the boy bowed to her, son to mother, as was proper. All that brilliance of goldwork felt wrong; as though she should be bowing to the floor, as she once had to Ichindar.

Then the boy straightened and gave an undignified whoop. "Mother!" he cried and ran forward.

Mara forgot her finery and reached. Her son rushed into her arms, taller, heavier now, fully and impressively coming closer to manhood. As his arms locked around her neck, she realized she did not have to bend down anymore to embrace him. His shoulders had started to broaden in a way that felt all too familiar. He was all Kevin's, Mara realized; he would have his father's great height. The jolt of that restored her to dignity.

As her son stepped back from her embrace, he regarded her levelly with eyes that were the image of his barbarian father's. "I am ready, Good Servant. The princess Jehilia awaits."

Mara's voice failed her. She had lost two children already, Ayaki, and the little one poisoned before his birth. Now her only living son stood resolutely ready to give his life for her honor. The moment was more than she could endure.

Then Justin's face broke into a grin of such insouciance, she was again recalled to past days, and to Kevin's irrepressible humor. "We'd better hurry," her son admonished. "The late Emperor's First Wife keeps having hysterics, and all of her makeup is going to run."

Mara rallied. "What of Jehilia? Did she have hysterics, too?"

Justin gave back a boy's shrug. "She shouted a lot. She locked herself in her room. Then somebody asked her if she would rather wed an Omechan with a paunch and grey hair, and she let the maids in to get her dressed."

The girl had sense, Mara thought, as she took her place at Justin's side and prepared to enter the great audience hall. Arakasi stood by her, to steady her other side, and no one seemed to notice that he yet wore the robes of a drudge as the iron-studded doors swung open and the musicians began the fanfare that announced the arrival of the groom.

Mara stepped resolutely ahead, aware of her own hand, sweating, where she gripped Justin's. She wondered as she passed through the ranked columns of the Priests of the Twenty Higher Orders whether the gods would strike her down for pride, and for the sheer arrogance of presumption that caused her to dare set her son on the throne as the next Light of Heaven, the ninety-second Emperor of Tsuranuanni. But the representative of the temple of Juran, God of Justice, did not look displeased, and the High Priest of Turakamu gave her a small smile of encouragement. Apart from the rest, behind the Red God's priest, stood three shrouded figures in black, the Sisters of Sibi, Goddess of Death. Even those chilling aspects seemed to reassure Mara with a slight inclination of their heads. The High Priest of Jastur, the God of War, slammed his gloved fist against his chest in salute, as Mara passed, his blow ringing on the precious iron of his breastplate.

Mara took another step, and another, her inner confidence rebounding. As she passed, the priests of the higher and lower orders began to arrange themselves before the dais, in pairs by their nature, the priests of Lashima, Goddess of Wisdom, falling in beside those of Salana, Mother of Truth. Priest of Turakamu partnered the Sister of Sibi, while the High Priest of Jastur was joined by the High Priest of Baracan, the Lord of Swords.

Ahead, on the imperial dais, waited a small, blond-haired girl in a sparkling veil of gold tissue. Jehilia, Mara identified, as her maids drew back her headdress; the girl still had freckles, from too much time playing truant in the imperial gardens. And if she looked pale beneath the paint and powder of her makeup, she saw the Good Servant, and grinned.

"Let the doors be closed, and the ceremonial matrimony begin!" intoned the priest of Chochocan, the Good God, in ritual opening. Behind him and to his right the High Priest of Tomachca, Lover of Children, began silent prayer. Mara stared at him a lingering moment, remembering that the lesser brother of Chochocan was also known as the Bringer of Peace. She prayed he would be so today.

Justin's fingers gave Mara's a last squeeze as she let him loose to take his place at his Princess's side. Mara moved to where Hokanu waited, and as the ceremony began, she slipped her hand into his.

* * *

The Imperial Palace was bustling. Messengers hurried by, and servants moved purposefully across the courtyards in an anxious rush to complete errands. Perched on an elbow by a windowsill, Shimone of the Assembly watched their industry with deep, unreadable eyes. His face was more than usually austere, and if anything, he was yet more spare with words. He moved his head slightly, calling attention to the unusual level of activity.

The gesture was noted by Hochopepa, who sat upon cushions before a low table and a tray of half-consumed sugared fruits. The stout magician acknowledged with a nod and spoke softly so that only Shimone could hear. "Something more than everyday business is afoot. I've counted five priests hidden under cowls, and by the smell on the air, the kitchens are baking a banquet. Odd fare, for a city under attack."

As if to punctuate his observation, a large rock fired from a siege engine sailed down from the air and shattered in a courtyard nearby. A stray dog fled, yelping. Hochopepa gazed through the cracked screen with narrowed eyes. "Those damned things are starting to irritate me. Another stone this close and I'll go out and . . ." His threat was cut off as he was distracted by another band of oddly dressed nobles hurrying past the window. "We expected an influx of Ruling Lords to convene in the old council chambers, but this seems something more."

Shimone stirred, standing straighter. "It is much more. Motecha will not be stayed much longer from taking action."

Hochopepa regarded the remains of his snack with wistful regret. "*I* will not be stayed much longer from taking action," he corrected in faint reproof. "I think the Lady is here already, and that we waste our time in this vigil."

Shimone said nothing, but his eyebrows raised, and he pushed himself away from the window. Not to be left behind as the taller, slenderer mage stalked from the chamber, Hochopepa lumbered up from his cushions and hurried after.

Servants engaged in nameless activities fled or prostrated themselves in fear as the pair made their way down the passage. If the palace corridors were a maze of constructions added one on top of another over the centuries, the Black Robes needed no directions. They proceeded without error to a red-painted door emblazoned with an enameled seal. They did not knock, but entered the office of the Imperial Chancellor.

Dajalo of the Keda stood resplendent in his regalia of office, red and black robes cut in layers, with gold trim flashing at collar and cuffs. His massive headdress was straight. He looked composed, if pale. His staff members seemed less poised. The secretary at his elbow trembled, half-sick with fear, while the runner slave by the outer screen cowered. The reason for so much nervous unrest was obvious: the cushions left out for audience with petitioners were all taken, occupied by a half-dozen Great Ones. Motecha was pacing. Looking far from pleased, he glanced up as his two colleagues entered, but continued the interrogation he had in progress. ''Any word of her?''

The subject of his reference needed no qualifier. ''None, Great One.'' Dajalo bowed to the new arrivals and, adroitly as any skilled courtier, used the movement to unobtrusively blot running sweat from his brow. He straightened up, stiffly formal in appearance. If as Imperial Chancellor he felt uneasy in the presence of so many Black Robes, he contrived to hide it well.

Hochopepa crossed behind the imposing desk, plucked the chancellor's own seat cushion from the floor, and removed it to the embrasure beneath the window, where a breeze refreshed the air; the room had been crowded throughout the morning, and the servants too timid to venture in and open the screens. Hochopepa sat down. He plucked a sweetmeat from a pottery urn left for guests and chewed, looking dangerously intent for a man with a round, merry face. ''Oh, she will be here, certainly,'' he murmured around his mouthful. ''The High Council is reconvening at this moment, and the Lady of the Acoma wouldn't miss it. Never has there been one to play the Great Game like Mara.''

''Quite,'' Motecha snapped irritably. ''She would die first. As she will, the second we discover her location.''

Shimone looked faintly distasteful. ''We all must die; it is a rule of nature.''

The Imperial Chancellor buried his discomfort behind a studied mask of urbanity.

Motecha glanced from one face to another, but said nothing. His colleagues were still. The suspicion that Mara was guilty of uncovering some of the most closely guarded secrets of the Assembly, secrets that for an outsider were a death warrant, seemed to color the very air with tension. Not even Hochopepa and Shimone had been able to deny that the willingness of the cho-ja to shelter her suggested worse: that she might have seeded a rebellion, a breaking of the treaty that had stood for thousands of years. As convincingly as Shimone and others had argued that the Servant of the Empire deserved a full hearing before her life became forfeit, this time their efforts had been overruled.

The Assembly had voted. Mara's execution was now beyond debate.

Few would presume to act alone against the Servant of the Empire, but

Tapek had, and the worst trouble had resulted. Black Robes were starting at shadows in the suspicion that their privileged status stood threatened. Now more critical issues were at hand than a brother Black Robe's rashness. Hochopepa and Shimone exchanged glances of understanding. They had, in their way, admired Mara, who had accomplished much good for the Empire.

But now she had dared too much. The stout magician felt drawn into conflict: his loyalty to the Assembly and the vows sworn there when he took the Black Robe, against the allure of fresh ideas, many of them prompted by the heresies that Milamber the barbarian had shared with him.

Hochopepa valued the legacy of his friendship with Milamber. Over the years the Tsurani-born Black Robe had increasingly employed his arts in the cause of the common people. Now, with changes in the wind too great for even his progressive thinking to encompass, he wished for more time. Hochopepa longed for clear conviction on which course was right to follow: to work with Motecha's faction for Mara's immediate destruction or to embrace her call for reform and consider the unthinkable, after a majority vote: to oppose the Assembly's resolve, even perhaps save her life.

Suddenly Shimone took a long, swift step toward the window. He accompanied his movement with a penetrating glance at Hochopepa, who swallowed his sweetmeat more suddenly than he had intended.

"You feel it, too," the fat magician said to Shimone.

"Feel what?" Motecha interrupted. And then he also fell silent, as he sensed what had alerted the others.

A creeping chill pervaded the air, not the simple cold of shadow, nor even the clammy feeling prompted by uneasiness. Each magician present knew the unmistakable subliminal tingle of powerful magic.

Shimone poised like a dog on point. "Someone sets wards!" he announced in clipped tones.

Hochopepa rose awkwardly to his feet. "No Black Robe creates this spell." His admission came with reluctance, as if he deeply wished to claim otherwise.

"The cho-ja!" shouted Motecha. His face deepened to purple. "She has brought mages from Chakaha!"

The small chamber erupted into chaos as the other Black Robes surged to their feet. Their expressions, to a man, were stormy. The Imperial Chancellor was forced cowering into the cranny behind his desk to stay clear of them, but no one heeded his discomfort.

"Mara will die for this!" Motecha continued. "Sevean, call at once for reinforcements."

Even Hochopepa did not protest this order. "Hurry," he urged Shimone, and while the outrage of the assembled magicians whipped to a boiling rage, the fat magician and his slender companion were the first out the door.

The corridor beyond was deserted. Even the servants had fled. "I don't like this." Hochopepa's words echoed off the vaulted ceiling of the now empty wing. "In fact, I have the distinct impression that more than the High Council has been seeking unsanctioned convocation."

Shimone said nothing, but reached for his teleportation device, activated it, and vanished.

"Hrrumph!" Hochopepa exclaimed in frustration. "Letting me know where you're going wouldn't exactly be idle chatter!"

Shimone's voice replied out of the air. "You imply there might be a choice?"

Disgusted that his robe belt seemed suddenly to be cinctured too tight, Hochopepa pawed through cloth until he found his pocket. He grasped his teleportation device and engaged it, just as Sevean, Motecha, and the others shouted from the antechamber of the Imperial Chancellor's office. As he disappeared from the hallway, Hochopepa felt his last disconcerting thought cut off by the disorientation of his transfer: which party would accomplish Mara's execution? He and Shimone, who acted only for the purpose of the Assembly's self-preservation, or the others, led by Motecha, who lusted after revenge?

"She has made fools of us, and worse!" Sevean's voice rang out just before the shift in Hochopepa's location became accomplished.

Worse, the fat magician concluded as he reappeared, puffing, in the sunlit splendor of the courtyard outside the antechambers of the imperial audience hall. Mara had brought power to battle absolute power, and now far more than civil war might tear the Empire asunder.

The courtyard too was deserted. The flowering trees that bordered the wall and the approach to the wide steps hung still in the noon air. No birds flew, and no insects droned around the flowers. The din of the armies that clashed at the walls and the unceasing battering of rocks from the siege engines seemed distant and faint. If the noise was inconvenient, none of the Black Robes made any move at this juncture to quell it.

The warriors who defended the Imperial Precinct were best off distracted at the walls, to keep them unaware of the pending storm that soon must break over the audience hall.

Shimone stood in the center of the square, his head cocked slightly. "Here," he said. "The ward starts here."

Nothing showed in the noon air that looked in the least arcane. "You can't break through?" puffed Hochopepa. He squinted, concentrated, and extended his senses to their utmost. At last he detected a faint shimmer that might have been due to heat; except that when he looked directly at it, the phenomenon disappeared. He pawed through his other pocket, pulled out a gaudy handkerchief, and mopped his streaming brow. "If that's a ward, it hardly seems substantial."

Shimone turned with an air of sharpened reproof. "You try and pierce it."

Hochopepa extended his might, then suddenly widened his eyes as a rainbow of color played through the air before him. As if brushed aside without effort, the potency of his magic dissipated along the barrier created by the cho-ja. Hochopepa's mouth sagged open in astonishment. Then a stray fragment of rock fired from without descended whistling toward his head. He recovered his poise and deflected it as casually as a man might bat aside a fly. Throughout, his attention remained focused on the cho-ja–wrought protections. "That strong, eh? Fascinating. A very subtle piece of work. The way it lets you probe, then siphons off your energies and weaves them with its own . . ." Immersed in scholarly study, he was slow to waken to the fact that the cho-ja had mages evolved considerably in their skills since the treaty had effected the ban. "This is unsettling."

"Very." Shimone chose not to elaborate as behind him other magicians arrived in the central square. More had joined the party that had stood vigil in the Imperial Chancellor's chamber. Their number was two dozen strong, and growing. "There can be no argument now except force," Shimone concluded sadly.

Motecha picked up this last statement. "We should flame this palace to the ground! Burn every mind to idiocy that has dared to raise rebellion against us!"

Sevean stepped forward. "I disagree. Collapse these unsanctioned wards, yes, this is necessity. We must also destroy the cho-ja mages who work in violation of the treaty, and execute the Lady Mara. But destroy the Imperial palace? That's excessive. We may be outside the law, but we are still answerable to the gods. I doubt that heaven would sanction the priests of every order in the Empire dying along with Mara."

"The Holy Orders could be accomplices!" accused one of the recently arrived Black Robes.

"Indeed," Shimone cut in. "Or they could have been pressed into service by force. Better we hear their motives before we do their holinesses any violence."

"The wards only, then," Hochopepa summed up. He hitched at his too tight sash, and blotted with his dampened handkerchief. For all his outward resolution, his eyes were troubled. "We must break in without risking the lives of those inside the audience hall."

The magicians banded together in silence, as carrion birds might who contemplated the spoils on a battlefield. They stilled in mind and body, and the air seemed shaken by a deep, subliminal vibration as they melded their efforts into one.

The sky darkened, though no cloud gathered. The garden courtyard lost clarity, seeming to brood with a greenish tinge.

"Now," Motecha cried out.

Power speared down, lightning-bright, a sizzling bolt that appeared to bisect the heavens. It struck in a crack of violet sparks, but the ward seized the power, deflected it along the curve of its surface, then absorbed it. Heat flew back in a scorching wave. The stone faces of the buildings opposite blackened and cracked. Trees singed, and an ornamental fountain boiled dry in a puff of steam.

Untouched by the backlash, protected by their own wards, the gathered magicians exchanged dark looks of astonishment. They gathered for a second blow. A rainbow play of energies cascaded down upon the cho-ja barrier. It flared back a black opaqueness.

The Assembly magicians increased the force of their attack. Sparks jagged and flew, and thunder rumbled. Fire rained from the sky, and then charges of incandescent force.

"Keep up the assault," shouted Sevean. "Spare no effort. The wards must eventually weaken."

Winds howled, and fires raged. Tremors shook the earth, and paving cracked as gaps opened in the courtyard. The protective bubble of spells that sealed off the audience hall seemed to buckle, and shrink slightly inward.

"Yes!" Motecha redoubled his efforts. Lightning scored the invisible surface, and the winds raised by disturbed forces screamed around the spires of the Imperial Precinct like the howl of demons released.

One of the Black Robes with lesser strength crumpled to the pavement. The rest stood firm, sure now: the wards must break, over time. No magical defense could withstand such a concentrated onslaught for very long. As power hammered down, and split, and the rush of the gusts drowned even the din of the armies besieging the outside walls, the Assembly magicians immersed themselves in spells. In their collective fury, only one objective remained: the hall of the imperial audience would be breached, now at the cost of any lives; even their own.

The high, vaulted skylights of the imperial audience hall went dark. Plunged into sudden gloom, gathered courtiers and priests shifted nervously in their places. The only remaining illumination was cast by the wildly flickering lamps kindled in honor of the Twenty Higher Gods. On the dais, the priest of Chochocan who presided over the imperial marriage ceremony faltered in his lines.

A bang of nearby thunder shook the walls. While many in the chamber trembled, and more than one priest made signs to ward off heaven's displeasure, Justin's voice arose over the early murmurs of confusion. "Proceed," he stated clearly.

Mara felt her heart nearly burst with pride. The boy would make a fine ruler! Then she bit her lip; first, he would have to survive his wedding and coronation.

The Princess Jehilia at his side looked white with fright. She fought to keep her chin high, as royalty ought; but more than anything, she wanted to cower behind her veils. Justin's hand stole out and clamped around hers in a desperate attempt to share comfort.

After all, they were only children.

The floor shook under another concussion. The priest of Chochocan glanced about, as if seeking safe refuge.

Mara straightened. All must not be abandoned because one fainting priest lost heart! She tensed, prepared to intervene, although to do so was a risk: their holinesses would perhaps resent any further pressure from her. If she drove them too hard, they might mistake her motives for ambition, or worse: they might withdraw in the power of their office and pronounce that Justin's wedding to Jehilia went against the will of heaven.

Time was too short, and circumstances were too dangerous, to allow for long-winded justifications that had only circumstantial proof that the strike upon the cho-ja's wards was effected by mortal men who happened to be magicians, and that their will was no more that of heaven than the actions of any Ruling Lord who murdered out of greed or ambition for power.

The noise from without reached another crescendo as yet another arcane assault battered the wards. Rainbows of fractured light played through the skylights, bathing the chamber in unnatural colors. Mara's discomfort increased as the priests and officials in attendance began to shuffle feet. Old Frasai of the Tonmargu was trembling outright, perhaps on the point of cracking.

Support arose from an unexpected source, as the Red God's High Priest pressed to the forefront of temple representatives gathered beneath the imperial dais. "Brother," he exhorted his wavering fellow priest, "we are all Turakamu's, in the end. Were heaven displeased, we should already be struck down, and my God is silent within me. Please, proceed with the ceremony."

The High Priest of Chochocan nodded. He licked sweat from his upper lip and drew a deep breath, and his sonorous voice resumed the next lines of the ritual.

Mara exhaled in relief. At her side, the High Priest of Juran flashed her a look of understanding. "Bide, my good Lady Servant. You have allies."

Mara returned a slight nod. She did have allies; many more than she knew. The magical assault might intensify, but not all of the priests would be easily cowed. The twists and reverses of state politics over the course of centuries had taught them to be canny. If their hold slipped now, if Justin's wedding did not proceed according to law, and if his subsequent coronation were not to go forward and stand, they understood how greatly the authority of the temples would be ceded to the Assembly. The Sisters of Sibi stood like creatures from the realm of the dead, untroubled by the possibility that the Imperial Palace might collapse upon their heads.

For any portion of heaven's due influence and power to fall under mortal dominion was a perilous course, one that invited divine displeasure. Then would the gods curse misfortunes upon mankind that could make the wrath of an aroused Assembly seem but the tantrums of children.

Justin's reply to the next ritual question rang strongly over the din of another attack. Thunder rumbled, a seemingly endless peal. An ornamental bead shook loose from the imperial throne and rattled down the pyramidal steps. The crystal in the skylights cracked, and shards tumbled sparkling in the lamplight to shatter against the marble floor.

No one, thankfully, was in harm's way.

Mara closed her eyes. Hold, my children, she prayed. Hokanu's hand tightened over hers.

She returned a half-smile that warmed as Jehilia replied to the priest. The Princess was subdued, demure as befit her station; if she also clung to her new husband, she was still royalty. Her bearing stayed straight as the wicker cages with the ritual marriage birds were raised for the blessing. The reed doors were solemnly cut by the High Priest's knife.

Mara bit her lip, fighting tears, as the pair of birds inside took wing at their offered freedom. Fly, she willed them, fly up and mate and find happiness.

The omen of the birds at her own first wedding had been unfavorable. With all of her heart, she longed for this one to be different. She and Hokanu might not rule their lives by portents and tradition, but there were elderly priests present who did.

The birds shot aloft just as another bolt of thunder slammed the air. They winged over in alarm and, as one, arrowed up and out, through the gap in the cracked skylight.

"Thank the gods," Hokanu murmured. His hand squeezed Mara's, while the tears spilled unabashed over her eyelids. She could not hold in her emotion. Neither could she see as two Imperial Whites in ceremonial Force Leaders' armor stepped forward with the cloak edged in gold and sarcat fur: the mantle of the Emperor of all Tsuranuanni, which they spread over Justin's shoulders.

Tall as he had grown, the boy looked lost in the garment. Mara wiped her eyes and was struck by a poignant recollection of Ichindar, who had been as slender, and who in the end had been bowed down by the weight of imperial office.

Justin bore up well. He took Jehilia's hand as if he had been born being gallant to ladies, and led her up the stairs to the dais.

"His father's son indeed," Hokanu murmured proudly.

Singing acolytes followed the newly wedded couple, along with the priest of Juran, who bore the jeweled golden cushion that supported the imperial crown. The singing was ragged, cut across and half drowned by the rumble of continuous arcane attack from without.

The blows came much more closely spaced.

A pillar near the rear of the hall cracked with a sound like a whip. Mara started. She forced herself to focus wholly on the tableau that unfolded on the dais. She could not ignore signs of impending peril: that the air was growing warmer. The wooden railing beneath the dais where petitioners came to kneel before their Light of Heaven showed peeling layers of varnish. The stone floor grew hot enough to raise blisters, and courtiers shifted from foot to foot, as the leather of their sandals failed to protect from the growing heat.

"The cho-ja mages are hard pressed," Hokanu murmured in Mara's ear.

Thunder slammed again, rocking the chamber. Priests reached out to steady their colleagues, and more than one of the High Ones presiding on the dais looked frightened. They held to their purpose, grimly.

Mara watched as the priest of Lashima, Goddess of Wisdom, stepped forward to anoint her son's temples with oil. His vestments were knocked askew, and his hands shook. Much of the holy oil spilled on the intricate border of Justin's mantle. Jehilia was on the verge of panic, her hand locked white around her husband's. The priest of Baracan came next and presented Justin with the ancient golden sword of the Emperor, which would be brought forth again only when another Emperor was crowned. Justin put out his hand and rested it upon the sacred blade, and Mara, anguished, could see his young fingers trembling.

She must not think of failure! Annoyed with herself, she raised her chin and risked a glance back. The cho-ja mages stood by the door, no longer towering with their magnificent wings raised high. Now, they crouched on the floor, incanting counter-spells with a buzz that was like a dissonance beneath the rumbling booms of outside blows. The insectoid's strength was great, but the powers of the united Assembly were more than even they could stand off indefinitely. No matter how greatly they were provoked or threatened, their stance had been made emphatically clear. Chakaha still ruled them. Under no circumstances would they use their magic to attack.

When at last the ward failed, the Assembly would be freed to exercise the extent of their wrath upon the convocation in the audience chamber.

Strangely, Mara felt no fear. Too much had been risked, and too much lost. As if the part of herself that had known consternation at the prospect of horrible death had been seared out by degrees since the events that had harrowed her in Thuril, she was beyond acknowledging risk. In her rock-deep state of confidence, she seemed to radiate unearthly power.

Even Hokanu regarded her with the beginnings of awe. She barely noted. She stepped back from the front rank participants in Justin's coronation, saying quickly, "Praise our new Light of Heaven for me, when the crown is at last in place."

Her husband showed surprise, even yet taken aback by Mara's poise, though he had thought he understood all there was to know of her character. "What are you going to do?" His voice was falsely firm; even he must acknowledge that the mages who defended them were failing.

Mara gave him a firm look. "Subterfuge," she murmured. "What else is left?"

He bowed to her. "Good Servant." And then he stared in amazement as she walked to the back of the hall. He would remember her in this moment, he resolved, and cherish her unflagging spirit, even as the spells of the Assembly burst the wards and all of them became consumed by arcane fires.

Mara did nothing extraordinary. She reached the arched doors of the hall and bowed her respect to each of the cho-ja mages. They were too hard pressed to acknowledge beyond the merest flick of a forelimb. Then she paused by the portals and touched the wrists of the two imperial heralds who stood stationed at either side.

She conferred briefly with them. Hokanu, watching, was mystified. What was she doing? Her glance flashed up, met his: watch the ceremony, she seemed to chide.

He gave her a half-shrug and faced forward.

The earth rocked. On the dais, the priests' incantation went raggedly out of rhythm, and yet, stubbornly, they persisted. Sparks shot across the closed screens. The wards were breached. They were failing. The next hard blow would shatter all protections.

The coronation was nearly completed. "Hail!" cried the priests. They bowed, as the floor shook in thunderous report. "Hail!" The crown was raised up by the High Priest of Chochocan. He frantically mouthed the blessing.

Lightning flashed. A stone fell from the domed skylight and struck the agate flooring with a crash. The crown slipped from the priest's nerveless fingers and dropped crookedly to rest upon Justin's red head.

The act was accomplished. The heir to the Acoma, child of a slave, wore the sacred imperial regalia of Tsuranuanni, and no power short of heaven could rescind his anointed authority.

"Hail!" shouted the priests in convocation. "Hail, Justin, ninety-two times Emperor, and new-made Light of Heaven!"

The words tangled with an annihilating crash of thunder and Mara's shout to the heralds: "Now!"

Glittering gold in their ceremonial tabards, and pressed by a howling gust of air, the officials moved. They stepped to the great doors even as the cho-ja mages crumpled, grasped the rings, and threw wide the doors.

Against an onrushing wall of Black Robes, they performed their bows in perfect mirror image. "Hail to the new Light of Heaven!" they rang out in unison. White-faced, but inarguably firm, they straightened and the one with the most imposing voice qualified. "Great Ones of the Assembly, hear me! You are hereby summoned to the Imperial Court."

The lead ranks of Black Robes stumbled and rocked to a stop.

"Summoned?" shrieked a stupefied Motecha. Soot streaked his habit, and his red face sparkled with sweat. "By whom?"

The imperial heralds were well versed in maintaining poise in the face of intransigent courtiers. They performed impeccable bows. "By the Light of Heaven, Great One."

"What!" Sevean shoved forward, his colleagues crowding on his heels.

The heralds held to their dignity. From the dais, beside the high priests, the imperial Seneschal called out, "Justin! Ninety-two times Emperor!"

Motecha spluttered. Sevean looked pole-axed. Hochopepa was for once in his life left speechless, and even the austere Shimone never thought to press the issue with magic, as every other man and woman in the hall bowed before their ultimate monarch.

Between the slowly rising forms of two utterly spent Chakaha mages, Mara smothered exultation. The heralds had handled themselves admirably. Their confidence had seemed so unimpeachable that even the Great Ones had not yet thought to question the implicit inference: that the defenses of her allies were not spent unto exhaustion, and that protective wards had not in fact collapsed, but had been dropped deliberately.

"We have no power left," the Chakaha mage to Mara's left murmured in a near-inaudible frequency.

Mara waved a placating hand. "The Great Game," she murmured. "Now we must all play, or die."

32. Emperor

The Black Robes gaped.

Flanking the entrance to the audience hall, Imperial Whites in gold-edged armor stood at smart attention. Nowhere were warriors in Acoma or Shinzawai colors in evidence, as the magicians had expected to find.

They had anticipated the aftermath of struggle, with triumphant soldiers guarding their claimant until such time as the losers swore fealty. That was how disputed successions had been resolved in the past. But the Good Servant had not used compulsion to achieve her triumph. None rushed forward to hurl themselves in prostration and beg the mercy of the Black Robes, pleading for a reversal of Mara's usurpation of authority. Quite the contrary, the magicians at the forefront noticed that any discomfort on the faces that greeted them stemmed instead from their own precipitous arrival. Everyone present seemed involved in conspiracy with the end Mara had achieved.

Drums thundered in tattoo, drowning Motecha's shout for silence. He waved his raised hands to no avail, while colleagues on either side looked disgruntled by the flourish of trumpets and horns that sounded over the city in a peal not heard since the death of Ichindar. The notes even drowned the thudding of rocks from the siege engines.

Not far behind the leading magicians, Hochopepa leaned over to speak to Shimone. ''Servants must have been creeping in here making preparations for hours.''

Though his words were intended to be private, Sevean overheard. ''You imply a great deal of planning.''

Shimone treated his colleague to a gaze that masked contempt. ''Of all rulers in the Nations, Mara of the Acoma has never achieved *anything* without a plan.''

The fanfare rang away, leaving silence. ''You are summoned,'' the imperial heralds repeated, stepping back to clear the entrance. A long corridor opened between the ranking courtiers and officials who waited inside. A glowering Motecha hastened ahead, the rest of the magicians crowding at his heels. All stared. The panoply of personages gathered at the head of the hall formed an impressive sight.

At the base of the Imperial dais, the High Priests and Priestesses of the Twenty Gods of the Higher Heaven and Twenty Gods of the Lower Heaven stood in full regalia. Only at the coronation or the death of an Emperor would such a convocation be called for.

High, curved headdresses framed their faces, sparkling with lacquer-work, precious stones, and rare metal. Attendant upon each was a pair of acolytes, bearing the ceremonial badges of office each prelate was entitled to display. These, too, were gem-studded or adorned with metal bands and silk streamers. Only the Sisters of Sibi were plain; their black, fea-tureless appearance in ominous contrast to the panoply of plumage and finery. The community of temples was represented in its entirety. A delegation of one hundred and twenty from the holy orders of every significant divinity in the Empire made an impressive sight.

The Great Ones gave way to reluctant awe.

Hochopepa sidled closer to Fumita and Shimone in reaction to this emphatic demonstration of temple support for Mara's intrigues. While no single priest could rival any magician in raw power, the High Father Superiors of Turakamu and Jastur, as well as the Sisters of Sibi, com-manded respect, even from Great Ones. Spellcraft had preserved the audience hall intact, despite the Assembly's mightiest conjury. Hochopepa was not so irreverent toward the will of heaven that he discounted the force of divine favor.

Caution, he decided, was called for.

Incense swirled on the air. The polished marble floor sparkled with dust from cracked plaster and powdered glass from the shattered skylight. Such signs of violence could not divert the magicians from noting further details on their approach to the high dais: two empty reed cages festooned with ribbons of imperial white. The carpet beneath the Imperial thrones lay heaped with veils, lately removed from the bride in ritual order, according to the time-honored rites of a Tsurani state marriage cere-mony.

As the dismayed delegation of Great Ones reached the supplicants' rail beneath, an imperial herald struck the floor three times with a bronze-shod staff, crying out, "Justin, ninety-two times Emperor!"

The gold-armored royal honor guard knelt in homage as a boy in shining robes arose from the throne. The gathered nobles dropped to their knees. The boy did not look cowed; his shoulders were straight and his chin high despite the weight of his golden armor and the massive crown of state with its topaz stones and fretwork. At his side arose Jihilia,

Princess no longer, but Empress in her own right, the diamond-set circlet of office fitted over her bridal headdress. As the magicians drew to a halt, Justin held out his hand to his Lady. She arose and stood beside him.

Motecha went white. Around him some magicians bowed from the waist in the obeisance a Great One traditionally offered the Light of Heaven. Shimone, Fumita, and Hochopepa were among the first to give the Emperor and his bride due acknowledgement, while still other Black Robes deliberated in stupefication.

Motecha found his voice. "What mummery is this?"

The High Priest of Juran advanced in stiff displeasure. "We come to honor the new Light of Heaven, Great One." Pointedly he added, "As is every man's proper duty."

Sevean cried, "Upon what claim does this . . . boy presume to rule the Empire?" He stabbed a finger at Justin, but his eyes sought out the Lady Mara, who had moved to the base of the dais among the priests, in robes as fine as her son's.

She did not deign to answer, but allowed the High Priest of Juran speech in her place: "Justin is of the blood imperial, his adoption into Ichindar's family formalized when his mother was named Servant of the Empire." With that, the priest bowed in respect toward Mara. "He is the chosen husband of the Empress Jihilia—Ichindar's direct blood heir—and the marriage just completed was sanctioned by the Imperial Consort, Lady Tamara. All has been done according to the laws of man and the higher Law of Heaven. If somewhat hurried, the wedding abided strictly by custom."

One of the most fervent traditionalists, Lord Setark of the Ukudabi, made his way in the wake of the Great Ones through the double doors, which remained open. He and his army had been sequestered inside the city, prepared to aid Jiro should the Omechan fail in their attack upon the walls. He overheard the Priest's recitation of protocols with disfavor and raised a contentious shout. "The High Council never ratified this choice!"

Priests and magicians faced one another in uneasy confrontation. Redoubled tension charged the atmosphere at Lord Setark's outburst, and now the lines were drawn: acknowledge Justin as the new Light of Heaven, or resort to force of arms as the strongest nobles contended through bloodshed to seize power.

With the walls under assault by the Omechan, the catastrophe of the latter decision would be immediately felt. And the staid majority of magicians were still reluctant to become embroiled in politics. They were not of the Great Game of the Council; they were above it.

Akani stepped to the fore, the swirl of his black robe the only movement in the frozen tableau. He took stance beside Motecha and raised his
orator's voice. "Your call for ratification is a moot point, I fear. According to record, the High Council was disbanded by the ninety-first Light of
Heaven and, despite repeated petitions, was *never again reconvened.*"

The High Priest of Chochocan swept into a bow as polite as it was
firm. "The forms have been observed. The succession is established.
Justin of the Acoma is ninety-second Light of Heaven, and the gods
themselves are his judge. His ascension to the golden throne will stand,
and the temples will cast out for heresy anyone who dares disrupt his
rule." He looked squarely at Motecha as he said, "Even if such were a
Great One."

Motecha's glower deepened. "You dare!"

Then a voice that grated upon the ears like a cry of pain said, "Do not
oppose us, Great One."

The timid cringed, while the boldest turned toward the shrouded
figure of the most senior Sister of Sibi, whose speech echoed from the
depths of her inky cowl. No light would ever reveal her features—it was
held the Sisters embraced death within themselves when they joined their
Goddess' order. "Would you have us unleash our Mad Dancers in your
City of Magicians?"

Many nobles shuddered at the mention of those warriors who served
death, whose mere touch was fatal, as they leaped and gyrated until
exhaustion claimed their lives.

The High Priest of Jastur struck his metal breast plate with his gauntlet. "And will you face my warrior priests? We have little to fear in your
magic, Great One, when our god is invoked as our shield. Can you face
our blessed war hammers with impunity as we smash the walls of your
city?"

Motecha felt as any ordinary Tsurani would in his position; beliefs
ingrained since childhood were not absolutely dispelled by the sureties of
his authority. In an effort to conciliate, he said, "We do not argue the
legitimacy of Emperor Justin." Irritation edged his manner as, in concession to this point, he bent his aged back in the bow he withheld earlier.
He straightened up and leveled an accusatory finger at the Lady who stood
at the foot of the dais, and whose actions had escaped all restraint. "Lady
Mara of the Acoma," he intoned, "you have flouted tradition until your
actions are a stink in the nostrils of our ancestors. You have hidden behind
your office, misused public opinion, and caused confusion in the Assembly's ranks, all for the purpose of breaking our edict against waging war
upon the Anasati. Your armies attacked on the Plain of Nashika, and Lord

Jiro died at the hand of your husband. I name you guilty, and as Great One of the Empire, I am mandated to do that which the Assembly has voted best for the Nations! Our kind are outside the law! Your son shall be Emperor, may he live long and rule wisely, but you shall not be left at large to stand as his regent!''

''Who would you appoint in Mara's place?'' Shimone called out acerbically. ''The Omechan?''

The comment was ignored. Unopposed by his colleagues, Motecha raised his arm high. Green energies sparked around his fist, and he chanted in a harsh language known only by the magicians.

Hochopepa and Shimone flinched at his utterance, and Akani stepped quickly away. Fumita cried out, ''No!''

Motecha continued his incantation, secure in his right as a Black Robe.

Lady Mara turned pale, but did not flinch or flee. The lights of Motecha's gathering spell flickered across her face and caught sparks of reflection in her eyes. Calmly, she murmured something inaudible to the bystanders.

Motecha's lip curled as he called out in contempt between phrases, ''Prayer will not save you, Lady! Neither can these priests, whatever powers they may have wielded in warding this hall against our entry! The gods themselves might save you, but they are the only power capable.''

''The priests had no part in the warding!'' Mara retorted clearly. ''You may hurl your spells at me, Motecha, but hear warning. Your magic shall harm none, least of all me.''

Motecha's features pinched with fury. The Lady was not even afraid! Her end would be painful, he vowed, as he drew breath to snap off the phrase that would release his gathered death spell. The retribution Lady Mara had more than earned would sear her to a husk where she stood.

Mara closed her eyes, shaken at last by the immediacy of her peril.

''No!'' intoned a voice with a resonance that held nothing human. Its tone shot chills through every person present. On either side of Mara, unseen where they crouched behind the enveloping vestments of the priests, two figures reared erect. Their bodies were patterned in intricate colors, and with a clap of disturbed air, they extended twelve feet of iridescent wings aloft. The majesty of the cho-ja mages made the most costly imperial raiment seem tawdry by comparison.

''The Lady Mara shall not be harmed!'' the creatures cried in unison. ''She is under the protection of the mages of Chakaha!''

Fumita cried out, speech wrenched from him in stupefied recognition. ''The Forbidden! Daughter, what have you done?''

Motecha stood frozen; the powers he had summoned crackled and dissipated into air, the spell incomplete as his concentration was disrupted by shock. Other magicians blanched as the significance of the creatures before them registered.

"Lady Mara is blameless," contradicted the cho-ja mages, their oratory locked in a fluting two-part harmony. "It was by your own deed, magicians, that the ancient pact was breached, for until you destroyed a hive our Queens within the Empire stayed bound to the requirements of the treaty. Never once were magical arts employed, or outside aid given to Mara, until you broke the covenant! The blame lies with you! It was cho-ja arts that protected this hall. In those lands outside Imperial borders, human, our arts have grown and flourished. In protection and preservation, you are not our equal. If we choose, the magicians of Chakaha can ward Lady Mara from your death spells for the rest of her life."

As one, the Black Robes hesitated. Never in history had any human not gifted with magic dared to defy the Assembly, and never with a plot so devious: to lure the magicians themselves into destroying the very treaty their predecessors had forged.

No Black Robe could doubt the abilities of the cho-ja mages; their kind could not lie. By their word, they held means to thwart the most destructive of spells the Great Ones could conjure. Each candidate for the Assembly had studied the old texts; not one who achieved his master's robe failed to understand the significance of the markings on a cho-ja magician. The complexity of their patterns grew with the ascendance of their mastery; the pair who allied with Lady Mara were old in their art, and powerful beyond imagining.

Still, some Black Robes remained unmollified. The High Priest of Chochocan made a sign of protection as Sevean shouted to the cho-ja, "You are foreigners! How *dare* you raise your arts to protect the condemned!"

"Wait." All eyes turned as Mara stepped forward, boldly claiming the authority in the new order she had dreamed to achieve. Her bullion-edged sash of office proclaimed her Imperial Regent, even if the appointment had not been official. "I have a proposal to make."

Those gathered in the hall stilled expectantly, and all eyes regarded the Lady who was Servant of the Empire as they waited to hear what she said.

Mara buried her doubt deep within her heart. Despite their inference to the contrary, the Chakaha mages had spent their powers in their warding of the great hall. After long rest, they might be able to defend her as they

had boldly led the Black Robes to presume. As their magic had improved
with the centuries, so had their understanding of their enemies. The cho-
ja had cleverly manipulated the truth, implying what Mara had every
reason to believe: that should the hive-home at Chakaha send reinforcements to Kentosani, she stood beyond harm from the Assembly for the
rest of her life.

But now appearances were all she had to keep her opposition off
balance. She dared not provoke any test of the cho-ja mages' abilities.
Between herself and a horrible death she had no weapons beyond words,
bluff, and the politics of the Great Game. And the Black Robes were no
fools. Mara took an inward grip on her poise and answered Sevean directly. "The cho-ja mages dare nothing, but act in the cause of justice!
This embassy from Chakaha has come to make amends for the oppression
of all our ancestors."

Motecha shook his fist. "This is Forbidden! Any Empire cho-ja who
supports uprising is forsworn! The Great Treaty Between Races has stood
for thousands of years."

"Thousands of years of cruelty!" Mara flung back. "Your precious
Forbidden! Your hideous crime against a civilization that did nothing more
than resist the rapacious conquest of their lands! I have journeyed to
Thuril. I have seen how the Chakaha cho-ja live. Which of you can say the
same, magician?" The lack of the honorific "Great One" was lost on few
in the room. Many Lords gasped in admiration. The Imperial Whites
stood sword-straight in their ranks, and Jehilia and Justin clasped hands.

The priests maintained solemn formality as Mara continued, "I have
explored the beauty of cities raised by magic, and the peace of this great
culture. I have seen what our vaunted Empire has stolen from the cho-ja,
and I am determined to give it back."

Hochopepa cleared his throat. "Lady Mara, you had allies within our
ranks, until now. But this . . . obscenity"—he gestured to the cho-ja
magicians—"will unite us to a man."

"You aren't united already?" Mara lashed back in sarcasm. "Did the
destruction of my litter and my closest retainers not indicate your Assembly's decision on my execution?"

Here a few of the Great Ones shifted their weight and looked abashed,
for Tapek's impulsive act had not been regarded with favor. But the
Assembly itself was Tsurani; that one of their number had shamed his
office must never be admitted in public.

Mara's eyes narrowed. "As for obscenity, that is a false charge! Why?"
Her wave encompassed the winged beings who flanked her. "Because

these gentle creatures, who harbor no ill will to any of you, despite your persecution of their race, practice arts greater than your own?'' She quieted her voice to a whisper of menacing accusation. ''Hochopepa, how can that be an obscenity to a body of men who kill children with power *because they are female?''*

At this disclosure, several Black Robes expelled breaths in frantic dismay. Motecha whirled and gestured to a nearby soldier. ''Kill her!'' he commanded. ''I order you.''

The Force Commander of the Imperial Whites stepped before Mara, his sword half-drawn. ''I will cut down the first man, soldier or magician, who threatens the Good Servant, even should I die in the attempt. My life and honor are pledged to protect the Imperial Family. Before the gods, I will not foreswear my first duty.''

Motecha did not shout, but power radiated in waves from his person as he demanded, ''Stand away!''

The Imperial Force Commander met the magician's authoritative gaze. ''I will not, Great One.'' He snapped a hand signal.

Other white-clad warriors closed on the dais. Their armor might be ceremonial, but the blades they carried were sharp, flashing in the gloom as they drew weapons in a single motion. Akani rushed out and stayed the single warrior who had moved to obey Motecha out of fear. ''No, wait.''

Motecha advanced on his colleague as if he faced an adversary sworn to murder. ''You deny the law!''

''I'd still rather not turn the Imperial Palace into a charnel house, if you don't mind.'' The young magician gave Mara a wry shrug. ''Good Servant, we have reached a difficult impasse.'' He indicated the Great Ones at his back, many of them eager to call down immediate attack on her person, a hundred Imperial Whites, and two cho-ja masters who might or might not have skills enough to defend. ''If we don't find a quick solution, many will die.'' He smiled in sour humor. ''I don't know if we must take your cho-ja friends at their word, or test to see whose magical prowess is the greater.'' He glanced at Motecha. ''But given the difficulty we had in entering this very chamber, I have an inkling of the disaster that might result.'' Again he considered Mara, not entirely without warmth. ''I have no doubt you wish to live and guide your son's steps to maturity.'' He sighed and admitted, ''There are those of the Assembly who would spend their lives to eradicate you for this rebellion immediately. Others would prefer peace, and use the opportunity to study what our cho-ja counterparts could offer to expand our knowledge of the great arts. I exhort every man and mage to step back and refrain from profitless destruction until we have exhausted *all* other options.''

The cho-ja magician at Mara's right hand furled its wings; its companion followed suit and said, "In this, perhaps we can assist." It added a cantrip in its native language and waved short forearms. An unseen disturbance seemed to pass across the chamber, and the tension between the combatants began to leach away.

Motecha fought to preserve his anger. "Creature!" he cried. "Cease your . . ." But speech died in his throat. Against his will, his contorted face relaxed.

The cho-ja magician chided gently, "Magician, your fury clouds reason. Let peace ever be my gift to you."

Akani studied the magnificently marked carapace, veiled now in a translucence of folded wings. His shoulders relaxed and settled. "Although I revere our tradition," he admitted, his regard encompassing his fellows, "I also recognize what I sense in these emissaries from Chakaha. Look well and deeply. They bring us something . . . rare." To Motecha he added, "Their presence is not an offense. We are fools to cling mindlessly to tradition and not explore the wonders we are offered."

Hochopepa pushed to the fore. "Yes, I feel this, too." He sighed. "I know both . . . wonderment and"—the admission came with difficulty—"Shame."

Mara broke the stillness. "Can any Great One deny that nothing of hate or anger motivates this act of kindness?"

Hochopepa allowed the wave of calmness to envelope him wholly. He smiled. "No." Then his pragmatism reasserted as he said, "First, your son's ascension to the Throne of Heaven may be proper according to law. But your transgressions are . . . unprecedented, Good Servant. We may never be moved to forgiveness, Lady Mara."

Muted muttering resumed among some of the Lords in the hall, but no open opposition arose. Motecha added, "The Assembly's course is clear. We cannot accept as Justin's regent a ruler who has defied us. The precedent is dangerous. We are outside the law for valid reasons." As he calmly studied Mara, all anger gentled from him by the workings of cho-ja magic, Motecha's clear reason stirred agreement among his colleagues. "I have accepted Justin's coronation, but that does not free Lady Mara of responsibility for her disobedience. When she opposed us, she repudiated the law!" Across the space before the Imperial dais, he locked gazes with Mara. "You dishonor your rank and heritage if you shelter behind alien magic, Lady of the Acoma! You must reject cho-ja protection and voluntarily embrace your due punishment. Justice must be served."

"Indeed," said Mara softly. Her shoulders stayed straight only out of habit. She had no more ploys left; she alone was near enough to perceive the fine tremors of exhaustion that played through the cho-ja mages. The calming spell had been called up from reserves that were already exhausted. They had no hidden miracles in them to offer. Too quietly for anyone but those closest to her and the cho-ja to overhear, she said, "You did your best. We have won a review of the terms of the great treaty, no matter what becomes of me."

The mage to her left stroked her wrist with a gentle forelimb. "My Lady," it intoned in her mind, "among our kind your memory will never die."

Mara forced her chin up. To all who were gathered in the audience hall she said, "I once thought to dedicate my life to service in the temple of Lashima. But fate decreed that I assume the mantle of the Acoma. I will be heard. The gods have given into my care more than my house and my family." Her voice strengthened, carrying into the farthest corners of the domed chamber. "I have undertaken to change traditions that have shackled us into stagnation. I have seen cruelty, injustice, and the profligate waste of worthy lives. For this have I set myself up as midwife to a rebirth, without which we as a people will die." No one interrupted while she drew breath. "You all know of the enemies I have defeated. They have varied in their cunning from base to brilliant."

She looked from face to face, seeing her appeal touch some of those before her. Motecha and many others simply listened. "Our Ruling Lords craved power for honor, for prestige, for the enjoyment of themselves, with no thought for the suffering of subjects under their sway. Our noble families and clans play the Game of the Council for stakes that spill blood to no purpose! To kill me in the name of justice, before my son has achieved manhood and can rule without guidance from a regent, would be to condemn the Nations to stagnation and ruin again. Our Empire will fall, for our flaws. That is the price of my death, Great Ones. That is the epitaph your justice will write on our future. That is the cost our people must pay for your *privilege* of acting outside the law!"

Silence claimed the audience hall while all present pondered the import of Mara's words. She herself stood rigid, while behind her the priests shuffled in their ranks and whispered among themselves. Pride forbade Mara to look around. She saw the concern on Hokanu's face. Mara dared not acknowledge his worry for her, not with so much as a glance. To meet her husband's eyes would be to lose her grip and break down weeping in public.

She stood statue-straight, as a Servant of the Empire and a daughter of the Acoma, and prepared to meet her fate.

The magicians were once more unsettled, the effects of cho-ja magic wearing thin.

"She's gone too far now," Shimone murmured. "No argument can save her, for our Assembly is answerable to no law. This *must* not be misconstrued as a privilege. It is our right!"

Fumita averted his face; Hochopepa looked troubled.

Sevean said, "You will die, Lady Mara. Cast off the alliance of your emissaries from Chakaha, or they will perish with you. I say they cannot defend you. When we destroy you, the priests will return to their rightful place in the temple and leave politics to others." Indicating the High Priest of Jastur and the Sisters of Sibi, he said, "Or let them challenge us if they feel they must. We are still supreme in our arts! Our powers broke the wards over this hall! Perhaps these cho-ja have learned to lie in the lands outside the Empire! I say you attempt to deceive, Lady Mara, and that you have no means of self-defense."

Motecha looked startled for a moment. Then his expression hardened. He studied the Chakaha magicians and saw they made no gestures to protect Lady Mara. His eyes narrowed as he felt Sevean's power manifest. Again Motecha raised his hands, and again his magic coalesced into a fiery lash of green light. He muttered a harsh incantation, fierce in his concentration.

This time nothing would stop him and his colleagues from striking down the Good Servant.

The priests seemed distressed. Many of them stepped back, as if trying to set distance between themselves and the Servant of the Empire. Hokanu looked anguished, until his First Adviser, Dogondi, stepped between, shielding his view of Mara's plight. "Don't look, my Lord," he murmured.

Enthroned on the Imperial dais, Jehilia gripped Justin's hand, while the boy stared at his mother with wide, hard eyes that had all the fear scoured out of them. "The Great Ones will pay," the young Emperor vowed in a monotone. "If they kill her, I will see them destroyed!"

Jehilia tugged his hand in anxiety. "Hush! They will hear you."

But the Great Ones had no attention to spare for the children who sat the thrones of power. As a body, they banded together, conjoining their powers with Motecha's spell. Only three remained apart, as the incantation for the death spell neared its climax: Hochopepa, looking miserable; Shimone, his stern face twisted with regret; and Fumita, who could not entirely release his ties to family and contribute in killing a woman who would have been his daughter-in-law.

Mara stood straight on the polished stone floor below the Imperial dais.

At her sides, the Chakaha mages crouched now with furled wings. Behind her stood the High Priest of Turakamu, leathery and old, but erect under his trappings of office. He laid a thin hand on her shoulder, as if in comfort to one who would shortly be greeting his divine master, just as Motecha flung out his arms.

Green light exploded in a blinding coruscation, and a report slammed the air that threw many notables at the forefront headlong onto the floor. Mara and the priest were lost in the raging heart of the mage fire that caused solid stone to glow red and run molten. A column collapsed like an overheated candle, and the stone paving puckered and puddled into lava.

"Behold the price of defying those who are outside the law!" Motecha cried. He clapped his hands together, and the spell died out with a snap.

The light vanished. Through stinging, tearful eyes, the onlookers beheld a circle of charred flooring, and waves of heat from stress-heated rock that caused the air to buckle and shimmer. Inside that expanse where the very forces of nature had been skewed into violence, the Lady stood untouched. Her robes were unmarked; not a hair on her head was out of place. The pair of Chakaha mages were both bowing in homage to the priest, who now raised his quavery voice in a paean of thanks to his god.

"What is this!" shouted Motecha. He was shaken, white to the roots of his hair. "She lives! How is this?"

The priest of Turakamu ceased his hymn. He stepped forward, patiently smiling. "Great One, you may claim to be outside the laws of mortal men. But you are yet answerable to the higher order of heaven."

"How?" Mara began weakly, and the cho-ja mages steadied her as she swayed.

The priest of the Red God turned his back on the baffled magicians and addressed her. "Lady Mara, you once visited the high father superior of Turakamu's temple in Sulan-Qu. He showed you his powers and explained that my god does not act out of turn. Your policies revitalize our people. You have never spurned the temples in your manipulation of politics—you have always been a respectful daughter of our faith, unlike those who mouth loyalty for tradition and spurn spiritual righteousness."

"But how?" Mara began, a little stronger, as her stunned mind accepted the impossibility that she still lived.

The High Priest grew solemn. "The temples support you. Our pledge was not merely political. It was agreed among us that my god, who holds all men's deaths, should determine whether this moment was your time. Had you lacked heaven's support, you would have died." He spun with a rattle of corcara skulls to face the ranks of the Great Ones. ''Which she did not!''

The chilling voice of the senior Sister of Sibi said, ''And should our Dark Lady's little brother not summon Lady Mara, our goddess refuses to send her to the Red Halls.'' The featureless opening of her robe moved, as she gave a rapacious survey of every soul in the room. ''There are others here my divine mistress would gladly dispatch.''

Even some of the magicians made signs of protection from evil. Unfazed, even amused by their posturing, the Priest of Turakamu pronounced, ''My God has awarded the Good Servant his divine protection. Her life is sacrosanct, by the will of heaven, and let any man, magician or otherwise, act against her at his peril!''

Motecha of the Assembly stiffly accepted his defeat, but his expression remained implacable. ''The Lady's life is not ours to take; this has been unequivocally proven. Yet her right to act as regent is contestable still. Lord Jiro of the Anasati also held forth a claim to the golden throne. He acted, as Mara has, to seize power whatever the cost. Are not the Lady's ambitions the same, if she rules as Justin's regent until his twenty-fifth year? Why not have an Omechan take the post, or a Xacatecas, or one of a lesser house with no claim upon the Warlordship, perhaps the Netoha or Corandaro?''

Recovered now from her close brush with death, and stern in her resolve, Mara cut off the chance for traditionalist supporters to sieze the opening. ''No. I give you a choice.''

Stillness rippled through the crowd of priests and courtiers, from the high dais and its new-made Light of Heaven, across the band of magicians packed in the broad central floor, to the double doors by the entry, still presided over by the requisite pair of heralds, and the stiff rows of Imperial Whites. All awaited upon Lady Mara to hear her unprecedented intent. Mara ascended one stair of the dais. Over the sea of watching faces, she raised her voice. ''I could stay within these halls, acting as my son's regent. His rule would be held stable by an alliance of Lords who understand, as all eventually must, that change must come to the Empire. The cho-ja would mediate willingly as allies to enforce a new order that will end the wrong done them centuries ago. Their warriors will stop internal bickering between noble houses and avert this civil war. For Justin's first action as ninety-second Emperor will be to free them from all constraints imposed by humans.''

Mara paused for a steadying breath. But before insurrection could stir the Ruling Lords to shout her down, she hurried on.

"I offer peaceful change! As senior adviser to the late Emperor, I know the workings of imperial government. As Servant of the Empire, I submit that I alone hold the power and the prestige among both Ruling Lords and the populace to quell the riots. The alternatives are plain. The Omechan have already taken the field against me, laying siege to Kentosani. They will soon be joined by allies of the late Lord Jiro, and other Lords who support the traditionalist party. If this trend is not stopped, we shall have civil war unmatched, to the very ruination of the Nations we profess to serve."

Hochopepa coughed dryly. "That justification has been offered in the past, my Lady. The bloodshed in most instances was none the less for the argument."

Mara gestured in repressed anger, that she should, even by implication, be apportioned the motives of her power-hungry past enemies. "Bloodshed, you say, magician? For what end? There is no Warlord's mantle left to be won. The High Council is abolished!"

Many Lords stirred in unsettled protest at this, but again Mara overrode them. "Our taste for murderous political infighting must be stopped. The Game of the Council shall no longer be a justification for war and assassination. Our concept of honor must be revitalized, and our traditions that endorse cruelty rejected. We shall be a nation of laws! Whatever the crime, from lowest to highest, *every* man and woman must be equally answerable to imperial justice. From this new code of decency not even our Light of Heaven's actions shall be exempt."

Motecha waved a fist. "But we are outside the law!"

Mara descended the stair and advanced until only the rail that separated the high dais from the Emperor's petitioners stood between her and the packed ranks of Great Ones. Her gaze met Motecha's squarely, then swept over his black-robed fellows who crowded on either side. "Every man and woman," she insisted firmly. "No Ruling Lord who does murder shall be applauded, even should the traditional forms be observed. No beggar, no slave, and no child of noble birth shall fail to be lawfully punished for criminal acts; you of the Assembly most of all. Your kind will no longer be free to keep hideous secrets: to kill baby girls and women who manifest the power."

Muttering arose as this time her accusation was loud enough to be fully public, and not only Black Robes were inflamed to a shifting of feet. "Yes!" Mara cried over the rising tumult that swept through the Lords and courtiers, "I speak the truth! The Assembly has done murder for years beyond counting, and for reasons our gods would never sanction."

The priest of Lashima brandished his staff of office, streamers and corcara shell tokens waving to garner attention. "Listen to the Lady. She does not lie to make her case. Last season a young woman who was to be tested as an acolyte was taken from the very temple courtyard. She has not been seen by our priests or her family since the day the Great One came for her."

Hokanu looked faintly sick; among the Black Robes, Fumita stared at the floor. He did not glance toward his son. More than a few noblemen of the court showed shock, that daughters called to serve by the Great Ones were not still alive in the City of Magicians. Angry eyes swung toward the Black Robes, while Mara continued her oratory quickly to redirect a mounting wave of ill feeling. "As a community, you should continue to govern yourselves—as must the Lords of each family. . . ." Relief visited the nobles at this assurance of their ruler's prerogatives. "Within the law!" Mara snapped. "But the Assembly will no longer be proprietors of privilege. The study of arcane arts will not be theirs to dictate. Any who practice magic must have license to freely pursue their art. Those lesser magicians, and women who develop arcane talent, may study under the Assembly or not, *as it pleases them!* Those that prefer to seek knowledge elsewhere may do so."

The Chakaha mage nearest to the Great Ones raised a forelimb. In gentle tones it offered, "We will be glad to teach any who seek wise use of their gifts."

Though the offer may have mollified some magicians, others looked vexed as Mara added, "I have walked in the shoes of a captive, in Thuril, and I have shared Imperial decisions, under Ichindar. I alone in this company can assert the validity of the claim that every man, woman, and child deserves protection. Only when this"—she frowned as she sought the term that her beloved Kevin had mentioned with such passion— "Great Freedom is bestowed upon us all will any one of us be safe. The Game of the Council has become both perilous and bloody beyond endurance, and I would see that end. True honor does not condone murder. True power must equally shield the weak that we, for centuries, have thoughtlessly trampled under our feet."

Motecha pressed forward, leaning across the railing in ferocious contention. Mara looked back at him in contempt. She addressed him alone, but her words carried to the farthest reaches of the crowded hall. "You Black Robes have no right to destroy that which is not pleasing to you. The gods did not gift you with magical talent so that you could take lives at whim."

The High Priest of Juran banged his white-striped staff on the floor. "The Good Servant speaks truth."

Another Black Robe, lately arrived with the last contingent from the City of Magicians pushed through the ranks of his brethren to join Motecha. Tapek shed the inhibition instilled by his recent disgrace. His hair was pushed back, and his cheeks inflamed in passionate repudiation. "You seek to strip us of ancient rights!"

"Power is used at the discretion of those who hold it," the Lady returned, unafraid, although she stood but an arm's reach away. "You should understand that above all others, magician. Your colleagues have been poor stewards, setting themselves up in arrogance, usurping the judgment that is the rightful province of heaven. With your attempt at my execution stayed—no, canceled!—by the power of the gods, today it is *I* who have the power."

The other magicians exchanged unsettled glances, but none had words to add. Their magic had been negated, rendered powerless over this woman who had handed them a failure they were ill prepared to reverse. They had no precept to fall back on; no point around which to rally.

Only Hochopepa's gaze remained upon Mara. "You mentioned a choice?"

Had the circumstances been of less import, and the chamber of audience's occupants been one whit less tense, Mara might have smiled at the stout magician's sharpness. "Yes, Great One, a choice," she announced loudly. "For centuries your Assembly has enjoyed authority without responsibilities. You Black Robes have done as you pleased for 'the Good of the Empire,' no matter how whimsical, perverse, or destructive the act may have been." Unmentioned behind her words were the memory of two young children, slaughtered by their Minwanabi father as a consequence of the disgrace forced upon him by Great Ones. Although Tasaio had been an enemy, Mara yet found the murder of his heirs abhorrent, a tragedy the more unforgivable because it might have been prevented by the very Assembly that had condemned the father. Sharply, she concluded, "Since your community of magicians has shown little inclination to self-discipline, now comes an accounting. You may do as I have bid, and be about your own affairs in your city of fearful, inward-looking men —the gods have mercy upon you—or you may take the only other course that will avert unbridled war."

Hochopepa's round face furrowed in distaste, and he tapped one foot uncomfortably. "I suspect what that may be."

"Do you?" Mara withdrew an ornate dagger from her robe sash and reversed it, pointing it toward her breast. "The gods may have declared it is not my time to die. But I can still exercise my free will as Lady of the Acoma. If you choose, I can take my own life, now, in expiation for breaking your stated edict. If I do this, Justin shall abdicate, and return home as Lord of the Acoma. Jehilia, his wife, will reign, and her husband will be consort only, taking vows never to raise his hand against you, or any other Black Robe." Mara's eyes narrowed as she delivered her final line, and the blade in her hand never quivered. "But then *you* must rule."

Hochopepa actually grinned. Shimone and Akani nodded, while Tapek appeared only befuddled. "Lady, what are you saying?" the redheaded magician asked.

"You only have the power to destroy, to wage war, or oppose," declared Mara. "My allies shall not resist. Before sundown, if you so command, I can honorably end my life by the blade." Her glance swept the hall, pausing only briefly to review the assorted nobles who strained to catch every word, who even yet hoped of catching some mis-step by which they could advance themselves over their neighbors. Her blade might be plunged home, and the Game of the Council resume as if she had never lived; as if the dreams of a murdered Emperor and a barbarian slave had never started to precipitate change. The moment was at hand to decide the future. The priests waited upon their gods, and prayed for fate to favor them. Focusing on Motecha and Tapek in particular, Mara delivered her summary. "Oh, you may find another willing to play Emperor or Warlord for a time. The Omechan would fall over themselves for the honor, never doubt—until an ambitious neighbor or rival decides it is time to upset the succession.

"But consider this: the illusion is ended. Men now know that the Assembly can be opposed. The temples will not be content to be relegated to a secondary role. Be assured that the last act of the Emperor Justin will be to emancipate the cho-ja, so that they may again use magic to raise their glass cities in the sun. Lacking willing soldiers, how will you magicians keep order? How will you stop the bickering and power plays between Lords to whom tradition has allocated the trappings of honor? The Game of the Council is a dead end, but our Ruling Lords for the most part are too contentious or too greedy to create a new order. Are you magicians prepared to put on armor and pick up a sword? Tapek? Sevean? Motecha?"

The confounded expressions upon the faces of the three so named were comical. Never had they considered the prospect of dirtying their hands in battle! And yet, with their weaknesses exposed, they recognized that magic by itself would no longer command awe. Others as bold as Mara would start uprisings, and the Assembly would be pressured by the politics and circumstance to take sides. They would have no choice but absent themselves from scholarly study to manage the mechanics of governance.

To a body accustomed to acting at the whim of the individual, the prospect was distastefully daunting.

Motecha looked distressed. Sevean edged unobtrusively behind Shimone, while Tapek masked dismay behind bluster. "We are not a council of Lords, given to haggling over trivia! Our calling is loftier than mandating the punishment of warring Houses!"

Hochopepa actually laughed.

Mara gave a demure bow. Still the blade remained in her hand, unswervingly pointed toward her breast. Her eyes were stony. "Those are your choices, Great One. Either administrate this Empire or cease interfering with those of us who must."

In the face of his colleagues' dumbfounded stillness, Hochopepa waved a weary arm. "It is over."

Tapek yet looked ready to argue, but Akani intervened. "I agree. The Assembly as a body will no more wish to govern the Empire than we have in the past. Gods above, our debates have extended for days in deciding a single issue!" Unable to restrain a loaded glance at Shimone and Hochopepa, he sighed, then bowed gravely to the Servant of the Empire. "Lady, you shall not take your life before sundown. The public would create too much outcry, and my colleagues are likely to be blamed. Our choice is clear: chaos or a new order. You were first to see that not all of us hold enough command of our nature to kill without hesitation. Most magicians, in fact, would be hard set to harm an insect. No, our might over the Empire has arisen from blind obedience over the years. Without that, we are . . . powerless."

"Powerless!" Tapek fumed. "Not I, Akani!"

Fumita restrained the red-haired magician with a crushing grip. "Tapek, one foolish act shamed you nearly beyond forgiveness. Listen to reason for a change! Mara does not act for herself. She never has, could you but see that. You will never win over the Assembly to endorse civil war and chaos. And bloodshed unequaled is what we would have if you and your cadre of young-bloods do not accept the inevitable. I strongly suggest that you start repairing your reputation by appearing on the walls and commanding the attacking armies to cease fire and lay down their weapons."

"I will go with Tapek," Shimone announced. He turned a stern, even pitiless look at his younger colleague, then grasped his teleportation device and disappeared. Few magicians in the Empire dared to cross Shimone when he was aroused. Still, Fumita showed no sign of releasing his hold until Tapek lowered his eyes and conceded the point. The young magician was then freed to vanish and rejoin Shimone.

Hochopepa managed an affable shrug before the panoply of religious orders and ranking Lords backing Mara. "I have no wish to govern, nor do I intend to attempt to murder wholesale the most powerful priests in the Empire." This statement was pointedly directed toward Motecha, who sought the support of other colleagues to back him, but found his cadre dissolving. In Shimone's absence, Sevean had sidled behind Fumita. Many more magicians were nodding agreement to the fat magician's capitulation. Gently Hochopepa reached out and removed the dagger from Mara's fingers.

Then he announced loudly, "A remarkable man, the magician Milamber, from Midkemia, once exhorted that our Empire had a stagnant culture brought into decline by our rigid adherence to our traditions. I think he was right"—the stout magician awarded Mara and the magnificence of the Chakaha mages a smile of admiration—"for why else would the gods have preserved this remarkable woman?"

To Mara he added, "Lady, if the Light of Heaven may allow, we will withdraw and meet formally, but you may rest assured what our official position will be." Then he was first among the Black Robes to step forward and repeat his bow of homage to emphasize that the boy on the dais was beyond dispute the ninety-second Light of Heaven.

The magicians as a group followed suit, most of them humiliated enough to do so quietly, though a few in the back were heard to grumble. Fumita gave these dissenters a stern glare, and the Chakaha mages fixed each with an agate black eye that reminded of the singular ability of the cho-ja hive mind to remember.

Mara felt a giddy relief sweep through her at the unequivocal capitulation of the most fearful enemies she had ever dared to provoke. As the Black Robes acknowledged her son's sovereignty, she went weak at the knees. Hokanu's heartwarming perception anticipated her need, and gratefully, Mara accepted his support as he stepped to her side and put his arm around her waist.

As the Great Ones filed out, and the central floor of the great hall slowly cleared, Lord Keda, Imperial Chancellor, swept forward in his glittering robes of office. Over his earlier bout of nerves, the old man had lost none of his command or his gifts as an orator as he announced, "As chancellor, let me be first among your nobles to swear my loyalty to Emperor Justin." He knelt and uttered the time-honored oaths, and tension seemed to flow from the crowd. Suddenly what might have been an armed camp was transformed into a hall of men kneeling, repeating the words of devotion to a boy who had been conceived as the get of a slave, and who had risen from being heir of the Acoma to become the ninety-second Emperor of Tsuranuanni.

When the newly sworn members of his court arose, Justin squirmed on the dais, distress obvious on his face. To his mother, and the father who had adopted him for his own, he whispered loudly, "You instructed me on everything else, but what do I do now?"

Jehilia looked mortified by his lapse.

Not a few of the priests stifled chuckles behind their ceremonial masks, while Hokanu pulled off his battle helm and laughed outright. "Tell your people, 'Let the celebration commence!' "

Justin jumped up from his throne, all but dislodging the heavy golden helm with its crown piece that denoted imperial majesty. Dragging his lady wife by the hand, he looked far from decorous—more like a boy who had mischief in mind the moment his elders were not looking. "Let the celebration commence!" he shouted.

A cheer rocked the great hall of audience, more deafening for the fact that the siege engines of the Omechan had fallen silent. No more rocks crashed down upon the Imperial Precinct. And when the voices and the clamor had quelled to a more tolerable level, the great gongs in the temples of the Twenty Gods pealed out, calling the populace into the streets to accept largesse in the name of Justin, ninety-two times Emperor of Tsuranuanni.

In the midst of the commotion as the great hall emptied, and the Imperial Heralds cried the news throughout the city, the small, mouselike figure of Jican descended upon the palace staff. The great bulk of the imperial hadonra caused him only the briefest pause. After an agitated argument, the immense official backed down, huffed words to the effect that royal propriety was going to be irretrievably ruined, and stalked off to his quarters. Jican turned his tongue-lashing on the rest of the palace staff, and within minutes the imperial household was turned upon its collective ear. They would produce a festival for their new Emperor, Jican commanded, whether it killed them all to the least of the pot boys and drudges. His determination proved infectious. Within hours the nobles in residence had exchanged battle armor for silk robes, and entertainers were converging upon the city officials, vying for the honor of providing music and poetry. Throughout the city, celebrations began as word spread that the new Light of Heaven had been chosen, and more, that Lady Mara, Servant of the Empire, had taken the stewardship of the Nations.

33. *Imperial Council*

Lamps burned.

Their light transformed the night into kaleidoscopic patterns of colors as silk-robed revelers danced in the streets and masked players staged joyous entertainment. The sounds of lacquered bells and laughter replaced the thudding impacts caused by siege engines. Within an ornate suite in the royal apartments of the Imperial Palace, Mara sat before a painted screen. The noise of the happy populace gave her deep satisfaction, but the half-smile of contentment that curved her lips was all for the small girl child who lay sound asleep in her lap. The Lady's expression of tranquillity was so profound that Hokanu, arriving at the door, hesitated to disturb her.

But she had always been sensitive to his presence. Though he made no sound, Mara looked up. Her expression flowered into a smile of welcome. "Hokanu." Her greeting expressed all, from tenderness to deep love to the ache of separation that had lasted through the late troubled times.

The Lord of the Shinzawai crossed the floor, his step a whisper on tile. He wore silk, not armor, and had replaced his studded battle sandals for leather-soled ones with cloth ties. He reached his wife's side, knelt, and offered his hand to Kasuma. The little one grasped his finger, comforted by his presence although she did not fully waken.

"She has grown so much!" Mara murmured. When she had left for Thuril, Kasuma had been but an infant. Now she was a toddler, already trying her first words. The Lady's finger traced the line of her daughter's brows. "She's going to have your scowl," Mara mused to her husband. "Probably that means she's inherited your stubbornness, also."

Hokanu chuckled. "She's going to need it."

Mara joined him in laughter. "Surely. She had better develop a sharp tongue, too, if she's to keep your cousin Devacai in line. Perhaps we should send her to Isashani of the Xacatecas for her finishing?"

Hokanu was unusually silent at this. Mara missed his moment of stillness, touched as she was by memories of Nacoya, the irascible nurse who had raised and schooled her to the skills of a Ruling Lady. Then reminiscence was abandoned as Hokanu's hands lifted Kasuma and settled her gently on her sleeping mat. He reached next for his wife, with the intent to perform the same office.

"Your battles have not depleted you, I see," Mara said as her husband settled beside her, and she began to work free the ties on his robe. "Thank the gods for that, for I have missed you sorely. I don't think I could have endured another night of lying awake wondering whether you were alive or dead, or whether our children were going to fall as the victims of politics. . . ." She paused, letting Hokanu's hands smooth away the unpleasant memory of dread. Somewhere in the city, a temple gong sang notes of felicity, and a laughing couplet of dancers ran on light feet past the window. Mara settled in the crook of her husband's arm. "You came from the imperial suite, I presume. How is our Justin handling himself?"

Hokanu muffled a snort of laughter in the warmth of his wife's hair. "The little barbarian," he said, when he could speak. "The boy came to me with the shakes, his face as red as his hair, asking if he was expected to perform his husbandly office with Jehilia. Tonight."

Mara grinned. "I should have thought he'd ask that before anybody else would have found time to inform him. He's stared down the shifts of the maids since he was big enough to climb up on the furniture. What did you say?"

"When I could keep a straight face, you mean?" Hokanu said. "I told him that he'd have to wait for the privilege until his manhood ceremony at twenty-five."

Playfully shoving her husband, Mara said, "You didn't!"

Hokanu grinned. "I don't think I've ever seen regret and relief so evenly mixed. Then I explained that Jehilia, being two years older than he, might decide she wished to visit his bedchamber when she came of age, and that as he would be only twenty-three, it would be her decision to make."

Now Mara exploded into merriment. "Oh, that's perfect! The poor boy thinks he's to remain a chaste husband for another eleven years!"

Hokanu shrugged. "He'll figure it out soon enough."

"Don't let Jehilia discover what you've told Justin. She'll make his life miserable."

Hokanu planted a kiss on Mara's forehead. "At least he'll think twice before he tries pushing the girl into a fishpond again."

"She's Empress." Mara chuckled. "She'd have every legal right to pull him in after her."

"And I expect one day, in a year or two, the rough play will turn friendly and Justin's concerns about husbandly duty will vanish." Moving so that his face was above hers, Hokanu said, "And speaking of husbandly duties . . ." Conversation died as Hokanu's lips found hers, and their embrace slowly blossomed into passion.

Much later, the lanterns still shone. The revelers in the streets were fewer, but no less joyously raucous. The Lady of the Acoma and the Lord of the Shinzawai lay twined close, replete with their lovemaking. Neither felt inclined toward sleep. Both had much on their mind, and this was the first peaceful moment they had gained in which to speak of personal issues.

Hokanu was first to broach the subject. "Lady, with Justin now responsible for continuing the imperial line, you are again left without any heir for the Acoma."

Mara turned in her husband's arms, her hands tracing the firmness of a shoulder yet muscled from the sword. She took a moment to reply. "I am content. If the line should end, there is no more honorable way. And it may be that Jehilia will be fecund, or that Justin will father sons on a later wife. His issue might be numerous enough that one can take on my mantle without harm to the imperial succession."

A moment later, she added, "I could also adopt a child."

But both husband and Lady knew this was not something she would do. Tradition required that the child have some connection to the adopting family, and no direct blood relatives survived the early days of the Minwanabi war upon the Acoma. Some distant linkage could be discovered, no doubt, but the Acoma line had too old and honorable a name to bestow upon a child of obscure descent.

Hokanu smoothed Mara's hair. "The problem has already been resolved," he murmured.

Mara felt the slight tension enter his body; she knew! He had done something irrevocable, which he was certain before he spoke that she would argue. "What have you done, Hokanu?" Her voice was sharp with fear, worry, and concern. And then, by his very reluctance to answer, she guessed. "Kasuma," she blurted. "You have—"

He stole her words, said them for her, but without her snap of outrage. "I have given her over to the Acoma."

Mara surged up, but he caught her. He stopped her rush of words with a gentle finger, and shook her, tenderly, to subside. "Wife, it has been done! You cannot revoke the oaths sworn this day. Fumita and the priests of a half-dozen orders were witnesses, and the altar of the Temple of Juran was the place where Kasuma's heirship to the Shinzawai was renounced. Then I swore her to the Acoma, as is my right as her father. She will continue your house and lineage, as is fitting and proper. You will know far better than anyone what instruction a girl needs to become a Ruling Lady.''

Hokanu's finger fell away, leaving Mara struck speechless—not with happiness, Hokanu understood, but with hurt and rage that was entirely for his own sake. "You will leave yourself heirless!" she said finally. "It's too dangerous in these times, with Devacai plotting to assume your mantle. The Omechan and other Ionani allies may relent and swear fealty to Justin, but many Lords with old jealousies will foment traditionalist rebellion. You will face their threats for years to come, Hokanu. Justin and Jehilia need every advantage we can give them, and that means a secure Shinzawai succession!" Her voice became half strangled by tears as she added, "Do not tempt our enemies to target you for murder! I could not bear to see you die like your father, struck down for someone else's venal ambition!"

Hokanu gathered her close. "You are right to fear," he murmured into her hair, "just as I was right to place Kasuma in custody of the Acoma heirship. She is my daughter!" The ring in his voice was all pride now; there never had been any rejection of the girl in his heart. Mara knew a pang of sorrow that she had ever known doubt.

"I am her father," Hokanu repeated. "And to my knowledge, there are still laws and traditions that support my right to make this decision." He traced the tense line of her jaw. "My Lady, you are overruled in this matter, perhaps for the first time in your life."

Mara's reply was an explosion of weeping. To have Kasuma as heir was a joy, yes, but she would feel that later. For now she was consumed by the hurt of knowing what Hokanu renounced to give her this supreme gift and sacrifice.

She could not help but know what he held back: that he would have no Shinzawai child of her loins to grow and inherit the blue.

"I have dozens upon dozens of cousins," he was saying, his voice compelled to lightness. "They are not all avaricious like Devacai. In fact, most are honorable and worthy. It might ease my family difficulties if I chose among my rivals for an heir. That would divide Devacai's faction."

Mara hoarsely found her voice. "You will take no concubine."

Her tone did not indicate a question. And her husband's steely stillness became answer in itself, until he acknowledged the truth. "My Lady, you are all the woman I could wish in this world. So long as you are at my side, I will have no other."

Mara bit her lip. In the undertones behind her husband's statement she heard the personal longings he had hardened himself to deny. A like hardness entered her own heart. But she said nothing of her inward resolves as Hokanu's arms closed around her and his lips sought hers in the light.

The doors to the grand audience hall boomed open, and trumpeters and drummers sounded fanfare. In the open square outside, those commoners still celebrating the new Emperor's accession fell silent out of respect. Two imperial heralds stepped to the entry, their matched voices pealing out the announcement that the inaugural council of the ninety-second Light of Heaven was officially called to session. They followed by shouting the list of names of those to appear before his Imperial Majesty, Justin.

First to be summoned were the high officials and servants who had held office under Ichindar. These all filed inside as they were named, dressed in dazzling finery, though their faces were sober or apprehensive. The Lord of the Keda led the procession. He advanced between the ranks of assembled Lords and made his bow before the railing that fronted the pyramidal dais.

Young Justin formally affirmed his continuance in the office of Imperial Chancellor. Lord Keda made deep obeisance, both to the boy ruler and to the Lady who sat on a cushion among the attending priests, five ranks up on the pyramid.

Lady Mara wore red, from the ceremony of remembrance held for her dead at dawn. Deep sorrow left her peaked, weary, and somewhat hollowed cheeked. Lord Keda felt a moment of compassion for her. She had won out over widespread contention to achieve an impossible victory: yet her triumph had come at grievous cost. Keyoke and her advisers Saric and Incomo had all given their lives; many more minor officers and warriors had fallen in the strife. House Acoma held but a handful of its ranking servants on this side of the Wheel of Life. Lord Keda offered the Lady his personal salute. Not many rulers in the Empire would have risked so much, or sacrificed nearly all they held dear, in the name of the common good.

The heralds pealed out another title, and Lord Keda made his bow and withdrew. He took his place amid the other Lords as, one by one, the ministers of the court were called forth. Many were given appointment to their former posts. A few were promoted. Others were sent away in shame, though no reason was given in public.

In time, Lord Keda noted that the boy Justin took his cues from a slight, dark figure who wore the armor of an Imperial White and was placed in the position of bodyguard at the boy's right hand. Lord Keda studied the man, whose face seemed to lose itself in shadow. He had never seen the officer before, which was odd. The ranking Imperial Whites were all known to him, in his long years of service to Ichindar. Lord Keda might have raised voice in concern, except that Lady Mara seemed complaisant.

At length the list of officials drew to its end. Next, rank after rank of Ruling Lords approached, to swear obedience to the Light of Heaven. For a few the moment was clearly joyous, while for others it was bitter. But when the last of the families of the Empire had knelt, Justin rose and spoke. "My Lords, you who were once the Council of the Nations, I welcome your acceptance of our assess"—He stumbled over the word, and the hovering imperial officer whispered to the boy—"accession to the Throne of Heaven. Some of you were our enemies, but are no longer. From this day forward, there is a general amnesty, and all rebellion against the Empire is forgiven. Let it be known also"—again the officer prompted the boy—"that all blood feuds and rivalries are abolished. He who raises his hand against his neighbor raises his hand against me, I mean us. The Empire." The boy flushed, but no one laughed at his awkwardness. For with that pronouncement, the young Light of Heaven had decreed that this Empire would indeed be run by laws, and that anyone who sought to rekindle the bloody Game of the Council would do so at peril of imperial wrath.

The Emperor nodded to his heralds, and a fiery lock of hair slipped out from under his golden helm. His freckled face burst into a smile as the Chief Herald called out, "Lujan, Force Commander of the Acoma! Come before your Emperor!"

Lujan made his appearance, looking half-stunned with surprise and embarrassment. He wore his best armor, for Mara's honor, but had never dreamed he would be formally presented at court. He knelt before the new Emperor and the mistress he had long served, who seemed a stranger with the tiara of regent pressed over her mourning headdress of red.

Mara spoke to her Force Commander in words that only the privileged few who occupied the foremost ranks might hear. "Saric, Keyoke, and Irrilandi all gave their lives in this, our greatest victory. You are summoned, Lujan, by your Emperor, to accept reward for your years of praiseworthy service. Let your deeds and your loyalty stand as example to all warriors in the Nations. None living has matched your steadfastness in our service."

Lujan still seemed stunned as Lady Mara arose and descended from her place of state. She took his hand, bade him rise, and led him down the rail to one side, where two Imperial Whites opened a small gate, and snapped him a crisp salute as the Lady drew him through. Force Commander Lujan, who had commanded armies against the express edict of the Assembly, turned pale with apprehension. He moved carefully, as if the air were too rare to breathe, and the floor under his sandals too highly polished to walk upon.

On the high dais, the Emperor Justin beckoned him onward, upward, to a height of exaltation he had never dreamed.

In the end he hesitated, and Lady Mara had to give him a surreptitious push.

He recovered himself short of a stumble; he, who was swordsman enough never to be caught off balance. He managed somehow to ascend the stair without mishap. At the top, he bowed at Justin's feet, his green plumes sweeping the carpet.

"Get up, Lujan." The boy was grinning with the same affection he had shown the first time he had touched his teacher with a lunge in training with his wooden sword.

Lujan seemed too stunned to respond. At length the Imperial White with the shadowy face prodded him on with a toe and murmured something nobody else could hear. The Force Commander of the Acoma shot upright as if kicked, and looked down on the face of his Emperor.

Justin's grin took on an insolent edge. "The Emperor hereby grants to Lujan, officer of the Acoma, official patent to commence his own house. Let it be heard by all: this warrior's children and servants and soldiers shall wear colors of his own designation, and swear upon the natami of House Lujan. The sacred stone awaits its new Lord and master in the Temple of Chochocan. The papers of patent will be given by the hand of the Good Servant, Mara." Justin's happiness threatened to brim over into laughter. "You may bow to your Emperor and swear fealty, Lord Lujan of the House of Lujan."

Lujan, who had never in his life been at a loss for a glib reply, could only gape like a fish. He made his bow, and somehow beat a decorous retreat down the stair. But when at the bottom he found himself confronted by Lady Mara, the eyes that met hers were suspiciously bright at the corners.

"My Lady," Lujan said huskily, disbelief holding him confounded.

Mara inclined her head. "My Lord." She caught his hand as he started to flinch back at the title, raised it, and placed in his palm three scrolls. Only one was tied off with ribbons of imperial gold. The other two were looped with green, and set with the shatra seal of the Acoma.

Mara smiled. "My first recruit, the boldest of the grey warriors ever to swear Acoma service, and my oldest living friend: I do formally release you now from your vows to the Acoma natami, with happiness, as you now go on to serve your own destiny. Today a great house is born. To the title of Ruling Lord that our Light of Heaven has seen fit to bestow, the Acoma add gifts of appreciation." She gave Lujan's hand a squeeze. "First, the House of Lujan shall have title to the estates that were mine by right of birth. All lands and livestock on the properties adjacent to Sulan-Qu are henceforward yours to manage and hold for your heirs, with the contemplation glade to be consecrated as setting for your house natami."

"My Lady," Lujan stammered.

Mara overrode him. "My Lord, with this estate, I as Lady of the Acoma grant you the service of five hundred warriors. These shall be made up, first, of all those who swore covenant to you in your band of grey warriors. The rest shall be of your choosing, from among those willing to serve you in the garrison already housed on the Sulan-Qu estate."

Lujan recovered enough of his rakish poise now to grin. "Gods," he murmured, "wait till the men hear. They started out robbing two needra for a meal, and now they will be officers of my house!" He chuckled, then shrugged, and might have broken protocol to laugh, when Mara stopped him with a touch to the last scroll in his hand.

"You are offered a place of honor in Clan Hadama, if you desire it," she finished. "Were Keyoke alive today, he would say that you learned well. He counted Papewaio as the son of his heart, after my brother Lanokota. You were his youngest son . . . and at the last, the one of whom he was proudest."

Lujan felt a poignant moment of loss for the old man who had always treated him fairly, and who had been among the first to recognize and reward his gifts of command. As if in salute to his former officer, he touched the scrolls to his forehead, accepting their contents with a flourish. "You are too generous," he murmured to Mara. "If every needra thief in this Empire realizes he might rise so high, you will be the ruler of mayhem." Then he turned serious and bowed. "In my heart, you shall ever be my mistress, Lady Mara. Let the colors of House Lujan be grey and green: grey in symbolic remembrance of my origin, and green, for my service to Acoma that has led me to this pinnacle of honor."

"Grey and green are the colors of House Lujan!" cried the imperial herald by the dais, that all Lords might hear and take note.

Mara smiled in pleasure at the tribute. "Now be off!" she whispered to her galliant former officer. "Keep the promise you made me swear to keep you to in Chakaha. Marry a fine woman, get children, and live to a white old age!''

Lujan snapped off a jaunty salute, spun on his heel, and marched back through the ranks of his peers, while the Imperial White at the Emperor's right hand murmured softly, ''I'll wager he'll be falling down drunk with celebration within the hour.''

Justin peered up into the familiar face of Arakasi. ''Don't sound so smug. Your turn will come in due course.''

Though the Acoma Spy Master tipped his young master a quizzical look, Justin refused to elaborate upon his statement. He looked straight ahead, his young shoulders stiffly square. Not all of the imperial grants made this day would be as pleasurable as Lujan's patent of Lordship. He nodded to his Herald, and the name of Hokanu of the Shinzawai was called across the audience chamber.

Now more than one in the ranks of Ruling Lords exchanged glances, many of which hinted at jealousy. Lady Mara had professed to be a fair regent, but now, not a few presumed, she would show her venality by having her husband appointed to some exalted station or office.

Yet if that were true, Hokanu's face as he approached the imperial dais was fixed in lines hard as rock. He looked neither pleased nor annoyed; only determinedly neutral as he made his bow before the Light of Heaven.

His obeisance was made to Justin; yet his eyes, as he arose, were turned immovably toward Lady Mara. Neither did she appear overjoyed to be the subject of her husband's scrutiny. Stiffly formal, even more pale than she had been earlier, she stared woodenly ahead as his Imperial Majesty formally made proclamation.

''Let all present hear and take heed: your Emperor does as he must for the Good of the Empire. It has been duly noted, according to a ceremony in Juran's temple yesterday, that the child Kasuma has been dedicated by her father to become the heir to the mantle of the Acoma.'' Justin paused, swallowed, and with a manhood beyond his years forced his voice to steadiness. ''This has drawn our attention to the Shinzawai, now an heirless house. By Lady Mara's bequest, for she has been pronounced barren by the priests of Hantukama, she has petitioned for divorce.'' Justin lowered his eyes and regarded his feet in discomfort. ''As Light of Heaven, for the Good of the Empire, I have seen fit to grant her request.''

Murmurs swept the packed chamber.

Hokanu looked stunned, but he did not change expression. Only his eyes, locked with Mara's, showed a silent scream of pain.

Justin made a noise behind one wrist that might have been a smothered sniffle. "Shinzawai is too great a house, and too important to this Empire, to invite internal strife by remaining heirless. Lord Hokanu is hereby commanded by his Emperor to seek out a bride, and remarry, for the purpose of begetting sound children."

It was Mara who descended the dais to deliver the divorce papers with their crust of imperial seals. She moved against a shocked silence, and then whispers: for all could plainly see that she loved her Lord. Her sacrifice stilled the petty thoughts of even the most ambitious Ruling Lords. She was not as they had presumed, but a true Servant of the Empire, acting selflessly even where necessity left her wounded.

Former Lady and husband met before the dais. Naked to public regard, they could not fall into each other's arms and weep. For this, Mara was grateful. Only the pride of her ancestors prevented her from shouting for appeal. Her heart wanted no part of this brutal choice. She yearned only to cast herself at Hokanu's feet and beg him to plead for a reversal of the papers Justin had tearfully signed that morning.

She had meant to say nothing, but words burst from her, without restraint. "I had to! Dear gods, I love you still, but this was—" She stopped, reining back tears.

"It had to be," Hokanu grated back, his voice as shaken as hers. "The Empire demands all our strength."

His clear understanding of necessity was a sword that cut, a gift that threatened to undermine all of her resolve. Mara held the scroll with its cruel words and official seals as if it were glued to her flesh.

Gently, Hokanu took the document from her. "You will ever be my Lady," he murmured. "I may breed my sons upon another, but my heart will always be yours." His hands were shaking, causing the gold ribbons to flutter and flash in the light. His eyes were hard with distance and pain, and he was recalling the priest of Hantukama, who had once accused him of loving his Lady too much: at the expense of himself, that gentle holy man had rebuked. Bitterly, and only now, Hokanu understood the extent of this truth. Almost, he had allowed his care for Mara to set House Shinzawai in jeopardy.

The Empire could ill afford any weakness, far less one caused by an affection of the heart. Mara was right, hurtful as her petition was to him in this their hour of triumph. She had recognized the need for this parting; he had unknowingly made her choice the more compelling by his own hard-headedness concerning his disposition of Kasuma.

His course was clear, if sorrowful. He must accept at once, lest courage fail him. For the Good of the Empire, he, too, must make his sacrifice. He reached out with a gentle finger, tipped up Mara's chin, and forced her eyes to meet his own. "Don't be a stranger, Lady Servant," he murmured. "You are always welcome to my company and my counsel, and you will ever be first in my affections."

Mara swallowed, speechless. As always, Hokanu's faultless understanding held the power to captivate her heart. She would miss his constant company, and his tender, solicitous presence in her bed. And yet she, too, knew: if she did not force this decision upon him, he would die without a son, heirless. That he should not pass on his gentleness, and his ability to choose right and merciful action when necessary, would be a crime against humanity.

"I love you," she whispered soundlessly.

But he had already bowed and taken his leave, his step as firm as if he marched into battle.

The watching Lords were awed. Hokanu's courage humbled them; and Mara's silent pain left them abashed to a man. The Empire was entering a new order, and it appeared that the remarkable couple who had arranged its renaissance were themselves to become a shining example to them all. Men who had greeted such change with resentment were forced to reexamination. They had just witnessed the epitome of honor. To fail to live up to the standards Lady Mara and Lord Hokanu set was to relearn the meaning of shame.

On the golden throne, a boy who had just renounced a beloved father swallowed a lump in his throat. He flashed a glance to his bride, Jehilia, and swallowed again. Then he straightened the shoulders that seemed suddenly weighed down by the drag of the imperial mantle, and waved to his herald.

Next to be summoned was Lady Mara of the Acoma, Servant of the Empire.

She seemed at first not to hear, her eyes fixed upon the empty aisle where Hokanu had lately departed. Then she, too, straightened, and climbed the stair of the high dais, to give her bow to the Light of Heaven.

Justin was through with practiced speeches. He could not bring himself to adhere to the forms he had rehearsed. "Mother!" he called out, a grin curving his impish mouth. "To you, who have surpassed every prior Servant of the Empire in service to our Nations . . ." Justin paused, and was elbowed in the ribs by Jehilia. He flashed her a surprised glance, and went on, "You will accept the regency of our rule until our twenty-fifth birthday."

Polite applause swept the audience hall, swelling in volume until a cheer erupted, first from the Acoma honor guard, then echoed by the Imperial Whites and the Shinzawai warriors. Then Lord after Ruling Lord surged to their feet and shouted in appreciation of Lady Mara. Justin waved to restore decorum, but order was a long time returning. Into the ripple of reluctantly suppressed admiration he called, "To you, Lady Mara, greatest among the Servants of the Empire, we see fit to create a new title." Justin rose to his feet, hands upraised. "We name Lady Mara, *Mistress of the Empire!*"

The noise became deafening. Mara stood at the center of all admiring eyes, looking stunned, and pleased, and saddened.

She had never asked for power or public adulation. All she had ever striven for was to keep her family name alive.

How strange it was that in the course of life the gods had given her, she had come to see all of the Nations as her family, and her son, child of a barbarian slave, take the supreme throne and title Light of Heaven.

Lord Keda's curiosity concerning the mysterious man who wore the armor of an Imperial White was not satisfied until afternoon, when the young Emperor called a select, closed meeting in his private study.

The room was no small chamber but a grand hall in itself, sparkling with gilt-trimmed screens, and appointed with ancient paintings. Justin had doffed his imperial armor. For this meeting he had donned a robe edged in gold, borrowed from the wardrobe of his predecessor. The fabric hung off his youthful frame, pinned up at the hem and shoulders with rare metal fastenings.

Lord Keda entered. He bowed before the low dais upon which the boy Light of Heaven reclined on cushions, then glanced with interest at the other assembled personages.

Lady Mara yet wore her mourning red. With her was the mysterious bodyguard, his hair damp from a recent bath, and his poised, gaunt body no longer disguised in white armor. He now wore a nondescript robe that was subtly bordered in green. The man's face was guardedly still. Clever hands were folded neatly in his lap. Only his eyes betrayed his intellect, and they watched, missing nothing. Quick the fellow would be, Lord Keda assessed; he had a talent for judging men. This one would react well in a crisis; except that about him at this moment was a haunted air of abstraction that made him seem one step removed from the people in his presence.

Mara noted Lord Keda's keen study. "Let me introduce you to Arakasi, a valued servant of the Acoma who commands our highest respect."

Lord Keda's interest sharpened. This nondescript man with his almost inhuman attentiveness: could he be the fabled Spy Master that had kept the Acoma so miraculously well informed?

The man answered directly, as if, uncannily, he could read Lord Keda's thoughts from the play of expressions on his face. "I have resigned from my former post," he admitted, his voice like velvet rubbed on stone. "Once I was Spy Master for the Acoma. Now I have discovered that life and nature hold secrets more profound than intrigues fashioned by men."

Lord Keda considered this remarkable statement, fascinated by the man who had uttered it.

But the Emperor they all attended was young yet for subtle nuances. He squirmed impatiently on his gilded cushions and clapped his hands to his runner. "Fetch in the prisoner."

Two Imperial Whites entered, flanking a slender man with bitten nails and shrewd eyes. Lord Keda recognized Chumaka, who had served the late Lord Jiro as First Adviser. The Imperial Chancellor frowned, wondering why he had been summoned to this private council, since his was not a judicial office. His appointment was more an administrator's than one of tribunal authority who could seal an accusation of treason.

For surely Lord Jiro had been behind the assassination of the Emperor Ichindar; Omechan had inherited the siege engines, and Omechan armies had been in place to back the Anasati plot to seize the throne. Chumaka could not have escaped involvement; all too likely, the deadly plan had been of his own design.

Mara responded to Lord Keda's trepidation. "You have been called here as witness," she explained quietly, then faced forward as Chumaka awarded the Emperor a deep bow. He followed with an obeisance to Mara, murmuring, "Great Lady, I have heard of your reputation. I cast myself at your mercy and humbly beg for my life."

Lord Keda frowned. The man had been Lord Jiro's adviser; he had surely been party to the murder of Hokanu's father, as well as to the poisoning of Lady Mara herself.

That Mara knew this was mirrored in her face. The expressionless line of her mouth hinted at underlying pain: but for this man's meddling, and a nearly successful attempt on her life, she might still be capable of childbearing. The husband she had been compelled to renounce might yet be at her side.

Chumaka held his pose of prostration, his hands trembling slightly. There was no arrogance in him; his humiliation seemed deeply genuine.

"Justin," Mara murmured, her tone husky.

The boy gave his mother a glance that hinted at rebellion.

Mara braced herself, but it was Arakasi who coached the boy in her place.

"Majesty," he said in a tone that grated like old rust, "there are times to hold grudges, and other times to grant clemency. I urge you to choose as a man, and as Emperor. Consider wisely. This man who throws himself on your mercy is the most brilliant foe I have ever known. You've already pardoned every other enemy in the Nations, but this one must be specially exempted. Either order him executed, banish him for life, or swear him to your service and give him a commission. He is far too dangerous to let run free inside the Empire."

Justin's red brows gathered into a frown. He thought long and hard. "I cannot decide," he said at last. "Mother, this man has been responsible for more pain than any other. His life is yours to dispose of as you will."

The Lady in her red of mourning stirred. She regarded the thinning hair of the man who crouched at her feet. It took her a long time to speak. "Rise, Chumaka."

The prisoner obeyed, all of his cleverness absent. He regarded the Lady whose choice would determine his fate, and by the deep stillness in his eyes, all in the chamber could see: he knew of no reason under heaven why she should grant him reprieve. "As my Lady wills," he murmured in a dead voice.

Mara's gaze bored into him. "Answer me on your honor; swear by your spirit that will be bound to the Wheel of Life after this existence shall end: why did you do it?"

She did not specify which of his crimes he should answer for. Perhaps naming them separately was too hurtful to her. More likely, she was too numbed by events to care; or else she was guileful, leaving the selection to Chumaka, that she could divine his deeper motives from his choice.

Chumaka's quick intellect floundered. He sighed, conceding her the match. As she had questioned, so he answered in general terms. And for the first time in his long and disingenuous life, he spoke the plain truth. "For my master's service, in part. But in the main, for my love of the Great Game, my Lady. In this, I served myself, not Jiro or Tecuma before him. I was loyal to the House of Anasati, yes, but also not; I did my Lord's bidding, but the joy of manipulating politics was always my own, private thing. You were the best the gods had placed upon the soil and under the sun, and to defeat you"—he shrugged—"would have been the most glorious triumph in the history of the Great Game."

Arakasi sucked in a breath. Too plainly he had understood the words of the antagonist who had come nearer than any man to beating him at subterfuge and wit, murder and plotting.

"That was my miscalculation," he murmured, as if he and Chumaka were alone. "I presumed that you acted for your master's honor. There was where you nearly had me: your motive was ever your own at heart, and Jiro's honor be damned."

Chumaka inclined his head. "To win, yes, was always the goal. The honor of the master *is* in victory." Then he turned back to Lady Mara. "No one understands this better than you, mistress. For the winner decides what is honor and what is not." He fell silent, awaiting pronouncement of his sentence.

The Mistress of the Empire clasped taut hands in her lap. She did not, in the end, speak for herself. "Would you serve the Empire, Chumaka?"

A fiery light shone in the former Anasati adviser's eyes. "Gladly, mistress. Despite vows of obedience and loyalty, many of those at your banquet drinking your wine tonight will be plotting your overthrow tomorrow. Keeping this new Empire from crumbling would be the greatest challenge any man could face."

Mara's gaze shifted to Arakasi. "Would you entrust your network to this man?"

The Spy Master of the Acoma narrowed his eyes and answered with barely a hesitation. "Yes. Better than I, he could run my agents. His pride in his work would keep them safer than I ever could, even before I lost my touch."

Mara nodded to herself. "So I thought. You had never found your heart. We need not fear this happening to Chumaka. He has none, save for his work."

She faced Chumaka. "You will take oath to serve your Emperor as Spy Master. As punishment for your past crimes against this Empire, and as penance, you will serve your new Light of Heaven to the last breath in your body. Lord Keda stands as witness." As Chumaka regarded the remarkable Lady who had large enough heart to forgive him for some of the greatest sorrows in her life, and as disbelief gave way to dawning joy, he lost the chance to thank her. She dismissed him summarily, in the care of Lord Keda, to swear his oath of fealty and set the words under the imperial seal.

As the Imperial Whites and the Chancellor left the chamber, Mara and Justin were left alone with Arakasi. The Lady regarded the remarkably talented man who had taken innumerable guises, from the lowest scabby beggar in the gutters, to the glittering gold-edged armor of an elite warrior in Justin's retinue. All that she had achieved she owed in part to him. His ability to perceive without prejudice had served her more than loyalty, more than duty, more than treasure or wealth. "There is only one post left unfilled,'' she said at last, her mouth showing signs of a smile. ''Will you take the mantle of Imperial First Adviser? I very much doubt there is any other man living with a fast enough mind to keep Justin out of mischief.''

Arakasi returned a grin that was startling for its spontaneity. ''What does Justin think?''

Mara and her former Spy Master glanced at the boy, whose face was utterly crestfallen.

''He thinks he will lose out in his escapades,'' Mara concluded with a laugh. ''Which decides the issue. Will you accept, Arakasi?''

''I would be honored,'' he replied solemnly. And then delight showed through his façade. ''More: I would be pleased.''

''Then prepare to begin your duties tomorrow,'' Mara finished. ''To-night is yours, to seek out your lady Kamlio.''

Arakasi quirked up one brow in an expression no one present had ever seen.

''What is it?'' Mara asked gently. ''Has the girl rejected your suit?''

Arakasi's manner became bemused. ''She has not. In fact, she has agreed I may pay court to her—for a former courtesan, she suddenly desires a large measure of propriety. Her moods are still changeable, but she is no longer the sullen child you took with you into Thuril.'' He shook his head a little in bemused wonder. ''Now she has discovered her self-worth, it remains to be seen whether I am a match for *her*.''

''You are,'' Mara assured him. ''I have seen. Do not doubt.'' Then she looked closely at the man whose thoughts had stimulated hers to new heights and long leaps of revelation. ''You wish to ask a favor,'' she guessed.

Arakasi looked uncharacteristically chagrined. ''As a matter of fact, yes, I do.''

''Name it.'' Mara said. ''If it is within my power to grant, it is already yours.''

The man in the unobtrusive green-bordered robe, who would soon wear the white and gold of imperial service, smiled shyly. ''I would ask you to assign Kamlio's service to Isashani of the Xacatecas,'' he said in a rush of embarrassed words.

Mara laughed outright. ''Brilliant!'' she said when next she could speak. ''Of course! No one, man or woman, has ever escaped the charm of the dowager Lady of the Xacatecas. Kamlio will do well with her, and you will gain a superbly trained wife.''

Arakasi's eyes glittered. ''She will certainly become a manipulator equal to my best effort.''

Mara waved him away. "You need a woman of wits to keep your acuity," she chided fondly. "Now go and tell Lady Isashani that the most difficult match in all the Empire is her bag of knots to untangle. She'll be delighted to oblige, I am sure."

"Why?" Justin demanded outright, as Arakasi made his graceful bow and habitually silent exit. "Do all women amuse themselves in such fashion?"

The Mistress of the Empire sighed and gazed fondly upon her son, whose frankness could be an embarrassment, for his ability to set words to truths that were a breach of good manners and all too often resulted in reddened ears. "Visit your predecessor's harem, sometime, and you will see," she said. Then, as Justin's eyes took on an unholy gleam of mischief, she added hastily, "On second thought, that part of your education can wait until you are grown. You are too like your father to be set loose among rival women at a tender age."

"What do you mean?" Justin demanded.

Mara gave her son a faraway smile. "When you are older, and I am no longer your regent, you will see."

The garden was secluded, a green haven of shade surrounded by flowers and fountains. Mara wandered its paths, seeking peace. Hokanu walked at her side, from time to time speaking, other times wrapped in silence. "I shall miss you," he said, in a heart-wrenching shift of subject.

"And I you," Mara said quickly, lest she lose her voice entirely. "More than I can say."

Hokanu gave her back a brave smile, his loss carefully walled away. "You have certainly enlivened the gossip and given Lady Isashani pause for thought. She will be busy writing letters, and I will have to fend off the results of her matchmaking."

Mara tried to smile at his humor. "You are the best a woman could wish for in a husband. You gave love without condition. You never held me back from my destiny."

"No man could," Hokanu admitted wryly. Unspoken behind his words was an anger for the works of Jiro's assassin: if not for the tong's ugly poison, he would not be losing the only woman who would ever match him in spirit.

Mara plucked a white flower, and Hokanu gently took it from her. As he had once done before, he wound it in her hair. There were light strands amid the black, now, that matched the hue of the petals.

"You gave me a beautiful daughter to follow after me," Mara said. "One day she will have brothers who are your sons."

Hokanu could only nod. After a long moment of just walking at the Lady's side, he said, "There is a certain elegance in your being succeeded by Kasuma as Ruling Lady." His smile was bittersweet. "Our daughter. My father would be pleased to know that our children will rule two great houses."

"He is," announced a voice.

Lord and Lady spun around in surprise. Deep in mystery in his black robes, Fumita offered them both a bow. "More than you know . . . my son." The admission of kinship was not wrung from him, but a glad pronouncement that the changed status of the Assembly now made possible. The magician's stern face broke into a startlingly brilliant smile. "Lady Mara, always think of yourself as my daughter." Then his manner became impassive, as he delivered his official message. "I asked to be the one to inform the Great Mistress that the Assembly has voted. The decision was reluctant, but the magicians concede to her demands. Our order will be answerable to the new law, as set down by the Emperor Justin over the Nations."

Mara inclined her head in respect. She half expected Fumita to effect the same abrupt departure that was his habit when he saw his part as finished.

But as if his admission of kinship with his son had opened the floodgates of change, this one time he lingered. "My son, my daughter, I wish you both to know that your courageous actions are approved. You have done Acoma and Shinzawai honor. I only wish my brother—Hokanu's foster father—were still alive to bear witness."

Hokanu kept an impassive face, but Mara could sense his great pride. A crooked smile finally cracked his warrior's façade, matched almost at once by a mirroring one from Fumita. "I guess none of the scions of House Shinzawai are adept at keeping tradition," the magician observed. To Mara he added, "You may never know how difficult it has been, sometimes, for our kind to give up the life we knew before our power was recognized. It is worse for those like myself, who were grown men with families when our power manifested. The Assembly's secrets have crippled our emotions, I sometimes think. That has been a tragic mistake. We were forced to wall away our feelings, and as a consequence, acts of cruelty seemed removed from us. As change refreshes us, we will reawaken to our humanity. In the end, we of the Assembly will grow to have cause to thank you, and to bless Lady Mara's memory."

The Mistress of the Empire embraced the magician with a familiarity she would never have dared before. "Visit the imperial court often,

Fumita. Your granddaughter must grow with the joy of knowing her grandfather.''

As if uncomfortable with the rush of feelings, for the gift of a family restored, Fumita bowed brusquely. A heartbeat later, he vanished in a breath of air, leaving Mara and Hokanu alone to share a last moment of each other's private company.

The fountains sang, and the flowers released their perfume on the deepening evening air. The page who arrived was an intrusion, as he made his bow and announced, ''My Lady, the Light of Heaven requests the presence of his father, and the Mistress of the Empire, for his council.''

''Politics,'' Mara said with a sigh. ''Is it the dance or ourselves that are the masters?''

''It is the dance that masters us, of course.'' Hokanu smiled. ''Else I should never be leaving you, Lady.'' Then he turned, and presented his arm to his former wife. With a dignity born of profound courage and unshakable inner peace, he escorted her toward the imperial suite, and her new role as Regent and Mistress of the Empire.

Epilogue. Reunion

The herald struck the gong.

Lady Mara, Mistress of the Empire, resettled her weight on the gilt-edged cushion that failed to soften the unyielding marble of her official seat on the imperial dais. Hers might be less brilliant a throne than Justin's gold-overlaid one, but it was no less uncomfortable. In two years of presiding over Justin's public duties, she had never grown used to it.

Mara's thoughts drifted. Gaining in his experience on the golden throne, Justin was more and more capable of managing the decisions presented on the Day of Appeals. He had his mother's talent for seeing the pattern in complex issues, and his father's ability to cut to the heart of the matter. Most of the time Mara served at his side more in the role of adviser than Regent; sometimes she sat lost in memories as she endured the lengthy hours of state councils, trusting Justin to let her know when her attention was needed.

Sundown was near, she saw by the slant of the light through the dome in the grand hall of audience. The Day of Appeals was at last drawing to a close. The last few of the Emperor's petitioners approached the rail on the floor below. Mara resisted the urge to rub tired eyes as Justin, ninety-two times Emperor, called out the traditional words that acknowledged his approaching subject's right to be heard.

"Lord Hokanu of the Shinzawai, know that you have the ear of the gods through our ear." Justin's voice was breaking to the baritone that would be his in manhood, but joy at the arrival of his foster father caused him to forget to blush at the roughness that had invaded his speech. "Heaven smiles down upon the felicity of your visit, and we bid you glad welcome."

Mara started sharply from reverie. Hokanu was here! Her heart leaped as she looked down to see how he fared. Months had passed since their paths had last crossed at a state function. The Shinzawai Lord had left the court, she recalled, to attend upon his lady wife, who had been pregnant with his heir.

Heirs, Mara was forced to correct herself, as the imperial herald called out two names, and she reviewed the pair of bundles born in the arms of their father. A nurse and two servants hovered nearby, and another, a slight, pretty girl whose eyes were downcast and shy before the presence of her Emperor.

Justin was grinning; another trait he had inherited from his outworld father was spurning the Tsurani bent for stiff-faced protocol. These days some of the younger nobles were imitating him, affecting his animated expressions and frank speech, as unmarried women might follow popular fashion, much to the discomfort of the older Ruling Lords. He gave his stately mother a mischievously unroyal poke in the ribs. "Mother, you must have words for this occasion."

Mara did not. She could only smile down on the proud father for a long minute, close to tears. The babies were beautiful, perfect; if they could not have been hers to bear, she blessed the gods that the quiet Elumani's fertility had granted her husband's fierce desire. "Sons?" Mara managed to whisper at last.

Hokanu nodded, speechless. His eyes mirrored the joy in her own, and also the aching regret. He missed Mara's quick mind, and the ease of her company. Elumani was a gentle girl, but she had not been chosen for fiery spirit. Still, she had given what Mara could not: the House of Shinzawai now had children for continuance of the line. Hokanu had his boys, and they would grow and come to replace the companionship he had lost.

The imperial herald cleared his throat. "Lord Hokanu of the Shinzawai, presenting to the Light of Heaven his heirs, Kamatsu and Maro."

Justin voiced the official acknowledgment of the children. "May they grow in joy and strength, with the blessing of heaven."

Mara found her voice. "I am happy for you both. Lady Elumani, I am especially flattered and proud." She paused, deeply touched by the unexpected gift of having a namesake of Hokanu's blood. She had to force herself not to weep as she continued. "When your sons are old enough, I would be pleased to have them visit the imperial nursery, and to enjoy making acquaintance with their half-sister, Kasuma."

The tiny, auburn-haired girl at Hokanu's side gave a graceful bow. She still did not raise her eyes, and the skin of her cheeks blushed pink at this royal recognition. "I am deeply honored," she said in a voice like a mellow songbird's. "The Mistress of the Empire is too kind."

All too soon the Shinzawai party were making bows of parting to the Emperor. Mara gazed wistfully after the blue-armored figure that strode out with all the warrior's grace she remembered. Then her emotions overcame her. She raised her ceremonial fan and tipped it open to hide her sudden tears. Sons for the Shinzawai: they were now a fulfilled wish, more than a dream for the future of the Empire. Twins! Mara shook her head, bemused. It seemed as if the bounty of the gods outdid itself to make up for the poor infant of hers who had died before birth.

Her loneliness was now well worth such rewards. Seeing Hokanu, spending time with him, was no longer possible, and she missed him, but a time would come when they could visit without pain, because deep friendship had formed the heart of their marriage.

Again the gong chimed. The imperial herald's voice rang out, announcing the presentation of the newly arrived ambassador from the Kingdom of the Isles, on the world of Midkemia.

Mara stole a peek at the group who approached, then raised her fan swiftly as her heart twisted yet again.

Never could she behold a group of men in outworld dress without thinking of the barbarian lover who had tossed her life tempestuously into change. Three of them were slender and tall, and one even walked with the barest hitch to his stride. That flawed movement tugged at her memory.

She chided herself. Too much, today, she had allowed herself to become maudlin over past affairs of the heart. She braced herself to endure greeting a man who would be a stranger, who might speak Tsurani with the odd, nasal twang of a Midkemian, and who, though tall, would not be Kevin. That these men did not wear slave's grey, but rather the fine silks and rich velvets, with the blazon of the King of Isle upon the tabards of the officers, made no difference. Mara looked away, avoiding even imperfect reminders of personal loss.

The ambassador from the Isles and his company reached the rail. An official who had visited repeatedly in establishing this exchange of envoys, Baron Michael of Krondor, addressed the court. "Your Majesty, it is my honor to present to you the ambassador of the Kingdom of the Isles—" The sudden silence caused Mara to look.

The ambassador had one hand half-raised to sweep off his plumed hat and bow, in the style of his homeland. But there he had frozen. His knuckles obscured his face. The watching courtiers stilled also; a few of the nearer Imperial Whites peculiarly struggled to hide amazement.

Then the barbarian ambassador doffed his hat and bowed, slowly, his eyes never leaving Justin's face. A murmur swept the court as he did so. Mara looked again at the new ambassador, and her heart again seemed to skip. The man who had reminded of her lost love was replacing his outlandish hat, with the white plume and gold badge. Her eyes again threatened to betray her, so she quickly fanned her face, lest rumors sweep the city this night that the Imperial Regent had been given over to unreasonable bouts of tears for no good reason. She heard Baron Michael finish the introduction: ". . . emissary from His Royal Highness Lyam, King of the Isles."

"You may approach," the Light of Heaven allowed, sounding all boyishly treble. Mara heard movement as the Imperial Whites stepped aside and opened the railing, inviting the ambassador onto the dais to present his credentials.

The Midkemian ascended the first stair. His booted footfall rang across a chamber arrested into stillness. Carefully Mara closed her fan, as the emissary from the Kingdom of the Isles mounted the last steps between them.

He paused three paces from the throne and swept into another bow. This time his hat stayed off as he straightened. Mara beheld his face.

A soft cry escaped her. The profile of the man, and that of her son in his gold-edged robes of state, were mirror images. But where the boy's features were yet unlined, and only lately beginning to mature into the firmness of adulthood, the man's were well scored with creases, as fair skin will age with years and too much sun. The once red hair was frosted now with white, and the eyes were wide, stunned.

The Mistress of the Empire saw fully. She was forced to confront what all the Lords in the court had seen, from the instant the ambassador had made his entry. Only the hat, and the high angle of the dais, and the weak moment of cowardice that had caused her to hide behind her fan had made her the last to discover just who stood before her with an air of exasperated startlement.

"Kevin," Mara mouthed soundlessly.

Arakasi, as Imperial First Adviser, stepped forward to receive the ambassadorial credentials. Showing an unusual grin, he said, "You've changed."

Recognition registered. With an answering laugh, Kevin said, "So have you. I didn't recognize you without a disguise."

With only the barest glance at the documents, Arakasi turned and said, "Your Majesty, before you stands the ambassador from the King of the Isles, Kevin, Baron of the Royal Court."

Justin nodded and said, "You are welcome," but his voice showed he, too, was close to losing decorum. For before him stood the blood father whom he had only heard about.

Mara's hand went to her mouth, as if to prevent words from escaping unbidden. That smallest motion from her caused a shiver to chase over Kevin's flesh. His eyes—so much bluer than she recalled—turned toward her. His smile warred with a frown on his familiar face that the years had changed little, after all. "I expected I might find you here," he said in husky, pent-back emotion that only those atop the dias could hear. "Who else in these nations could fit the title 'Mistress of the Empire'? But this, your Light of Heaven"—his large, capable hand indicated Justin, and his eyes brightened to a knifepoint of intensity—"Lady, why ever didn't you tell me?"

The pair who had once been lovers might have been alone in that vast hall.

Mara swallowed. Too clearly she recalled their last parting: this man in the street, scuffed and half-beaten, as he resisted the slave handlers who had acted on her orders to send him by force back to his homeworld.

She had lacked the capacity for speech then. Now words came to her in a rush. "I didn't dare tell you. A son would have kept you this side of the rift, and that would have been a crime against all that you taught me to profess. You would never have married, never have lived for yourself. Justin has been raised knowing who his father was. Are you angry with me?"

"Justin," Kevin repeated, trying the name out on his tongue. "After my father?" As Mara gave back a timid nod, he shot a glance that glowed at the boy who sat straight on the golden throne. Then he shivered again. "Angry?"

Mara flinched. He always had spoken at inopportune moments, in a tone that rang too loud.

He looked at her, quieting his voice, though his inflection was no less harsh. "Yes, I am angry. I've been robbed. I'd have liked to watch my boy grow."

Mara blushed. He had lost none of his ability to throw her off balance. Forgetting to show demure Tsurani poise, she defended herself. "You would never have had any other children had I done so."

Kevin slapped his hand against his knee. While still low, his rejoinder was starting to carry to those standing at the bottom of the dais. "Lady, what is this talk of children? I have none! I never did marry. I took service in my Prince Arutha's court—for a dozen years I've been fighting goblins and dark elves with the border barons at Highcastle and Northwarden. Then out of nowhere, I'm summoned to Krondor, and told to my chagrin that when the Emperor of Tsurannuani requested an exchange of ambassadors, I was overqualified for the post—I'm noble born, but beyond any chance of inheritance with older brothers and near a dozen nephews, and I speak fluent Tsurani. So my King commanded—or rather, Prince Arutha appointed on his brother's behalf—and suddenly I'm a beribboned court baron, bowing like some sort of trained monkey before my own son!''

Here the Midkemian ambassador turned to regard the Emperor. His irritation modulated as he said, ''He does look like me, doesn't he?'' Then he grinned and tossed a wink at Justin. The gaze he turned back to Mara was edged as ice as his merriment faded again. ''I hope that your husband doesn't come after me with a sword for this!'' he finished in that tone of dry mocking that could either delight or enrage Mara.

The Mistress of the Empire blinked, realizing how little Kevin would know of the past fourteen years. ''Hokanu fostered the boy, knowing the truth of his conception.''

Now Kevin looked dumbfounded in turn. ''Didn't I just see the Lord of the Shinzawai outside, with a child bride, and two babies?''

Mara nodded, past speech.

Never one to be caught speechless, Kevin said, ''You're not married?'' Mara could only shake her head no. ''Yet you had a husband. What Tsurani convolution of traditions is this?''

''It's called divorce on grounds of barrenness. Hokanu needed heirs, for the stability of Justin's reign, and the Good of the Nations. You just observed the result.'' Mara shook off the play of feelings that threatened to knock her dizzy. She was in public, in full view of the court; her image as a Lady and a Tsurani must be laughable at this moment.

Taking his cue from Mara, Arakasi called out, ''The Day of Appeals is at an end. Let all retire and give thanks for our Light of Heaven.'' Then began a very slow withdrawal, as most of the court nobles lingered, curious to overhear the strange exchange taking place atop the imperial dais. The cadre of Midkemian nobles who had accompanied Kevin exchanged uncertain signals, unsure if they should wait for their leader or withdraw without him.

Mara saw a hundred pairs of eyes turned toward her, to see how she would react next. And then, suddenly, she did not care. She assumed her most dignified, formal posture. ''Kevin, Baron of the Court, Ambassador of the Midkemian King of the Isles, I have been remiss in my duties as a mother. I present to you your blood son: Justin, ninety-two times Emperor, and Light of Heaven of Tsurannuani. I humbly pray he is fair in your sight, and an honor to your family pride.''

The senior imperial herald, eyes wide in astonishment at what he had just heard, glanced at Arakasi for instruction. The Imperial First Adviser shrugged and nodded, and the herald raised his voice to ring out over the assembled Tsurani nobles. "Kevin of Rillanon, ambassador of King Lyam, and father of our own Light of Heaven!"

Lady Mara was jolted almost out of her skin by the noise of a resounding cheer from the younger nobles of the court, who were halfway to the great outer doors. They flooded back toward the railing and began stamping and clapping their approval. More than any other thing, that impressed upon Mara how swiftly two short years of changed policies were taking deeper root: for there was but one way for a Midkemian to have become the father of a fourteen-year-old boy: if he had visited the Empire previously as a slave and a prisoner of war.

It had not been long in the past when the idea of a slave's child becoming Emperor would have been cause for bloody rebellion, a war over insult and honor that had no point beyond an excuse for each Lord who harbored secret ambitions to see his house triumph over his enemies.

But as Mara studied the faces on the floor below, she saw mostly bemusement, surprise, and honest admiration. To all but a narrow-minded few, the Laws of the Great Freedom were already coming to replace the Game of the Council. More sons of nobles sought out imperial duty rather than serving with their family's forces. It was these young men, breaking free of the traditions of their ancestors, who cheered the loudest.

Once again, Mara had done the unthinkable. Her people of the Empire were coming to expect that of her, so adept had they grown at taking such turns in their stride.

And then Justin was off his throne, discarding his mantle and headdress into the care of his body servant. He flung himself into the arms of the father he had never known, but whose name had become a legend spoken in awed tones by the older Acoma servants.

Mara looked on, new tears brightening her eyes, until Kevin's huge arm hooked out and hauled her off her cushions to share in a three-way embrace.

The Lady was startled into laughter. She had forgotten how impulsive he was, and how overwhelmingly strong.

"Mistress of the Empire," he murmured over a redoubled volume of cheers. "You are a Lady of surprises! I trust I will have the chance to spend time in the imperial suite, getting to know my son, and renewing old acquaintance with his mother?"

Mara took a deep breath, smelling the odd taint of off-world fur, and strange spices, and velvets that were woven on looms far away, in a colder land that someday she must journey across the rift to visit. Her blood quickened to a beat of passion that all but swept her from her feet. "You will have a lifetime to share with your son," she murmured to Kevin so that only he could hear. "And all the years you could desire in the company of his mother, so long as your King permits."

Kevin laughed. "Lyam's glad to be rid of me, I think. Things are too quiet on the border for a troublemaker like me." Then he pulled her tight against him, for the simple joy of holding her.

The temple gongs rang out over the Holy City at that moment. Sweet music sounded over the Imperial Precinct, as the Priests of the Twenty Greater Gods sang their devotions at evening. Officially, the Day of Appeals was at an end.

Kevin drew back and smiled upon the Lady who had never for a day lost her hold upon his heart. "You are mistress of far more than this Empire," he said, laughing, and the cheers from the Lords of Tsurannuani did not stop as he led her and his Emperor son, hand in hand, down from the high dais.